# THE RUTH
# RENDELL
# OMNIBUS

*By the same author*

To Fear a Painted Devil
Vanity Dies Hard
The Secret House of Death
One Across, Two Down
A Demon in My View
A Judgement in Stone
Make Death Love Me
The Lake of Darkness
Master of the Moor
The Killing Doll
The Tree of Hands
Live Flesh
Talking to Strange Men
The Bridesmaid
Going Wrong

*Chief Inspector Wexford novels*

From Doon with Death
A New Lease of Death
Wolf to the Slaughter
The Best Man to Die
A Guilty Thing Surprised
No More Dying Then
Murder Being Once Done
Some Lie and Some Die
Shake Hands for Ever
A Sleeping Life
Put On by Cunning
The Speaker of Mandarin
An Unkindness of Ravens
The Veiled One
Kissing the Gunner's Daughter

*Short Stories*

The Fallen Curtain
Means of Evil
The Fever Tree
The New Girl Friend
The Copper Peacock

*Omnibuses*

Collected Short Stories
Wexford: An Omnibus
The Second Wexford Omnibus
The Third Wexford Omnibus
The Fourth Wexford Omnibus
The Fifth Wexford Omnibus

*Novella*

Heartstones

*Non-fiction*

Ruth Rendell's Suffolk

# THE RUTH RENDELL OMNIBUS

The Face of Trespass,
A Demon in My View,
A Judgement in Stone

## Ruth Rendell

LONDON   NEW YORK   SYDNEY   TORONTO

## For Don

I have peace to weigh your worth, now all is over,
   But if to praise or blame you cannot say.
For, who decries the loved, decries the lover;
   Yet what man lauds the thing he's thrown away?

Be you, in truth, this dull, slight, cloudy naught,
   The more fool I, so great a fool to adore;
But if you're that high goddess once I thought,
   The more your godhead is, I lose the more.

Dear fool, pity the fool who thought you clever!
   Dear wisdom, do not mock the fool that missed you!
Most fair,—the blind has lost your face for ever!
   Most fool,—how could I see you while I kissed you?

So . . . the poor love of fools and blind I've proved you,
For, foul or lovely, 'twas a fool that loved you.

*Rupert Brooke*

# Before

The new Member of Parliament finished his after-dinner speech and sat down. He was not, of course, unaccustomed to public speaking but the applause of these men who had been his schoolfellows brought him a slightly emotional embarrassment. Accepting the cigar which the chairman of the Feversham Old Boys' Society was offering him covered for a moment this disturbance of his poise and by the time it was lit for him he was more at ease.

'Did I do all right, Francis?' he said to the chairman.

'You were absolutely splendid. No platitudes, no dirty stories. Such a change to hear a crusader against social outrage! It almost seems a pity we don't have capital punishment any more so that you could abolish it.'

'I hope I wasn't a prig,' said the new Member quietly.

'My dear Andrew, you left-wingers always are, but don't let it worry you. Now do you want another brandy or would you like to – er, circulate?'

Andrew Laud refused the brandy and made his way to one of the tables where his former housemaster sat. But before he reached it someone tapped him on the shoulder and said, 'Congratulations, Andy, on the speech and your success in the by-election.'

'Jeff Denman,' said the M.P. after a moment's thought. 'Thank God for someone I know. I thought I was going to be stuck with old Scrimgeour there and that foul fellow Francis Croy. How are you? What are you doing these days?'

Jeff grinned. 'I'm fine. Now that I'm knocking thirty my family are getting over the disgrace of my driving a van for a living, so if you ever feel like moving house to live among your constituents I'll be happy to oblige.'

'I might at that. Come and have a drink? You know, everyone here seems so *young*. I can't see a soul I know. I thought Malcolm Warriner might be here or that bloke David Something I used to have those fierce arguments with at the debating society.'

'Mal's in Japan,' said Jeff as they went up to the bar. 'He'd be one of your constituents, as a matter of fact, if he were at home. Which brings me to one who isn't here but *is* a Waltham Forest constituent. Remember Gray Lanceton?'

The Member, to whose back this had been addressed, turned and emerged from the crush with two halves of lager in his hands. 'He'd have been a year behind us. Tall dark bloke? Wasn't there a bit of a fuss when his mother remarried and he threatened suicide? I heard he's written a novel.'

'*The Wine of Astonishment*,' said Jeff. 'It was obviously autobiographical, about a sort of hippie Oedipus. He shared my flat in Notting Hill with me and Sally for a bit but he didn't write anything more and when he started to feel the pinch he took Mal's place for somewhere to live rent-free. There was some sort of messy love affair too, I gather.'

'He's living in my constituency?'

Jeff smiled. 'You said "my constituency" like a bridegroom saying "my wife", with shyness and great pride.'

'I know. For weeks I've been thinking, suppose I lose the election and still have to come and talk to you lot? What a fool I'd have felt. Does he like living there?'

'He says the Forest gets him down. I've been out there and I was surprised that there are such remote rural corners left only fifteen miles out of London. It's a weatherboard cottage he lives in, at the bottom of a forest road called Pocket Lane.'

'I think I know it,' said the M.P. and, reflectively, 'I wonder if he voted for me?'

'I'd be very much surprised if Gray even knew there was a by-election, let alone voted. I don't know what's happened to him but he's turned into a sort of hermit and he doesn't write any more. In a way, he's one of those people you've committed yourself to help, the misfits, you know, the lost.'

'I should have to wait till he asked for that help.'

'No doubt you'll have enough on your plate without Gray Lanceton. I see Scrimgeour bearing down on us with the headmaster in tow. Shall I melt away?'

'Oh, God, I suppose so. I'll give you a ring, Jeff, and maybe you'll come and have a meal with me at the House?'

The Member set down his glass and composed his features into that earnest and slightly fatuous expression which, generally reserved for babes in arms and the senile, seemed to do equally well for those pedagogues who had once awed him into terrified submission.

# 1

It was sometime in early May, round about the fifth. Gray was never sure of the date. He had no calendar, he never bought a paper and he'd sold his radio. When he wanted to know the date he asked the milkman. The milkman always came on the dot of twelve, although he had no difficulty about knowing the time because he still had the watch she'd given him. He'd sold a lot of things but he wasn't going to sell that.

'What day is it?'

'Tuesday,' said the milkman, handing over a pint of homogenised. 'Tuesday, May the fourth, and a lovely day. Makes you feel glad to be alive.' He aimed a kick at the young bracken shoots, hundreds of them all tightly curled like pale green question marks. 'You want to get them ferns out of your garden, plant annuals. Nasturtiums'd do well there and they grow like weeds.'

'Might as well keep the weeds.'

'Them ferns'd get me down, but we can't all be the same, can we? Be a funny old world if we were.'

'It's a funny old world now.'

The milkman, who was easily amused, roared with laughter. 'I don't know, you are a scream, Mr L. Well, I must be off down the long long road that has no turning. See you.'

'See you,' said Gray.

The forest trees, which came very close up to the garden, weren't yet in full leaf but a green sheen hung over them, and this bright veil made a dazzlement against the sky. It was prematurely, freakishly hot. Gleaming in the sunshine, the beech trunks were the colour of sealskin. A good metaphor that, he thought, and thought too how once when he was a writer he would have noted it down for future use. Maybe some day, when he'd got himself together and got some money and rid himself finally of her and . . . Better not think of it now.

7

He'd only just got up. Leaving the front door open to let some warmth and fresh air into the dank interior, he carried the milk into the kitchen and put the kettle on. The kitchen was small and very dirty with a slightly sunken floor of stone flags covered with a piece of linoleum curling at its edges like a slice of stale bread. All around him, as he waited for the kettle to boil, were those kitchen appointments which had been the latest mod cons in eighteen-ninety or thereabouts: an earthenware sink, a disused range, an enamel bathtub with a wooden cover on it. The kettle took a long time to boil because it was coated with burnt-on grime and the gas burner wasn't very clean either. Inside the oven it was even worse. When he opened the oven door a black cavern yawned at him. A good many times last winter, sitting in front of the lighted oven in the Windsor chair, sitting in front of the black cave with the gold-tipped blue flames quivering in its heart, he'd been tempted to put out the flames, lay his head within that open door and wait. Just wait for death – 'do something foolish', as Isabel would put it.

He wouldn't do it now. The time for that was past. He would no more kill himself over her than he would over his mother and Honoré, and the time would come when he'd think of her as he did of them – with irritable indifference. Not yet, though. Memories of her still in the forefront of his mind, lying down with him at night, meeting him when he first woke, clinging to him through the long empty days. He drugged them down with cups of tea and library books but they were a long way from being exorcised.

The kettle boiled and he made the tea, poured milk over a couple of Weetabix and sat down to eat his breakfast on the bath counter. The sun was high, the kitchen stuffy because the window hadn't been opened for about a hundred years. Motes of dust dancing in it turned the beam of sunshine into a solid shaft that burned his neck and shoulders. He ate his breakfast in the destruction that wasteth at noonday.

This was her most usual time for phoning – this and, of course, Thursday evenings. While he'd adjusted more or less to not seeing her, he still couldn't manage the problem of the phone. He was neurotic about the phone, *more* neurotic, that is, than he was about other things. He didn't want to talk to her at all but at the same time he passionately wanted to talk to her. He was afraid she'd phone but he knew she wouldn't. When the tension of wanting and not wanting got too bad he took the receiver off. The phone lived in the horrible little parlour Isabel referred to as the 'lounge'. He thought of it as 'living' there rather then standing or just being because, although for days on end it never rang, it seemed alive to him when he looked at it, vibrant, almost trembling with life. And when he took the receiver off on Thursday evenings it seemed baulked, frustrated, peevish at being immobilised, its mouth and ears hanging useless from the dangling lead. He only went into the 'lounge' to answer the phone – he couldn't afford actually to make calls – and sometimes he left the receiver off for days.

Finishing his breakfast and pouring himself a second cup of tea, he wondered if it was still off. He opened the 'lounge' door to check. It was on. Saturday or Sunday he must have replaced it, turning the phone to stare at him like a squat, smug little Buddha. His memory had got very bad since the winter. Like an old man, he could remember the past but not the immediately recent past; like an old man, he forgot the date and the things he had to do. Not that there were many of those. He did almost nothing.

He opened the window on to the greening sunlit forest and drank his tea, sitting in an armchair covered with some early, perhaps the very earliest, prototype of plastic, a brown shiny fabric worn down to its cloth base at the arms and on the seat. There was only one other armchair. Between the two chairs was a low table, its legs made of moulded iron, its top burned by cigarettes from the days when he'd been able to afford cigarettes and marked with white rings from the base of the hot teapot. A stained Turkey rug, so thin that it wrinkled and rucked when he walked on it, lay in the middle of the floor. Apart from these, the only furnishings were Mal's golf clubs resting against the wall under the phone shelf and the paraffin heater on which she'd broken the perfume bottle and which, throughout the winter, had mingled her scent, evocative and agonising, with the reek of its oil each time it was lighted.

He pushed away the thought. He finished his tea, wishing he had a cigarette or, preferably, a whole packet of twenty king-size. Almost hidden by the golf bag under which he'd concealed it, he could see the grey cover of his typewriter. It wouldn't be true to say he hadn't used it since he came to this cottage Mal called the hovel. He'd used it for a purpose he liked thinking about even less than he liked thinking about her, although the two were one and inextricably linked. To think of one was to think of the other. Better dwell instead on Francis's party, on getting away from this hole to London if only for a weekend, to meeting there some girl who would replace her – 'with eyes as wise but kindlier and lips as soft but true, and I daresay she will do'. To getting money together too, and finding a room, to sloughing off this dragging depression, this nothingness, even to writing again . . .

The phone gave the nasty little prefatory click it always made some ten seconds before it actually rang. Ten seconds were quite long enough for him to think in, to hope it was going to ring and at the same time to hope the click wasn't from the phone at all but from the worm-eaten floorboards or something outside the window. He still jumped when it rang. He hadn't learned how to control that, although he had managed to regard his reaction very much as a convalescent regards the headaches and tremors he still has. They will pass. His reason and his doctor have told him so, and meanwhile they must be borne as the inevitable aftermath of a long illness.

Of course it wasn't she. The voice wasn't husky and slow, but squeaky. Isabel.

'You do sound tired, dear. I hope you're eating properly. I just rang to find out how things are.'

'Just the same,' he said.

'Working hard?'

He didn't answer that one. She knew he hadn't done a day's work, an hour's, for three years; they all knew it. He was a bad liar. But even if he lied and said he was working, that didn't help. They only asked brightly when 'it' was coming out and what was it about and said how marvellous. If he told the truth and said he wasn't they told him never to say die and would he like them to try to help get him a job. So he said nothing.

'Are you still there, dear?' said Isabel. 'Oh, good. I thought they'd cut us off. I had a lovely letter from Honoré this morning. He's really wonderful with your mother, isn't he? It always seemed so much worse somehow, a man having to care for an invalid.'

'Don't see why.'

'You would if you had to do it, Gray. It's been a great blessing for you, your mother having got married again and to such a wonderful man. Imagine if you had the looking after of her.'

That was almost funny. He could scarcely look after himself. 'Isn't that a bit hypothetical, Isabel? She married Honoré when I was fifteen. You might as well say, imagine if my father had lived or I hadn't been born or mother'd never had thrombosis.'

As always when the conversation became what Isabel called 'deep', she switched the subject. 'What d'you think? I'm going to Australia.'

'That's nice. What for?'

'My friend Molly that I used to have my typing bureau with, she lives in Melbourne now and she wrote and asked me. I thought I might as well go before I get past it. I've fixed on the beginning of the first week in June.'

'I don't suppose I'll see you before you go,' Gray said hopefully.

'Well, dear, I might drop in if I have a spare moment. It's so lovely and peaceful where you are. You don't know how I envy you.' Gray gritted his teeth. Isabel lived in a flat over shops in a busy Kensington street. Maybe . . . 'I always enjoy a quiet afternoon in your garden. Or wilderness,' she added cheerfully, 'as I should call it.'

'Your flat will be empty, then?'

'Not a bit of it! The decorators are moving in to do a mammoth conversion job.'

He wished he hadn't asked, for Isabel now began to describe, with a plethora of adjectives, precisely what alterations, electrifications and plumbing work were to be undertaken in her absence. At least, he thought, laying the receiver down carefully on the shelf, it kept her off nagging him or harking back to the days when his life had looked promising. She hadn't questioned him about his finances or asked him if he'd had his hair cut. Making sure

11

that the blether issuing distantly from the phone was still happily going on, he eyed himself in the Victorian mirror, a square of glass that looked as if it had just been breathed on or, possibly, spat on. The young Rasputin, he thought. Between shoulder-length hair and uneven beard – he'd stopped shaving at Christmas – his eyes looked melancholy, his skin marked with spots, the result presumably of a diet that would have reduced anyone less healthy to scurvy.

The mirrored face bore little resemblance to the photograph on the book jacket of *The Wine of Astonishment*. That had looked rather like a latter-day Rupert Brooke. From Brooke to Rasputin in five months, he thought, and then he picked up the phone again to catch the breathless tail end of Isabel's sentence.

'. . . And double glazing in every single one of my rooms, Gray dear.'

'I can't wait to see it. D'you mind if I say good-bye now, Isabel? I have to go out.'

She never liked being cut short, would have gone on for hours. 'Oh, all right, but I was just going to tell you . . .'

Hollowly through the phone he heard her dog barking. That would fetch her. 'Good-bye, Isabel,' he said firmly. With a sigh of relief when she had finally rung off, he put his library books into a carrier bag and set off for Waltham Abbey.

Drawing a cheque to cash was the traumatic highspot of his week. For half a year he'd been living on the royalties he'd received the previous November, a miserable two hundred and fifty, drawing at the rate of four pounds a week. But that didn't take into account the gas and electricity bills he'd paid and Christmas expenses at Francis's. There couldn't be much left. Probably he was overdrawn already and that was why he waited, tense and uncomfortable by the bank counter, for the cashier to get up and, having flashed him a look of contempt, depart into some nether regions to consult with higher authority.

This had never happened and it didn't happen now. The cheque was stamped and four pound notes handed over. Gray spent one of them at the supermarket on bread and margarine and cans of glutinous meat and pasta mixtures. Then he went into the library.

On first coming to the hovel, he'd determined, as people do when retiring temporarily from the world, to read all those books he'd never had time for: Gibbon and Carlyle, Mommsen's *History of Rome* and Motley's *Rise of the Dutch Republic*. But at first there had been no time, for she had occupied all his thoughts, and then when she'd gone, when he'd driven her away, he'd fallen back on the anaesthesia of old and well-loved favourites. *Gone with the Wind* would just about be readable again after four months' abstinence, he thought, so he got that out along with Dr James's ghost stories. Next week it would probably be *Jane Eyre*, Sherlock Holmes and Dr Thorndyke.

The librarian girl was new. She gave him the sort of look that indicated she liked unwashed bearded men who had nothing better to do than loaf around libraries. Gray hazarded a return of the look but failed in mid-glance. It was no use. It never was. Her hands were stubby, the nails bitten. She had a ridge of fat round her waist and, while he was among the shelves, he had heard her strident laugh. Her lips were soft but she wouldn't do.

The books and the cans were heavy to carry and he had a long way to go back. Pocket Lane was a deep hole through the forest, a long tunnel to nowhere. The signpost at this end said 'London 15', a fact which still amazed him. He was in the depths of the country but the heart of London was only fifteen miles distant. And it was quieter than the country proper, for here no men worked in the fields, no tractors passed and no sheep were pastured. A bright still silence, broken only by the twitter of birds, surrounded him. He wondered that people actually lived here from choice, voluntarily bought houses here, paid rates, *liked* it. Swinging his carrier bag, he passed the first of these houses, the Willises' farm – so-called, although they farmed nothing – with its exquisite lawns and florist's shop borders, tulips in red and gold uniforms standing in precise rows as if on parade. Next came Miss Platt's cottage, smart brother of the hovel, showing what fresh paint and care could do for weatherboard; lastly, before the rutted clay began and the forest closed in, the shuttered withdrawn abode of Mr Tringham. No one came out to talk to him, no curtain moved. They might all have died. Who would know? Sometimes he wondered how long it would be before they found him if he were to die. Well, there was always the milkman . . .

The hawthorn hedges, fresh green and pearled with buds, ended at the end of the metalled road, and tall trees crowded in upon Pocket Lane. Nothing but bracken and brambles was strong enough to grow under the shade of those trees, in the leaf-mould-crusted clay their roots had deprived of nourishment. Just at this point she had always parked her car, sliding it under the overhanging branches away from the eyes of those most incurious neighbours. How frightened she had always been of spies, of watchers existing only in her imagination yet waiting, she was sure, to relay her movements back to Tiny. No one had ever known. For all the evidence there was of their meetings, their love, none of it might ever have happened. The lush grass of spring had grown over the impress of her car tyres, and the fragile branches which had been broken by that car's passage were healed now and in leaf.

He had only to lift the phone and ask her and she'd come back to him. He wouldn't think of that. He'd think of *Gone with the Wind* and making a cup of tea and what to have for supper. It would be better to think about phoning her after six o'clock when, on account of Tiny, it would be impossible to do so, not now when it was practicable.

They said bracken made a comfortable bed and they were right. He lay on the springy green shoots reading, occasionally going into the hovel for fresh tea, until the sun had gone and the sky behind those interlaced branches was a tender melted gold. The birds and their whispered song disappeared before the sun and the silence grew profound. A squirrel slid down a branch on to the verge where it began to chew through the stem of a small doomed sapling. Gray had long ago got over thinking he was mad because he talked to squirrels and birds and sometimes even to trees. He didn't care whether he was mad or not. It hardly seemed important.

'I bet,' he said to the squirrel, 'you wouldn't mess about drinking tea or, in your case, eating plants, if you knew there was a beautiful lady squirrel panting for you not four miles away. You'd go right off and pick up the phone. You're not messed in your mind like humans and you wouldn't let a lot of half-baked principles get between you

14

and the best lay in Metropolitan Essex. Especially if the
lady squirrel had a whole treeful of luscious nuts stored
away, now would you?'

The squirrel froze, its jaws clamped round the stem.
Then it leapt up the trunk of an enormous beech. Gray
didn't go near the phone. He immersed himself in the Old
South until it grew too dark to read and too cold to lie any
longer on the ground. The sky above him was indigo now
but in the south-west over London a glowing plum-red. He
stood by the gate as he always did at this hour on fine
evenings, looking at the muted blaze of London.

Presently he went into the house and opened a can of
spaghetti. At night the sleeping wood seemed to stir in its
slumber and embrace the hovel entirely in great leafy arms.
Gray sat in the Windsor chair in the kitchen under the
naked light bulb, dozing, thinking, in spite of himself, of
her, finally reading almost a third of *Gone with the Wind*
until he fell asleep. A mouse running over his foot awakened him and he went upstairs to bed in the silent close
blackness.

It had been a typical day, varying only in that it had been
warm and sunny, from the hundred and fifty or so that had
preceded it.

# 2

The Post Office, Gray thought, ought really to pay him a
fee for causing them so little trouble. It couldn't be above
once a week that the postman had to make the long trek
down Pocket Lane to the hovel and then he brought only
bills and Honoré's weekly letter. That had come the previous Thursday in company with the gas bill, a demand for
nine pounds which Gray didn't want to pay until he was
more certain of his financial position. He'd be a whole lot
more certain when he received from his publishers his
royalty statement, currently due. It must be, he reflected,
somewhere about May the twelfth or thirteenth now and
surely that statement would arrive any day.

Meanwhile, he ought to write to Honoré before he did his shopping. *M. Honoré Duval, Petit Trianon* – God, he could never write that without squirming – *Bajon*, followed by the number that signified the department, *France*. He did the envelope first while he thought what to say, always a difficult task. Two cups of tea had been drunk before he started. *Cher Honoré, je suis très content de recevoir votre lettre de jeudi dernier, y inclus les nouvelles de maman . . .* His French was bad but no worse than Honoré's English. If his stepfather insisted on writing in a language of whose grammar and syntax he was abysmally ignorant – just, Gray was sure, to annoy – he would get as good, or as bad, as he gave. A few remarks on the weather followed. What else was there to say? Ah, yes, Isabel. *Imaginez-vous, Isabel va visiter Australie pour un mois de vacances . . . Donnez mes bons voeux à maman, votre Gray.*

That would shut him up for a bit. Gray took *Gone with the Wind* and the ghost stories and set off for the town where he posted his letter, bought half a pound of tea, a giant packet of Weetabix (this week's cheap offer) and two cans of Swedish meatballs. *Jane Eyre* was out and they'd only got one copy. He glowered at the fat girl, feeling ridiculously disappointed, almost paranoid. Didn't they realise he was one of their best customers? If Charlotte Brontë were still alive she'd be short of income through their incompetence.

He took out *The Man in the Iron Mask* and the first of the Herries Chronicles, cast a glance of dislike at the grey pile of the Abbey, and walked gloomily back along Pocket Lane. A cigarette would have done a lot to mitigate the misery of these walks. Perhaps he could give up milk, cut down his tea, and use the resulting savings to buy forty cigarettes a week. Of course it was all absurd, this life. He could easily do something about it. Well, not *easily* but he could do something. Get a labouring job, for instance, or train as a G.P.O. telephonist. Half the telephonists in London were failed authors, broken lovers, unappreciated poets, intellectuals *manqué*. Only a little energy was needed, a scrap of drive . . .

The sun was unseasonably hot and, because of the humidity in this wooded place, unpleasant. In the shadowy gaps between the bushes gnats buzzed in clouds. Sparrows chattered, bathing in dust pockets in the dry clay of the path, and occasionally a jay screamed. The lane was sylvan, unspoilt countryside really, but it had something about it of a dusty room. And no matter what time of the year it was, the dead leaves lay everywhere, brown on the surface, falling to dust and decomposition below.

It was Friday, pay day, so the milkman was late, trundling back along the ruts, his work done.

'Lovely day, Mr L. Makes you feel glad to be alive. May I trouble you for forty-two pee?'

Gray paid him, leaving himself with one eighty to last till he went to the bank next week.

'That's a couple of great books you've got there,' said the milkman. 'Studying, are you? Doing one of them external degrees?'

'The University of Waltham Holy Cross,' said Gray.

'University of Waltham Holy Cross! You are a scream. I must tell the wife that one. Don't you want to know what day it is?'

'Sure. You're my calendar.'

'Well, it's Friday, May the fourteenth, and I reckon you need reminding you've got a date. There's a car parked outside your place, one of them Minis, red one. You expecting some beautiful bird?'

Isabel. 'My fairy godmother,' said Gray glumly.

'Best of luck, Cinderella. See you.'

'See you – and thanks.'

Bloody Isabel. What did she want? Now he'd have to find something to give her for her tea. You couldn't give a sixty-two-year-old Kensington lady ravioli or Weetabix at three in the afternoon. It was some months since he'd possessed a bit of cake. And she was bound to have brought that dog of hers, that Dido. Gray didn't at all dislike Isabel's labrador bitch – in fact, he preferred her to her owner – but his godmother had a nasty way of forgetting to bring anything for the dog's evening meal and of raiding his meagre store of corned beef.

He found her sitting in the Mini's passenger seat, the door open. The labrador was digging a hole among the bracken, snapping sometimes at the flies. Isabel was smoking a king-size cigarette.

'There you are at last, dear. I poked around the back a bit but you hadn't left a window open so I couldn't get in.'

'Hallo, Isabel. Hallo, Dido. When you've dug that lot up you can get planting nasturtiums like the milkman said.'

Isabel gave him rather a funny look. 'Sometimes I think you're alone too much, dear.'

'Could be,' said Gray. Dido came up to him, got up on her hind legs and licked his face, putting her large, clay-filled paws around his neck. He thought she had a beautiful face, much nicer than most human faces – except one, always except one. Her nose was shrimp-pink and ice-cold. She had deep brown eyes – kind eyes, Gray thought, which was a funny thing to think about a dog. 'I'll go and make us some tea.' Dido, who was intelligent in matters of food, wagged her long frondy tail.

Isabel followed him. She pretended not to see the dirty plates or the flies and fixed her eyes on Gray instead.

'I won't ask you why you don't have your hair cut,' she said, laughing merrily and sitting on the back step which she first dusted with her handkerchief.

'Good.' Gray put the kettle on.

'No, but really, dear, you're not a teenager any more. Your hair's down on your shoulders.'

'Since you're not going to ask me why I don't have it cut,' said Gray, 'we may as well talk about something else. I'm afraid I don't have any cake. There's bread.' He considered. 'And Stork.'

'Oh, but I brought a cake.' Isabel creaked to her feet and loped off towards the car. A small fat woman, she wore turquoise trousers and a red sweater. Gray thought she looked like one of Honoré's garden gnomes. When she came back she was smoking a fresh cigarette. 'I won't offer you one. I remember you said you'd given it up.'

Experience should have taught him the cake wouldn't be the large home-made Dundee, marzipanned and iced, which he had been hungrily envisaging. He took the bakewell tart out of its packet. It was already in a foil case so he didn't bother with a plate. The dog walked in and shoved her nose between his hand and the bath cover.

'Now, darling, don't be tiresome.' Isabel always called her dogs darling, reserving this endearment for canines

18

exclusively. 'Perhaps we could go into your lounge. I do like to sit down properly to my tea.'

The phone was still off the hook from the night before. Tiny went to his masonic thing on Thursday nights and if she was going to phone, Thursday evening was the most likely time. Maybe she'd tried. Maybe she often tried on Thursday nights. He put the receiver back on the Buddha's knees, wondering what he'd say or do if she phoned now while Isabel was there. He fancied that today he could smell a faint breath of *Amorce dangereuse*, brought out perhaps by the warmth. Isabel watched him dealing with the phone. She preserved a tactful, heavily curious silence that was scarcely more endurable than her questions. She had armed herself, he noticed, with a box of tissues as might someone suffering from a heavy cold. Isabel didn't have a cold. She dusted the seat of her armchair with one tissue, spread another on her lap and asked him finally how he was getting on.

Gray had given up placating the old. It necessitated too many lies, too much elaborate subterfuge. Life might have been easier if he had deceived Isabel and Honoré into believing he was actually writing another novel, that the place was filthy because he couldn't get a cleaning woman, that he lived in Pocket Lane because he liked it. But he told himself that the approval of people he didn't himself approve of wasn't worth having so, accordingly, he replied that he wasn't, in the accepted meaning of the phrase, getting on at all.

'What a pity that is, dear. You were such a lovely little boy and you used to have such marvellous school reports. And when you got your degree your mother and I had such high hopes of you. I don't want to say anything to hurt you, but if anyone had asked me to predict your future in those days, I'd have said you'd be at the top of the tree by now.'

'You won't hurt me,' said Gray truthfully.

'And then you wrote that book. Not that I liked it myself. I don't care for books without a proper story. But all the people who know about these things forecast a wonderful career for you. And, oh, Gray dear, what has it come to?'

'Pocket Lane and Swedish meatballs,' said Gray, blessing Dido for causing a diversion by sweeping her tongue across his plate.

19

'Take your face off the table, darling. Cake isn't good for doggies.' Isabel lit a fresh cigarette and inhaled dizzily. 'What you need,' she said, 'is some outside interest, something to take you out of yourself.'

'Like what?'

'Well, that's really why I've come. No, I must be honest. I've come to ask you a favour but it would be very good for you as well. You'd admit you need something to do?'

'I'm not taking a job, Isabel. Not your sort of job, anyway. I can't be a clerk or a salesman or a market researcher, so can we get that clear from the start?'

'My dear, it's nothing like that. This isn't *paid*. It isn't a job in that sense. I only want you to do something for *me*. I may as well come straight to the point. What I want you to do is look after Dido for me while I'm in Australia.'

Gray said nothing. He was watching a fly which was either eating, or laying eggs on, a lump of icing that had fallen on to the rug. Dido was looking at it too, her eyes going round in wild circles when the fly rose sluggishly from the crumb and drifted about in front of her nose.

'You see, dear, I've never left her since she was a puppy and she's five now. I couldn't put her in kennels. She'd fret and I shouldn't enjoy myself knowing she was fretting.'

London, Kensington, just to get away, and so easily. 'You mean, look after her in your flat?'

'*No*, dear. I told you I was having builders in. Look after her here, of course. She loves it here and your not having a job means she wouldn't be left alone. You could take her out for lovely walks.'

It wouldn't be too bad, he supposed. He liked Dido better than he liked most people. And Isabel would provide her food with possibly a little extra in the shape of actual money.

'How long for?'

'Just four weeks. I go on Monday, June the seventh. My aircraft leaves Heathrow at three-thirty. What I thought was I could bring Dido to you on the Sunday evening.'

'Sunday the sixth?'

'That's right.'

'Sorry, Isabel,' said Gray firmly. 'Not possible. You'll have to find someone else.'

20

He wasn't going to give up Francis's party, especially for Isabel. Francis's party was the only thing he had to look forward to, the only thing that kept him going, he thought sometimes. He'd planned ahead for it, deciding to go up on the Sunday morning, wander round the Park, look at the street vendors in the Bayswater Road and arrive at Francis's by about four. That would mean helping to get food ready and hump crates of booze, but he didn't mind that, particularly as it would get him into Francis's good books and secure him the offer of a bed for the night. Well, not the night but the period of from five in the morning till he woke up somewhere around noon. He had had fantasies about this party, real people to talk to, unlimited drink and cigarettes, the new girls, one of whom might be the one to make him forget and with whom he might even share that bed or couch or carpet or patch of floor. The idea of sacrificing this for anything less than severe illness or his mother's dying or something equally seismic made him feel almost sick.

'Sorry, but I'm doing something that Sunday.'

'Doing what? You never do anything.'

Gray hesitated. It was one thing to resolve not to placate the old, quite another to stick this system out. He could tell Isabel he'd be dining with his publishers but that was improbable on a Sunday night and, knowing he hadn't published anything for three years, she was unlikely to believe it. Again he decided on the truth.

'I'm going to a party.'

'On a *Sunday*? Oh, Gray dear, I do find that strange. Unless you're going to see someone there you might – well, who might give you a helping hand?'

'Very possibly,' said Gray, thinking of the imaginary girl. Not wanting to be jesuitical, he added, 'This party's just for pleasure, no strings. But I want to go. I'm sorry, Isabel. I see you think it's selfish and maybe immoral – yes, you do – but I can't help that. I'm not putting off this party for you or Dido or anyone.'

'All right, dear, don't. I can manage to bring Dido the next morning. I can bring her at twelve and go on from here to the airport.'

Christ, he thought, that was persistence for you. No

wonder she'd made a fortune bludgeoning executives into employing her illiterate little typing pool rejects.

'Isabel,' he said patiently, 'this is not going to be a cocktail party where nice middle-aged fuddy-duddies eat twiglets and drink martinis from six till eight. This is going to be more in the nature of an all-night orgy. I shan't get to bed till five or six and, naturally, I shan't want to leap up again at nine to get back here and receive you and your dog.'

'You're very frank!' Isabel tossed her head and coughed in a futile effort to prevent his seeing how deeply she had blushed. 'I should have thought a little natural shame about carryings-on of that kind wouldn't be out of place. You might have had the decency to think up some excuse.'

They didn't even want you to be truthful. They knew you liked sex and liquor – in fact, they thought you liked them a hell of a lot more than you did – but you were supposed to put up some Victorian pretence that a simple Westbourne Grove rave-up was really a conference at the Hyde Park Hotel.

'Can I have one of your cigarettes?'

'Of course you can. I would have offered, only I thought you'd given it up. Now, dear, why shouldn't I bring Dido at twelve and just put her in the house – shut her in the kitchen, say, till you get home?'

'O.K., you can do that.' There was evidently no escape. 'I'll be back around three. I suppose she'll be all right for three hours?'

'Of course she will. I'll leave her some water and I'll leave you enough tins and money for fresh meat to last you out.' Isabel went off into a long string of instructions for Dido's proper care, while the dog, unobserved by her owner, though not by Gray, removed the remains of the bakewell tart from the table. 'Now what about a key?'

When he first came to the hovel there had been three keys. One he carried about with him, one hung on a nail above the kitchen sink, and the third – probably she had thrown it away by now, along with anything else she had to remember him by. Gray went out and fetched the spare key.

'I'll shut her in the kitchen because, though she's very clean *normally*, she might have a little accident if she's alone in a strange place.'

22

Gray said that little accidents would make small difference to the general grot in the hovel, but he agreed to this, telling Isabel the kitchen window didn't open.

'That won't matter for three hours, as long as you make a fuss of her when you come in and take her for a nice walk. I'll put the key back on the hook, shall I?'

Gray nodded. While Isabel wiped her mouth and brushed her lap with fresh tissues, he put out his hand to the dog who gambolled over at once, licked his fingers and sat down beside him, leaning her soft golden weight against his knees. He let his arm fall over her as it might encircle a woman's shoulders. The warmth of flesh, of blood pulsing, was a strange sensation to him, new in a way. This wasn't human flesh and blood; there was no infinity of mind under that shapely skull. But the very touch of warmth, and the pressure of what seemed like real affection, brought him a sudden sharp pain, brought home to him the agony of his loneliness. And at that moment he was terribly near to tears for loss, for unconquerable apathy, for waste and for his own feeble self.

But it was in his normal voice that he said, 'We'll be all right, won't we, Dido, my old love? We'll get on fine.'

Dido lifted her head and licked his face.

# 3

At some sleepy hour, about eight perhaps, he heard a letter flop on to the front-door mat. It couldn't be another one from Honoré, not yet. The electricity bill – too small to distress his bank account – was paid; the final demand for the gas wasn't due yet, surely. It must be that royalty statement at last. And about time too. Not that it would announce some huge windfall, but if it was only a hundred, only fifty . . . Just a tiny bit of capital like that would give him the incentive to get away from here, find a room in London, take a job working in a bar or washing-up till he got himself together to write again.

The bedroom was filled with pale light, moving as wind tossed the beech branches. He lay there, thinking about London, about Notting Hill, Ladbroke Grove switchbacking up to Kensal Green, people in the streets all night. No branches, no clay, no leaves crepitating and rustling wherever you walked, no more vast blank days. Although he didn't expect to sleep again, he dozed off into a dream – not of London, as might have been expected, but of her. In the weeks following their separation he had dreamed of her every night, had been afraid to sleep because of those dreams, and they still came often, once or twice a week. Now she was in the room with him, this very room, the wind blowing her hair that was neither red nor gold nor brown but a fox-fur blend of all three. And her eyes, the colour of smoky crystal, were on him.

She said holding out a little hand the rings shackled, 'We'll talk about it. There's no harm in just talking.'

'There's no point either.'

She didn't listen to his reply. Perhaps he hadn't made it aloud. Who knows in dreams? 'It's been done before,' she said. 'Lots of people in our sort of situation have done it. You'll say they got caught.' He said nothing, only gazed into those eyes. 'You'll say that, but we don't know about all the ones who didn't get caught. They're the kind we'll be.'

'Yes, darling, yes, Gray . . .' Closer now, her hair blown against his skin. He put out his arms to hold her, but her flesh was hot and that flying hair flames. He shrank, pushing away the fire, crying out as he surfaced from the dream, 'I couldn't do it, I couldn't kill a fly . . . !'

There was no staying in bed after that. Shivering from the effect of her presence – for is a dream woman less a presence than a real one? – he got up and pulled on jeans and faded tee-shirt. Gradually his body stopped shaking. Reality splashed back in hard light and loneliness and the dull hopeless safety of being without her. He looked at his watch. Half past eleven. He wondered what day it was.

Almost the first thing he saw when he got downstairs was a cow's face, white and gingery brown, looking at him through the kitchen window. He opened the back door and went out into the patch of stinging nettles, birch saplings and hawthorn that was supposed to be a garden. It was full

24

of cows milling about under the sagging greyish washing he'd left hanging on the line since Sunday. The Forest wasn't fenced and farmers could let their cattle wander about as they pleased, which was a cause of misery and frustration to the garden-proud. Gray approached the cows, patting several of them on their noses which had much the same feel as Dido's and addressing them aloud on the virtues of anarchy and contempt for property. Then he remembered the letter, the royalty statement, and he went in to fetch it. But before he picked it up, the stamp on the envelope – that bloody affected Marianne strewing flowers or whatever – told him he'd been wrong.

'My dear son . . .' Gray was used to that by now but it still made him wince. 'My dear son, I try to telephone to you thursday last evening but the line is occupied and again friday and the line still occupied. How gay the life you have with many friends! You must not be unquiet but mummy is again not well and the doctor Villon say she have an other attack of paralyse. There is much work here for me who is habituate to be just a poor infirmier and work all day and night making care of your mummy.

'Now it will be good if you come. Not today I mean but be ready to come if mummy is not so well. For that when you must come I will talk to you with the telephone to tell you now is the time you must come my son. You will say you have no money to pay the train or the avion company but I will send you the money not in a letter as that is against law which I will not but to your bank that is Midland in Waltham Abbey as you have said where you can take it when you must come. Arrangements for this I make. Yes you say this is funny. Honoré pay money to me when he is caring so for his little saved money but old Honoré know the duty of a son for his mummy and for this he break the rule of sending no money to a son who work not at all make arrangement for the bank to have thirty pounds of money.

'Do not be unquiet. Doctor Villon say the good God take mummy not yet and no need to send to Father Normand but tell you who is her one son and child. Be calm my boy. Your loving papa Honoré Duval. P.S. I have borrowed to the mayor the french traduction of your book you have gave me and he read when he has leisure. You will like to

25

have the critique of a man of reason what the mayor is.
H.D.'

Gray knew that the mayor of Bajon's sole claim to literary judgement was the fact of his great-aunt's having been maid to a cousin of Baudelaire. He screwed the letter up and threw it behind the bath. Honoré knew perfectly well he could read French without difficulty but he insisted on writing in the horrible dining-room English he had picked up while a waiter in Chaumont. Gray didn't suppose his mother's life was really in danger and he wasn't prepared to rely on the word of Dr Villon, another one of Honoré's cronies along with the mayor at Bajon's local, the Écu d'Or.

He wouldn't go so far as to say he didn't care whether his mother lived or died, and he certainly intended to fly over to France if she were really on her deathbed, but he hadn't much feeling for her left. It would be false to say that he loved her. It had been a great shock to him when, touring through France with Isabel, his mother had fallen in with – Gray wasn't prepared to say fallen in love with – one of the waiters at the Chaumont hotel. He had been fifteen, his mother forty-nine and Honoré probably about forty-two. Honoré even now never revealed his true age, making out he was a poor old man on whom the duties of nursing weighed heavily. They had got married very quickly after that, Honoré being well aware, Gray knew, that his betrothed owned the car she was travelling in as well as, far more important, a fairly large house on Wimbledon Common. Whatever its effects on the bride's relatives, the marriage had apparently worked out wisely and well. The Wimbledon house had been sold and Honoré had built a bungalow in his native village of Bajon-sur-Lone, where they had lived ever since. Mme Duval had become a Catholic on her marriage, another departure which Gray found hard to forgive. He had no religion himself, largely due to his mother's having taught him agnosticism from his cradle. All that had gone when she remarried. Now she had the priest to tea and put ashes on her forehead on mercredi-des-cendres, or had done when she had been well enough. The first stroke had hit her four years before. Gray had gone over then, paying his own fare out of money earned by selling short stories, and again when she had the

26

next one, relying this time on part of the handsome advance on his novel. Sometimes he wondered how he was going to make it when the *attaque de paralyse* struck again, perhaps fatally. Now he knew. Honoré would stump up.

Honoré *had* stumped up. It was quite pleasant to think of the money being there, waiting for him, making his own waiting for that statement less fraught with worry. He mixed some packet curry with water, heated it in a saucepan and ate it on the front doorstep while watching the cows who had begun to wander off in search of richer pastures than Mal's nettle bed. At twelve sharp the milkman arrived.

'I've got my own dairy,' said Gray, who sometimes felt obliged to live up to his reputation as an entertainer. 'You'd better watch out or you'll find yourself redundant.'

'Got your own dairy? You're a real comedian, you are. Them cows is all bullocks, or hadn't you noticed?'

'I'm just a simple Londoner and proud of it.'

'Well, it takes all sorts to make a world. Wouldn't do if we was all the same. Just for the record, it's Thursday, May the twentieth.'

'Thanks,' said Gray. 'See you.'

'See you,' said the milkman.

Gray did a mammoth wash-up, his first for four or five days, read the last chapter of *Rogue Herries* and set off down the lane. Rain had fallen at the beginning of the week and the clay was soggy, churned up by the hooves of the twenty or so bullocks who had left behind them steaming pats of dung from which rose a sour scent. He caught up with them outside the gate to the farm. He didn't know much about Willis except that he had a hatchet-faced wife and a red Jaguar. But cows live on farms; these cows evidently wanted to get into this farm; obviously it was the place for them. He opened the gate, a fancy affair of cartwheels stuck between bars, and watched the cows canter clumsily in the way cows have, up the gravel drive and across Mr Willis's lawn. This was a sheet of glistening green velvet on to which a sprinkler scattered a fine cascade of water drops. He leant against the gatepost, interested by the cows and amused at their antics.

Three of them began immediately to devour tulips, stalks and vermilion blooms sprouting from their jaws in a way

27

that Gray thought rather delightful and reminiscent of some Disney cartoon. The others jostled each other about the lawn and one began to make its way round the back of the house. He was just moving off again, shifting his books to his other arm, when a bedroom window of the farmhouse was flung open and a voice screamed at him:

'Did you open that gate?'

The hatchet-faced Mrs Willis.

'Yes. They wanted to come in. Aren't they yours?'

'*Ours?* When did we ever keep cattle? Can't you see what you've done, you stupid man? Look what you've done.'

Gray looked. The exquisite moist turf was mashed by the indentations of some eighty cloven feet.

'I'm sorry, but it's only grass. It'll heal up or whatever the right term is.'

'Heal up!' yelled Mrs Willis, leaning out and shaking her arms at him. 'Are you mad? D'you know what it's cost my husband to get his lawn like that? Years and years of labour and hundreds of pounds. You ought to be made to pay for what you've done, you – you long-haired layabout. I'll see to it my husband makes you pay if he has to take you to court.'

'Oh, piss off,' said Gray over his shoulder.

Screeches of reproach, threats of retribution and of shocked disgust at his language pursued him down the lane. He felt rather cross and shaken, a state of mind which wasn't improved by finding, when he got to the bank five minutes before they closed, that he had just two pounds, forty-five pence in his account. This he drew out, remembering Honoré's thirty which should arrive any day. It wouldn't do, however, to splash out on any fancy tins. He returned *Rogue Herries* and *The Man in the Iron Mask* and took out *Anthony Absolute, The Prisoner of Zenda* and *No Orchids for Miss Blandish*, all in paperback treated with the sort of fortifying process the library went in for. They were light to carry and on the one day he didn't need a lift he got one. He had just entered Pocket Lane when Miss Platt's car pulled up beside him.

'I'm so glad I saw you, Mr Lanceton, because I want to ask you if you'll come to my little party on Tuesday fortnight.'

Gray got into the car. 'Your what?' he said. He hadn't meant to be rude, for he liked what he knew of Miss Platt, but the idea of anyone of seventy giving a party and out here was so novel as to be shocking.

'Just a few friends and neighbours in for drinks and a sandwich at about seven on June the eighth. I'm moving, you see. I've sold the house and I'm moving out on the ninth.'

Gray muttered something about being sorry to hear that. They passed the farm which the cows had now left. Mrs Willis was on the lawn, prodding at the broken turf with a rake.

'Yes, I sold it the same day I advertised it. Really, I thought the price the agent told me to ask was quite ridiculous – fifteen thousand pounds for a cottage! Can you imagine? – but the man who's bought it didn't turn a hair.'

'It's a lot of money,' Gray said. He could hardly believe it. Miss Platt's place was just like the hovel, only smartened up a bit. Fifteen thousand . . .

'House prices have trebled around here in the past few years. The Forest can't be built on, you see, and yet it's so near London. I've bought the flat above my sister's in West Hampstead because she's really getting past looking after herself. But it seems dreadful after this lovely spot, doesn't it?'

'I wouldn't say that,' said Gray sincerely. 'You'll have a great time.'

'Let's hope so. But you will come?'

'I'd like to.' A thought struck him. 'Will the Willises be there?'

'I haven't asked them. Are they particular friends of yours?'

'I think Mrs Willis is my particular enemy. I let the cows into her garden.'

Miss Platt laughed. 'Oh, dear, you must be unpopular. No, there'll just be me and my sister and Mr Tringham and a few friends from Waltham Abbey. Do you often hear from Malcolm Warriner?'

Gray said he'd had a postcard with a picture of Fujiyama at Easter, thanked Miss Platt for the lift and got out. He made a pot of tea and sat in the kitchen reading *The Prisoner of Zenda* and eating slices of bread and Stork. The wind had risen, blowing the clouds and making the place quite dark, though it was still early. He lit the oven and opened it to give him some warmth.

It wasn't till the phone started ringing that he remembered the milkman had said it was Thursday, the night he always took the receiver off. His watch said ten past seven. Tiny would have been off to his masonic thing an hour ago. Every Thursday night she tried to get him, but she'd never been able to because the receiver was always off. It wasn't off tonight and she was succeeding. Of course it was she. She would speak to him, he would speak to her, and in half an hour she would be here. He moved towards the 'lounge', the phone, not rushing but walking slowly and deliberately as a man may walk to an inevitable, hated, yet desired, fate. His heart was thudding, it actually hurt. She was in that phone like a genie in a lamp, waiting to be released by his touch, to flow into and fill the room, red-gold, crystal green, *Amorce dangereuse*.

He was so certain it was she that he didn't say hallo or give Mal's number but said what he'd always said when he knew it was she phoning, 'Hi,' miserably, resignedly, longingly, in a very low voice.

'Gray?' said Francis. 'I want to speak to Graham Lanceton.'

Relief? Despair? Gray hardly knew what he felt unless it were the beginning of a coronary. 'This is me, you fool. Who did you think it was? D'you think I keep a staff?'

'It didn't sound like you.'

'Well, it was. It is.'

'Really, this is getting ridiculous. You sound as if you're messing your mind properly out in that dump. Look, I'm phoning about this party. Could you possibly come up on the Saturday?'

Ten minutes before he'd have been excited at the very idea. 'Yes, if you like,' he said.

'I've got to meet this aged relative at Victoria on the Saturday morning and I want someone to be here when the blokes come to fix up some rather fancy electric wiring I'm having done for the party. A sort of blink arrangement that has quite an alarming psychedelic effect.'

'I'll be there. I can get to you by ten.' His heart had stopped pounding. As he put the phone down, he felt limp, sick. He sat in the brown plastic armchair, in the dusk, and

30

stared at the silent secretive phone, the detached self-confident phone that had snapped shut its organs like a sea anemone, and squatted on its seat, not returning his gaze but withdrawn now as if it were asleep.

Christ, but he mustn't start investing the thing with a personality. That was real neurosis. That could lead to only one end, to a ward in a mental hospital and E.C.T. or something. Better anything than that. Better dial her number now, talk to her, establish once and for all that there was never again to be any contact between them.

But they'd established that at Christmas, hadn't they?

'If you phone me, I'll put the receiver down.'

'We'll see about that,' she'd said. 'You wouldn't have the will-power.'

'Don't try me then. I've told you till I'm sick of it, if you can't leave off getting at me about that obsession of yours, it's no use any more. And you can't obviously.'

'I do what I want. I always do what I want.'

'All right, but I don't have to do what you want. Goodbye. Go away now, please. We shan't see each other again.'

'You're bloody right there,' she'd said.

So it had been a pact, hadn't it? I've loved you faithfully and well two years or a bit less, it wasn't a success. . . . If it had been a pact, why did he hope and fear? Why did he take the receiver off? Because she'd been right and if she phoned he wouldn't have the will-power to resist. Because he knew confidently, proudly, that five months' separation wouldn't be long enough to stop her loving him. But, as a woman, maybe she wouldn't risk the humiliation of phoning him and being repulsed. He could phone her . . .

Tiny wouldn't be home before eleven. She was alone there, he alone here. It was all ridiculous. He was making himself ill, ruining his life. He jerked out of the chair and stood over the phone.

Five-O-eight . . . He dialled that bit fast but paused before going on with the rest of the number, the four-digit bit. Then he dialled it more slowly, dialled three of the numbers. He inserted his finger in the nine hole, let it linger there, trembling, pulled it out with a soft 'Oh, Christ', and banged the side of his hand down on the receiver rest. The receiver dropped, swinging, knocking against the golf clubs.

31

It wasn't any good. For one evening, maybe for a whole week, he'd have her in peace, but it would start again, the nagging, the one topic of conversation that filled the spaces between love-making. And he couldn't keep on stalling the way he'd stalled last summer and last autumn because in the end he'd have to tell her he couldn't do it. He'd have to say, as he'd said at Christmas, that if it was doing that or not seeing her he'd choose not seeing her.

He went out of the front door and stood among the bracken the cows had flattened into a prickly mattress. Black branches whipped against a sky of rushing cloud. Over there, behind him, lay Loughton, Little Cornwall, Combe Park. It was ironic, he thought wearily, that he was longing for her and she for him, that only four miles separated them, that the phone would link them in a second; that neither had qualms about betraying Tiny or revulsion for adultery, but they could never meet again because she wouldn't stop demanding what he wouldn't do, and he couldn't, under any circumstances, agree to do it.

# 4

He didn't sleep much that night. Probably this was due to his not following his usual sleep-inducing method, the writer's resource, of telling himself a story as soon as he laid his head on the pillow. Instead, he did what he'd done those sleepless nights of January, thought about her and their first meeting.

Yet he'd hardly intended to get on to it. He lay there, examining the curious results of haphazard chance, how some tiny alteration of purpose or a word spoken by a friend, a delay or a small change in the day's routine, may ineluctably dictate the course of a life. Such had happened when his mother and Isabel, awakened in the small hours by the phone ringing – a wrong number, of course – and unable to sleep again, had set off earlier than they'd intended and reached Dover in time to catch the first boat. Because of this they were down as far as Chaumont by the evening, although they shouldn't really have been there till the next night when Honoré would have been off duty. Who had made that phone call? What careless unthinking arbiter had misdialled at four in the morning and so made a marriage and changed a nationality?

In his own case, he knew his arbiter's identity. Jeff had helped himself to the last twenty sheets of typing paper – for what? To make out some removals bill? Some list of household goods? – and he'd had to go out to Ryman's and get a fresh ream. The branch in Notting Hill were out of stock. Why hadn't he walked across the Park to the branch in Kensington High Street? Because the 88 bus had stopped at the red light. At that moment the traffic lights had turned red, the bus had stopped and he had got on it. So was it the light that had made his fate, or the buyer who hadn't got the paper in, or Jeff, or the householder who had to have a list of tables and chairs made before he could move? Useless to go on. You could get back to Adam that way, back and back, trying to learn who spun, who held the scissors and who cut the thread.

The 88 took him down Oxford Street and he'd gone to Ryman's in Bond Street. He'd always felt good with a fresh ream of paper under his arm. It wasn't daunting but a challenge, that virgin pack he would fill with richness. And because he'd been dwelling on this, looking down and not where he was going, he'd crashed into her before he even saw her face, cannoned right into the girl who was walking towards him, so that her parcels tumbled on to the pavement and her scent bottle broke against a shop window-ledge.

He could smell it now, the same smell that had lingered so long in the hovel. It rose in a hot heady cloud, steaming on the crisp January air.

'Can't you look where you're going?'

'The same applies to you,' he'd said, not very politely, and then, softening because she was beautiful, 'I'm sorry about your perfume.'

'So you bloody should be. The least you can do is buy me another bottle.'

He shrugged. 'O.K. Where do we get it?' He thought she'd refuse then, say it didn't matter. The impression he had of her as they stood close together, picking up parcels, was that she wasn't at all badly off. A red fox coat, the same colour as her hair, cream leather boots – at least thirty quid's worth – rings bulging through the fine leather gloves.

'In here,' she'd said.

He didn't mind. At that time, though not rich, he was richer than he'd ever been before or since. He followed her into the hot crowded store, holding his small square packet of paper.

'What's it called, that stuff of yours?'

They were at a vast series of cosmetic counters.

'*Amorce dangereuse.*'

It cost him nearly six pounds. The price was so ridiculous, her childlike simple acceptance of it so straightforward – she happily dabbed some of it on his wrist as well as on her own – that he burst out laughing. But he stopped laughing abruptly when she brought her face close to his, laid a hand on his arm and said, whispering, 'D'you know what it means, the name of that perfume?'

'Dangerous bait, dangerous allure.'

'Yes. Rather apt.'

'Come on. I'll buy you a coffee or a drink or something.'

'I can't. I have to go. Get me a taxi.'

He hadn't much liked being commanded, but he hailed a taxi and gave the driver some address in the City she'd told him. While he was holding the door open for her, holding it rather ironically because she took so much for granted, took and tempted and withdrew, she almost floored him with a farewell remark thrown casually over her shoulder.

'Tomorrow, seven, New Quebec Street. O.K.?'

Certainly it was O.K. It was fantastic, also absurd. The taxi moved off, lost itself in the traffic. His hand smelt of *Amorce dangereuse*. Tomorrow, seven, New Quebec Street. He didn't know where New Quebec Street was but he'd find it and he'd be there. An adventure wouldn't do him any harm.

Had he really thought of it like that before it had begun, as an adventure? He remembered that he had and also that it would very likely come to nothing. Arrangements like that which gave the parties thirty hours to think in so often came to nothing . . . But that was how it had happened. Jeff had pinched the last of his paper and, godlike, sent him to Bond Street and to her. Jeff had ruined him, kind Jeff who wouldn't hurt a fly. By rights, then, Jeff ought to save him, though no one, of course, could do that except himself.

For he had been ruined. The ream had been started on but only about a hundred of the sheets used up. How can you complete a novel whose purpose is to explore the intricacies of love as you know them when halfway through you find your whole conception has been wrong? When you find that the idea of love on which you based it is vapid and false because you've discovered its true meaning?

Dreaming of her, thinking about her, all night, he was purged of her by the morning. But he knew this wasn't a full catharsis. Possessing him again, his succubus would come to him again in the day and the next night.

A strong furious gale howled about the hovel. No post had come for days. Pushing her firmly out of a mind that felt excoriated, he began worrying about his royalty statement. Why hadn't it come? The last one had arrived early in November, stating the income he'd made up to the previous June, and he'd had the cheque by the end of the month. By now, well by now, he ought to have had the statement for his earnings from June till December. *Maybe there wasn't anything to come.* In the days when the cheques had been for several hundreds he'd never considered whether they'd bother to tell him if there wasn't any money to pay out. Perhaps they didn't. Perhaps their accountants or cashiers or whatever just went heartlessly through a list of names and when they came to him, said, 'Oh, Graham Lanceton? Nothing for him. We can forget him.'

He hunted out the November statement which he kept in a strong-box in the spare bedroom. There was a phone number on the top of it, the number of their accounts department which was somewhere out in Surrey, miles from the London office. Gray knew that any responsible practical author would simply dial that number, ask to speak to someone in authority and enquire what the hell had happened to his money. He wasn't keen on doing this. He didn't feel he could take, at this period of his life, after the night he'd spent, the brusque voice of some accountant living on a safe three thousand a year telling him his coffers were empty. What he'd do, he decided, was wait one more week and if it still hadn't come he'd phone Peter Marshall. Peter was his own editor and a very nice bloke who'd been charming and hospitable when *The Wine of Astonishment* was born into a waiting world and still charming and kind, though wistful, when it was clear *The Wine of Astonishment* was to have no siblings. Of course, he'd ask if Gray was writing anything and remind him they had the first option on any full-length work of fiction he might produce, but he wouldn't nag or be unpleasant. He'd promise very kindly and reassuringly to look into the matter for him and maybe ask him to lunch.

This decision made, he examined his larder. It was obvious that even he couldn't exist until the end of the month on two cans of Mincemeat, a packet of raspberry jelly and the rock-hard end of a Vienna loaf. Money must be acquired. He thought vaguely of touching Francis (fairly hopeless), of the Social Security (if he was going to do that he'd pack up and do it in London), of selling his watch to the shop near the Abbey which was already in possession of his lighter. He didn't want to part with that watch. The only thing would be to use Honoré's money or part of it. The sheer awfulness of using money sent to one for the reaching of one's mother's deathbed chilled him, but he told himself not to be stupid. Presumably even Honoré wouldn't want him to starve.

It had begun to rain, was now pouring with rain. He put on Mal's oilskins which hung in the cellar and trudged off through the rain to the bank. There he drew out ten pounds which he meant to spend very sparingly indeed, reducing himself if necessary to a diet of milk, bread and cheese till the cheque came. He had stuffed the money into a pocket of the oilskins and when he fished in it for a pound he brought out with it a crumpled sheet of paper. Reading it, Gray could hardly believe his eyes. It was nearly six months since he'd worn these oilskins – generally he stayed in when it rained – and he must have shoved the letter from his publishers' contracts manager into this pocket sometime in December. It was dated just before Christmas – Oh, Drusilla, that Christmas! – and it informed him that the Jugoslavian serial rights of *The Wine of Astonishment* had been sold for fifty pounds. A measly sum, but money. He must be going to get a cheque, they hadn't forgotten him. Right, he wasn't going to stint himself. He bought fresh meat, frozen vegetables, bread, real butter and forty cigarettes, one of which he lit as soon as he was outside the shop.

It made him feel a bit faint. Apart from the one he'd had off Isabel, it was the first he'd smoked since the autumn when he'd always helped himself out of her packets of King-sized.

'I'll have to give it up,' he'd said then. 'It gets on my conscience, Tiny keeping me in fags, because that's what it amounts to.'

'It needn't be that way.'

'Don't start. Let's have one day of rest.'

'You mentioned him. You brought Tiny up.'

There had been no talk of Tiny that first time, no ridiculous diminutive bandied between them, only the hint of a husband somewhere in the background.

'Mrs Harvey Janus? My God, if I were Mr Harvey Janus I wouldn't be too happy about this, but since I'm not . . .'

Waiting for her in New Quebec Street, in the complex that lies behind Marble Arch, he hadn't even known her name. She was late and he'd begun to think she wasn't coming. The taxi drew up at twenty past seven when he was on the point of giving up, of realising that it wasn't any use wondering where he was going to take her, whether they were going to walk about or go into a pub or what. A hand was thrust out of the window, beckoning him. She sat in the middle of the seat, dressed in white trousers, a fur jacket, a huge black hat and huge black sun-glasses. Sun-glasses in January . . .

'Hi. Get in.'

He looked at the driver who was staring deadpan in front of him.

'Come on, get in.' She tapped on the glass. 'The Oranmore Hotel, Sussex Gardens. You don't know it? Can't say I'm surprised. Keep going down Sussex Gardens, it's nearly halfway down on the right.'

To say he was flabbergasted was an understatement. He got in, raising his eyebrows at her, and then closed the glass panel between them and the driver. 'You might put me in the picture.'

'Oh, isn't the picture clear? There's an old girl and her husband keep this place. You just register when we get there, and she'll say you want to pay now, don't you, in case you're leaving early in the morning.'

'Well, well.' He couldn't get over the speed of it, the lack of preamble. 'We don't have to leave too early in the morning, do we?'

'We have to leave at nine-thirty tonight, ducky. Just two hours we've got. She'll tell us to leave the key on the dressing table when we go. For God's sake, you don't know much about it, do you?'

'My women usually have flats or rooms.'

'Well, I'm a married lady and just for your information I'm supposed to be at my yoga class.' She giggled and in that giggle he heard a note of childlike triumph. 'It's not everyone I'd sacrifice my yoga class for.'

'I'll do my best to make it worth your while.'

The Oranmore turned out to be an early nineteenth-century house that had probably once been a brothel. It had its name in blue neon over the front door, but both the Os were blacked out. He registered as Mr and Mrs Browne – not so much because the name is common as through association with the title of a peerage – and was given a key for number three. The old woman behaved exactly as had been predicted.

On the stairs Gray said, 'Do you have a first name, Mrs Browne?'

'It's Drusilla,' she said.

He unlocked the door. The room was small with twin beds, Junk City furniture, a washbasin, a gas ring. Drusilla pulled down the window blind.

'Drusilla what?' he said, going up to her, putting his hands on her waist. It was a very narrow fragile waist and when he touched it she thrust her pelvis forward. 'Drusilla what?'

'Janus. Mrs Harvey Janus.'

'My God, if I were Mr Harvey Janus I shouldn't be too happy about this, but since I'm not . . .' He unfastened the fur jacket. Underneath it she was naked. He had expected that somehow. Already he was beginning to assess her, the kind of things, daring, provocative, direct, she would do. But he gasped just the same and stepped back, looking at her.

38

She began to laugh. She took off her hat, the knot of pearl strings from her neck, the jacket, sure, he thought, that she had the situation under control, that it was going to be her way. But he'd had enough of her running things.

'Shut up,' he said. He picked her up, lifting her bodily, and she stopped laughing, but her lips remained parted and her moonstone eyes grew very wide. 'That's better. Two hours, I think you said?'

She had hardly spoken again for those two hours. That time she hadn't told him anything about herself, hadn't asked his name till they were downstairs again, passing the old woman who, playing her part, had wished them a pleasant evening and reminded them not to forget their key. He took her to the Tube at Marble Arch and at the entrance, between the newspaper vendors, she said, 'Next Thursday? Same time? Same place?'

'Kiss?'

'You've got an oral fixation,' she said, but she put up her lips which were thin, delicate, unpainted.

He'd bought a packet of cigarettes, lit one and begun to walk all the way back to Notting Hill. How had that cigarette tasted? He couldn't remember. The one he was inhaling on now was ash-flavoured, a hot rasping smoke. He threw it away among the bracken, half-hoping it would start a fire and the whole of lonely silent Pocket Lane go up in flames.

That day he hadn't even seen the milkman and he didn't see anyone else to talk to throughout the weekend. No trippers, no picnickers, penetrated so far down the lane. Only old Mr Tringham passed the hovel, taking his Saturday evening walk, apparently his only walk of the week. Gray saw him from the window, strolling slowly, reading from a small black book as he walked, but he didn't lift his head or glance to either side of him.

The phone, still off its hook, hung dumb.

# 5

In the middle of the week he got the final demand from the Gas Board and, by the same post, a card from Mal. 'Coming home August. Not to worry. We can share the hovel till you find another place.' Mal wouldn't like if it he came back to find they'd cut off the gas, which they'd certainly do if the bill wasn't paid by the weekend. No royalty statement had arrived.

Friday morning and as bitterly cold as November. He'd saved one cigarette and he lit it as he dialled his publishers' London number.

'Mr Marshall is out for the day,' said the girl they'd put him on to. 'Can I help?'

'Not really. I'll phone him on Monday.'

'Mr Marshall starts his holiday on Monday, Mr Lanceton.'

That, then, was that. For the rest of the day he debated whether to phone the Surrey department but by half past five he still hadn't done so and then it was too late. He decided to write to them instead, a good idea which he couldn't understand not having thought of before. When he'd finished the letter and its carbon copy, he sat with his fingers resting on the typewriter keys, thinking about the last time he'd used the machine. The ribbon was nearly worn clean. He'd worn the ribbon out writing those letters to Tiny. The absurdity, the grotesquerie, of that business made him wince. How had he ever been such a fool as to let her persuade him so far, to type those dreadful letters with her standing over him? He'd better make sure he remembered that next time he was tempted into phoning her.

The phone was on its hook, but it had a passive look as if it were asleep. It hadn't made a sound since it had opened its mouth more than a week ago to let Francis speak through it, and he hadn't again contemplated ringing that Loughton number. He took his letter and stuck it on the hall window-sill. Tomorrow he'd buy a stamp for it.

Saturday was bath day. Until he came to the hovel he'd hardly ever passed a day without a bath. Now he understood why the poor smell and he saw how insensitive are those bathroom owners who won't sympathise with the dirty because washing is free and soap cheap. When you wanted a bath at the hovel you had to heat water up in two saucepans and a bucket and then you didn't get enough hot to cover your knees. Back in the days when he was Drusilla's lover he went through this ritual quite often or stood up at the sink and washed himself all over in cold water. You needed an incentive to do that. After the parting there wasn't much incentive. The milkman never got very close to him and he was past caring what the librarian thought, so these days he had a bath on Saturday and washed his hair in the bath. Then he used the same water to wash his jeans and tee-shirt.

All the week he used the bath as a repository for dirty sheets, chucking them on to the floor as a sort of absorbent mat when he was actually in the water. He hadn't been to the launderette for ages and they were getting mildewed. He washed his hair and was just rinsing it, dipping it into the scummy water, when the phone belched out its warning click. Ten seconds later it began to ring. It couldn't be Drusilla, who went shopping with Tiny on Saturdays, so he let it ring till he was out of the bath and wrapped in a grey towel.

Cursing, leaving footprints on the stone hall floor, he went into the 'lounge' and picked up the phone. Honoré.

'I disarrange you, I think, my son.'

For once, his choice of a word was apt. Gray gathered the damp folds around him, forgetting to talk French in the slight anxiety the call had caused.

'How's Mother?'

'That is for why I call. Mother goes better now so I say, I call to Gray-arm and give him these good news so he is no more unquiet.'

Wants his money back, more like, thought Gray. '*Que vous êtes gentil, Honoré. Entendez, votre argent est arrivé dans la banque. Il paraît que je n'en aurai besoin, mais . . .*'

Trust Honoré to interrupt before he'd reached the point of asking whether he could keep the money a little longer.

41

'Like you say, Gray-arm, you need my money no more and old Honoré know you so well.' Gray could see the brown finger wagging, the avaricious knowing smile. 'Ah, so well! Better for you and me you send him back, *hein*? Before you spend him for wine and women.'

'This call,' said Gray, whose French wasn't adequate for what he wanted to say, 'is going to cost you a lot.'

'Very sure, so I say good-bye. You send him back today and I get you again if Mummy go less good.'

'Right, but don't phone next weekend as I'll be at Francis Croy's place. *Vous comprenez?*'

Honoré said he understood very well and rang off. Gray ran the water out of the bath. It was evident his mother wasn't dying and the money wasn't going to be needed for any trip to France, but it was absurd Honoré wanting it back at once. What difference could it make to him whether he got it now or in, say, a fortnight? Didn't he own his own house and car, all bought out of Gray's father's life assurance? Now he knew his mother wasn't dying, Gray allowed himself to dwell on a usually forbidden subject – her will. Under that, he and Honoré were to have equal shares. When she died ... No, he'd let himself sink into enough deep dishonour without that. She wasn't going to die for years and when she did he'd have a flat of his own in London and a string of successful novels behind him.

Because it had begun to rain, he draped his wet clothes over a line he put up in the 'lounge' and read *Anthony Absolute* dejectedly till the milkman came. The lane had turned bright yellow in the wet, the colour of gamboge in a paint-box, and the wheels of the van were plastered with it.

'Lovely weather for ducks. Pity we're not ducks.'

Gray said savagely, 'God, how I hate this place.'

'Don't be like that, Mr L. There's some as likes it.'

'Where do you live?'

'Walthamstow,' said the milkman stoically.

'I wish I lived in Walthamstow. Beats me how anyone can live out here from choice.'

'The Forest's very desirable residentially like. Some of them big houses Loughton way are fetching prices you wouldn't believe. Real high-class suburbia, they are.'

'Christ,' said Gray feelingly. He didn't like to see the milkman look so bewildered and crestfallen, and to know he'd been the cause of it. But his words had gone in like a knife teasing an already open wound.

'Where do you live?' he'd said, drawing one finger down the smooth white body, white as lily petals, blue-veined. 'I don't know anything about you.'

'Loughton.'

'Where's that, for God's sake?'

She made a face, turning her shoulder, giggling. 'Real high-class suburbia. You keep going for ever down the Central Line.'

'D'you like that?'

'I have to live where Tiny lives, don't I?'

'*Tiny*?'

'It's just a nickname, everyone calls him that.' She put up her arms, holding him, saying, 'I like you a lot, Mr Browne. Let's keep this going a bit longer, shall we?'

'Not in this dump. Can't I come to your suburb?'

'And have all my neighbours dropping hints to Tiny at bridge parties?'

'Then you'll have to come to Tranmere Villas. Will you mind other people being in the flat?'

'You know,' she said, 'I think I'll like it.'

His eyebrows went up. 'That doesn't quite go with the Loughton housewife bit.'

'Damn you, I married him when I was eighteen, that's six years ago. I didn't know then. I didn't know a thing.'

'You don't have to stay with him.'

'I have to stay,' she said. 'God, who asked you to criticise my life style, Mr Justice Browne? That's not what I miss my yoga class for. That's not what I strip off for. If you don't want it I'll soon find someone who does.'

Toughness, sophistication, hung on her like a call girl's see-through dress on an *ingénue*. For that's what she was, an *ingénue*, a green girl, a late starter and he was only her second lover. She didn't admit she knew the Oranmore because she'd been there with her first, or New Quebec Street because she'd once bought a vase in the pottery shop. She didn't admit it but he was a writer and he could tell. He could tell she got that smart wisecracking talk of hers out of books, bought her Harrods' clothes because

43

she'd seen them advertised in magazines at the hair-dresser's, her hard brittle manner out of films seen at Essex Odeons. He wanted to find the little girl that existed some-where underneath it all and she wanted equally hard to stop him knowing the little girl was there.

When he met her at the station he knew at once she'd never been to Notting Hill before. If he hadn't stopped her she'd have crossed the street to the Campden Hill side. No one else seeing her would have guessed the under-lying naivety from her appearance, the long purple dress, the silver chains, the purple paint on her mouth, for her face was made up that night. He took her to the flat and it was he, not she, who was put off by the bedroom door being accidentally opened and as quickly closed again. So he took her for a walk up through the drab, exotic, de-caying streets of North Kensington, into little pubs with red plush and gilded saloon bars. They saw a sad skeletal boy giving himself a fix in a telephone box. She didn't find it sad; her eyes were greedy for what she called life and she made out so well that he almost forgot how innocent she was.

'That cinema,' he said, 'they smoke in there. The air hangs blue with it.'

'They what? Everyone smokes in cinemas.'

'I meant pot, Drusilla.'

The little girl turned on him furiously. 'Damn you! I can't help not knowing. I want to know. I want to be free to know things and you – you bloody laugh at me. I want to go home.'

And then he had really laughed at her, poor little child in adult's clothes, who wanted both to be free and to be safe at home; little sheltered girl, protected all her life. Tantalised by innocence that should, but didn't, go hand in hand with prudery, thinking only of the delight she gave him, he hadn't considered the full significance of a child in a grown-up body. He hadn't thought then what it must mean – to have an adult's subtlety, command of language and sensual capacity without an adult's humanity.

'I didn't know you owned a house,' Gray said when Mal dropped in at Tranmere Villas one night, a fortnight before he left for Japan.

44

'It's just a hovel, no hot water, no mod cons. I had a Premium Bond come up about five years ago and someone said property was the thing, so I bought this place. I go to it sometimes at weekends.'

'Where is it, for God's sake?'

'Epping Forest, near Waltham Abbey. I was born near there. I mention it because I was wondering if you'd like to take it on while I'm away.'

'Me? I'm a Londoner. It's not my scene.'

'It's just the place for you to write your masterpiece. Isolated, dead quiet. I wouldn't want rent. But I do want someone to see it doesn't fall into rack and ruin.'

'Sorry. You've come to the wrong shop.'

'Maybe the right shop,' said Mal, 'would be an estate agent's. I'd better try and sell it. I'll get hold of an agent in Enfield or Loughton.'

'*Loughton?*'

'It's four miles from there. D'you know it?'

'In a sort of way I do.'

So he'd agreed to take care of the hovel because it was only four miles from Loughton. . . .

'A funny sort of lane east of Waltham Abbey?' said Drusilla when he told her.

' "The beds i' the East are soft." '

'Beds, floor, stairs, kitchen table, it's all the same to me, ducky. I expect I could pop over quite often.'

The beds were no longer soft. There is no bed so hard as the one deserted by one's lover. For her sake he had come here and now she was gone there was no longer anything to keep him but poverty.

He paid the gas bill, went to the library (*The Sun is My Undoing, The Green Hat, King Solomon's Mines*) but forgot to buy a stamp. Well, he'd buy one on Monday, post the letter, and soon as the money came – as soon as there was a definite prospect of the money – he'd shake the dust of this place off his feet for ever.

Mr Tringham went by at six-thirty, reading his book. He too could become like that one day, Gray thought, a hermit who has grown to love his solitude and who jealously preserves it. He must get away.

45

and no Thursday ever passed without his thinking of her alone, perhaps taking her own receiver off as he was doing now. He stood looking at the deadened instrument for some time, just standing there and looking at it. Alexander Graham Bell had a lot to answer for. There was something sinister, frightening, dreadful, about a telephone. It seemed to him as if all the magic which in ancient times had manifested itself in divination, in strange communions across land and ocean, in soul-binding spells, conjurations, fetishes that could kill by the power of fright, were now condensed and concentrated into the compact black body of this instrument. A night of sleep might depend on it, days of happiness; its ring could break a life or raise hilarity, wake the near-dead, bring to the tense body utter relaxation. And its power was inescapable. While you possessed one of its allotropes – or it possessed you – you were constantly subject to it, for though you might disarm it as he had just done, it wasn't really gagged. It always retained its ultimate secret weapon, the braying howl, the long-drawn-out crescendo cry of an encaged but still dangerous animal, which was its last resort. Hadn't she once put the howlers on him when, by chance – no leaving the receiver off deliberately in those days – he'd replaced it imperfectly?

'Playing hard to get, lovey? You can't get away from me as easily as that.'

But he had got away and into his miserable high-principled freedom, though not easily, not easily – how long would it take before it got easier? He slammed the door shut on the muck and dust and the immobilised phone and went upstairs to look out some gear to wear at Francis's party. His one decent pair of trousers, his one good jacket, were rolled up in the bottom of the bedroom cupboard where he'd slung them after that London weekend with Drusilla. He took out the cream silk shirt, dirty and creased, breathing from its creases as he unfolded it *Amorce dangereuse*. In the darkening bedroom with its low ceiling, rain pattering overhead on the slates, he knelt on the haircord, on the tea stains, and pressed the silk against his face, smelling her smell.

'Shall I wear your shirt to go out in? Do I look good?'

'You look great,' he'd said. Fox-gold hair cloaking the cream silk, blood-red fingernails like jewels scattered on it,

48

her naked breasts swelling out the thin, almost transparent stuff. 'What am I supposed to wear? Your blouse?'

'I'll buy you another shirt, ducky.'

'Not with Tiny's money, you won't.'

Tiny had gone on a business trip to Spain. That was how they'd managed the weekend. Until then he'd never had a whole night with her. He'd wanted Cornwall but she'd insisted on London, the Oranmore.

'I want to go to way-out places and do decadent things. I want to explore vice.'

'Doriana Gray,' he said.

'Damn you, you don't understand. You've been free to do what you like for ten years. I had my father keeping me down and I went straight from him to Tiny. There's always been someone bloody looking after me. I can't go out without publishing where I'm going or making up lies. I'll have to phone Madrid in a minute to keep him quiet. You don't know what it's like never to do *anything*.'

'Darling,' he'd said very tenderly, 'they're nothing, these things, when you're used to them. They're boring, they're ordinary. Imagine the people who think living in your place and having your clothes and your car and your holidays the acme of sophistication. But to you it's all – ordinary.'

She took no notice of him. 'I want to go to awful places and smoke pot and see live shows and blue films.'

Christ, he'd thought, she was so *young*. That's what he'd thought then, that it was all bravado, and they'd quarrelled because his London wasn't the London she said she wanted; because he wouldn't take her round Soho or to the drag ball she'd seen advertised, but to little cinemas with mid-thirties kitsch décor, Edwardian pubs, the Orangery in Kensington Gardens, the Mercury Theatre, the mews and the canal at Litle Venice. But she'd enjoyed it, after all, making him laugh with her shrewd comments and her flashes of surprising sensitivity. When the weekend was over and he back at the hovel, he'd missed her with a real aching agony and it wasn't just laziness that made him not wash out the shirt. He kept it unwashed for the scent that imbued it, knowing even then when their affair was a year old and almost at its zenith that the time would come when he'd need objects to evoke memory, objects in which life is petrified, more present (as he'd read somewhere) than in any of its actual moments.

Well, the time had come, the time to remember and the time to wash away memories. He took the clothes downstairs, washed the shirt and went down into the cellar. He hadn't got an electric iron but there was an old flat-iron in the cellar, left there by the occupant before Mal.

The cellar steps were steep, leading about fifteen feet into the bowels of the Forest. It was a brick-walled, stone-flagged chamber where he kept his paraffin and where former owners had left a broken bike, an antique sewing machine, ancient suitcases and stacks of damp yellowish newspapers. The iron was among these newspapers along with the thing Gray thought was called a trivet. He took it up to the kitchen and put it on the gas.

Now that he'd made up his mind to leave the hovel, he no longer had to pretend to himself that this kitchen where he'd spent the greater part of two years was less horrible and squalid than it was. In all the time he'd never really cleaned it and the condensation of cooking and gas fumes had run unchecked, unwiped, down the pea-green painted walls. The sink was scored all over with brown cracks and under it was a ganglion of grime-coated pipes, hung with dirty cloths. An unshaded bulb, hanging from the veined and cobwebby ceiling, illuminated the place dully, showing up the cigarette burns and the tea stains on the lino. Mal had asked him to see it didn't go to rack and ruin, so it was only fair to Mal to clean it up. Next week he'd have a real spring clean.

It was pitch-dark outside, soundless but for the faint pattering of rain, He got up out of the Windsor chair and spread his velvet trousers on top of the bath cover. He'd never handled the flat-iron before, only electric irons with insulated handles. Of course, he knew very well you needed a kettle holder or an old sock or something before you got hold of a hot iron bar, but he'd acted instinctively, without thought. The pain was violent, scarlet, roaring. He dropped the iron with a shout, cursing, clutching his burnt hand and falling back into the chair.

When he looked at his hand there was a bright red weal across the palm. And the pain travelled up his wrist, his arm, a pain that was almost a noise in the silence. After a while he got up and held his hand under the cold tap. The shock was so great that it brought tears to his eyes, and when he'd turned off the tap, and dried his hand, the tears didn't stop. He began to cry in earnest, abandoning himself to a storm of weeping, sobbing against his folded arms. He knew he wasn't crying because he'd burnt his hand, though that had caused the first tears. Full release had never come to him before, the release of all that pent-up pain. He was crying now for Drusilla, for obsession unconquered, for loneliness and squalor and waste.

His hand was stiff and painful. It felt enormous, a lump of raw flesh hanging from the end of his arm. He hung it outside the bed, the sour sweat-smelling sheets, and lay, tossing and turning, until the birds started their dawn song and pale grey waterish light came through the faded curtains. Then at last he slept, falling at once into a dream of Tiny.

He'd never seen Drusilla's husband and she'd never described him to him. She hadn't needed to. He knew very well what a forty-year-old rich property dealer would look like, a man whose facetious parents or envious schoolfellows had called Tiny because even as a child he'd been huge and gross. A vast man with thinning black hair, who drank hard, smoked heavily, was vulgar, taciturn and jealous.

'What does he talk about? What do you do when you're alone together?'

She giggled. 'He's a man, isn't he? What d'you think we do?'

'Drusilla, I don't mean that.' (Too painful to think, or imagine, then or now.) 'What have you got in common?'

'We have the neighbours in for drinks. We go shopping on Saturdays. He's got his old mum that we go and see once a week after the shopping, and that's a right drag. As a matter of fact, he collects old coins.'

'Oh, *darling*!'

'It's not my bloody fault. He's got his car, it's a red Bentley, and we go out in that to eating places with his dreary middle-aged mates.'

Tiny was in that car, the red Bentley he'd never seen, when he dreamed about him. He was standing by the side

Moonstone eyes, the colour of transparent cloud through which the blue sky shows; white skin, blue-veined at the temples; hair like the pale hot flames that warmed them.

'I'd like you to be a kept man. I'd like Tiny to die so that we could have all that loot for us.'

'What, marry me, d'you mean?' The thought had never before crossed his mind.

'To hell with marriage! Don't talk about it.' She shuddered, speaking of marriage as some people speak of cancer. 'You don't want to get married, do you?'

'I'd like to live with you, Dru, be with you all the time. Marriage or not, I shouldn't mind.'

'The house alone'd fetch a fortune. He's got hundreds of thousands in the bank and shares and whatever. Be nice if he had a coronary, wouldn't it?'

'Not for him,' he said.

The watch she'd given him just ten months before the end of it all told him now it was twelve noon. But it was Friday, so the milkman wouldn't get there till nearly three. He went down into Waltham Abbey, returned the library books but took out no fresh ones, and at the bank drew out seven pounds, thus emptying his account. On the way back he met the milkman who gave him a lift to the hovel on his van.

'Going to be a scorcher tomorrow, I reckon,' said the milkman. 'If you're out when I come I'll pop the milk in the shade, shall I?'

'I shan't want any milk till Monday, thanks. Come to think of it, I shan't want any more milk ever. I'm moving out next week.' That would spur his going. He could always buy milk when he went into Waltham Abbey for the few days that remained to him of next week. 'Getting out of here for good,' he said.

The milkman looked quite upset. 'Well, it'll make my work lighter. I shan't have to come all the way down here. But I'll miss you, Mr L. No matter how I felt, I could always count on you to cheer me up.'

One of the Pagliacci, Gray thought, one of the sad clowns. All the time he'd been so wretched the milkman had seen him as a light-hearted joker. He'd have liked to have achieved just one last mild wisecrack – very little wit was ever needed – but he couldn't manage it. 'Yes, well, we've had a good laugh, haven't we, one way and another?'

'It's what makes the world go round,' said the milkman. 'Er – you won't mind me pointing out you owe me forty-two pee?'

Gray paid him.

'When are you going?'

'Tomorrow, but I'll be back again for a few days.'

The milkman gave him his change and then, unexpectedly, held out his hand. Gray had to take it and have his own blistered hand shaken agonisingly. 'See you, then.'

'See you,' said Gray, though the chances were he'd never see the milkman again.

He had nothing to read and his burnt hand kept him from starting on the spring clean. Instead, he passed the rest of that hot day sorting through his papers, some of which were in the strong-box, the rest in an untidy heap on top of the disused range. It wasn't a task calculated to cheer him. Among the pile on the range, he found four old royalty statements, each one showing a smaller amount than its predecessor, a demand for back tax he hadn't paid, and – most troubling of all – a dozen drafts of, or attempts at, letters to Tiny.

Re-reading them made him feel a little sick. They were only pieces of paper, creased, soiled, thumb-marked, some bearing no more than two or three lines of typed words, but the motive behind them had been destructive. They had been designed to lure a man to that holocaust, realised, as it happened, only in dreams of fire.

Each one was dated, and the whole series spanned a period from June to December. Although he'd never really intended that any one of them should be sent, although he'd typed them only to humour her, he felt that he was looking at a side of himself which he didn't know at all, at a cruel and subtle *alter ego* which lay buried deep under the layers of idleness, talent, humanity and saneness, but was nevertheless real. Why hadn't he burned them long ago? At any rate, he'd burn them now.

In a space that was clear of nettles down by the back fence he made a little fire and fed it with the letters. A thin spire of smoke, sequinned with red sparks, rose into the night air. It was all over and dead in five minutes.

He'd never before seen the Forest in its golden cloak of morning mist, it was so rare for him to be up this early. The squirrel was sitting where the fire had been.

'You can move in if you like,' Gray said. 'Be my guest. You can keep your nuts in the cellar.'

He bathed and put on a tee-shirt and the velvet trousers, hoping the hole didn't show. The silk shirt was to be saved for Sunday night and he packed it into his bag along with his toothbrush and a sweater. There was no point in going into the 'lounge' before he left or changing the filthy sheets, but he washed the dishes and left them to drain. By nine he was on his way to the station at Waltham Cross.

The Tube didn't come out this way. You had to catch a train that went from Hertford (or somewhere equally remote) to Liverpool Street. The powers that be, he often thought, had been singularly narrow in their attitude to the travel requirements of the residents of Pocket Lane and its environs. It was possible to go to London or Enfield or places no one would want to go to in Hertfordshire, extremely difficult to get to Loughton or anywhere in that direction except by car or on foot. The only time he'd been to Loughton he'd walked to the Wake Arms and caught the 20 bus that came from Epping.

'I can't think why you want to see my place,' she'd said, 'but you can if you want. You could come on Thursday evening. Just this once though, mind. If the neighbours see you I'll say you came selling encyclopaedias. They think I have it off with the tradesmen, anyway.'

'I hope you'll have it off with this tradesman.'

'Well, you know me,' she said.

Did he? The Thursday they'd chosen was in early spring when the trees of the Forest weren't yet in leaf but hazed all over with the golden brown of their buds, when the flowers were on the blackthorn but the holly berries still scarlet. He caught the bus to one of the fringe-of-the-Forest ponds, a water-filled gravel pit, overlooked by the large houses that sprang up in this district on every bit of land they'd let you build on. Everywhere there were trees, so that in summer the houses would seem to stand in the Forest itself. It would be, he'd decided, in such a one that she lived, a four-bedroomed, Tudor-style villa.

56

She'd drawn him a little plan and told him which way to go. The sun had gone but it would be an hour yet before it was dark. He walked along a road on one side of which open green land, dotted with bushes, fell away into a valley. Beyond this valley the Forest rose in blue-black waves. On the other side were old cottages of weatherboard and slate like the hovel, new houses, a pub. They called the district he was approaching, the part where she lived, Little Cornwall, because it was exceptionally hilly and from its hills, she'd said, you could look down into Loughton which lay in a basin below, and then on and on over Metropolitan Essex, over the 'nice' suburbs, the distant docks, and see sometimes the light shining on the Thames.

It was too dark for that by the time he'd reached the top of the hill. Lights were coming out everywhere over the blue spread of land. He turned off along Wintry Hill and found himself in a lane – gates in high fences, trees overhanging, long drives disappearing into shrubberies and leading to distant hidden houses. The Forest hung behind them, densely black against a primrose sky. And he felt that this was very different from the area around the pond. This was grandeur, magnificence and, in a way, awesome. Her house (Tiny's house) was called Combe Park, a name which she'd got haughty and self-conscious about when she'd mentioned it and which he'd laughed at as absurdly pretentious.

But it wasn't pretentious. He came to the end of the lane to face wrought-iron gates which stood open. The name Combe Park was lettered on these gates and he saw at once that it hadn't been bestowed with the intention to impress on some detached three-bedroomed affair. The grounds were enormous, comprising lawns and flower-beds and an orchard which was a mass of daffodils, a pond as large as a small lake and ringed with rockeries on which cypresses, twice as tall as a man, were dwarfed by overhanging willows and cedars. The neighbours would have needed periscopes as well as binoculars to see the house through those tree screens. Not that the house itself wasn't large. He saw an enormous box, flat-roofed and balconied, part of white stucco, part cedar-boarded, with a kind of glass sun lounge on its roof and a York stone terrace spreading away from front door and plate-glass picture windows. The terrace was set about with white metal furniture and evergreens in marble urns.

At first he'd thought it couldn't be hers, that he couldn't know (let alone, love) anyone that affluent. But this was Combe Park all right. The triple (quadruple? quintuple?) garage, a large house in itself, had its doors wide open and inside he could see the E-type, reduced to Mini scale by the vastness of its shelter. There was no red Bentley to keep it company but, just the same, he didn't move from the position he'd taken up and in which he felt frozen outside the gate. He didn't want to go in, he wasn't going in. He forgot then that it was he who'd invited himself, who'd insisted, and thought only of his poverty, her wealth, and that if he set foot on that drive, and began to walk up it under her eye, he'd feel like the village boy sent for by the squire's lady. And he might start getting greedy too. He might start thinking of that coronary she'd wished on Tiny.

So he'd walked back to the bus-stop, caught the bus after half an hour's wait, walked back to Pocket Lane, and before he'd been in the house five minutes the phone started.

'Damn you! I saw you at the gate and I came down to open the door and you'd bloody gone. Were you scared?'

'Only of your money, Drusilla.'

'God,' she'd said, drawling then, the little girl voice submerged in the lady-who-picks-up-men voice. 'It could all be yours if he had a heart attack or a car crash. Yours and mine. Wouldn't that be super?'

'That's just pointless fantasy,' he'd said.

He got on the Circle at Liverpool Street and out at Bayswater. Queensway, very lively with its clothes shops and fruit shops, Whiteley's Cupola, the interesting trendy people, cheered him up. And the weather was perfect, the bright blue sky giving Porchester Hall an almost classical look to his London-starved eyes.

Francis lived in one of those old streets of Victorian houses each one separate and each one different, each in its garden of very old London shrubs and town flowers that seem faded to pale pinks and golds by dust and hard light, which lie to the north of Westbourne Grove. Francis's flat was the conservatory of one of these houses, a red and blue crystal palace partitioned off into two rooms with bath-room and kitchen added.

He opened the crimson glass door to Gray and said, 'Hallo, you're late. Just as well I don't have to meet my aunt after all. We can get on with moving the furniture. This is Charmian.'

Gray said, 'Hi,' and wished he hadn't because Hi was what he said to Drusilla. Charmian, who in any case was probably booked for Francis, wasn't the girl to rid him of Drusilla, being plump, snub-nosed and ungainly. She had a lot of jolly fair curls and she wore a very short skirt which showed her fat thighs. While she looked on, sitting cross-legged on a window-sill and eating a banana, Gray helped Francis move the enormous Victorian sideboard and tall-boy from the living room into the bedroom, and moved beds out to make divans for exhausted, lecherous or stoned guests. His hand was thickly bandaged but it throbbed, sending shafts of pain up his arm.

Francis said discouragingly, 'I tried to phone you to tell you not to bother to come till tomorrow but your line's always engaged. I suppose you leave the receiver off. What are you scared of? Your creditors?'

Charmian laughed shrilly. The receiver was still off, Gray realised. It had been off since Thursday evening.

Presently the men arrived to fix up the winking lights. They took hours about it, drinking very inferior tea made by Charmian with tea bags. Gray wondered when they were going to get a meal, as both Francis and the girl had said they were on diets. At last the men went and the three of them went down to the Redan where Francis and Char-mian drank orange juice in accordance with their diets and Gray drank beer. It was nearly six o'clock.

'I hope you've got some money on you. I've left mine in my other jacket.'

Gray said he had. He thought Francis lucky to possess another jacket. 'When you've had that orange juice, maybe you'll go back and fetch it and then we can eat somewhere.'

'Well, actually, Charmian and I are dining with some people we don't know very well. I only mention that about our not knowing them to show we can't exactly take a stranger with us.'

'Not very well,' said Charmian. She had been staring fixedly at Gray for some minutes and now she launched

59

with Tiny, the room that overlooked those black waves of forest. Tiny would be there too, asleep possibly; possibly sitting up reading one of those books he was so fond of, memoirs of some tycoon or retired general, and she'd be reading a novel. Although he'd never been in the bedroom, he could see them, the gross bloated man, curly black hair showing at the open neck of red and black silk pyjamas, the slim girl in white frills, her fiery hair loose, and around them all the lush appointments of a rich man's bedroom, white pile rugs, white brocade curtains, Pompadour furniture, ivory and gold. Between them, the white, silent, threatening phone.

He could phone her but not speak to her. That way he'd hear her voice. When she didn't know who was calling, when it wasn't someone to say 'Hi' to, she just said 'Yes?' with cool indifference. She'd say 'Yes?' and when there wasn't any reply, 'Who the hell *is* that?' But he couldn't phone her now, not at midnight.

He walked down past the Odeon Cinema to Marble Arch. The last of the queue was going in for the midnight movie. There were still a lot of people about. He knew he was going to have to phone her. It was as if it was too late to go back, though he'd done nothing, taken no decisive step, only thought. He went into Marble Arch Tube station and into a phone booth. For two pence he could buy her voice, a word or two, whole sentences if he was lucky and got a bargain. His heart was thudding and his hands were wet with sweat. Suppose someone else answered? Suppose they'd moved? They could be on holiday, taking the first of those two or three annual holidays which in the past had brought him postcards and loneliness. With a sweaty hand he lifted the receiver and placed a finger in the five slot on the dial.

Five-O-eight, then all the four digits including the final nine. He leant against the wall, the receiver cold as ice against his branded palm. I am a little mad, he thought, I'm breaking down . . . They might have gone out with those friends to a roadhouse, they might . . . He heard the whistling peep-peep that told him he was through and, trembling, he pressed in his coin. It fell through the machinery with a hollow crash.

'Yes?'

Not Tiny, not some newcomer, but she. The single monosyllable was repeated impatiently. 'Yes?'

He'd resolved not to speak to her but he needed no resolve. He couldn't speak, though he breathed like one of those men who phone women in the night to frighten them. She wasn't easily frightened.

'Who the hell's that?'

He listened, not as if she were speaking to him – as indeed she wasn't – but as though this were a tape someone was playing to him.

'Listen,' she said, 'whoever you are, some bloody joker, you've had your kick, you pervert, so just piss off!'

The phone went down with a crack like a gunshot. He lit a cigarette with shaking fingers. Well, he'd had what he wanted, her voice, the last of her to remember. She'd never speak to him again and he'd be able to remember for ever her parting words, the positively last appearance of the prima donna – 'piss off, you pervert'. He went back into the street, swaying like a drunk.

It was about ten in the morning when Francis appeared by his bed with an unexpected cup of tea. Francis had slept in the bedroom, Gray on one of the beds that had been moved into the main room where the sun now penetrated in red, blue and golden rays through the glass and made dancing blobs on the floor.

'I owe you an apology for that carry-on in the pub yesterday. Charmian's a wonderful girl but she is impulsive.'

'That's all right.'

'I Spoke To Her About It,' said Francis rather pompously. 'After all, what you'd take from an old mate like me doesn't come too well from someone you've just met. But she's a marvellous girl, isn't she?'

Gray smiled neutrally. 'Are you and she . . . ?'

'We aren't yet having a sexual relationship, if that's what you mean. Charmian views these things very seriously. Time will tell, of course. It might be as well for me to consider marriage quite soon.'

'Quite soon?' said Gray, alarmed at possible interference with his plans. 'You and Charmian mean to marry quite soon?'

63

'My God, no. It may not even be with Charmian. It's just that I think marriage should be the next big event I plan for in my life.'

Gray drank his tea. Now was the moment and he'd better seize it. 'Francis, I want to come back to London.'

'Of course you do. I've been telling you for ages.'

'I'll get paid quite soon and when I do – well, could I come here for a bit while I look for a room?'

'Here? With me?'

'It wouldn't be for more than a month or two.'

Francis looked rather sour. 'It'll be very inconvenient. I'd have to have help with the rent. This place costs me eighteen a week, you know.'

There'd be at least fifty when the cheque came . . . 'I'd go halves.'

Maybe it was his guilt over the lecture he'd exposed Gray to the night before that made Francis put aside his usual scepticism when his friend mentioned making monetary contributions to anything. 'Well, I suppose so,' he said ungraciously. 'Let's say you'll stay six weeks. When d'you want to come? Charmian and I are going down to Devon to her people tomorrow for a few days. How about next Saturday?'

'Saturday,' said Gray, 'would suit me fine.'

After he'd had a bath – in a proper bathroom with hot water coming out of a tap – he walked over to Tranmere Villas. Jeff was still in bed and it was the tenant of Gray's old room, the room where just once he'd made love to Drusilla, who admitted him to the flat.

'Sally out?' he said when Jeff appeared, sleepy, gloomy and myopic without his glasses.

'She's left me. Walked out a few weeks back.'

'God, I'm sorry.' He knew how it felt. 'You'd been together a long time.'

'Five years. She met this bloke and went off with him to the Isle of Mull.'

'I *am* sorry.'

Jeff made coffee and they talked about Sally, the bloke, loneliness, the Isle of Mull, a man they'd been at school with who was now Gray's M.P. and then about various people they'd known in the old days, all of whom seemed to have gone off to remote places. Gray told his friend about the move.

'Yes, I could shift your stuff on Saturday. There isn't much of it, is there?'

'Some books, a typewriter, clothes.'

'Say mid-afternoon, then? If you change your plans you can give me a ring. By the way, there's a letter here for you, came about a month back just when Sally went. It looked like a bill, so what with Sally and everything, I never got around to sending it on. I know I should have done but I was in a hell of a mess. Thank God I'm getting myself together again now.'

Gray wished he could do the same. He took the envelope, knowing what it was before he opened it. How could he forget so much that was important when he remembered everything that was past and dead and useless? She'd left him and he'd gone to London for Christmas with Francis, resolving then never to go back to the hovel, never to set foot within ten miles of her. And he'd written to his publishers asking them to send the next statement to Tranmere Villas because that was the one address he could be sure of being permanent. How could he have forgotten? Because he'd felt so hopeless and disorientated that he'd drifted back to Pocket Lane, fleeing from the tough members of his tribe like a wounded animal seeking the shelter of its lair?

He slit open the envelope. *The Wine of Astonishment*: Sales, home, £5; 75% sales, French, £3.50; 75% sales, Italian, £6.26. Total, £14.76.

'Since you're not doing anything,' said Charmian, 'you can give me a hand with the food. We're not having a real lunch, just picking at bits from this lot.' 'This lot' was a heap of lettuces, tomatoes, plastic-wrapped cheese, envelopes of sliced meat and French loaves. 'Unless you feel like treating us to a meal.'

'Now then, lovey,' said Francis.

Gray wasn't annoyed with her. He was too shattered by the royalty statement to feel anything much. On the way to Jeff's he'd bought a bottle of Spanish Chablis for the party and now he'd got just two pounds of the seven left.

'There's plenty of food here,' said Francis kindly. 'My God, there goes the phone again.'

The phone had been ringing ever since Gray got back. People couldn't come or wanted to know if they could bring friends or couldn't remember where Francis lived.

'So you're moving in here,' said Charmian, vigorously washing tomatoes.

Gray shrugged. Was he? 'Only for a few weeks.'

'My mother invited a friend for the weekend once and she stayed three years. You're very neurotic, aren't you? I notice you jump every time the phone rings.'

Gray cut himself a piece of cheese. He was just thinking what a snorter of a letter he'd write them about those Jugoslavian rights when Francis came back into the kitchen, his expression concerned, rather embarrassed. He came up to Gray and laid a hand on his shoulder.

'It's your stepfather. Apparently, your mother's very ill. Will you go and talk to him?'

Gray went into the living room. Honoré's broken English rushed excitedly at him out of the receiver. 'My son, I try to find you at your house but always the telephone is occupy, so I remember me you go to the house of Francis and I find the number . . . Oh, the difficulty of finding him!'

'What is it, Honoré?' said Gray in English.

'It is Mummy. She die, I think.'

'You mean, she's *dead*?'

'No, no, *pas du tout*. She have a grand *paralyse* and the doctor Villon he is with her now and he say she die very soon, tomorrow, he didn't know. He wish her go to the hospital in Jency but I say no, no, not while old Honoré have breath and force to make care of her. You come, *hein*? You come today?'

'All right,' said Gray, a hollow feeling at the pit of his stomach. 'Yes, sure I'll come.'

'You have the money, you carry him with you? I give you sufficient money to go with the plane for Paris and then the bus for Bajon. So you fly with him this day from Eetreau and I see you tonight at Le Petit Trianon.'

'I'll come straight away. I'll go home and get my passport and then I'll come.'

66

He walked back into the kitchen. The others were sitting at the table, silent, wearing long faces as suitable to the occasion.

'I say, I'm awfully sorry about your mum,' said Charmian gruffly.

'Yes, well, of course,' said Francis, 'I mean, if there's anything we can do . . .'

There was something he could do but Gray postponed asking him for a few minutes. He knew very well that people who make this offer at times of bereavement or threatened bereavement seldom intend to do anything beyond producing sympathy and a drink.

'I'll have to miss the party. I'd better go now if I've got to get to the hovel before going to the airport.'

'Let me give you a drink,' said Francis.

The whisky, on a more or less empty stomach, gave Gray courage. 'There is one thing you could do,' he said.

Francis didn't ask him what it was. He sighed slightly. 'I suppose you haven't got the money for your fare.'

'All I've got between me and the dole is about two quid.'

Charmian said, but not unkindly, 'Oh, God.'

'How much would it be?'

'Look, Francis, I'm expecting a cheque any day. It'll only be a short-term loan. I know I've got money coming because I've sold some Jugoslavian rights.'

'You can't get money out of Communist countries,' said Charmian briskly. 'Writers never can. My mother's got a friend who's a *very famous* writer and he says publishers have to pay so much tax or something that they just leave the money in banks in places behind the Iron Curtain.'

It was like a jet of cold water hitting him in the face. It didn't occur to him to doubt what she said. He remembered now hearing remarks very like hers from Peter Marshall at one of those convivial lunches, only Peter had added, 'If you do sell in Jugoslavia, say, we'll leave the money in our account in Belgrade and maybe you can have a holiday there sometime and spend it.' Pity Honoré didn't live in Belgrade . . .

'Christ, I'm in a hell of a mess.'

Francis said again, 'How much would it be?'

'About thirty-five pounds.'

'Gray, you mustn't think I'm not sympathetic, but how the hell d'you think I'm going to lay my hands on thirty-five quid on a Sunday? I don't have more than five in the flat. Have you got any money, lovey?'

'About two fifty,' said Charmian. Having apparently decided that the period of empathetic grieving was over, she had resumed her eating of ham and lettuce.

'I suppose I'll have to go down to the tobacconist and see if he'll cash me a cheque.'

Gray phoned the airport and was told there was a flight at eight-thirty. He felt stunned. What was going to happen when he got back from France? When the cheque came he'd have about sixteen pounds but he'd owe thirty-five to Francis, and then there was going to be the business of giving Francis another nine pounds a week to share this bloody greenhouse. Oblivious of the girl, he put his head in his hands and closed his eyes . . .

Inevitably, he began to think how different his situation would have been if he'd agreed to what Drusilla had required of him a year ago. Of course he'd still be going to Bajon, that and that only would be the same. But he wouldn't have been dependent on other people's charity, despised by this girl, the object of Francis's contempt, always worried out of his wits over money . . .

A touch on his shoulder jerked him out of this reverie. 'Bear up,' said Francis. 'I've got you the thirty-five.'

'Thanks. I'm very grateful, Francis.'

'I don't want to press you at a time like this but the thing is it doesn't leave me much to spare, and what with these few days in Devon and the rent and everything, if you could see your way . . . ?'

Gray nodded. It seemed pointless to make promises about quick repayment. He wouldn't be able to put conviction into his voice and Francis wouldn't believe him if he did.

'Have a good party.'

'We'll drink to you,' said Francis. 'Absent friends.'

Charmian lifted her head and managed a half-hearted farewell smile. And Francis's own expression was indulgent but impatient too. They'd both be glad to get rid of him. The red glass door closed with a relieved bang before he was halfway down the path.

If he'd done what she'd asked, he thought, he'd be in a taxi now, proceeding from his luxury flat to a first-class seat in an aircraft, his pigskin luggage up there beside the driver, his pockets full of money. He'd be like Tiny, who, she'd once said, always carried huge sums about on him, ready to pay cash for what he wanted. And in Bajon the chambermaids would be preparing for him the best bedroom with private bath at the Écu d'Or. Above all, he'd have been free from worry.

It seemed to him as he waited for his train that all his troubles had come upon him because he hadn't done what she'd asked and conspired with her to kill her husband.

# 9

Although he'd been preoccupied with thoughts of money throughout that long journey, it wasn't until he was back at the hovel that he remembered his mother's will. Under it, he was to inherit half her property. Well, he wouldn't dwell on that, it was too base. Pushing away the thought with all its attractions and all its attendant guilt, he packed some clothes, put his royalty statement into the strong-box and got out his passport. There didn't seem any point in locking the strong-box, so he just closed the lid, leaving the key in. Was there anything else he had to do before leaving for France, apart from putting the phone back on the hook? He did this, but at the back of his mind there remained something else. What? Not put Jeff off. He'd be back by next Saturday, and Francis would take him in all right when he knew he was heir to half his mother's money. No, this was some engagement, some duty. . . . Suddenly he remembered – Miss Platt's party. On his way back down the lane he'd call on Miss Platt and tell her he wouldn't be able to go.

Seen from the gate, the hovel looked as if it hadn't been inhabited for years. It's weatherboard soaked by seasons of rain, scaled and bleached by sun to the texture of an oyster shell. It lay deep in its nest of bracken, a decaying shack behind whose windows hung faded and tattered cotton curtains. Silver birches, beeches with trunks as grey as steel, encroached upon it as if trying to conceal its decrepitude. It had a lost abandoned look as of a piece of rubbish thrown into the heart of the Forest along with the rest of the tripper's litter. But it was worth fifteen thousand pounds. Miss Platt had said so. If Mal were to put it up for sale, he'd get rid of it that same day for this huge, this unbelievable, sum.

He found the lucky vendor in her front garden, cutting early roses.

'Aren't we having a lovely warm spell, Mr Lanceton? It makes me more sorry than ever I have to leave.'

Gray said, 'I'm afraid I shan't be able to come to your party. I've got to go to France. My mother lives there and she's dangerously ill.'

'Oh, dear, I *am* sorry. Is there anything I can do?' Miss Platt put down her scissors. 'Would you like me to keep an eye on The White Cottage?'

But for the letters to Tiny, Gray might have forgotten this was the hovel's real name. 'No, thanks. I haven't anything worth pinching.'

'Just as you like, but it wouldn't be any trouble and I'm sure Mr Tringham would take over from me. I do hope you'll find your mother better. There's no one like one's mother, is there? And worse for a man, I feel.'

As he went down the lane, past the Willises' churned-up lawn, past the new estate and out into the High Beech Road, he thought about what she'd said. There's no one like one's mother . . . Since Honoré's phone call, he'd thought a lot about money, about Drusilla and money, about his mother's money but he hadn't really thought about his mother herself at all. Did he care for her? Did it matter to him at all whether she lived or died? In his mind he had two mothers, two separate and distinct women, the woman who had rejected her son, her country and her friends for an ugly little French waiter, and the woman who, since her first husband's death, had kept a home for her son, loving him, welcoming his friends. It was of this woman – lost to him, dead for fourteen years – that Gray tried to think now. She had been a friend and companion rather than a parent and he had mourned her with the

70

bitter bewilderment of a fifteen-year-old, unable to understand – he understood now all right – the power of an
obsessive passion. Understanding doesn't make for love,
only for indifferent forgiveness.

He'd mourned her then. But, because she wasn't really
two women but only one, he couldn't grieve now for the
broken creature who was dying at last, not his but Honoré's, the property of Honoré and of France.

Flying to Paris was nothing to Tiny, no more than driving
down to Loughton High Road. He flew to America, Hong
Kong, Australia; to Copenhagen for lunch and back home
for dinner. Once, Gray remembered now, he'd flown to
Paris for the weekend . . .

'You'll be able to come and stay with me at the hovel.
We can have the whole weekend together, Dru,' he'd said.

'Yes, and it'll give us a chance to take the acid.'

'I thought you'd forgotten all about that.'

'How little you know me. I never forget anything. You
can get some, can't you? You said you could. I hope you
weren't just bragging to impress.'

'I know a bloke who can get me some acid, yes.'

'But you're going to be all moralistic and bloody upstage
about it? Damn you, you make me sick! What's the harm?
It's not addictive, it's anti-addictive. I know all about it.'

From reading pop paperbacks he'd thought, with sec-
tions entitled *The Weed* and *Club des Haschischins* and *A
New Perception*. 'Look, Dru, I just happen to believe it's
wrong to use a drug like L.S.D. just for playing, for sensa-
tion-seeking. It's quite another thing when it's used in
psycho-therapy and under supervision.'

'Have you ever taken it?'

'Yes, once, about four years ago.'

'Christ, that's marvellous! You're like one of those crappy
old saints who went to orgies every night until they were
about forty and then turned on everybody else and told
them sex was sin just because they'd got past it themselves.
*God!*'

'It wasn't a nice experience. It may be for some people
but it wasn't for me.'

'Why shouldn't I try it? Why you and not me? I've never
done anything. You're always stopping me when I want to

71

have experiences. I shan't come here at all if you won't get the acid. I'll go to Paris with Tiny and, my God, won't I live it up while he's at his stupid old seminar. I'll pick up the first guy that makes a pass at me.' She leaned towards him then, wheedling, 'Gray, we could take it together. They say it makes sex wonderful. Wouldn't you like that, me even more wonderful than I am?'

Of course he'd got the acid. There was very little he wouldn't have done for her except that one thing. But he wasn't going to take it himself. That was dangerous. One to take it, one to be there and watch, to supervise and, if necessary, to restrain. For, although the stable personality may react no more than to see distortions (or realities?) and experience a heightening of certain senses, the unstable may become violent, manic, wild. Drusilla, whatever she was, however much he might love her, was hardly stable.

It was early May, just over a year ago, the east wind sharp and chill. On the Saturday morning they had gone into his bedroom and he'd given her the acid while the wind howled around the hovel and, up above them somewhere, Tiny's plane flew away to France. Massive Tiny in his eighty-guinea suit leaned back in his first-class lushly cushioned seat, taking his double Scotch from the air hostess, opening his *Financial Times*, reading, having no idea, no idea at all, of what was taking place those thousands of feet below him. Serene, innocent Tiny, who had never for a moment suspected . . .

'And many a man there is, even at this present,
Now while I speak this, holds his wife by th'arm,
That little thinks she has been sluiced in's absence,
And his pond fished by his next neighbour,
By Sir Smile, his neighbour . . .'

Gray felt a shiver run through him. It was ugly when put like that, for he had been Tiny's neighbour, in the geographical as well as the ethical sense, had even pointed out the fact in the first of those letters. He'd been Sir Smile, Tiny's neighbour, who had fished his pond in his absence – how coarse and clinical was that Jacobean imagery! – and had scarcely considered the man as a person except when it came to drawing the line at the furthest limit.

Well, it was past now, and he and Tiny, the sparer and the spared, perhaps both betrayed in their absence by a neighbour, that smiling tennis player . . .

Gray blocked off his memories. Beneath him now he could see the lights of Paris. He fastened his seat belt, put out his cigarette and braced himself for further ordeals ahead.

The aircraft was late and the one available bus took him only as far as Jency, ten miles from Bajon, but he thumbed an illegal hitch the rest of the way. The only lights still on in Bajon were those of the Écu d'Or, haunt of Honoré, the mayor and M. Reville, the glass manufacturer. Honoré, however, would hardly be there now. Gray looked at his watch, striking a match to do so, and saw it was close on midnight. Strange to think that at this time twenty-four hours before he'd been in Marble Arch Tube station phoning Drusilla.

He went past the clump of chestnut trees, past the house called Les Marrons and down the little side road which would, after the bungalows, finally peter out as miserably as Pocket Lane itself into fields, woods and the farm named Les Fonds. Honoré's was the fourth bungalow. A light was on in a front room. By this light Gray could see the sheet of green concrete spread over and crushing every growing thing that might have protruded its head, the plastic-lined pond, and around the pond, the brightly coloured circus of gnomes, frogs fishing, coy naked infants, lions with yellow staring eyes and fat ducks, which was Honoré's great pride. Mercifully, the light was too dim to show the alternating pink and green bricks of which the bungalow was built.

Not for the first time Gray reflected on this extraordinary anomaly in the French nation, that they who have contributed more to the world's art in music, in literature, in painting, than perhaps any other race and have been the acknowledged arbiters of taste, should also possess a bourgeoisie that exhibits the worst taste on earth. He marvelled that the French who produced Gabriel and Le Nôtre should also have produced Honoré Duval, and then he went up to the door and rang the bell.

Honoré came running to answer his ring.

'Ah, my son, at last you come!' Honoré embraced him, kissing him on both cheeks. He smelt, as usual, very powerfully of garlic. 'You have a good fly? Don't be unquiet now, *ce n'est pas fini.* She lives. She sleeps. You see her, no?'

'In a minute, Honoré. Is there anything to eat?'

'I cook for you,' said Honoré enthusiastically. It was a fervour, Gray knew, which would soon wane and be replaced by wily suspiciousness. 'I make the omelette.'

'I only want a bit of bread and cheese.'

'What, when I not see you three, four years? You think I am that bad father? Come now to the kitchen and I cook.'

Gray wished he hadn't mentioned food. Honoré, though French and an ex-waiter, one who had moved for two-thirds of his life among French *haute cuisine* and in the ambience of its tradition, was an appalling cook. Aware that French cooking depends for much of its excellence on the subtle use of herbs, he overdid the rosemary and basil to an inedible degree. He also knew that cream plays an important part in most dishes but he was too mean to use cream at all. This would have been less unbearable if he had cooked egg and chips or plain stews but these he scorned. It must be the time-honoured French dishes or nothing, those traditional marvellous delicacies which the world venerates and copies – only with the cream and wine left out and packet herbs thrust in by spoonfuls.

'Extinguish, please,' said Honoré as Gray followed him tiredly into the kitchen. This was Honoré's way of telling him to put the light out. Every light had to be put out when one left a room to keep the electricity bills down. Gray extinguished and sat down in one of the bright blue chairs with scarlet and blue plastic seat. It was very quiet, nearly as quiet as in the hovel.

In the middle of the kitchen table was a pink plastic geranium in a white plastic urn and there were plastic flowers all over the window-sill. The wall clock was of orange glass with chrome hands and the wall plates which ringed it showed châteaux in relief and glorious Technicolor. All the tints of a tropic bird were in that kitchen and every surface was spotless, bathed in the rosy radiance of a pink strip light.

Honoré, who had tied an apron round himself, began beating eggs and throwing in pinches of dried parsley and dried chives until the mixture turned a dull green. Cooking demanded concentration and a reverend silence and

74

neither man spoke for a while. Gray eyed his stepfather thoughtfully.

He was a thin spare man, rather under middle height, with brown skin and hair which had been black but now was grizzled. His thin lips were permanently, even when relaxed, curled up into a sickle-shaped smile, but the small black eyes remained shrewd and cool. He looked what he was, a French peasant, but he looked more so: he looked like a French peasant in a farce written by an Englishman.

Gray had never been able to fathom what his mother had seen in him but now, after three years' separation, he began to understand. Perhaps this was because he was older or perhaps it was because he had only in those years really known the power of sex. To a woman like his mother, sheltered, refined even, this dark and certainly vital little man with his sharp eyes and his calculating smile, might have been what Drusilla had been to him, Gray, the embodiment of sex. He always reminded Gray of one of those onion sellers from whom his mother used to buy when they called at the house on Wimbledon Common. Could it be that Enid Lanceton, outwardly cool and civilised, had been so drawn to these small brown men with onion strings hanging from their bicycles that she longed to find one for herself? Well, she'd found him, Gray thought, looking at Honoré, his plastic flowers and his curtains patterned with yellow pots and pans, and she'd paid very dearly for her find.

'*Voilà!*' said Honoré, slapping the omelette down on a green and red checked plate. 'Come now, eat her quick, or she grow cold.'

Gray ate her quick. The omelette looked like a cabbage leaf fried in thin batter but it tasted like a compost heap and he gobbled it down as fast as he could, hoping in this way to avoid those pauses in eating in which the full flavour might make itself felt. There was a faint sound in the bungalow which reminded him of the regular whirr, rising and falling, of a piece of machinery. He couldn't think what it was but it was the only sound apart from the clatter Honoré was making at the sink.

'Now for some good French coffee.'

Good coffee was the last thing one got at Le Petit Trianon. Honoré scorned instant which all his neighbours now used but his avarice jibbed at making fresh coffee each time it was needed. So once a week he boiled up a saucepanful of water, coffee and chicory, and this mixture, salt and bitter, was heated up and served till the last drop was gone. Gray's stomach, which digested Swedish meatballs, ravioli and canned beef olives with impunity, revolted at Honoré's coffee.

'No, thanks. I shan't be able to sleep. I'll go in and see Mother now.'

Her bedroom – their bedroom – was the only room she had managed to keep unscathed from her husband's taste. The walls were white, the furniture plain walnut, the carpet and covers sea-blue. On the wall above the bed hung a painted and gilded icon of a Virgin and Child.

The dying woman lay on her back, her hands outside the counterpane. She was snoring stertorously, and now Gray knew what was the dolorous, regular sound he had heard. It had been machinery, the machinery of Enid Duval's respiration. He approached the bed and looked down at the gaunt, blank face. He had thought of her as two women, but now he saw that there were three: his mother, Honoré's wife, both absorbed in this third and last.

Honoré said, 'Kiss her, my son. Embrace her.'

Gray took no notice of him. He lifted one of the hands and held it. It was very cold. His mother didn't stir or change the rhythm of her breathing.

'Enid, here is Gray-arm. Here is your boy at last.'

'Oh, leave it,' said Gray. 'What's the point?'

His English deserting him, Honoré burst into an excited Gallic tirade. Gray caught only the gist of it, that Anglo-Saxons had no proper feelings.

'I'm going to bed. Good night.'

Honoré shrugged. 'Good night, my son. You find your room O.K., *hein*? All day I run up and down, the work is never done, but I make time for arranging clean drapes for you.'

Used to Honoré's curious and direct rendering of French terms into English, Gray knew this meant he had put clean sheets on the bed. He went into 'his' room which Honoré had furnished as suitable for the son of the house. It was mainly blue – blue for a boy – magenta roses on the blue carpet, yellow daffodils on the blue curtains. The one picture, replacing a *pietà* Gray had once told his stepfather he loathed, showed Mme Roland in a blue gown standing on the steps of a red and silver guillotine and uttering, according to the caption beneath, *O Liberté, que de crimes on commis en ton nom!*

The truth of this was evident. Many crimes were commited in the name of liberty, his mother's marriage for instance. For liberty Drusilla had contemplated a crime far more horrible. Gray thought he would probably stay awake dwelling on this, but the bed was so comfortable – the best thing about Le Petit Trianon, the most comfortable bed he ever slept in, vastly superior to the one at the hovel or Francis's or the one by the window at the Oranmore – that he fell asleep almost immediately.

# 10

He was awakened at seven by a racket so furious that at first he thought his mother must have died in the night and Honoré have summoned the whole village to view her. Surely no one could make so much noise getting breakfast for three people. Then, under the cacophony, as it were, he heard the rhythm of her snoring and understood that Honoré, who never seemed tired, was using this method of indicating it was time to get up. He rolled over and, though he couldn't get back to sleep, lay there defiantly till eight when the door flew open and a vacuum cleaner charged in.

'Early to bed and early to rise,' said Honoré merrily, 'make him wealthy, healthy and wise. There, I know the English proverb.'

Gray noticed he'd put 'wealthy' first. Typical. 'I didn't get to bed early. Can I have a bath?'

At Le Petit Trianon you couldn't count on there being hot water. A bathroom there was, with fishes on the tiles and a furry peach-coloured cover on the lavatory seat; a large immersion heater there was also, but Honoré kept this switched off, washing up from heated kettles. If you wanted a bath you had to book it some hours or even days in advance.

'Later,' said Honoré. In very colloquial French he went on to say something about electricity bills, the folly of too much bathing and – incredibly, Gray thought – that he had no time at present to turn on the heater.

'Sorry, I didn't get that.'

'Aha!' His stepfather wagged a finger at him while energetically vacuuming the room. 'I think you don't know French like you say. Now you are here you practise him. Breakfast waits. Come.'

Gray got up and washed in water from a saucepan. The cheap cheese-coloured soap Honoré provided stung his hand so that he almost cried out. In another saucepan was coffee, on the table half a *baguette*. The custom of the French is to buy these sticks freshly each morning but Honoré never did this. He couldn't bear to throw anything away and old *baguettes* lingered till they were finished up, even though by then they looked and tasted like petrified loofahs.

After Dr Villon had called and pronounced no change in his patient, Gray went down to the village to get fresh bread. Bajon hadn't altered much since his last visit. The Écu d'Or was still in need of painting, the brown-grey farm buildings still slumbered like heavy old animals behind brown-grey walls. The four shops in the post-war parade, wine shop, baker, butcher and general store-post office, were still under the same management. He walked to the end of the village street to see if the bra advertisement was still there. It was; a huge poster on a hoarding showing two rounded mountains encased in lace, and the words, *Desirée*, Votre *Soutien-gorge*. He retraced his steps, went past Honoré's turning, past two new shops, past a hairdresser ambitiously called *Jeanne Moreau, Coiffeur des Dames*, and came to the road sign, *Nids de poule*. When he'd first come to Bajon he'd thought this really meant there were hen's nests in the road, not just potholes, but Honoré had corrected him, laughing with merry derision.

The day passed slowly and the slumbrous heat continued. Gray found some of the books his mother had brought with her from Wimbledon and settled down in the back garden to read *The Constant Nymph*. The back garden

78

was a lawn ten metres by eight on which Honoré had erected three strange objects, each being a tripod of green-painted poles surmounted by a plaster face. Three chains hung from the poles bearing a kind of urn or bucket filled with marigolds. Gray couldn't get used to these elaborate and hideous devices, designed with such care and trouble to display very small clusters of flowers, but the sun was warm and this a way of passing the time.

At about eight Honoré said that a poor old man who was on his feet from morning till night, worn out as cook, nurse and general manager, deserved a little relaxation in the evenings. Gray, he was sure, would stay with Enid while he went to the Écu for a *fine*. Several neighbours had called during the day to offer their services as sitters, but Honoré had refused them, saying Gray would like to remain with his mummy.

Enid maintained her regular unbroken snoring while Gray sat beside her. He finished *The Constant Nymph* and began on *The Blue Lagoon*. Honoré came in at eleven, smelling of brandy and with a message from the mayor that he longed to meet the author of *Le Vin d'Étonnement*.

In the morning Father Normand appeared, a stout and gloomy black figure whom Honoré treated as if he were at least an archbishop. He was closeted for a long time with Gray's mother, only leaving the bedroom on the arrival of Dr Villon. Neither priest nor doctor spoke to Gray. They had no English and Honoré had assured them that Gray had no French. The week-old concoction was served and the two elderly men drank it with apparent pleasure, complimenting Honoré on his selfless devotion to his wife and pointing out to him (Fr Normand) that he would find his reward in heaven, and (Dr Villon) that he would find it on earth in the shape of Le Petit Trianon and Enid's savings. Since Gray wasn't supposed to be able to understand a word of this, they spoke freely in front on him of Enid's imminent death and Honoré's good fortune in having married, if not for money, where money was.

Gray wouldn't have put it past him to help Enid towards her end if she lingered on much longer. He showed no grief, only a faint unease at the mention of money. The priest and the doctor praised him for his stoical front, but Gray didn't think it was stoicism. Honoré's eyes flashed

79

with something like loathing when he was feeding Enid or sponging her face, and when he thought Gray wasn't looking.

How many husbands and wives were capable of murder in certain circumstances? A good many, maybe. Gray had hardly thought of Drusilla since he'd arrived in France. There was nothing here to evoke her. He hadn't been to France since becoming her lover, so he hadn't even the memory of remembering her while there. Nor had she ever been near the place. She and Tiny holidayed in St Tropez and St Moritz – those patron saints of tourism – or further and more exotically afield. But he thought of her now. When he considered spouses as murderers he could hardly fail to think of Drusilla.

When had she first mentioned it? In March? In April? No, because she hadn't taken the acid till May . . .

It took about half an hour to work. Then she began to tell him what she saw, the old beamed bedroom vastly widened and elongated so that it seemed to have the dimensions of a baronial hall. The clouds outside the window became purple and vast, rolling and huge as she had never seen clouds before. She'd got up to look more closely at them, distressed because the window wasn't a hundred feet away but only two yards.

She was wearing an amethyst ring, its stone a chunk of rough crystal, and she described it to him as a range of mountains full of caves. She said she could see little people walking in and out of the caves. He wouldn't make love – it seemed wrong to him, unnatural – and she didn't seem to mind, so they went downstairs and he cooked her lunch. The food frightened her. She saw the vegetables in the soup as sea creatures writhing in a pool. After that she sat still for a long time, not telling him any more until at last she said:

'I don't like it. It's bending my mind.'

'Of course. What did you expect?'

'I don't feel sexy. I've got no sex any more. Suppose it doesn't come back?'

'It will. The effects will wear off quite soon and then you'll sleep.'

'What would happen if I drove the car?'

'For God's sake, you'd crash! Your sense of distance would be all messed up.'

80

'I want to try. Just in the lane.'

He had to hold her back by force. He'd known something like that might happen but he hadn't realised she was so strong. She struggled, striking him, kicking at his legs. But in the end he got the car key away from her, and when she was calmer they went for a walk.

They walked in the Forest and saw some people riding ponies. Drusilla said they were a troop of cavalry and their faces were all cruel and sad. He sat down with her under a tree but the birds frightened her. She said they were trying to get at her and peck her to pieces. Early in the evening she'd fallen asleep, waking once to tell him she'd dreamed of birds attacking Tiny's aircraft and pecking holes in it till Tiny fell out. One of the birds was herself, a harpy with feathers and a tail but with a woman's breasts and face and long flowing hair.

'I can't understand people taking that for *fun*,' she said when she left for home the next night. 'Why the hell did you give it to me?'

'Because you nagged me into it. I wish I hadn't.'

Many times he'd wished he hadn't, for that wasn't the end of the nagging but only the beginning. That was when it had begun. But it didn't matter now; it was all the same now . . .

'Raise yourself, my son. You are having the dream?'

Honoré spoke jovially but with a hint of reproof. He expected young people – especially young people without means of support – to leap to their feet whenever their seniors entered or left a room. Dr Villon and Fr Normand were leaving, lost in admiration apparently of Honoré's linguistic ability. Gray said *au revoir* politely but remained where he was. Out in the hall he could hear Honoré waving away their compliments with the explanation that anyone who had been for years in a managerial situation in the international hotel business was bound to have several languages at his tongue's end.

After the evening meal – canned lobster bisque with canned prawns and bits of white fish in it that Honoré called *bouillabaisse* – he went for a walk down the road as far as Les Fonds. There were nearly as many gnats and flies as in Pocket Lane. In fact, the place reminded him of Pocket Lane except for the persistent baying of the farmer's chained dog. Gray knew that French country people like to keep their dogs chained. Presumably the animals get used to it, presumably this one would be let loose at night. But for some reason the sight and sound disquieted him deeply. He didn't know the reason. He couldn't think why this thin captive sheepdog, straining at its chain, barking steadily, hollowly and in vain, awakened in him a kind of chilly dread.

When he got back Honoré was spruce in dark jacket, dark cravat and beret, ready for his *fine*.

'Give my love to the mayor.'

'Tomorrow he come here to call. He speak good English – not so good as me, but good. You must stand when he come in, Gray-arm, as is respectable from a young boy to an old man of honour and reason. Now I leave you to give Mummy her coffee.'

Gray hated doing this, hated supporting Enid, who smelt and who dribbled, on one arm while with the other hand he had to force between her shaking lips the obscene feeding cup with its spout. But he couldn't protest. She was his mother. Those were the lips that had said – long, long ago – 'How lovely to have you home again, darling,' those the hands that had held his face when she kissed him good-bye, sewn the marking tags on his school clothes, brought him tea when he awoke late in the holidays.

As he fed her the hot milk with a trace of coffee in it, watching perhaps a quarter of the quantity go down her throat while the rest slopped on to the coverlet, he thought she was weaker than she had been on the previous evening, her eyes more glazed and distant, her flesh even less pliant. She didn't know him. Probably she thought he was some-one Honoré had got in from the village. And he didn't know her. She wasn't the mother he'd loved or the mother he'd hated, but just an old Frenchwoman for whom he felt nothing but repulsion and pity.

The relationship between mother and son is the most complete that can exist between human beings. Who had said that? Freud, he thought. And perhaps the most easily destroyed? She and Honoré and life itself had destroyed it and now it was too late.

He took away the cup and laid her down on the pillows. Her head lolled to one side and she began to snore again,

82

but unevenly, breathily. He'd never seen anyone die but, whatever Honoré or the doctor might say, whatever false alarms, reassurances, anticlimaxes, there had been in the past, he knew she was dying now. Tomorrow or the next day she would die.

He sat by her bed and finished *The Blue Lagoon*, relieved when Honoré came back and she was still alive.

All the next day, Wednesday, Enid went on dying. Even Honoré knew it now. He and Dr Villon sat in the kitchen, drinking coffee, waiting. Honoré kept saying something which Gray interpreted as meaning he wouldn't wish it prolonged, and he was reminded of Theobald Pontifex in *The Way of All Flesh* who had used those words when his own unloved wife lay on her deathbed. Gray found *The Way of All Flesh* among his mother's books and began to read it, although it was a far cry from his usual reading matter, being a great novel and such as he used to prefer.

Fr Normand came in and administered Extreme Unction. He left without taking coffee. Perhaps yesterday's dose had been too much for him or else he thought it a frivolous drink and unsuitable to the occasion. The Mayor didn't come. By now the whole village knew that Enid was really dying at last. They hadn't loved her. How could they love a foreigner and an Englishwoman? But they all loved Honoré who had been born among them and who, when rich, had returned humbly to live in the village of his birth.

That night Honoré didn't go to the Écu, though Enid slept a little more peacefully. He vacuumed the whole house again, made more green omelettes and finally switched on the heater for Gray's bath. Wrapped in a dragon-decorated dressing gown belonging to his step-father, Gray came out of the bathroom at about eleven, hoping to escape to bed. But Honoré intercepted him in the hall.

'Now we have the chat, I think. We have no time till now for the chat, *hein*?'

'Just as you like.'

'I like, Gray-arm,' said Honoré, adding as Gray followed him into the living room: 'Extinguish please.'

Gray turned off the hall light behind him. His stepfather lit a Disque Bleu and re-corked the brandy bottle from which he had been drinking while Gray was in the bath.

'Sit down, my son. Now, Gray-arm, you know of – how do you say? – Mummy's legs?'

Gray stared at him, then understood. For one grotesque moment he'd thought Honoré was referring to Enid's lower limbs, the French for legacy having eluded him.

'Yes,' he said warily.

'Half for you and half for me, yes?'

'I'd rather not talk about it. She's not dead yet.'

'But, Gray-arm, I do not talk of it, I talk of you. I am unquiet only for what become of you without money.'

'I shan't be without money after . . . Well, we won't discuss it.'

Honoré drew deeply on his cigarette. He seemed to ponder, looking sly and not altogether at ease. Suddenly he said loudly and rapidly, 'It is necessary for you only to write more books. This you can do, for you have talent. I know this, I, Honoré Duval. Just a poor old waiter, you say, but a Frenchman, however, and all the French, they *know*.' He banged his concave chest. 'It is in-built, come in the birth.'

'Inborn,' said Gray, 'though I doubt that.' He'd often noticed how Honoré was a poor old waiter when he wanted something and an international manager when out to impress.

'So you write more books, come rich and undependant again, *hein*?'

'Maybe,' said Gray, wondering where all this was leading and determined to let it lead nowhere. 'I'd rather not talk about any of this. I'm going to bed in a minute.'

'O.K., O.K., we talk of this at other time. But I tell you it is bad, bad, to hope for money come from anywhere but what one works. This is the only good money for a man.'

People who live in glasshouses shouldn't throw stones, thought Gray. 'We were going to talk of something else.'

'O.K., very good. We talk of England. Only once I visit England, very cold, very rainy. But I make many friends. All Mummy's friends love me. So now you tell me, how goes Mrs Palmer and Mrs 'Arcoort and Mrs Ouarrinaire?'

Resignedly, Gray told him that while the first two ladies were no longer within the circle of his acquaintance, Mal's mother was, as far as he knew, still well and happy in Wimbledon. Honoré nodded sagely, his composure recovered. He stubbed out his cigarette and lit another.

'And how,' he said, 'goes the good Isabel?'

# 11

Gray too had been lighting a cigarette. He'd taken the match from Honoré and held it downwards to steady the flame. Now he let it fall into the ashtray and took the cigarette from his lips.

'Isabel?' he said.

'You look unquiet, Gray-arm, like you see the phantom. Perhaps you have too much hot water in your bath. Take a blanket from your bed or you will be enrheumed.'

Gray said automatically, the words having no meaning or sense for him, 'I'm not cold.'

Honoré shrugged at the folly of the young who never take advice. Speaking French, he began to extol Isabel, praising her English strength of character, her intrepidity as a spinster *d'un certain âge* in going by herself to Australia.

Getting up stiffly, Gray said, 'I'm going to bed.'

'In the centre of our chat? I see. O.K., Gray-arm, do as please yourself. Manners make man. Another English proverb. Strange that these English proverbs make nonsense to English persons.'

Gray went out and banged the door, ignoring Honoré's command to extinguish the hall light. He shut himself in his room and sat on the bed, his body really cold now and convulsed with gooseflesh.

Isabel. Christ, how had he come to forget about Isabel? And he'd only just forgotten. He'd almost remembered as he was leaving the hovel. He'd known there was something to remember and he'd thought it was Miss Platt's party. As if it mattered a damn whether he went to her party or not. All the time it was Isabel. Shades of memory had flitted across his mind, making him faintly cold and sick, as when he'd walked down to the farmyard at Les Fonds. Was it possible he'd made another mistake, got the wrong weekend?

In the kitchen there was an old copy of *Le Soir*, Friday's. He went out there and found it lining the scarlet pedal bin. *Vendredi, le quatre juin*, and there the photograph of the floods in some remote antipodean city that had certainly been last Friday's main news. If Friday was the fourth, today, the following Wednesday, was June the ninth and Monday had been the seventh. Anyway, it was pointless checking. Isabel's day was the day he'd been due back from Francis's party.

He slumped down at the table, pressing his hands so hard against his head that the burnt palm began to throb again. What the hell was he going to do, trapped here in Bajon, without money, with his mother dying?

He tried to think coolly and reasonably about what must have happened. At midday on Monday, June the seventh, Isabel must have driven down Pocket Lane in her Mini. She'd have let herself into the hovel with the key he'd given her, opened the kitchen door, left on the bath cover a dozen or so cans of meat, placed on the floor a small pan of water and, after kisses and farewells, gentle pats and promises to return after not too long a time, left Dido, the labrador bitch, alone and waiting.

Gray will be back soon, she'd have said. Gray will take care of you. Be a good dog and sleep till he comes. And then she'd have hung the key up on the hook, shut the kitchen door and driven to Heathrow, to an aircraft, to Australia . . .

It was unthinkable, but it must have happened. What was there to have stopped it happening? Isabel knew she'd find an empty house, closed up, neglected, shabby. That was how she'd expect to find it. He'd left nothing to indicate he'd gone to France, told no one but Miss Platt who, even if she'd been in her garden, wouldn't know Isabel, still less accost a stranger to gossip about her neighbours.

The dog, that was the important thing. Dido, the dog with the lovely face and what he'd thought of as kind eyes. God, they wouldn't be kind now, not after she'd been locked in that hole without food and only about half a pint

86

of water for more than two days, but wild and terrified. There was food beside her, food ironically encased in metal which even the most persistent fangs and claws couldn't reach. At this moment those fangs and claws would be tearing at the bolted back door, the larder door, the cellar door, until in exhaustion she took refuge in baying, roaring with far more need and agony than the farmer's chained dog.

There was no one to hear her. No one would come down the lane till Mr Tringham passed on Saturday evening . . . Gray got up and went back to the living room where Honoré was still sitting, the brandy bottle once more uncorked.

'Honoré, can I use the phone?'

This was a request far more momentous than merely asking for a bath. Honoré used the phone to speak to his stepson perhaps three times a year on matters of urgency and, almost as rarely, to summon Dr Villon. It stood in his and Enid's bedroom, between their beds. Actually getting one's hands on it was more difficult than obtaining the use of the phone trolley in a crowded hospital.

Having cast upon him a look of reproachful astonishment, Honoré said in elementary slow French that the phone was in Enid's room, that to disturb Enid would be a sin, that it was ten minutes to midnight and, lastly, that he had thought Gray was asleep.

'It's urgent,' said Gray, but without explanation.

Honoré wasn't going to let him get away with that. Whom did he wish to phone and why? Answering his own question, he suggested it must be a woman with whom Gray had made a date he now realised he couldn't keep. In a way this was true, but Gray didn't say so. Honoré proceeded to tell him, first, that calls to England were of a cost *formidable* and, secondly, that any woman one could phone at midnight couldn't be virtuous and the relationship he supposed Gray was having with her must therefore be immoral. He, Honoré Duval, wouldn't give his support to immorality, especially at midnight.

Gray thought, not for the first time, how absurd it is that the French whom the English think of as sexy and raffish should in fact be morally strict while believing the English sexy and depraved. 'This,' he said, trying to keep his patience, 'is something I've forgotten to do in the rush of coming here, something to do with Isabel.'

'Isabel,' said Honoré, 'has gone to Australia. Now go to your bed, Gray-arm, and tomorrow we see, *hein*?'

Gray saw it was useless. Whom could he phone, anyway? In his panic he hadn't thought of that. At this hour there wasn't anyone he could phone and he told himself, still feeling sick and cold, that there was nothing to be done till the morning.

He couldn't sleep. He tossed from side to side, sometimes getting up and going to the window until the dawn came and the chained dog began to bark. Gray flung himself face-downwards on the bed. A doze that was more dream than sleep came to him at about five, the dream he often had in which Drusilla was telling him she wanted to marry him.

'Will you ask Tiny to divorce you?' he'd said as he was saying now in the dream.

'How can I? He wouldn't, anyway.'

'If you left him and stayed away for five years he'd have to whether he wanted to or not.'

'*Five years*? Where'll we be in five years? Who's going to keep me? You?'

'We'd both have to work. They talk about unemployment, but there's plenty of work if you don't mind what you do.'

Her white hands, beringed, that had never done heavier work than put flowers in a vase, whisk cream, wash silk . . . She stared at him, her thin pink mouth curling.

'Gray, I can't live without money. I've always had it. Even before I was married I always had everything I wanted. I can't imagine what life'd be if I couldn't just walk into a shop and buy something when I wanted it.'

'Then we go on as we are.'

'He might die,' she said. 'If he dies it'll all be mine. It's in his will, I've seen it. He's got hundreds of thousands in shares, not a million but hundreds of thousands.'

'So what? It's his. What'd you do with it if it were yours, anyway?'

'Give it to you,' she said simply.

'That's not my tough little Dru talking.'

'Damn you! Damn you! I *would*.'

'What can I do about it? Kill him for you?'

88

'Yes,' she said.

He lurched awake, bathed in sweat, muttering, 'I couldn't kill anyone, anything. I couldn't kill a fly, a wasp . . .' and then he remembered. He couldn't kill anything but he was now, at this moment, killing a dog. With that thought came simultaneously a tremendous relief, a knowledge, sudden and satisfying, that it was all right, that Isabel wouldn't have left Dido there, after all. Because she'd have met the milkman. She was coming at twelve and she was always punctual; the milkman too was always punctual and came at twelve, except on Fridays when he was later. The milkman knew he was away and would have told Isabel. She'd have been very cross and put out but she wouldn't have left the dog.

He fell at once into a profound and dreamless sleep from which he was awakened at about eight by the pompous measured tones of Dr Villon. The snoring was no longer audible. Gray got up and dressed quickly, rather ashamed to be so relieved and happy when his mother was dying and perhaps now dead.

Enid wasn't dead. A spark of life clung to that otherwise lifeless body, showing itself in the faint rise and fall of her chest under the bedclothes. He did what Honoré had urged him to do but what he wouldn't do in his stepfather's presence, kissed her gently on the sunken yellowish cheek. Then he went into the kitchen where Honoré was repeating to the doctor that he wouldn't wish it prolonged.

'*Bonjour*,' said Gray. '*Je crois qu'il fera chaud aujourd'hui.*'

The doctor took this to indicate Gray's having received a miraculous gift of tongues and burst into a long disquisition on the weather, the harvest, tourism, the state of French roads and the imminence of drought. Gray said, 'Excuse me, I'm going out to get some fresh bread.'

His stepfather smiled sadly. 'He does not understand, *mon vieux*. You are wasting your breath.'

Bajon lay baked in hard white sunlight. The road was dusty, showing in the distance under the bra advertisement (*Desirée*, Votre *Soutien-gorge*) shivering mirages above the potholes. He bought two bread sticks and turned back, passing a milkman on a cart. This milkman wore a black tee-shirt and a black beret but, in spite of his Gallic air, he had something of the look of Gray's own milkman, and this impression was enhanced when he raised one hand and called out, '*Bonjour, Monsieur!*'

Gray waved back. He'd never see his own milkman again and he'd miss him more than anyone else in Pocket Lane. It had been rather nice and touching the way his milkman had shaken hands with him when they'd said good-bye and . . .

God! He'd forgotten that. Of course Isabel wouldn't have seen the milkman because he wasn't calling any more. Gray had paid him and said good-bye. And he wouldn't even be down that end of the lane. He'd said that was the one good thing about losing Gray's custom, not having to go all the way down the lane again. Oh, *God*. He'd snatched those few hours of sleep on the strength of utter illusion. Things were just as they'd been last night, only worse. Dido *was* in the hovel and now – it was half past nine – she'd been there for nearly seventy hours.

He felt almost faint, standing there in the heat, the *baguettes* under his arm, at the enormity of it. He wanted to run away and hide somewhere, hide himself for years on the other side of the earth. But it was ridiculous thinking like that. He had to stay and he had to phone someone and *now*.

But who? Miss Platt, obviously. She lived nearest. She was a nice kindly woman who probably loved animals but wasn't one of those censorious old bags who'd relish lecturing him on his cruelty and then broadcasting it about. And she was practical, self-reliant. She wouldn't be afraid of the dog who had by now very likely lost all her gentleness in fear and hunger. Why had he been such a fool as to stop Miss Platt when she'd offered to keep an eye on the hovel? If only he'd agreed none of this would have happened. Useless thinking of that now. The only thing to think of was somehow getting hold of Miss Platt's number.

'How pale is your face!' said Honoré when he put the bread down on the kitchen table. 'It's the shock,' he said in French to Dr Villon. 'He mustn't be ill. What will become of me if I have two *malades* on my hands?'

'I'd like the phone, Honoré, please.'

'Ah, to telephone the bad lady, I think.'

'This lady is seventy years old and lives next door to me in England. I want her to see to something at my house.'

90

'*Mais le téléphone se trouve dans la chambre de Mme Duval!*' exclaimed Dr Villon who had picked up one word of this.

Gray said he knew the telephone found itself in the room of his mother but the lead on it was long and could be taken out into the hall. Muttering about *formidable* expense, Honoré fetched the phone and stuck it on the hall floor. Gray was getting directory enquiries when he remembered that Miss Platt wouldn't be there. Today was Thursday and she'd moved.

He mustn't despair over a thing like that. There were other people. Francis, for instance. Francis wouldn't like it but he'd do it. Anyone but a monster would do it. No, on second thoughts, Francis couldn't because he'd gone to Devon with Charmian. Jeff, then. Jeff had the van to get him there fast. Good. After a long delay, Gray heard the distant burr-burr of the phone ringing in Tranmere Villas. Jeff was the perfect person to ask, not censorious or thick either, not the kind to want a string of explanations or to make a fuss about breaking in. Whoever went would have to do that as he, Gray, had one key, the other was on the hook and the third . . .

When he'd heard twenty burr-burrs and got no answer, he gave up. No use wasting time. Jeff must be out with the van. Who else was there? Hundreds of people, David, Sally, Liam, Bob . . . David would be at work and God knew where he worked; Sally had gone to Mull; Liam among the dozens of friends Jeff said had left London; Bob would be at a lecture. There was always Mrs Warriner. He'd heard of her from Mal but not actually seen her for three years. He couldn't bring himself to phone a sixty-year-old Wimbledon lady who had no car and ask her to make a twenty-mile journey.

Back to Pocket Lane, review the scene there. Pity he hadn't chatted up the library girl or got to know some of the people on the estate. Mr Tringham had no phone. That left the Willises. His courage almost failed him, but there was no help for it. A quickly flashing picture of Dido collapsed on the floor, her swollen tongue extended from bared teeth, and he was asking the operator to find him Mrs Willis's number.

91

leaves – you'll have to time that carefully – he'll crash. He'll go over the top of the Wake roundabout.'

'Apart from the fact that I wouldn't, it's absurd. It's so old-hat, freaking people out with acid for a joke.'

'Damn you, it's not a joke! It'd work.'

He'd laughed as one laughs with embarrassment at other people's fantasies, and said with a shrug, shifting out of the light into sane cool shadow, 'You do it, then, if that's the kind of thing you fancy. He's your bloke. You give him acid and let him crash his car in Loughton High Road, only don't expect me to get it for you.'

'Gray . . .' The hand in his, the thin scented lips against his neck, his ear. 'Gray, let's talk about it. As a joke, if you like but let's *see* if it could be done. We'll pretend we're the sort of unhappy wife and her lover you read about in murder books. Mrs Thompson and Bywaters or Mrs Bravo and her old doctor. Let's just talk, Gray.'

He jerked to his feet and out of the blazing light as his mother's own old doctor came out of the sickroom. Dr Villon threw up his hands, sighed and went into the kitchen. Gray squatted down again, took off the phone receiver and immediately replaced it. He couldn't talk to her. How could he even have considered it? There must be other people, there must be someone. . . . But he'd been through all that before and there wasn't.

The only thing to do was to put the whole thing into cold practical terms, to forget all those dreams he'd had of her and those total recall reconstructions, and tell himself plainly what had happened and what he was doing. Well, he'd had a love affair and a very satisfying one, much as most people do sometime in their lives. It had ended because the two of them weren't really compatible. But there wasn't any reason why they couldn't still be friends, was there? If he was going to go through life being afraid of meeting every woman he'd had any sort of relationship with, it was a poor look-out. It was ridiculous to get neurotic over talking to an old friend.

An old friend? *Drusilla?* No more of that . . . He could sit here all day arguing with himself and all the time the dog was in there, starving, maybe going mad. Once more he'd talk to her, just once. In some ways it might actually do him good to talk to her. Very probably hearing her voice

– talking to him, not like that Marble Arch one-sided thing – and hearing the stupid ignorant things she'd say would cure him of her once and for all.

With a half-smile, blasé, a little rueful (the rake giving his discarded mistress a ring for old times' sake) he picked up the receiver and dialled her number. He dialled the code and the seven digits. It was all so simple. His hand was trembling which was rather absurd. He cleared his throat, listening to the number ringing, once, twice, three times . . .

'Yes?'

His heart turned over. He put his hand to it as if, stupidly, he could steady its turbulence through ribs and flesh. And now the temptation to do what he'd done on Saturday night, to breathe only, to listen and not to speak, was nearly overpowering. He closed his eyes and saw the sunshine as a scarlet lake, burning, split by meteors.

'Yes?'

Again he cleared his throat which felt bone dry yet choked with phlegm.

'Drusilla.' That one word was all he could manage but it was enough. Enough to cause utter deep silence, broken at last by her sigh, a long rough sound like a fingernail drawing across silk.

'You took your time,' she said slowly, enunciating each word with great care; then briskly, shockingly, and in her old way, 'What d'you want?'

'Dru, I . . .' Where was the rake, the casual caller-up of old girl friends? Gray made a grab at this errant Don Juan who had never really been an *alter ego*, tried to speak with his voice. 'How are you? How have you been all these months?'

'All right. I'm always all right. You didn't ring me up to ask that.'

Don Juan said, 'No, I rang you as an old friend.'

'An old what? You've got a nerve!'

'Dru . . .' Firmly now, remembering nothing but the dog, 'I'm ringing you to ask you to do me a favour.'

'Why should I? You never did me any.'

'Please listen, Dru. I know I've no right to ask anything of you. I wouldn't do this if it wasn't – terribly urgent. There's no one else I can ask.' It was easy after all, easy after the first initial shock. 'I'm in France. My mother's –

well, dying.' And then he told her about it, as he'd told Honoré but more succinctly.

A sort of soft vibrant moan came down the line. For a moment he thought she was crying, not at the pathos of the story, but for them, for what they'd lost. There came a gasp and he knew she was laughing.

'What a fool you are! You make a mess of everything.'

'But you will go there, won't you?'

A pause. A gust of smothered laughter. He was talking to her quite ordinarily and pleasantly and she was laughing also quite ordinarily and pleasantly. It was hard to believe.

'I'll go,' she said. 'Haven't much choice, have I? What am I supposed to do with it when I get it out?'

'Could you get her to a vet?'

'I don't know any bloody vets. Oh, I'll find one. I think you've lost your mind.'

'Quite possibly. Dru, could you – will you call me back at this number? I can't call you because my stepfather freaks out if I keep using the phone.'

'I'll phone you. Tonight some time. I'm not surprised about your stepfather. You haven't any money, that's your trouble, and when people haven't any money other people treat them like children. It's a rule of life.'

'Dru . . . ?'

'Yes?'

'Nothing,' he said. 'You'll call me back?'

'Didn't I say I would?' The phone went down hard. He hadn't had a chance even to say good-bye. She never said it. Not once could he remember her ever saying the word good-bye. He scrambled to his feet, went into the bathroom and was sick down the loo.

Enid was snoring irregularly. Otherwise the house was silent. Gray lay on his bed in the blue room whose closed curtains couldn't shut out the blaze of noon. Mme Roland remarked to him scornfully, aloof in the face of the scaffold, 'O Liberty, what crimes are committed in thy name!'

Well, he'd done it and it hadn't been too bad. The sickness was only natural after the release of so much tension. He'd spoken to his discarded mistress and the dog

96

would be rescued. Cool and practical, he was becoming almost what Honoré or Isabel would call a mature grown-up person. Well, well. *C'est le premier pas qui coûte*, as Honoré might say, and he'd got over the first step which counted. No harm would be done at this juncture, however, in reminding himself by another one of those reconstructions of the ugliness he'd escaped and the pitfall there still might be.

'Suppose we were serious,' he'd said, 'I don't see how we'd get him here.'

'That's easy. You write him a letter.'

'What sort of letter? "Dear Tiny, if you'll pop over one afternoon, I'd like to give you some acid to make you crash your car. Yours truly, G. Lanceton."?'

'Don't be so bloody stupid. He collects coins, doesn't he? He's always advertising for coins in some rag called *Numismatists' News*. Get the typewriter, go on.'

So he'd got the typewriter to humour her.

'Now I'll dictate. Put your address and the date, June the sixth.' She'd looked over his shoulder, her hair against his face. 'Now write, "Dear Sir, As a fellow numismatist . . ." No, that won't do. "Dear Sir, in reply to your advertisement . . ." Sometimes he advertises in *The Times*. Oh, God, get a fresh bit of paper.'

How many attempts had they made before they got the letter that satisfied her? Three? Four? At last, the final, perfect one. 'Dear Sir, in reply to your advertisement in *The Times*, I think I have just what you are looking for. Since my home is not far from yours, would you care to come over and see it? Four o'clock on Saturday would be a suitable time. Yours faithfully . . .'

'And how am I supposed to sign it?'

'Better not put your real name.'

He signed it Francis Duval. She folded it up and made him type the envelope: 'Harvey Janus Esq., Combe Park, Wintry Hill, Loughton, Essex.'

His indulgent smile growing rather stiff, rather sick, he'd said, 'I don't have any old coins, Dru.'

'I'll give you one. He's got lots of worthless coins he keeps in a box, things he thought were valuable when he first started collecting. I'll give you a Roman denier.'

'Then he'd know I wasn't serious.'

97

'Of course. So what? He'll think you just don't know. He'll say that's not what he wants and you'll say you're sorry but now he's here can you give him a cup of tea?'

'Dru, I'm getting a bit tired of this game.'

O, Liberty, what crimes . . . The doorbell was ringing. Gray got off the bed because no one was answering it. There was a note on the hall table: 'Depart to village for shopping. Make care of mummy. Honoré.' He opened the door. A stout elderly man in a grey suit and grey Homburg stood there. Gray recognised the mayor whom Honoré on some previous occasion had pointed out to him across the street.

'*Entrez, Monsieur, je vous en prie.*'

The mayor said in English which was very beautifully pronounced, very nearly perfect, 'Mr Graham Lanceton? I saw your stepfather in the village and he told me it would be convenient to call. How is your poor mother?'

Gray said there was no change. He showed the mayor into the living room. After what Honoré had said, the mayor's command of English struck him almost dumb. But that was typical of Honoré who, with unbounded arrogance, had probably convinced himself he was the superior linguist. Sensing his astonishment, the mayor said, with a smile, 'Many years ago I spent a year in your country. I was attached to a company in Manchester. A beautiful city.'

Gray had heard otherwise but he didn't say so. 'I believe you – er, wanted to give me your views on my book.' Might as well get it over at once.

'I should not presume, Mr Lanceton. I am not a literary critic. I enjoyed your novel. It recalled to me happy memories of Manchester.'

Since *The Wine of Astonishment* was set exclusively in Notting Hill, Gray couldn't quite understand this, but he was relieved to be spared the criticism. The mayor sat silent, smiling, apparently perfectly at ease.

Gray said, 'Would you care for some coffee?'

'I thank you, no. If there were perhaps some tea?'

If only there were! No packet of tea had ever found its way into Le Petit Trianon. 'I'm afraid not.'

'It is of no importance. It was not for coffee or tea or the discussion of contemporary literature that I came.'

Why had he come, then? The mayor sat in easeful silence for quite a minute. Then he leant forward and said slowly,

98

'Your stepfather is a gentleman of great vitality. Ebullience is, I think, the word.'

'Well, it's *a* word.'

'A man of impulse and one who, I think I may say, is inclined somewhat to our national vice, common among our peasantry of – shall I name it? – avarice. What matters one small vice among so many virtues?'

The mayor's English grew more expert and semantically involved with every sentence. It recalled to Gray the speech of solicitors in Victorian novels. He listened, puzzled but fascinated.

'A desire too to acquire something for nothing or almost nothing, a need to cast bread upon the waters and harvest whole loaves.'

'I'm afraid I don't follow you, Monsieur.'

'Ah, perhaps not. I will abandon metaphor, I will make a long story short. You expect, I understand, when something happens to your mother – this English euphemism I find so tactful, so gentle – to be her heir?'

Taken aback, Gray said, 'I shall inherit half, yes.'

'But half of what, Mr Lanceton? Listen, if you will be so good. Let me explain. Half of what your poor mother leaves when she passes on – you see, I know you English do not care for the strict cold expression – half will be, to put it bluntly, half of this bungalow!'

Gray stared. 'I don't understand. My mother had a good deal of money invested when she remarried and . . .'

' "Had" ', interrupted the mayor urbanely, 'is the operative word. Let me be quite open and above-board with you. M. Duval reinvested this money, speculated, if you will. There was a mine, I believe, a railway to be built that, alas, was not built. You may imagine.'

Gray imagined. He knew nothing about the stock market except what everyone knows, that it is easier to lose there than to gain. But he didn't feel at all sick or angry or even very disappointed. How had he believed there would ever be any real money from any source for him?

'So you see, Mr Lanceton,' said the Victorian solicitor, 'that were you to claim your inheritance, as you would be within your rights to do, you would only deprive an ageing man of the very roof over his head. This, I am sure, you would not do.'

'No,' said Gray rather sadly, 'no, I wouldn't do that.'

'Good. Excellent.' The mayor got up, still smiling. 'I was sure my words would be effectual. We speak,' he added with a slight pedantic laugh, 'the same language.'

'How will he live?' asked Gray, shaking hands.

'He had the forethought, poor gentlemen, to purchase a small annuity.'

He would. 'Good-bye,' said Gray.

'I will not be so optimistic as to wish your mother recovered health, Mr Lanceton, but say only that we must hope her suffering will not be prolonged.'

They must have arranged to meet somewhere and chew over the results of the interview, for when Honoré returned with his full shopping bag, he was truly, to use the mayor's word, in an ebullient mood. He actually embraced Gray.

'My son, my boy! How goes the bad lady? You make contact with her? And the poor animal?'

Gray said, with a sense of unreality, that everything was all right now.

'Then I make the lunch. *Croque Monsieur* for us today.'

'No, I'll do it.' Even this simple, though grandly named, dish wasn't safe in the hands of Honoré, who would be sure to add herbs and garlic to the cheese. 'You go and sit with Mother.'

Poor Honoré. Poor, indeed. Slicing up cheese, Gray reflected on the strange calm he felt, the lightness of heart even. Honoré while rich had been hateful to him, a kind of king to his Hamlet. For Honoré poor he had a fellow-feeling. The bath-water watching, the shouts of 'Extinguish, please!', the phone fanaticism – weren't they, after all, only the sort of economies he too was forced to practise? It amused him to think of those two, Honoré and the mayor, screwing up their courage to tell him the truth, afraid of his righteous anger. But it hadn't angered him at all. Probably he'd have done the same in Honoré's place, blued all his money on a bubble and then sent some braver deputy to confess it to his judge.

No, he wasn't angry. But he was a bit ashamed of himself for mentally accusing Honoré of wanting to make away with his wife. Not every marriage partner was a Drusilla.

'Drusilla,' he'd said, 'I've had enough of this. It's as stupid as mooning over what you'd do if you won the pools.'

'No, it isn't. You can't fix the pools. You can fix this. Just let me post that letter. I've still got it.'

'It's out of date.'

'Write another, then. What's the date? July the first. "Dear Sir, In reply to your advertisement . . ." '

'I'm going out. I'm going for a walk. It's no fun being with you if all you can do is play this stupid game.'

'It's not a game, it's serious.'

'All right,' he'd said. 'So it's serious. Once and for all, will you listen to me? Leaving morality out of it, it wouldn't work. Probably he wouldn't die. He'd feel strange, see distortions and park the car. He'd ask the first motorist he saw to go to the police and the first person they'd come to'd be me.'

'You don't know him. He always drives very fast. He wouldn't be able to stop in time. And they wouldn't know about you because I'd get hold of the letter and burn it.'

'Burn it now,' he'd said.

He shook himself and looked at Honoré who sat at the opposite side of the table, eating toasted cheese. His eyes were bright and darting but not, Gray suddenly realised, the malicious eyes of a potential killer. Honoré lacked the intelligence to be wicked. And Gray realised too that all the time he'd been at Le Petit Trianon he hadn't done a thing to help until today when he'd made the lunch. Honoré had done it all and, on the whole, done it well.

'Why don't you go out for a bit?' he said. 'You need a change. Take your car.'

The Citroën was hardly ever used. It lived in the garage under a nylon cover, coming out once a week to be polished. But Gray understood that now too.

'Where will I go?'

'See a friend. Go to the cinema. I don't know.'

Honoré threw up his hands, smiled his monkey smile. 'I don't know too, Gray-arm.'

So they sat together in Enid's room, waiting for her to die. Gray read *The Way of all Flesh* intermittently. He held his mother's hand, feeling very calm, very tranquil. His mother was dying but he no longer had any reason to hope for her death. He had no money to keep him from working, to lull him into idle security. The dog would be safe now. Drusilla would phone him soon, he'd thank her and they'd say their last dignified good-byes. Even she would say good-bye. It was wonderful to feel so free, to know that no crimes need be committed to secure liberty.

The evening was close as if a storm threatened – not tonight perhaps or tomorrow but soon. Honoré had gone to the Écu, assured by Gray that this would be good for him, that no useful purpose could be served by his staying with Enid.

Gray, who had been at peace since noon, as if his physical sickness had provided a more than physical catharsis, began to feel a gradual mounting of tension. He had meant to sit outside among the gnomes or the tripods. Provided he left the doors open, he'd hear the phone when it rang, for he'd placed it on the hall floor near the kitchen door. But, although he went into the garden, he couldn't concentrate on the last chapters of his book.

It was Thursday and Tiny went to his Masons on Thursdays at about six. She could have phoned him then. Why hadn't she? He told himself that it was only the dog's fate that was worrying him. He was concerned only for the dog and for Isabel. Drusilla was what he'd called her that morning, a discarded mistress, interesting only as an old friend might be when doing him a favour.

It was Thursday. Very likely she still turned her Thursday evenings to good account, possibly with what's-his-name, the tennis guy, Ian Something. Perhaps she was with him now and wouldn't phone till he'd gone. Gray pondered this idea, found it particularly unpleasant and went back into the house. The farmer's dog had stopped barking. No doubt it had been let off its lead. It was almost too dark to make out the shape of the phone which, dog-like, was also attached to a lead, a wire stretched through the crack in the door.

Ten o'clock. He looked in on his mother who had ceased to snore, who lay on her back with her mouth open. Suppose Drusilla didn't phone? Suppose, in order to be revenged on him, she'd promised to see about the dog and then deliberately done nothing? He could phone her. If he was going to he'd better be quick, for another half-hour

102

and it would be too late for safety. But she'd phone him. She never changed her mind and she always did what she undertook.

He stood over the phone, directing his will on it, telling it to ring, ring. He clenched his fists, tensed his muscles, said to it, 'Ring, damn you. Ring, you bastard!'

It obeyed him immediately and rang.

# 13

When he had coped with the stream of idiomatic French which issued from the receiver, when he had told M. Reville, the glass manufacturer, that his mother remained the same and that Honoré had gone to the Écu, he uncorked the brandy bottle and drank some. Honoré was getting everything else, after all. He oughtn't to grudge him a drop of brandy.

If she didn't phone he wouldn't be able to sleep. That was ridiculous, though, because if she hadn't been to the hovel Dido would be dead by now and all further worry pointless. He had some more brandy and put the bottle away. He wished he knew exactly what he was worrying about. Honoré was out and he could easily phone her. There was a good half-hour, before danger time and Tiny got home. He'd phoned her before, twice if you counted the Marble Arch time, and it was the first step that counted.

Surely he wasn't still afraid of getting involved with her again? Or maybe afraid of *not* getting involved with her? Remember what she is, he told himself, remember what she wanted you to do. . . .

' "Dear Sir, In reply to your advertisement . . . !" Put the date. It's November the twenty-first. Oh, come on, Gray. Get up then and I'll do it. Any fool can type, I suppose. My God, it's freezing in here. When he's dead and we're together all the time we'll never be cold again. We'll have a flat in Kensington and if the central heating doesn't go up to eighty we'll have it all taken out and new in.'

'We aren't going to be together all the time and you know it. We're going to go on like this till one of us gets tired of the other.'

'What's that supposed to mean? I didn't see any signs of tiredness upstairs just now.'

He'd turned away, warming his hands at the oil heater, looking wearily at the window scummed with frost, the skeletal trees beyond rooted in pools of water thinly crusted with ice. Round her shoulders she'd slung the red fox, coarser and brighter than her hair.

'There's more to life than sex,' he said.

'Like what? Like living in a frozen slum? Like brooding about the books you don't write and the money you can't make. I'm going to do this letter and by the spring – March, say – we can be living together with all his money in a joint account. God, but my fingers are too cold to type. You do it.'

'Dru, you said just now you didn't see any signs of tiredness. All right, I'm not tired of sex. I don't think I'd ever get tired of sex with you. But I'm sick and tired to my soul of you ballsing on about killing your husband. It's grotesque.'

She'd crashed her hands down on the keys so that they tangled and stuck together. Her eyes were white fire.

'D'you mean me? D'you mean I'm grotesque?'

'I didn't say that but – yes, you're grotesque and stupid and a bit mad when you talk of making that poor bloke crash his car.'

'Damn you! Damn you!' He'd had to hold her off, seize her hands and force them behind her to stop her long nails tearing at his face. She'd crumpled and softened, the fur falling from her shoulders, leaving her vulnerable in the thin clinging dress that was so unsuitable for the hovel. And then, of course, the inevitable. Because this was Drusilla who, naked, warm and sinuous under the piled blankets, was anything but grotesque, anything but stupid . . .

The tape that was playing in his brain switched off sharply. Stop, stop, remember the bad times. Forget that the bad times always ended in good times until that last time. Twenty past ten. She wasn't going to phone. That bloody thing, straining on the end of its wire leash, wasn't going to ring again tonight.

104

He was halfway back to the cupboard where the brandy was when the bell brayed at him. He jumped, and the jump was so galvanic that it actually pained him. Then he was on the phone at a leap, crouched over it, gasping out, 'Yes, Dru, yes?

'Hi,' she said.

The coolness of her voice chilled memories, blew away longing and dreading. 'What happened?' he said. 'Did you find her?'

'I found her.' There was a long pause. 'God, Gray,' she said with an almost refined distaste, quite unlike her, 'God, how *could* you?'

'Is she dead?' He sat on the floor, resting his head against the wall.

'No. She was alive – just.'

He exhaled on a long sigh. 'What happened?' he said again.

'I took some milk and chicken with me. I was a bit scared to open the kitchen door but I needn't have been, she was too weak to move. God, the stink and the muck in there! She'd got up on the sink and plastered the window with her muck and saliva – the lot.'

'Oh, Dru . . .' His head had begun to bang. It was the brandy partly, and partly the shock, though he ought to have been relieved. This was the best that could have happened.

She said harshly, 'Someone ought to lock you up in a cell for three days without food or water and see how you'd like it. Why didn't you phone the police, anyway?'

Why hadn't he? It was the obvious thing. 'I never thought of it.'

'You haven't phoned them today?'

'No, of course not.'

'You just left it to me? Typical. D'you want to hear the rest? I carried her out to the car and, Christ, was she heavy. In the car I gave her some milk but she couldn't take the chicken. Then I got her to this vet.'

'Which vet?'

'A guy in Leytonstone.'

'*Leytonstone?* Why on earth . . . ?'

'Because I was going up to town.'

105

'I see,' he said. She always left her car in the car park at Leytonstone Tube station when she was going to London. But to have gone today? It seemed heartless, too casual. And why had she gone? To buy clothes? To – meet someone? 'You went to London?'

'Why not? It's not my dog, as I hastened to tell the vet. I didn't want him thinking I'd do a thing like that. You'd better have his address and see him as soon as you get back. It's twenty-one George Street. Got that?'

'Yes. Thanks. I'm very very grateful, Dru. I ought to have phoned the police, of course. I ought . . .' He broke off, fumbling in his mind for suitable words to end the conversation. She'd done the favour he'd asked of her and now was the time for those dignified good-byes. Thanks, no hard feelings, maybe we'll meet again someday, and meanwhile thanks . . . 'Well, Dru, maybe after all this trauma we'll be able to meet one of these days and – well, you know what I mean. I'll never forget what you – I mean I'll never . . .'

'After I got back from town,' she said as if he hadn't spoken, 'I went in and cleaned up a bit for you.'

'You did what?' He remembered once having told her that the only brush she ever lifted was the one she used for mascara. And now she, those white hands of hers, had cleaned up his filthy kitchen. He could hardly believe it. 'Why did you do that?'

'Why did I get the dog? Why do I do anything for you? Don't you know yet?'

Good-bye, Drusilla. Good night, sweet lady, good night. Say it, say it, Don Juan hissed at him. A tremor rose in his throat, choking him, taking away the power of speech. He rested his cheek against the wall to cool his blood-heated face.

'You don't know, do you?' Her voice was very soft now. 'You don't think about my feelings. I'm O.K. when you want someone to get you out of a mess, that's all. As far as you're concerned, the rest is over and done with.'

'And you know why,' he whispered, 'it had to be over and done with.' Clinging to a shred of sanity, he said, 'We had to split up. I couldn't take it.'

'That? I've given all that up. It would never have worked. I see that now.' She paused and said in a very low childlike

106

voice, almost as if reluctantly, 'I tried to phone you a lot of times.'

His heart was pounding. 'On Thursday nights?'

'Of course.'

'I left the receiver off.'

'Oh, you fool,' she sighed. 'You hopeless fool. I wanted to tell you back in January I'd given all that up. God, I was so lonely. I wanted to talk to you so much. The line was always engaged, always engaged. I thought . . . Never mind.'

'Why didn't you come to me?'

'And find you with another girl?'

'There's been no other girl, there's been no one. I was alone too.'

'Then we've been a pair of hopeless fools, haven't we? Frightened of each other when all the time we really . . . Oh, what's the use? You're in France and I'm here and Tiny'll be in in a minute. We'd better stop this before we say too much.'

His voice returned to him powerfully and he almost shouted at her. 'Too much? How could we say too much? Don't you see we've been apart all this time over a stupid misunderstanding? We've tortured ourselves over nothing . . .'

'I've got to ring off. I can hear Tiny's car.'

'Don't ring off, please. No, you must. Of course you must. Listen, I'll phone you in the morning. I'll phone you at nine as soon as he's gone. God, Dru, I'm so happy . . .'

A sighing whisper cut him short. 'Tomorrow, then,' and the phone slid delicately into silence. In the dark warm hall he sat on the floor, cradling the receiver in his hands, hearing still an echo or a memory of her voice. His heart quietened, his body relaxed like a taut spring set free to uncoil, and as happiness, pure joy, swamped him he wanted to dance and shout, run outside and sing, embrace the tripods, yell to the whole of sleeping Bajon that his love had come back to him.

Instead of doing that, he got to his feet and went into his mother's room. Enid lay on her back, breathing shallowly, her eyes closed. Once, when he'd had nothing much to tell, he'd been able to tell her everything, and she'd listened and understood. If she were aware now, conscious, would she understand? Wouldn't her own experience of passion give her empathy?

He bent over her. He said, 'Mother, I'm so happy. Everything has come right for me.'

Her lids moved. The wrinkled black-stained hoods lifted and half-showed her eyes. In his euphoric state he fancied he saw recognition there, comprehension even, and in that moment he loved her again, forgiving her entirely. He took her face in his hands and pressed his lips against the corner of her mouth, kissing her as he hadn't kissed her since he was a little boy.

Mme Roland gave him a cynical glare and he turned her picture to the wall. He didn't want her shouting her pre-decapitation liberty nonsense at him any more. He knew all about liberty, he'd had enough of it in the past six months. He'd taken his liberty to avoid committing a crime and now he thought he'd committed a crime against himself and Drusilla. Let Mme Roland make what she liked of that with her histrionic *salon* philosophy.

He got into bed naked because of the heat. How long was he going to have to stay here? Days? Weeks? If only he'd got money he could fly home and see her and then come back again. That wasn't possible – but to wait here on and on while she was in England longing for him as he was longing for her? It was a pity, he thought, that uncomplicated joy lasts so short a time, that it must always give way rapidly to practicalities and plans. In the morning when he phoned her they'd have to start making plans. In the morning, too, he'd phone Jeff and tell him not to come on Saturday. Maybe he wouldn't be moving now, after all.

In a couple of weeks' time, perhaps less, she'd be visiting him at the hovel again just like she used to before Christmas. And they'd discuss the dead months with laughter at their own folly, reducing Christmas, as they looked back on it, to a row not much bigger than any of their rows, a momentary frown on the face of love.

In the hot stuffy bedroom where no wind lifted the curtains at the open window, where the air was warm and dry at midnight, it was hard to imagine snow. But snow had come before Christmas, and on the night before the Eve Drusilla, the red fox lady, had pelted him with snowballs, screaming, laughing, as they walked in the frozen forest. He caught her in his arms and, mouth to mouth, the snow crystals melting on warm lips, they'd fallen to make love in the drifts under the sealskin branches of the beech trees.

That was a good memory, one to hold on to now, one he wouldn't have dared recall till now when she was back with him. But the quarrel that came after? How many times had he played that tape over and over, following as it did their final act of love? The last time, he'd thought, the last time. Now it wasn't going to be the last time. It would even cease to be associated with the quarrel, and the quarrel itself would fade down one of the alleys which debouch from the avenue of time.

He turned over, spreadeagled under the crumpled sheet. A Thursday, of course. Exactly twenty-four weeks ago to-night. No Christmas decorations at the hovel, for Christmas was to be spent in London with Francis. But the present she'd given him on the bath cover in the kitchen, the present of a silver chain on which hung a silver Hand of Fortune (since sold) and all around it the red and gold wrappings he'd torn off in his love and gratitude. He'd drawn out a ridiculous amount, far more than he could afford, to buy her *Amorce dangereuse* and she'd laughed with delight, spraying it on her red fur, although she could have bought gallons of the stuff herself and not noticed.

Into the hovel to take her perfume before driving back to Combe Park. He'd worn the chain to go out in the forest and it had fallen icy against his chest, but now, under his shirt and Arran, it was warm with his body warmth. Tiny, of course, had paid for it. Her father didn't send her a cheque more than once a year.

'So what?' she'd said, and that had been the beginning. No, for it had begun long before, but just the beginning of the final quarrel, of the end. 'I'm entitled to some of what he makes, I suppose? You could look on it as wages. Don't I keep house for him and cook and sleep with him. He only pays me two thousand a year and I'm cheap at the price.'

'*Two thousand?*' One year he'd managed to make almost that himself, but never before and never after.

'Ah, come on, Gray. Five pounds for a silver neck thing? It's only an advance, anyway. It'll all be yours soon.'

'Don't start that again, Dru. Please don't.'

Don't start that, he warned himself, reaching out for the glass of water he'd put by the bed. Why remember that quarrel now? She'd given it all up, she'd said so. He'd never hear her say those things again.

'Look, Gray, you sit down and listen to me. You never thought that was a game I was playing. You were as serious as me, only you haven't got as much guts as I have.'

'Please don't come the Lady Macbeth bit, Drusilla.'

'Well, he did it in the end, didn't he? And so will you. We'll do another letter and you can buy the acid while you're up in town.'

' "Up in town". You sound like the chairman of the Women's Institute off for her annual shopping spree.'

She was more sensitive to this kind of insult than any other, but she took no notice. 'I'll give you the money.'

'Thanks. The poor bastard's going to pay for his own poison, is he? I like that. It reminds one of the Borgias. A judge'll make a lot of that: "The unfortunate Harvey Janus, murdered by his wife and her lover with a hallucinogen purchased out of his own money." Charming.'

In her red fur, water drops gleaming on its spikes, she sat down at the typewriter to compose another letter. The oil heater on, blue flame, incandescent; snow falling thickly, silently, against the dirty window-pane.

'Dru, will you give up this idea now? Will you promise me never to mention it again?'

'No. I'm doing it for you. You'll thank me afterwards. You'll be grateful to me all the rest of your life.'

The watch she'd given him showing ten past ten; the Hand of Fortune she'd given him warm against his breastbone; melted snow lying on the floor in pools.

'It's no good, Gray. I'll never give this up.'

'Will you give me up?'

She was folding the letter, sliding it into an envelope. 'What's that supposed to mean?'

'That I can't go on like this. It doesn't matter what we're doing, what we're talking about. With you all roads lead to killing Tiny.'

'You can put a stop to that by killing him.'

'No, there's another way.' He didn't look at her. 'I can put a stop to it by not seeing you.'

110

'Are you trying to say you're tired of me?'

'No, I can't imagine any man being tired of you. I'm tired of *this*. I've had it, Drusilla. As it is, I'll never be able to look back on what we had, you and me, without this poisoning it all.'

'You're just a spineless coward!'

'That's true. I'm too much of a coward to kill anyone and too much of a coward to stay being your lover. You're too much for me. I hate it ending like this but I knew it would. I've known it for weeks, I shan't see you again, Dru.'

'Christ, you bastard! I hate you. That's what I think of your filthy Christmas present!' The flagon broke against the heater, glass flying, scented steam rising. 'I was going to make you rich. I was going to give you everything you wanted.'

He felt sick. The perfume made him feel sick.

'Good-bye, Drusilla. It was nice – once. It was the best I ever had.'

'You bloody liar! You ungrateful, bloody liar!'

Good-bye, Drusilla, good night, sweet, sweet lady, good night, good night . . .

'Good night, Drusilla,' he said aloud. 'Good night, my love. I'll talk to you in the morning.'

He fell at once into a dream. He was with Tiny in the fast red car. There wasn't much room for him because Tiny was so huge, filling up his own seat and half the passenger seat, and he was driving fast, zigzagging the car from side to side of the forest road. Gray tried to make him slow down but no voice came when he tried to speak. He couldn't speak and when he put fingers to his tongue, he found it – Oh, horrible! – divided and forked like a snake's tongue, dumb, speechless, unhuman. Then the green hillock of the roundabout was upon them, green but capped with snow, and Tiny was going over it. The red car and Tiny were going over the mountain and he, Gray, was going with them. He too was trapped in the hurtling burning car, the fire engulfing him as he struggled to get out. And now someone was hammering on the roof of the car, not a rescuer but she. Drusilla was pounding on the roof of the red Bentley to make sure that both of them were dead . . .

He gasped, 'Don't, don't . . . I've had enough. I want you to give me up,' and then, as the dream and the flames and the snow faded, as French smell and light and stuffiness burst back, 'What . . . ? Who is it? What is it?'

Broad daylight in the bedroom and someone knocking on the door. He wrapped himself in the twisted sheet. He staggered to the door and opened it. Honoré stood outside in the dragon dressing gown, his face yellow and drawn.

'What . . . ?'

'*C'est fini.*'

'I don't . . . I was asleep.'

'*C'est fini. Elle est morte.*'

'She can't be dead,' he said stupidly. 'It can't be finished, it's only just beginning . . .' And then he knew that Honoré meant his mother, that Enid Duval had died at last.


# 14


In a thin high voice Honoré said, 'You come and see her?'

'All right. If you like.'

The yellowness had gone from Enid's skin and death had erased most of the lines. Already she looked waxen, her open eyes glazed blue china.

'You ought to close her eyes,' Gray began, and then he looked at Honoré who stood at the opposite side of the bed, dulled, silent, tears falling weakly down his cheeks. 'Honoré, are you all right?'

Honoré said nothing. He fell across the bed and took the dead woman in his arms. He lay there and clung to her, making soft animal moans.

'Honoré . . .'

Gray lifted him up gently and helped him into the living room. His stepfather huddled into an armchair, shaking, his head turned against the lapel of his dressing gown. Gray gave him brandy but Honoré choked on it, sobbing. 'What shall I do?' he said in French. 'What will become of me?'

And then Gray saw that he'd been wrong, that his stepfather had loved her. The love hadn't been all on his mother's side but had been reciprocated to the full. Not a cynical purchase but true love. And that hatred, that disgust, he'd seen in Honoré's eyes while feeding her? Wasn't that what any man would feel? Disgust not for her but for life, for the world in which such things happened, in which the woman he loved became a helpless dribbling animal. He had loved her. He wasn't a caricature, a sick joke, but a man with a man's feelings. Gray forgot that he'd resented Honoré, hated him. He felt a great surge of guilt for misunderstanding, for laughing and despising. He forgot too, just for a moment, that he wasn't Honoré's son and – although he'd never before held a man so – he took Honoré in his arms and pressed him close against himself and forgot everything but Honoré's grief.

'My son, my son, what shall I do without her? I knew she was dying, I knew she must die, but death . . .'

'I know. I understand.'

'I loved her so. I never loved any woman like her.'

'I know you loved her, Honoré.'

Gray made coffee and phoned the doctor and then, when it was nine and the Marseilles shop where she worked would be open, he phoned Honoré's sister. Mme Derain agreed to come. Trilling r's, swallowed vowels assaulted Gray along a crackly line, but he gathered that she'd come by Monday when she'd made arrangements with her employer.

The day was going to be close and oppressive but cooler, the sun veiled by cloud. The doctor came, then Fr Normand, then an old woman, a very French little old woman looking like something out of Zola, whose job was to lay Enid Duval out. Gray, who had always been treated in this house as if he were a recalcitrant fifteen-year-old, fixed in Honoré's estimation at the age he'd been when Honoré had first met him, now found himself forced to take charge. It was he who received the mayor and M. and Mme Reville, he who interviewed undertakers, prepared meals, answered the phone. Broken, weeping intermittently, Honoré lay on the sofa, calling to him sometimes, begging him not to leave him. His English, of which he had been so proud and which he had used as a means of defying his stepson and demonstrating his authority, deserted him. He spoke only French. And now, using his native tongue exclusively, he ceased to be a farce Frenchman. He was the dignified bereaved who commanded respect. To Gray his stepfather appeared quite different and he realised he had never known him.

'You will stay with me, my son? Now she is gone you are all I have.'

'You'll have your sister, Honoré.'

'Oh, my sister! Forty years have passed since we lived in the same house. What is my sister to me? I want you to stay, Gray-arm. Why not? Stay here where you have a home.'

'I'll stay till after the funeral,' Gray promised.

He was surprised at the intensity of his own grief. Even last night, when he'd loved his mother again and fully forgiven her, he'd thought that her death, when it came, wouldn't touch him. But he was weighed down, as he busied himself with the hundred and one things that needed doing, by a quite irrational feeling. He realised that during all those years there had existed at the back of his mind a hope that one day he'd be able to have it all out with her. He'd put his case and she hers, they'd explain to each other, and in those explanations their pain would be resolved. Now she was dead and he mourned her because that day could never come. He could never tell her now how she'd hurt him and she could never tell him why.

Drusilla seemed very far away. He hadn't forgotten to phone her but only deferred it. Later in the day, when all these people had gone, when the phone had stopped ringing and he'd finished the letters to England Honoré had asked him to write, then . . .

'Mrs 'Arcoort and Mrs Ouarrinaire and our dear Isabel.'

'Isabel's in Australia, Honoré. I'll be back in England before she is.'

'Change your mind. Stay here with me.'

'I can't but I'll stay while you need me.'

He took his letters to the post. It had begun to rain. The great *camions* travelling along the road to Jency splashed muddy water against his legs. The funeral had been fixed for Monday, so he could go home on Tuesday and maybe see Drusilla that same night. It was getting a bit late to phone her now, nearly half past five, and the weekend was coming. Maybe it would be better to delay phoning her till Monday morning – she'd understand when she knew about his mother. But would she? Wasn't the real reason for his not phoning her a fear that he couldn't take the sharp comment he was likely to get? The 'So she's popped off at last' or 'Has she left you anything?' He couldn't quite take that now, not even though it came from his Dru that he loved, his Dru who had changed and was going to be his for ever.

He heard the phone bell before he was inside the house. Another local sympathiser probably. Honoré wasn't in any fit state to answer it. He went quickly into the room where the phone was, not looking at the empty bed whose blue cover was drawn taut and straight over a bare mattress. The window was open to blow in rain and blow out the smell of death. He picked up the receiver.

'Hi.'

'Dru?' he said, as if it could be anyone else. 'Dru, is that you?'

'You didn't phone,' she said in a voice that seemed to contain a world of desolation.

'No.' He knew his tone sounded clipped but he couldn't help it. He was bracing himself for the unkind retort. 'No, I couldn't,' he said. 'Dru, my mother died this morning.'

Not an unkind retort but silence. Then, as if she had received a shock, almost as if the dead woman had been someone she had known and loved, she said, 'Oh, *no!*'

He was moved, warmed, by the consternation in her voice. All day, strangely when they were on the point of renewing their love affair, she had been more removed from him, less present, than at any time since Christmas. She'd been – he confessed it to himself now – almost a burden, an extra problem to cope with. But that appalled 'Oh, *no!*' which seemed to contain more feeling and more sympathy than any long speech of condolence, touched his heart and brought a tremor to his voice.

'I'm afraid so, Dru. My stepfather's taken it very hard and I . . .'

She wailed, 'You won't be able to come home now!' She sounded sick, despairing. 'I can tell by your voice, you're going to stay for the funeral!'

It was wonderful, of course, to be wanted, to know she needed him so much. But he'd have felt happier if her sympathy had been pure and simple, without strings. Yet for her to be sympathetic at all . . .

'I must, Dru darling,' he said. 'Try to understand. Honoré needs me till his sister comes. I've promised to stay till Tuesday.'

'But *I* need you!' she cried, the imperious child whose wishes must always be paramount.

'God, and don't I need you? But we've waited six months. We can wait four more days. You must see this changes things.'

Please God, let her not be difficult about it, not now. Let her not make a scene *now*. His happiness at rediscovering her couldn't take storms just yet. He felt he needed to carry that happiness undisturbed, unalloyed, through the next few days like a talisman; to have it there as a quiet place to retreat to when the sadness of bereavement grew sharp and the practical tasks exasperating. He listened to her ominous silence that seemed charged with protest, petulance, resentment.

'Dru, don't ask me to break my promise.'

He dreaded the phone going down, the angry crash as she hung up on him. But there was no crash, no stormy outburst, and when she broke the silence her voice had grown hard with the chill of Thursday morning.

'I'm afraid,' she said, 'I'll have to. I haven't told you why I phoned yet.'

'Did we ever need a reason?'

'No, but this time there happens to be one. This vet wants to see you.'

'Vet?' he said obtusely.

'Yes, *vet*. Remember?'

Dido. He hadn't forgotten Dido but somehow he'd thought that now she'd been rescued from the hovel and fed and given attention, everything would be all right.

'Why does he want to see me?'

'I phoned him today to check up. He says the dog's got something wrong with her liver, something bad, and she's in a very bad way. He has to talk to the owner or someone taking the place of the owner before he operates on her. Gray, you can't just leave all this to me. Don't you see, you have to take the responsibility?'

Gray sat down heavily on Honoré's bed. He was remembering Dido as he'd last seen her, so vigorous, so vital, rippling with health. There was something sickeningly ugly in the idea that he'd destroyed all that by his lack of responsibility.

116

'How can she have something wrong with her liver?' he said. 'I mean, malnutrition, I could understand that. But something wrong with her liver? What can I do about it? How can I help by coming home?'

'He wants to see you tomorrow,' she persisted. 'Gray, I said you'd come. I didn't see why not. It isn't very far just to come to London. Tiny often flies to Paris and back in a day.'

'Dru, don't you see how fantastic it is? You can tell him to go ahead and operate, do anything to save the dog's life. I'll pay. I'll manage to borrow the money somehow and I'll pay.'

'You'll do that but you won't come home and see to it yourself? Not even if I promise to meet you at the hovel afterwards?'

His hand closed hard on the receiver and a long thrill that was almost pain passed through his body. But it was impossible . . . 'I don't have the money to go in for this jet-set flying about. All I have is about three quid.'

'I'll pay your fare. No, don't say you won't take Tiny's money. It won't be his. I've sold my amethyst ring. And Tiny didn't give it me, my father did.'

'Dru, I don't know what . . .'

'I told the vet you'd be there at about three. Go and ask your stepfather if it'll be all right to leave him for a day. I'll hold on.'

Dry-mouthed, he laid the receiver on the pillow and went into the living room. 'Honoré, I've got to go home tomorrow. I'll go in the morning and be back by night.'

A bitter but very non-farcical argument ensued. Why did he have to go? Where was the money to come from? What would Honoré do on his own? Finally, why didn't Gray get a job, settle down (preferably in France) marry and forget about mad, bad Englishwomen who loved animals more than people?

'I promise I'll be back by midnight and I'll stay till after the funeral. Your friends will be with you. I'll ask Mme Reville to come to you for the whole day.'

Gray left him, feeling sick because Honoré was crying again. He picked up the phone.

'All right, Dru, I'll come.'

'I knew you would! Oh, God, I can't believe it. I'm going to see you tomorrow. I'm going to see you!'

117

'I've got to see this vet first and that won't be pleasant. You'd better tell me the set-up.'

'You've got the address. Just go there and talk to him at three.'

'And when and where do I see you?'

'If it were only a weekday,' she said, 'I could come to the airport. That's not possible on a Saturday. Tiny's going to look at some house he wants to buy for his mother in the afternoon. I'll get out of that and I'll see you at the hovel at five. O.K.?'

'Can't you – can't you meet me at the vet's?'

'I'll try, but don't count on it. I should be able to drive you back to Heathrow.'

'But we will have . . .' He couldn't frame what he wanted to say in the right words, the words that would make her understand. 'We will have a little time together?'

She'd understood. She gave an excited chuckle. 'You know me,' she said.

'Ah, Dru, I love you! I'd go a thousand miles to be with you. Say you love me and that everything that's happened doesn't matter any more.'

He held his breath, listening to her silence. A long long silence. He could hear her breathing shallowly as he'd breathed that night he rang her from Marble Arch. Suddenly, coolly and steadily, she spoke:

'I love you. I've decided, if you still want me, I'll leave Tiny and come and live with you.'

'My darling . . .'

'We'll talk about it tomorrow,' she said.

Bang, the phone went down and he was left holding the emptiness, savouring the fulness, hardly daring to believe what she'd said. But she had, she had. And he was going to see her tomorrow.

At the end of the long lane she'd be waiting for him. He'd run the length of it. He'd let himself in by the front door and the scent of her would meet him, *Amorce dangereuse*. And she'd come out to him, her arms outstretched, her hair like a bell of gold, her white hand bare of the ring she'd sold to fetch him back to her . . .

Honoré had stopped crying but he looked very sad.

'I have been thinking, you must take the car. *Si, si, j'insiste*. It is the quickest way to fetch you back soon.'

'Thank you, Honoré, it's kind of you.'

'But you must remember that in France we drive on the *correct* side of the road and . . .'

'I'll take great care of your car.'

'*Seigneur!* It is not of the car that I am thinking but of you, my son, you who are all I have left.'

Gray smiled, touched his shoulder. Yes, he must stop seeing the worst in everyone, attributing to people self-seeking motives. He must try to understand the power of love. Drusilla would have killed for love, was leaving Tiny for love just as he was abandoning Honoré for love. O Love, what crimes are committed in thy name . . .

'Let us have a little glass of *cognac*,' said Honoré.


# 15


The plane got to Heathrow at one-fifteen. Gray bought a London A-Z Guide, leaving himself with just enough money for his Tube fare to Leytonstone and his train fare to Waltham Abbey. By ten to three he was at Leytonstone station, one of those pallid, desert-like and arid halts that abound on the outer reaches of the Tube lines, and had walked round the curving tunnel into the street.

Drusilla had said nothing about a chance of meeting him there and he didn't expect her, but he couldn't help eyeing the cars parked by the kerb in the faint hope that the E-type might be among them. Of course it wasn't there. He thought of how often her feet must tread this very spot where he now was, how often she must come to this tunnel entrance on her way to London, and then he began to walk down the long street of biggish late Victorian houses, his A-Z in his hand.

Taking the back doubles that filled the area between the road where the station was and the last far-flung finger of Epping Forest, he found George Street, a curving, respectable-looking terrace, which lay under the shadow of an enormous Gothic hospital. Number twenty-one bore no brass plate or anything else to indicate that a vet occupied it, but he went up the steps and rang the bell. Expecting that at any minute the door would open and an aggressive middle-aged man in a white coat, his pockets bristling with syringes and steel combs, would fall upon him with threats of the R.S.P.C.A. and certain prosecution, Gray mentally rehearsed his defence. But when the door did open – after he'd rung twice more – no mingled smells of dog and disinfectant rolled out, no veterinary veteran was waiting to excoriate him with his tongue. Instead, a smell of baking cakes and a girl holding a baby.

'I've an appointment with the vet at three o'clock.'

'What vet?' said the girl.

'Isn't there a vet has his . . .' What did they call it? '. . . his surgery here?'

'You want the place up the road. It's on this side. I don't know the number. You'll see the name up.'

Surely Drusilla had said twenty-one? But maybe she hadn't. He hadn't after all, written it down. Perhaps she'd said forty-nine which was, in fact, the number of the house on which the vet's name-plate was. He was quite used to forgetting things and he no longer really wondered at his forgetfulness. His lapses were all due, he thought, to psychological blocks, defences put up by his unconscious, and these would soon go away now. The really important things he never forgot. Nothing could have made him forget his date with Drusilla at five.

The doggy smell was here all right, a thick animal reek. Finding the door on the latch, he'd walked in without ringing and was standing in the waiting room, contemplating the copies of *The Field* and *Our Dogs* and wondering what the correct procedure was, when a woman in a khaki smock came in to ask what he wanted.

'Mr Greenberg doesn't have a surgery on Saturday afternoons,' she said curtly. 'We're only open for clipping and stripping.'

Distant squeaks and grunts, coming from the upper regions, testified that these operations were at present being performed.

'My name is Lanceton,' he said, pausing to allow for the expression of hatred and disgust which would cross her face, when she realised she was in the presence of an animal torturer. 'My dog – well, a dog I was looking after – you've

120

got it here.' Her face didn't change. She simply stared. 'A yellow labrador called Dido. She was brought to Mr – er, Greenberg last Thursday.'

'Brought here? We don't board dogs.'

'No, but she was ill. She was left here. She was going to have an operation.'

'I will check,' said Khaki Smock.

She came back after quite a long time, more than five minutes. 'We've no records of what you say happened. What time on Thursday?'

'Around lunchtime.'

Khaki Smock said triumphantly, 'Mr Greenberg wasn't here after twelve on Thursday.'

'Could you phone him or something?'

'Well, I could. It's very inconvenient. It won't be any use. He wasn't here.'

'Please,' said Gray firmly.

He sat down and leafed through *The Field*. Twenty-five past three. He'd have to get out of here in five minutes if he was going to make it to the hovel by five. He could hear her phoning in another room. Was it possible he'd got the name of the street wrong as well as the number? She came back at last, looking exasperated.

'Mr Greenberg knows nothing about it.'

He had to accept that. He went back into the street, utterly at a loss. The E-type wasn't there. Drusilla hadn't managed to come and meet him. Or was she, at this moment, waiting somewhere else for him, parked outside another vet's in another street? There must be dozens of vets in Leytonstone. Well, not dozens but several. As he walked down the street the way he'd come he had the sensation of being in a dream, one of those nightmares in which one is already late for an urgent meeting or rendez-vous, but everything goes wrong. Transport is irregular or delayed, people antagonistic, addresses mistaken and simply reached goals hideously elusive.

The obvious thing was to try and get Drusilla on the phone. Tiny would be out house-hunting and maybe she'd be there and alone. He dialled her number but no one answered, so he looked through the yellow page directory for veterinary surgeons. Immediately he saw the mistake he'd made, a mistake possible only when two suburban and contiguous townships have closely similar names. Greenberg was a vet at 49 George Street, Leytonstone; Cherwell a vet at 21 George Street, Leyton. Dido was in Leyton, not Leyton*stone*.

Twenty to four. Well, he'd come over for the sake of the dog, hadn't he? That was the real purpose of his trip, and it was no good giving up just because time was getting on. Yet even now, if he gave up now, he wouldn't get to the hovel before five-fifteen. He was aware of that pressure, engendering panic, which affects us when we know we shall be late for an all-important, longed-for appointment. The air seems to swim, the ground drags at our feet, people and inanimate things conspire to detain us.

He opened his A-Z. George Street, Leyton, looked miles away, almost in Hackney Marshes. He didn't know how to get there but he knew it would take at least half an hour. That wasn't to be thought of, out of the question when Drusilla would already be dressing for him, scenting herself, watching the clock. Instead, he dialled Cherwell's number. Nothing happened, no one replied. Vets, obviously, didn't work this late on Saturdays.

But the dog . . . Surely this Cherwell guy would act on his own initiative? Surely, if an operation were necessary, he'd operate with or without consent? All he, Gray, could do was phone him from France first thing on Monday morning. And now put all this vet business behind him, waste no more time on it, but get to Liverpool Street fast.

There must be, he thought, a quicker way of making this trans-forest journey of seven or eight miles than by going all the way back into London and out again via sprawling northern suburbs. There must be buses, if only he knew their routes and their stops. If he'd had money he could have phoned for a mini-cab. As it was, he had just enough for his train fare.

The Tube seemed to go exceptionally slowly and he had to wait fifteen minutes for a train to Waltham Cross. By the time it came and he was in the carriage his watch he had kept checking with station clocks to make sure it wasn't fast, showed twenty-five minutes to five.

Only once had she ever been late for a date with him and that had been that first time in New Quebec Street. She

122

wouldn't be late now. By now she'd have been waiting half an hour for him, growing bewildered perhaps, distressed, as she paced the rooms, running to the window, opening the front door to look up the lane. Then, when he hadn't come and still he hadn't come, she'd say, I won't look, I'll go away and count a hundred and by then he'll have come. Or she'd go upstairs where she couldn't see the lane and scrutinise herself again in the mirror, once more comb her flying fiery hair, touch more scent to her throat, run her hands lightly, in sensuous anticipation, over the body she'd prepared for him. Count another hundred, go slowly down the stairs, walk to the window, lift the curtain, close her eyes. When I open my eyes I shall see him coming . . .

At half past five he was at the Waltham Abbey end of the lane. There had been an accident on the corner and the police signs were still up, the police cars still there. In the middle of the road black skid marks met and converged on a heap of sand, flung down perhaps to cover blood and horror. He didn't stop to look or enquire but quickened his pace, telling himself that a man of his age ought to be able to run two miles in twenty minutes.

He ran on the hard flat surface of the metalled road, avoiding the soggy grass verges. Pocket Lane had never seemed so long, and the twists and turns in it, the long straight stretches, with which he was so familiar, seemed multiplied as if the lane were made of elastic which some hostile giant had stretched out to frustrate him. The blood pounded in his head and his throat was parched by the time he came to the point where the tarmac petered out into clay.

Under the trees where the E-type should have been was a big dark green Mercedes. So she'd changed her car. Tiny had bought her a new one. Gray was exhausted with running but the sight of her car brought him a new impetus and he raced on, his trousers covered with yellow mud. The rain that had fallen on the other side of the Channel had fallen here too, and in the deep ruts the clay was almost liquid. This last stretch of the lane – how short it had always seemed on those nights when he had walked her back to her car! Had it really been as long as this, hundreds of yards long surely? But he could see the hovel now, the pallid hulk of it, white as the overcast sky. The gate was

123

open, swinging slightly in the faint breeze that set all those millions of leaves trembling. He stopped for a moment at the gate to get his breath. The sweat stood on his face and he was gasping, but he'd made it, he'd done it in just under twenty minutes.

He unlocked the front door, calling before he was inside, 'Dru, Dru I'm sorry I'm so late. I ran all the way from the station.' The door swung to and clicked shut. 'Dru, are you upstairs?'

There was no sound, no answer, but he thought he could smell her scent, *Amorce dangereuse*. For a second he was sure he smelt it, and then it was gone, lost in the hovel smells of dust and slowly rotting wood. Breathing more evenly now, he dumped his case and shed his jacket on to the floor. The 'lounge' was empty and so was the kitchen. Of course she'd be upstairs, in bed even, waiting for him. That would be like her, to tease him, to wait for him silently, giggling under the bedclothes, and then, when he came into the bedroom, break into a gale of laughter.

He ran up the staircase two at a time. The bedroom door was shut. He knew he'd left it open – he always did – and his heart began to drum. Outside the door he hesitated, not from shyness or fear or doubt, but to let himself feel fully the excitement and the joy he'd been suppressing all day. Now, when he'd reached his goal at last, he could yield to these emotions. He could stand here for ten seconds, his eyes closed, rejoicing that they were together again; stand on the threshold of their reunion, savour it and what it would mean to the full, then open the door.

Opening his eyes, he pushed the door softly, not speaking.

The bed was empty, the dirty sheets flung back as he'd left them, a cup half full of cold tea dregs on the bedside table as he'd left it, as he'd left it . . . The breeze fluttered the strips of rag that served as curtains and swayed a dust-hung cobweb. A hollowness where that full pounding heart had been, he surveyed the empty room, unable to believe.

The spare room was empty too. He went downstairs and out into the garden where the bracken now grew as high as a man and where little weeds already greened the ash patch of his fire. No sun shone out of the white sky. There was no sound but the muted twitter of songless birds. A gust of wind ruffled the bracken tops and rustled away into the Forest.

But she must be here, her car was here. Perhaps she'd got tired of waiting and gone for a walk. He called her name once more and then he walked back down the lane, splashing through the yellow mud.

The car was still there, still empty. He went up to it and looked through its windows. On the back seat was a copy of the *Financial Times* and, lying on top of it, a spectacles case. Drusilla wouldn't have those things in her car. She wouldn't have a black leather head-rest for her passenger or a pair of very masculine-looking string-backed driving gloves on the dashboard shelf.

It wasn't her car. She hadn't come.

'You won't come? Not even if I promise to meet you at the hovel afterwards?'

That's what she'd said.

'Oh, God, I can't believe it. I'm going to see you tomorrow. I'm going to see you!'

He resisted a temptation to kick the car, the innocent inanimate thing that had nothing to do with her but probably belonged to some bird-watcher or archaeologist. Dragging his feet, his head bent, he didn't see Mr Tringham until the old man was almost upon him and they had nearly collided.

'Look where you're going, young man!'

Gray would have gone on without making any answer but Mr Tringham, who was for once not carrying a book and who had apparently come out of his cottage especially to talk to him, said rather accusingly, 'You've been in France.'

'Yes.'

'There was a man in your garden earlier on. Little short chap, walking round the place, looking up at the windows. Thought you ought to know. He could have been trying to break in.'

What did he care who broke in? What did it matter to him who'd been there if she hadn't? 'I couldn't care less,' he said.

'Hmm. I went out for my walk early, thinking it might rain later. There was this rough-looking long-haired chap sitting under a tree and this other one in your garden. I'd have called the police only I haven't got a telephone.'

'I know,' Gray said bitterly.

'Hmm. You young people take these things very lightly, I must say. Personally, I think we should use your phone – or Mr Warriner's, I should say – and get on to the police now.'

Gray said with irritable savagery, 'I don't want the police messing about the place. I want to be left alone.'

He walked away sullenly. Mr Tringham grunted something after him about decadence and modern youth, after the manner of Honoré. Gray slammed the hovel door shut and went into the lounge, aiming a kick at the golf clubs which fell over with a clang.

She hadn't come. He'd travelled all this way to see her, travelled hundreds of miles, run the last bit till he'd felt his lungs were bursting, and she hadn't come.


# 16


The phone clicked, then began to ring. He lifted the receiver dully, knowing it would be she, not wanting her voice or any part of her, but the whole of her.

'Hi.'

'What happened?' he said wearily.

'What happened to *you*?'

'Dru, I got here at five to six. I ran like hell. Couldn't you have waited for me? Where are you?'

'I'm at home,' she said. 'I just got in. Tiny said he'd be home at six and I couldn't think of an excuse for not being home too. I left it till the last moment and then I had to go. He's out in the garden now but we'd better be quick.'

'Christ, Dru, you promised me. You promised you'd be here. You were going to drive me to the airport. That doesn't matter but if you could have made the time for that, surely you could have . . . I wanted you so much.'

'Can't be helped. I did what I could. I should have known you're always late and you always make a mess of things. You didn't even find the vet, did you?'

'How can you know that?'

'Because I rang Mr Cherwell myself to check if you'd been.'

'So it *was* Cherwell . . . ?'

'Of course it was. Twenty-one George Street, Leyton. I told you, didn't I? It's no use, anyway. The dog's had to be destroyed.'

'Oh, Dru, *no!*'

'Oh, Gray, *yes*. You couldn't have done anything if you had seen Cherwell, so it's no good worrying about it. What are you going to do now?'

'Lie down and die too, I should think. I've come all this way for nothing and I haven't got a bean. If ever anyone made a pointless journey, this is it. I haven't had anything to eat all day and I haven't got my fare back. And you ask me what I'm going to do.'

'You haven't found the money, then?'

'Money? What money? I've only been here ten minutes. I'm plastered with mud and dead tired.'

'My poor Gray. Never mind, I'll tell you what you're going to do. You're going to change your clothes, take the money I left you – it's in the kitchen – and get the hell out of that hole back to France. Just write the day off, don't think about it. Quick now, I can see Tiny coming back up the garden.'

'*Tiny?* What the hell do we care about Tiny now? If you're joining me next week, if you're coming to live with me, what does it matter what Tiny thinks? The sooner he knows the better.' He cleared his throat. 'Dru, you haven't changed your mind? You are going to come to me next week?'

She sighed, a fluttery trembly sound. Her words were firm but not her voice. 'I never change my mind.'

'God, I feel sick when I think I've come all this way and I'm not going to see you after all. When will I see you?'

'Soon. As soon as you get back. Tuesday. I'm going to ring off now.'

'No, don't. Please don't.' If the receiver went down now, if she ended as she always did without a farewell . . . But she always ended like that. 'Dru, please!'

For the first time she said it. 'Good-bye, Gray. Good-bye.'

On the bath counter he found the electricity bill, the phone bill, the cheque from his publishers – the first two cancelling out the third – a postcard from Mal and, strangely enough, one from Francis and Charmian in Lynmouth. Beside all this correspondence she'd left the money for him in an untidy heap. It seemed a small heap until he looked again, saw that the notes were all tenners and that there were ten of them. He'd expected thirty pounds and found a hundred.

There was no loving note with them. She'd left a hundred pounds in a careless heap as someone else might have left twenty pence in small change; she'd sold her amethyst ring to get him money and he felt a warm, heart-beating gratitude, but he'd have liked a letter. Just a word to tell of her love for him, her distress at not seeing him. He'd never received a letter from her in all their time together and he didn't know what her handwriting looked like.

Still, he wouldn't need handwriting, mementoes, recorded evidence of her, after next week. It was getting on for half past six and he ought to be on his way. Change these filthy clothes first, though. He went upstairs, wondering what he could find to put on, for he'd left everything dirty just as he'd taken it off.

He hadn't looked round the bedroom at all beyond looking at the bed itself. Now he saw that his dirty jeans and shirt had been washed and actually ironed and were draped over the back of the bedroom chair with his clean Arran. She'd done that for him. She'd cleaned up his kitchen and washed his clothes. Changing quickly, he wondered if she'd done that to show him she could do it, that she wouldn't be helpless, the bewildered rich girl uprooted from luxury, when she came to him. He rolled up his clay-spattered trousers and thrust them under the bath cover. The window had been polished, the paintwork washed in places. She'd done all that for him and sold her precious ring too. He ought to be on top of the world with happiness, but disappointment at not seeing her still weighed him down. Nothing she could do for him or give him made up for the lack of her.

But once back in France, he'd phone her and ask her to be waiting for him when he got home on Tuesday night. She still had her key. The one he could see hanging over the sink must be Isabel's, left there when she'd brought Dido – guilt for the dog's death welled up inside him. His own absent-mindedness had brought that about and led him to make a mistake that almost amounted to criminality. But once Drusilla was with him all that would be changed. He'd have to plan, remember, make decisions.

Just time for a pot of milkless tea and something out of a tin before he set off back to the station. The phone was on the hook, his correspondence examined, the back door bolted. Now was there anything he ought to remember? Perhaps he'd better take that spare key with him. If the little man Mr Tringham had seen had really been a burglar, the key was in a very vulnerable position. Break one pane of glass in the window, insert a hand and reach for the hook, and the hovel, Mal's hovel, would be anyone's to do as he liked with. Mal wouldn't be too happy to have his golf clubs pinched or any of that tatty old furniture which was, after all, all he had.

Congratulating himself on this unprecedented prudence, Gray unhooked the key and was slipping it into his pocket when he paused, surprised to see how bright and shiny it was. Surely he'd given Isabel the spare key Mal had left him? This key looked more like the one he'd had specially cut for Drusilla when she'd been visiting him so often that there was a chance she'd have to let herself in before he got back from the shops. But perhaps he hadn't given her the new one. Perhaps, in fact, she'd had the old one and the shiny key had been kept for spare. He couldn't remember at all and it didn't seem to matter.

He drank his tea and left the dirty crockery on the draining board. The hundred pounds in his pocket, the two keys, he closed the front door behind him. A thin drizzle, not much more than a mist, was falling and heavier drops popped rhythmically from waterlogged beech leaves. He walked on the wet grass to avoid the paintbox mud.

The green car was still there. Probably it was a stolen car, abandoned in this out-of-the-way spot. Or its owner had gone on some nature ramble in the forest depths. Both the Willises were in their front garden, standing on their lawn which now looked as good as new to Gray, arguing about something or commiserating perhaps with each other over a case of mildew or leaf blight. They saw Gray and turned away very stiffly, ramrod-backed.

At the corner the police cars had gone and the sand been removed. He walked quickly on towards the station.

Over France the moon was shining. Had the sky cleared in England too and was this same moon shining down on Epping Forest and Combe Park? She and Tiny would be in bed, the gross man in his black and red pyjamas reading some company chairman's memoirs or maybe the *Financial Times*, the slender girl in white frills, reading a novel. But this Saturday night there wouldn't be a phone call from a strange man, saying nothing, breathing heavily. And she wouldn't be lonely any more but thinking about how she'd have to tell the husband in the next bed she'd be leaving him next week. Dream of me, Drusilla . . .

He drove past the last *nids de poule* sign and entered sleeping Bajon, skirting the clump of chestnut trees and the house called Les Marrons. The moon gave him enough light to see by as he covered the car once more in its protective nylon. But the hall of Le Petit Trianon was pitch dark. He felt for the light switch and stumbled over something that was standing just inside the door, a bouquet of funeral lilies in a plastic urn. Afraid that the noise might have awakened his stepfather, he pushed open the bedroom door which Honoré had left ajar.

The thin moonlight, which had transformed the gnome circus into a ghostly ballet, edged the furniture with silver and made little pale geometric patterns on the carpet. Honoré, his greyish-black hair spiky and tousled, lay curled in his own bed but facing the one where Enid had slept, one arm bridging the space between, his hand tucked under her pillow. He was deeply asleep, serene, almost smiling. Gray supposed that they had always slept like that, Honoré's hand holding Enid's, and he saw that his stepfather, reality and its awfulness alienated by dreams, made belief that she lay there still and still held his hand under her cheek.

Touched, awed by the sight, Gray thought how he and Drusilla would sleep like that but in same the bed, always together. And he dreamed of her, the most tender untroubled dreams he'd ever had of her, throughout the night until the baying of the farmer's dog awoke him at eight.

Then he got up and took coffee to Honoré who was neither smiling nor serene in the mornings now and whose methodical early-to-rise habits seemed to have died with Enid's death.

Mme Reville called and carried Honoré off to Mass. Gray had the house to himself and he was alone with the phone. What did she and Tiny do on Sundays? Searching in his mind for some recollection, some account she might have given him of their usual Sunday activities, he found only a blank. Certainly they wouldn't go to church. Did Tiny perhaps play golf or drink with some equally affluent cronies in the pub that crowned the summit of Little Cornwall? There was just a chance she might be alone, or a chance even that she'd told Tiny by now and would be glad of a call from him to back her up and give her confidence.

Without further hesitation, he dialled the number. It rang and rang but no one answered. He was trying again an hour later when Mme Reville's car drew up outside and he had to abandon the attempt. Well, he'd said Monday and surely he could wait till Monday?

The day passed slowly. Every hour now that he was away from her seemed endless. He kept thinking of the scene which might at this moment, at any moment, be taking place at Combe Park with Drusilla declaring her intention to leave and Tiny his intention of stopping her at all costs. He might even use violence. Or he might throw her out. Still, she had her key and she could take refuge at the hovel if necessary.

Honoré lay on the sofa, reading the letters Enid had written to him during the short period between their meeting and their marriage. Weeping freely, he read bits of them aloud to Gray.

'Ah, how she loved me! But so many doubts she had, my little Enid. What of my boy, she writes here, my friends? How shall I learn to live in your world, I who speak only the French I learned in school?' Honoré sat bolt upright, pointing a finger at Gray. 'I crushed all her doubts with my great love. I am master now, I said. You do as I say and I say I love you, so nothing else can matter. Ah, how she adapted herself! She was already old,' he said with Gallic frankness, 'but soon she speaks French like a French-

131

woman born, makes new friends, leaves all behind to be with me. With true love, Gray-arm, it can be so.'

'I'm sure it can,' said Gray, thinking of Drusilla.

'Let us have a little *cognac*, my son.' Honoré bundled up his letters and rubbed at his eyes with his sleeve. 'Tomorrow I shall be better. After the funeral I shall – what is it you English say? – pull me together.'

After the funeral, while the company drank wine and ate cake in the living room, Gray slipped away to phone Drusilla. She'd be waiting impatiently for his call, he thought, had possibly tried to phone him earlier while they were at the church. Very likely she'd be sitting by the phone, feeling lonely and frightened because she'd had a terrible row with Tiny and now might think, because she hadn't heard from him, that her lover had deserted her too. He dialled the code and the number and heard it start to ring.

After about six double peals the receiver was lifted.

'Combe Park.'

The coarse voice with its cockney inflexion, the voice that obviously wasn't Drusilla's, almost floored him. Then he realised it must be the daily woman. He and Drusilla had always had an arrangement that if he phoned and the woman answered he was to put the phone down without speaking. But not any longer surely? That didn't apply any longer, did it?

'Combe Park,' she said again. 'Who's that?'

Better try again later. Better not do anything now to interfere with what might be a delicate situation. He put the receiver back very carefully and quietly as if by so doing he could make believe he hadn't called Combe Park at all, and then he went back into the room where they were all talking in hushed voices, sipping Dubonnet and nibbling at *Chamonix oranges*. Immediately the mayor took him to one side and questioned him closely as to his visit to England. Had he been able to watch a Test match or, better still, managed a trip to Manchester? Gray answered no to both, very conscious of the glare Mme Derain had fixed on him. Her eyes were beady like her brother's and her skin as brown, but in her case the small Duval bones were concealed under a mountain of hard fat and her features buried in dark wrinkled cushions.

'*Ici.*' she said like a notice in a shop window, '*on parle français, n'est ce pas?*'

She had taken over the management of the household. It was evident that she intended to stay, to give up her job and her flat over the Marseille fish shop, for the comparative luxury and peace of Le Petit Trianon. Even more parsimonious than Honoré, she was already making plans to take in a lodger, already talking of removing the marigolds and the tripods and growing vegetables in the back garden. And English stepsons who contributed nothing to the household expenses weren't welcome to her.

One glass of Dubonnet per head was all she allowed and then the mourners were hustled away. Gray tried to phone Drusilla again and again the daily woman answered. His third attempt, made at five-thirty, the last safe moment, didn't stand a chance, for Mme Derain actually wrested the phone from his hand. She didn't moan at him or talk of *formidable* expense but said stonily that she planned to have the apparatus disconnected as soon as possible.

He'd have to try again in the morning while she was out buying bread, he thought, but when the morning came, when Honoré was drinking coffee in the kitchen, he entered the bedroom to find her already there. Ostensibly removing signs from it which would be painful to her brother, she was in fact, Gray thought, sorting out which of Enid's clothes she could convert to her own use. Gray guessed he was the type of man who would have liked to keep his dead wife's room as a shrine, each little possession of hers treasured as a reminder of their happiness. But this wasn't Mme Derain's way. She had allowed her brother to keep Enid's wedding ring – although suggesting it would be more prudent to sell it – and Honoré held the ring loosely in his horny brown hands. It was too small to go on any of his fingers.

'I want to give you back the money you sent me,' Gray said. 'Here it is, thirty pounds. I want you to have it.'

Honoré expostulated, but feebly and not for long. Gray foresaw his stepfather's future life as a way of crafty deception in which money would have to be slyly wrested from his sister and windfalls concealed. This was the first of them. Honoré slipped the money into his pocket, but not

before he had glanced, already surreptitiously, already fearfully, towards the door.

'Stay another week, Gray-arm.'

'I can't. I've got a lot of things to do. For one thing, I'm
going to move.'

'Ah, you will move and forget to give old Honoré your
new address and he will lose you.'

'I won't forget.'

'You'll come back for your holidays?'

'There won't be room for me when you've got your lodger.'

Gray wondered suddenly if he should tell Honoré about
Drusilla, give him an expurgated version perhaps, tell him
there was a girl he hoped to marry when she'd got her
divorce. And that was true. One day they'd be married. He
wanted it that way now, open, above-board for all the
world to see, no more secrets. He glanced at Honoré who
was eating and drinking mechanically, whose thoughts
were obviously with his dead wife. No, let it remain a secret
for now. But it struck him as strange that he'd even contemplated telling his stepfather, his old enemy. All those
years when they might have had a happy relationship they
had gone out of their way each to antagonise the other,
each obstinately insisting on speaking the other's language.
And now, when the relationship was ending, when it was
probable – and both knew it – that they would never meet
again, Honoré spoke French and he English and they
understood each other and something that was almost love
had grown up between them.

Still, one day he might come back. He and Drusilla could
have their honeymoon in France, drive through Bajon –
hitch through more likely, he thought – and call and see
Honoré . . .

Should he try to phone her from the village? Call at the
Écu and use the phone in the bar? That way they'd be able
to fix a definite time for their meeting and he could have
a meal ready for her and wine when she came at last to her
new home and her new life.

But it would be hard to explain this action to Honoré
who seemed to have an *idée fixe* that his stepson had formed
a liaison with an elderly dog-breeder. Why go to all that
trouble, anyway, when in three of four hours he'd be in
London?

'You will miss your plane,' said Mme Derain, coming in with one of Enid's scarves over her arm, a scarf that Honoré winced at the sight of. 'Come now, the bus leaves in ten minutes.'

'I will drive you to Jency, my son.'

'No, Honoré, you're not up to it. I'll be O.K. You stay here and rest.'

'*J'insiste*. Am I not your papa? Now, you do as I say.'

So the nylon cover was removed from the Citroën and Honoré drove him to Jency. There they waited, drinking coffee at a little pavement café and, when the bus came, Honoré embraced him tenderly, kissing his cheeks.

'Write to me, Gray-arm.'

'Of course I will.'

And Gray waved from the bus until the little figue in the dark beret, the French onion seller, the waiter, the thief of his happy adolescence, the killer of his dream, had dwindled to a black dot in the wide dusty square.


# 17


London lay under a heavy, almost unbreathable, humidity. Like November, Gray thought, but warm. The sky was uniformly pastel grey and it seemed to have fallen to lie on roofs and tree tops like a sagging muslin bag. There was no wind, no breath of it to move a leaf or flutter a flag or lift a tress from a woman's head. The atmosphere was that of a greenhouse without its flowers.

He dialled her number from the air terminal and got no reply. Probably she was out shopping. She couldn't be expected to stay in all day just on the chance that he'd phone. At Liverpool Street he tried again and again at Waltham Cross but each time the bell rang into a void. Once, maybe twice, she could have been out shopping or in the garden – but every time? He hadn't said he'd call her but surely she'd guess he would. There was no point, though, in getting into a state about it, rushing into every phone box he saw on every stage of his journey. Better wait now till he got home.

Pocket Lane had attracted to its moist dim shelter what seemed like all the buzzing insects in Essex. Slumbrously they rose from leaf and briar, wheeled and sang. He brushed them off his face and off the carrier bag of food he'd bought at a delicatessen in Gloucester Road, cold meat and salad for their supper, and a bottle of wine. Maybe she was out because she'd done what he'd wistfully envisaged, taken refuge from Tiny at the hovel. She might be there waiting for him. But no, he wasn't going to let himself in for that one again, for the hideous Saturday nightmare of half-killing himself running to her and then finding she wasn't there.

Until he was inside the house and had been upstairs he couldn't rid himself of the very real hope of it. Hope doesn't die because you tell yourself it is pointless. He dropped the food on to the iron-legged table and lifted the phone. Then, before he dialled, he saw that the golf clubs were standing up, resting once more against the wall. But he'd kicked them over and left them in a scattered heap. . . . So she had been there? Five-O-eight, then the four digits. He let the bell ring twenty times and then he put the receiver back, resolving to keep calm, to be reasonable and not to try her number again for two hours.

She'd said Tuesday but she hadn't said anything about getting in touch with him before she came. And there were all sorts of explanations to account for her absence from Combe Park. She might even have gone to the airport to meet him and they had missed each other. He went out into the front garden and lay down in the bracken. It was slightly less stuffy than the house, slightly less claustrophobic. But the atmosphere, thick, still, warm, was charged with the tension characteristic of such weather. It was as if the weather itself were waiting for something to happen.

No birds sang. The only sound was that of the flies' muted buzzing as they rose and fell in their living clouds. And the trees stood utterly immobile around the hovel, their green cloaks motionless, their trunks like pillars of stone. He lay in the bracken thinking about her, crushing down each doubt as it rose, telling himself how resolute she was, how punctual, how she never changed her mind. The front door was ajar so that he would hear the phone when it rang. He lay on his side, staring through the bracken trunks, through this forest in miniature, towards the lane, so that he would see the silver body of her car when it slid into the gap between thrusting fronds and hanging leaves. Presently, because it was warm and he had lulled himself into peace, he slept.

When he awoke it was nearly half past five but the appearance of the Forest and the light were unchanged. No car had come and the phone hadn't rung. Half past five was the last safe time to ring her. He went slowly back into the house and dialled but still there was no answer. All day long she'd been out, for the whole of this day when she was due to leave her husband for her lover, she'd been out. Those reassuring excuses for her absence, her silence, which had lulled him to sleep began to grow faint and a kind of dread to replace them. 'I never change my mind,' she'd said. 'I'll leave Tiny and come and live with you. Tuesday,' she'd said, 'when you get back.' But she'd also said good-bye. She'd never said that before. Two or three hundred times they'd talked to each other on the phone; they'd met hundreds of times, but she'd never terminated their conversations or their meetings with a true farewell. See you, take care, till tomorrow, but never good-bye . . .

But wherever she was, whatever she'd been doing all day, she'd be bound to go home in the evening. Tiny demanded her presence in the evenings except when he was out on Thursdays. Well, he'd try again at six-thirty and to hell with Tiny. He'd try every half-hour throughout the evening. If she hadn't come, of course. There was always the possibility she'd promised Tiny to wait till he came home before leaving.

Although he hadn't eaten since he left Le Petit Trianon, he wasn't hungry and he didn't fancy starting on the wine he'd bought. Even the idea of a cup of tea didn't attract him. He lay back in the chair, watching the inscrutable phone, chain-smoking, lighting, smoking and crushing out five cigarettes in the hour that passed.

Tiny'd have been in half an hour by now. Whatever happened, unless he was away on a business trip – and if he'd been going away she'd have said – Drusilla's husband drove the Bentley through the Combe Park gates just before six. Perhaps he'd answer the phone. So well and good. He, Gray, would say who he was, give his name and ask to speak to Drusilla, and if Tiny wanted to know why he'd tell him why, tell him the lot. The time for discretion was past. Five-O-eight . . . He must have made a mess of it, for all he got was a steady high-pitched burr. Try again. Probably his hand hadn't been very steady. Five-O-eight . . .

The bell rang, twice, three times, twenty times. Combe Park was empty, they were both out. But it wasn't possible she'd go out with her husband, the husband she was on the point of leaving, on the very day he and she were due to start their life together.

'I love you. If you still want me I'll leave Tiny and come and live with you. As soon as you get back, soon, Tuesday . . .'

He went to the window. Standing there, gazing through a web of unmoving, pendulous branches, he thought I won't look out of the window again till I've counted a hundred. No, I'll make a cup of tea and smoke two cigarettes and count a hundred and then she'll be here. He'd do what he'd thought of her as doing while she waited for him on Saturday.

But instead of going into the kitchen he sat down once more in the chair and, closing his eyes, began to count. It was years since he'd counted up so high, not since he was a little boy playing hide-and-seek. And he didn't stop when he reached a hundred, but went obsessively on, as if he were counting the days of his life or the trees of the Forest. At a thousand he stopped and opened his eyes, frightened by what was happening to his mind, to himself. It was still only seven o'clock. He lifted the phone, dialled the number that was more familiar to him than his own, making the movements that were so automatic now that he could have made them in the dark. And the bell rang as if it were echoing his counting, on and on, emptily, pointlessly, meaninglessly.

Tiny must have taken her away. She'd told Tiny and he, aghast and angry, had shut up the house and taken away his wife from the lures of a predatory young lover. To St Tropez or St Moritz, to the tourists' shrines where miracles

138

took place and in the glamour of high life women forgot the life they had left behind. He dropped the receiver and pushed his hand across his eyes, his forehead. Suppose they were away for weeks, months? There seemed no way to find out where they'd gone. He couldn't very well go questioning the neighbours and he didn't know Tiny's office number or her father's address. The thought came to him horribly that if she died no one would tell him; no news of her illness, her death, could reach him, for nobody in her circle knew of his existence and no one in his knew of hers.

There was nothing he could do but wait – and hope. After all, it was still Tuesday. She hadn't said *when* on Tuesday. Perhaps she'd postponed telling Tiny till the last minute, was telling him now, and their quarrel was so intense, their emotions running so high, that they scarcely heard the phone, still less bothered to answer it. In a little while she'd have said all there was to say and then she'd fling out of the house, throw her packed cases into the car, drive furiously down the Forest roads . . .

He was seeing it all, following the phases of their quarrel, the two angry frightened people in their beautiful loveless house, when the phone, so dead and silent that he had thought it would never ring again, gave its preliminary hiccup. His heart turned over. He had the receiver to his ear before the end of the first peal and he was holding his breath, his eyes closed.

'Mr Graham Lanceton?'

Tiny. Could it be Tiny? The voice was thick, uncultured, but very steady. 'Yes,' Gray said, clenching his free hand.

The voice said, 'My name is Ixworth, Detective Inspector Ixworth. I should like to come over and see you if that's convenient.'

The anticlimax was so great, so sickening – far worse than when he had answered Honoré's phone to M. Reville – that Gray could hardly speak. It was as hard to find words as to find, from his dry constricted throat, the voice with which to speak them. 'I don't . . .' he began thinly. 'Who . . . ? What . . . ?'

'Detective Inspector Ixworth, Mr Lanceton. Shall we say nine o'clock?'

Gray didn't answer. He didn't say anything. He put the phone down and stood shivering. It was fully five minutes before he could get over the shock of simply realising it hadn't been she. Then, wiping the sweat off his forehead, he made his way towards the kitchen where at least he'd be out of the sight of that phone.

On the threshold he stopped dead. The window had been broken and forced open and the cellar door stood ajar. All his papers were now stacked in as neat a pile as a new ream of typing paper. Someone had been here and not she. Someone had broken into the house. He shook himself, trying to get a grip on reason, on normalcy. Vaguely he began to understand the reason for that policeman's phone call. The police had discovered a burglary.

Well, he had to fill in the time till she phoned or came, and he might as well look round to see if anything had been pinched. It would be something to do. His typewriter was still there, though he had a feeling it had been moved. He couldn't remember where he'd left the strong-box. Having searched the downstairs rooms, he went up to the bedrooms. Everywhere smelt musty, airless. He opened windows as he went across the landing and his own bedroom but there was no breeze to blow stale air out and fresh in. There was no fresh air. He longed to draw into his lungs great gulps of oxygen – something to relieve this tightness in his chest. But when he put his head out of the window the thick atmosphere seemed to stick at the rim of his throat.

The strong-box wasn't in either of the bedrooms. He no longer retained much faith in his own memory, but he was certain he'd left the box somewhere in the house. What else would he have done with it? If it wasn't there, the intruder must have taken it. He searched the 'lounge' again and the kitchen and then went down the cellar steps.

Someone had disturbed and turned over those mounds of rubbish and the iron was gone. Its trivet stood on a heap of damp newspapers but the iron which had burnt him, which had left a still clearly visible scar on his hand, had disappeared. He kicked some of the coal aside, mystified by this strange robbery, and saw at his feet on the moist flagstones, a spattered brown stain.

The stain looked as if it might be blood. He remembered Dido again and thought that perhaps she'd succeeded in getting into the cellar and had fallen from the steps or wounded herself against one of the oil drums or the old unusable bicycle. It was an ugly thought that made him wince and he went quickly back up the steps. The box wasn't there, anyway.

The garden was crushed now by rising mist, cottony white and oppressive, hanging immobile on nettle and fern bract. The broken window made the kitchen look more derelict than ever. He put the kettle on for tea but he went out of the kitchen while he waited for it to boil. After what had happened there, he was never going to be able to bear that kitchen for long. Dido's ghost would be behind him. He'd fancy he could hear her padding steps or the touch of her moist nose against his hand.

Shivering, he reached for the phone again and dialled carefully but fast. They said that if you dialled too slowly or left too long a pause between two of the digits, something could go wrong and you'd get the wrong number. They said a hair across the mechanism or a grain of dust . . . suppose he'd been dialling the wrong number all this time? It could happen, some Freudian slip could make it happen. He put the receiver back, lifted it again, and dialled with calculated precision, repeating the seven figures over to himself aloud. The ringing began, and yet from the first double peal he knew it would be useless. Give up now till ten. Try again at ten and at midnight. If they weren't there at midnight he'd know they were away.

He'd made a cup of tea and carried it into the 'lounge' – for all his resolve, he couldn't bear to be more than a yard from that phone – when he heard the soft purr of a car. At last. At last, at twenty past eight, a perfectly reasonable time, she'd come to him. The long and terrible waiting was over, and like all long and terrible waiting times would be forgotten immediately now that what he had waited for had happened. He wouldn't run to the door, he wouldn't even look out of the window. He'd wait till the bell rang and then he'd go there slowly, hoping he could maintain this calm façade even when he saw her, white and gold and vital

141

in the closing twilight, keep his rushing emotion down until she was in his arms.

The bell rang. Gray set down his tea cup. It rang again. Oh, Drusilla, at last . . . ! He opened the door. Appalled, every muscle of his body flexing into rigidity, he stared, for it was Tiny who stood there. In every imagined detail – now proved correct by the too real reality – this man was Drusilla's husband. From the black curly hair, cropped too short and crowning, with coarse contrast, a veined dusky-red face, to the gingery suede shoes, this was Tiny Janus. He wore a white raincoat, belted slackly over a belly made thick with rich living.

They eyed each other in a silence which seemed im-measureable but which probably lasted no more than a few seconds. At first Gray, by instinct rather than by thought, had supposed the man was going to strike him. But now he saw that the mouth, which had been so grim and so bellig-erent, was curling into an expression of mockery, too faint to be called a smile. He stepped back, losing his sense of conviction, because the words he was hearing were wrong, were the last conceivable words in these circumstances.

'I'm a bit early.' A foot over the threshold, a briefcase swung. 'Nothing wrong, I hope?'

Everything was wrong, everything unbalanced. 'I wasn't expecting . . .' Gray began.

'But I phoned you. My name's Ixworth.'

Gray held himself still then nodded. He pulled the door wider to admit the policeman. There is a limit to how long anticlimaxes remain anticlimactic. One grows to accept them, to take them as part and parcel of nightmare. It was better, probably, that this man should be anyone but Tiny, intolerable, just the same, this his caller was anyone but Drusilla.

'Just got back from France, have you?' They had got themselves into the 'lounge' – Gray hardly knew how – and Ixworth moved confidently as if he were familiar with the place.

'Yes, I was in France.' He had spoken mechanically, had simply answered the question, but there must have been in his reply some note of surprise.

'We talk to friends and neighbours, Mr Lanceton. That's our job. All part of the job of investigating this sort of thing.

You went to France to see your mother before she died, isn't that it?'

'Yes.'

'Your mother died on Friday and you came home on a flying visit on Saturday, going back again that same night. You must have had a very pressing reason for that trip.'

'I thought,' said Gray, remembering, recalling the least significant shocks of the day, 'you came to talk about my house being broken into.'

'Your house?' The thick black eyebrows went up. 'I understood this cottage was the property of a Mr Warriner who is at present in Japan.'

Gray shrugged. 'I live here. He lent it to me. Anyway, there's nothing missing.' Why mention the strong-box, when to mention it would only keep the man here? 'I didn't see anyone. I wasn't here.'

'You were here on Saturday afternoon.'

'Only for about half an hour. Nobody'd been here then. The window wasn't broken.'

'We broke the window, Mr Lanceton,' said Ixworth with a slight cough. 'We entered this house with a warrant yesterday and found the body of a man lying at the foot of the cellar steps. He'd been dead for forty-eight hours. The wristwatch he was wearing had broken and the hands stopped at four-fifteen.'

Gray, who had been standing limply but with a kind of slack indifferent impatience, lowered himself into the brown armchair. Or, rather, the chair seemed to rise and receive him into its lumpy uneven seat. The stunning effect of what Ixworth had said blanked his mind, but into this blankness came a vision of a little man prowling round the hovel garden.

The burglar or burglars, the brown stain . . . Who were these intruders who had forced their way into his own nightmare and made, with a kind of incongruous sub-plot, a littler yet greater nightmare of their own?

'This man,' he said, because he had to say something, 'must have fallen down the steps.'

'He fell, yes.' Ixworth was looking at him narrowly, as if he expected so much more than Gray could give. 'He fell after he'd been struck on the head with a flat-iron.'

143

Gray looked down at his right hand, at the blister which had become a cracked and yellow callous. He turned his hand downwards when he saw that Ixworth was looking at it too.

'Are you saying this man was killed here? Who was he?'

'You don't know? Come outside a minute.' The policeman led him into the kitchen, as if the house were his, as if Gray had never been there before. He opened the cellar door, watching Gray. The switch for the cellar light didn't work, and it was in the thin pale glow from the kitchen that they looked down into the depths and at the brown stain.

It was strange that he should feel so threatened, so impelled to be defensive, when none of this was anything to do with him. Or was it a case of any man's death diminishes me? All he found to say was, 'He fell down those steps.'

'Yes.'

Suddenly Gray found he didn't like the man's tone, the expectancy, the accusatory note in it. It was almost as if Ixworth were trying to tease him into some sort of admission; as if, fantastically, the police could do no more unless he confessed to some defection or omission of his own – that he hadn't, for instance, taken proper precautions against this kind of thing or was deliberately failing to give vital information.

'I know nothing about it. I can't even imagine why he'd come here.'

'No? You don't see any attractions in a charming little weatherboard cottage set in unspoilt woodland?'

Gray turned away, sickened at this inept description. He didn't want to know any more, he couldn't see the point. The intruder's identity or business was nothing to him, his death an ugliness Ixworth seemed to use only as an excuse for curious glances and cryptic words. And Ixworth had been so suave, so teasing, that Gray felt a jolt shake him when, after a brief silence, the policeman spoke with a clipped brutality.

'Why did you come home on Saturday?'

'It was because of a dog,' Gray said.

'A *dog*?'

'Yes. D'you think we could go back into the other room?' He wondered why he was asking Ixworth's permission. The

144

policeman nodded and closed the cellar door. 'I went to France, forgetting that someone had left a dog, a yellow labrador, shut up in my kitchen. When I realised what I'd done I phoned a friend from France and got them to let the dog out and take her to a vet.' Silently, Gray blessed English usage which permitted him to say 'them' instead of 'her' in this context. Drusilla wouldn't thank him for involving her in all this. 'It was a stupid mistake to make.' Suddenly he saw just how stupid all this would sound to someone else. 'The dog died,' he went on, 'but – well, before that, on Saturday, the vet wanted to see me. He's called Cherwell and he lives at 21 George Street, Leyton.'

Ixworth wrote the address down. 'You spoke to him?'

'I couldn't find him. I spoke to a woman at 49 George Street, Leyton*stone*. That would have been just after three.'

'You aren't making yourself very clear, Mr Lanceton. Why did you go to Leytonstone?'

'I made a mistake about that.'

'You seem to make a lot of mistakes.'

Gray shrugged. 'It doesn't matter, does it? The point is I didn't get here till six.'

'*Six*? What were you doing all that time? Did you have a meal, meet anyone? If you left Leytonstone at half past three, a bus or buses would have got you here in three-quarters of an hour.'

Gray said more sharply, 'It's a long walk and I can't afford taxis. Besides, I went back into London and caught a train.'

'Did you meet anyone, talk to anyone at all?'

'I don't think so. No, I didn't. When I got here I spoke to an old boy called Tringham who lives up the lane.'

'We've interviewed Mr Tringham. It was five past six when he spoke to you, so that doesn't help much.'

'No?' said Gray. 'Well, I can't help at all.'

'You haven't, for instance, any theory of your own?'

'Well, there were two men, weren't there? There must have been. Mr Tringham said he saw another bloke.'

'Yes, he told us.' Ixworth spoke casually, laconically, returning to his old manner. Once more it was as if he had ceased to take Gray seriously. 'The Forest,' he said, 'is full of picnickers at this time of year.'

'But surely you ought to find the other man?'

'I think we should, Mr Lanceton.' Ixworth got up. 'Don't you worry, we shall. In the meantime, you won't go popping off to France again, will you?'

'No,' said Gray, surprised. 'Why should I?'

He saw the policeman to the gate. When his car lights had died away, the Forest was impenetrably black. And the moonless starless sky was densely black except on the horizon where the lights of London stained it a dirty smoky red.

It was nearly ten o'clock. Gray made tea, and as he drank it the interview with Ixworth, irritating and humiliating rather than alarming, began to fade, becoming a distant instead of a recent memory. It seemed less real now than those dreams of his, for that which supremely mattered had returned to engulf him.

The light bulb in the 'lounge', one of the last in the hovel that still worked, flickered, shone briefly with a final bold radiance, fizzed and went out. He had to dial her number in the dark but it was as he'd thought, his fingers slipped automatically into the right slots.

There was no reply, and none at midnight when he tried for the last time and Tuesday was over.

# 18

Gray and Tiny and Drusilla were travelling together in a tourist coach along a road that led through a thick dark forest. The husband and wife sat in front and Gray behind them. She wore her cream lawn dress and on her finger the amethyst ring. Her hair was a red flower, a chrysanthemum with fiery points to its petals. He touched her shoulder and asked her how she came to be wearing the ring she'd sold but she took no notice, she couldn't hear him.

The forest thinned and opened on to a plain. He knew they were in France from the road signs, but when they came to Bajon it wasn't the Écu outside which they stopped but the Oranmore in Sussex Gardens. In one hand Tiny held the case containing his coin collection, with the

146

other he grasped a passive and meek Drusilla, shepherding her up the steps, under the neon sign and into the hotel. He was going to follow them in but the glass doors slid closed against him and, although he beat on the glass begging to be admitted, Drusilla turned her head only once before going up the stairs. She turned her head once and said, 'Good-bye, Gray. Good-bye.'

After that he woke up and couldn't get to sleep again. Soft hazy sunshine filled the room. It was half past eight. He got up and looked out of the window. The mist was still there but thin now, diaphanous, shot through with shafts of gold and veiling a blue sky.

Gradually the events of the previous day came back to him, the events and the non-events. He stretched, shivered, quite unrefreshed by his eight hours of uneasy, dream-filled sleep. He went downstairs. The kitchen was beginning to fill with leaf-filtered sunshine and for the first time it didn't smell stale. Fresh air came in with the sunlight through the broken window. Gray put the kettle on. It was strange, he thought, how, since Christmas, day had followed day without anything ever happening in a terrible monotony, and then had come a week filled with ugly violent action. Wasn't it Kafka who'd said, no matter how you lock yourself away, shut yourself up, life will come and roll in ecstasy at your feet? Well, it was hardly ecstasy, anything but. And it was very far from the kind of life and ecstasy he'd envisaged.

He couldn't see how the intruders had got in. The doors had been locked and the spare key hanging at that time over the sink. Probably the police wouldn't bother him any more now they knew he hadn't been here and couldn't assist them. Strange to remember how bitterly disappointed he'd been at not finding Drusilla here on Saturday. He was glad now, he thanked God, she hadn't been here when the men had broken in.

He'd try her number just once more and if he got no reply think of ways and means to get hold of her. Why not ask her neighbours, after all? Someone would know where she and Tiny had gone. The daily woman would come in whether they were there or not and she'd be bound to know. He dialled the number just before nine, listened this time without much disappointment and no surprise to the ringing tone, put the receiver back and made tea. While he

147

was eating some of the bread he'd bought, spreading it with vinegar-tainted melting butter, the phone rang.

It must be she. Who else would know he was home? He gulped down a mouthful of bread and answered it.

A woman's voice, a voice he didn't begin to recognise, said, 'Mr Lanceton? Mr Graham Lanceton?'

'Yes,' he said dully.

'Oh, *hallo*, Graham! It didn't sound a bit like you. This is Eva Warriner.'

Mal's mother. What did she want? 'How are you, Mrs Warriner?'

'I'm fine, my dear, but I was so distressed to hear about your mother. It was nice of you to write to me. I'd no idea she was as ill as that. We were very close in the old days, I always thought of her as one of my dearest friends. I hope she didn't suffer much?'

Gray didn't know what to say. It was a struggle to speak at all, to make a recovery from the bitterness of knowing this wasn't Drusilla. 'She did for a while,' he managed. 'She didn't know me.'

'Oh, dear, so sad for you. You said you'd be back at the beginning of the week so I just thought I'd phone and tell you how sorry I am. Oh, and I rang Isabel Clarion and told her the news too. She said she hadn't heard from you at all.'

'*Isabel?*' he almost shouted. 'You mean she's come back from Australia already?'

'Well, yes, Graham,' said Mrs Warriner, 'she must have. She didn't mention Australia but we only talked for a couple of minutes. The builders that are doing her flat were making so much noise we couldn't hear ourselves speak.'

He sat down heavily, pushing his fingers across his hot damp forehead. 'I expect I'll hear from her,' he said weakly.

'I'm sure you will. Isn't it wonderful Mal coming home in August?'

'Yes. Yes, it's great. Er – Mrs Warriner, Isabel didn't say anything about . . . ? No, it doesn't matter.'

'She hardly said anything, Graham.' Mrs Warriner began to reminisce about her past friendship with Enid but Gray cut her short as soon as he politely could and said good-bye. He didn't replace the receiver but left it hanging as it had so often hung in the past. That would stop Isabel for a while, at any rate, Isabel who'd stayed in Australia barely a week. Probably she'd quarrelled with her old partner or hadn't liked the climate or something. Vaguely he remembered reading in Honoré's newspaper, on that dreadful night when he'd realised Dido was at the hovel, about floods in Australia. That would be it. Isabel had been frightened or made uncomfortable by those floods and had got on a plane as soon as she could. She'd very likely got home yesterday and today she'd want her dog back . . .

Well, he'd known he'd have to tell her sometime and it would be as well to get it over. But not today. Today he had to sort out his life and Drusilla's, find where Drusilla was and get her back. He eyed the receiver that was still swinging like a pendulum. Better make one more attempt to phone. By now the daily woman would have arrived.

Five-O-eight and then the four digits. The double burrs began. After the fifth the receiver was lifted. Gray held his breath, the fingers of his left hand curling into the palm and the nails biting the flesh. It wasn't she. Still, it was someone, a human voice coming out of that silent place at last.

'Combe Park.'

'I'd like to talk to Mrs Janus.'

'Mrs Janus is away. This is the cleaner. Who's that speaking?'

'When will she be back?'

'I'm sure I couldn't tell you. Who's that speaking?'

'A friend,' Gray said. 'Have Mr and Mrs Janus gone away on holiday?'

The woman cleared her throat. She said, 'Oh, dear . . .' and 'I don't know if I should . . .' and then, gruffly, 'Mr Janus passed away.'

It didn't register. All it did was bring back a flashing memory of the mayor and his euphemisms, those idiomatic polished understatements. 'What did you say?'

'Mr Janus passed away.'

He heard the words but they seemed to take a long while to travel to his brain, as such words do, as do any words that are the vehicles of news that is unimaginable.

'*You mean he's dead?*'

149

'It's not my place to talk about it. All I know is he's passed away, dead like you say, and Mrs Janus has gone to her mum and dad.'

'Dead . . .' he said and then, steadying his voice, 'D'you know their address?'

'No, I don't. Who's that speaking?'

'It doesn't matter,' Gray said. 'Forget it.'

He made his way very slowly to the window but he seemed half-blind and, instead of the forest, all he saw was a blaze of sun and hollows of blue shadow. Tiny Janus is dead, said his brain. The words travelled to his lips and he spoke them aloud, wonderingly: Harvey Janus, the rich man, the ogre, is dead. Drusilla's husband is dead. The phrases, the thoughts, swelled and begun to take on real meaning as the shock subsided. He began to feel them as facts. Tiny Janus, Drusilla's husband, is dead.

When had it happened? Sunday? Monday? Perhaps even on Tuesday, the day she was to join him. Now her absence was explained. Even her failure to phone was explained. Dazed but gradually coming to grips with the news, he tried to imagine what had occurred. Probably Tiny had had a coronary. Heavy fat men like Tiny, men who drank too much and lived too well, men of Tiny's age, often did have coronaries. Perhaps it had happened at his office or while he was driving the Bentley, and they had sent her a message or the police had come to her. She hadn't loved Tiny but still it would have been a shock and she would have been alone.

She'd have sent for her parents, the father she loved and the mother she never mentioned. It was hard to imagine Drusilla having a mother, Drusilla who seemed man-born. They must have carried her off to wherever they lived. He realised he didn't know their name, her maiden name, or anything about where they lived except that it was some-where in Hertfordshire. But her failure to phone him was explained. He would just have to wait.

'Wouldn't it be nice if he died?' she'd said. 'He might die. He might have a coronary or crash his car.'

Well, she'd got what she wanted. Tiny was dead and Combe Park and all that money hers. He thought how she'd said that when she got it she'd give it to him, that they would share it, put it into a joint account and live happily on it for ever. And he'd wanted it, if it could have been his more or less legitimately, reaching a zenith of desire for it when he'd stood outside the gates of Combe Park in the spring and seen the daffodils that seemed made of pure gold. Strange that now the impossible had happened and Tiny was dead, now it would all be his and hers, he no longer cared at all about possessing it.

He tested his feelings. No, he wasn't happy, glad that a man was dead. Of course, he had nothing to do with Tiny's death, no more than he had to do with the death of the man who had fallen down his cellar stairs, yet he felt a heavy weight descend on to his shoulders, something like despair. Was it because in his heart he'd really wanted Tiny to die? Or for some other reason he couldn't define? The two deaths seemed to merge into one and to stand between him and Drusilla like a single ghost.

His body smelt of the sweat of tension. He went back to the kitchen and began heating water for a bath. All the time he was waiting for happiness and relief to dispel his depression, but he could only think of the repeated shocks to which he'd been exposed. He couldn't take any more. Another shock would send him over the edge.

He lifted the lid of the bath cover and tugged out the tangle of mould-smelling sheets and towels. The mud-stained trousers he'd put in there on Saturday were gone but he didn't worry about their disappearance. Too many strange things were happening in his world for that. He poured the boiling water into the bathtub, chucked in a bucketful of cold. Getting into the bath, soaping himself, he thought of Tiny dead. At the wheel of his car perhaps? In so many dreams he'd seen Tiny crash in his car, blood and flames pouring scarlet over the green turf. Or had he died in bed after a drinking bout while Drusilla, unaware and dreaming of her lover, slept a yard from him?

There were many other possibilities. But the only one that came vividly to Gray, the only one he could see as a real picture, was of Tiny lying crumpled at the foot of a flight of stairs.

If he went up the lane just before twelve, he might be able to catch the milkman and buy a pint off him. Tea was the only sustenance he felt he could stomach. The food in the

151

carrier bag smelt unpleasant, and the sight of it brought him a wave of nausea. Downstairs the hovel seemed full of death, the intruder's, Tiny's, the dog's, and yet the rooms gleamed with sunlight. Gray could never remember the place so bright and airy. But he longed to get out of it. If once he got out, would he have the courage to come back? Or would he wander through the glades of the Forest, on and on until weariness overcome him and he lay down to sleep or die?

The chance of her phoning seemed to have grown very remote. Days might pass before he heard from her. He couldn't envisage those empty days and himself passing through them, waiting, waiting, and all the time this tension mounting until, before she phoned, it cracked.

He went upstairs and put on the dirty shirt he'd taken off the night before. The sound of a car engine a long way up the lane froze him as he was combing his hair. Holding the comb poised, utterly still, he listened for the whisper of sound to grow into the powerful purr of a Jaguar sports. He'd passed beyond feeling joy at her coming. All these deaths, anticlimaxes, shocks, blows to his mind had removed the possibility of delight at their coming meeting. But he would fall into her arms and cling to her in silence when she came.

It was not to be yet. The engine noise had become the thinner jerkier rattle of a small car. He went to the window and looked out. Much of the lane was obscured by bracken at ground level and by branches above, but there was a space between wide enough to make out the shape and colour of a car. The Mini, small and bright red, edged cautiously along the still sticky surface and slid to a halt.

Isabel.

His first instinct was simply to hide from her, go into the spare room, lie on the floor and hide till she went away. Inside each one of us is a frightened child trying to get out. The measure of our maturity is the extent to which we are able to keep that child quiet, confined and concealed. At that moment the child inside Gray almost broke loose from its bonds, but the man who was nearly thirty held it down, just held it down. Isabel might go away but she'd come back. If not today, tomorrow, if not tomorrow, Friday.

152

Weak as he was, trembling now, he must face her and tell her what he'd done. No hiding, defiance, blustering, could make his act less of an outrage than it was.

She was getting out of the car. In the bright, sun-flooded segment between dark green fern and lemon-green leaves, he saw her ease her thick body in pink blouse and baby-blue trousers out of the driving seat. She was wearing big sun-glasses with rainbow frames. The black circles of glass levelled themselves upwards towards the window and Gray turned quickly away.

He retreated to the door, to the top of the stairs, and there he stood, trying to command himself, clenching his hands. He was still a child. For more than half his life he'd fended for himself; he'd got a good degree, written a successful book, been Drusilla's lover, but he was still a child. And more than ever he was a child with these grown-ups, with Honoré, with dead Enid, Mrs Warriner, Isabel. Even in telling himself he wouldn't conciliate them or play things their way but be honest and himself, he was a child, for his very defiance and rebellion was as childish as obedience. In a flash he was aware of this as never before. One day, he thought, when the present and all its horrors were the past, when he'd got over or through all this, he would remember and grow up . . .

Sick, already tasting the nausea on his tongue, he went down and slowly pulled open the front door. Isabel, still at the car, bending over to take milk and groceries out of the boot, lifted her head and waved to him. He began to walk towards her.

Before he was halfway down the path, before he could fetch a word out of his dry throat, the thicket of bracken split open. It burst with a crack like tearing sacking and the big golden dog leapt upon him, the violence of her embrace softened by the wet warmth of her tongue and the rapture in her kind eyes.

# 19

The bright air shivered. The myriad leaves, lemony-green, silk-green, feathery, sun-filtered, serrated, swam in swirling, parabolas, and the ground rose in a hard wave to meet him. He just kept his balance. He shut his eyes on the green-gold trembling brightness and thrust his fingers into warm fur, embracing the dog, holding her against his shaking body.

'Dido!' Isabel called. 'Leave Gray alone, darling.'

He couldn't speak. Shock stunned him. All his feeling, all thought, were crystallised into one unbelievable phrase: she is alive, the dog is alive. He drew his hands over Dido's head, the fine bones, the modelling, as a blind man passes his fingers over the face of the woman he loves.

'Are you all right, Gray? You do look peaky. I suppose you're just beginning to feel what this loss means.'

'Loss?' he said.

'Your *mother*, dear. Mrs Warriner told me last night and I made up my mind to come over first thing this morning. You ought to sit down. Just now I thought you were going to faint.'

Gray had thought so too. And even now, when the first shock had passed, he seemed unable to get his bearings. Following Isabel into the house, he tried to feel his way along that other path that should have led into the reaches of his mind. But he came against a blank wall. Experience and memory had become a foreign country. Logic had gone, and lost too were the processes of thought by which one says, this happened so, therefore, this and this happened too. His mind was an empty page with one phrase written on it: the dog is alive. And now, slowly, another was being inscribed alongside it: the dog is alive, Tiny Janus is dead.

Isabel was already sitting down in the 'lounge', pouring out platitudes on life, death and resignation. Gray lowered himself carefully into the other chair as if his body, as well as his mind, must be guardedly handled. Speed, roughness, would be dangerous, for, lying beneath the surface, was a scream that might burst out. He rubbed his hands over the dog's pelt. She was real, he knew that for certain now. Perhaps she was the only real thing in a tumbling, inside-out world.

'When all's said and done,' Isabel was saying, 'it was a merciful release.' Gray lifted his eyes to her, to this fat pink and blue blur that was his godmother, and wondered what she was talking about. 'You haven't got your receiver off now, I see. Really, there's no point in having a phone if the receiver's always off, is there?'

'No point at all,' he agreed politely. He was surprised that he could speak at all, let alone form sentences. He went on doing it, pointlessly, just to prove he could. 'I wonder sometimes why I do have one. I really wonder. I might just as well not have one.'

'There's no need,' Isabel said sharply, 'to be sarcastic. You've no right to be resentful, Gray. The first thing I did was try to phone you. As soon as I knew I couldn't go to Australia – I mean, when I read about the floods and Molly cabled me to say she'd literally been washed out of her home – I made up my mind there was no point in trying to go. I tried to phone you that Friday and goodness knows how many times on the Saturday, and then I gave up in sheer despair. I thought you'd realise when I didn't turn up with Dido.'

'Yes,' said Gray. 'Oh, yes.'

'Well, then. Really, it was a blessing I didn't go to Molly's. All the responsibility of getting Dido boarded would have been on your shoulders, and you had quite enough with your poor mother, I'm sure. (Lie down, darling. You're just making yourself hot.) I shall write to Honoré today, poor man, and tell him I've seen you and how upset you are. It cheers people to knowing others are unhappy, don't you think?'

This crass expression of *schadenfreude*, which once would have made Gray laugh, now washed over him with most of the rest of Isabel's words. While she continued to burble, he sat as still as stone, his hands no longer caressing the dog who had sunk into a somnolent heap at his feet. Memory was beginning to come back now, returning in hard thrusts of pain.

'Is she dead?' he'd asked, relying on her, utterly in her hands.

'No, she was alive – just.'

His hand fell again to fumble at the dog's coat, to feel her reality. And Dido turned her head, opened her eyes and licked his hand.

'I took some milk and chicken with me. I was a bit scared to open the kitchen door but I needn't have been. She was too weak to move. Someone ought to lock you up in a cell and see how you'd like it.'

Oh, Drusilla, Drusilla . . .

'It's no use, anyway, the dog's had to be destroyed.'

Oh, Dru, no . . .

'Anyway, dear,' said Isabel, drawing breath, 'you can have your key back now. Here you are. I'll go and hang it on the hook, shall I?'

'I'll take it.'

An old blackened key, twin of the one he always carried.

'And put the kettle on, Gray. I brought some milk in case you didn't have any. We'll have a cup of tea and I'll run into Waltham Abbey and get us something for our lunch. I'm sure you're not fit to take care of yourself.'

Not fit . . .

'I went in and cleaned up for you,' she'd said.

'Why did you do that?'

'Why do I do anything for you? Don't you know yet?'

The bright key that had been Drusilla's hung on the hook, glittering like gold in the sun. She'd left her key and said good-bye. Alone, free of Isabel for a moment, he laid his face, his forehead, against the damp cold wall and the scream came out into the stone, agonising, uncomprehending, silent.

'I love you. If you still want me I'll leave Tiny and come and live with you.'

I love you . . . No, he whispered, no, no. Good-bye, Gray, good-bye. I never change my mind. Punctual, relentless, unchanging in any fixed course, she never wavered. But this . . . ? Red fur, red fox hair, perfume rising like smoke, that low throaty laugh of hers – the memories spun, crystallised into a last image of her, as hard and unyielding as the stone against his face.

156

'A watched pot never boils, dear,' said Isabel brightly from the doorway. She peered inquisitively at his numb blind face. 'There's a car pulled up at your gate. Are you expecting anyone?'

He had been so adept at optimism, at supposing with uncrushable hope that every car was hers, every phone bell ringing to bring her to him. This time he had no hope and in realising his deep stunned hopelessness, he knew too that he was living reality. He'd never see her again. She'd left her key and said good-bye. Betraying him systematically and coldly for perhaps some purpose of revenge, she'd brought him to this climax. Without speaking, he pushed past Isabel and opened the door to Ixworth. He gazed speechlessly but without dismay or even surprise at the policeman whose coming seemed the next natural and logical step in this sequence of happenings. He didn't speak because he had nothing to say and felt now that all words would be wasted effort. Why talk when event would now, in any case, pile upon event according to the pattern she had designed for them?

Ixworth looked at the flattened bracken. 'Been sunbathing?'

Gray shook his head. This, then, was what it felt like to have the mental breakdown he'd feared all those months. Not manic hysteria, not fantasy unbridled or grief too strong to bear, but this peaceful numb acceptance of fate. After the liberating silent scream, just acceptance. It was possible even to believe that in a moment he would feel almost happy . . . Gently he held the dog back to keep her from springing lovingly at Ixworth.

'*Another* yellow labrador, Mr Lanceton? D'you breed them?'

'It's the same dog.' Gray didn't trouble to consider the implication of his words. He turned away, indifferent as to whether Ixworth followed him or not, and almost collided with Isabel who was saying in sprightly tones:

'Aren't you going to introduce me?'

Grotesquely girlish, she fluttered in front of the dour inspector. Gray said, 'Miss Clarion, Mr Ixworth.' He wished vaguely that they would both go away. If only they would go away and leave him with the dog. He'd lie down

157

somewhere with kind Dido, put his arms round her, bury his face in her warm, hay-scented fur.

Ixworth ignored the introduction. 'Is that your dog?'

'Yes, isn't she gorgeous? Are you fond of dogs?'

'This one seems attractive.' Ixworth's eyes flickered over Gray. 'Is this the animal you were supposed to be looking after?'

'I'm sure he will when I do finally go away.' Isabel seemed delighted that the conversation was taking such a pleasant sociable turn. 'This time my trip fell through and poor Dido didn't get her country holiday.'

'I see. I rather hoped I'd find you alone, Mr Lanceton.'

Quick to warm, equally quick to take offence, Isabel tossed her head and stubbed out her cigarette fiercely. 'Please don't let me intrude. The last thing I want is to be in the way. I'll run into Waltham Abbey now, Gray, and get our lunch. I wouldn't dream of keeping you from your friend.'

Ixworth smiled slightly at this. He waited in patient silence till the Mini had gone.

Gray watched the car move off down the lane. Dido began to whine, her paws on the windowsill, her nose pressed against the glass. This, Gray thought, was how it must have been when Isabel left her alone here that Monday . . . Only that had never happened, had it? None of that had happened.

'None of that really happened, did it?' Ixworth was saying. 'Your whole story about the dog was untrue. We know, of course, that no animal answering this one's description was ever taken to Mr Cherwell on Thursday.'

Gray pulled the dog down gently. The sun's glare hurt his eyes and he pulled the chair away from the slanting dazzling rays. 'Does it matter?' he said.

'Tell me,' said the policeman in a tone which was both puzzled and bantering, 'what you think does matter.'

Nothing much now, Gray thought. Perhaps just one or two small things, questions to which he couldn't supply the answers himself. But his brain was clearing, revealing cold facts to which he seemed to have no emotional reaction. The dog had never been there. Working onwards from that, recalling certain phrases of hers in this new context – 'I never change my mind, Gray' – he began to see the pattern

158

she had designed. He saw it without pain, dully, almost scientifically. 'I thought,' he said, 'that Harvey Janus was a big man, but then I'd never seen him, and I thought he had a Bentley still, not the Mercedes he left in the lane. Strange, I suppose they called him Tiny because he *was* tiny. Would you like some tea?'

'Not now. Right now I'd like you to go on talking.'

'There was no need to drug him, of course. I see that now. It was only necessary to get him here. That was easy because he was looking for a house in the Forest to buy his mother. And easy to overpower such a small man. Anyone could have done it.'

'Oh, yes?'

'She had her key then. But I don't quite see . . .' He paused, sticking at betraying her even though she'd betrayed him. 'But I suppose you've talked to Mrs Janus? Even . . .' He sighed, though there was very little feeling left to make him sigh.

'Even arrested her?' he said.

Ixworth's face changed. It hardened, grew tough like that of some cinema cop. He reached for his briefcase and opened it, taking out a sheet of paper from a thin file. The paper fluttered in the sunbeam as he held it out to Gray. The typed words danced but Gray could read them. He'd typed them himself.

His address was at the top: The White Cottage, Pocket Lane, Waltham Abbey, Essex. Underneath that was the date: June the sixth. No year. And at the foot, under those terrible words he'd thought he'd never see again: Harvey Janus Esq., Combe Park, Wintry Hill, Loughton, Essex.

'Have you read it?'

'Oh, yes, I've read it.'

But Ixworth read it aloud to him, just the same.

' "Dear Sir, In reply to your advertisement in *The Times*, I think I have just what you are looking for. Since my home is not far from yours, would you care to come over and see it? Four o'clock on Saturday would be a suitable time. Yours faithfully, Francis Duval." '

The letter was the first they'd written.

'Where did you find it?' Gray asked. 'Here? In this house?'

'It was in his breast pocket,' said Ixworth.

159

'It *can't* have been. It was never posted. Look, I'll try to explain . . .'

'I wish you would.'

'It's very difficult to explain. Mrs Janus . . .' He didn't wince at her name, but he hesitated, searching for a form into which to fit his sentence. 'Mrs Janus,' he began again, wondering why Ixworth was frowning, 'will have told you we were close friends. At one time she wanted me to . . .' How to describe what she'd wanted to this hard-faced inscrutable judge? How make him understand where fantasy ended and reality began? '. . . To play a trick on her husband,' he said, lying awkwardly, 'to get money from him. She had no money of her own and I'm always broke.'

'We are aware of the state of your finances.'

'Yes, you seem to be aware of everything. I did write that letter. I wrote a whole lot more which were never sent and I've still got them. They're . . .'

'Yes?'

'I burnt them. I remember now. But that one must have got . . . Why are you looking at me like that? Mrs Janus . . .'

Ixworth took the letter and re-folded it. 'I thought we were really getting somewhere, Lanceton, till you brought Mrs Janus's name up. Leave her out of this. She doesn't know you. She's never heard of you either as Duval or Lanceton.'

The dog moved away from him. It seemed symbolic. She lay down and snored softly. Ixworth hadn't stopped talking. Steadily, he was outlining details of the events of Saturday afternoon. They were precise circumstantial details and they included his, Gray's, arrival at the hovel just before four, his greeting of Tiny Janus, their subsequent journey round the house and to the head of the cellar stairs. There was nothing wrong with the account except that it was inaccurate in every particular.

But Gray didn't deny it. He said flatly, 'She doesn't know me.'

'Leave her out of it. On Saturday afternoon she was playing tennis with the man who coaches her.'

'We were lovers for two years,' Gray said. 'She's got a key to this house.' No, that wasn't true any more . . . 'Does she say she doesn't even know me?'

'Can you produce witnesses to prove she did?'

He was silent. There was no one. Nobody had ever seen them together so it had never happened. Their love had no more happened than the dog's death had happened. And yet . . .

Without heat or the least emotion, he said slowly, 'Why would I have killed Janus except to get his wife?'

'For gain, of course,' said Ixworth. 'We're not children, Lanceton. You're not a child. Credit us with a little intelligence. He was a rich man and you're a very poor one. I'll tell you frankly we have it from the French police you didn't even gain by your mother's death.'

The hundred pounds . . . Had there been more hidden in the house? 'He brought the deposit with him.'

'Of course. You banked on that. Mr Janus was very unwisely in the habit of carrying large sums of money on him, and these things get around, don't they? Even without seeing it, he was pretty sure he'd want this place and he was going to secure it – with cash.' Ixworth shrugged, a heavy contemptous gesture. 'My God, and it wasn't even yours to sell! I suppose you worked out the sort of price it would fetch from looking in estate agents' windows.'

'I know what it's worth.'

'You knew what it would *fetch*, say. And you knew a good deal about human greed and need too. We found the three thousand pounds Mr Janus brought with him in your strong-box with a copy of *The Times* and his advertisement marked. The box was locked and the key gone, but we broke it open.'

Gray said, 'Oh, God,' very softly and hopelessly.

'I don't know if you're interested in knowing how we got on to you. It's obvious, really. Mrs Janus knew where her husband had gone and how much money he was carrying. She reported him missing and we found his Mercedes in the lane.'

Gray nodded at the inexorability, the neatness of it. 'Someone ought to shut you up in a cell,' she'd said. And perhaps there was a rightness in it somewhere, a harsh justice. He felt too weak, too unarmed, to argue and he knew he never would. He must accept. In writing the letters at all, he must always have hoped for an outcome of this kind; only his higher consciousness had struggled,

161

deceiving him. He'd hoped for Tiny's death and, caught in her net, done as much as she to bring it about. Who spun, who held the scissors and who cut the thread? Had the traffic light made his fate, or Jeff, or the buyer who hadn't got the paper in? Who made Honoré's marriage but the night phone caller? And who had made Tiny's death but he by meeting on that winter's day Tiny's wife? Who but Sir Smile, his neighbour?

'You'll want to make a statement,' Ixworth said. 'Shall we go?'

Gray smiled, for blank peace had returned. 'If we might just wait for Miss Clarion?'

'Put the door on the latch and leave her a note.' Ixworth spoke understandingly, almost sympathetically. His eye, satisfied now, no longer mocking, glanced on the sleeping Dido. 'We can – er, shut the dog up in the kitchen.'

# After

There were only six beds in Alexander Fleming Ward. The Member hesitated in the doorway and then made for the one bed around which the curtains were drawn. But before he reached it a nurse intercepted him.

'Mr Denman's visitors are restricted to ten minutes. He's still in a serious condition.'

Andrew Laud nodded. 'I won't stay long.'

The nurse lifted one of the curtains for him and he ducked under it apprehensively, wondering what he was going to see. A hideously scarred face? A head swathed in bandages?

Jeff Denman said, 'Thank God you could come. I've been on tenterhooks all day,' and then the Member looked at him. He was as he had always been, apart from his pallor and his hair which had been cropped to within an inch of his head.

'How are you, Jeff?'

'I'm much better. I'll be O.K. It's a strange sensation to wake up in the morning and find that yesterday was six months ago.'

The bed was covered with newspapers which the nurse stacked into a neat pile before swishing out through the curtains. The Member saw his own face staring out from the top one and the headline: 'M.P. Acts in Forest Murder Appeal.'

'I haven't acted very much,' he said. 'They've let me see Gray a couple of times but he seems to have a kind of amnesia about the whole thing. He either can't or won't remember. All he talks about is getting out and starting to write again but that, of course, unless this Appeal . . .'

Jeff interrupted him. 'I haven't got amnesia, surprisingly enough.' He shifted in the bed, lifting his head painfully from the pillow. 'But first I'd better tell you how I come to be here.'

'You explained that in your letter.'

'I had to get the sister to write that and I couldn't get my thoughts straight. You see, when I recovered consciousness and saw the papers it was such a shock. I couldn't believe Gray had got fifteen years for murder and I dictated that letter very incoherently. I just prayed you'd take me seriously and come. Give me a drink of water, will you?'

Andrew Laud put the glass to his lips and when Jeff had drunk, said, 'I've gathered that your van crashed into a lorry somewhere in Waltham Abbey on June the twelfth and you were seriously injured. As soon as I read that I knew you might have something important to tell me, but you didn't explain what you were doing there.'

'My job,' Jeff said. 'Moving furniture, or trying to.' He coughed, holding his hands to his ribs. 'The Sunday before that Gray asked me to move his stuff for him on the following Saturday. He said he'd phone if anything went wrong – things are liable to go wrong for him – and when he didn't I drove over there like I promised. It was the day after I'd had that letter from you asking me to dinner. You must have wondered why I didn't accept your wife's invitation.'

'Never mind that. Tell me what happened.'

Jeff said slowly, but quite clearly and coherently, 'I got there about three. I left the van on the metalled part of the lane because it was muddy and I thought the wheels might get stuck. When I got to the cottage there was a key in the lock and a note pinned up beside it. It was typed on Gray's typewriter – I know that typewriter – but it wasn't signed. It said something like *Have to go out for a while. Let yourself in and have a look round.* I thought it was meant for me.

'I went in, made a sort of mental note of the things he'd want me to move – which is what I thought he'd meant in the note – and sat down to wait for him. Oh, and I went all over the house. If there's any question of Gray's having been there then, I can tell you he wasn't.'

'You remember everything very clearly.'

'Not the accident,' said Jeff, and he winced slightly. 'I can't remember a thing about that. But what happened before is quite clear to me. The place was very stuffy and musty-smelling,' he went on after a pause, 'and when it got to be nearly four o'clock I decided to go outside again, leaving the key and the note where they were. I thought I'd

164

sit in the garden but it was so overgrown that I went into the Forest and walked about a bit. But the point is I never went out of sight of the cottage. I was pretty fed-up with Gray by this time and I wanted to get the job over and done with as soon as he got back.'

'He didn't come?'

Jeff shook his head. 'I sat down under a tree. I decided to give him ten minutes and then I'd go. Well, I was sitting there when I saw two people come down the lane.'

'Did you now?' The Member leaned closer towards the bed. 'In a car? On foot?'

'On foot. A little short bloke of about forty and a much younger woman. They went up to the door, read the note and let themselves in. They didn't see me, I'm sure of that. I realised then that the note was meant for them, not me. And I felt very strange about that, Andy. I just didn't know what to do.'

'I don't quite follow you there,' said the M.P.

'I recognised the girl. I knew her. I recognised her as a former girl friend of Gray's. And I couldn't understand what she was doing there with a bloke I was somehow certain must be her husband. He *looked* like a husband. I wondered if they'd come to have some sort of a scene with Gray. No, don't interrupt, Andy. Let me tell you the rest.' The sick man's voice was beginning to flag. He rested back against his pillows and gave another painful dry cough. 'I can tell you precisely when and where I'd seen her before. Gray brought her back to Tranmere Villas. Sally was living with me then. Gray had forewarned her and she kept out of the way when he and this girl came in, she never even saw them. But I'd been at work, I didn't know, and I opened the door of his room without knocking as soon as I got in. There was a review of his book in the evening paper and I was so pleased I rushed in to show him. They were on the bed making love. Gray was so – well, lost, I suppose you'd say – that he didn't even know I'd come in. But she did. She looked up and smiled a sort of look-how-daring-and-clever-I-am smile. I got out as fast and quietly as I could.'

Andrew Laud said over his shoulder as the curtain was drawn aside, 'Just two more minutes, Nurse. I promise to go in two minutes.'

'Mr Denman mustn't get excited.'

'I'm the one that's getting excited, Jeff,' said the Member when they were alone again. 'Go back to June the twelfth now, will you?'

'Where was I? Oh, yes sitting under that tree. After a while an old boy came along the lane, reading a book, and then the bloke I'd seen go into the cottage came out and walked around the place, looking up at the windows. I thought they were going and I waited for her to come out too. Well, the bloke went back into the house and about ten minutes later the girl came out alone. She didn't put the key back in the door and the note had gone. I thought she looked a bit shaken, Andy, and she wasn't walking very steadily. I nearly called out to her to ask if she was all right, but I didn't, though I was beginning to think the whole thing was a bit odd. She walked away into the Forest and when she'd gone I went too. I thought I'd drive down to Waltham Abbey to see if I could find Gray and tell him about it. There was a big green car parked near the van. I didn't notice the make or the number.

'It must have been about half past four then because they tell me I had the crash at twenty to five. And that's all. Since then I've been asleep and what I've told you has been asleep with me. Christ, suppose I'd died?'

'You didn't and you won't now. You'll have to get well fast so that you can tell all that to the Appeal Court. It's a pity you don't know who the girl was.'

'But I do. Didn't I say?' Jeff was lying down now, exhausted, his face grey. But he spoke with a feeble intensity. 'I'd know that face anywhere and I saw it again yesterday. There was a picture in the paper of Mrs Drusilla Janus, or Mrs McBride, as I suppose I should call her. The *Standard* said she got married to some tennis coach last month. You'll have to go now, Andy. Keep in touch?'

Smiling, a little dazed, the Member got up. Jeff reached out from under the bedclothes and, silently, rather formally, the two men shook hands.

166

# A DEMON IN MY
# VIEW

**For Margaret Rabbs**
**With Love**

From childhood's hour I have not been
As others were; I have not seen
As others saw; I could not bring
My passions from a common spring.
From the same source I have not taken
My sorrow; I could not awaken
My heart to joy at the same tone;
And all I loved, I loved alone.
Then – in my childhood, in the dawn
Of a most stormy life – was drawn
From every depth of good and ill
The mystery which binds me still . . .
And the cloud that took the form
(When the rest of Heaven was blue)
Of a demon in my view.

*Edgar Allan Poe*

The cellar was divided into rooms. Each of these caverns except the last of them was cluttered with the rubbish which usually encumbers the cellars of old houses: broken bicycles, old mould-grown leather cases, wooden crates, legless or armless chairs, cracked china vessels, yellowing newspapers bundled up with string, and in heaps, the nameless unidentifiable cylinders and tubes and rods and rings and spirals of metal which once, long ago, bolted or screwed or linked something on to something else. All this rubbish was coated with the thick black grime that is always present in cellars. The place smelt of soot and fungus.

Between the junk heaps a passage had been cleared from the steps to the first doorless doorway, on to the second doorway and thence to the bare room beyond. And in this room, unseen as yet in the pitch blackness, the figure of a woman leaned against the wall.

He came down the steps with a torch in his hand. He switched on the torch only when he had closed and bolted the door behind him. Then, led by its beam, he picked his way softly along the path that was hedged by rubbish. There was no sound but the shuffle of his slippers on the sooty stone, yet as he entered the second room he told himself he had heard ahead of him an indrawn breath, a small gasp of fear. He smiled, though he was trembling, and the hand which held the torch shook a little.

At the second doorway he raised the beam and let it play from the lower left-hand corner of the room upwards and then downwards, moving it languidly towards the right. It showed him pocked walls, a cracked ceiling hung with cobwebs. It showed him old broken long-disused electric wires, a trickle of viscous water running from the fissure in a split brick, and then playing in a downward arc, it showed him the woman's figure.

Her white face, beautiful, unmarked by any flaw of skin or feature, stared blankly back at him. But he fancied, as the torch shivered in his hand, that she had cringed, her slim body in its short black dress pressing further into the wall which supported it. A handbag was hooked over one of her arms and she wore scuffed black shoes. He didn't speak. He had never known how to talk to women. There was only one thing he had ever been able to do to women and, advancing now, smiling, he did it.

First he rested the torch on a brick ledge at the level of his knees so that she was in shadow, so that the room took on the aspect of an alley into which a street lamp filters dimly. Then he approached her, paralysed as she was, and meeting no resistance – he would have preferred resistance – he closed his hands on her throat.

Still there was no resistance, but what happened next was almost as satisfactory. His hands squeezed till the fingers met, and as forefinger pressed against thumb, the beautiful white face changed, crumpled, twisted in agony and caved in. He gave a grunting gasp as her body fell sideways. He released his hold, swaying at the earthquake inside him, and he let her fall, prone and stiff into the footmarked soot.

It took him a few minutes to recover. He wiped his hands and the corners of his mouth on a clean white handkerchief. He closed his eyes, opened them, sighed. Then he picked up the plastic shop window model and set her once more against the wall. Her face remained caved-in. He wiped the dust from it with his handkerchief and, inserting his fingers through the split in her neck, a split which grew wider each time he murdered her, pushed out sunken nose and crumpled eyes and depressed chin, until she was blank and beautiful again.

He straightened her dress and replaced the handbag, which had come unhooked, once more on her arm. She was ready to die for him again. A week, a fortnight, might go by but she would wait for him. It was good, the best thing in his life, just knowing she was there, waiting till next time . . .

# 1

The houses were warrens for people, little anthills of discomfort. Almost each one, built to accommodate a single family, had been segmented into four or five separate units. Ungracious living was evinced by a row of doorbells, seven in an eight-roomed house, by the dustbins that had replaced rose bushes in the front gardens, by the slow decay that showed in a boarded window, a balcony rail patched with chicken wire, a latchless gate that tapped ceaselessly, monotonously, against its post.

On the odd-numbered side of Trinity Road the houses were tall and with high basements so that the flights of steps mounting to their front doors seemed to assault the very hearts of these houses like engines of siege. They faced terraces of brown brick, humbler-looking and only three floors high. Outside number 142 was parked a large shiny car, a green Jaguar. A toy dog that nodded its head at the slightest vibration rested inside the rear window, and hanging from the centre of the windscreen was a blonde doll in a two-piece bathing suit.

The car looked incongruous in Trinity Road, along which such vehicles generally passed without stopping. Just inside the low wall that bounded the front garden of number 142 grew two lopped-off lime trees, stumps bearing on their summits excrescences of leathery leaves that gave them the look of prehistoric vegetation. Behind them was a small patch of brown turf. On the ground floor was a bay window, curtained in orange; above that two windows curtained in floral green – frayed curtains these, with a rent in one of them; on the top floor brown velvet curtains which, parted, disclosed a white frilly drapery like the bodice of a woman's nightgown.

A shallow flight of steps, of pink granite but grazed instead of polished, led to a front door whose woodwork might have been of any colour, green, brown, grey, it was so long since it had been painted. But the glass panels in

171

it kept the dim glow they had always had, rubber plant green and the dull maroon of sour wine, the kind of stained glass found in chapel windows of the last century.

There were five bells, each one but the lowest labelled. A psychologist would have learned much from the varied and distinctive labelling of these bells. The topmost bore below it a typewritten slip, framed in a plastic container clearly designed for this purpose, which stated: Flat 2, Mr A. Johnson. Beneath this and the next bell, on a scrap of card secured with adhesive tape, was scrawled in a bold reckless hand: Jonathan Dean. While under the third bell two labels seemed to quarrel with each other for pre-eminence. One was of brown plastic with the letters on it in relief: Flat 1, B. Kotowsky. Its rival, jostling it, stuck to the corner of it with a gob of glue, announced in felt-tipped pen: Ms V. Kotowsky. Last came a frivolous oval of orange cardboard on which, under a pair of Chinese characters done with a brush, the caller might read: Room 1, Li-li Chan.

The space beneath the lowest bell was vacant, as was Room 2 with which it communicated.

Between the door of the vacant room and the long diagonal sweep which was the underside of the staircase, a shabby windowless space, Stanley Caspian, the landlord, had his office. It was furnished with a desk and two bentwood chairs. On top of the shelves, bristling with papers, which lined the rear wall, stood an electric kettle and a couple of cups and saucers. There was no other furniture in the hall but a rectangular mahogany table set against the banisters and facing the ground floor bathroom.

Stanley Caspian sat at the desk, as he always did when he came to a hundred and forty-two for his Saturday morning conference with Arthur Johnson. Arthur sat in the other chair. On the desk were spread the rent books and cheques of the tenants. Each rent book had its own brown envelope with the tenant's name printed on it. This had been an innovation of Arthur's and he had done the printing. Stanley wrote laboriously in the rent books, pressing his pen in hard and making unnecessary full-stops after every word and figure.

'I'll be glad to see the back of that Dean,' he said when he had inked in the last fifty pence and made the last full-stop. 'Middle of next month and he'll be gone.'

'And his gramophone,' said Arthur, 'and his wine bottles filling up our little dustbin. I'm sure we'll all be devoutly thankful.'

'Not Kotowsky. He won't have anyone to go boozing with. Still, thank God he's going off his own bat, is what I say. I'd never have been able to get rid of him, not with this poxy new Rent Act. Put the kettle on, me old Arthur. I fancy a spot of elevenses.'

And tenses and twelveses, Arthur thought. He plugged in the electric kettle and set out the cups. He wouldn't have dreamed of eating anything at this hour, but Stanley, who was enormously fat, whose belly almost burst open the front of his size seventeen collar shirt, opened one of the packages he had brought with him and began devouring sandwiches of bread rolls and processed cheese. Stanley spluttered crumbs all over his shirt, eating uninhibitedly like some gross superannuated baby. Arthur watched him inscrutably. He neither liked nor disliked Stanley. For him, as for everyone, he had no particular feeling most of the time. He wished only to be esteemed, to keep in with the right people, to know where he stood. Inclining his head towards the door behind him, he said:

'A little bird told me you'd let that room.'

'Right,' said Stanley, his mouth full. 'A little Chinese bird, was it?'

'I must confess I was a bit put out you told Miss Chan before telling me. You know me, I always believe in speaking out. And I was a little hurt. After all, I am your oldest tenant. I *have* been here twenty years, and I think I can say I've never caused you a moment's unease.'

'Right. I only wish they were all like you.'

Arthur filled the cups with instant coffee, boiling water and a dribble of cold milk. 'No doubt, you had your reasons.' He lifted cold eyes, of so pale a blue as to be almost white. 'I mustn't be so sensitive.'

'The fact is,' said Stanley, shovelling spoonfuls of sugar into his cup, 'that I wondered how you'd take it. You see, this new chap, the one that's taking Room 2, he's got the same name as you.' He gave Arthur a sidelong look and then he chortled. 'You have to laugh. Coincidence, eh? I wondered how you'd take it.'

'You mean he's also called *Arthur Johnson*?'

173

'Not so bad as that. Dear, oh, dear, you have to laugh. He's called Anthony Johnson. You'll have to take care your post doesn't get mixed up. Don't want him reading your love letters, eh?'

Arthur's eyes seemed to grow even paler, and the muscles of his face tightened, tensed, drawing it into a mask. When he spoke his accent smoothed into an exquisite, slightly affected, English. 'I've nothing to hide. My life is an open book.'

'Maybe his isn't. If I wasn't in a responsible position I'd say you could have a bit of fun there, me old Arthur.' Stanley finished his sandwiches and fetched a doughnut from the second bag. '*The Sexual Behaviour of the Human Male*, that's the sort of open book his life'll be. Good-looking young devil, he is. Real flypaper for the girls, I shouldn't wonder.'

Arthur couldn't bear that sort of talk. It made him feel sick. 'I only hope he's got a good bank reference and a decent job.'

'Right. He's paid two months' rent in advance and that's better than all your poxy bank references to me. He's moving in Monday.' Stanley got heavily to his feet. Crumbs cascaded on to desk, envelopes and rent books. 'We'll just have a look in, Arthur. Mrs Caspian says there's a fruit bowl in there she wants and young Anthony'll only smash it.'

Arthur nodded sagely. If he and his landlord were in agreement about anything, it was the generally destructive behaviour of the other tenants. Besides, he enjoyed penetrating the rooms, usually closed to him. And in this one he had a special interest.

It was small and furnished with junk. Arthur accepted this as proper in a furnished room, noting only that it was far from clean. He picked his way over to the window. Stanley, having secured his fruit bowl, of red and white Venetian glass, from heterogeneous stacks of crockery and cutlery on the draining board, was admiring the only object in the place less than twenty years old.

'That's a bloody good washbasin, that is,' he remarked, tapping this article of primrose-coloured porcelain. 'Cost me all of fifteen quid to have that put in. Your people did it, as I remember.'

'It was a reject,' said Arthur absently. 'There's a flaw in the soap dish.' He was staring out of the window which overlooked a narrow brick-walled court. Above an angle of wall you could see the topmost branches of a tree. The court was concreted and the concrete was green with lichen, for into the two drains on either side of it flowed – and sometimes overflowed – the waste water from the two upstairs flats and Jonathan Dean's room. In the wall which faced the window was a door.

'What are you looking at?' said Stanley none too pleasantly, for Arthur's remark about the washbasin had perhaps rankled.

'Nothing,' said Arthur. 'I was just thinking he won't have much of an outlook.'

'What d'you expect for seven quid a week? You want to remember *you* pay seven for a whole flat because the poxy government won't let me charge more for unfurnished accommodation. You're lucky, getting your hooks on that when I didn't know any better. Oh, yes. But times have changed, thank God, and for seven quid a week now you look out on a cellar door and lump it. Right?'

'It's no concern of mine,' said Arthur. 'I imagine my namesake will be out a lot, won't he?'

'If he's got any sense,' said Stanley, for at that moment there crashed through the ceiling the triumphant chords of the third movement from Beethoven's Eighth. 'Tschaikowsky,' he said learnedly. 'Dean's at it again. I like something a bit more modern myself.'

'I was never musical.' Arthur gravitated into the hall. 'I must get on with things. Shopping day, you know. If I might just have my little envelope?'

His shopping basket in one hand and an orange plastic carrier containing his laundry in the other, Arthur made his way along Trinity Road towards the launderette in Brasenose Avenue. He could have used the Coinerama in Magdalen Hill, but he went to Magdalen Hill every weekday to work and at the weekends he liked to vary his itinerary. After all, for good reason, he didn't go out much and never after dark.

So instead of cutting through Oriel Mews, past the Waterlily pub and making for the crossroads, he went down past All Souls' Church, where as a child he had passed two hours each Sabbath Day, his text carefully committed to memory. And at four o'clock Auntie Gracie had always been waiting for him, always, it seemed to him, under an umbrella. Had it invariably rained on Sundays, the granite terrace opposite veiled in misty grey? That terrace was now gone, replaced by barrack-like blocks of council flats.

He followed the route he and Auntie Gracie had taken towards home, but only for a little way. Taking some pleasure in making the K.12 bus stop for him alone, Arthur went over the pedestrian crossing in Balliol Street, holding up his hand in an admonitory way. Down St John's Road where the old houses still remained, turn-of-the-century houses some enterprising but misguided builder had designed with Dutch façades, and where plane trees alternated with concrete lamp standards.

The launderette attendant said good morning and Arthur rejoined with a cool nod. He used his own soap in the machine. He didn't trust the blue stuff in the little packet you got for five pence. Nor did he trust the attendant to put his linen in the drier nor the other customers not to steal it. So he sat patiently on one of the benches, talking to no one, until the thirty-five minute cycle was completed.

It afforded him considerable satisfaction to note how superior were his pale blue sheets, snowy towels, underwear and shirts, to the gaudy jumble sale laundry in the adjacent machines. While they were safely rotating in the drier, he went next-door to the butchers and then to the greengrocers. Arthur never shopped in the supermarkets run by Indians, in which this area of Kenbourne Vale abounded. He selected his lamb chops, his small Sunday joint of Scotch topside, with care. Three slices off the roast for Sunday, the rest to be minced and made into Monday's cottage pie. A pound of runner beans, and pick out the small ones, if you please, he didn't want a mouthful of strings.

A different way back. The linen so precisely folded that it wouldn't really need ironing – though Arthur always ironed it – he trotted up Merton Street. More council flats, tower blocks here like pillars supporting the heavy overcast sky. The lawns which separated them, Arthur had often

176

noticed with satisfaction, were prohibited to children. The children played in the street or sat disconsolately on top of bits of sculpture. Arthur disapproved of the sculptures, which in his view resembled chunks cut out of prehistoric monsters for all they were entitled *Spring* or *Social Conscience* or *Man and Woman*, but he didn't think the children ought to sit on them or play in the street for that matter. Auntie Gracie had never allowed him to play in the street.

Stanley Caspian's Jaguar had gone, and so had the Kotowskys' fourth-hand Ford. A fistful of vouchers, entitling their possessor to three pence off toothpaste or free soap when you bought a giant size shampoo, had been pushed through the letter box. Arthur helped himself to those which might come in handy, and mounted the stairs. There was a half-landing after the ten steps of the first flight where a pay phone box was attached to the wall. Four steps went on to the first floor. The door of the Kotowskys' flat was on his left, that to Jonathan Dean's room facing him, and the door to the bathroom they shared between the other two. Dean's door was open, Shostakovitch's Fifth Symphony on loud enough to be heard in Kenbourne Town Hall. The intention apparently was that it should be loud enough merely to be audible in the bathroom from which Dean, a tall red-haired, red-faced man, now emerged. He wore nothing but a small mauve towel fastened round him loincloth-fashion.

'The body is more than raiment,' he remarked when he saw Arthur.

Arthur flushed slightly. It was his belief that Dean was mad, a conviction which rested partly on the fact that everything the man said sounded as if it had come out of a book. He turned his head in the direction of the open door.

'Would you be good enough to reduce the volume a little, Mr Dean?'

Dean said something about music having charms to soothe the savage breast, and beat his own which was hairy and covered with freckles. But, having slammed his door with violence but no animosity, he subdued Shostakovitch and only vague Slavic murmurs reached Arthur as he ascended the second flight.

And now he was in his own exclusive domain. He occupied the whole second floor. With a sigh of contentment,

177

resting his laundry bag and his shopping basket on the mat, he unlocked the door and let himself in.

# 2

Arthur prepared his lunch, two lamb cutlets, creamed potatoes, runner beans. None of your frozen or canned rubbish for him. Auntie Gracie had brought him up to appreciate fresh food, well-cooked. He ended the meal with a slice from the plum pie he had baked on Thursday night, and then, without delay, he washed the dishes. One of Auntie Gracie's maxims had been that only slatternly housekeepers leave dirty dishes in the sink. Arthur always washed his the moment he finished eating.

He went into the bedroom. The bed was stripped. He put on clean sheets, rose pink, and rose pink pillow cases. Arthur couldn't sleep in a soiled bed. Once, when collecting their rent, he had caught a glimpse of the Kotowskys' bed and it had put him off his supper.

Meticulously he dusted the bedroom furniture and polished the silver stoppers on Auntie Gracie's cut-glass scent bottles. All his furniture was late-Victorian, pretty though a little heavy. It came up well under an application of polish. Arthur still felt guilty about using spray-on polish instead of the old-fashioned wax kind. Auntie Gracie had never approved of short cuts. He gave the frilly nets, with which every window in the flat was curtained, a critical stare. They were too fragile to be risked at the launderette, so he washed them himself once a month, and they weren't due for a wash for another week. But this was such a grimy district, and there was nothing like white net for collecting every bit of flying dust. He began to take them down. For the second time that day he found himself facing the cellar door.

The Kotowskys had no window which overlooked it. It could be seen only from this one of his and from the one in Room 2. This had long been known to Arthur, he had known it for nearly as long as the duration of his tenancy.

Very little in his own life had changed in those twenty years. The cellar door had never been painted, though the bricks had darkened perhaps and the concrete grown more green and damp. No one had ever seen him cross that yard, he thought as he laid the net curtains carefully over a chair, no one had ever seen him enter the cellar. He continued to stare down, considering, remembering.

He had been at school with Stanley Caspian – Merton Street Junior – and Stanley had been fat and gross and coarse even then. A bully always.

'Auntie's baby! Auntie's baby! Where's your dad, Arthur Johnson?' And with an inventiveness no one would have suspected from the standard of Stanley's school work: 'Cowardy, cowardy custard, Johnson is a bastard!'

The years civilise, at least inhibit. When they met by chance in Trinity Road, each aged thirty-two, Stanley was affable, even considerate.

'Sorry to hear you lost your aunt, Arthur. More like a mother to you, she was.'

'Yes.'

'You'll be wanting a place of your own now. Bachelor flat, eh? How about taking the top of a hundred and forty-two?'

'I've no objection to giving it the once over,' said Arthur primly. He knew old Mrs Caspian had left her son a lot of property in West Kenbourne.

The house was in a mess in those days and the top flat was horrible. But Arthur saw its potential – and for two pounds ten a week? So he took Stanley's offer, and a couple of days later when he had started the re-decorating he went down into the cellar to see if, by chance, it housed a stepladder.

She was lying on the floor of the furthest room on a heap of sacks and black-out curtains left over from the war. She was naked and her white plastic flesh was cold and shiny. He never found out who had brought her there and left her entombed. At first he had been embarrassed, taken aback as he was when he glimpsed likenesses of her standing in shop windows and waiting to be dressed. But then, because he was alone with her and there was no one to see them, he approached more closely. So that was how they looked? With awe, with fear, at last with distaste, he looked at the

179

two hemispheres on her chest, the soft swollen triangle between her closed thighs. An impulse came to him to dress her. He had done so many secret things in his life – almost everything he had done that he had wanted to do had been covert, clandestine – that no inhibition intervened to stop him fetching from the flat a black dress, a handbag, shoes. These had belonged to Auntie Gracie and he had brought them with him from the house in Magdalen Hill. People had suggested he give them to the W.V.S. for distribution, but how could he? How could he have borne to see some West Kenbourne slattern queening it in her clothes?

His white lady had attenuated limbs and was as tall as he. Auntie Gracie's dress came above her knees. She had yellow nylon hair that curled over her cheekbones. He put the shoes on her feet and hooked the handbag over her arm. In order to see what he was doing, he had put a hundred-watt bulb in the light socket. But another of those impulses led him to take it out. By the light of the torch she looked real, the cellar room with its raw brick walls an alley in the hinterland of city streets. It was sacrilege to dress her in Auntie Gracie's clothes, and yet that very sacrilege had an indefinable rightness about it, was a spur . . .

He had strangled her before he knew what he was doing. With his bare hands on her cold smooth throat. The release had been almost as good as the real thing. He set her up against the wall once more, dusted her beautiful white face. You do not have to hide or fear or sweat for such a killing; the law permits you to kill anything not made of flesh and blood . . . He left her and came out into the yard. The room that was now Room 2 had been untenanted then as had the whole house but for his flat. And when a tenant had come he had been, as had his successor, on night work that took him out five evenings a week at six. But before that Arthur had decided. She should save him, she should be – as those who would like to get hold of him would call it – his therapy. The women who waited in the dark streets, asking for trouble, he cared nothing for them, their pain, their terror. He cared, though, for his own fate. To defy it, he would kill a thousand women in her person, she should be his salvation. And then no threat could disturb him, provided he was careful never to go out after dark, never to have a drink.

After a time he had come to be rather proud of his solution. It seemed to set down as nonsense the theories of those experts – he had, in the days of his distress, studied their works – that men with his problem had no self-control, no discipline over their own compulsions. He had always known they talked rubbish. Why shouldn't he have the recourse of the members of Alcoholics Anonymous, of the rehabilitated drug addict?

But now? Anthony Johnson. Arthur, who made it his business to know the routines and life-styles of his fellow-tenants, hoped he would soon acquire a thorough-going knowledge of the new man's movements. Anthony Johnson would surely go out two or three evenings a week? He must. The alternative was something Arthur didn't at all want to face.

There was nothing for it but to wait and see. The possibility of bringing the white lady up into the flat, installing her here, killing her here, occurred to him only for him to dismiss the idea. He disliked the notion of his encounters with her taking on the air of a game. It was the squalor of the cellar, the dimness, his stealthy approach that gave to it its reality. No, she must remain there, he thought, and he must wait and see. He turned from the window and at the same time turned his mind, for he didn't much care to dwell upon her and what she truly was, preferring her to stand down there forgotten and unacknowledged until he needed her again. This, in fact, he thought as he took away the curtains to put them in to soak, was the first time he had thought of her in those terms for many years.

Dismissing her as a man dismisses a compliant and always available mistress, Arthur went into the living room. The sofa and the two armchairs had been re-upholstered since Auntie Gracie's death, only six months after, but Arthur had taken such good care of them that the covers still looked new. Carefully he worked on the blue moquette with a stiff brush. The cream drawn-thread antimacassars might as well go into the water with the nets. He polished the oval mahogany table, the mahogany tallboy, the legs and arms of the dining chairs; plumped up the blue and brown satin cushions, flicked his feather duster over the

181

two hand-painted parchment lamp-shades, the knobs on the television set, the Chelsea china in the cabinet. Now for the vacuum cleaner. Having the flat entirely covered with wall-to-wall carpet in a deep fawn shade had made a hole in his savings, but it had been worth it. He ran the cleaner slowly and thoroughly over every inch of the carpet, taking his time so that its droning zoom-zoom wouldn't be lost on Jonathan Dean, though he had little hope of its setting him an example. Finally, he rinsed the nets and the chair backs and hung them over the drying rack in the bathroom. There was no need to clean the bathroom or the kitchen. They were cleaned every morning as a matter of course, the former when he had dried himself after his bath, the latter as soon as breakfast was over.

At this point he sat down in the chair by the front window and, having left all his doors open, surveyed the flat along its spotless length. It smelt of polish, silver cleaner, soap and elbow grease. Arthur recalled how, when he was about eleven and had neglected to wash his bedroom window as thoroughly as Auntie Gracie demanded, she had sent him round to Winter's with threepence.

'You ask the man for a pound of elbow grease, Arthur. Go on. It won't take you five minutes.'

The man in the shop had laughed himself almost into a fit. But he hadn't explained why he had no elbow grease, and Arthur had to take the threepenny bit – a threepenny joey, they called them then – back home again.

'I expect he did laugh,' said Auntie Gracie. 'And I hope you've been taught a lesson.' She rubbed Arthur's arm through the grey flannel shirt. 'This is where your elbow grease comes from. You can't buy it, you have to make it yourself.'

Arthur hadn't borne her any malice. He knew she had acted for the best. He would do exactly the same by any child in his charge. Children had to be taught the hard way, and it had set him on the right path. Would she be pleased with him if she could see him now? If she could see how well he kept his own place, his bank balance, how he ordered his life, how he hadn't missed a day at Grainger's in twenty years? Perhaps. But she had never been very pleased with him, had she? He had never reached those heights of perfection she had laid before him as fitting for

182

one who needed to cleanse himself of the taint of his birth and background.

Arthur sighed. He should have washed the Chelsea china. It was no good telling himself a flick with that duster would serve as well as a wash. Tired now but determined to soldier on, he put the shepherdesses and frock-coated gentlemen and dogs and little flower baskets on to a tray and carried them into the kitchen.

# 3

Arthur was a sound sleeper. He fell asleep within five minutes of laying his head on the pillow and hardly ever awoke before the alarm went off at seven-thirty. This ability to sleep was something to confound those silent critics, that invisible army of psychiatrists whose words he had read but never yet heard, and who would, he suspected, categorise him disagreeably. Which was absurd. Neurotic people don't sleep well, nor do hysterics. Arthur knew he was a perfectly normal man who happened (like all normal men) to have a small peculiarity he was well able to keep under control.

He was always the last to leave for work and the first to get home. This was because the others all worked further afield than he. Jonathan Dean went first. He left at five past eight while Arthur was still in his bath. This Monday morning his room door was slammed so loudly that the bath water actually rocked about like tea in a joggled cup. The front door also crashed shut. Arthur dried himself and, for decency's sake, put on his towelling robe before washing down bath, basin and floor. As soon as he was dressed, he opened his own front door and left it on the latch.

The Kotowskys burst out of their flat while he was pouring out his cornflakes. As usual, they were quarrelling.

'All right, I get the message,' he heard Brian Kotowsky say. 'You've told me three times you won't be in tonight.'

'I just don't want you ringing up all my friends, asking where I am.'

'You can settle that one, Vesta, by telling me where you'll be.'

They clumped down the stairs, still arguing, but Arthur couldn't catch Vesta Kotowsky's reply. The front door closed fairly quietly which meant Vesta must have shut it. Arthur went to his living room window and watched them get into their car which was left day in and day out, rain, shine or snow, parked in the street. He was sincerely glad he had never taken the step of getting married, had, in fact, taken such a serious step to avoid it.

As he was returning to his kitchen he heard Li-li Chan come upstairs to the half-landing and the phone. Li-li spoke quite good English but rather as a talking bird might have spoken it. Her voice was high and clipped. She was always giggling, mostly about nothing.

She giggled now, into the receiver. 'You pick me up soon? Quarter to nine? Oh, you are nice, nice man. Do I love you? I don't know. Yes, yes, I love you. I love lots, lots of people. Good-bye now.' Li-li giggled prettily all the way back down the stairs.

Arthur snorted, but not loudly enough for her to hear. London Transport wouldn't get rich out of her. Don't suppose she ever spends a penny on a train or bus fare, Arthur thought, and darkly, I wonder what she has to do to make it worth their while? But he didn't care to pursue that one, it was too distasteful.

He heard her go out on the dot of a quarter to. She always closed the doors very softly as if she had something to hide. A well set-up, clean-looking young Englishman had come for her in a red sports car. A wicked shame, Arthur thought, but boys like that had only themselves to blame, they didn't know the meaning of self-discipline.

Alone in the house now, he finished his breakfast, washed the dishes and wiped down all the surfaces. The post was due at nine. While he was brushing the jacket of his second-best suit and selecting a tie, he heard the dull thump of the letter box. Arthur always took the post in and arranged the letters on the hall table.

But first there was his rubbish to deal with. He lifted the liner from the wastebin, secured the top of it with a wire fastener and went downstairs, first making sure, with a quick glance into the mirror, that his tie was neatly knotted and that there was a clean white handkerchief in his breast pocket. Whether there was anyone in the house or not, Arthur would never have gone downstairs improperly dressed. Nor would he set foot outside the house without locking the doors behind him, not even to go to the dustbin. Once more, the bin was choked with yellowish decaying bean sprouts, not even wrapped up. That wasteful Li-li again! He would have to make it clear to Stanley Caspian that one dustbin was inadequate for five people – six when this new man came today.

Unlocking the door and re-entering the house, he picked up the post. The usual weekly letter, postmarked Taiwan, from Li-li's father who hadn't adopted Western ways and wrote the sender's name as Chan Ah Feng. Poor trusting man, thought Arthur, little did he know. Yet another bill for Jonathan Dean. The next thing they'd have debt collectors round, and a fine thing that would be for the house's reputation. Two letters for the Kotowskys, one for her and one for both of them. That was the way it always was.

He tidied up the circulars and vouchers – who messed them about like that out of sheer wantonness he didn't know – and then he arranged the letters, their envelope edges aligned to each other and the edge of the table. Ten past nine. Sighing a little, because it was so pleasant having the house to himself, Arthur went back upstairs and collected his briefcase. He had no real need of a briefcase for he never brought work home, but Auntie Gracie had given him his first one for his twenty-first birthday and since then he had replaced it three times. Besides, it looked well. Auntie Gracie had always said that a man going to business without a briefcase is as ill-dressed as a lady without gloves.

He closed his door and tested it with his hand to make sure it was fast shut. Down the stairs once more and out into Trinity Road. A fine bright day, though somewhat autumnal. What else could you expect in late September?

Grainger's, Contractors and Builders' Merchants, weren't due to open until nine-thirty and Arthur was early. He lingered to look at the house where he had lived with Auntie Gracie. It was on the corner of Balliol Street and Magdalen Hill, at the point where the hill became Kenbourne Lane, a tall narrow house, condemned to demolition but still waiting along with its neighbours to be demolished. The front door and the downstairs bay were sealed up with gleaming silvery corrugated iron to stop squatters and other vagrants getting in. Arthur often wondered what Auntie Gracie would say if she could see it now, but he approved of the sealing up. He paused at the gate and looked up to the boarded rectangle on the brick façade which had once been his bedroom window.

Auntie Gracie had been very good to him. He could never make up to her for what she had done for him if he struggled till the day of his death. He knew well what she had done, for, apart from the concrete evidence of it all around him, she had never missed an opportunity of telling him.

'After all I've done for you, Arthur!'

She had bought him from his mother, her own sister, when he was two months old.

'Had to give her a hundred pounds, Arthur, and a hundred was a lot of money in those days. We never saw her again. She was off like greased lightning.'

How fond Auntie Gracie had been of grease! Elbow grease, greased lightning – 'You need a bit of grease under your heels, Arthur.'

She had told him the facts of his birth as soon as she thought him old enough to understand. Unfortunately, Stanley Caspian and others of his ilk had thought him old enough some months before, but that was no fault of hers. And she had never mentioned his mother or his father, whoever he may have been, at all. But in that bedroom – with the door open, of course. She insisted on his always leaving the door open – he had spent many childhood hours, wondering. How foolish children were and how ungrateful . . .

Arthur shook himself and gave a slight cough. People would be looking at him in a moment. He deplored anything that might attract attention to oneself. And why on earth had he been mooning away like this when he passed the house every day, when there had been no unusual circumstance to give rise to such a reverie? But, of course, there was an unusual circumstance. The new man was coming to Room 2. It was only natural that today he should dwell a little on his past life. Natural, but governable too.

He turned briskly away from the gate as All Souls' clock struck the half-hour. Grainger's yard was next door but one to the sealed-up house, next to that a half-acre or so of waste ground where houses had been demolished but not yet replaced; beyond that Kenbourne Lane tube station.

Arthur unlocked the double gates and let himself into the glass and cedarwood hut which was his office. The boy who made tea and swept up and ran errands and whose duty it was to open the place, hadn't yet arrived. Typical. He wouldn't be late like this morning after morning if he had had an Auntie Gracie to put a spot of grease under his heels.

Raising the venetian blinds to let sunshine into the small neat room, Arthur took the cover off his Adler standard. Plenty of post had come since Friday, mostly returned bills with cheques enclosed. There was one irate letter from a customer who said that a pastel blue sink unit had been installed by Grainger's in his kitchen instead of the stainless steel variety he had ordered. Arthur read it carefully, planning what diplomatic words he would write in reply.

He called himself, when required to state his occupation, a surveyor. In fact, he had never surveyed anything and wouldn't have known how to go about it. His work consisted simply in sitting at this desk from nine-thirty till five, answering the phone, sending out bills and keeping the books. He knew his work back to front, inside out, but it still caused him anxiety, for Auntie Gracie's standards were always before him.

'Never put off till tomorrow what you can do today, Arthur. Remember if a job's worth doing, it's worth doing well. Your employer has reposed his trust in you. He has put you in a responsible position and it's up to you not to let him down.'

Those, or words like them, had been the words with which she had sent him off to be Grainger's boy a week after his fourteenth birthday. So he had swept up better than anyone else and made tea better than anyone else. When he was twenty-one he had attained his present responsibility, that of seeing to it that every customer of Grainger's got his roof mended better than anyone else's roof and his kitchen floor laid better than anyone else's kitchen floor. And he had seen to it. He was invaluable.

187

*Dear Sir,* Arthur typed, *I note with regret that the Rosebud de Luxe sink unit (type E/4283, pastel blue) was not, in fact*

Barry Hopkins slouched into the office, chewing bubble gum.

'Hi.'

'Good morning, Barry. A little late, aren't you? Do you know what time it is?'

'Round half nine,' said Barry.

'I see. Round half nine. Of all the lackadaisical, feckless . . .' Arthur would have liked to advise him to go over to the works and ask for a pound of elbow grease, but the young were so sophisticated these days. Instead he snapped, 'Take that filthy stuff out of your mouth.'

Barry took no notice. He blew an enormous bubble, like a balloon and of a pale shade of aquamarine. Leaning idly on the window sill, he said:

'Old Grainger's comin' across the yard.'

Arthur was galvanized. He composed his face into an expression suggestive of a mixture of devotion to duty, self-esteem and simpering sycophancy, and applied his hands to the typewriter.

# 4

Anthony Johnson had no furniture. He possessed nothing but a few clothes and a lot of books. These he had brought with him to 142 Trinity Road in a large old suitcase and a canvas bag. There were works on sociology, psychology, his dictionary of psychology, and that essential textbook for any student of the subject, *The Psychopath* by William and Joan McCord. Whatever else he needed for reference he would obtain from the British Museum, and from that excellent library of criminology – the best, it was said, in London – housed in Radclyffe College, Kenbourne Vale. In that library too he would write the thesis whose subject was *Some Aspects of the Psychopathic Personality*, and which he hoped would secure him from the University of London his doctorate of philosophy.

188

Part of it, he thought, surveying Room 2, would have to be written here. In that fireside chair, presumably, which seemed to be patched with bits from a woman's tweed skirt. On that crippled gate-leg table. Under that hanging lamp that looked like a monstrous, joke shop, plastic jellyfish. Well, he wanted his Ph.D and this was the price he must pay for it. Dr Johnson. Not, of course, that he would call himself doctor. It was Helen who had pointed out that in this country, the land of such anomalies, the bachelor of medicine is called doctor and the doctor of philosophy mister. She too had seen the funny side of being Dr Johnson and had quoted epigrams and talked about Boswell until he, at last, had seen the point. But it was always so. Sometimes he thought that for all his Cambridge First, his Home Office Social Science diploma, his wide experience of working with the poor, the sick and the deprived, he had never woken up to awareness and insight until he met Helen. She it was who had turned his soul's eye towards the light.

But as he thought this, he turned his physical eye towards Stanley Caspian's green-spotted fingermarked mirror and surveyed his own reflection. He wasn't a vain man. He hardly ever thought about the way he looked. That he was tall and slim and strongly-made with straight features and thick fair hair had never meant much to him except in that they denoted health. But lately he had come to wonder. He wondered what he lacked that Roger had; he who was good-looking and vigorous and – well, good company, wasn't he? – hyper-educated with a good salary potential, and Roger who was stupid and dull and possessive and couldn't do anything but win pistol shooting contests. Only he knew it wasn't that at all. It was just that Helen, for all her awareness, didn't know her own mind.

To give her a chance to know it, to choose between them, he had come here. The library, of course, was an advantage. But he could easily have written his thesis in Bristol. The theory was that absence made the heart grow fonder. If he had gone to his parents in York she could have phoned him every night. He wasn't going to let her know the phone number here – he didn't know it himself yet – or communicate with her at all except on the last Wednesday in the month when Roger would be out at his gun club. And he couldn't write to her at all in case Roger intercepted the

189

letter. She'd write to him once a week. He wondered, as he unpacked his books, how that would work out, if he had been wise to let her call the tune, make all the arrangements. Well, he'd given her a deadline. By November she must know. Stay in prison or come out with him into the free air.

He opened the window because the room smelt stale. Outside was a narrow yard. What light it received came from a bit of sky just flicked at its edges by leaves from a distant tree. The sky was a triangular patch because most of it was cut off by brick wall meeting brick wall diagonally about four yards up. In one of these walls – they were festooned with pipes betwigged with smaller pipes like lianas – was a door. Since there was no window beside it or anywhere near it, Anthony decided it must lead down to a cellar.

Five o'clock. He had better go out and get himself something to cook on that very old and inefficient-looking Baby Belling stove. The hall smelt vaguely of cloves, less vaguely of old unwashed fabrics. That would be the bathroom, that door between his and Room I, and that other one to the right of old Caspian's table, the loo. Wondering what sort of a woman or girl Miss Chan was and whether she would get possession of the bathroom just when he wanted to use it, he went out into the street.

Trinity Road. It led him via Oriel Mews into Balliol Street. The street names of London, he thought, require an historical treatise of their own. Someone must know why this group in Hampstead are called after Devon towns and that cluster in Cricklewood after Hebridean islands. Were the Barbara, the Dorinda and the Lesley, after whom roads are named just north of the City, once the belles of Barnsbury? Did a sorcerer live in Warlock Road, Kilburn Park, and who was the Sylvia of Sylvia Gardens, Wembley, what is she, that all our maps commend her? In that corner of Kenbourne Vale, to which his destiny had drawn Anthony Johnson, someone had christened the squalid groves and terraces after Oxford colleges.

A cruel joke cannot have been intended. The councillor or town planner or builder must have thought himself inspired when he named Trinity Road, All Souls' Grove, Magdalen Hill, Brasenose Avenue and Wadham Street.

190

What was certain, Anthony thought, was that he hadn't been an Oxford man, had never walked in the enclosed quadrangles of that city or even seen its dreaming spires.

Such a fanciful reverie would once have been alien to him. Helen had taught him to think like this, to see through her eyes, to associate, to compare, and to dream. She was all imagination, he all practical. Practical again, he noted mundane things. The Vale Café for quick cheap snacks; Kemal's Kebab House, smelling of cumin and sesame and fenugreek, for when he wanted to splash a bit; a pub – the Waterlily, it was called. Just opening now. Anthony saw red plush settees, a brown-painted moulded ceiling, etched glass screens beside and behind the bar.

The pavements everywhere were cluttered with garbage in black plastic sacks. A dustmen's strike, perhaps. The kids were out of school. He wondered where they played. Always on these dusty pavements of Portland stone? Or on that bit of waste ground, fenced in with broken and rusty tennis court wire, between Grainger's, the builders, and the tube station?

Houses marked here for demolition. The sooner they came down the better and made way for flats with big windows and green spaces to surround them. Not many truly English people about. Brown women pushing prams with black babies in them, gypsy-looking women with hard worn faces, Indian women with Marks and Spencers woolly cardigans over lilac and gold and turquoise saris. Cars parked everywhere, and vans double-parked on a street that was littered with torn paper and bruised vegetables and silvery fish scales where a market had just packed up and gone. Half-past five. But very likely that corner shop, Winter's, stayed open till all hours. He went in, bought a packet of ham, a can of beans, some bread, eggs, tea, margarine and frozen peas. Carried along by a tide of home-going commuters, he returned to 142 Trinity Road. The house was no longer empty.

A man of about fifty was standing by the hall table, holding in his hand a bundle of cheap offer vouchers. He was tallish, thin, with a thin, reddish and coarse-skinned face. His thin, greyish-fair hair had been carefully combed to conceal a bald patch and was flattened with Brylcreem. He

191

wore an immaculate dark grey suit, a white shirt and a maroon tie dotted with tiny silver spots. On his rather long, straight and quite fleshless nose, were a pair of gold-rimmed glasses. When he saw Anthony he jumped.

'These were on the mat,' he said. 'They come every day. You wouldn't think there was a world paper shortage, would you? I tidy them up. No one else seems to be interested. But I hardly feel it's my place to throw them away.'

Anthony wondered why he bothered to explain.

'I'm Anthony Johnson,' he said. 'I moved in today.'

The man said, 'Ah,' and held out his hand. He had a rather donnish look as if he perhaps had been responsible for the naming of those streets. But his voice was uneducated, underlying the pedantic preciseness Kenbourne Vale's particular brand of cockney. 'Moved into the little room at the back, have you? We keep ourselves very much to ourselves here. You won't use the phone after eleven, will you?'

Anthony asked where the phone was.

'On the first landing. My flat is on the second landing. I have a *flat*, you see, not a room.'

Light dawned. 'Are you by any chance the other Johnson?'

The man gave a severe, almost reproving, laugh. 'I think you must mean *you* are the other Johnson. I have been here for twenty years.'

Anthony could think of no answer to make to that one. He went into Room 2 and closed the door behind him. On this mild, still summery day the room with its pipe-hung brick ramparts was already growing dark at six. He switched on the jellyfish lamp and saw how the light radiated the whole of that small courtyard. Leaning out of the window, he looked upwards. In the towering expanse of brick above him there was only one other window, and that on the top floor. The frilly net curtains behind its panes twitched. Someone had looked down at him and at the light, but Anthony's knowledge of the geography of the house was as yet insufficient to tell him who that someone might be.

Every morning for the rest of that week, Arthur listened carefully for Anthony Johnson to go off to work. But Jonathan Dean and the Kotowskys always made so much noise

192

over their own departures that it was difficult to tell. Certain it was, though, that Anthony Johnson remained at home in the evenings. Peering downwards out of his bedroom window, Arthur saw the light in Room 2 come on each evening at about six, and could tell by the pattern of two yellow rectangles divided by a dark bar, which the light made on the concrete, that Anthony Johnson didn't draw his curtains. It was a little early for him to feel an urge to visit the cellar again, and yet he was already growing restless. He thought this restlessness had something to do with frustration, with knowing that he couldn't go down there however much he might want to.

On the Friday morning, while fetching in the post, he saw Anthony Johnson come out of Room 2 and go into the bathroom, wearing nothing but a pair of jeans. Didn't the man *go* to work? Was he going to stop in there all day and all night?

Among that particular batch of letters was the first one to come for Anthony Johnson. Arthur knew it was for him as it was postmarked York and written on the flap was the sender's name and address: Mrs R. L. Johnson, 22 West Highamgate, York. But the front of the envelope was addressed, quite ambiguously, to A. Johnson Esq., 2/142 Trinity Road, London W15 6HD. Arthur sucked in his lips with an expression of exasperation. And when, a minute or so later, Anthony Johnson re-emerged, smelling of toothpaste, Arthur pointed out to him the possible consequences of such impreciseness.

The young man took it very casually. 'It's from my mother. I'll tell her to put Room 2, if I think of it.'

'I hope you will think of it, Mr Johnson. This sort of thing could lead to a great deal of awkwardness and embarrassment.'

Anthony Johnson smiled, showing beautiful teeth. He radiated health and vigour and a kind of modest virility to an extent that made Arthur uncomfortable. Besides, he didn't want to look at bare brown chests at ten past nine in the morning, thank you very much.

'A great deal of awkwardness,' he repeated.

'Oh, I don't think so. Let's not meet trouble half-way. I don't suppose I'll get many letters, and the ones I do get will either be postmarked York or Bristol.'

193

'Very well. I thought I should mention it and I have. Now you can't blame me if there is a Mix Up.'

'I shan't blame you.'

Arthur said no more. The man's manner floored him. It was so casual, so calm, so poised. He could have coped with defensiveness or a proper apology. This cool acceptance – no, it wasn't really cool, but warm and pleasant – of his reproach was like nothing he had ever come across. It was almost as if Anthony Johnson were the older, wiser man, who could afford to treat such small local difficulties with indulgence.

Arthur was more than a little irritated by it. It would have served Anthony Johnson right if, when Arthur took the post in on the following Tuesday, he had torn open the letter from Bristol without a second thought. Of course he didn't do so, although the postmark was so faint as to be almost illegible and there was no sender's name on the flap. But this one, too, was addressed to A. Johnson Esq., 2/142 Trinity Road, London W15 6HD. The envelope was made of thick mauve-grey paper with a rough expensive-looking surface.

Arthur set it on the table on the extreme right-hand side, the position he had allotted to Anthony Johnson's correspondence, and then he went into the front garden to tidy up the mess inside, on top of and around the dustbin. The dustmen had now been on strike for two weeks. In the close sunless air the rubbish smelt sour and fetid. When he went back into the house the mauve-grey envelope had gone.

He didn't speculate about its contents or the identity of its sender. His concern with Anthony Johnson was simply to get some idea of the man's movements. But on the following evening, the last Wednesday of the month, he was to learn simultaneously partial answers to all these questions.

It was eight o'clock and dusk. Arthur had long finished his evening meal, washed the dishes, and was about to settle in front of his television. But he remembered leaving his bedroom window open. Auntie Gracie had always been most eloquent on the subject of night air and its evil effects. As he was pulling down the sash, taking care not to catch up the fragile border of the net curtain, he saw the light,

194

shed on the court below, go out. Quickly he went to his front door, opened it and listened. But instead of leaving the house, Anthony Johnson was coming upstairs.

Arthur heard quite clearly the sound of the phone dial being spun. A lot of digits, not just the seven for London. And presently a lot of coins inserted . . .

Anthony Johnson's voice: 'I'm taking it that the coast is clear, he's not listening on this extension and he won't come up here and shoot me in the morning.' A pause. Then, 'Of course I'm teasing you, my love. The whole business is sick.' Arthur listened intently. 'I had your letter. Darling, I need footnotes. You must be the only married lady who's ever quoted *The Pilgrim's Progress* in a letter to her lover. It was *Grace Abounding*? Then I do need footnotes.' A long, long pause. Anthony Johnson cursed, obviously because he had to put more money in.

'Shall I transfer the charges? No, of course I won't. Roger would see it on the bill and so on and so on.' Silence. Laughter. Another silence. Then: 'Term starts a week today, but I'll only be going to a few lectures that touch on my subject. I'm here most of the time, working and – well, thinking, I suppose. Go out in the evenings? Lovey, where would I go and who would I go with?'

Arthur closed his door, doing this in the totally silent way he had cultivated by long practice.


# 5


The air of West Kenbourne, never sweet, stank of rubbish. Sacks and bags and crates of rubbish made a wall along the pavement edge between the Waterlily and Kemal's Kebab House. Factory refuse and kitchen waste, leaking from broken cardboard boxes, cluttered Oriel Mews, and in Trinity Road the household garbage simmered, reeking, in the sultry sunlight.

'And we've only got one little dustbin,' Arthur said peevishly to Stanley Caspian.

195

'Wouldn't make any difference if we'd got ten, they'd be full up now. Can't you put your muck in one of those black bags the council send round?'

Arthur changed his tack. 'It's the principle of the thing. If these men insist on striking, other arrangements should be made. I pay my rates, I've got a right to have my waste disposed of. I shall write to the local authority. They might take notice of a strongly-worded letter from a ratepayer.'

'Pigs might fly if they'd got wings and then we shouldn't have any more pork.' Stanley roared with laughter. 'Which reminds me, I'm starving. Put the kettle on, me old Arthur.' He opened a bag of peanuts and another of hamburger-flavoured potato crisps. 'How's the new chap settling in?'

'Don't ask me,' said Arthur. 'You know I keep myself to myself.'

He made Stanley's coffee, asked for his envelope and went back upstairs. The idea of discussing Anthony Johnson was distasteful to him, and this was partly because any conversation in the hall might easily be overheard in Room 2. Stanley Caspian, of course, would be indifferent to that. Arthur wished he too could be indifferent, but there had crept upon him in the past few days a feeling that he must ingratiate himself with Anthony Johnson, not on any account offend him or win his displeasure. He now rather regretted his sharp words about the imprecise addressing of letters. Vague notions of having to become *friendly* – the very word distressed him – with Anthony Johnson were forming in his mind. For in this way he might perhaps persuade Anthony Johnson to draw his curtains when his light was on, or provide himself with a Venetian blind as an ostensible heat-retaining measure (Stanley Caspian would never provide one) or even succeed – and this would take much subtle and weary work – in convincing him that he, Arthur, had some legitimate occupation in the cellar, developing photographs, for instance, or doing carpentry.

But as he gathered up his laundry and stuffed it into the orange plastic carrier, he felt a fretful dismay. He didn't want to get involved with the man, he didn't want to get involved with anyone. How upsetting it was to have to *know* people, and how unnecessary it had been for twenty years!

196

*The psychopath is asocial – more than that, he is in positive conflict with society. Atavistic desires and a craving for excitement drive him. Self-centred, impulsive, he disregards society's taboos* . . . Anthony had been making notes all the morning, but now as he heard Stanley Caspian leave the house, he laid down his pen. Was there any point in beginning on his thesis before he had attended that particular lecture on criminology? On the other hand, there was so little else to do. The music from upstairs, which had been hindering his concentration for the past half-hour, now ceased and two doors slammed. So far he had met none of the other tenants but Arthur Johnson and, as fresh sound broke out, he went into the hall.

Two men were sitting on the stairs, presumably so that one of them, smallish with wild black hair, could do up his shoelaces. The other was chanting:

> 'Then trust me, there's nothing like drinking,
> So pleasant on this side the grave.
> It keeps the unhappy from thinking,
> And makes e'en the valiant more brave!'

Anthony said hallo.

His shoelaces tied, the small dark man came down the stairs, extended his hand and said in a facetious way, 'Mr Johnson, I presume?'

'That's right. Anthony. The "other" Johnson.'

This remark provoked laughter out of all proportion to its wit. 'Put that on your doorbell, why don't you? Brian Kotowsky at your service, and this is Jonathan Dean, the best pal a man ever had.'

Another hand, large, red and hairy, was thrust out. 'We are about to give our right arms some exercise in a hostelry known to its habitués as the Lily, and were you to . . .'

'He means, come and have a drink.'

Anthony grinned and accepted, although he was already wondering if he would regret this encounter. Jonathan Dean slammed the front door behind them and remarked that this would shake old Caspian's ceilings up a bit. They crossed Trinity Road and entered Oriel Mews, a cobbled passage whose cottages had all been converted into small factories and warehouses. The cobbles were coated with a

197

smelly patina of potato peelings and coffee grounds, spilt from piled rubbish bags.

Anthony wrinkled his nose. 'Have you lived here long?'

'For ever and a day, but I'm soon to depart.'

'Leaving me alone with that she-devil,' said Brian. 'Without your moderating influence she'll kill me, she'll tear me to pieces.'

'Very right and proper. All the best marriages are like that. Not beds of roses but fields of battle. Look at Tolstoy, look at Lawrence.'

They were still looking at, and hotly discussing, Tolstoy and Lawrence, when they entered the Waterlily. It was crowded, smoky and hot. Anthony bought the first round, the wisest measure if one wants to make an early escape. His tentative question had been intended as a preamble to another and now, in the first brief pause, he asked it.

'What is there to do in this place?'

'Drink,' said Jonathan simply.

'I don't mean in here. I mean Kenbourne Vale.'

'Drink, dispute, make love.'

'There's the Taj Mahal,' said Brian. 'It used to be called the Odeon but now it only shows Indian films. Or there's Radclyffe Park. They have concerts in Radclyffe Hall.'

'Christ,' said Jonathan. 'Better make up your mind to it, Tony, there's nothing to do but drink. This place, the Dalmatian, the Hospital Arms, the Grand Duke. What more do you want?'

But before Anthony could answer him, a woman had flung into the pub and was leaning over them, her fingers whose nails were very dirty, pressed on the table top. She addressed Brian.

'What the hell are you doing, coming here without me?'

'You were asleep,' said Brian. 'You were dead to the world.'

'In the rank sweat,' remarked Jonathan, 'of an enseamed bed.'

'Shut up and don't be so disgusting.' She levelled at him a look of scorn, such as women often reserve for those friends of their husbands who may be thought to exercise a corrupting influence. For that Brian was her husband Anthony was sure even before he waved a feeble hand and said, 'My wife, Vesta.'

She sat down. 'Your wife, Vesta, wants a drink, G. and T., a big one.' She took a cigarette from her own packet and Dean one from his, but instead of holding out his lighter to her, he lit his own cigarette and put the lighter away. Turning her back on him, she struck a match and inhaled noisily. Anthony regarded her with interest. She seemed to be in her mid-thirties and she looked as if she had come out without attempting to remove the 'rank sweat' of Jonathan Dean's too graphic description. Her naturally dark hair was hennaed and strands of the Medusa locks – it was as wild and unkempt as her husband's but much longer – had a vermilion metallic glint. A greasy-skinned, rather battered-looking face. Thin lips. Large red-brown angry eyes. A smell of patchouli oil. Her dress was long and of dark dirty Indian cotton, hung with beads and chains and partly obscured by a fringed red shawl. When Brian brought her gin, she clasped both her hands round the glass and stared intensely into the liquid like a clairvoyant looking into a crystal.

Three more beers had also arrived. Jonathan, having directed several more insulting but this time ineffectual remarks at Vesta – remarks which seemed to gratify rather than annoy her husband – began to talk of Li-li Chan. What a 'dish' she was. How he could understand those Empire builders who had deserted their pallid dehydrated wives for Oriental mistresses. Like little flowers they were. He hoped Anthony appreciated his luck in sharing a bath-room with Li-li. And so on. Anthony decided he had had enough of it for the time being. Years of living in hall and rooming houses and hostels had taught him the folly of making friends for the sake of making friends. Sooner or later the one or two you really want for your friends will turn up, and then you have the problem of ridding yourself of these stopgaps.

So when Brian began making plans for the evening, a mammoth pub crawl, he declined firmly. To his surprise, Jonathan also declined, he had some mysterious engage-ment, and Vesta too, suddenly becoming less zombie-like, said she was going out. Brian needn't start asking why or who with and all that. She was free, wasn't she? She hadn't got married to be harassed all the time and in public.

Anthony felt a little sorry for Brian whose spaniel face easily became forlorn. 'Some other time,' he said, and he meant it.

The sun was shining and the whole afternoon lay ahead of him. Radclyffe Park, he thought, and when the K.12 bus came along he got on it. The park was large and hardly any of it was formally laid-out. In a green space where the grass was dappled with the shadows of plane leaves, he sat down and re-read Helen's letter.

*Darling Tony, I knew I'd miss you but I didn't know how bad it would be. I feel like asking, whose idea was this? But I know we both came to it simultaneously and it's the only way. Besides, neither of us is the sort of person who can be happy in a clandestine thing, an intrigue. Being discreet seems pointless to you, doesn't it, a squalid bore, and as for me, I always hated lying to Roger. When you said – or was it I who said it? – that it must be all or nothing, I, you, we, were right.*

*But I can't be very good at lying because I know Roger has sensed my defection. He has always been causelessly jealous but he never actually did things about it. Now he's started phoning me at work two or three times a day and last week he opened two letters that came for me. One of them was from mother and the other was an invitation to a dress show, but I couldn't get all upstage and affronted virtue with him. How could I? After all, I do have a lover, I have deceived him. . . .*

A child, playing some distance off, gave his ball a massive kick so that it landed at Anthony's feet. He bowled it back. Funny, how people thought it was only women who wanted to marry and have children of their own.

*I remember all the things you taught me, principles on which to conduct one's life. Applied Existentialism. I tell myself I am not responsible for any other adult person and that I am not in this world to live up to Roger's expectations. But I married him, Tony. Didn't I, in marrying him, go a long way towards promising to be responsible for his happiness? Didn't I more or less say that he had a right to expect much from me? And he has had so little, poor Roger. I never even pretended to love him. I haven't slept with him for six months. I only married him because he pressed me and pressed me and wouldn't take my no . . .*

Anthony frowned when he came to that bit. He hated her weakness, her vacillations. There were whole areas of her soft sensitive personality he didn't begin to understand. But here was the Bunyan passage – that made sense.

200

*So why don't I just tell him and walk out? – Leap off the ladder even blindfold into eternity, sink or swim, come heaven, come hell . . . Fear, I suppose, and compassion.* But sense that was too short-lived. *It's because at the moment compassion is stronger than passion that I'm here and you're alone in London* . . . He folded the letter and put it back in his pocket. He wasn't downcast, only rather lonely, more than rather bored. In the end she would come to him, her own feelings for him were too strong to be denied. There had been things between them she would remember in his absence, and that memory, that hope of renewal, would be stronger than any pity. In the meantime? He threw back the child's ball once more, rolled over on his side on the warm dry grass and slept.

The tube took Anthony one stop back to Kenbourne Lane. At the station entrance a boy of about ten came up to him and asked him for a penny for the guy.

'In *September*? A bit premature, aren't you?'

'Got to make an early start, mister,' said the boy, 'or someone else'll get my patch.'

Anthony laughed and gave him ten pence. 'I don't see any guy.'

'That's what me and my friend are collecting for. To get one.'

The children, those in the park, and the two at the station, gave him an idea. A job for the evenings and the occasional weekend afternoon, a job for which he was admirably and thoroughly trained . . . It was six o'clock. He let himself into Room 2, wrote his letter, addressed an envelope and affixed a stamp to it. The whole operation took no more than ten minutes, but by the time it was done the room was so dark that he had to put the jellyfish light on. Emerging, he encountered Arthur Johnson in the hall, and Arthur Johnson was also holding a letter in his hand. Anthony would have passed him with no more than a smile and a 'good evening', but the 'other' Johnson – or was that he? – turned, almost barring his passage, and fixed him with an intense, anxious and almost hungry look.

'May I enquire if you are going out for the evening, Mr Johnson, or merely to the post?'

'Just to the post,' Anthony said, surprised.

The hopeful light in the other man's eyes seemed to die. And yet why should he care one way or the other? Perhaps, on the other hand, that was the answer he had wanted, for now he held out his hand, smiling with a kind of forced bonhomie, and said ingratiatingly:

'Then, since I am going there myself, let me have the pleasure of taking your letter.'

'Thanks,' Anthony said. 'That's nice of you.'

Arthur Johnson took the letter and, without another word, left the house, closing the front door silently and with painstaking care behind him.

# 6

The dustmen's strike had ended, Arthur read in his paper, on the last Monday of September. Two days later, on the first Wednesday of October, he heard the crashing of lids, the creak of machinery and the (to his way of thinking) lunatic ripostes of the men, that told him Trinity Road was at last being cleared of refuse. He might have saved himself the trouble of writing to the local authority. Still, such complaints kept them on their toes; they had replied promptly enough. The brown envelope was marked: London Borough of Kenbourne and addressed to A. Johnson Esq., 2/142 Trinity Road, London W15 6HD. Arthur put it in his pocket. The rest of the post, a shoe shop advertising circular for Li-li Chan and a mauve-grey envelope, postmarked Bristol, for Anthony Johnson, he arranged in their appropriate positions on the hall table.

They were all out but for himself. From the phone call he had overheard, Arthur knew Anthony Johnson would be going off to college or whatever it was today, but he was relieved to have had assurance made doubly sure by the sight of the 'other' Johnson, viewed from his living room window, departing at five past nine for the tube station. Not that it was of much practical assistance to him, as he too must go to work in ten minutes; it was simply comforting to know the man went out sometimes. It was a beginning.

He went back upstairs and slit the letter open with one of Auntie Gracie's silver fruit knives. *London Borough of Kenbourne, Department of Social Services.* Well, he'd have expected to hear from the sanitary inspector but you never could tell these days. *Dear Sir, in reply to your letter of the 28th inst., requesting information as to the availability of work in children's play centres within the Borough, we have to inform you that such centres would come under the auspices of the Inner London Education Authority and are not our . . .*

Arthur realized what had happened and he was appalled. That he – he out of the two of them – should be the one to open a letter in error! It would have mattered so much less if it had been someone else's letter, that giggly little Chinese piece, for instance, or that drunk, Dean. Obviously the letter must be returned. Arthur was so shaken by what he had done that he couldn't bring himself to write the necessary note of apology on the spot. Besides, it would make him late for work. It was nearly a quarter past nine. He put the envelope and its contents into his empty briefcase and set off.

The demolition men were at work and Auntie Gracie's living room – brown lincrusta, marble fireplace, pink linoleum – all exposed to the public view. There on the ochre-coloured wallpaper was the paler rectangle marking where the sideboard had stood, the sideboard into whose drawer he had shut the mouse. His first killing. Auntie Gracie had died in that room, and from it he had gone out to make death . . . Why think of all that now? He felt sick. He unlocked the gates and let himself into his office, wishing there was some way of insulating the place from the sounds of hammer blows and falling masonry, but by the time Barry lounged in at a quarter to ten, he was already composing the first draft of a note to Anthony Johnson.

Fortunately, there was very little correspondence for Grainger's that day, the books were in apple pie order and well up to date. Arthur found the task before him exacting, and one draft after another went into the wastepaper basket. But by one o'clock the letter – handwritten, as typewritten notes were discourteous – was as perfect a specimen of its kind as he could achieve.

*Dear Mr Johnson, please accept my heartfelt apologies for having opened your letter in error. Considering the gravity of this intrusion into your private affairs, I think it only proper to give you a full explanation. I was myself expecting a letter from the council of the London Borough of Kenbourne in reply to one of my own requesting action to be taken with regard to the disgraceful situation concerning the cessation of a regular refuse collection. Reading the Borough's name on the envelope, I opened it without more ado only to find that the communication was intended for your good self. Needless to say, I did not read more than was strictly necessary to inform me that I was not the proper recipient. In hopes that you will be kind enough to overlook what was, in fact, a genuine mistake, I am, Yours sincerely, Arthur Johnson.*

Who could tell what time Anthony Johnson would return? Arthur let himself into a hundred and forty-two at 1.15. The house was silent, empty, and the mauve-grey envelope was still on the hall table. Beside it, neatly aligned to it, Arthur placed the Kenbourne council letter and his own note, the two fastened together with a paper clip. When he returned from work just before 5.30 all the letters were still there and the house was still empty.

Alone in his flat, he began to speculate as to Anthony Johnson's reaction. Perhaps the whole incident would turn out to be a blessing in disguise. Anthony Johnson would read his note, be moved by its earnest rectitude, and come immediately upstairs to tell Arthur he quite understood and not to give it another thought. This would be his chance. He put the kettle on, set a tray with the best china, and left his front door on the latch so that Anthony Johnson would know he was expected and welcomed. For, irksome as it was to entertain someone and make conversation, it was now of paramount importance. And how wonderful if, in the course of that conversation, Anthony Johnson should announce his intention of securing an evening job – as the letter had intimated he might.

He sat by the window, looking down. Li-li Chan was the first to get home. She arrived with a different young man in a green sports car, and ten minutes after they got into the house Arthur heard her on the phone.

'No, no, I tell you I very sorry.' Li-li almost, but not quite, said 'velly'. 'You give theatre ticket some other nice girl. I wash my hair, stay in all night. Oh, but you are so

204

silly. I don't love you because I wash my hair? I say I do love you, I love lots, lots of people, so good-bye now!'

Arthur craned his neck to see her and her escort leap into the car and roar off in the direction of Kenbourne Lane. He waited. Vesta Kotowsky came in alone, looking sulky. There was one, Arthur thought, who could do with an evening at home to get that draggled greasy hair washed. At five past six Anthony Johnson emerged from under the arched entrance to Oriel Mews. And as Arthur watched him approach, the tall well-proportioned figure, the firm-featured handsome face, the mane of hair crowning a shapely head, he felt a stirring of something that was part envy, part resentment. Yet this wasn't evoked by the 'other' Johnson's good looks – hadn't he, Arthur, had just as great a share of those himself? – or by his occupancy of Room 2. Rather it was that there, in the process of its mysterious unfair workings, fate had been kinder. Fate hadn't saddled this man with a propensity that placed his life and liberty at constant risk . . .

The front door of the house closed with a thud mid-way between Arthur's pernickety click and Jonathan Dean's ceiling-splitting crash. Ten minutes went by, a quarter of an hour, half an hour. Arthur was on tenterhooks. It was getting almost too late for tea. Time he started cooking his meal. The idea of anyone even tapping at the door, let alone coming in, while he was eating was unthinkable. Should he go down himself? Perhaps. Perhaps he should reinforce his note with a personal appearance and a personal apology.

A car door slammed. He rushed back to the window. It was the Kotowsky car, and Brian Kotowsky and Jonathan Dean got out of it. There followed a resounding crash of the front door. A long pause of silence and then a single set of footsteps mounted the stairs. Could it be at last . . . ? But, no. Dean's door banged beneath him.

Very uneasy now, Arthur stood at the window. And again Brian Kotowsky appeared. Arthur caught his breath in sharply as he saw Anthony Johnson also emerge from the house. He looked reluctant, even irritable.

'All right,' Arthur heard him say, 'but it'll have to be a quick one. I've got work to do.'

They crossed the road, bound for the Waterlily. Arthur crept down the first flight. A low murmur of voices could be heard from Jonathan Dean's room and then a soft throaty laugh. He went on down. From over the banisters he saw that the hall table was bare but for the inevitable cheap offer vouchers. Li-li Chan's shoe shop circular and the two envelopes for Anthony Johnson had gone. Arthur stood by the table, nonplussed. Then some screws of paper lying in Stanley Caspian's wastepaper basket caught his eye. He picked them out. They were the note he had written with such care and anxiety to Anthony Johnson and the envelope in which the council's letter had been contained.

The Inner London Education Authority told Anthony that they couldn't possibly say over the phone whether they had a vacancy for him or not. Would he write in? He wrote and got a very belated reply full of delaying tactics which amounted to telling him that he had better apply again at Christmas. At least the Kenbourne authority had replied promptly. Anthony smiled ruefully to himself when he recalled the evening on which he had received their reply. It had been fraught with annoyance.

Firstly had come that letter from Helen, a letter which was more like an essay on Roger's miseries. *I sit reading escapist literature and every time I look up I find his eyes on me, staring accusingly, and every little innocent remark I make he takes me up on ('What's that supposed to mean?' 'What are you getting at?') so that I feel like some wretched shoplifter being interrogated by the great detective. I started to cry last night and – Oh, it was awful – he began to cry too. He knelt at my feet and begged me to love him* . . . Anthony had been so exasperated by this letter which, in his delight at receiving it, he had stood reading out in the hall by the table, that it was some minutes before he had even noticed that there was another one for him. And when he did, when he opened and read that ridiculous note from Arthur Johnson, his impatience had reached such a pitch that he had screwed it up and tossed it into the wastepaper basket. It was at this point that Brian Kotowsky had arrived and, deserted by the best pal a man ever had, had pressed him to accompany him to the Waterlily. There Anthony had been obliged to listen to a dissertation on the horrors of matrimony, the undesirable independence having a job of her own gave to a wife, and what Brian would do after Jonathan's departure he honestly didn't know. Obliged to listen, but not for more than half an hour.

Returning alone to a hundred and forty-two Anthony considered going upstairs to reassure Arthur Johnson. The man obviously had an acute anxiety neurosis. A better-adjusted person would simply have scribbled *Sorry I opened your letter* and left it at that. The circumlocutions, the polysyllabic words were pathetic. They breathed a tense need for the preservation of an immaculate ego, they smelt of paranoia, fear of retribution, a desire to be thought well of by all men, even strangers. But men like that, he thought, cannot be reassured, their deepseated belief in their own worthlessness is too great and too long-established at fifty for self-confidence ever to be implanted in them. Besides, Arthur Johnson liked to keep himself to himself, and would probably only be further perturbed by an invasion of his privacy. Much better wait until they happened to meet in the hall.

In the week which followed he didn't encounter Arthur Johnson but he was again accosted by the children at Kenbourne Lane station.

'Penny for the guy, mister?'

'Where are you going to have your bonfire?' asked Anthony. 'In Radclyffe Park?' He handed over another ten pence.

'We asked. The park keeper won't let us, rotten old bastard. We could have it in our back yard if my dad lets us.'

'Old Mother Winter,' said the other boy, 'got the cops last time your dad had a bonfire.'

Anthony went off down Magdalen Hill. The kids and their parents called it Mag-da-lene, just as they called Balliol Street Bawlial. How stupid these pseudo-intellectuals were – Jonathan Dean was one of them – to sneer at mispronunciations. If the people who lived here hadn't the right to call their streets what they wanted, who had? His eye was caught by the piece of waste ground, enclosed by its rusty tennis court netting. The authorities wouldn't let him do official social work, but why shouldn't he do some privately and off his own bat? Why not, in fact, think about organizing November 5th celebrations on that bit of ground? The idea was suddenly appealing. He gazed through the wire at the hillocky weed-grown wilderness. On one side of it was the cutting through which the tube ran down to London, on the other the mountains of brown brick, broken woodwork and yellow crumbled plaster which was all that remained now of the demolished houses. Backing on to the ground rose the grey-brown rears of Brasenose Avenue terraces, tall tenements hung with Piranesi-like iron stairways. A man seen building a bonfire there would soon attract all the juvenile society in the neighbourhood. And he could rope in the parents, mothers especially, to organise a supper. The great Kenbourne Vale Guy Fawkes Rave-up, he thought. Why, he might set a precedent and they'd start having one there every year.

It was six o'clock on a Friday evening, Friday, October 10th. If he was going to do it he'd better start on the organisation tomorrow. Work tonight, though. Seated at the table in Room 2, its gateleg propped up with Arieti's *The Intrapsychic Self*, Anthony assembled and read his notes.

*Not to be classified as schizophrenic, manic-depressive or paranoid. Condition cannot strictly be allied to any of these. Psychopath characteristically unable to form emotional relationships. If these are formed – fleetingly and sporadically – purpose is direct satisfaction of own desires. Guiltless and loveless. Psychopath has learned few socialized ways of coping with frustrations. Those he has learned (e.g. a preoccupation with 'hard' pornography) may be themselves at best grotesque. For his actions . . .*

With a sudden fizzle, the light bulb in the jellyfish shade went out.

Anthony cursed. For a few moments he sat there in the dark, wondering whether to appeal for help from Jonathan or the Kotowskys. But that would only involve him in another drinking session. The gentle closing of the front door a minute or two before had told him of Li-li's departure. He'd have to go out and buy another light bulb. Just as well Winter's didn't close till eight.

Making for the front door, he was aware of footsteps on the landing above him. Arthur Johnson. But as he hesitated,

208

glancing up the stairs – now might be an opportunity for that belated reassurance – he saw the figure of which he had only caught a glimpse retreat. Anthony shrugged and went off in search of his light bulb.

# 7

Arthur was certain he had given mortal offence to Anthony Johnson and thus had wrecked his own hopes. Now there was nothing for it but to watch and wait. Sooner or later the 'other' Johnson must go out in the evening. He went out by day on Saturdays and Sundays all right, but what was the use of that? It was darkness that Arthur needed, darkness to give the illusion that the side passage, the courtyard, the cellar, were the alley, the mews, the deserted shadowed space that met his desires. Darkness and the absence of noisy people, car doors slamming, interference . . .

He could remember quite precisely when this need had first come upon him. The need to use darkness. He was twelve. Auntie Gracie had had two friends to tea and they were sitting in the back round the fire, drinking from and eating off that very china he had set out in vain for Anthony Johnson. Talking about him. He would have liked, as he would often have liked, to retreat to his own bedroom. But this was never allowed except at bedtime when, as soon as he was in bed, Auntie Gracie would turn off the light at the switch just inside the door and forbid him on pain of punishment to turn it on again. The landing light was always left on, so Arthur wasn't afraid. He would have preferred, in fact longed for, enough light to read by or else total darkness.

Mrs Goodwin and Mrs Courthope, those were the friends' names. Arthur had to sit being good, being a credit to Auntie Gracie. They talked a lot about some unnamed boy he supposed must be himself from the mysterious veiled way they spoke and the heavy meaningful glances exchanged.

'Of course it puts a stigma on a child he can never shake off,' Mrs Goodwin said.

Instead of answering, Auntie Gracie said, 'Go into the other room, Arthur, and get me another teaspoon out of the sideboard. One of the best ones, mind, with the initial on.'

Arthur went. He didn't close the door after him but one of them closed it. The hall light was on so he didn't put on the front room light, and as a result he opened the wrong drawer by mistake. As he did so a mouse scuttered like a flash across the sideboard top and slithered into the open drawer. Arthur slammed it shut. He took an initialled spoon out of the other drawer and stood there, holding the spoon, his heart pounding. The mouse rushed around inside the drawer, running in desperate circles, striking its head and body against the wooden walls of its prison. It began to squeak. The cheep-cheep sounds were like those made by a baby bird, but they were sounds of pain and distress. Arthur felt a tremendous deep satisfaction that was almost happiness. It was dark and he was alone and he had enough power over something to make it die.

Strangely enough, the women didn't seem to have missed him, although he had been gone for quite five minutes. They stopped talking abruptly when he came in. After Mrs Goodwin and Mrs Courthope had gone, Auntie Gracie washed up and Arthur dried. She sent him to put the silver away which was just as well, because if she had gone she would have heard the mouse. It had stopped squeaking and was making vague brushing, scratching sounds, feeble and faint. Arthur didn't open the drawer. He listened to the sounds with pleasure. When he did at last open it on the following evening, the mouse was dead and the drawer, which contained a few napkin rings and a spare cruet, spattered all over with its blood. Arthur had no interest in the corpse. He let Auntie Gracie find it a week or so later, which she did with many shrieks and shudders.

Darkness. He thought often in those days of the mouse afraid and trapped in the dark and of himself powerful in it. How he longed to be allowed out in the streets after dark! But even when he was at work and earning Auntie Gracie wanted him to come straight home. And he had to please her, he had to be worthy of her. Besides, defiance of her was too enormous an enterprise even to consider. So he went out in the evenings only when she went with him, and once a week they went together to the Odeon that was now Indian and called the Taj Mahal. Until one night when old Mr Grainger, catching him in the yard as he was sweeping up at five-thirty, sent him over to the other side of Kenbourne to pick up an electric drill some workman had been careless enough to leave behind in a house where he was doing a re-wiring job. He'd tell Miss Johnson on his way home, he told Arthur, and he was to cut along as fast as he could.

Arthur collected the drill. The darkness – it was mid-winter – was even lovelier than he thought it would be. And how very dark it was then, how much darker than nowa-days! The blackout. The pitch darkness of wartime. In the dark he brushed against people, some of whom carried muffled torches. And in a winding little lane, now de-stroyed and lost, replaced by a mammoth housing com-plex, he came up against a girl hurrying. What had made him touch her? Ah, if he knew that he would know the answer to many things. But he had touched her, putting out his hand, for he was already as tall as a man, to run one finger down the side of her warm neck. Her scream as she fled was more beautiful in his ears than the squeaking of the mouse. He stared after her, into the darkness after her, emotion surging within him like thick scented liquid boiling. He knew what he wanted to do, but thought inter-vened to stay him. He had read the newspapers, listened to the wireless, and he knew what happened to people who wanted what he wanted. No doubt, it was better not to go out after dark. Auntie Gracie knew best. It was almost as if she had known why, though that was nonsense, for she had never dreamed . . .

His own dreams had been troubling him this past fort-night, the consequence of frustration. Each evening at eleven, before going to bed, he had taken a last look out of his bedroom window to see the courtyard below aglow with light from Room 2. It seemed a personal affront and, in a way, a desecration of the place. Moreover, Anthony Johnson hadn't been near him, had avoided all contact with him. Arthur wouldn't have known he was in the house but for the arrival, and the subsequent removal from the hall table, of another of those Bristol letters, and of course that ever-burning light.

Then, on a Friday evening just before eight, it went out. Carrying his torch, Arthur let himself out of his flat and came softly down the top flight. He had heard the front door close, but that might have been Li-li Chan going out. Both she and Anthony Johnson closed it with the same degree of moderate care. And it must have been she, for as Arthur hesitated on the landing he saw Anthony Johnson appear in the hall below him. Arthur stepped back and immediately the front door closed. Through its red and green glass panels the shape of Anthony Johnson could be seen as a blur vanishing down the marble steps. No one, Arthur reasoned, went out at this hour if he didn't intend to stay out for some time. He descended the stairs and, delaying for a moment or two to let the occupant of Room 2 get clear, left the house, crossed the lawn and entered the side passage.

There was no moon. The darkness wasn't total but faintly lit by the far-reaching radiance of street lamps and house lights, and the sky above, a narrow corridor of it, was a gloomy greyish-red; the darkness, in fact, of any slum backwater. And this passage resembled, with the colouring of Arthur's imagination, some alleyway, leading perhaps from a high road to a network of shabby streets. The muted roar of traffic was audible, but this only heightened his illusion. He crossed the little court, all the muscles of his body tense and tingling, and opened the cellar door.

It was three weeks since he had been here, and being here at last after so much dread and anguish brought him a more than usually voluptuous pleasure. Even more than usual, it was nearly as good as the real thing, as Maureen Cowan and Bridget O'Neill. So he walked slowly between the jumbled metal rubbish, the stacks of wood and newspapers, his torch making a quivering light which snaked ahead of him. And there, in the third room, she was waiting.

His reactions to her varied according to his mood and his tensions. Sometimes she was no more than the instrument of his therapy, a quick assuagement. But there were times, and this was one of them, when strain and memory had so oppressed him and anticipation been so urgent that

212

the whole scene and she in it were altered and aggrandized by enormous fantasy. So it was now. This was no cellar in Trinity Road but the deserted, seldom-frequented yard between a warehouse, say, and a cemetery wall; she no lifesize doll but a real woman waiting perhaps for her lover. The light of his torch fell on her. It lit her blank eyes, then, deflecting, allowed shadows to play like fear on her face. He stood still, but he could have sworn she moved. There was no sanctuary for her, no escape, nothing but the brick wall rising behind her to a cracked cobweb-hung sky. His torch became a street lamp, shining palely now from a corner. On an impulse he put it out. Absolute silence, absolute darkness. She was trying to get away from him. She must be, for as he felt his way towards the wall he couldn't find her.

He touched the damp brickwork, and a trickle of water fell between his fingers. He moved them along the wall, feeling for her, grunting now, making strong gruff exhalations. Then his hand touched her dress, moved up to her cold neck. But it felt warm to him and soft, like Bridget O'Neill's. Was it he or she who gave that choking stifled cry? This time he used his tie to strangle her, twisting it until his hands were sore.

It took Arthur a long time to recover – about ten minutes, which was much longer than usual. But the deed had been more exciting and more satisfying than usual, so that was only to be expected. He restored her to her position against the wall, picked up the torch and made his way back to the cellar door. Cautiously he opened it. The window of Room 2 was still dark. Good. Excellent.

He stepped out into the yard, turned to close the door behind him. As he did so the whole court was suddenly flooded with light. And this light was as terrifying to him as the beam of a policeman's torch is to a burglar. He wanted to wheel round, but he forced himself to turn slowly, expecting to meet the eyes of Anthony Johnson.

At first he saw only the interior of Room 2, the pale green flecked walls, the gateleg table propped by and piled with books, the primrose washbasin and that light glowing inside the pink and green polythene shade which, for some reason, was swinging like a pendulum. Then Anthony

Johnson appeared under the swinging lamp, crossing the room; now, at last, staring straight back at him. Arthur didn't wait. He hastened across the court, his head bent, a burning flush mounting across his head and neck. He scuttled through the passage, let himself into the house and went swiftly upstairs.

There, in his own flat, he sat down heavily. Vesta Kotowsky had come up in his absence and pushed her rent under his door, but he was so upset he let the envelope lie there on the doormat. His hands were trembling. Anthony Johnson had returned within less than half an hour of going out. It almost looked as if the whole exercise had been a plot to catch Arthur. But how could he know? He would know now or know something. Probably he was looking for some way of getting back at him for opening that letter. On the face of it, that letter hadn't seemed very private, not like the ones postmarked Bristol would be, but you never could tell. It might be that this college of his had some sort of rule about students not taking jobs – Arthur admitted to himself that he knew very little about these things – and that he would be expelled or sent down or whatever they called it for attempting to do so. After all, what else could explain Anthony Johnson's enraged rejection of his note, his deliberate shunning of him, his sneaking out like that followed by his purposeful illumination of the courtyard just as Arthur was emerging from the cellar?

The euphoria he felt after one of his killings totally ruined, Arthur passed a bad night. He sweated profusely so that he fancied the pink sheets smelt bad, and he stripped them off in a frenzy of disgust. Li-li had put her rent envelope under his door at some time in the small hours. By half-past nine he had assembled hers, the two envelopes of the Kotowskys' – Vesta insisted on paying her half-share separately from that of her husband – and his own and was seated downstairs waiting for Stanley Caspian. No more rent from Jonathan Dean who would be leaving today, thank God, and none to collect (thank God again) from Anthony Johnson who had paid two months in advance.

The hall was cold and damp. It was a foggy morning, an early harbinger of the winter to come. Stanley stumped in at ten past ten, wearing a checked windcheater that looked as if it was made from a car rug, and carrying a huge cellophane bag containing cheese puff cocktail snacks. Arthur began to feel queasy because the cheese puffs, orangey-brown, fat and curvy, reminded him of overfed maggots.

Stanley split the bag open before he had even sat down, and some of the cheese larvae spilt out on to the desk.

'Put the kettle on, me old Arthur. Have a Wiggly-Woggly?'

'No, thank you,' said Arthur quietly. He cleared his throat. 'I was down the cellar last night.' Forcing the carefully planned lie out with all the casualness he could muster, he said, 'Looking for a screwdriver, as a matter of fact. The wires had come out of one of my little electric plugs.'

Stanley looked at him truculently. 'You're always grumbling these days, Arthur. First it was the dustbin, now it's the electricity. I suppose that's your way of saying I ought to have the place re-wired.'

'Not at all. I was simply explaining how I happened to be in the cellar. In case – well, in case anyone might think I was snooping.'

Stanley picked cheese puff crumbs off the bulge of his belly whose ridges seemed as if they had been artfully designed to catch everything their possessor spilt. 'I couldn't care less if you go down the cellar, me old Arthur. Have yourself a ball. Ask some girls round. If you like spending your evenings in cellars that's your business. Right?'

Somehow, though he had intended wit, Stanley had got very near the truth. Arthur blushed. He was almost trembling. It was all he could do to control himself while Stanley filled in his rent book, banging in the full stops until it looked as if he would break his pen. Arthur put it back in its envelope himself and, muttering his usual excuse about Saturday being a busy day, made for the stairs. Half-way up them, he heard Anthony Johnson come out of Room 2 and use to Stanley – in mockery? He must have been listening behind the door – his own words of a few moments before:

'I was down your cellar last night.'

215

# 8

Winter's being out of stock of all but forty watt light bulbs, Anthony had been obliged to go as far as the open-till-midnight supermarket at the northern end of Kenbourne Lane. This unsettled him for work, and when he saw Arthur Johnson coming out of the cellar its possibilities intrigued him. He had penetrated no further than the first room, but that was enough.

Stanley Caspian burst into gales of laughter. 'I suppose you were looking for a screw?'

Anthony shrugged. Bawdy talk from a man of Caspian's age and girth disgusted him. 'You've got a lot of wood and cardboard and stuff down there,' he said. 'If you don't want it, can I have it? It's for a Guy Fawkes bonfire.'

'Help yourself,' said Stanley Caspian. 'Everyone's got very interested in my cellar all of a sudden, I must say. You weren't planning to have this here bonfire on my premises, I hope?'

Anthony said no, thanks, it wasn't suitable, which didn't seem the reply to gratify Caspian, and left him to his rents. He walked over to the station where the little boys were once more at their post, and with them this time a black child. The white children knew him by now. Instead of asking for money, they said hallo.

'Why don't we have a bonfire on that bit of waste ground?' But even as he spoke he checked himself. Wasn't that the insinuating approach a child molester would use? 'If you like the idea,' he said quickly, 'we'll go and talk to your parents about it.'

Leroy, the coloured boy, lived with his mother in a groundfloor flat in Brasenose Avenue. Linthea Carville turned out to be a part-time social worker, which gave her an immediate affinity with Anthony, though he would in any case have been drawn to her. He couldn't help staring at her, this tall daughter of African gods, with her pearly-bloomed dark face, and her black hair, oiled and satiny,

216

worn in a heavy knot on the crown of her head. But he remembered his plan, explained it, and within ten minutes they had been joined by white neighbours, the chairman of the Brasenose Tenants' Association, and by the mother of Leroy's taller friend, Steve.

The chairman was enthusiastic about Anthony's idea. For months his association had been campaigning for the council to convert the waste ground into a children's playground. This would be a feather in its cap. They could have a big party on 5th November and maybe invite a council representative to be present. Linthea said she would make hot dogs and enlist the help of another friend, the mother of David, the third boy. And when Anthony told them about the wood, Steve said his elder brother had a box barrow which he could bring over to a hundred and forty-two on the following Saturday.

Then they discussed the guy Steve's mother said she would dress in a discarded suit of her husband's. Linthea made lots of strong delicious coffee, and it was nearly lunchtime before Anthony went back to Trinity Road. He had forgotten that this was the day of Jonathan Dean's departure. The move, he now saw, was well under way. Jonathan and Brian were carrying crates down the stairs and packing them into Brian's rather inadequate car. Vesta was nowhere to be seen.

'I'll give you a hand,' Anthony said, and regretted the offer when Brian slapped him on the back and remarked that after Jonathan had deserted him he would know where to turn for a pal.

Jonathan, like Anthony, possessed no furniture of his own but he had hundreds of records and quite a few books, the heaviest and most thumbed of which was the *Oxford Dictionary of Quotations*. While they worked and ate the fish and chips Brian had been sent out to buy, the record player remained on, and the laughter sequence from Strauss's *Elektra* roared out so maniacally that Anthony expected Arthur Johnson to appear at any moment and complain. But he didn't appear even when Jonathan dropped a crate of groceries on the stairs and collapsed in fits of mirth at the sight of egg yolk and H.P. Sauce and extended life milk dripping from the treads.

They had to make several journeys. Jonathan's new home was a much smaller room than the one he had occupied at a hundred and forty-two, in a squalid run-down house in the worst part of South Kenbourne. And this alternative to Trinity Road seemed to perplex Brian as much as it did Anthony. What had possessed Jonathan? he kept asking. Why not change his mind even at this late stage? Caspian would surely let him keep his old room if he asked.

'No, he wouldn't,' said Jonathan. 'He's let it to some Spade.' And he added, like Cicero but less appositely, '*O tempora! O mores!*'

The record player was the last thing to be shifted. A container was needed in which to transport it so Brian and Anthony went down to Anthony's room where Anthony said he had found a cardboard box in the wardrobe. The books impressed Brian and soon he had found out all about Anthony's thesis, taking up much the same attitude to it as he would have done had he learned Anthony was writing a thriller.

'There's a study for you,' he said as they drove past the cemetery. 'You could use that in your writing. Twenty-five years ago last month that's where the Kenbourne Killer strangled his first victim. Maureen Cowan, she was called.'

'What, in the cemetery?'

'No, in the path that runs along the back of it. A lot of people use that path as a short cut from the Hospital Arms to Elm Green station. She was a tart, soliciting down there. Mind you, I was only a kid at the time but I remember it all right.'

'Kid?' said Jonathan. 'You mean you're *kidding*. You were thirteen.'

Brian looked hurt but he made no response. 'They never caught the chap. He struck again' – he employed the journalese quite unconsciously as if it were standard usage – 'five years later. That time it was a student nurse called Bridget Something. Irish girl. He strangled her on a bit of open ground between the hospital and the railway bridge. Now would he be a psychopath, Tony?'

'I suppose so. Was it the same man both times?'

'The cops thought so. But there were never any more murders – not unsolved ones, I mean. Now why, Tony, would you say that was?'

218

'Moved out of the district,' said Anthony who was getting bored. 'Or died,' he added, for he had been less than a year old when that first murder was committed.

'Could have been in prison for something else,' said Brian. 'Could have been in a mental home. I've often wondered about that and whether he'll ever come back and strike again.' He parked the car outside Jonathan's new home. 'What a dump! You could still change your mind, Jon old man. Move in with Vesta and me for a bit. Have our couch.'

'Christ,' said Jonathan. 'There's one born every minute.' He delivered this platitude as if it were a quotation, as perhaps, Anthony thought, it was.

They invited him to accompany them to the Grand Duke for an evening's drinking, but Anthony refused. It was nearly five. He went home and read J. G. Miller's doctoral dissertation: *Eyeblink Conditioning of Primary and Neurotic Psychopaths*, remembering at ten to put his clock and his watch back. It was the end of British Summertime.

Watching from his eyrie, his living room window, Arthur saw the new tenant of Room 3 arrive on Sunday afternoon. At first he thought this must be some visitor, a disreputable friend perhaps of Li-li or Anthony Johnson, for he couldn't recollect any previous tenant having arrived in such style. The man was as black as the taxi from which he alighted, and not only black of skin and hair. He wore a black leather coat which, even from that distance, Arthur could see had cost a lot of money, and he carried two huge black leather suitcases. To Arthur's horrified eyes, he resembled some Haitian gangster-cum-political bigwig. He had seen such characters on television and he wouldn't have been surprised to learn that a couple of revolvers and a knife were concealed under that flashy coat.

Staying here obviously, but as whose guest? Arthur put his own front door on the latch and listened. The house door closed quietly, footsteps crossed the hall, mounted the stairs. He peeped out in time to see a sepia-coloured hand adorned with a plain gold signet ring insert a key in the lock of Room 3. He was incensed. Once again Stanley Caspian hadn't bothered to tell him he'd let a room. Once again he had been slighted. For two pins he'd write a strongly-worded letter to Stanley, complaining of ill-usage. But what would be the use? Stanley would only say Arthur hadn't given him the chance to tell him, and it was vain to grumble about the new man's colour with this Race Relations Act restricting landlords the way it did.

On Tuesday Arthur learned his name. He took in the letters, a whole heap of them this morning. One for Li-li from Taiwan sender Chan Ah Feng; two for Anthony Johnson, one postmarked York, the other, in a mauve-grey envelope, Bristol. *Her* letters, Arthur had noted, always came on a Tuesday or a Wednesday, and were still addressed to A. Johnson Esq., 2/142 Trinity Road. Mrs R.L. Johnson, however, had learned sense and put Room 2. All the other correspondence, five official-looking envelopes, was for Winston Mervyn Esq., 3/142 Trinity Road. Winston! The cheek of it, some West Indian grandchildren of slaves christening their son after the greatest Englishman of the century! It seemed to Arthur an added effrontery that this presumptuous black should receive letters so soon after his arrival – five letters to fill up the table and make him look important.

But he didn't see the new tenant or hear a sound from him, though nightly he listened for voodoo drums.

As Anthony had expected, the departure of Jonathan Dean was the signal for Brian to put on the pressure. He was marked to succeed Jonathan, and evening after evening there came a knock on the door of Room 2 and a plaintive invitation to go drinking in the Lily.

'I do have to work,' Anthony said after the fourth time of asking. 'Sorry, but that's the way it is.'

Brian gave him his beaten spaniel look. 'I suppose the fact is you don't like me. I bore you. Go on, you may as well admit it. I *am* a bore. I ought to know it by now, Vesta's told me often enough.'

'Since you ask,' said Anthony, 'yes, it'd bore me going out and getting pissed every night. And I can't afford it.' He relented a little. 'Come in here for a while tomorrow night, if you like. I'll get some beer in.'

Brightening, Brian said he was a pal, and turned up at seven sharp on the Friday with a bottle of vodka and one of French vermouth which made Anthony's six cans of beer look pathetic. He talked dolefully about his job – he sold antiques in a shop owned by Vesta's brother – about the horrors of living always in furnished rooms, Vesta's refusal to have children even if they got a house, her perpetual absences in the evenings – worse than ever this week – his drink problem, and did Anthony think he was an alcoholic?

Anthony let him talk, replying occasionally in monosyllables. He was thinking about Helen's latest letter. It was all very well to talk of absence making the heart grow fonder, but 'out of sight, out of mind' may be just as true a truism. He hadn't expected her letters to concentrate quite so much on Roger's woes. Roger had scarcely been mentioned during that summer of snatched meetings, that clandestine fortnight of love when a shadowy husband had been away somewhere on a business trip. Now it was Roger, Roger, Roger. *I ask myself if it wouldn't be better for both of us to try and forget each other. We could, Tony. Even I, whom you have called hyper-romantic, know that people don't go on loving hopelessly for years. The Troilus and Cressida story may be beautiful but you and I know it isn't real. We should get over it. You'd marry someone who is free and trouble-free and I'd settle down with Roger. I just don't think I can face Roger's misery and violence, and not just for a while but for months, years. I'd know for years that I'd ruined his life . . .* Stupid, Anthony thought. Illogical. He and she wouldn't go on loving hopelessly for years, but Roger would. Of all the irrational nonsense . . .

He said 'Yes' and 'I see' and 'That's bad' for about the fiftieth time to Brian and then, because he couldn't take any more, he bundled him out with his two half-empty bottles under his arm. Having drunk no more than a pint of beer himself, he set to work and was still writing at two in the morning. The coarse talking-with-his-mouth-full voice of Stanley Caspian woke him at ten, and he waited until he and Arthur Johnson had gone before going to the bathroom. It was lucky he happened to be in the hall when Linthea Carville, her son and Steve and David arrived, for it was Arthur Johnson's bell they rang. Anthony saw them silhouetted behind the red and green glass and, making a mental note that sometime he must put his own name under his own bell, he went outside and took them

221

round the back to the cellar. Linthea had brought a torch and two candles, and the boys had the box barrow. They didn't take the barrow down but carried the wood up in armfuls.

He was impressed by Linthea's strength. She had a perfect body, muscular, but curvy and lithe as well, and the jeans and sweater she wore did nothing to impede those graceful movements which he found himself watching with a slightly guilty pleasure.

'There's more wood here than I thought,' he said hastily when he realised she was aware of his gaze. 'We'll have to make a second journey,' and he pushed the door as if to shut it.

'Don't forget my boy's still down there,' said Linthea. 'They all are. And they've got your torch.'

The training they had in common had prevented them from falling into the adult trap of doing all the work themselves on the grounds that they could do it faster and more efficiently than the children. But once the barrow was filled, they had left the boys to explore the rest of the cellar. Linthea called out, 'Leroy, where are you?' and there came back a muffled excited call of 'Mum!' which held in it a note of thrill and mischief.

David and Steve were sitting on an upturned box, the torch between them, in the first room of the cellar. They giggled when they saw Linthea. Carrying a candle, she went on through the second room, walking rather fastidiously between the banks of rubbish. Anthony was just behind her and when, at the entrance to the last and final room, her candle making the one tiny puddle of light in all that gloom, she stopped and let out a shriek of pure terror, he caught her shoulders in his hands.

Her fear was momentary. The shriek died away into a cascade of West Indian merriment, and she ran forward, shaking off Anthony's hands, to catch hold of the boy who was hiding in a corner. Then and only then did he see what she had seen and which had sent that frightened thrill through her. As the candlelight danced, as the woman caught the laughing boy, the torch beam levelled from behind him by Steve, showed him the pale figure leaning against the wall, a black handbag hooked over one stiff arm.

'You wanted to give your poor mother a heart attack, I know you,' Linthea was saying, and the boy: 'You were scared, you were really scared.'

'They were all in it,' said Anthony. 'I wonder how on earth that thing came to be down here.'

He went up to the model, staring curiously at the battered face and the great rent in its neck. Then, hardly knowing why, he touched its cold smooth shoulders. Immediately his fingertips seemed again to remember the feel of Linthea's fine warm flesh, and he realized how hungry he had been to touch a woman. There was something obscene about the figure in front of him, that dead mockery of femaleness with its pallid hard carapace as cold as the shell of a reptile and its attenuated unreal limbs. He wanted to knock it down and leave it to lie on the sooty floor, but he restrained himself and turned quickly away. The others were waiting for him, candles and torch accounted for, at the head of the steps.

# 9

November was the deadline Anthony had given Helen for making up her mind. It was nearly November now and he was due to make his phone call to her on Wednesday, 30 October. The letter he had received from her on the previous Tuesday had dwelt less on Roger's feelings and more on her own and his. In it she had written of her love for him and of their love-making so that, reading it, he had experienced that curious pit-of-the-stomach *frisson* that comes exclusively when nostalgia is evoked for a particular and well-remembered act of sex. With this in mind, he knew he would want to refer to it in their telephone conversation, would use it to reinforce his pressures on her, and he didn't want that conversation overheard by the Kotowskys, Li-li Chan or the new tenant of whom he had once or twice caught a glimpse.

Why not ask Linthea Carville if he could make the call from her flat? This seemed to have a twofold advantage.

He would have complete privacy and, at the same time, the very making of such a request, involving as it would an explanation of his situation with Helen, would reinforce the friendship that was growing between Linthea and himself.

But by Tuesday, 29 October, that situation had changed again. He retrieved Helen's letter from under the huge pile of correspondence for Winston Mervyn which had fallen on top of it, and tore open the envelope only to be bitterly disappointed. *On Wednesday when you phone I know you will ask me if I've come to a decision. Tony, I haven't, I can't. We have had a terrible weekend, Roger and I. First of all he started questioning me about my movements during that fortnight he was away in the States in June. I'd told him before that I'd spent one weekend with my sister and apparently he's now found out from my brother-in-law that I was never there. He made a lot of threats and raved and sulked but in the evening he became terribly pathetic, came into my room after I'd gone to bed and began pouring out all his miseries, how he'd longed for years to marry me, served seven years like Jacob (of course he didn't, I'm not old enough) and now he couldn't bear to be frozen out of my life. This went on for hours, Tony. I know it's blackmail but most people give in to blackmail, don't they?*

He was glad now he hadn't made that request to Linthea. Hedging his bets? Maybe. But the West Indian girl had seemed more attractive to him than ever when he had had lunch with her and Leroy after they had collected the wood and when they had met again at the Tenants' Association last Saturday afternoon. And if, as it would seem, he was going to lose Helen, be dismissed in favour of that sharp-shooting oaf . . . ? Was it so base not to want to jeopardise his chances with Linthea – her husband, at any rate, was nowhere in evidence – by making her think herself a second choice, a substitute?

Rather bitterly he thought that he didn't now much care who overheard his phone call, for there would be no reminiscing over past love passages. One who wouldn't overhear it, anyway, was Vesta Kotowsky who rushed past him in a floor-length black hooded cloak as he was coming up the station steps. He went to the kiosk and bought a box of matches with a pound note, thus ensuring a supply of tenpence pieces for his phone call. He was going to need them, all of them.

224

Her voice sounded nervous when she answered, but it was *her* voice, not heard for a month, and its effect on him was temporarily to take away his anger. That voice was so soft, so sweet, so civilised and gentle. He thought of the mouth from which it proceeded, heart-shaped with its full lower lip, and he let her talk, thinking of her mouth.

Then he remembered how crucial this talk was and what he must say. 'I got your letter.'

'Are you very angry?'

'Of course I'm angry, Helen. I'm fed up. I think I could take it even if you decided against me. It's probably true what you said in your other letter, that we'd forget each other in time. What I can't take is being strung along and . . .' He broke off. The Kotowskys' door opened and Brian came out. Brian started making signals to him, ridiculous mimes of raising an invisible glass to his lips. 'Can't,' Anthony snapped. 'Some other night.'

Helen whispered, 'What did you say, Tony?'

'I was talking to someone else. This phone's in a very public place.' He shouted, 'Oh, Goddamnit!' as the pips sounded. He shovelled in more money. 'Helen, couldn't you call me on this number? I'll give it to you, it's . . .'

She interrupted him with real fear in her voice. 'No, please! I'll have to explain it when the bill comes.'

He was silent. Then he said, 'So you're still going to be there when the bill comes?'

'Tony, I don't *know*. I thought if you could come here at Christmas, stay in an hotel here, and we could see each other again and talk properly and I could make you understand how difficult . . .'

'Oh, no!' he exploded. 'Come for a week, I suppose, and see you for half an hour a day and maybe one evening if you can get out of jail? And at Easter perhaps? And in the summer? While you keep on vacillating and I keep on trying to understand. I won't be any married woman's lap dog, Helen.'

The pips went. He put in more money. 'That was the last of my change,' he said.

'I do love you. You must know that.'

'No, I don't know it. And stop crying, please, because this is important. Your next letter is going to be very important, maybe the most important letter you'll ever write.

If you'll come to me we'll find a place to live and I'll look after you and you needn't be afraid of Roger because I'll be with you. Roger will divorce you when he sees it's no use and then we'll get married. But your next letter's your last chance. I'm fed up, I'm sick to death of being kicked around, and it'll soon be too late.' Anger made him rash, that and the threat of the pips going again. 'There are other women in the world, remember. And when I hear you tell me your husband's so important to you that you're afraid of him seeing phone bills three months hence, like someone in a bloody French farce, I wonder if it isn't too late already!'

A sob answered him but it was cut off by the shrilling peep-peep-peep. He dropped the receiver with a crash, not bothering to say good-bye. But in the silence he leant against the wall, breathing like someone who has run a race. In his hand was one last twopence piece. His breathing steadied, and on an impulse he dialled Linthea's number.

As soon as she heard who it was she asked him round for coffee. Anthony hesitated. His conversation with Helen had become a jumble in his mind and he couldn't remember whether he had given her this number or not. If he had and she phoned back . . . ? No, he wouldn't go to Linthea's, but would Linthea come to him? She would, once she had got the upstairs tenant to listen for Leroy.

Arthur had overheard it all, or as much of phone conversations as a listener can hear. Because he hadn't heard the woman's replies he wasn't sure whether or not Anthony Johnson was going out. Please let him go out, he found himself praying. Perhaps to that God whose portrait with a crown of thorns hung in All Souls' church hall where his Sunday school had been, though neither he nor Auntie Gracie had ever really believed in Him. Please let him go out.

But the light from Room 2 continued to illuminate the lichen-coated court. He heard the front door opened and closed and then he saw what he had never seen before, the shadows of two heads, one Anthony Johnson's, the other sleekly crowned with a pin-pierced chignon, cast on the lighted stone. Arthur turned away, his whole body shaking.

226

He threw back the pink floral eiderdown and seized the pillows one after the other in his hands, strangling them, digging his fingers into their softness, tossing them and grasping them again so savagely that his nails ripped a seam. But this brought him no relief and, after an excess of useless violence, he lay face-downwards on the bed, weeping hot tears.

Linthea wore a long black wool skirt embroidered with orange flowers. The upper part of her body was covered with a yellow poncho and she had small gold pins in her hair.

'I dressed up,' she said, 'because you're expecting other guests. A party?'

He was a little disappointed because she hadn't dressed up for him. 'I'm not expecting anyone. What made you think so?'

She raised eyebrows that were perfect arcs, black crescents above white moons. 'You wouldn't come to me. Oh, I *see*. You're so fond of this exquisite little room with all its antiques and its lovely view of an old-world cellar that you can't bear to leave it. Do you know, that lampshade looks exactly like a Portuguese Man o' War?'

He laughed. 'I knew it was a jellyfish but I didn't know what kind. The fact is, I may be going to get a phone call.'

'Ah.'

'Not "ah" at all.' Anthony put the kettle on, set out cups. 'I'll tell you about it sometime. But now you tell me about you.'

'Nothing much to tell. I'm twenty-nine, born in Kingston. Jamaica, not the By-pass. I came here with my parents when I was eighteen. Trained as a social worker here in Kenbourne. Married a doctor.' She looked down at her lap, retrieved a fallen gold pin. 'He died of cancer three years ago.'

'I'm very sorry.'

'Yes.' She took the cup of coffee Anthony gave her. 'Now you,' she said.

'Me? I'm the eternal student.' As he said it, he remembered it was Helen who had dubbed him so, quoting apparently from some Chekhov play. She wasn't going to phone back. Not now. He began telling Linthea about his thesis, but took his notes gently from her when she started to read them. That sort of thing – *For his actions, cruelty to*

227

*children and animals, even murder, he feels little, if any, guilt.*
*His guilt is more likely to be felt over his failure to perform*
*routine or compulsive actions which are, taken in the context of*
*benefit to society, virtually meaningless* – no, that wasn't what
he wanted to talk about tonight. Pity there wasn't a sofa in
the room but just the tweed-patched fireside chair and the
upright chairs and the thing he thought was called a pouffe.
He sat on that because he could surreptitiously, and apparently artlessly, edge it closer and closer to her. He had got
quite close, and quite close too, to unburdening himself
about his whole disillusionment over the Helen affair, when
there came a sharp rap on the door.

Phone for him. Come to think of it, he wouldn't be able
to hear the phone bell in here. . . . He flung the door open.
On the threshold stood the new occupant of Room 3, a tall
handsome man who looked rather like Muhammad Ali.

'I'm extremely sorry to disturb you,' said Winston
Mervyn in impeccable academic English quite different
from Linthea's warm sun-filled West Indian. He held out
a small cruet. 'I wonder if you would be so kind as to lend
me a little salt?'

'Sure,' said Anthony. 'Come in.' No phone call. Of
course he hadn't given her the number. He remembered
quite clearly now.

Winston Mervyn came in. He walked straight up to Linthea who – if this is possible in a Negress – had turned pale.
She half-rose. She held out her hand and said:

'This is unbelievable. It's too much of a coincidence.'

'It is not,' said the visitor, 'entirely a coincidence. The
salt was a ploy. I saw you come to the door.'

'Yes, but to be living here and in this house . . .' Linthea
broke off. 'We knew each other in Jamaica, Anthony. We
haven't met for twelve years.'


# 10


On the doormat lay three letters for Winston Mervyn, a bill
for Brian Kotowsky and the mauve-grey envelope from

Bristol addressed to Anthony Johnson. Arthur, holding it in his hand, speculated briefly as to its contents. Had the woman decided to leave her husband or to stay with him? But he couldn't summon up much interest in it, for he was obsessed to the exclusion of all else by his need to secure absolute private possession of the cellar.

It had been frosty, the night preceding 5 November, and a thick white rime stuck like snow to walls and railings and doorsteps. The yellow leaves which clogged the gutters were each edged with a tinsel rim. He put his hand to Grainger's gate and found that it was already unlocked. For once, Barry was in before him. Arthur saw him over by a load of timber, about to set a match to a jumping cracker.

'Stop that,' Arthur said in a chilly, carrying voice. 'D'you want to set the place on fire?'

He let himself into the office. Barry came and stood sulkily in the doorway.

'When I was your age I'd have been severely punished if I'd so much as touched a firework.'

Barry blew an orange bubble gum bubble. 'What's pissing you off this morning?'

'How dare you use such language!' Arthur thundered. 'Get out of here. Go and make a cup of tea.'

'What, at half-nine?'

'Do as you're told. When I was your age I'd have thought myself lucky to have *got* a cup of tea in the morning.'

When I was your age . . . Looking out of the window at the white desolation, Arthur thought of that lost childhood of his. Would he have been punished for touching a firework? Perhaps, by the time he was Barry's age, he had already been deterred from doing anything so obviously venal. Yes, he had been strictly brought up, but he had no quarrel with the strict upbringing of children.

'Until you are grown-up, Arthur,' Auntie Gracie used to say, 'I am the master of this house.'

Laxity on her part might have led to his growing up weak, slovenly, heedless about work and punctuality. And a greater freedom would have been bad for him. Look what he did with freedom when he had it – things which would, if unchecked, deprive him of freedom altogether. Like the incident with Mrs Goodwin's baby. . . . But before he could dwell on that one, Barry had come in with the tea.

229

'You see that bonfire they're going to have on the bit of ground?'

'I like my tea in my cup, not in my saucer,' said Arthur. 'No, I cannot say I have seen it. Who might "they" be?'

'People, kids, I don't know. It's a bleeding great pile of wood they got there. I reckon it'll be the best fire in Kenbourne. It's no good you looking out of the window, it's right up against them fences in Brasenose.'

Arthur sipped his tea. 'Let us hope there won't be any catastrophes. I imagine the fire brigade will have a busy night of it. Now when you've finished helping yourself to Mr Grainger's sugar, perhaps you'll condescend to empty my wastepaper basket.'

A formidable pile of correspondence awaited him. He began opening envelopes carefully. Once, hurrying, he had torn a cheque for a large sum in half. But this morning a proper concentration was almost impossible to achieve. He knew, from the images which kept moving in procession across his mental eye, from memories arising out of a past he had been used to think eradicated, from the pressure and buzzing in his head, that he was reaching the end of his tether.

Those images included, of course, dead faces; that of Auntie Gracie, those of the two girls. He saw the mouse, stiff, stretched, bloody. And now he saw the baby and heard again its screams.

Auntie Gracie had been minding that baby for its mother. There had been some sick relative, Arthur remembered, whom Mrs Goodwin was obliged to visit.

'If I have to pop out to the shops,' Auntie Gracie had said, 'Arthur will be here,' and with a loaded look, 'It will be good for Arthur to be placed in a position of trust.'

Once she was out of the house, he had gone and stood over the baby, scrutinising it with curious desire. It was about six months old, fat, fast asleep. He withdrew the covers, lifted the woolly jacket it wore, and still it didn't wake. A napkin, white and fleecy, secured with a large safety pin, was now visible above its leggings. Safety was a strange word to apply to so obviously dangerous a weapon. Arthur removed the pin and, taut now with joy and power, thrust it up to its curled hilt into the baby's stomach. The baby woke with a shattering scream and a great bubble of

230

scarlet blood welled out as he removed the pin. For a while he listened to its screams, watching it and exulting, watching its wide agonised mouth and the tears which washed down its red face. He watched and listened. Auntie Gracie was away at the shops quite a long time. Fortunately. He had to make things right to avoid her anger. Fortunately, too, the pin seemed to have struck no vital part. He changed the napkin which was now wet with urine as well as blood, washed it – how Auntie Gracie had congratulated him and approved of that! – and by the time she returned the baby was only crying piteously as babies do cry, apparently for no reason.

No harm ever came to the baby. It was, he supposed, a man in his mid-thirties by now. Nor had he or Auntie Gracie ever been blamed for the wound, if indeed that wound had ever been discovered. But he was glad for himself that he had known Auntie Gracie wouldn't be long away, for where else, into how many more vulnerable soft parts would he have stuck that pin had the baby been his for hours? No, she had been his guardian angel and his protectress, succeeded at her death by that other protectress, his patient white lady, garbed in her clothes. . . .

By one o'clock he hadn't replied to a single letter. Perhaps, when he had a good lunch inside him . . . He put on his overcoat of silver-grey tweed, a shade lighter than his steel-grey silk tie, which he tightened before leaving the office until it stood out like an arch of metal. On his way to the Vale Café, he paused for a moment to view the stacked wood. The pile stood some fifteen feet high and someone had flanked it with a pair of trestle tables. Arthur shook his head in vague undefined disapproval. Then he walked briskly to the café, having an idea that the crisp air, inhaled rhythmically, would clear his pulsing head.

Returning, he was accosted by a young woman in a duffel coat who was collecting information for a poll. Arthur gave her his name and address, told her that he supported the Conservative Party, was unmarried; he refused to give his age but gave his occupation as a quantity surveyor. She took it all down and he felt a little better.

Grainger's correspondence still awaited him and, thanks to his idleness of the morning, it looked as if he might have to stay late to get it all done. During the winter, when dusk had come by five, he liked to leave the office promptly at the hour. The streets were crowded then and he could get home, safe and unobserved, before dark. But he comforted himself with the thought that the streets would be crowded till all hours tonight. Already he could see flashes of gold and scarlet and white fire shooting into the pale and still sunlit sky.

But from a perverse wish to see the evening's festivities spoiled, he hoped for rain and went outside several times to study the thermometer. There had been a few clouds overhead at lunchtime. Since then the clouds had shrunk and shivered away as if chilled out of existence by the increasing cold, for the red column of liquid in the thermometer had fallen steadily from 37 to 36 to 35 until now, at five-thirty, it stood at 29 degrees.

The sun had scarcely gone when stars appeared in the blue sky, as hard and clear as a sheet of lapis. And the stars remained, bright and eternal, while those false meteors shot and burst into ephemeral galaxies. Arthur pulled down the blind so that he could no longer see them, though he could hear the voices and the laughter of those who were arriving for the bonfire and the feast.

At ten past six he completed his last letter and typed the address. Then, leaving his replies in the 'Out' tray for Barry to post in the morning he put on his overcoat, gave yet another tug to his tie, and left the office. He locked the gates. The Guy Fawkes celebrants were making what Arthur thought of as a most unseemly din. He came out into Magdalen Hill and approached the wire-netting fence.

A small crowd of home-going commuters were already gathered there. Arthur meant to walk past, but curiosity mixed with distaste and some undefined hope of disaster, impelled him to join them.

The tables had been laid with paper cloths on which were arranged mountains of sandwiches, bread rolls, hot dogs and bowls of soup. The steam from this soup hung on the air. There were, Arthur estimated, about a hundred people present, mostly children, but many women and perhaps half a dozen men. All were wrapped in windcheaters or thick coats with scarves. Already the grass was frosted and their boots made dark green prints on the frost. The lights in the houses behind shed a steady orange refulgence over the moving figures, the silvered grass, the ponderous mountain of wood, the whole Brueghel-like scene.

One of the women brought to the stacked woodpile a box barrow filled with potatoes which she tipped out. These, Arthur supposed, were to be roasted in the embers of the fire. And very nasty they would taste, he thought, as he saw a man – a black man, they all looked the same to him – tip paraffin over wood and cardboard and paper and then splash it over the guy itself. The guy, he had to admit, was a masterpiece, if you cared for that sort of thing, a huge lifelike figure dressed in a man's suit with a papier mâché mask for a face and a big straw hat on its head. He was about to turn away, sated and half-disgusted with the whole thing, when he saw something – or someone – that held him frozen and excited where he stood. For a man had come out of the crowd with a box of matches in his hand, a tall man with a blaze of blond hair hanging to the collar of his leather jacket, and the man was Anthony Johnson.

Arthur didn't question what he was doing there or how he had come to be involved in this childish display. He realised only that no man can be in two places at once. If Anthony Johnson was here – from the way the children cheered, an evident master of ceremonies – he couldn't also be at 142 Trinity Road. It looked as if he would be here for hours, and during those hours the cellar would be private and unobserved. It would be dark and very cold, solitudinous but, on this night of sporadic violent sound, sufficiently within the world to touch his fantasy with a greater than usual measure of reality.

A kind of joy that was both intense and languid filled his whole being. Until that moment he had hardly realised to the full how insistently urgent his need for the woman in the cellar was. None of his dreams, none of his frustration, had brought it home to him as the sight of Anthony Johnson, striking his first match, applying it to the timber, now did. But as he savoured his anticipation and felt it mount, he knew he must let it mount to its zenith. He had time, a lot of time. The culmination and the release would be all the greater for being sensuously deferred.

He stood there, trembling again but now with ecstasy. And he had no fear of the dark or its temptations. Happiness, contentment, was in watching Anthony Johnson apply match after match to that stack of wood until the flames began to leap, to crackle and to roar through the pyramid. As the fire became established, a sheet of it licking the feet of the guy, the first fireworks went off. A rocket rose in a scream of sparks, and along the fence, under the supervision of the black man, a child ignited the first in a long row of Catherine Wheels. One after another they rotated in red and yellow flames. And those paler stronger flames climbed across the guy's legs, shooting long tongues across the black suit in which it was clothed, until they leapt to its face and head, spitting through its eye sockets, catching the straw hat and roaring through its crown.

The hat toppled off. The suit burned and fell away. There was a grotesque indecency in the way white limbs, long and smooth and glossy, lashed from under the burning material until the fire caught them and began to consume them also. Arthur came closer to the wire. His hands gripped the rusty cold wire. The mask was now a glowing mass that flew suddenly from the face and rose like a firework itself before eddying in sparks to the ground. A child screamed and its mother pulled it clear.

The flames teased the naked face. It wasn't a man's face but a woman's, pale, blank, even beautiful in its utter dead calm expressionlessness. It seemed to move and come close to Arthur until he could see nothing, no people, no cascading colour, no smoke, nothing but that familiar and beloved face. Then it was still and calm no longer. It arched back as if in parody of those burned at the stake. The great rent under its chin opened, gaped wide like a razor-made slash, and the fire took it, bursting with a hiss through the tear and roasting with a kind of lust the twisted face.

His white lady, his Auntie Gracie, his guardian angel . . .


# 11


The house at 142 Trinity Road was unlit, every street-overlooking window a glaze of blackness between dim drifts of curtain. The curtains on the top floor shimmered whitely like the lacy ball gowns of women who wait in vain to be asked to dance. Inside the house there was total, breathless silence. Arthur, leaning against the banisters, his hot forehead against cold smooth wood, thought he had never known it so silent – no tap of heels, no soft giggles, mutter of words, whistle of kettles, trickle of water, throb of heaters, thud of door, heart-beat of life. It was as if it had retreated into sleep, but the sleep of an animal which is awakened at once by the smallest sound or movement. He could awaken the house by going upstairs and setting in motion all the processes of a routine evening. He could switch lights on, fill his kettle, turn on the television, turn down his bed, close the bedroom window – and look down into that court, at last unlighted, but dispossessed for ever of its lure.

Rage seized him. He put on the hall light and took a few steps towards the door of Room 2. To destroy property was foreign to his nature, property was what he respected, but now if he could get into that room, he would, he thought, destroy Anthony Johnson's books. One after another he pulled open the drawers in Stanley Caspian's desk. Stanley had been known to leave duplicate keys lying about there, but they were empty now of everything except screwed-up pieces of paper and bits of string. Yet he must have revenge, for he had no doubt that Anthony Johnson had performed an act of revenge against him. All these weeks Anthony Johnson had been harbouring against him a grudge – hadn't everything in his behaviour shown it? – because he had opened that letter from the council. Now it was his turn, he who had done his best to make amends. Now some act must be performed of like magnitude. But what?

Turning away from the desk and the door of Room 2, his eye fell on the hall table. Something seemed to clutch at his chest, squeezing his ribs. All the letters were still there, undisturbed; the bill for Brian Kotowsky, the official-looking correspondence for Winston Mervyn, the mauve-grey envelope from Bristol for Anthony Johnson. No one had returned to the house since that morning, no one had removed a letter. Arthur put his hand over the Bristol envelope, covering it. A light constant tremor animated his hand, a tremor that had been there, electrifying his hands and his body with a delicate frenetic throb from the moment he had witnessed that fire and its consequences. Blood beat in his head as if it were feeding an engine.

He thought now of the telephone call he had overheard. 'Your next letter's our last chance, . . .' Her next letter. It lay under his trembling hand. Arthur lifted it up, holding it by its edge as if its centre were red-hot. Words of Auntie Gracie's trickled across his brain.

'Other people's correspondence is sacrosanct, Arthur. To open someone else's letter is the action of a thief.'

But she was gone from him, never more to guard him, never more to watch and save . . . He ripped open the envelope, splitting it so savagely that it tore into two pieces. He pulled the letter out. It was typewritten, not on mauve-grey paper but on flimsy such as is used for duplicates, and the machine was an Adler Standard like the one in his office at Grainger's.

*Darling Tony, I think I've changed a lot since I spoke to you. Perhaps I've grown up. Suddenly I realised when you put the phone down that you were right. I can't hover and play this insane double game any more. It came quite clearly to me that I have to choose directly between you and Roger. I would have called you back then and there, but I don't know your number – isn't that absurd? I only know your landlord's got a name like a river or a sea.*

*I have chosen, Tony. I've chosen you, absolutely and finally. For ever? I hope so. But I promised for ever once before, so I'm chary of making that vast dreadful promise again. But I will leave Roger and I will marry you if you still want me.*

*Don't be angry, I haven't told Roger yet. I'm afraid, of course I am, but it isn't only that. I can't tell him I'm leaving him without having anywhere to go or anyone to go to. All you have to do for me to tell him is to write – write to me at work – and let me know where and when to meet you. If my letter gets to you by Tuesday, you should be able to get yours to me by Friday at the latest. Of course, what I really mean is I want word from you that you aren't too disgusted with me to need me any more. I will do whatever you say. Command me.*

*Tony, forgive me. I have played fast and loose with you like 'a right gypsy'. But no longer. We could be together by Saturday. Say we will be and I will come even if I have to run from*

236

*Roger in my nightdress. I will be another Mary Stuart and follow you to the ends of the earth in my shift. I love you. H.*

Arthur felt a surge of power. Just as the control of his destiny, his peace, had lain in Anthony Johnson's hands, so the other man's now lay in his. An eye for an eye, a tooth for a tooth. Anthony Johnson had taken away his white lady; now he would take from Anthony Johnson *his* woman, rob him as he had been robbed of his last chance.

He screwed up the letter and envelope and thrust them into his pocket. He walked down the hall and came to the foot of the stairs. How terrible and beautiful the silence was! With something like anguish, he thought of the cellar, unguarded, unwatched. Wasn't it possible he could still get some relief from it, from its atmosphere that had fed his fantasy, from an imagination that could still perhaps provide, furnishing her absence with vision and empty air with flesh? He turned off the light, left the house and made his way down the side passage. But he had no torch, only a box of matches in his pocket. One of these he lit as he passed through the first and second rooms. He lit another and in its flare saw the heap of clothes on the floor, Auntie Gracie's dress, the bag, the shoes, and scattered all of them like so much trash as if they had never clothed a passion.

It was the death of a fantasy. His imagination shrivelled, and he was just an embittered man in a dirty cellar looking at a pile of old clothes. The match burned down in his fingers; its flame caught the box which suddenly flared into a small brilliant fire. Arthur dropped it, stamped on it. He caught his breath on a sob in the darkness, stumbled back through the thick darkness, feeling his way to the steps.

Through the passage to the front he walked. He turned to the right, crossed the grass, set his foot on the bottom step. Like others before him, he would have been safe if he had not paused and looked back. The mouth of the dark opened and called him. The jaws of darkness received him, the streets received him, taking him into their arteries like a grain of poison.

The tables were bare, the fire had burned out, and the only fireworks which remained were those sparklers which are safe for children to hold in their hands. Only they and the stars now glittered over the frosty debris-scattered

237

ground. Linthea had stacked her crockery into the barrow and now, having collected her son and Steve, left them with a wave and one of her radiant smiles.

Anthony and Winston Mervyn began dismantling the trestle tables which they would return to All Souls' hall. The last of the fire, a fading glow, dying into handfuls of dust, held enough heat to warm them as they worked. Winston, who seemed preoccupied, said something in a language Anthony recognised for what it was, though the words were unintelligible.

'What did you say?'

Winston laughed and translated. 'Look at the stars, my star. Would I were the heavens that I might look at you with many eyes.'

'Amazing bloke, you are. I suppose you'll turn out to be a professor of Greek.'

'I thought of doing that,' Winston said seriously, 'but there's more money in figures than in Aristotle. I'm an accountant.' Anthony raised his eyebrows but he didn't say what he wanted to, why was an accountant living at that grotty hole in Trinity Road? 'Easy does it,' said Winston. 'You take that end and I'll go ahead.'

They carried the tables up Magdalen Hill and along Balliol Street. A Roman Candle, ignited outside the Waterlily, illuminated in a green flash the cave-like interior of Oriel Mews. Anthony, walking behind Winston, realised that although he had been told what Winston had quoted, he hadn't been told why he chose to quote it. All Souls' caretaker took the tables from them, and Winston suggested a drink in the Waterlily. Anthony said all right but he'd like to go home first as he was expecting an important letter.

A hundred and forty-two was a blank dark smudge in a street of lighted houses. Winston went in first. He picked up his letters from the table. There was nothing for Anthony. Well, Helen's letter didn't always come on a Tuesday. It would come tomorrow.

'That's more like it,' said Winston. 'I might get along and look at that tomorrow.' He passed a printed sheet to Anthony who saw it was an estate agent's specification of a house in North Kenbourne, the best part. The price was twenty thousand pounds.

'You're a mystery,' he said.

'No, I'm not. Because I'm coloured you expect me to be uneducated, and because I live here you expect me to be poor.'

Anthony opened his mouth to say this was neither true nor fair, but he knew it was so he said, 'I reckon I do. Sorry.'

'I came to live here because my firm moved to London and now I'm looking for a house to buy.'

'You're not married, are you?'

'Oh, no, I'm not married,' said Winston. 'Let's go, shall we?'

Going out, they met Brian Kotowsky coming in.

'You look thirsty,' said Brian. 'Me, I'm always thirsty. How about going across the road and seeing if we can find an oasis?'

There was no way of getting rid of him. He trotted along beside them, talking peevishly of Jonathan Dean whom, he said, he hadn't seen since the other man moved away. This was because Jonathan and Vesta disliked each other. Brian was positive Jonathan had phoned, but Vesta had always taken the calls and refused to tell him out of spite. They walked through the mews which smelt of gunpowder and entered the Waterlily just before nine o'clock.

In another public house, the Grand Duke, in a distant part of Kenbourne, Arthur sat alone at a table, drinking brandy. A small brandy with a splash of soda. When first he had set out on this nocturnal walk he had been terrified – of himself. But gradually that fear had been conquered by the interest of the streets, by the changes which had come to them, by the squalid glitter of them, by the lonely places at which alley mouths and mews arches and paths leading to little yards hinted like whispers in the dark. He hadn't forgotten, in twenty years, the geography of this place where he had been born. And how many of the warrens, the labyrinths of lanes twisting across lanes, still remained behind new soaring façades! The air was smoky, acrid with the stench of fireworks, but now, at half-past nine, there were few people about. It excited Arthur to find himself, during that long walk, often the only pedestrian in some wide empty space, lividly lighted, swept by car lights, yet sprawled over with shadows and

239

bordered with caverns and passages penetrating the high frowning walls.

The pattern, twice before experienced, was repeating itself without his volition. On both those previous occasions he had walked aimlessly or with an unadmitted aim; on both he had entered a pub; on both ordered brandy because brandy was the one alcoholic drink he knew. Auntie Gracie had always kept some in the house for medicinal purposes. Sipping his brandy, feeling the unaccustomed warmth of it move in his body, he began to think of the next repetition in the pattern . . .

# 12

There were strangers in the Waterlily, men with North Country accents wearing green and yellow striped football scarves. Brian Kotowsky struck up acquaintance with one of them, a fat meaty-faced man called Potter, and that would have suited Anthony very well, enabling him to discuss houses and house-buying with Winston, but Brian kept calling him 'Tony, old man' and trying hard to include him in the conversation with Potter. Before Helen's tuition, Anthony wouldn't have noticed the way greenish-ginger hairs grew out of Potter's ears and nostrils, nor perhaps been able to define Potter's smell, a mixture of onions, sweat, whisky and menthol. But he would have known Potter was very drunk. Potter had one arm round Brian's shoulders and, having listened to the saga of Jonathan Dean's defection and Vesta's knack of losing her husband all his friends, he said:

'Rude to him, was she?' He had a flat West Riding accent. 'And he were rude to her? Pickin' on her like? Ay, I get the picture.'

'You've got one of her kind yourself, have you?'

'Not me, lad. I never made the mistake of putting my head in the noose. But I've kept my eyes open. When a woman's rude to a man and he's rude to her, it means but one thing. He fancies her and she fancies him.'

'You have to be joking,' said Brian.

'Not me, lad. You mark my words, you haven't set eyes on him because him and your missus is out somewhere now being rude.' And Potter gave a great drunken guffaw.

'I'm going,' said Anthony. 'I'm fed up with this place.' He got to his feet and glanced at Winston who replaced the specifications in their envelopes.

They turned into the mews and were very soon aware that Brian and Potter were following close behind them. It was a little after ten.

'This is going to be splendid,' said Winston in his cool precise way. 'They'll be drinking and rioting next door to me half the night.'

But as it happened, Potter was unable to make the stairs. He sat down on the bottom step and began to sing a bawdy agricultural ballad about giving some farmer's daughter the works of his threshing machine. Anthony had noticed that Li-li wasn't in and that all the upstairs lights were off. That meant Arthur Johnson must already be in bed. Sound asleep too, he hoped.

'You'd better get him out of here,' he said to Brian. 'He's your friend.'

'Friend? I never saw him before in my life, Tony old man.' Brian had brought a half-bottle of vodka back with him from the off-licence and this he raised to his lips, drinking it neat. 'Where am I supposed to put him? Out in the street? He comes from Leeds.'

'Then he can go back there. On the next train out of King's Cross.'

Brian looked helplessly at Potter who was humming now and conducting an imaginary orchestra. 'He doesn't want to go back there. He's come down for tomorrow's match.'

'What Goddamned match?' said Anthony, who rarely swore. 'What the hell are you on about?' He knew nothing of football and cared less.

'Leeds versus Kenbourne Kingmakers.' Brian waved his bottle at Anthony. 'Want some Russian rotgut? O.K., be like that. I'd never have brought him here if I'd known he was that pissed. I suppose we couldn't put him in your . . . ?'

'No,' said Anthony, but as he was about to add something rude and to the point, Potter staggered to his feet and waved his arms, swivelling his head about.

241

'He wants the lavatory,' said Winston. He took Potter's arm and propelled him down the passage. Anthony unlocked the door of Room 2 and, without waiting to be asked, Brian followed him in and sat down on the bed. He was flushed and truculent.

'I didn't like what he was insinuating about Vesta.'

'He doesn't know her,' Anthony said. 'What's the use of listening to stupid generalisations about behaviour? They're always wrong.'

'You're a real pal, Tony, the best pal a man ever had.'

The lavatory flush went, and Winston came in with Potter who looked pale and smelt even worse than in the pub. Potter sat down in the fireside chair and lay back with his mouth open. Outside a rocket going off made them all jump except Potter, who began to snore.

'Give him half an hour,' said Winston, 'then we'll get some black coffee into him. In my ambulance driving days I saw a lot of them like that.'

'You've crowded a lot into your life,' said Anthony. 'Greek, accountancy, a bit of medical training. You'll be telling me you're a lawyer next.'

'Well, I did read for the bar but I was never called,' said Winston, and taking Ruch's *Psychology and Life* from the bedside table, he was soon immersed in it.

'I didn't like what he said about my wife,' said Brian. The vodka bottle was half-empty. He glared at Potter and gave one of his shoulders a savage shake. Potter sat up, groaned and staggered off once more to the lavatory. 'He shouldn't have said that about Jonathan. Jonathan's the best friend I ever had.'

Winston looked at him severely over the top of his book. 'Make some coffee,' he snapped. 'Get on with it. You need it as much as he does.'

Brian obeyed, whimpering like a little dog. He put the kettle on while Anthony got out coffee and sugar. Feeling suddenly tired, Anthony sat on the floor because there wasn't anywhere else to sit, and closed his eyes. The last thing he noticed before he fell into a doze was that Brian was crying, the tears trickling down his sagging red cheeks.

Arthur went into the gents' where he tore the Bristol letter into small pieces and flushed them down the pan. There

242

was a finality in this act which both pleased and frightened him. No going back now, no possibility of restoring the letter with another explanatory note. The deed was done and his revenge accomplished. Would the knowledge of that be sufficient to sustain him till he was home again? Could he get home in safety? As he emerged once more into the cocktail bar, the fear of himself began to return. But all the same, he bought another small brandy. He was deferring his departure from the Grand Duke until the last possible moment. It was twenty minutes to eleven. In his absence, someone had taken his seat and he was obliged to stand in a corner by the glass partition which divided this section from the saloon. The glass was frosted but with a flower pattern on it of clear glass. Glancing through a clear space, the shape of a petal, Arthur saw a familiar profile some three or four yards away.

Fortunately, it was the profile and not the full face of Jonathan Dean that he saw, for he was sure Dean hadn't seen him. He moved away quickly, elbowing through the crowd. Dean's mouth had been flapping like the clapper of a briskly-rung handbell, so he was obviously talking to an unseen person. Very likely, unseen *people*. Brian Kotowsky and maybe Anthony Johnson and that black man as well. Birds of a feather flock together. He must get out.

It was only when he was out in the street that he questioned that compulsion of his. If he meant to go straight home, what did it matter who saw him or what witnesses there were to his absence from 142 Trinity Road? Or didn't he mean to go straight home, but to wander the streets circuitously, the pressure in his head mounting, until the last permutation of the pattern was achieved? Arthur shivered. There was a bus stop a few yards down the High Street from the Grand Duke, but he didn't want a bus which would take him no nearer Trinity Road than the Waterlily. A taxi, on the other hand, would deposit him at his door.

Taxis came down this way, he knew, returning to the West End after dropping a fare in North Kenbourne. But the minutes passed and none came. Ten to eleven. Soon the Grand Duke would close and disgorge its patrons on to the pavement. On the opposite side of the street Arthur could see the edge of the thickly-treed mass of Radclyffe

Park. Its main gate was closed, but the little iron kissing gate, the entry to a footpath which skirted the park, couldn't be closed. He saw a woman pass through this gate, her shadow, before she entered the dark path, streaming across the lighted pavement. His heart squeezed and he clenched his hands. Maureen Cowan, Bridget O'Neill. . . .

At last a taxi appeared. He hailed it feverishly and asked the driver for Trinity Road.

'Where might Trinity Road be?'

Arthur told him.

'Sorry, mate. I'm going back to town and then I'm going to my bed. I've been at the wheel of this vehicle since nine this morning, and enough is enough.'

'I shall note down your number,' Arthur said shrilly. 'You're obliged to take me. I shall report you to the proper authority.'

'Screw you and the proper authority,' said the driver and moved off.

The last K.12 bus would pass at two minutes to eleven. Arthur decided he had no choice but to get on it, but at the Waterlily stop avoid Oriel Mews and walk home by the bright lighted way of Magdalen Hill. Yet it took all his self-control to remain at that bus stop and not set off on foot, to take the way the woman had taken or to follow the serpentine course of Radclyffe Lane which, passing at one point between acres of slum-cleared land, at another between terraces of squat houses and mean little shops, at last came to the hospital, the bridge and the grey-grassed embankment of Isambard Kingdom Brunel's railway. But as the temptation to do this became intolerable, the K.12 appeared over the brow of the rise from the direction of Radclyffe College.

Arthur went inside and the bus began to move. But it slowed again and stopped for the flying figure of a woman in a long black hooded cloak who had rushed from the Grand Duke to catch it. There were no more seats inside and she went upstairs.

The bus moved along fast because there wasn't much traffic at that time of night. It passed the cemetery where Maureen Cowan had plied her trade and where Auntie Gracie lay in the family plot beside her father and mother.

It detoured along a one-way street and returned briefly to the High Street before turning up Kenbourne Lane. And still, all along the route, red and green and silver flashes pierced the cold dark curtain of sky, breaking at their zeniths into tumbling cascades of sparks.

They took the right-hand turn into Balliol Street and Arthur – who seldom rode on buses but who, when he did, was always ready to get off them a hundred yards before his stop – began to edge out of his seat. The black hooded shape was already waiting on the platform. Like a monk or a great bird, he thought. She was the first to alight, as if nervously anxious to get home.

The Waterlily was closed. All the shops were closed, and as he looked along the length of Balliol Street, he saw the light in the window of Kemal's Kebab House go out. But lights there were in plenty, amber squares dotted haphazardly across house fronts, street lights like wintergreen drops, the high rise tower a pharos with a hundred twinkling eyes. Scattered on the pavement were the blackened paper cases of used fireworks. But there were no people, no one but he and the cloaked woman who fluttered away across the mews entrance towards Camera Street. An occasional car passed.

Arthur stood still. He looked through the window of the public bar of the Waterlily, but he watched the woman from the corner of his eye. A cruising car had drawn up beside her, delaying her. The driver was saying something. Arthur thought he would count up to ten, by which time she would have turned into Camera Street or gone with the man, be lost to him, he and she safe, and then he would turn and make for Magdalen Hill. But before he had got to five, he saw her recoil sharply from the car and begin to run back the way she had come. His heart ticked, it swelled and pounded. There were three white posts under the mews arch. No car could pass into it from this end. But she passed into it. The car seemed to give a shrug before it slid away down the hill, leaving her for easier, more complaisant prey.

Arthur too went into Oriel Mews, walking softly as a cat. It was dark in there, sensuously, beautifully dark. She was walking fast – he could just make out the grotesque flapping shape of her – but he walked faster, passing her and hearing the sharp intake of her breath as he brushed the skirts of her cloak.

Then, behind him, she fell back, as he had known she would. She would linger until she saw his silhouette against the lighted mouth at the Trinity Road end, until she saw him disappear. He let her see him. But instead of stepping out into the light, he pressed himself against the cold bricks of the mews wall and eased back a yard, two yards. He smelt her. He couldn't see her.

His tie was very tightly fastened and he had to wrench at it to get it off. His strength was such that if it had indeed been made of the metal it resembled he would still have possessed the power to get it free. Fireworks were hissing and breaking in his head now. The last of them fell into a million stars as the flapping hooded creature closed upon him and he upon her.

She didn't cry out. The sound she made came to his acute ears only, the gurgle of ultimate terror, and the smell of her terror was for his nostrils alone. He never felt the touch of her hands. She fell on the stones like a great dying bird, and Arthur, rocking with an inner tumult, let her weight rest heavily on his shoes until at last, precisely and fastidiously, he shifted his feet away.

# 13

When Anthony opened his eyes it was twenty past eleven. Winston was still reading *Psychology and Life*, Potter was still asleep. Both bars of the electric fire were on and the room was very hot.

'Where's Brian?'

Winston closed the book. 'He went off about half an hour ago. Said he was going to find this Dean character and have it out with him.'

'Oh, God,' said Anthony. 'Let's get rid of Potter.'

'When you like,' said Winston equably. 'I looked through his pockets while you were asleep. He's got plenty of money and he's staying at the Fleur Hotel in Judd Street.'

'Well done, sergeant. You'll go far.' A thought struck Anthony. 'You were never in the police, were you?'

Winston grinned. 'No, I never was. Shall we get him a cab?'

Anthony nodded and they managed to wake Potter. But, as always on waking, Potter had a call of nature or wanted to be sick. He departed for the lavatory and Anthony and Winston waited for him in silence. They had to wait a long time as it was fully ten minutes before Potter reappeared, green-faced, unsteady and drooling.

Arthur came through the front door of 142 Trinity Road at twenty-five to twelve. He held his coat collar high up against his throat so that the absence of a tie wouldn't be noticed. The bitter cold made such an action natural in someone who might be thought bronchial. But there was no one to see him and he wasn't afraid.

At first the house appeared as dark as when he had left it all those hours before. No light showed in Li-li Chan's window or in that of Winston Mervyn. The hall was dark and silent, but, pausing at the foot of the stairs, he saw a line of light under the door of Room 2, and the ill-fitting lavatory door had a narrow rim of light all the way round its rectangle. Anthony Johnson. It could be no one else. Arthur moved soundlessly up the stairs, but before he reached the first landing, six steps before, he heard the lavatory door open and saw a blaze of light stream into the hall below. It seemed to him that Anthony Johnson must have paused, must be looking up the stairs – for why else should he hang about in the hall? He didn't look down and by the time he was on the landing, he heard the door of Room 2 close.

Light flooded the courtyard below his bedroom window. But it was of no importance. The only danger to him lay in his being actually caught in the act of a killing, for he had been a stranger to the woman he had strangled as he had been a stranger to Maureen Cowan and Bridget O'Neill. No one would care what time Arthur Johnson had come home that night because no one would think it necessary to enquire.

There was nothing to worry about. These were perhaps the only moments in his life when he had nothing to worry

247

about. He savoured them, excluding thought, feeling an exquisite peace, an animal's well-being. Not bothering, for once, to wash, he stripped off his clothes, leaving on top of the heap of them the stretched twisted silver tie, and fell beneath the blue floral quilt. In seconds he was asleep.

It was always, as Winston pointed out, next to impossible to secure a taxi in Trinity Road which wasn't a through road and whose inhabitants in general couldn't afford cabs.

'We could get him up to the rank by the station.'

'No, we couldn't,' said Anthony. It had been bad enough lugging the somnolent smelly Potter from Room 2 out into the street. He must have weighed at least sixteen stone. Now he sat where they had placed him, on the low wall that divided the patch of grass from the street, his head resting against the stump of a lime tree. The heavy frost that made them shiver had no effect on Potter who began once more to snore.

'I'll go to the rank,' said Winston, 'if you'll stay here and see he doesn't fall off on to the grass.' But as he spoke a taxi cruised out of Magdalen Hill and came to a stop outside a hundred and forty-two. Li-li Chan, in a green satin boiler suit and pink feather boa, skipped out of it and thrust a pound note at the driver.

'Ninety-eight, lady,' said the driver, giving her back two pence.

'You keep change,' said Li-li, waving it away. While the driver stared after her in gloomy disbelief, she uttered a 'Hallo, it's fleezing,' to Anthony and Winston and danced off up the steps.

'You wouldn't believe it,' said the driver, 'if you hadn't seen it with your own eyes.' He scrutinised the coin as if he feared it might vanish in the wake of its bestower.

Winston grabbed Potter under one arm while Anthony took the other. They shoved him into the back of the cab. 'This one's loaded and he's in no state to argue about your tip. Fleur Hotel, Judd Street. O.K.?'

'Long as he don't throw up,' said the driver.

The night was growing quiet now and there had been no sound of fireworks for half an hour.

It took nearly an hour to air Room 2. Anthony was a long time getting to sleep and, as a result, he overslept. Waking at eight-thirty, he hadn't time to shave or wash much, for he was determined to get down to work in the college library by half-past nine. There was a stranger in the hall, a nondescript middle-aged man who nodded and said good morning in what seemed a deliberate and calculating way. Anthony had made up his mind he must be a plainclothes policeman even before he saw the police car parked outside the house, and at once he wondered if this visit had any connection with Brian Kotowsky. Brian had gone out the previous night, intent on quarrelling with Jonathan Dean – intent perhaps on fighting Dean?

But none of the occupants of the car attempted to speak to him, so he crossed the road towards Oriel Mews. Here his passage was barred. The mews entrance was blocked off by a tarpaulin sheet, erected on a frame some eight feet high, and none of its interior was visible.

The sound of knocking had awakened Arthur just before his alarm was due to go off. Someone was hammering on one of the doors, Kotowskys' or Mervyn's, on the floor below. Then he heard voices, Mervyn's and another's, but he was used to all sorts of unnecessary wanton noise, made at uncivilized hours, so he didn't take much notice. Ten minutes later, when all the noise had stopped, he got up and had his bath. He cleaned bath and basin carefully, mopped the floor, plumped up the blue pillows and shook out the quilt, took a clean shirt and clean underwear from the airing cupboard.

A tramping up and down the stairs had begun. Perhaps someone else was moving out. It would be just like Stanley Caspian not to have told him. He went into the kitchen and plugged in his kettle, wondering in a detached kind of way if the body of the woman had yet been found. Imprudent of him really to have done the deed so near home, but prudence, of course, hadn't entered into it. The evening newspaper would tell him, reveal to him as to any other stranger, the known facts. And this time he wouldn't collapse and be ill from the culminating traumas of it, but would watch with relish the efforts of the police to find the killer.

A good strong pot of tea, two eggs, two rashers of bacon, two thin piping hot pieces of toast. If they had found the body, he thought as he washed up, they would in some way cordon off the mews. Its entrance was just visible from his living room window. His curiosity irresistible, he peered out between the crossover frilled net curtains. Yes, Oriel Mews was cordoned off, its arch blanked out with a big opaque sheet of something. A van had probably gone in to load or unload and the driver had found her. He scanned the area for police cars, found nothing until, focussing closer, he saw one where he least expected it, right under the window at the kerb.

Arthur's heart gave a great lurch, and suddenly his chest seemed full of scalding liquid. But they couldn't know, they couldn't have come for him . . . No one had seen him go into the mews and there was nothing to connect him with the dead woman. Pull yourself together, he told himself in the admonishing Auntie Gracie voice he kept for moments like this. Not that there ever had been a moment like this before.

He had slumped into a chair and now, looking down at his hands, he saw that he was holding the dish cloth just as he had held that silver tie last night, taut, his fingers flexed at its ends. He relaxed them. Was it possible the police car was parked outside because earlier there had been no other space in which to park? Again he looked out of the window. Anthony Johnson was crossing the road towards the closed mews. The long thrill of his doorbell ringing seemed to go through the soft tissues of Arthur's brain like a knife. He swayed. Then he went to the door.

'Mr Johnson?'

Arthur nodded, his face shrivelling with pallor.

'I'd like a word with you. May I come in?'

The man didn't wait for permission. He stepped into the flat and showed Arthur his warrant card. Detective Inspector Glass. A tall lean man was Inspector Glass with a broad flat bill of a nose and a thin mouth that parted to show big yellow dentures.

'There's been a murder, Mr Johnson. In view of that, I'd be glad if you'd tell me what your movements were last evening.'

'My movements?' Arthur had rehearsed nothing. He was totally unprepared. 'What do you mean?'

'It's quite simple. I'd just like to know how you spent last evening.'

'I was here, in my flat. I was here from the time I got in from work at six-thirty. I didn't go out.'

'Alone?'

Arthur nodded. He felt faint, sick. The man didn't believe him. A blank, almost disgusted, incredulity showed in his face, and his lip curled above those hideous teeth.

'According to my information, you spent the evening with Mr Winston Mervyn, Mr Brian Kotowsky and a man called Potter.'

And now Arthur didn't understand at all. Fleeting images of the Grand Duke, of Dean's profile, appeared on his mind's eye, but surely . . . Then came light.

'I think you are mistaking me for Mr *Anthony* Johnson who lives on the ground floor. Room 2.' Firmly now, as he saw he had been right, that Glass had made a mistake, he added, 'I was at home on my own all evening.'

'Sorry about that, Mr Johnson. An understandable confusion. Then you can't help us as to the whereabouts of Mr Kotowsky?'

'I know nothing about it. I hardly know him. I keep myself to myself.' But Arthur had to know, had to discover before Glass departed, why he had come to this house – why here? 'This murder – you're connecting Mr Kotowsky with it?'

'Inevitably, Mr Johnson,' said Glass, opening the front door. 'It is Mrs Vesta Kotowsky who has been murdered.'

# 14

Anthony spent the day in the college library and it was nearly five when he reached Kenbourne Lane tube station on his way home. There on the newsboards he read: *Murder of Kenbourne Woman* and *Kenbourne Killer slays again?* Though he was necessarily interested in what leads men to kill, murder itself fascinated him not at all, so he didn't buy a paper. Helen's letter would be waiting for him, and since leaving the library his whole mind had been possessed by speculating as to what she would say.

251

The hall table was piled with correspondence, a heap of it, for once not carefully arranged. Anthony leafed through it. Three specifications from estate agents for Winston, Li-li's Taiwan letter, a bill for Brian, a bill for Vesta, a bill that would have to be re-directed for Jonathan Dean. Nothing for him. Helen hadn't written. For the first time since he had moved into 142 Trinity Road, a Tuesday and a Wednesday had gone by without a letter from her. But before he could begin to wonder about this omission, whether he had been too harsh with her, whether she was afraid to write, the front door opened and Winston Mervyn and Jonathan Dean – who as far as he knew didn't know each other, had never met – came into the hall together.

'When did they let you off the hook?' said Winston. 'We must have missed you.'

'Hook?' said Anthony.

'I mean we didn't see you at the police station.'

Anthony thought he had never seen Jonathan Dean look so grim, so spent, and at the same time so much like a real person without pose or role. 'I'm not following any of this.'

'He doesn't know,' said Jonathan. 'He doesn't know a thing. Vesta was murdered last night, Tony, strangled, and Brian's disappeared.'

They went up to Winston's room because it was bigger and airier than Anthony's. Jonathan looked round his old domain with sick eyes, and finding no hackneyed line of verse or prose to fit the situation, stretched himself full-length on the old red sofa. A freezing fog, white in the dusk, pressed smokily against the window. Winston drew the sparingly-cut curtains.

'The police came here at half-past seven this morning,' he said. 'They couldn't get an answer from Brian, so they came to me. They wanted to know when I'd last seen Brian and what sort of a mood he was in. I told them about last night. I had to.'

'You told them about all those insinuations of Potter's, d'you mean?'

'I had to, Anthony. What would you have done? Said Brian was sober and calm and went off to bed in a happy frame of mind? They rooted Potter out, anyway. He must have missed his match. Presumably, after that, they thought they wouldn't bother with you. And Potter must have remembered, hangover or not, because they got me down to the station and asked me if Brian had been in a jealous rage. I had to say he'd gone off looking for Vesta and *him*.' Winston waved his hand in the direction of the recumbent Dean.

'But it was rubbish,' said Anthony. 'It was Potter's drunken fantasy. There wasn't any foundation for it, we all know that.'

'But there was,' said Jonathan Dean.

'You mean, you and Vesta . . . ?'

'Oh, God, of *course*. That's why I moved away. We couldn't do it here, could we? In the next room to the poor old bastard. Christ, I was with her yesterday. We spent the afternoon and most of the evening together and then we went off for a drink in the Grand Duke. She left me just before eleven to get the last bus.'

Anthony shrugged. He felt cold, helpless. 'You said Brian had disappeared?'

Jonathan ran his fingers through his untidy ginger hair. 'I haven't been living in that bloody awful hole for the past week. It stinks and it's over-run with mice. My sister said I could stay in her place while she's away in Germany. She's got a flat in West Hampstead. I went back there last night from the Duke. I got there about midnight and Brian turned up around half-past. He was pissed out of his mind and he was making all sorts of threats and accusations, only he passed out and I put him to bed.'

'But how did he know you'd be there?'

'God knows. I've gone there before when my sister's been away.' Jonathan shivered. 'The thing is, Vesta could have told him before he . . .'

'Then where is he now?'

Jonathan shook his head. 'I left him there and went to work. The fuzz got hold of me at about midday and I told them everything, but when they got to my sister's Brian had gone. They're searching for him now. It's no good looking like that, Tony old man, he must have done it. Why else would he vanish?'

'He could have gone out and seen an evening paper and panicked. I don't believe him capable of murder.'

253

'D'you think I do? D'you think I like thinking that way about my old pal? We were like – like two red roses on one stalk.'

Perhaps it was the crass ineptitude of this quotation, or the fact that, in these circumstances, Jonathan had quoted anything at all, which made Winston round on him. 'If he did do it, it's your fault. You shouldn't have messed about with his wife.'

'You lousy black bastard!' Jonathan turned his face into the sofa arm and his body shook. 'God, I could do with a drink.'

Not at all put out by the offensive epithets, Winston said calmly, 'I wonder how many thousand times the ears of these walls have heard those words?' He shook Jonathan vigorously. 'Why I didn't leave you on the steps of the nick for the dustmen to pick up I'll never know. Get up, if you want that drink. But we're not showing our faces in the Waterlily till all this fuss has died down.'

'They say,' said Barry, 'as that bird as was done in lived in your house. Is that a fact?'

'Yes,' said Arthur.

'Only they don't give you no number in the paper, just Trinity.' Barry spooned sugar from the basin into his mouth and crunched it. 'Here,' he said, and thrust the *Evening Standard* under Arthur's nose.

*The body of a woman, Mrs Vesta Kotowsky, 36, of Trinity Road, Kenbourne Vale, West London, was found in Oriel Mews, Kenbourne Vale, early this morning. She had been strangled. Police are treating the case as murder.*

The print swam. Other words were superimposed on it. *The body of a woman, Maureen Cowan, 24, of Parsloe Street, Kenbourne Vale, West London, was last night found on a footpath adjacent to Kenbourne Vale Cemetery. Police are treating the case . . . The body of a woman, Bridget O'Neill, 20, student nurse . . .*

Strangers to him, utter strangers. He had never even looked into their faces. Had he ever looked into any woman's face but Auntie Gracie's and Beryl's?

Beryl was Mrs Courthope's daughter. When he came home and found her there one evening, drinking tea with Auntie Gracie out of those china cups he now possessed

254

and cherished, he had been jealous of her presence. Who was she to break in on their cloistered world? And she had been there again and again after that, sometimes with her mother, sometimes alone. It was better when her mother was there because then Auntie Gracie stayed in the room too instead of leaving Arthur and Beryl together. He had never known what to say when he was alone with Beryl, and now he couldn't remember whether he had so much as uttered a word. He couldn't remember whether Beryl was pretty or plain, talkative or silent, and he doubted whether he had known at the time. He was indifferent to her.

But she liked him, Auntie Gracie said.

'Beryl likes you very much, Arthur. Of course, that's not surprising. You're steady, you've got a good job, and though I shouldn't tell you so, you're a very nice-looking young man.'

Beryl started coming with them to the Odeon. Auntie Gracie always arranged it so that Beryl sat between them. He dared to say he had liked things better before they knew Beryl and had been alone together.

'There's no reason why we should ever be apart, Arthur. This is a big house. I have always intended you to have the top floor to yourself one day.'

He didn't know what she meant or why she was hoarding her clothes coupons or examining so closely the best of the linen she had kept packed away for so long or talking of furniture being so hard to get in this aftermath of wartime. He didn't like being left with Beryl and talked about among Auntie Gracie's particular friends as if Beryl were his particular friend.

The night it had happened was the night Auntie Gracie had such a bad headache she couldn't face the Odeon and the film about American soldiers in the Pacific. Arthur said that in that case he wouldn't go either.

'You must, Arthur. You can't let Beryl down. She's been looking forward to going out with you all the week. You don't realize how fond of you she is. I know you're fond of her too, only you're shy. You haven't been friendly with any other girls, I'm glad to say.'

Friendly . . . Beryl came to the house in Magdalen Hill and they set off together in silence. But when they had to

255

cross the road she took his arm and held on to it all the way to the cinema. Her body was warm and clinging. Suddenly she began to talk. Her talk was madness. He thought she was mad.

'I've never had a boy friend before, Arthur. Mother wouldn't let me go out with boys till you came along. I know I'm not very attractive, nothing special, but I could have had boy friends. Now I'm glad I waited. Mother's told me, you see.'

He said hoarsely, 'Told you what?'

'That you like me very much, only you're too shy to say so. I like shy boys. I've been hoping and hoping for weeks you'd ask me to go out with you alone and now you have.'

'My aunt's ill. That's why she hasn't come, because she's ill.'

'Oh, *Arthur*. You don't have to pretend any more. I know you've been trying to put her off coming with us for weeks and weeks.'

They went into the cinema. Sweets were just coming back into the shops. He bought her a bag of things called Raspberry Ruffles and muttered to her that he had to go to the gents'. 'I want to be excused,' was what he said like you said in school. There was an emergency exit between the foyer and the lavatory. Arthur walked straight out of it into the street. He walked and walked until he had put two miles between himself and Beryl, and then, for the first time in his life, he went into a pub. There he drank brandy because he didn't know what else to order.

Soon after ten he left and began to walk home along the path that bordered the cemetery. There was a girl standing near the end of the path, and as he came up to her she said good evening. Later, he had learned she was a prostitute, waiting for the pubs to turn out, though at the time he had scarcely known of the existence of prostitutes.

He went up to her and put his hand into his pocket where he had stuffed his scarf. Perhaps she thought he was feeling for his wallet, for she moved towards him and put her hand on his arm. He strangled her then, and she was too surprised to struggle or cry out. Afterwards, when he understood what he had done, he knew he would be caught, tried, hanged – but nothing had happened. The police never came to the house in Magdalen Hill, and if they had they would have discovered nothing, for Beryl told neither his aunt nor her mother that he had left her alone in the Odeon. She gave them the impression that it was she who had jilted him, left him finally at eleven that night and never wanted to see him again. Auntie Gracie was hot against her for her ingratitude and her fickleness, and of course she understood why Arthur, disappointed in love, fell ill suddenly from some virus the doctors couldn't diagnose and was off work for six weeks. He never saw Beryl again, though later he heard that she had married a greengrocer and had two children . . .

'Reckon her old man done it,' said Barry.

Arthur couldn't summon the energy necessary to rebuke Barry for this slangy, coarse and ungrammatical usage. He digested the sense behind the words. They would suppose Kotowsky had done it. Glass, evidently, already supposed so. But Arthur was still unable to struggle out of the paralysis of fear in which he had been gripped since eight-thirty. Impossible to get over the fact – yet equally impossible to grasp the full significance of it – that he had not only killed a woman he knew but one who lived in the same house. Impossible too to forget or come to terms with another aspect. He had lied to Inspector Glass, that piranha-faced man, lied under the pressure of panic and forgetting that his lie could easily be detected. Anthony Johnson could show the police he had lied. Anthony Johnson, emerging from the lavatory at twenty to twelve, had seen him creeping up the stairs in the dark.

He could, of course, say he had merely been down to deposit rubbish in the dustbin. He? At that hour? In his overcoat? No, whatever he said, Anthony Johnson's testimony would be enough to draw their attention to him. And naturally Anthony Johnson would tell them. By now they would know, would perhaps be waiting for him at 142 Trinity Road.

Arthur went back there because he had nowhere else to go. No police car, no policeman in the hall. He stood in the hall, listening, wondering if they were up there on the top landing. A door above him crashed for all the world as if Jonathan Dean were back. And he was. Arthur stared. Jonathan Dean was coming downstairs with that black man and Anthony Johnson.

He managed to say good evening. Winston Mervyn said good evening back, but Jonathan Dean said nothing. He was drunk perhaps. He looked drunk, leaning on Mervyn's arm, his face grey and puffy. They went out into the street. Anthony Johnson said, 'I'll be with you in a minute,' and turned away to the hall table where he began sifting through the heap of letters Arthur hadn't felt capable of arranging methodically that morning. Arthur couldn't leave him to it and go upstairs. He edged along the hall almost shyly, but his heart was pounding with terror.

Anthony Johnson was looking annoyed. He said rather absently to Arthur, 'An awful thing, this murder.'

Arthur found a voice, a husky weak voice that came from somewhere in the back of his neck. 'Have the police – have they interviewed you?'

And now Anthony Johnson turned round to face him, his blue eyes very penetrating. 'No, they haven't, oddly enough. I'm surprised because I do have things to tell them.'

'I see.' Arthur could hear his own voice as strange, as throaty. 'Will you – will you go and tell them off your own bat, as it were?'

'I shouldn't think so. They can come to me if they want me. I don't see myself as the instrument of justice or the means of shutting a man up for life. Except, maybe, in very special circumstances. I mean, if an injury were done to me or mine, for instance.'

Arthur nodded. Relief caused sweat to break over him, flushing him with heat. Anthony Johnson's meaning was unmistakable, hardly veiled, and as if to reinforce it, as Arthur began to walk away, he called:

'Mr Johnson?'

'Yes?'

'I've been meaning to thank you for that note you left me. It was weeks ago but we don't seem to have met since. You remember? When you opened my letter by mistake?'

'Yes.'

'It was thoughtful of you to leave that note.' Anthony Johnson's voice was very gentle now, very considerate. Was he imagining the hint of menace that underlay it or was that menace really there? 'I wouldn't like you to think I'd bear a grudge. It wasn't as if it was a very personal letter.'

'Oh, no.' Arthur stammered. 'No, indeed. A personal letter – that would be a dreadful intrusion.' He cleared his throat. 'An injury,' he said.

# 15

Brian Kotowsky was the only son of Polish Jews, now dead, who had emigrated to this country in the nineteen thirties. Stanley Caspian told Arthur that Jonathan Dean and Vesta's brother were the only close associates Brian had had. They had been, therefore, closely questioned by the police as to his possible hiding place. The brother-in-law remembered hearing of an aunt of Brian's, his mother's sister, who lived in Brighton, but when the police went to her house they found that she had been in hospital for a minor operation since the day before Vesta's death.

'I don't know.' By this Arthur meant he didn't know how Stanley could know so much. Some grass roots system, perhaps, that had often proved reliable in the past.

'He'll have skipped off to South America,' said Stanley, jabbing full stops into Li-li Chan's rent book. 'They must have had a fortune stashed away, him and her, considering they were both working and not paying me more than a poxy fourteen quid a week for that flat.'

'Two rooms,' said Arthur absently.

'A two-roomed flat with fridge and immersion heater. Cheap at the price. Put the kettle on, me old Arthur. Mrs Caspian's sister's mother-in-law's got a pal who knows a chap that keeps a papershop up West Hampstead, West End Lane, and he told the pal he'd been helping the police in their enquiries on account of Kotowsky going in there Wednesday morning to get some fags and a paper. Identified him, this papershop chap did, from photos. And he's the last living soul to have set eyes on him. Have a bit of pie?'

'No, thank you,' said Arthur.

'God knows what he was doing in Hampstead. It's more than I can understand, a chap killing his own wife, me and

Mrs Caspian having been a pair of real lovebirds all our married life. A cream passionate is what they call it. Thank God it wasn't under my roof. There's nothing like that to give a place a bad name. What's worrying me is when I'll be able to re-let the flat. I can't afford to take a drop in my income at this juncture, I can tell you.'

'I shouldn't wonder,' said Arthur with malice, 'if the authorities don't seal it up for months and months. And now, if I might have my little envelope?'

In his pocket was another, mauve-grey, postmarked Bristol, which he had picked up from the doormat ten minutes before. Who could have suspected that she would write again, having been turned down, or apparently turned down, and send a letter to arrive on a Saturday? However, because Stanley Caspian was already parking his car at the kerb, he had snatched it up. Now he wondered why, for he intended no further revenge on Anthony Johnson. Far from it. Just as Anthony Johnson had forgiven him for opening that letter from the council, so he would forgive Anthony Johnson for that act of destruction by fire. *Must* forgive him, because now he was entirely in Anthony Johnson's power.

Dropping the Bristol letter on his kitchen table, Arthur forced himself to think clearly. Anthony Johnson had said plainly that he wouldn't pardon the theft of a personal letter. No letter could be more personal than last Tuesday's. Therefore, he must never know that Arthur had taken it. He would surely go to the police and tell what he had seen if he suspected Arthur of interfering with his correspondence. So Anthony Johnson must have this letter. But what if H. mentioned in it that she had written before? Arthur plugged in his electric kettle. The envelope flap reacted obediently to the jet of steam and curled easily away. With extreme care, he took out the sheet of flimsy.

*Darling Tony, Why haven't I heard from you? I couldn't believe it when the post brought me nothing from you. Letters don't go astray, do they? But the alternative is that you didn't want to write, that you're angry with me, making me wait now as I made you wait in the past. Or is it that you need time to think in, to make plans for where we shall live and so on? I see you may need time to adjust to a new life and disrupt the new one you have already made. But if you need weeks, if you want* to wait till your term ends, can't you understand that I'll understand? I'm so entirely yours now, Tony, that I'll do anything you ask. Only don't let me endure suspense, don't leave me in fear.

But there isn't any real need to be frightened, is there? I know you'll write. Is it possible that someone living in your house would take your letters by mistake? Surely, no one who did that would keep a letter like mine, a true love letter. And yet I hope and hope this is what happened. Or that this murder in your street I've read about in the newspapers has somehow made the police take people's post.

Because I have to believe you didn't get my letter, I'll repeat what I said in it, that I'll leave Roger and come to you whenever you like. Your most devoted and loving, H.

Arthur read it several times. He wondered at the emotion conveyed in it. Strange that anyone could put such exaggerations, such drama, on paper. But her guesswork was correct. Her previous letter had been purloined by someone living in the house, and therefore Anthony Johnson must no more receive this one than he had received the last. He must never be allowed to receive any letter in a mauve-grey envelope, postmarked Bristol. . . .

When nothing had arrived from Helen by the weekend, Anthony's attitude towards her wavered between resentful anger and the more reasonable feeling that her letter had got lost in the post. She would, in any case, write again next week. It brought him a small bitter pleasure to think she might have written to say she had made up her mind in his favour. How ironical if it were that letter which had got lost and she now be wondering if he were paying her back in her own coin. But he didn't really think she would have decided for him. The likeliest answer was that she had written with her usual ambivalence, given the letter to some colleague or friend to post, and it lay even now in that friend's pocket or handbag.

On Saturday night he phoned Linthea, but she was out and Leroy's sitter answered. However, on Sunday evening she was free and Anthony was invited to the flat in Brasenose Avenue.

The Sunday newspapers all had photographs of Brian Kotowsky, dog-faced Brian with his wild hair and his unhappy eyes. *Police Mount Massive Search for Vesta's Husband.* She was Vesta now to everyone, a household word, her christian name on the lips of strangers enough to summon up immediate images of violence, terror, passion, death. But, keeping their options open, the less genteel of the Sundays also carried whole page spread stories entitled in one case, *Was Vesta Kenbourne Killer's Victim?* and in another, echoing poor Brian's own words, *Kenbourne Killer Strikes Again?*

Linthea, in the kitchen making Chicken Maryland, talked about the murder practically, logically, like a character in a detective story. 'If Brian Kotowsky did kill her, he can't have gone straight to find this Dean because he left your house at a quarter to eleven and she didn't leave the Grand Duke till ten minutes later. So they're saying he hung about in the street on a freezing cold night on the chance she'd come that way and at that time. When she did come they didn't go home to quarrel but quarrelled in a pitch-black mews where he killed her. And that's ridiculous.'

'We don't know what they're saying.'

'The police always think murdered wives have been murdered by their husbands, and considering what I see in my work every day almost, I know why.'

He thought how Helen would have spoken of it, with intuition, using her rich imagination to clothe that night and the players in its drama. But Linthea looked coolly and prosaically at things as he did. Linthea had more in common with him than Helen had. Strange that the girl gifted with the delicate perception, the passionate imagination, should look so cool and fair, the calm and practical one so exotic. Tonight Linthea's long black hair hung loose down her back. She wore a heavy gold chain about her neck which threw a yellow gleam up against her throat and chin. He wondered about that dead husband of hers and whether she now lived a celibate life.

Later, when they had eaten and she had exhausted the subject of the Kotowskys, completed her analysis of times and circumstances and likelihood, he felt an overpowering urge to confide in her about Helen. But that brought him back to where he had been once before. Can you, if you want to make love to a woman, confess to her your present,

262

strong and angry love for another woman? Certainly not with her son in the room, pressing you to a game of Scrabble.

'You're keeping him up late,' he said at last.

'He's on half-term. No school tomorrow, no work for me.' She had a merry laugh, evoked by very little, as some West Indians have. 'Scrabble's good for him, he can't spell at all. How will you grow up,' she said, hugging the boy, 'to be a big important doctor like Anthony if you can't spell?'

So they played Scrabble till midnight when Leroy went to bed and Linthea said very directly, 'I shall send you home now, Anthony. You must be fresh for your psychopaths in the morning.'

He didn't feel very fresh on Tuesday morning because he had awakened at four and been unable to sleep again. All day he wondered if a letter would be waiting for him when he got home, though he refused to give way to the impulse that urged him to go home early and find out. But when he returned at five there was no letter. No post had come that day for the occupants of 142 Trinity Road and the table was bare. So, on the following morning, beginning now to feel real anxiety, he waited at home until the post came, and at nine he took it in himself. Two letters, one for Li-li, one for Winston. It was now two whole weeks since he had heard from Helen.

Two of her letters couldn't have gone astray. He considered breaking her rule and phoning her at work. She was assistant to the curator of a marine art museum. But why give her what she wanted, a lover content to hang on, playing the *amour courtois* game, while she gave him nothing? No, he wouldn't phone. And maybe he wouldn't phone on the last Wednesday of the month either. By that time, anyway, he might have managed to console himself. Linthea, he thought, Linthea who had no ties, who lived in and worked for a society he understood, who wasn't effete with poetry and dream and metaphor and a jelly-like sensitivity that melts at a hard touch. Above all, this mustn't affect his thesis. He had begun to write it in earnest and it was going well. Now, having dealt in depth with the findings of various psychometric tests, he wrote:

263

*In the survey it was suggested that the majority of psycho-
paths feared their own aggression and were as guilt-and
anxiety-ridden about their acts as were the normal subjects. In
their manner of relating to female and authority figures, a
greater disturbance was found in psychopaths than in non-psy-
chopaths, but whereas more guilt feelings were present in the
former, further analysis shows that the guilt feelings of psychopaths were indicative rather of their difficult and disagreeable
situation than of true remorse. The psychopath, when offered a
choice between selfish forms of conduct and those which seem
self-denying and are therefore socially acceptable, may be
shrewd enough to choose the latter. When obliged to be guided
solely by his own judgement, his choice is directed primarily by
personal need. . . .*

A tap on the door, discreet and somehow insinuating,
interrupted Anthony. Arthur Johnson stood outside,
dressed as usual in one of his silver-sheened suits and a shirt
as white as that in a detergent commercial. He gave a small
deprecating cough.

'I do most sincerely apologise for this intrusion, but
I have to trouble you about the little matter of the rent.
Your – er, first weekly payment in advance falls due tomor-
row.'

'Oh, sure,' said Anthony. 'Will a cheque do?'

'Admirably, admirably.'

While Anthony hunted out his cheque book which was
sandwiched between Sokolov's *The Conditioned Reflex* and
Stein's *Role of Pleasure in Behaviour*, Arthur Johnson, in a
finicky manner, waved at him a small red rent book and a
brown envelope on which was printed with a touching
attention to detail: Mr Anthony Johnson, Room 2, 142
Trinity Road, London W15 6HD.

'If you would be good enough to place your cheque
inside your rent book each Friday and the book inside this
little envelope? Then I will either collect it or you may leave
it on the hall table.'

Anthony nodded, wrote his cheque.

'Thank goodness, the police have ceased to trouble us.'

'They haven't troubled me at all yet,' said Anthony.

'Of course, there can be no doubt in anyone's mind that
Mr Kotowsky is guilty. He's known to be in South America
but he will be extradited.'

'Oh, rubbish,' said Anthony rather more roughly than he intended. 'And there's plenty of doubt in my mind. I don't believe for a moment he did it.'

Arthur had been rather perturbed during the previous week to observe that on two mornings the post had been taken in by someone else. But that hadn't happened since Saturday – thanks to his watching from his living room window for the postman to appear round the corner of Camera Street, and taking care to be down in the hall in good time. In any case, no further mauve-grey envelopes had arrived. The woman wouldn't write again. She had now been twice rebuffed and she wouldn't risk a further snub. Tuesday, 19 November, and Wednesday, 20 November, went by. Those were crucial days, but they brought Anthony Johnson only a letter from York from his mother. Arthur felt more relaxed and peaceful than he had done since the night of 5 November, and although it gave him a certain bitterness to notice, now when it was too late and unimportant, that twice this week already no light had fallen from the window of Room 2 on to the courtyard in the evenings, the cause of Anthony Johnson's absence from the house pleased him. Very little that went on escaped Arthur. He had seen that black woman call at the house with her black child. He had seen her call alone. Sometimes he had seen their silhouetted faces cast on the green stones of the yard. And when he saw Anthony Johnson depart with a bottle of wine under his arm, he knew whose home he was bound for. Much as Arthur deplored the idea of a clean fair-haired young Englishman getting involved with a black woman, it would divert Anthony Johnson's attention from Bristol.

Friday, 22 November, dawned cold and wet. Arthur saw Anthony Johnson leave the house at eight-thirty and Winston Mervyn follow him five minutes later. Then Li-li Chan emerged. She stood at the front gate under a red pagoda umbrella, scanning the cars that turned into Trinity Road from Magdalen Hill. Then the front door slammed with a Dean-like crash and Arthur heard her platform soles clumping up the stairs. He opened his door and put it on the latch.

Li-li was on the phone.

'You say you come at eight-thirty. You are oversleeping? Why don't you buy alarm clock? I am late for my work.

265

You would not oversleep if I sleep with you?' Arthur clicked his tongue at that one. 'Perhaps I will, perhaps I won't. Of course I love you. Now come quick before I get sack from my job.'

It was five to nine before the car came for her, an ancient blue van this time. Arthur went down to take in the post. There was nothing on the mat, so presumably the postman hadn't yet come. But as he turned back into the hall, he saw that the table which on the previous night had been bare even of vouchers, now held a pile of envelopes. The post must have come early and while he was listening to Li-li's phone conversation. She had taken it in herself.

His own new Barclaycard, two circulars for Winston Mervyn and – unbelievable but real – a mauve-grey envelope postmarked Bristol. H. had written again. Was there no stopping her? Arthur held the envelope in his fingertips, held it at arm's length as if it might explode. Well, he had decided no Bristol letter must ever be allowed to reach Anthony Johnson and that decision should stand. Better burn the thing immediately as he had burned the last. And yet . . . A thrill of fear touched him. Li-li had taken that letter in, might or might not have noticed it. But how could he be sure she hadn't? If Anthony Johnson began to wonder why no letter had come for him for three weeks and started asking around – following up, in fact, H's suggestion, though it had never been communicated to him – then Li-li would remember.

Again he steamed open the envelope.

*Darling Tony, What have I done? Why have you rejected me without a word? You begged me to make up my mind and let you know as soon as I could. I did let you know by the Tuesday. I told you I was willing to leave Roger as soon as I heard from you and that I'd come to you. That was November 5th and now it's November 21st. Please tell me what I did and where I went wrong. Is it because I said I couldn't promise to love you for ever? God knows, I've wished a thousand times I'd never written those words. Or is it because I said I hadn't told Roger? I would have told him, you must believe me, as soon as I'd heard from you.*

*I think I've lost you. In so far as I can think rationally at all, I think I shall never see you again. Tony, you would have pity on me if you knew what black despair I feel, as if I can't go on another day. I would even come to you, only I'm terrified of your anger. You said there are other women in the world. I am afraid to come and find you with another girl. It would kill me. You said I was the only woman you had ever felt real passion for, apart from wanting them as friends or to sleep with. You said you thought 'in love' was an old-fashioned meaning-less expression, but you understood it at last because you were in love with me. These feelings can't have been destroyed be-cause I wrote tactless silly things in my first letter. Or weren't they ever sincere?*

*Roger has gone to Scotland on business. He's to be there at least a fortnight and wanted me to go with him, only I can't get time off from work till next Wednesday. Tony, while I'm alone here, please will you phone me at home? At any time during the weekend – I won't leave the house – or next week in the evenings. I beg you to. If I ever meant anything to you in the past, if only for what we once were to each other, I beg you to phone me. If it's only to say you don't want me, you've changed your mind, I want to hear you saying it. Don't be so cruel as to let me wait by the phone all the weekend. I can take it – I think – if you say you've changed. What I can't take is this awful silence.*

*But, Tony, if you don't phone, and I have to face the possi-bility that you won't, I shan't write again. I don't know what I shall do, but what little pride I have left will keep me from throwing myself at you. So whatever happens now, this is my last letter. H.*

That, Arthur thought, re-reading the last sentence, was at any rate something to be thankful for. But if Anthony Johnson saw this letter he'd be on the phone at once, tonight. And in their conversation it would all come out, the dates she'd written and the things she'd written. Yet Anthony Johnson must see this letter because Li-li Chan had already seen it.

By now it was almost twenty past nine. Arthur con-sidered not going to work, phoning Mr Grainger and saying he'd got this gastric bug that was going about. He seemed to see Auntie Gracie loom before him, shaking her head at his deceit and his cowardice. Besides, he'd have to go back tomorrow or the next day. Shivering as if he were really ill, he dragged on his raincoat and took his umbrella from the rack in the hall. What to do with H's letter? Take

267

it to work and try to think of some solution. He could come home at lunchtime, anyway, in good time to restore it if he could find no alternative but to deliver it and himself into Anthony Johnson's hands.

He was late, of course, late for the first time in years. Drizzle speckled the office window, then rain gushed in sheets against the glass. In a wretched state that was intensely nervous and at the same time apathetic, Arthur opened Grainger's post, though he felt he never wanted to see another envelope as long as he lived. The handwriting of potential customers who wanted roofs re-tiled and central heating installed danced before his eyes. He typed two replies, full of errors, but at last there was nothing for it but to take H's letter out of his briefcase and scrutinise it once more.

Should he take a chance on Li-li's having failed to notice it? The chances were she hadn't noticed it among so much other stuff. Since there seemed no alternative, this was a risk he would have to take. Destroy the letter now and hope Anthony Johnson either wouldn't bother to ask her or that she wouldn't remember. He had closed his fist over the two sheets of flimsy paper when he realised, with a new terror, that even if Anthony Johnson didn't get this latest of H's letters, he would still discover the injury that had been done him. For on Wednesday, 27 November, next Wednesday, the last Wednesday in the month, he would phone H as he always did and the whole thing would come out.

Arthur ground two sheets of paper into his typewriter and struggled with a reply to a Mr P. Coleman who wanted Grainger's advice on the conversion of his nineteenth century coach-house into a dwelling for his mother-in-law. H's letter would have to go back to 142 Trinity Road by one and it was eleven now. He'd brazen it out, that was all. He'd deny in his most severe manner ever having touched Anthony Johnson's correspondence. Useless to keep turning things over in his mind like this when there was no help for it. He glanced at the sheet on which he was typing and saw he had put an H instead of a P before Coleman and 'convict' instead of 'convert'. The paper was torn out and a fresh sheet inserted. Anthony Johnson would go at once to the police. The police would stop hunting for Brian

Kotowsky and start thinking seriously about Arthur Johnson who never went out at night but who had been out that night; who was a resident of Kenbourne Vale at the time of the murder of Maureen Cowan and at the time of the murder of Bridget O'Neill: who had unaccountably lied to them. . . . He flexed his hands to try and prevent their trembling.

A mammoth effort, a mammoth concentration, and a passable letter advising Mr Coleman to consult a certain firm of Kenbourne Vale architects had been achieved. But as soon as he had done it and read it through, it struck him that if this reply came to the notice of Mr Grainger he would be very displeased indeed. Mr Grainger would expect him, while possibly mentioning the architects, to suggest that Grainger's themselves would be happy to carry out the work. The displeasure of the whole world, of everyone who mattered, loomed before him. He gave a shuddering sigh. Another, and very different, letter must be composed.

Fresh sheets of paper were in the machine before Arthur realised the significance of the words he had spoken under his breath. Another, and very different, letter must be composed. . . .

# 16

For her letters H always used the same flimsy paper Grainger's used for their carbon copies. And she used a similar typewriter to Arthur's. Suppose he himself were to type a letter to Anthony Johnson and insert it in that mauve-grey envelope? The envelope would be the original one, the postmark and its date correct, and it could be placed on the hall table in good time for Anthony Johnson to find it. Only the contents would be different.

Arthur, who had spent half a day composing with fear and extreme care that note of apology, was appalled by the magnitude and the danger of the task. And yet the letter wouldn't have to be a long one. His purpose, already half-formulated, was to make it as short as possible. He could imitate H's hysterical style – he had seen enough of it – and make the sort of errors she made, not depressing that key properly so that it made an eight instead of an apostrophe, depressing this one too long so that the second as well as the initial letter came out as upper case. And he could make the H with his own blue-black ballpoint pen.

He put two sheets of flimsy into the typewriter. The date first: 21 November, and the O of November a capital as well as the N. *Darling Tony* – no, she wouldn't call him darling for the kind of letter he meant to write. What would she call him? The only personal letters Arthur had written in his whole life were to a certain cousin of Auntie Gracie's who had sent him five-shilling postal orders on his birthdays. *Dear Uncle Alfred, Thank you very much for the postal order. I am going to save the money up in my money box. I had a nice birthday. Auntie Gracie gave me a new school blazer. With love from Arthur.* Dear Tony? In the end, not having the least idea whether people ever wrote that way, Arthur typed *Tony*. Just *Tony*.

How to begin? She was always asking him to forgive her. *Forgive me.* That was good, convincing. *I'm sorry*, he went on, taking care that an eight instead of an apostrophe appeared, *not to have written to you before as I promised.* Why hadn't she written? *I knew you would be angry if I said I couldn't make up my mind.* Good, he was doing well. But he must get on to the nub of it. *I have made it up now and I am going to stay with Roger. I am his wife and it is my duty to stay with him.* Arthur didn't like that much, it wasn't H's style, but he couldn't better it and still make her say what he meant her to say. There ought to be some love stuff. He racked his brains for something from the television or from one of those old films. *I never really loved you. It was just infatuation.* Now for the most important thing, the point of writing this letter that was primarily designed to put an end to all further communication between H and Anthony Johnson.

Barry loafed in just before one to say he had had his lunch and would be around to answer the phone while Arthur was out. It was still teeming with rain. Arthur put up his umbrella and set off for Trinity Road via the mews.

270

He passed the spot where he had strangled Vesta Kotow-sky, feeling a tickle of nostalgia and a fretful resentment against a society which had given him the need to commit such acts yet would condemn him with loathing for yield-ing to them.

The house was empty. Nothing on the table had been disturbed. Arthur checked that the flap of the mauve-grey envelope was securely gummed down, and then he placed it in the very centre of the glossy mahogany table.

The house was semi-detached, with the uncluttered lines of sixties building, of pale red bricks with big windows to let in ample light. The family who had lived there since it was new had planted each January in its front garden their Christmas trees, and these Norway spruces, ten of them, stood in a row, each one a little taller than its predecessor. Anthony, as he left the house with Winston, thought of Helen and the delight she would have taken in those Christmas trees, seeing in their arrangement the almost ritualistic placing of them, evidence of domestic harmony, quietude and a sense of permanent futurity.

The street was very quiet, a cul-de-sac. Children could play there in safety. But there were no children playing now, for it was dark, dark as midnight at six o'clock.

'What d'you think?' said Winston.

'Very nice, if you've got twenty thousand pounds. But you'll have to get married. It's no place for a bachelor. You must get married, have children, and with luck you'll be able to plant at least forty more Christmas trees.'

'Do I detect a note of sarcasm?'

'Sorry,' said Anthony. Viewing the house had made him bitter. It wasn't his ideal, too bourgeois, too dull, too sheltered, and yet – could you find a better place in which to build a marriage and raise a family? Relationships are hard to come by, and one woman may make a man very discriminating, very selective. He saw his youth wasted in hanging after Helen, their dream children vanishing in their dream mother's vacillations.

Winston said, 'I think I shall buy it. I shall come and live here among the nobs.' He pointed as they turned the cor-ner to a grander street. 'Caspian lives in one of those mini-mansions, and all made out of grinding our faces.'

They walked towards the K.12 stop. A thin cold drizzle was falling. It laid a slimy sheen on pavements and on the darker tarmac of the roadway, which threw back glittering yellow and red reflections of lamps. The neighbourhood changed abruptly as London neighbourhoods do. Once again they were among the tenements, the dispirited rows of terraced cottages without gardens or fences, the corner shops, the new housing blocks.

'You can always tell council flats by the smallness of their windows,' said Anthony. 'Have you noticed?'

'And their hideous design. It comes of giving second-rate architects a chance to experiment on people who can't afford to refuse.'

'Unlike lucky you.'

'In a filthy temper tonight, aren't you? Excuse me, I'm going in here to get a paper.'

Anthony waited at the door. What was happening to him that he could be rude and resentful to this new friend he liked so much? He stood in the now fast-falling rain, feeling depression settle on him. Friday night, Friday, 22 November. He had to get through another five days of this, five days till the last Wednesday of the month. But then he would phone her, certainly he would. He thought of her face that he hadn't seen for two months. It appeared before his eyes like a ghost face in mist, delicate, sensitive, contrite, wistful. The last time he had made love to her – he remembered it now, her eyes open and watching his eyes, her smile that had nothing to do with amusement. To have that again, even impermanently, even deferred, wasn't it worth sacrificing his pride for that, his ideal of himself as strong and decisive, for that? Yes, on Wednesday he would beg and persuade all over again, he would begin again. . . .

Winston came out of the shop, holding the paper up, reading the front page. He came up to Anthony, thrust the paper at him.

'Look.'

The first thing Anthony saw was the photograph of Brian, the uncompromising passport photograph that had appeared so many times already, day after day, in every newspaper. The mop of hair, the wizened yet flaccid face, the eyes that ever seemed to implore, ever to irritate with their silliness. First the picture, then the headline: *Vesta's Husband Found Drowned*. The account beneath those huge black letters was brief.

*The body of a man washed up on the beach at Hastings, Sussex, was today identified as that of Brian Kotowsky, 38, husband of Vesta Kotowsky, strangled on Guy Fawkes Day in Kenbourne Vale, West London. Mr Kotowsky had been missing since the day following his wife's death.*

*Mr Kotowsky, an antique dealer, of Trinity Road, Kenbourne Vale, was known to have relatives in Brighton.*

*His aunt, Mrs Janina Shaw, said today that she had not seen her nephew for nine years.*

*'We were once very close,' she said. 'We lost touch when Brian married. I cannot say if my nephew visited my house prior to his death as I have been ill in hospital.'*

*An inquest will be held.*

Anthony looked at Winston. Winston shrugged, his face closed and expressionless. The rain fell on to the newspaper, darkening it with great heavy splashes.

On the way home they hardly spoke. With a kind of delicacy but without communicating that delicacy to each other, they avoided the mews and walked to Trinity Road by the long way round. Then Winston said:

'I shouldn't have let him go out. I should have dissuaded him and put him to bed and then none of this would have happened.'

'No one is responsible for another adult person.'

'Can you define an adult person?' said Winston. 'It isn't a matter of years.'

Anthony said no more. Entering the hall, he remembered meeting Brian there for the first time. Brian had been sitting on the stairs doing up his shoelaces and he had come up to him and said, 'Mr Johnson, I presume?' Now he was dead, had walked out into the wintry sea until he drowned. He heard Winston say, as from a long way off, that he had a date at seven-thirty, that he must hurry.

'And I must do some work. Have a good time.'

'I'll try. But I wish I hadn't seen a paper till tomorrow morning.'

Winston set his foot on the bottom stair, then, having glanced over the banisters, turned and walked up to the table. He picked up three envelopes. 'Now I've decided on

273

my house, I must remember to tell these agents to stop sending me stuff.' He handed a fourth envelope to Anthony, a mauve-grey one with a Bristol postmark. 'Here's one for you,' he said.

At last, after so long, she had written. To say she wanted his patience a little longer? That she had been ill? Or, wonder of wonders, that she was coming to him? He unlocked his door and kicked on the switch of the electric fire. A single thumb thrust split open the flap of the envelope. He pulled out the sheet of flimsy. Just one sheet? That must mean she had hardly anything to say, that she had settled in his favour. On the brink of a happy upheaval of his life, of consummation, he read it.

*Tony, Forgive me. I'm sorry not to have written to you before as I promised. I knew you would be angry if I said I couldn't make up my mind. I have made it up now and I am going to stay with Roger. I am his wife and it is my duty to stay with him.*

*I never really loved you. It was just infatuation. You must forget me and it will soon be as if you hadn't known me.*

*Do not phone me. You mustn't try to get in touch with me at all. Not ever. Roger will be angry if you do. So remember, this is final. I shall not see you again and you must not contact me. H.*

Anthony read it again because at first he simply couldn't believe it. It was as if a letter for someone else and written by someone else had got into one of those envelopes whose colour and shape and texture had always held a magic of their own. This – this obscenity – couldn't be intended for him, couldn't have been written by her to him. And yet it had been. Her typewriter had been used, those distinctive errors were hers. He read it a third time, and now rage began to conquer disbelief. How dare she write such hideous cliché-ridden rubbish to *him*? How dare she keep him waiting three weeks and then write this? The language appalled him almost as much as the sentiments it expressed. Her duty to stay with Roger! And then that lonelyhearts novelette word 'infatuation'. 'Contact' too – journalese for approach or communicate. He examined the letter, analysing it, as if close scrutiny of semantics could keep him from facing the pain of it.

274

The truth flashed upon him. Of course. She had begun it and the remainder had been dictated by Roger. Instead of serving to pacify him, this realisation only made him angrier. She had confessed to Roger and he had compelled her to write like this. But what sort of a woman was it who would let a man take her over to that extent? And when did she think she was living, she who was self-supporting and had the franchise and was strong and healthy? A hundred years ago? A deep humiliation enclosed him as he imagined them composing that letter in concert, the woman abject and grateful for forgiveness, the man domineering, relegating him, Anthony, to the status of some gigolo.

'You give that presumptuous devil his marching orders. Let him know whose wife you are and where your duty lies. And put in something about not contacting you if he values his skin. For God's sake, Helen, make him see it's final. . . .'

Final.

He screwed the letter up, then unscrewed it and tore it into tiny shreds so that the temptation to read it again was removed.


# 17


The news of Brian Kotowsky's death reached Arthur at nine o'clock that night by way of the television. The announcer didn't say much about it, only that a drowned corpse had been identified and that there would be an inquest. But Arthur was satisfied. He had never even considered that honourable promptings of conscience might bring him qualms when Brian was tried for Vesta's murder. Brian Kotowsky was nothing to him, his indifference towards the dead man tempered only by a natural dislike of someone who got drunk and was noisy. But Kotowsky might have been acquitted. Nothing could now acquit him. His self-dealt death marked him as plainly a murderer as any confession or any trial could have done. The police would consider the case as closed.

He slightly regretted his forgery of the morning. So much of his life had been ruined by terror, so much of his time wasted by gruelling anxiety. All of it in vain. But he consoled himself with the thought that, at the time, he had no choice. Undoubtedly, Kotowsky's death hadn't appeared in the early editions of the evening papers so, even if he had bought one, he still wouldn't have known in time to avoid the substitution of the letter. But now, if Anthony Johnson were to find him out, there was no damaging action he could take. The police had a culprit, dead and speechless.

And so to get on with the business of living. Arthur watched a very old film about the building of the Suez Canal, starring Loretta Young as the Empress Eugénie and Tyrone Power as de Lesseps, till eleven. He enjoyed it very much, having seen it before with Auntie Gracie when he was thirteen. Those were the days. In euphoric mood, he really thought they had been. Saturday tomorrow. The new attendant at the launderette was Mr Grainger's nephew's wife, earning a bit of pin money, and he thought he could safely leave his washing with her while he went to the shops. Maybe he'd treat himself to a duck for Sunday by way of celebration.

There are ways and ways of ending a love affair. Anthony thought of the ways he had ended with girls in the past and the ways they had ended with him. Cool discussions, rows, pseudo-noble renunciations, cheerful let's-call-it-a-day farewells. But it had never been Helen's way. No one had rid herself of him with a curt note. And yet any of those other girls would have been more justified in doing so, for he had claimed to love none of them and offered none of them permanency. A last meeting he could have taken, a final explanation from her or even an honest letter, inviting him to phone her for a last talk. What he had received was more than he could take and he refused it. There still remained the last Wednesday of the month. Tomorrow. He would ask Linthea for the use of her phone so that there wouldn't be that hassle with the change. And Helen should learn she couldn't dismiss him as if he were some guy she'd picked up and spent a couple of nights with.

Leroy was still at school when he called at Linthea's on his way home from college. 'You're welcome,' she said,

276

'but I have to go out around eight, so when you've done your phoning, would you sit with Leroy for an hour or two?'

This wasn't exactly what Anthony had envisaged. He had seen himself needing a little comfort after speaking his mind to Helen. On the other hand, this way Linthea wouldn't have to know whom he was phoning and why. And there would be plenty of time later in the week, next week, the week after, for consolation. All the time in the world. . . .

Linthea was ready to go out when he got there and Leroy was playing Monopoly in his bedroom with Steve and David. Because it was still only ten to eight, Anthony passed the time by reading the evening paper's account of the inquest on Brian Kotowsky. Evidence was given of the murder of Brian's wife three weeks before, of his disappearance, but not a hint was breathed that Brian might have been responsible for that murder. The body had been in the sea for a fortnight and identification had been difficult. No alcohol had been present, but the cumulative effects of alcohol were found in the arteries and the liver. The verdict, in the absence of any suicide note or prior-to-death admission of unhappiness on Brian's part, was one of misadventure. In a separate paragraph Chief Superintendent Howard Fortune, head of Kenbourne Vale C.I.D., was quoted as saying simply, 'I have no comment to make at this stage.'

Eight o'clock. He would give it till ten past. Steve and David went home, and Anthony talked to Leroy, telling him stories about a children's home where he had once worked and where the boys had got out of the windows by night and gone off to steal cars. Leroy was entranced but Anthony's heart wasn't in it. At eight-fifteen he put the television on, gave Leroy milk and biscuits and shut himself up in Linthea's bedroom where she had a phone extension.

He dialled the Bristol number and it began to ring. When it had rung twelve times he knew she wasn't going to answer. Would she, after all there had been between them, just sit there and let the phone ring? She must know it was he. He dialled again and again it rang unanswered. After a while he went back to Leroy and tried to watch a quiz

277

programme. Nine o'clock came and he forgot all about sending Leroy off to bed as he had promised. Again he dialled Helen's number. She had gone out, he thought, guessing he would phone. That was how she intended to behave if he tried to 'contact' her. And when Roger was at home and the phone rang they would have arranged it so that he answered. . . . He put the receiver back and sat with a contented little boy who didn't get sent to bed until five minutes before his mother came home with Winston Mervyn.

'I don't owe you anything for the call,' said Anthony. 'I couldn't get through.'

He went home soon after and lay on his bed, thinking of ways to get in touch with Helen. He could, of course, go to her house. He could go on Saturday, it was only two hours to Bristol in the train. Roger would be there, but he wasn't afraid of Roger, his guns and his rages. But Roger would be *there*, would possibly open the door to him. With Roger enraged and belligerent, Helen frightened and obedient according to what she had the effrontery to call her duty, what could he say? And nothing would be said at all, for Roger wouldn't admit him to the house.

He could phone her mother if he knew what her mother was called or where she lived. The sister and brother-in-law? They had hardly proved trustworthy in the past. In the end he fell into an uneasy sleep. When he awoke at seven it occurred to him that he could phone her at the museum. He had never done so before because of her absurd neurosis about Roger's all-seeing eye and all-hearing ear, but he'd do it now and to hell with Roger.

He had planned to spend the day in the British Museum library but it didn't much matter what time he got there. At nine he went out and bought a couple of cans of soup at Winter's in order to get some change. On the way back he passed Arthur Johnson in a silver-grey overcoat and carrying a briefcase, the acme of respectability. Arthur Johnson said good morning and that the weather was seasonable, to which Anthony agreed absently. A hundred and forty-two was quite empty, totally silent. The seasonableness of the weather was evinced by a high wind, and little spots of coloured light cast through the wine red and sap green glass danced on the hall floor.

He went upstairs to the phone and dialled. Peep-peep-peep, and in went the first of his money. A girl's voice but not hers.

'Frobisher Museum. Can I help you?'

'I want to speak to Helen Garvist.'

'Who is that calling?'

'It's a personal call,' said Anthony.

'I'm afraid I must have your name.'

'Anthony Johnson.'

She asked him to hold the line. After about a minute she was back. 'I'm afraid Mrs Garvist isn't here.'

He hesitated, then said, 'She must be there.'

'I'm afraid not.'

Then he understood. She would have come to the phone if he hadn't given his name, if he had insisted on anonymity. But because she didn't want to talk to him, was determined at any cost not to talk to him, she had got the girl to tell this lie.

'Let me speak to the curator,' he said firmly.

'I'll see if he's available.'

The pips started. Anthony put in more money.

'Norman Le Queux speaking,' said a thin academic voice.

'I'm a friend of Mrs Helen Garvist and I'm speaking from London. From a call box. I want to speak to Mrs Garvist. It's very urgent.'

'Mrs Garvist is taking a fortnight of her annual leave, Mr Johnson.'

How readily the name came to him. . . . He had been forewarned. 'In November? She can't be.'

'I beg your pardon?'

'I'm sorry, but I don't believe you. She told you to say that, didn't she?'

There was an astonished silence. Then the curator said, 'I think the sooner we terminate this conversation the better,' and he put the receiver down.

Anthony sat on the stairs. It is very easy to become paranoid in certain situations, to believe that the whole world is against you. But what if the whole world, or those significant members of it, truly are against you? Why should Helen go away now in the cold tail end of the year? She would have mentioned something about it in her last

279

letter if she had planned to go away. No, it wasn't paranoid, it was only feasible to believe that, wanting no more of him, she had asked Le Queux and the museum staff to deny her to a caller named Anthony Johnson. Of course they would co-operate if she said this was a man who was pestering her. . . .

'Kotowsky's being cremated today.' Said Stanley Caspian.

Arthur put the rent envelopes on the desk in front of him. 'Locally?' he said.

'Up the cemetery. Don't suppose there'll be what you'd call a big turn-out. Mrs Caspian says I ought to put in an appearance but there are limits. Where did I put me bag of crisps, Arthur?'

'Here,' said Arthur, producing it with distaste from where it had fallen into the wastepaper basket.

'Poxy sort of day for a funeral. Eleven-thirty, they're having it, I'm told. Still, I should worry. I'm laughing, Arthur, things are looking up. Two bits of good news I've got. One, the cops say I can re-let Flat 1 at my convenience, which'll be next week.'

'It could do with a paint. A face-lift, as you might say.'

'So could you and me, me old Arthur, but it's not getting it any more than we are. I've no objection to the new tenant getting busy with a brush.'

'May I know your other piece of good news?'

'Reckon you'll have to, but I don't know how you'll take it. Your rent's going up, Arthur. All perfectly legal and above board, so you needn't look like that. Up to four-fifty a year which'll be another two quid a week in that little envelope, if you please.'

Arthur had feared this. He could afford it. He knew the Rent Act made provision for just such an increase in these hard times. But he wasn't going to let Stanley get away with it totally unscathed. 'No doubt you're right,' he said distantly, 'but I shall naturally have to go into the matter in my own interest. When you let me have the new agreement it would be wise for my solicitors to look at it.' As a parting shot he added, 'I fear you won't find it easy letting those rooms. Two violent deaths, you know. People don't care for that sort of thing, it puts them off.'

He took his envelope and went upstairs, his equilibrium which had prevailed, though declining, for a week, now shaken. He hoped that any prospective tenants of the Kotowskys' flat would come round while he was at home, in which case he would take care to let them know all. A gloomy day of thin fog and fine rain. Not enough rain, though, for his umbrella. The orange plastic bag of laundry in one hand, the shopping basket in the other, he set off for the launderette.

Mr Grainger's nephew's wife promised to keep an eye on his washing and pleased Arthur by commenting favourably on the quality of his bedlinen. He bought a Dover sole for lunch, a pound of sprouts, a piece of best end of neck for Sunday. The K.12 bus drew up outside the Waterlily and, on an impulse, Arthur got on it. It dropped him at the cemetery gates.

This was the old part, this end, a necropolis of little houses, the grey lichen-grown houses of the dead. Some years back a girl had been found dead on one of these tombs, a family vault. Arthur paused in front of the iron door which closed off the entrance to this cavern. He had been there before, had been inside, for the girl had been strangled and he had wondered if the police would regard her as the third of his victims, though he had been safe in those days with his white lady. Her murderer had been caught. He walked under the great statue of the winged victory, past the tomb of the Grand Duke who had given his name to the pub, on to the crematorium. The chapel door was closed. Arthur opened it diffidently.

A conversation seemed to be taking place inside, for what else can you call it when one man is speaking to one other? The man who was speaking was a clergyman and the man who was listening, sole member of that congregation, was Jonathan Dean. Brian Kotowsky had only one friend to mourn him. Music began to play, but it was muzak really, as if the tape playing in a supermarket had suddenly taken a religious turn. The coffin, blanketed in purple baize, began to move, and silently the beige velvet curtains drew together. Brian Kotowsky, like Arthur's white lady, had gone to the fire.

Arthur slipped out. He didn't want to be seen. He walked back towards the gates along another path, much over-

281

grown, this one, by brambles and the creeping ivy and long-leaved weeds the frost hadn't yet killed. Droplets of water clung to stone and trembled on leaf and twig. Presently he came to the red granite slab on which was engraved: *Arthur Leopold Johnson, 1855–1921, Maria Lilian Johnson, 1857–1918, beloved wife of the above, Grace Maria Johnson, 1888–1955, their daughter. Blessed are the dead which die in the Lord.* No room for him there, no room for his mother, though perhaps she too was dead. Perhaps that was why she hadn't come to Auntie Gracie's funeral. . . .

In his best dark suit and new black tie, he had sat in the front room of the house in Magdalen Hill, reading the paper. The paper was full of some journalist's theorizing about the Kenbourne Killer and his latest victim. He had read it while he waited for the mourners, Uncle Alfred who had sent him the birthday postal orders, the Winters, Beryl's mother, Mrs Goodwin from next door. It was she who had told him of Auntie Gracie's death.

A cold Monday in March it had been. His bedroom was icy, but no one in his milieu and at that time thought of heating bedrooms. Auntie Gracie awakened him at seven-thirty – he never questioned why he should get up at seven-thirty when he only worked next door and didn't have to be there till half past nine – awakened him and left for him in the cold bathroom a jug of hot water for shaving. Then into clean underwear because it was Monday.

'If you keep yourself clean, Arthur, you don't need clean underclothes more than once a week.'

But a fresh white shirt each day because a shirt goes on top and shows. Downstairs to the kitchen where the boiler was alight and the table laid for one. Since he became a man Auntie Gracie had put away childish things for him. She ate her breakfast before he came down and waited on him because he was now master of the house. A bowl of cornflakes, one egg, two rashers of collar bacon, it was always the same. And she had been just the same that morning, her grey hair in tight curls from the new perm she hadn't yet combed out, dark skirt, lilac jumper, black and lilac crossover overall, slippers that were so hard and plain and unyielding that you could have thought them walking shoes.

'It looks like rain.' As he emptied a plate she took it and washed it. Between washing, she stood at the window, studying the sky above the rooftops in Merton Street. 'You'd better take your umbrella.'

Once he had protested that he didn't need an umbrella to walk twenty yards through light rain or a hat to withstand ten minutes' chill or a scarf against the faintly falling snow. But now he knew better. By keeping silent he could avoid hearing the words that aroused in him impotent anger and shame: 'And when you get ill like you were last time, I suppose you'll expect me to work myself into the ground nursing you and waiting on you.'

So he kept silent and didn't even attempt to argue that he might have spent a further hour in bed rather than on a stool in front of the boiler reading the paper. She bustled about the house, calling to him at intervals, 'Ten to nine, Arthur,' 'Nine o'clock, Arthur.' When he left, allowing himself ten minutes to walk next door, she came to the front door with him and put up her cheek for a kiss. Arthur always remembered those kisses when, in his introspective moments, he reminded himself how happy their relationship had been. And he felt a savage anger against Beryl's mother for a comment she had once made.

'You give that boy your cheek like you were showing the doctor a boil on your neck, Gracie.'

That morning he had kissed her in the usual way. Many times since he had wished he had allowed his lips to linger or had put an arm round her heavy shoulders. But thinking this way was a kind of fantasising, identifying with characters from films, for he had no idea how to kiss or embrace. And he blocked off the picture at this point because, after the image of that unimaginable closeness, came a frightening conclusion of the embrace, the only possible ending to it. . . .

At eleven, when he was doing Grainger's accounts in the room at the side of the works – no little cedarwood and glass office in those days – Mr Grainger had walked in with Mrs Goodwin. He could see them now, Mr Grainger clearing his throat, Mrs Goodwin with tears on her face. And then the words: 'Passed away . . . her heart . . . fell down before my eyes . . . gone, Arthur. There was nothing anyone could do.'

Someone had been in and laid her out. Arthur wouldn't let the undertakers take the body till the following day. He knew what was right. The first night after death you watched by the dead. He watched. He thought of all she had done for him and what she had been – mother, father, wife, counsellor, housekeeper, sole friend. The large-featured face, waxen and calm, lay against a clean white pillowcase. He yearned towards her, wanting her back – for what? To be better than he had been? To please her as he had never pleased her? To explain or ask her for explanation? He didn't think it was for any of those things and he was afraid to touch her, afraid even to let one of his cold fingers rest against her colder cheek. The hammering in his head was strong and urgent.

Not for nearly six years had he been out alone at night. But at half past nine he went out, leaving Auntie Gracie on her own. He slipped through the passage into Merton Street and then he walked and walked, far away to a pub where they wouldn't know him – the Hospital Arms.

There he drank two brandies. A stretch of weed-grown bomb site separated the hospital from the embankment, the railway line and the footbridge that crossed it. Arthur didn't need to cross the line. His way home was by way of the long lane that straggled through tenements and cottages to the High Street. But he went on to the bomb site and lingered among the rubble stacks until the girl came hurrying over the bridge.

Bridget O'Neill, 20, student nurse. She screamed when she saw him, before he had even touched her, but there was no one in that empty waste land to hear her. A train roared past, letting out its double-noted bray. She ran from him, tripped over a brick, and fell. With his bare hands he strangled her on the ground, and then he left her, returning through the dark ways to Magdalen Hill. Soon he slept, falling into a sleep almost as deep, though impermanent, as that which enclosed Auntie Gracie in her last bed.

He had never tended her grave. Thick grass grew above the sides of the slab, and her christian name was obliterated by tendrils of ivy. Death surrounded him, cold, musty, mildewed death, not the warm kind he wanted. He knew he had begun to want it again, and frightened, wearied by this urge which only death itself could end, he went back to the bus, the launderette and the eternal cleaning of the flat.

Love is the cure for love. Anthony knew that, whatever might happen between him and Linthea it could at best be a distraction. But what was wrong with distractions? His love for Helen had been deep, precious, special. It was absurd to suppose that that could be replaced at will. But many activities and many emotions go under the name of love, and almost any one of them will for a while divert the mind from the real, true and perfect thing.

So he set off for Brasenose Avenue, if not a jolly thriving wooer, at least a purposeful one. In his time he had received very few refusals. His thoughts, embittered, took a base turn. Was it likely that a widow, lonely, older than himself, would turn him down? And when he rang the doorbell it was answered almost at once by Linthea herself who drew him without a word into the flat and threw her arms round his neck. Afterwards he was thankful he hadn't responded as he had wanted to. Perhaps, even at that moment, he sensed that this was a kiss of a happiness so great as to include any third party.

Winston was in the sitting room. They had been drinking champagne. Anthony stuck his bottle of Spanish Graves on top of the cupboard where it wouldn't be noticed.

'You can be the first to congratulate us,' Winston said. 'Well, not the first if you count Leroy.'

'You're getting married.' Anthony uttered it as a statement rather than a question.

'Saturday week,' Linthea said, embracing him again. 'Do come!'

'Of course he'll come,' said Winston. 'We'd have told you before, we decided a week ago, but we wanted to make sure it was all right with Leroy first.'

'And was it?'

Winston laughed. 'Fine, only when Linthea said she was marrying me he said he'd rather have had you.'

So Anthony also had to laugh at that one and drink some champagne and listen to Winston's romantic, but not sentimental, account of how he had always wanted Linthea, had lost her when she married and had later pursued her half across the world in great hope. Helen had once quoted to Anthony that it is a bitter thing to look at happiness through another man's eyes. He told himself that her quotations and her whole Eng. Lit. bit bored him, she was as

285

bad as Jonathan Dean, and then he went home to do more work on his thesis.

*Though the psychopath may suffer from compulsive urges or an obsessional neurosis, his condition is related to a lowered state of cortical arousal and a chronic need for stimulation. He may therefore face the warring elements of a routine-driven life and an inability to tolerate routine in the absence of exciting stimuli. . . .*

He broke off, unable to concentrate. This wasn't what he wanted to write. He wanted – needed – to do something he had never done before, write a letter to Helen.

# 18

He wouldn't send it to her home, that would be worse than useless. To the museum then? Although she hadn't a secretary, he remembered her telling him there was a girl who opened the incoming post for herself and Le Queuex. Her mother would do if only he knew her mother's address. He tried to remember the names of friends she had spoken of when they were together. There must be someone to whom he could entrust a letter that was for her eyes only.

Re-reading her old letters in search of a name, a clue, was a painful exercise. *Darling Tony, I knew I'd miss you but I didn't know how bad it would be. . . .* That was the one with the bit in it about an invitation to a dress show. If he'd known the name of the dress shop . . . The people she'd been to school with, to college with? He recalled only christian names, Wendy, Margaret, Hilary. Suppose he wrote to her old college? The authorities would simply forward the letter to her home. Anyone would do that unless he put in a covering letter expressly directing them not to. And could he bring himself to do that? Perhaps he could, especially as the letter he intended to write wasn't going to be a humble plea.

He wrote it. Not simply, just like that, but draft after draft until he wondered if he was as mentally unstable as the sick people he studied. The final result dissatisfied him but he couldn't improve on it.

*Dear Helen, I love you. I think I loved you from the first moment we met, and though I would give a lot to blot this feeling out and maybe be free of you, I can't. You were my whole hope for the future and it was you who gave me a purpose for my life. But that's enough of me. I don't mean to go in for maudlin self-pity.*

*This letter is about you. You led me to believe you loved me in the same way. You told me you had never loved anyone the way you loved me and that Roger was nothing to you except an object of pity. You made love with me many times, many beautiful unforgettable times, and you are not – I can tell this, you know – the kind of woman who sleeps with a man for fun or diversion. You almost promised to come away and live with me. No, it was more than that. It was a firm promise, postponed only because you wanted more time.*

*Yet you have ditched me in such a cold peremptory way that even now I can hardly believe it. When I think of that last letter of yours it takes my breath away. I don't mean to reproach you for the pain you have caused me but to ask you what you think you are doing to yourself? Have you, in these past weeks, ever asked yourself what kind of woman can live your sort of ambivalent life, pretending and lying to a husband and lover equally? What happens to that woman as she grows older and begins to lose any idea of what truth is? Life isn't worth living for someone who is a coward, a liar and has lost self-respect, particularly when she is sensitive as, God knows, you are.*

*Think about it. Don't think about me if you don't want to but think about the damage fear and woolly mindedness and that sort of confusion are going to do to whatever there is under that pretty exterior of yours.*

*If you want to see me I'll see you. But I won't commit myself to more than that now. I think I would be wilfully damaging my own self if I were ever to get back into a relationship with the kind of person you are. A.*

But who could he send it to? Who could be his go-between?

It was talking about Christmas with Winston that brought him what could be a solution. Helen had told him of friends in Gloucester with whom she and her mother and, since her marriage, Roger as well, spent every Christmas. He had never heard their address and their name eluded him, though Helen had mentioned it. She had told him, he remembered, that it was Latin for a priest. . . .

'Linthea and I,' Winston said, 'will still be on our honey-moon. Lovely having Christmas in Jamaica, only I feel a bit bad about Leroy. Maybe we ought to take him. On our *honeymoon*? Perhaps I'm being too conventional, per-haps . . .'

'What's the Latin for a priest?' said Anthony abruptly.

Winston stared at him. 'Sorry if I'm boring you.'

'You're not boring me. I hope you'll have a fabulous honeymoon. I should be so lucky. Take the whole Merton Street Primary School with you if you like, but just tell me the Latin for a priest.'

'*Pontifex, pontificis*, masculine.'

He knew it was the right name as soon as he heard it. Pontifex. He'd go to the public library, the main branch in the High Street, where they kept telephone directories for the whole country. 'Thanks,' he said.

'You're welcome,' said Winston. 'Just a dictionary, I am. Mr Liddell or Mr Scott.'

There were three Pontifexes (or *pontifices*, as Winston would have put it) in the city of Gloucester. But A.W. at 26 Dittisham Road was obviously the one, Miss Margaret and Sir F. being unlikely candidates. Anthony prepared an envelope: Mrs Pontifex, 26 Dittisham Road, Gloucester, and on the flap: Sender, A. Johnson, 2/142 Trinity Road, London, W15 6HD. The letter to Helen went into a blank, smaller envelope to be inserted inside it. But there would have to be a covering letter.

Anthony knew he couldn't write to a woman he had never met, instructing her to pass an enclosure to another woman without the knowledge of that woman's husband. But that wouldn't be necessary. Helen and Roger would arrive at the Pontifex home on, say, Christmas Eve. Mrs Pontifex would hand his letter over to Helen either when they were alone together – perhaps in Mrs Pontifex's bed-room immediately after their arrival – or else, and more likely, in public and full view of a company of festive relatives. Did that matter? Anthony thought not. This way, even if Roger were to demand to see it, Helen would see it first.

*Dear Mrs Pontifex, I know that Mrs Garvist will be spending Christmas with you and I wonder if you would be kind enough to give her the enclosed when you see her. I have mislaid her present address, otherwise I would not trouble you. Yours sincerely, Anthony Johnson.*

It looked, he thought, peculiar, to say the least. He had mislaid the address of someone with the rare name of Garvist whom he obviously knew well, but was in possession of the address of someone with the equally rare name of Pontifex whom he didn't know at all. If one name could be found in the phone book so could the other. He stuck a stamp on the envelope. He looked at this result of so much complicated effort. Was it worth it? Would any possible outcome mitigate the depression which enclosed him? The letter need not, in any case, be sent till a few days before Christmas. Pushing it to one side with a heap of books and papers and notes, he wondered if, in the end, he would send it at all.

When Arthur spoke of 'my solicitor' he meant a firm in Kenbourne Lane who had acted for him twenty years before in the matter of proving Auntie Gracie's meagre will. Since then he had never communicated with this firm or been inside its offices, but he went there now and it cost him fifteen pounds to be told that unless there were any repairs outstanding to the fabric of his flat, he hadn't a leg to stand on against Stanley Caspian in the matter of the rent increase. Although, as he put it to himself exaggeratedly, the rest of the place was falling down, Flat 2 was in fact in good order. Almost wishing that the roof would spring a leak, Arthur managed some petty revenge by telling a young couple whom he found waiting in the hall before Stanley Caspian's Saturday arrival that Flat 1 had macabre associations and that its rent could be knocked down to eight pounds a week by anyone who cared to try it on. The young couple argued with Stanley but they didn't take the Kotowskys' flat.

The police had not reappeared. Everyone took it for granted Brian Kotowsky had murdered his wife. But Arthur remembered the case of John Reginald Halliday Christie. Christie had murdered, among others, another man's wife and that man had been hanged for it. But in the end that murder had been brought home to the true perpetrator. Arthur never relaxed his surveillance of the post or failed to put his door on the latch when he heard

289

anyone use the telephone. Wednesday, 27 November, had been a bad evening but it had passed without Anthony Johnson making a call. No letters from Bristol had come for more than a fortnight. Surely there would be none? Arthur observed Anthony Johnson coming and going at his irregular hours, a little dejected perhaps as if some of that youthful glow and vigour which he had noticed on their first meeting, had gone out of him. But we all have to grow up and face, Arthur thought, the reality and earnestness of life. Once, passing beneath his window, Anthony Johnson raised a hand and waved to him. It wasn't a particularly enthusiastic wave, but Arthur would have distrusted it if it had been. It signified to him only that Anthony Johnson bore him no malice.

On the morning of Saturday, 7 December, he wrote a stiff letter to his solicitor, deprecating the high cost of such negative advice but neverthless enclosing a cheque for fifteen pounds. He always paid his bills promptly, having an undefined fear of nemesis descending should he be in debt to anyone for more than a day or two. At nine he saw the postman cross the street and he went down to take in the mail. Nothing but a rates demand for Stanley Caspian which shouldn't, by rights, have come to Trinity Road at all.

Li-li Chan's rent envelope was on the hall table and so was Winston Mervyn's. Anthony Johnson's, however, was missing. Arthur listened warily outside the door of Room 2. Silence, then the clink of a tea cup against a saucer. He knocked softly on the door and gave his apologetic cough.

'Yes?'

'It's Mr Johnson, Mr Johnson,' said Arthur, feeling this was ridiculous, but not knowing how else to put it.

'One minute.'

About a quarter of a minute passed and then the door was opened by Anthony Johnson in jeans and a sweater which had obviously been pulled on in haste. The room was freezing, the electric fire having perhaps only just been switched on. From the state of the bed and the presence on the bedside table of a half-consumed cup of tea, it was evident that Anthony Johnson had been having a lie-in. And to his caller's extreme disapproval, he intended to resume it, for, having offered Arthur a cup of tea which was refused, he got back into bed fully-clothed.

290

'I hope you'll excuse the intrusion, but it's about the little matter of the rent.'

'You needn't have bothered. I'd have put it out before Caspian came.' Anthony Johnson finished his tea. 'It's on the table,' he said casually, 'among all that other stuff.'

'All that other stuff' was a formidable array (or muddle, as Arthur put it to himself) of books, some closed, some open and face-downwards, scattered sheets of foolscap, dog-eared notebooks and a partially completed manuscript.

'With your permission,' Arthur said, and delicately picked about in the mess as if it were a pile of noxious garbage. He came upon the brown rent envelope under a weighty tome entitled *Human Behaviour and Social Processes*.

'The rent book and my cheque are in there.'

Arthur said nothing. Under the rent envelope was another, stamped and addressed, but without his glasses he was unable, from this distance, to read the address. At once it occurred to him that this letter might be to H in Bristol. He thought quickly, said almost as quickly:

'I have to go to the post with a letter of my own. Would you care for me to take this one of yours?'

Anthony Johnson's hesitation was unmistakeable. Was he remembering that other occasion on which Arthur had posted a letter for him and the unfortunate antagonism that action had led to? Or did he perhaps suspect a tampering with his post? Anthony Johnson threw back the bed covers, got up and came over to the table. He picked up the envelope and looked at it in silence, indecisively, deep in thought. Arthur managed a considerate patient smile, but inwardly he was trembling. It must be to her, it must be. Why else would the man linger over it like this, wondering, no doubt, whether posting it would risk a violent confrontation with the woman's husband.

At last Anthony Johnson looked up. He handed the letter to Arthur with a funny swift gesture as if he must either be rid of it quickly or not at all.

'O.K.,' he said. 'Thanks.'

Once more in the hall and alone, Arthur held the envelope up to within two inches of his eyes. Then he put on his glasses to make absolutely sure. But it was all right. The letter was addressed to a Mrs Pontifex in Gloucester. He was savouring his relief when Stanley Caspian banged in, sucking a toffee. Arthur put the kettle on without waiting to be asked and handed Stanley his rents. Stanley opened Winston Mervyn's envelope first.

'Well, my God, if Mervyn's not going now! Given in his poxy notice for the first week of Jan.'

'A little bird told me he's getting married.'

Stanley munched ill-temperedly, jabbing so hard into Arthur's rent book that his pen made a hole in the page. 'That'll be the whole of the first floor vacant. Makes you wonder what the world's coming to.'

'The rats,' said Arthur, 'might be said to be leaving the sinking ship.'

'Not you, though, eh? Oh, no. Those as have unfurnished tenancies don't go till they're carried out feet first. You'll die here, me old Arthur.'

'I'm sure I hope so,' said Arthur. 'Now, if I could have my little envelope?'

He took it and set off with his laundry, pausing outside Kemal's Kebab House to drop both letters in the pillar box.

# 19

During the week which followed Arthur was oppressively aware of the emptiness of 142 Trinity Road. Li-li had never been at home much, was flying to Taiwan for Christmas, and now Winston Mervyn was out every night. Soon he too would be gone. Then, if the pressure of the London housing shortage wasn't strong enough to overcome people's semi-superstitious distaste for a hundred and forty-two, he and Anthony Johnson would in effect be the sole tenants. He would once have welcomed the idea. Once he had savoured those moments when he had had the house to himself, when the last of them to leave in the mornings had given the front door a final bang. And he had dreamed of being its only occupant, living high on the crest of silent emptiness, while she who inhabited the depths below awaited the attentions and whims of her master.

But now that empty silence disturbed him. For three nights out of the seven no light fell on to the court from the window of Room 2, and the dark well he could see below him when he drew his curtains brought him temptations he had no way of yielding to. It frightened him even to think of them, but these suppressed thoughts blossomed in dreams like tubers which, put away in the dark, throw out sickly, slug-like shoots. Not since he was a young man had he dreamed of that act he had three times performed. But he dreamed of it now and awoke one morning hanging half out of bed, his hands clenched as if in spasm round the leg of his bedside table which, unknowingly, he had dragged towards him.

The postman had ceased to call. In all the years Arthur had been there no such week as this, without a single letter, had passed. It was as if the Post Office were on strike. Of course it was easily explicable. Winston Mervyn had seldom received any post except that from estate agents; Li-li's father wouldn't write when he expected to see his daughter next week; little had ever come for Anthony Johnson but those mauve-grey Bristol envelopes. And yet this also seemed to contribute to Arthur's feeling that all the forces of life were withdrawing from the house and leaving it as a kind of mausoleum for himself.

But on the morning of Saturday, 14 December, something resembling a convulsion took place in it, like a death throe. The phone ringing wakened him. It rang for Winston Mervyn three times before nine o'clock. Then he heard Winston Mervyn running up and downstairs, Anthony Johnson in Mervyn's room, Anthony Johnson and Mervyn talking, laughing. He went down to see if there was, by chance, any post. There wasn't. The door of Room 1 was open, music playing above the whine of the vacuum cleaner. Li-li had decided, unseasonably and uniquely, to springclean her room. And Stanley Caspian, usually so mindful of the fabric of his property, added to the noise by slamming the front door so hard that plaster specks lay scattered on his car coat like dandruff.

Stanley detained him so long with moans about the rates, the cruelty of the government towards honest landlords and the fastidiousness of prospective tenants, that he was late in getting to the shops. Every machine at the launderette was taken. He had to leave his washing in the care of Mr Grainger's nephew's wife who was distant with him and demanded an extra twenty pence for service.

'I never heard of such a thing,' said Arthur.

'Take it or leave it. There's inflation for me same as for others.'

Arthur would have liked to say more but he was afraid it might get back to Mr Grainger, so he contented himself with a severe, 'I'll call back for it at two sharp.'

'Four'd be more like,' said the woman, 'what with this rush,' and she paid Arthur no compliments as to the superiority of his linen.

It was a June-skied day but hazeless and clearer than any June day could be, and the sunlight was made icy by a razor wind. Angrily, Arthur shouted at the children who were climbing on the statues. They took no notice beyond shouting back at him a word which, though familiar to any resident of West Kenbourne, still brought a blush to his face.

A taxi stood outside a hundred and forty-two, and as he approached, Winston Mervyn and Anthony Johnson came out of the house and went up to it. Arthur thought how awkward and embarrassed he would feel if called upon to say to a taxi driver what Winston Mervyn now said:

'Kenbourne Register Office, please.'

He said it in a bold loud voice as if he were proud of himself, and favoured everyone with a broad smile. Arthur would have liked to pass on up the steps without a word, but he knew better than to neglect his social obligations particularly as Stanley Caspian had told him this coloured fellow, obviously well-off, was buying a house in North Kenbourne.

'Let me offer you my best wishes for your future happiness, Mr Mervyn,' he said.

'Thanks very much.'

'A fine day for your wedding,' said Arthur, 'though somewhat chilly.'

He went indoors and passed Li-li going out, her rare effort at cleaning finished or abandoned. Again he was alone. He cooked his lunch, scoured the flat, watched

Michael Redgrave in *The Captive Heart* on television. It wasn't till darkness began to close in and lights came on in the tall houses opposite that he remembered he still had to collect his washing.

Winston had engaged one of the dining rooms at the Grand Duke for his wedding reception, and there at one-thirty the bride and groom, Leroy, Anthony, Winston's brother and sister-in-law and Linthea's sister and brother-in-law sat down to lunch. Linthea gave Anthony a rose from the bouquet she was carrying.

'There, that means you'll be the next to marry.'

He felt a painful squeeze of the heart. But he smiled down at the beautiful girl in her apple green silk dress and said, 'That's only for bridesmaids.'

'For best men too. It's an old West Indian custom.'

Cries of denial, gales of laughter greeted this. Anthony made a speech which he felt was feeble, though it was received with applause. He could hardly bear to look at Winston and Linthea whose exchanged glances and secret decorous smiles spoke of happiness enjoyed and anticipated.

At four they all went back to Brasenose Avenue to collect Linthea's luggage and then to Trinity Road for Winston's. From the call box on the landing Winston phoned London Airport to check his honeymoon flight to Jamaica and was told it had been delayed three hours. By this time Leroy had already been carried off by his aunt with whom he was to stay, and Linthea felt a dislike of going back to the empty flat. At a loose end, they were debating how they should kill the intervening time when the front door, which had been left on the latch, crashed heavily, and a voice called up the stairs:

'The wedding guest, he beat his breast!'

Jonathan Dean.

'Thought I'd try and catch you before you left, old man. Wish you God speed and all that.' He showed, Anthony thought, no scars from grief over his dead friend, but seemed stouter and ruddier. Half-way up the stairs he met them coming down. 'Did I hear someone mention killing time? How about a quick one or a few slow ones up the Lily?'

'It's not five,' said Winston.

Jonathan agreed but said it wanted only ten minutes and that tempus was fugitting as usual. At this point Li-li emerged from Room 1 to be met by a look of frank lechery from Jonathan who made a joke with heavy play on her name and that of the pub which evoked screams of merriment from Winston's sister-in-law. And so, without much show of enthusiasm on the part of either bride or groom, the whole party, now swelled to seven, made their way towards the Waterlily.

When they reached the corner of Magdalen Hill and Balliol Street – by common unspoken consent, they avoided Oriel Mews – Anthony saw, standing on the other side of the street, waiting for the lights to change, a familiar lean figure in silver-grey overcoat and carrying an orange plastic laundry bag. The man's face had the sore reddish look he had noticed before, and there was something prickly and resentful in his whole bearing as if he took the persistent greenness of the traffic light and the stream of vehicles as an affront aimed personally at him. In that crowd, London working class, hippy-costumed drop-outs, brown immigrants, his clothes and his air set him apart and enclosed him in loneliness. Time and change had passed him by. He was a sad and bitter anachronism.

Anthony touched Winston's arm. 'Should we ask old Johnson to join us for a drink? It's up to you, it's your party, but it seems a bit cold not to . . .'

Before he could finish, Winston had hailed Arthur Johnson who had begun to cross the road. 'I'm glad you saw him,' he said to Anthony. 'He was rather nice to me this morning with his good wishes, and seeing everyone else in the house is here, it's the least we can do. Mr Johnson!' he called. 'Can you spare a few minutes to come and celebrate with us in the Waterlily?'

Anthony wasn't surprised to see that Arthur Johnson was flummoxed, even shocked, by the suggestion. First came the mottled flush, then a stream of excuses. 'I couldn't possibly – most kind but out of the question – a busy evening ahead of me – you must count me out, you really must, Mr Mervyn.'

It seemed definite enough. But Anthony – and evidently Arthur Johnson – had reckoned without West Indian hospitality and West Indian enthusiastic pressure. In argument, Arthur Johnson would perhaps have won, but he was given no chance to argue, the situation being managed by Winston's brother, a man of overpowering bonhomie. And Anthony who in the past had been irritated by and sorry for Arthur Johnson, now felt neither anger nor pity. It was all he could do to stop himself laughing aloud at the sight of this finicky and austere-looking man propelled into the saloon bar of the Waterlily between Perry Mervyn and Jonathan Dean. Arthur Johnson looked amazed and frightened. Still clutching his carrier bag, he had the air of some gentleman burglar of fiction apprehended by plainclothes policemen, the bag, of course, containing the spoils of crime. And now it was Li-li who took the bag from him, ignoring his protests and thrusting it under the settle on which she and Jonathan sat down with their victim between them.

It was a violation, a kidnapping almost, Arthur thought, too affronted to speak. He had never before entered the Waterlily which, in his youth, had been pointed out to him by Auntie Gracie as a den of iniquity. Bewildered, crushed by shyness, he sat stiff and silent while Jonathan Dean paid Li-li compliments across him and Li-li giggled in return. The stout and very black woman who faced him added to his discomfiture by asking him in rapid succession what he did for a living, if he was married and how long had he lived in Trinity Road. He was saved from answering her fourth question – didn't he think her new sister-in-law absolutely lovely? – by Anthony Johnson's asking him what he would drink. Arthur replied, inevitably, that he would have a small brandy.

'Claret is the liquor for boys, port for men, but he who aspires to be a hero must drink brandy.' Having quoted this, Dean roared with laughter and said it was by Dr Johnson.

Arthur didn't know what he meant but felt he was getting at him personally and perhaps also at Anthony Johnson. He wondered how soon he could make his escape. The brandy came and with it a variety of longer, less strong, drinks for the others, which made Arthur wonder if he had made a too expensive choice or even committed some gross social error. Two entirely separate conversations began to be conducted round the table, one between Li-li, Dean and Mervyn's sister-in-law, the other between the bridal couple and Mervyn's brother. And Arthur was aware of the isolation of himself and the 'other' Johnson, both of whom were left out of these exchanges. Anthony Johnson looked rather ill – had drunk too much, Arthur supposed, at whatever carousing had been going on since lunchtime – and he began turning over in his mind various opening gambits for a conversation between them. As the only English people present, for the loathsome Dean didn't count and was very likely an Irishman, anyway, it was their duty to present some sort of solid front. And he had opened his mouth to speak of the severe frost which the television had forecast for that night, when Dean, raising his glass in what he called a nuptial toast, launched into a speech.

For some moments this was listened to in silence, though Winston Mervyn seemed fidgety. Didn't like someone else stealing his thunder, Arthur thought. And Dean was certainly airing his education, spouting streams of stuff which couldn't have been thought up on the spur of the moment but must have been written down first. It was all about love and marriage, and Arthur actually chuckled when Dean levelled his gaze on Mervyn's stout brother-in-law and said that in marriage a man becomes slack and selfish and undergoes a fatty degeneration of his moral being. At the same time he was aware that under the table a heavily shod foot was groping across his ankles to find a daintily shod foot. He drew in his knees.

'To marry,' said Dean, 'is to domesticate the Recording Angel. Once you are married there is nothing left for you, not even suicide, but to be good.'

Only Li-li laughed. The Mervyn relatives looked blank. Winston Mervyn got up abruptly and stalked to the bar while Anthony Johnson, with a violence which alarmed Arthur because he couldn't at all understand it, said:

'For God's sake, shut up! D'you ever stop and think what you're saying?'

Dean's face fell. He blushed. But he leaned across Arthur almost as if he wasn't there and whispered on beery breath into Li-li's face, 'You like me, don't you, darling? You're not so bloody fastidious.'

298

Li-li giggled. There was some awkward dodging about and then Arthur realised she was kissing Dean behind his back.

'Perhaps,' he said, 'you'd care to change places with me?'

Why this should have caused so much mirth – general laughter after awkwardness – he was unable to understand, but he thought he could take it as his chance to leave. And he would have left had not Mervyn returned at that moment with another tray of drinks including a second small brandy. He edged along the settle, leaving Li-li and Dean huddled together.

It was a pity, in a way, about the brandy because it necessarily brought memories and associations. But without it he couldn't have borne the party at all, couldn't even have looked on the conviviality or withstood the incomprehensible warring tensions. Now, however, when he had drunk the last vaporous fiery drop of it, he jumped to his feet and said rather shrilly that he must go. He must no longer trespass on their hospitality, he must leave.

'Stand not upon the order of your going, but go at once,' said Dean.

Such rudeness, even if it came out of a book, wasn't to be borne. Arthur made a stiff little bow in the direction of Mervyn and the new Mrs Mervyn, gave a stiff little nod of the head in exchange for their farewells, and escaped.

The joy of getting out was heady. He hurried home through the mews, that dark throat where once, in its jaws, he had made death swallow a woman who flitted like a great black bird. A mouse, a baby, Maureen Cowan, Bridget O'Neill, Vesta Kotowsky. . . . But, no. Home now, encountering no one.

At the top of the empty house he settled down to watch John Wayne discharging yet again the duties of a United States Cavalry Colonel. He leaned against the brown satin cushion, cool, clean, luxurious. The film ended at half past eight. Rather late to begin on his ironing, but better late than on Sunday. For twenty years he had done his ironing on a Saturday.

Entering the kitchen to get out the ironing board and the folded linen, he looked in vain for the orange plastic bag. It wasn't there. He had left it behind in the Waterlily.

# 20

The first to leave the party was Jonathan Dean. Anthony, aware that for the past half-hour Jonathan had been busy entangling his legs with Li-li's under the table, supposed they would remain after he and the Mervyns had gone and that the evening would end for them by Li-li's becoming Vesta's successor. Things happened differently. Li-li departed to the passageway that housed the ladies' lavatory. It also housed a phone, and when she came back she announced that she must soon go as she had a date at seven-thirty. Junia Mervyn, a woman who seemed to take delight in the general discomfiture of men, laughed merrily.

'What about me?' said Jonathan truculently.

Li-li giggled. 'You like to come too? Wait and I go call my friend again.'

'You know very well I didn't mean that.'

'Me, I don't know what men mean. I don't try to know. I love them all a little bit. You like to go on my list? Then when I come back from Taiwan I make you number three, four?' She and Junia clutched each other, laughing. Jonathan got up and without a backward look or a word to his hosts, banged out of the pub.

The men were heavily, awkwardly, silent. Anthony, suddenly and not very aptly identifyingly, felt through his depression a surge of angry misogyny. And he said before he could stop himself:

'As a connoisseur of bad behaviour in woman, I'd give you my prize.'

Li-li pouted. She sidled up to him, opening her eyes wide, trying her wiles. He wondered afterwards if he would actually have struck her, at least have given her a savage push, had Winston not interrupted by announcing it was time to leave for the airport.

He interposed his body, spoke smoothly. 'Feel like coming with us, Anthony? My brother will give you a lift back.'

Anthony said he would. In a low voice he apologised to Linthea. She kissed his cheek.

'Have women really behaved so badly to you?'

'One has. It doesn't matter. Forget it, Linthea, please.'

'I'm not to bother my pretty little head about it?'

Anthony smiled. This description of her head, goddess-like with its crown of coiled braids, was so inept that he was about to correct her with a compliment when Winston's brother said:

'Your friend left his shopping behind.'

'He's not our fliend,' said Li-li, 'and it's not shopping, it's washing.' She pulled it out from under the settle, pointing to and giggling at the topmost item it contained, a pair of underpants. 'You,' she said imperiously to Anthony, 'take it back for him.'

'Suppose you do that? I'm going to the airport.'

'Me take nasty old man's washing out on my date?'

'You've got time to take it home first,' said Winston. 'It's only a quarter past seven.' Always a controller of situations, he closed her little white hand round the handles of the orange plastic bag and placed her firmly but gently back on the settle. A fresh glass of martini in front of her, she sat silenced, looking very small and young. 'That's a good girl,' said Winston.

The night was cruelly cold, its clarity turning all the lights to sharply cut gems. Linthea took Winston's arm and shivered against him as if, now she was going home, she could allow herself to feel the cold of an English winter for the first time. As they crossed the street, Anthony saw a familiar red sports car draw up outside the Waterlily.

The contents of the bag were worth, Arthur calculated, about fifty pounds – all his working shirts, his underwear, bed-linen. . . . It was unthinkable to leave them in that rough public house which would fill up, on a Saturday night, with God knew what riff-raff. But to go out at this hour into darkness?

One of them might, just might, have brought the bag back for him. He went out on to the landing, and the light from his own hall shed a little radiance as far as the top of the stairs. But below was a pit of blackness. There was nothing outside his door, nothing at the head of the stairs.

301

He put on lights, descended. First he knocked on Li-li's door, then on that of Room 2. But he knew it was in vain. Slits of light always showed round the doors when the occupants of the rooms were in.

If only he dared forget about it, leave it till the Waterlily opened in the morning. But, no, he couldn't risk losing so much valuable property. And it was only a step to the pub, less than five minutes' walk. He went back upstairs and put on his overcoat. He walked rapidly up Camera Street, keeping his eyes lowered. But Balliol Street was full of people, corpses in brown grave clothes, their faces and their dress turned pallid or khaki by the colour-excluding sodium lamps. Yellow-brown too was the sports car parked outside Kemal's Kebab House, but Arthur recognised it as belonging to one of Li-li's young men. Only the traffic lights were bright enough to compete with that yellow glare. Their green and scarlet hurt his eyes and made him blink.

Entering the Waterlily on his own recalled to him those three previous occasions on which he had gone into a public house alone. He pushed away the memory, reminding himself how near he was to Trinity Road. The pub was crowded now and Arthur had to queue. He asked for a small brandy, though he hadn't meant to buy a drink at all. But he needed the warmth and the comfort of it to combat the agonies of embarrassment he passed through while the licensee asked the barman and the barman asked the barmaid – in bellowing amused voices – for a Mr Johnson's laundry bag.

'You were with those people who'd got married, weren't you?' Arthur nodded.

'An orange-coloured bag? That Chinese girl took it. I saw her go out of the door with it.'

He gave a gasp of relief. Li-li was in Kemal's, and his laundry, no doubt, was in that very car he had walked past. He almost ran out of the Waterlily. He crossed the mews entrance. There were so many cars lining the street and all their paintbox colours reduced to tones of sepia. But the sports car wasn't among them. Li-li and her escort had gone.

Arthur stood shaking outside the restaurant, and the hot spicy smell that wafted to him from its briefly opened door brought a gust of nausea in which he could taste the sting-ing warmth of brandy. And for support he rested one arm along the convex frosted top of the pillar box. All he wanted, he told himself, was to get his washing, secure it from those who, with reasonless malice, had taken it and were keeping it from him.

Where did people go when they went out in the evening? To pubs, restaurants, cinemas. Li-li had already been to a pub, a restaurant. Arthur considered, his head beginning to drum. Then he crossed the road in the direction of Magdalen Hill and the Taj Mahal.

Now the whole corner was boarded up, the waste ground as well as the area where the demolished houses had been, where Auntie Gracie's house had been. It was fenced in blankly with a row of those old doors builders save and use for this purpose. As Arthur passed close by he could see through the yellow glare that each was painted in some pale bathroom shade, pink, green, cream. Closed, nailed together, they seemed to shut off great epochs of his life. He went past Grainger's and the station. A train running under the street made strong vibrations run up through his body.

The film showing at the Taj Mahal wasn't truly Indian but something from further east. The slant-eyed faces, the heads crowned with jewelled, pagoda-shaped head-dresses, on the poster outside told him that. And this gave force to his feeling that it was here Li-li had come. But there was no parking space in Kenbourne Lane with its double yellow band coursing the edge of the pavement. Suppose she was inside? He wouldn't be able to find her or fetch her out. Still he lingered at the foot of the steps, looking almost wistfully in at the foyer, so much the same as ever yet so dreadfully changed. Hundreds of times he had passed through those swing doors with Auntie Gracie, but it was more than twenty years since he had visited any cinema except that which his own living room afforded.

He wouldn't go in there now. Behind the cinema was a vast council car park. He would go into that car park and find the red sports car. It was unlikely to be locked, for the young were all feckless and indifferent to the value of property. He made his way down the path between shops and cinema, hearing the oriental music which reached him

303

through the tall cream-painted ramparts of the Taj Mahal. It made a huge pale cliff, overshadowing the car park which was unlit, though semi-circled at its perimeter with many of those yellow lights and with silvery white ones as well. There was no one in the attendant's hut at the entrance, there was no one anywhere. Arthur passed beside the barrier, the sword-shaped arm that would rise to allow the passage of a vehicle.

Cars stood in long regular rows. Underfoot it wasn't tarmac or concrete but a gravelly mud, beginning now to freeze into hardness. He could walk on it with soundless footfalls. Slowly he crept along, scanning car after car, pausing sometimes to stare along the lines of car roofs that gleamed dully like aquatic beasts slumbering side by side on some northern moonlit coast. But it was a false moonlight, the heavy purple sky suffused only by street lamps.

When he reached the southernmost point of the great irregular quadrangle, a sense of the absurdity of what he was doing began gradually to penetrate his brandy haze. He wasn't going to find the sports car, or if he did he wouldn't dare to touch it. He had no evidence that Li-li had ever passed this way or entered the Taj Mahal. Not for this purpose had he come into the solitary half-dark of this place. He had come for the reason he always ventured into the dark and the loneliness. . . .

But there were no women here. None of those creatures who threatened his liberty, were always a danger to him, was here. And he could only find one of them if he left the car park by the narrow gate behind him, impassable to vehicles, that led to a path into Brasenose Avenue. With painful lust he envisioned that little defile, but he turned his back on it, turned from its direction, and forced his legs to push him back towards the hut between the ranks of cars.

Then, as he emerged into a wider aisle, he saw that he was no longer alone. A car, one of those tinny, perched-up little Citroëns, had nosed in and was searching for a space. Arthur drew himself up, narrowing and trimming his body so as to present a respectable and decorous air. Almost greater than that growing, not-to-be-permitted desire was the need to appear to any watcher as a law-abiding car owner with legitimate business here. The Citroën dived into a well of darkness between two larger cars. Arthur was

304

only a dozen yards away from it. He saw the driver get out, and the driver was a woman.

A young girl, tallish and very slender, wearing jeans and an Afghan coat with furry edges and embroidery which gleamed a little in the light from pale distant lamps. Her hair was a golden aureole, a mass of metallic-looking filaments that hung below her shoulders. The car door open, she was bending over the interior, adjusting to the steering column some thief-proof locking device. He saw her high-heeled boots, the leather wrinkling over thin ankles, and he felt a constriction in his throat. He could taste brandied bile.

Now, soft-footed, he was a yard behind her. The girl straightened and closed the car door. But it refused to catch. She pulled it wide and shut it with a hard slam. The noise made a vast explosion in Arthur's ears as he raised his hands and leapt upon her from behind, digging his fingers into her neck.

The earth rocked as he held on to that surprisingly strong and sinewy neck, and the huge purple sky blazed at him, burning his eyes. The girl was resisting, strong as he, stronger. . . . She gave a powerful twist and her elbow thrust back hard into his diaphragm. He staggered at the sudden pain, slackening his hold, and a fist swung into his face, hard bone against his teeth. With a strangled grunt he fell back against the next car, sliding down its slippery bodywork. Her face loomed over his, contorted, savage, and Arthur let out a cry, for it was the face of a young man with a hooked nose, stubble on his upper lip and a cape of coarse hair streaming. The fist swung again, this time to his eye. Arthur slid down on to the frozen mud and lay there, half under the oil-blackened chassis of the other car.

He didn't move, although he was conscious. A hand turned him over, a sharp-toed boot kicked his ribs. He made no sound, but lay there with his eyes closed. The boy was standing over him, breathing heavily, making sucking sounds of satisfaction and triumph. Then he heard footsteps pounding away towards the hut and the barrier and there was a terrible deep silence.

Arthur hauled himself up, clinging to the wings of both cars. His face was wet with blood running from his upper lip and his head was banging as it had never banged from desire. He forced his eyes into focus so that he could see the shining, sleeping cars, the glittering frosted ground. No attendant coming, no one. He crawled between the cars, clutching here at a wing mirror, there at a door handle, until at last the strength that comes from terror brought him to an upright stance. He staggered. The icy air, unimpeded, was like a further blow to his face. He tasted the salt blood trickling between his teeth.

Still the hut was empty, the path between cinema and shops deserted. Covering his face with the clean white handkerchief he always carried, he made himself walk down that path, walk slowly, although he wanted to run and scream. Kenbourne Lane. No crowd was gathered, no huddle of passers-by stood staring in the direction taken by a running boy with golden hair. No one looked at Arthur. It was the season for colds, for muffled faces. He went on past the station until he came to Grainger's gates. Thank God they weren't padlocked but closed with a Yale lock. Holding up the handkerchief, he unlocked the gates, the conscientious surveyor who works Saturday nights despite a cold in the head. They closed behind him and he sank heavily against them.

But he must reach his own office. There, for a while, he would be safe. The little house of glass and cedarwood was an island and a haven in the big bare yard. He crawled to it because his legs, which had carried him so well when their strength had most been needed, had buckled now and were half-paralysed. From the ground, slippery with frost, he reached up and unlocked the door.

It was cold inside, colder than in the open air. The Adler stood on the desk, shrouded in its cover; the waste-paper basket was empty; the place smelt faintly of bubble gum. Arthur collapsed on to the floor and lay there, his body shaking with gasping sobs. He staunched the blood, which might otherwise have got on to the carpet, first with his handkerchief, then with his scarf. As the handkerchief became unusable, black with blood, he heard the wail of sirens, distant and keening at first, then screaming on an ear-splitting rise and fall as the police cars came over the lights into Magdalen Hill.

# 21

West Kenbourne was populated with police. It seemed to Anthony, returning from the airport in Perry Mervyn's car, that every other pedestrian in Balliol Street was a policeman. Since they had turned from the High Street up Kenbourne Lane, he had counted five police cars.

'Maybe someone robbed a bank,' said Junia.

It was half past eleven, but lights were still on in the Dalmatian and the Waterlily and their doors stood open. Police were in the pubs and standing in the doorways, questioning customers as they left. From behind the improvised fence that shut off the waste ground, the beams from policemen's torches cut the air in long pale swaying shafts.

'Must have been a bank,' said Perry, and he and his wife offered sage opinions – they were in perfect agreement – as to the comparative innocuousness of bank robbery. It could hardly be called morally wrong, it harmed no one, and so on. Anthony, though grateful for the lift, wasn't sorry when they arrived at 142 Trinity Road.

He thanked them and they exchanged undertakings not to lose touch. Anthony supposed, and supposed they supposed, that they would never meet again. Waving, he watched the car depart, its occupants having declared they would drive around for a while and try to find out what was going on.

Nothing was going on in Trinity Road. A hundred and forty-two was in total darkness. He went indoors and walked slowly along the passage towards Room 2. The police hunt afforded him no interest, brought him no curiosity. Nothing was able to divert him from the all-enclosing grey misery which had succeeded disbelief, anger, pain. The wedding, the happiness of Winston and Linthea, had served only to vary his depression with fresh pain. And in the airport lounge, where they had sat drinking coffee, a horrible aspect of that pain had shown itself. For that busy place, with its continual comings and goings, was peopled for him with Helens, with versions of Helen. Every fair head, turned from him, might turn again and show him her face. One girl, from a distance, had her walk; another, talking animatedly to a man who might be Roger – how would he know? – moved her hands in Helen gestures, and her laugh, soft and clear, reached him as Helen's laugh. Once he was certain. He even got to his feet, staring, catching his breath. The others must have thought him crazy, hallucinated.

He put his key into the door lock. But before he could enter Room 2 the front door opened and Li-li came in, carrying Arthur Johnson's washing bag.

'Have you been carting that round all night?' said Anthony disagreeably.

'Is not all night. Is only twelve.' She waved the bag at him. 'There, you shall take it to him now. He will be so pleased to have it safe.'

'Knowing him, I should think he's nearly gone out of his mind worrying about it. And you can take it to him yourself.'

But, as Li-li with a pout and a giggle disappeared round the first bend of the stairs, Anthony thought he had better follow her. He caught up with her as she was mounting the second flight.

'He'll be asleep. He always goes to bed early. Leave it outside his door.'

'O.K.' Li-li dropped the bag on the landing. 'Nasty, nasty, to be old and go to bed at midnight.' She gave Anthony a sweet provocative smile. 'You like some Chinese tea?'

'No, thanks. I go to bed at midnight too.' He walked into Room 2 and closed the door firmly. It was some time before he fell asleep, for Li-li, preparing for her journey on the following day, revenged herself by packing noisily, banging her wardrobe door and apparently throwing shoes across the room, until after three.

Arthur heard the police get Grainger's doors open half an hour after he had hidden himself in the office. He saw the beams of their torches searchlighting the yard. They came up to the office and walked round it, but because the door hadn't been forced and no window was broken, they went away. He heard the gates clang behind them.

His lip had stopped bleeding. When it was safe to get up from the floor, he wrapped his handkerchief in a sheet of flimsy paper and thrust it into his coat pocket. Very little light was available to him, only a distant sheen from the lamps of Magdalen Hill. He didn't dare put the light on or even the electric fire, though it was bitterly cold. His scarf was patched and streaked with blood, but not so badly stained that he couldn't wear it. It was of the utmost importance to leave no blood on the haircord or as finger-prints. But the yellow twilight was sufficient to show him that the haircord was unmarked. He licked his fingers till they were free of the salty taste.

Then he lay down again on the floor, sleepless, letting the long slow hours pass. His ribs ached on the left side but he didn't think the kick had broken a bone. Outside they would comb the whole area. When they couldn't find him they would leave the area and look further afield. Perhaps they wouldn't come to Trinity Road at all.

Would it never get light? Light would show any passer-by his injured face – if only he had the means to see how injured it was! – but a man walking solitary in the dark small hours would attract more attention. When the yel-lowness retreated into the milky grey of dawn, he dragged himself to his feet and looked out of the window on to the deserted yard. His body was stiff, every limb aching, and a sharp fluctuating pain teased his left side.

His watch had broken in the fall and the hands still showed twenty past nine. It must now be about eleven hours later than that. His watch had broken but not his glasses, which remained intact in their case. He put them on, although they were reading glasses that threw the world out of focus, but they would help disguise his eye. As to his lip – he licked a corner of his scarf and worked blindly at the cut, wincing because the rough fibres prickled the edges of the wound. But the morning was very cold and now he saw that a thin sleet had begun to fall, little gra-nules of ice that melted as they struck the ground. The kind of day, he thought, when a man with a muffled face is accepted as normal.

Shaking a little, controlling his shaking as best he could, he went out of the office, locking the door behind him. He had left no vestige of his presence. As he approached the gates, the falling sleet thickened into a storm. Snow, the first of the year, swirled about him, flakes of it stinging his lip. He pulled the scarf up to cover his mouth and, with lowered head, took what was a kind of plunge into Magdalen Hill.

There was no one about but a boy delivering Sunday papers. His encounter with the girl-boy in the car park had happened too late at night for there to be anything about it in the papers, and this little boy in thick coat and balaclava didn't look at him. A man walking a retriever in Balliol Street didn't look at him, nor did the cleaning woman who was letting herself into the public bar of the Waterlily. She too had a scarf swathing the lower half of her face. Arthur entered the mews as All Souls' clock struck eight.

Someone had left a newspaper, last evening's, on top of a dustbin in the mews. He picked it up and tucked it under his arm so that anyone who saw him would think he had been out to buy it. But no one saw him. Li-li's curtains were drawn. He crept upstairs through the sleeping house. On the lop landing, resting against his door, was the orange laundry bag. At some point Li-li had brought that bag up the stairs. Had she knocked on his door? And if she had, would she have assumed he was asleep? Or had she left it downstairs, and had Anthony Johnson, the only other occupant of the house, been responsible for bringing it here? There was no way of knowing. If Anthony Johnson were awake now light would show from his window on to the court, for Room 2 was dark in winter till nine. But there was no cross-barred cast of light to be seen on the green stone. Snow whirled down the well, flying against the cellar door and streaming down it as rivulets of water.

Arthur cut up his handkerchief and flushed the pieces down the lavatory. He washed his scarf and, pulling it out from the lining, washed too the pocket of his overcoat. Then, and only then, did he dare look at his face in the mirror.

His eye socket was the colour of meat that has lain exposed, a dark glazed red, and the lid was almost closed. And his lip was split, a cut running up unevenly at the centre join of the upper lip. He looked quite different, this wasn't his face, not his this sore bulbous mouth. Would it scar? It didn't seem bad enough to need stitching. He washed it carefully with warm water and antiseptic. It couldn't be stitched. Every casualty department in every hospital in London would be alerted to watch for a man coming in with a wounded mouth.

He mustn't show himself at all. At any cost, he must remain here, hidden, until his lip and his eye healed. It was hours since he had eaten or drunk anything, hours since he had slept, but he knew he could no more sleep than he could eat a crumb of bread. He drank some water and gagged on it, its coldness burning his throat.

Shrouded by the nightdress frills of the net curtains, he crouched at the window. If the police did a house-to-house search he would be lost. He watched people go by, expecting always to see the piranha face of Inspector Glass. The church bells rang for morning service and a few elderly women went by, carrying Prayer Books, on their way to All Souls'. At lunchtime he put on the television, and the last item in a news bulletin told him, as only this high authority could really tell him, what he had done and where he stood.

'A man was attacked last night in a car park near Kenbourne Lane tube station in West London. . . .' And there, on the screen, was the car park overhung by the ramparts of the Taj Mahal. Arthur trembled, clenching his hands. He half-expected to see himself emerge from behind a row of cars, caught by those cameras like a stalked animal. 'From the circumstances of the attack, police believe his assailant mistook him for a woman and are speculating as to whether the attacker could be the same man who, for a quarter of a century, has been known by the name of the Kenbourne Killer. A massive hunt in the area has so far been unsuccessful. . . .'

Arthur switched off the set. He went once more into the bathroom and looked in the mirror at the face of the Kenbourne Killer. Never, in the past, when he had thought of the things he had done, had he ever really considered that title and that role as belonging to him. But the television had told him so, it was so. Those marks had been put upon his face so that he and the world should know it. Looking at his face made him cry so he went back to his window where the nets veiled his face. The television remained off,

311

blank, though an early Rogers-Astaire film was showing, until five when there was more news.

An Identikit picture appeared on the screen, a hard cold face, sharply lined, vicious, elderly. The subject had a hare lip and a blind eye. Was that how he, so spruce and handsome, had looked to the boy with the Citroën? He felt faint and dizzy when the boy himself appeared and seemed to stare penetratingly into his own eyes. The boy put a hand up to that deceiving hair and smiled a little proudly.

'Well, I reckon this guy thought I was a girl, you know, on account of me being skinny and having long hair.'

The interviewer addressed him with earnest approval. 'Would you be able to identify him, Mr Harrison?'

'Sure, I would. Anyway, I knocked his face about a bit, didn't I? Anyone'd be able to identify him, not just me.'

And now Inspector Glass himself. Arthur shivered because his enemies were being ranged before him through this medium, once so friendly, once the purveyor of his second best delight.

The lips curled back and the great teeth showed. 'You can take it as certain that the police won't rest until we've got this chap and put him out of harm's way. It's only a matter of time. But I'd like to tell the public that this man is highly dangerous, and if anyone has the slightest suspicion of his identity, if he or she feel they're only going on what you might call intuition, they must call this number at once.'

The telephone number burned in white letters on a black ground. And the voice of Inspector Glass, the voice of a devourer of men, came heavy and grim.

'At any time of the day or night *you* can call this number. And if you hesitate, remember that next time it could be you or your wife or your mother or your daughter.'

The diesel rattle of a taxi called Arthur back to the window. Li-li came out of the house carrying two suitcases. There was another gone who might see his face and not hesitate. Snow had begun to fall again through the bitter cold darkness. He watched her get into the taxi.

And now he was alone in the house with Anthony Johnson.

312

# 22

That Sunday it was nearly noon before Anthony got up.
Room 2 was icy and he had to use powdered milk in his
tea because he had run out of fresh. The courtyard was
wet, although it wasn't raining, and the triangle of sky had
the yellowish-grey look snow clouds give.

It was so dark that he had to keep the lamp on all day.
He sat under it, leafing through the draft of his thesis,
wondering if it was any good, but into his concentration,
or what passed for concentration, fragmented images of
Helen kept breaking. He found himself recalling conversations they had had in the past, reading duplicity into
phrases of hers that had once seemed beautifully sincere.
And this obsession displaced everything else. He sat staring
dully at the pink and green translucent shade that swayed
with a slow gentle rhythm in the draught from the window
frame crack, hypnotised by it, subdued into apathy. Soon
after five, when he had heard Li-li leave, he put on his coat
and set off for Winter's.

The relief barman from the Waterlily was in the shop and
he and Winter were talking about the police activity of the
night before. Anthony had forgotten all about it. Now,
waiting to be served, he learned its nature.

'Young fellow of nineteen, student at Radclyffe College.
What I say is, if they will get themselves up like girls,
they're asking for it. Not that he didn't stand up for himself. Bashed the fellow's face up something shocking. You
see the news?'

The barman nodded. 'Funny thing, I got a black eye myself
last week. All above board, got it at my judo. But if it wasn't
better I wouldn't fancy showing myself on the street.'

'You didn't get a cut lip as well, though, did you? Mind
you, that'd be a turn up for the books, all the locals finding
out the Kenbourne Killer'd been serving them their booze.'
Winter laughed. He turned to Anthony. 'And what can I
do for you, sir?'

'Just a pint of milk, please.'

'Homogenized, Jersey or silver top?'

Anthony took the silver top. As he was closing the door behind him he heard them say something about his hair and prowling stranglers who couldn't tell the boys from the girls, and who could blame them? He went past the lighted windows of the Waterlily, for only drunks and potential pick-ups go into pubs on their own in the evenings. The snow had settled in little drifts between the cobbles of Oriel Mews where there was no light or heat to melt it. It floated thinly over Trinity Road, making a thinner webbier curtain over the draped nets at Arthur Johnson's window behind which Anthony thought he could vaguely make out a watcher.

Room 2 had grown cold again in his absence. He kicked on the electric fire, drank some milk straight out of the bottle. It was so cold it made his teeth chatter. He crouched over the fire, and into his mind came a clear and sweet vision of Helen as she had been in the summer, running along the platform at Temple Meads to meet his train when he came to her from York. He felt, closing his eyes, her hands reach up to hold his shoulders, her warm breath from her parted lips on his lips. And he felt real pain, a shaft of pain in his left side, as if he had been kicked where his heart was.

Then he lay face-downwards on the bed, hating himself for his weakness, wondering how he would get through the time ahead, the long cold winter of isolation with only Arthur Johnson for company.

Upstairs, on the landing, the telephone began to ring.

Arthur heard the phone but didn't answer it. The only people who were likely to receive phone calls had gone away. He went into the bedroom and looked again at his face. Impossible to consider going to work tomorrow. The phone had stopped ringing. He looked out of the window down to the court below. Anthony Johnson's light was on, and Arthur wondered why he hadn't answered the phone.

There was plenty of food in his fridge, including the Sunday joint he hadn't been able to face and couldn't face now. The food he had would last him for days. He managed to swallow a small piece of bread and butter. Then he looked at his face again, this time in the bathroom mirror. While he was wondering if ice would ease the swelling, if anyone would believe him if he said he had cut himself shaving – and, presumably, also knocked his eye with the razor – the phone started ringing again. He opened his front door and emerged on to the dark landing. Obscurely he felt that, whoever this might be phoning, it would be safer were he to answer it himself.

He lifted the receiver and Stanley Caspian's voice said, 'That you, Arthur? About time too. I buzzed you five minutes ago.'

Light flooded him suddenly from the hall below. He turned, covering his mouth with his left hand, and called in a muffled voice, 'It's all right. It's Mr Caspian for me.'

Anthony Johnson said, 'O.K.,' and went back into Room 2. Arthur wished the light would go out. He hunched over the phone.

'Listen, Arthur, I've got a chap coming to have a dekko at Flat 1 tomorrow around five. Can you let him in?'

'I'm not well,' Arthur said, sick with panic. 'I've got a – a virus infection. I shan't be going to work and I can't let anyone in. I'm going to have the day in bed.'

'My God, I suppose you can get out of your poxy bed just to open the front door?'

'No, I can't,' Arthur said shrilly. 'I'm ill. I should be in bed now.'

'Charming. After all I've done for you, Arthur, that's a bit thick. I suppose I'll have to fix it a bit earlier with this chap and come myself.'

'I'm sorry. I'm not well. I have to go and lie down.'

Stanley didn't answer but crashed down the receiver. Arthur stumbled up to his own door. It was almost closed. A slight draught, a tiny push, and he would have been locked out. He who never never neglected such precautions had forgotten to drop the latch. Shivering at the thought of what might have happened, he went into the bathroom to contemplate his lip and his eye. Tears began to course down his face, stinging the bruised flesh.

The second time the phone rang Anthony got off his bed to answer it. But the hopes he had had, hopes that were against all reason, were dissipated by the voice calling from the landing, 'It's Mr Caspian for me.'

Because the voice sounded thick and strange, Anthony, who in his disappointment would otherwise simply have drifted back into Room 2, glanced up at the figure on the landing. Arthur Johnson was covering his mouth with his left hand, and he turned away quickly, huddling over the phone, but not before Anthony had noticed one of his eyes was swollen and half-closed. The phone conversation went on for a few moments, Arthur Johnson protesting that he was ill, but from a virus infection, not some sort of facial injury. Anthony closed the door. He sat on the bed. An hour before he would have given a lot for some subject to come overpoweringly into his mind and crowd Helen out of it. But this? Did he want this and could he cope with it?

A series of images now. A man, evidently nervous, paranoid, repressed, saying, 'You are the *other* Johnson. I have been here for twenty years.' In the cellar a shop window model with a rent in her neck. Fire burning that figure, and that very night, the night of 5 November . . . Anthony looked out of the window and up to that other window two floors above. No light showed, though that was Arthur Johnson's bedroom and he had said he was ill and ought to be in bed. Perhaps he was, in the dark. Anthony went out into the street and looked up. There was light up there, orange light turning the draped muslin stuff to gold, and behind that shimmering stuff a light flickering movement.

He went quickly indoors and up the two flights of stairs. He had thought of no excuse for knocking on Arthur Johnson's door, but excuses seemed base and dishonest. Besides, once he had seen, he would need no excuse. But there was no answer to his knock, no answer when he knocked again, and that told him as much as if the damaged face had presented itself to him, six inches from his own. To knock again, to insist, would be a cruelty that revolted him, for in the silence he fancied he could sense a concentrated breath-held terror behind that door.

He knew now. He would have laughed at himself if this had been a laughing matter, for the irony was that he who was writing a thesis on psychopathy, who knew all about psychopaths, had lived three months in the same house as a psychopath and not known it. So, of course, he must go to the police. Knew? Did he? Well, he was sure, certain. When we say that, Helen had once said, we always mean we are not quite sure, not quite certain. He shivered in the hot fuggy yet draughty room. It had been a shock. Presently he began looking through his books, finding Arthur Johnson or aspects of him in every case history, finding what he well knew already, that if hardly anything is known of the causes of psychopathy, even less has been discovered of ways to cure it. For ever a prison for the criminally insane then, for ever incarceration, helplessly inflicted and helplessly borne. But he would go to the police in the morning. . . .

At last he undressed and got into bed. The triangle of sky was a smoky red scudded with black flakes of snow. He found it impossible to sleep and wondered if the man upstairs, lying in bed some twenty feet above him, also lay sleepless under his far greater weight of care.

At eight-thirty in the morning Arthur phoned Mr Grainger at home. He wouldn't be coming in, would have to take at least three days off. While he was on the phone he heard Anthony Johnson go into the bathroom, but the man didn't come to the foot of the stairs. Why had he knocked on his door last night? To borrow something, to get change for the phone? Still fresh with him, still aching in his bruised ribs, was the terror those repeated knocks had brought. But nothing would have made him let Anthony Johnson in to see his face. For hours he had hunched over the window ledge, intermittently leaving his post to look at his face, to listen by the door for Anthony Johnson to phone the police, watching for Anthony Johnson to go out and fetch the police. By midnight, when nothing had happened and the little court had gone dark, he had lain down, spent but sleepless.

The last of four lectures by a distinguished visiting criminologist was to be given at the college that morning. Anthony had attended them all, been rather disappointed that they were more elementary than he had hoped, and now he took notes abstractedly. He was tired and uneasy.

317

Still he hesitated to go to the police, although he had noted where the nearest station was, having passed its tall portals, its blue lamp, on his way to college on the K.12. One o'clock came and he was in the canteen, vacillating still, nauseated at the idea of betraying a man who had done him no injury. He seldom had much to say to the students. They were all younger than he and they seemed to him not much more than children. But now a girl who had sat next to him in the lecture room brought her tray to his table and pointed out to him a long-haired boy who was holding court at the far end of the room, surrounded by avid listeners.

'That's Philip Harrison.'

'Philip Harrison?'

'The guy who was attacked in the car park on Saturday.'

Anthony didn't look at him. He looked at the young girls who were his audience, one of whom was distressingly like Helen. If that girl had been in the car park she wouldn't be here now, listening with innocent relish. She would be dead. He had only to go to the police station and tell them what he knew, so little that he knew, so tenuous as it was, yet so true a pointer. Dully, he pushed away his plate. He had eaten nothing. A great weariness overcame him and he wanted nothing so much as to lie down and sleep. He remembered how, once in the summer, he and Helen had lain in each other's arms in a field in the West Country and for an hour he had slept with her hair against his cheek and the scent coming to him of seeded grass and wild parsley. Since then, it seemed, he had never slept so sweetly as during that hour. But the summer was past, in every sense, and the sweet hours of sleep. He got his coat, walked down the long hall, through the swing doors, out into the snow.

The police station was perhaps ten minutes' walk away. The college grounds were empty and barren as if the cold had shaved all vegetation away but for the clipped turf and swept up all people like so much litter. There was no one in the grounds but himself and a girl whom he could see in the extreme distance coming in by the main gates. He walked towards her and she towards him down the long gravel drive.

And now he began collecting together his knowledge and suspicions of Arthur Johnson for a coherent statement

318

to the police. But he was distracted by the sight of the approaching girl. By now he ought to be used to the deceptions practised on him by his eyes and his mind. He wasn't going to catch his breath this time because a strange girl walked like Helen, moved her head like Helen, and now that she came nearer could be seen to have Helen's crisp golden hair. He trudged on, looking down at the gravel, refusing any longer to contemplate the girl who was now only some twenty or thirty yards from him.

But, in spite of himself, he was aware that she had stopped. She had stopped and was staring straight at him. He swallowed hard and his heart thudded. They stared at each other across the cold bare expanse. As he saw her lift her arms and open them, and as she began to run towards him, calling his name, 'Tony, Tony!' he too ran towards her with open arms.

Her mouth was cold on his mouth but her body was warm. As he held her he knew he hadn't been warm like this for weeks. The warmth was wonderful and the feel of her, but he was afraid to look at her face.

'Helen,' he said, 'is it really you?'

# 23

They sat on a bench on College Green, not feeling the cold. Anthony held her face in his hands. He smoothed back a lock of hair that had fallen over her forehead, re-learning the look and the feel of her. 'I don't believe it,' he said. 'I really can't yet believe it.'

'I know. I felt like that.'

'You won't go away? I mean, you won't say in a minute that you've got a train to catch or anything like that?'

'I've nowhere *to* go. I've burned my boats. Tony, let's eat. I'm hungry, I'm starving. You know I always want to eat when I'm happy.'

The Grand Duke was crowded. They went into a café that was humble and clean and almost empty.

'I don't know whether to sit opposite you or next to you. One way I can look, the other way I can touch you.'

'Look at me,' she said. 'I want to look at you.'

She sat down and fixed her eyes on his face. She reached across the table and took his hand. They held hands on the cloth, hers covering his. 'Tony, it's all right now, it will always be all right *now*, but why didn't you answer my letters?'

'Because you told me not to. You told me never to write to you.'

'Not my last three. I begged you to write to me at the museum. Didn't you *get* them?'

He shook his head. 'Since the end of October I've only had one letter from you and that was the one where you told me you never wanted to see me again.'

She drew back, then leaned forward, clutching his hand. 'I never wrote such a thing!'

'Someone did. Roger?'

'I don't know. I don't – well, it's possible, but . . . I wrote and told you I was leaving him and coming to you. But how could I come when you didn't answer? I was crazy with misery. Roger went to Scotland and I waited at home alone night after night for you to phone.'

'I phoned,' he said, 'on the last Wednesday of November.'

'By then I'd gone to my mother's. I'd got a fortnight's holiday owing to me and I went to my mother because I couldn't bear being alone any more and being with Roger in Scotland would have been worse. I thought I'd never see you again.'

Just as he had thought he would never again see her. But now he had no wish to solve the mystery. It paled into insignificance beside the joy of being with her.

'Helen,' he said, 'why are you here now?'

'But you know that,' she said, surprised. 'I'm here because you wrote to me.'

'*That* letter? That stupid letter?'

'Was it? I never saw it. I only know you said you loved me in the first line of it, so I – I ran away!'

She leaned across the table and kissed him. The waitress gave a slight cough and, as they drew apart, placed their plates in front of them.

320

'I went to work this morning, my first day back. As soon as I got in the phone rang and it was Roger. A letter had come for me with your name and address on the flap and he – he opened it.'

'My name and address on the flap? But I . . .' He explained how he had enclosed his letter to her in one to Mrs Pontifex.

'Oh, I see. We never meant to go there for Christmas this year. She must have copied your name and address from the letter to her and forwarded it. I don't know. I told you, I didn't see it. I went out before the post came. Roger was – he was *frightening* with rage. I've heard him in some rages, I've seen him, when he's threatened to kill me and himself, but I've never heard him like that. He just read that first line, and then he sort of spat out, "From your lover." He said, "You're to go downstairs and wait outside the building for me, Helen. If you're not there I'll come up, but you'd better be there unless you want a public scene. I shan't flinch from telling everyone in that building what you are."

'He said he'd be there in the car in five minutes, Tony. I knew it couldn't take him more than five minutes and I was terrified of what he'd do. I grabbed my coat and my handbag and I rushed out and down the stairs. I remember calling out I'd had bad news and had to go.

'When I got into the street I was afraid to wait there even for a second. I crossed the road and ran down a side street, and then a taxi came and I said, "Temple Meads!" because I knew I must go to London and you. You loved me, you'd said you did, so everything was all right at last.

'I didn't bother to queue up for a ticket. I could hear an announcer saying, "The train standing at platform two is the nine fifty-one for London, calling at Bath, Swindon and Reading." It was nine-fifty then and I jumped on that train. I had to buy a ticket when the man came round and it took all the money I'd got but for five pence. I hadn't got a cheque book or a bank card or anything. Oh, Tony, I'm entirely skint, I've got just what I stand up in.

'When I got to Paddington I found a bus going to Kenbourne Vale Garage but I hadn't got enough money to get further than to Kensal Rise. So I walked the rest.'

321

'You *walked*? Here from Kensal Rise?'

She smiled at his dismay. 'Out in the cold, cold snow and without any money. All I needed was a baby in my arms. I went into a newsagent's and looked up the route in a guide. I was going to go to Trinity Road but then I thought you might be here. So I came here and here I am.' Her eyes were bright, the pupils mirrors in which, at last, he could see his own face reflected. 'Are you pleased?' she said.

'Helen, I was half-dead with misery and loneliness and you ask me if I'm *pleased*?'

'I only wish,' she said, 'that I'd seen your letter. I don't suppose I ever shall now and I'd waited so long for it. Can you remember what you wrote?'

'No,' he lied. 'No, only that it was nonsense. You had the only good bit in the first line.'

She sighed, but it was a sigh of happiness. 'Tony, what are we going to do? Where shall we go?'

'Who cares? Somewhere, anywhere. We shall survive. Right now we'll go to Trinity Road.'

As he spoke the name he remembered. It was nearly three o'clock and he had delayed long enough. He put an arm round her shoulders, helped her to her feet. 'Come along, my love, we're going to Trinity Road, but we'll take in an errand I have to do on the way.'

Behind the curtains Arthur had sat all day, breaking his vigil every half-hour or so to examine his face in the bathroom mirror. Now, at three o'clock, he saw Stanley Caspian's car draw up and park in front of one of the houses on the odd-numbered side. A man was coming to view Flat 1, and in a moment this man and Stanley would come into the house. Arthur watched the car but he could only see Stanley in it, sitting in the driving seat, his bulk and the bikini doll impeding further view. Perhaps he had brought the man with him or perhaps he was simply waiting for the new tenant to arrive for his appointment. Arthur went back to the bathroom. Already, so early, the winter light was beginning to fade. If Stanley did happen to call on him, if he had to show his face, perhaps those dreadful marks would pass unnoticed. . . .

As he came out of the bathroom his doorbell rang. The sound reverberated through Arthur's body and he gave a tremendous start. He stood stock still in the hall. It was evident what had happened. Stanley had forgotten his key. Let him go home and fetch it then. The bell rang again, insistently, and Arthur could picture Stanley's fat finger pressed hard and impatiently on the push. He forced himself to go back into the living room and look out of the window. Stanley's car was empty. At any rate, it must be he. No police cars anywhere, no parked vehicles but Stanley's and a couple of vans and a grey convertible. Another long ring fetched him back into the hall. He must answer it, for it would look odder if he didn't. But he was supposed to be ill and must give the appearance of having been got out of bed. Quickly, though he was shaking, he slipped off his jacket and took his dressing gown from the hook behind the bedroom door. A handkerchief to his face, he let himself out of the flat and went downstairs.

Outlined behind the red and green glass panels was the shape of a heavy thickset man. It must be Stanley. Arthur stood behind the door and pulled it open towards him. The man marched in, looked to the right, then to the left where Arthur stood, took the edge of the door in both hands and slammed it shut as violently as Jonathan Dean had slammed it in the past.

He was youngish, dark, and he was in the grip of an emotion greater even than Arthur's fear. Arthur didn't know what this emotion was, but he knew a policeman wouldn't look like this, stand trembling and wide-eyed and wild like this. Because the hall was shadowy, lit with a misty redness and greenness, he took the handkerchief away from his face and stepped back.

'Is your name Johnson?'

'Yes,' said Arthur.

'*A.* Johnson?'

Arthur nodded, mystified, for the man peered at him incredulously. 'My God, an old man! It's unbelievable.' But he did believe and when he said hoarsely, 'Where is she?' Arthur also knew and believed.

Once it would have been threatening, dreadful. Now it was only a relief. 'You want the other Johnson,' Arthur said

323

coldly and stiffly. 'Sit down and wait for him if you like. It's no business of mine.'

'The *other* Johnson? Don't give me that.' His eyes travelled over Arthur's dressing gown. He clenched his fists and said again, '*Where is she?*'

Arthur turned his back and climbed the stairs. He must get to his flat, shut himself in and pray that Stanley would soon come to turn this intruder out before violence drew the police. And now, realising what could happen, he ran up the second flight to push open his own front door. A cry of dread broke from him. He had no key, hadn't dropped the latch, and the door had closed fast behind him.

He stood shaking, his back to the door, his hands creeping to shield his face. Out here what chance had he when Stanley came with the new tenant, when trouble broke out between Anthony Johnson and H's husband? And now the man had reached the head of the stairs and was facing him. Arthur looked into the barrel of a small gun – a pistol or a revolver, he didn't know which. Television hadn't taught him that.

'Open that door!'

'I can't. I've no key. I've left my key inside.'

'My wife is in there. Open that door or I'll shoot the lock off. I'll give you thirty seconds to open that door.'

His front door shattered, swinging on its hinges, would be worse than his front door locked against him. Arthur, who had moved aside when he saw the gun, brought his gaze first to the smooth circle of metal surrounding the keyhole, then, with greater dread, to the smooth metal cylinder pointed at that keyhole. A voice like a woman's, a victim's, screamed out of him.

'I can't! I tell you I can't. Go away, get out, leave me alone!' And he threw his body, arms upraised, against the door.

Something struck him a violent blow on his back, on the lower left side. The pain was unimaginable. He thought it was his heart, a heart attack, for he felt the pain long before he heard the report as of a bursting firework, and heard too his own cry and that of another, aghast and terrified. Arthur fell backwards, his hands clutching his ribs. The pain roared in a red stream out of his mouth.

Heavily he rolled down the stairs, blood wrapping his body like a long scarlet scarf. The momentum flung him against Brian Kotowsky's door and there he felt the last beat of his heart in blood against his hand.

**For Gerald Austin
With Love**

# A JUDGEMENT IN STONE

# 1

Eunice Parchman killed the Coverdale family because she could not read or write.

There was no real motive and no premeditation; no money was gained and no security. As a result of her crime, Eunice Parchman's disability was made known not to a mere family or a handful of villagers but to the whole country. She accomplished nothing by it but disaster for herself, and all along, somewhere in her strange mind, she knew she would accomplish nothing. And yet, although her companion and partner was mad, Eunice was not. She had the awful practical sanity of the atavistic ape disguised as twentieth-century woman.

Literacy is one of the cornerstones of civilisation. To be illiterate is to be deformed. And the derision that was once directed at the physical freak may, perhaps more justly, descend upon the illiterate. If he or she can live a cautious life among the uneducated all may be well, for in the country of the purblind the eyeless is not rejected. It was unfortunate for Eunice Parchman, and for them, that the people who employed her and in whose home she lived for nine months were peculiarly literate. Had they been a family of philistines, they might be alive today and Eunice free in her mysterious dark freedom of sensation and instinct and blank absence of the printed word.

The family belonged to the upper middle class, and they lived a conventional upper-middle-class life in a country house. George Coverdale had a degree in philosophy, but since the age of thirty he had been managing director of his late father's company, Tin Box Coverdale, at Stantwich in Suffolk. With his wife and his three children, Peter, Paula and Melinda, he had occupied a large nineteen-thirtyish house on the outskirts of Stantwich until his wife died of cancer when Melinda was twelve.

Two years later, at the wedding of Paula to Brian Caswall, George met thirty-seven-year-old Jacqueline Mont.
She also had been married before had divorced her husband for desertion, and had been left with one son.
George and Jacqueline fell in love more or less at first sight
and were married three months later. George bought a
manor house ten miles from Stantwich and went to live
there with his bride, with Melinda and with Giles Mont,
Peter Coverdale having at that time been married for three
years.

When Eunice Parchman was engaged as their housekeeper George was fifty-seven and Jacqueline forty-two.
They took an active part in the social life of the neighbourhood, and in an unobtrusive way had slipped into playing
the parts of the squire and his lady. Their marriage was
idyllic and Jacqueline was popular with her stepchildren,
Peter, a lecturer in political economy at a northern university, Paula, now herself a mother and living in London, and
Melinda, who, at twenty, was reading English at the
University of Norfolk in Galwich. Her own son, Giles, aged
seventeen, was still at school.

Four members of this family, George, Jacqueline and
Melinda Coverdale and Giles Mont, died in the space of
fifteen minutes on 14 February, St Valentine's Day. Eunice
Parchman and the prosaically named Joan Smith shot them
down on a Sunday evening while they were watching opera
on television. Two weeks later Eunice was arrested for the
crime – because she could not read.

But there was more to it than that.

# 2

The gardens of Lowfield Hall are overgrown now and
weeds push their way up through the gravel of the drive.
One of the drawing-room windows, broken by a village
boy, has been boarded up, and wisteria, killed by summer
drought, hangs above the front door like an old dried net.
Bare ruined choirs where late the sweet birds sang.

It has become a bleak house, fit nesting place for the birds that Dickens named Hope, Joy, Youth, Peace, Rest, Life, Dust, Ashes, Waste, Want, Ruin, Despair, Madness, Death, Cunning, Folly, Words, Wigs, Rags, Sheepskin, Plunder, Precedent, Jargon, Gammon and Spinach.

Before Eunice came, and left desolation behind her, Lowfield Hall was not like this. It was as well kept as its distant neighbours, as comfortable, as warm, as elegant, and, seemingly, as much a sanctuary as they. Its inhabitants were safe and happy, and destined surely to lead long secure lives.

But on an April day they invited Eunice in.

A little blustery wind was blowing the daffodils in the orchard, waves on a golden sea. The clouds parted and closed again, so that at one moment it was winter in the garden and at the next an uneasy summer. And in those sombre intervals it might have been snow, not the blossom of the blackthorn, that whitened the hedge.

Winter stopped at the windows. The sun brought in flashes of summer to match the pleasant warmth, and it was warm enough for Jacqueline Coverdale to sit down to breakfast in a short-sleeved dress.

She was holding a letter in her left hand on which she wore her platinum wedding ring and the diamond cluster George had given her on their engagement.

'I'm not looking forward to this at all,' she said.

'More coffee, please, darling,' said George. He loved watching her do things for him, as long as she didn't have to do too much. He loved just looking at her, so pretty, his Jacqueline, fair, slender, a Lizzie Siddal matured. Six years of marriage, and he hadn't got used to the wonder of it, the miracle that he had found her. 'Sorry,' he said. 'You're not looking forward to it? Well, we didn't get any other replies. Women aren't exactly queueing up to work for us.'

She shook her head, a quick pretty gesture. Her hair was very blonde, short and sleek. 'We could try again. I know you'll say I'm silly, George, but I had a sort of absurd hope that we'd get – well, someone like ourselves. At any rate, a reasonably educated person who was willing to take on domestic service for the sake of a nice home.'

'A "lady", as they used to say.'

Jacqueline smiled in rather a shamefaced way. 'Eva Baalham would write a better letter than this one. E. Parchman! What a way for a woman to sign her name!'

'It was correct usage for the Victorians.'

'Maybe, but we're not Victorians. Oh dear, I wish we were. Imagine a smart parlourmaid waiting on us now, and a cook busy in the kitchen.' And Giles, she thought but didn't say aloud, obliged to be well mannered and not to read at table. Had he heard any of this? Wasn't he the least bit interested? 'No income tax,' she said aloud, 'and no horrible new houses all over the countryside.'

'And no electricity either,' said George, touching the radiator behind him, 'or constant hot water, and perhaps Paula dying in childbirth.'

'I know.' Jacqueline returned to her original tack. 'But that letter, darling, and her bleak manner when she phoned. I just know she's going to be a vulgar lumpish creature who'll break the china and sweep the dust under the mats.'

'You can't know that, and it's hardly fair judging her by one letter. You want a housekeeper, not a secretary. Go and see her. You've fixed this interview, Paula's expecting you, and you'll only regret it if you let the chance go by. If she makes a bad impression on you, just tell her no, and then we'll think about trying again.'

The grandfather clock in the hall struck the first quarter after eight. George got up. 'Come along now, Giles, I believe that clock's a few minutes slow.' He kissed his wife. Very slowly Giles closed his copy of the *Baghavad Gita* which had been propped against the marmalade pot, and with a kind of concentrated lethargy extended himself to his full, emaciated, bony height. Muttering under his breath something that might have been Greek or, for all she knew, Sanscrit, he let his mother kiss his spotty cheek.

'Give my love to Paula,' said George, and off they went in the white Mercedes, George to Tin Box Coverdale, Giles to the Magnus Wythen Foundation School. Silence settled upon them in the car after George, who tried, who was determined to keep on trying, had remarked that it was a very windy day. Giles said 'Mmm'. As always, he re-

332

sumed his reading. George thought, Please let this woman be all right, because I can't let Jackie keep on trying to run that enormous place, it's not fair. We shall have to move into a bungalow or something, and I don't want that, God forbid, so please let this E. Parchman be all right.

There are six bedrooms in Lowfield Hall, a drawing room, a dining room, a morning room, three bathrooms, a kitchen, and what are known as usual offices. In this case, the usual offices were the back kitchen and the gun room. On that April morning the house wasn't exactly dirty, but it wasn't clean either. There was a bluish film on all the thirty-three windows, and the film was decorated with fingerprints and finger smears: Eva Baalham's, and probably, even after two months, those of the last and most lamentable of all the *au pairs*. Jacqueline had worked it out once, and estimated that six thousand square feet of carpet covered the floors. This, however, was fairly clean. Old Eva loved plying the vacuum cleaner while chatting about her relations. She used a duster too, up to eye level. It was just unfortunate that her eyes happened to be about four feet nine from the ground.

Jacqueline put the breakfast things in the dishwasher, the milk and butter in the fridge. The fridge hadn't been defrosted for six weeks. Had the oven *ever* been cleaned? She went upstairs. It was awful, she ought to be ashamed of herself, she knew that, but her hand came away grey with dust from the banisters. The little bathroom, the one they called the children's bathroom, was in a hideous mess, Giles's latest acne remedy, a kind of green paste, caked all over the basin. She hadn't made the beds. Hastily she pulled the pink sheet, the blankets, the silk counterpane up over the six-foot-wide mattress she shared with George. Giles's bed could stay the way it was. She doubted if he would notice anyway – wouldn't notice if the sheets all turned purple and there was a warming pan in it instead of an electric blanket.

Attention to her own appearance she didn't skimp. She often thought it was a pity she wasn't as house-proud as she was Jacqueline-proud, but that was the way it was, that was the way *she* was. Bath, hair, hands, nails, warmer dress, sheer tights, the new dark green shoes, face painted to look *au naturel.* She put on the mink George had given her for Christmas. Now down to the orchard to pick an armful of daffodils for Paula. At any rate, she kept the garden nice, not a weed to be seen, and there wouldn't be, even in the height of summer.

Waves on a golden sea. Snowdrops nestling under the whiter hedge. Twice already, this dry spring, she had mown the lawns, and they were plushy green. An open-air lady I am, thought Jacqueline, the wind on her face, the thin sharp scents of spring flowers delighting her. I could stand here for hours, looking at the river, the poplars in the water meadows, the Greeving Hills with all these cloud shadows racing, racing. . . . But she had to see this woman, this E. Parchman. Time to go. If only she turns out to like house-work as much as I like gardening.

She went back into the house. Was it her imagination, or did the kitchen really not smell at all nice? Out through the gun room, which was in its usual mess, lock the door, leave Lowfield Hall to accumulate more dust, grow that much more frowsty.

Jacqueline put the daffodils on the back seat of the Ford and set off to drive the seventy miles to London.

George Coverdale was an exceptionally handsome man, classic-featured, as trim of figure as when he had rowed for his university in 1939. Of his three children only one had inherited his looks, and Paula Caswall was not that one. A sweet expression and gentle eyes saved her from plainness, but pregnancy was not becoming to her, and she was in the eighth month of her second pregnancy. She had a vigorous mischievous little boy to look after, a fairly big house in Kensington to run, she was huge and tired and her ankles were swollen. Also she was frightened. Patrick's birth had been a painful nightmare, and she looked forward to this coming delivery with dread. She would have preferred to see no one and have no one see her. But she realised that her house was the obvious venue for an interview with this London-based prospective housekeeper, and being en-dowed with the gracious manners of the Coverdales, she welcomed her stepmother affectionately, enthused over the daffodils and complimented Jacqueline on her dress. They had lunch, and Paula listened with sympathy to Jacqueline's doubts and forebodings about what would ensue at two o'clock.

However, she was determined to take no part in this interview. Patrick had gone for his afternoon sleep, and when the doorbell rang at two minutes to two Paula did no more than show the woman in the navy blue raincoat into the living room. She left her to Jacqueline and went upstairs to lie down. But in those few seconds she spent with Eunice Parchman she felt a violent antipathy to her. Eunice affected her in that moment as she so often affected others. It was as if a coldness, almost an icy breath, emanated from her. Wherever she was, she brought a chill into the warm air. Later Paula was to remember this first impression and, in an agony of guilt, reproach herself for not warning her father, for not telling him of a wild premonition that was to prove justified. She did nothing. She went to her bedroom and fell into a heavy troubled sleep.

Jacqueline's reaction was very different. From having been violently opposed to engaging this woman, till then unseen, she did a complete about-face within two minutes. Two factors decided her, or rather her principal weaknesses decided for her. These were her vanity and her snobbishness.

She rose as the woman came into the room and held out her hand.

'Good afternoon. You're very punctual.'

'Good afternoon, madam.'

Except by assistants in the few remaining old-fashioned shops in Stantwich, Jacqueline hadn't been addressed as madam for many years. She was delighted. She smiled.

'Is it Miss Parchman or Mrs?'

'Miss Parchman. Eunice Parchman.'

'Won't you sit down?'

No repulsive chill or, as Melinda would have put it, 'vibes' affected Jacqueline. She was the last of the family to feel it, perhaps because she didn't want to, because almost from that first moment she was determined to take Eunice Parchman on, and then, during the months that followed, to keep her. She saw a placid-looking creature with rather too small a head, pale firm features, brown hair mixed with grey, small steady blue eyes, a massive body that seemed neither to go out nor in, large shapely hands, very clean with short nails, large shapely legs in heavy brown nylon, large feet in somewhat distorted black court shoes. As soon as Eunice Parchman had sat down she undid the top button of her raincoat to disclose the polo neck of a lighter blue-ribbed jumper. Calmly she sat there, looking down at her hands folded in her lap.

Without admitting it even to herself, Jacqueline Coverdale liked handsome men and plain women. She got on well with Melinda but not so well as she got on with the less attractive Paula and Peter's *jolie laide* wife, Audrey. She suffered from what might be called a Gwendolen Complex, for like Wilde's Miss Fairfax, she preferred a woman to be 'fully forty-two and more than usually plain for her age'. Eunice Parchman was at least as old as herself, very likely older, though it was hard to tell, and there was no doubt about her plainness. If she had belonged to her own class, Jacqueline would have wondered why she didn't wear make-up, undergo a diet, have that tabby-cat hair tinted. But in a servant all was as it should be.

In the face of this respectful silence, confronted by this entirely prepossessing appearance, Jacqueline forgot the questions she had intended to ask. And instead of examining the candidate, instead of attempting to find out if this woman were suitable to work in her house, if she would suit the Coverdales, she began persuading Eunice Parchman that they would suit her.

'It's a big house, but there are only the three of us except when my stepdaughter comes home for the weekend. There's a cleaner three days a week, and of course I should do all the cooking myself.'

'I can cook, madam,' said Eunice.

'It wouldn't be necessary, really. There's a dishwasher and a deep freeze. My husband and I do all the shopping.' Jacqueline was impressed by this woman's toneless voice that, though uneducated, had no trace of a cockney accent. 'We do entertain quite a lot,' she said almost fearfully.

Eunice moved her feet, bringing them close together. She nodded slowly. 'I'm used to that. I'm a hard worker.'

At this point Jacqueline should have asked why Eunice was leaving her present situation, or at least something about her present situation. For all she knew, there might not have been one. She didn't ask. She was bemused by those 'madams', excited by the contrast between this woman and Eva Baalham, this woman and the last pert too-pretty *au pair*. It was all so different from what she had expected.

Eagerly she said, 'When could you start?'

Eunice's blank face registered a faint surprise, as well it might.

'You'll want a reference,' she said.

'Oh, yes,' said Jacqueline, reminded. 'Of *course*.'

A white card was produced from Eunice's large black handbag. On it was written in the same handwriting as the letter that had so dismayed Jacqueline in the first place: Mrs Chichester, 24 Willow Vale, London, S.W. 18, and a phone number. The address was the one which had headed Eunice's letter.

'That's Wimbledon, isn't it?'

Eunice nodded. No doubt she was gladdened by this erroneous assumption. They discussed wages, when she would start, how she would travel to Stantwich. Subject, of course, Jacqueline said hastily, to the reference being satisfactory.

'I'm sure we shall get on marvellously.'

At last Eunice smiled. Her eyes remained cold and still, but her mouth moved. It was certainly a smile. 'Mrs Chichester said, could you phone her tonight before nine? She's an old lady and she goes to bed early.'

This show of tender regard for an employer's wishes and foibles could only be pleasing.

'You may be sure I shall,' said Jacqueline.

It was only twenty past two and the interview was over.

Eunice said, 'Thank you, madam. I can see myself out,' thus indicating, or so it seemed to Jacqueline, that she knew her place. She walked steadily from the room without looking back.

If Jacqueline had had a better knowledge of Greater London, she would have realised that Eunice Parchman had already told her a lie, or at least acquiesced in a misapprehension. For the postal district of Wimbledon is S.W.

337

19 not S.W. 18 which designates a much less affluent area in the Borough of Wandsworth. But she didn't realise and she didn't check, and when she entered Lowfield Hall at six, five minutes after George had got home, she didn't even show him the white card.

'I'm sure she'll be ideal, darling,' she enthused, 'really the kind of old-fashioned servant we thought was an extinct breed. I can't tell you how quiet and respectful she was, not a bit pushing. I'm only afraid she may be too humble. But I *know* she's going to be a hard worker.'

George put his arm round his wife and kissed her. He said nothing about her *volte face*, uttered no 'I told you so's'. He was accustomed to Jacqueline's prejudices, succeeded often by wild enthusiasm, and he loved her for her impulsiveness which, in his eyes, made her seem young and sweet and feminine. What he said was, 'I don't care how humble she is or how pushing, as long as she takes some of the load of work off your hands.'

Before she made the phone call Jacqueline, who had an active imagination, had formed a picture in her mind of the kind of household in which Eunice Parchman worked and the kind of woman who employed her. Willow Vale, she thought, would be a quiet tree-lined road near Wimbledon Common, number 24 large, Victorian; Mrs Chichester an elderly gentlewoman with rigid notions of behaviour, demanding but just, autocratic, whose servant was leaving her because she wouldn't, or couldn't afford to pay her adequate wages in these inflationary times.

At eight o'clock she dialled the number. Eunice Parchman answered the phone herself by giving the code correctly followed by the four digits slowly and precisely enunciated. Again calling Jacqueline madam, she asked her to hold the line while she fetched Mrs Chichester. And Jacqueline imagined her crossing a sombre over-furnished hall, entering a large and rather chilly drawing room where an old lady sat listening to classical music or reading the In Memoriam column in a quality newspaper. There, on the threshold, she would pause and say in her deferential way:

'Mrs Coverdale on the phone for you, madam.'

The facts were otherwise.

338

The telephone in question was attached to the wall on the first landing of a rooming house in Earlsfield, at the top of a flight of stairs. Eunice Parchman had been waiting patiently by it since five in case, when it rang, some other tenant should get to it first. Mrs Chichester was a machine-tool operator in her fifties called Annie Cole who sometimes performed small services of this kind in exchange for Eunice agreeing not to tell the Post Office how, for a year after her mother's death, she had continued to draw that lady's pension. Annie had written the letter and the words on the card, and it was from her furnished room, number 6, 24 Willow Vale, S.W. 18, that Eunice now fetched her to the phone. Annie Cole said:

'I'm really very upset to be losing Miss Parchman, Mrs Coverdale. She's managed everything so wonderfully for me for seven years. She's a marvellous worker, and excellent cook, and so house-proud! Really, if she has a fault, it's that she's too conscientious.'

Even Jacqueline felt that this was laying it on a bit thick. And the voice was peculiarly sprightly – Annie Cole couldn't get rid of Eunice fast enough – with an edge to it the reverse of refined. She had the sense to ask why this paragon was leaving.

'Because I'm leaving myself.' The reply came without hesitation. 'I'm joining my son in New Zealand. The cost of living is getting impossible here, isn't it? Miss Parchman could come with me, I should welcome the idea, but she's rather conservative. She prefers to stay here. I should like to think of her settling in a nice family like yours.'

Jacqueline was satisfied.

'Did you confirm it with Miss Parchman?' said George.

'Oh, darling, I forgot. I'll have to write to her.'

'Or phone back.'

Why not phone back, Jacqueline? Dial that number again now. A young man returning to his room next to Annie Cole's, setting his foot now on the last step of that flight of stairs, will lift the receiver. And when you ask for Miss Parchman he will tell you he has never heard of her. Mrs Chichester, then? There is no Mrs Chichester, only a Mr Chichester who is the landlord, in whose name the phone number is but who himself lives in Croydon. Pick up the phone now, Jacqueline. . . .

'I think it's better to confirm it in writing.'

'Just as you like, darling.'

The moment passed, the chance was lost. George did pick up the phone, but it was to call Paula, for the report on her health he had received from his wife had disquieted him. While he was talking to her, Jacqueline wrote her letter.

And the other people whom chance and destiny and their own agency were to bring together for destruction on 14 February? Joan Smith was preaching on a cottage doorstep. Melinda Coverdale, in her room in Galwich, was struggling to make sense out of *Sir Gawain and the Green Knight*. Giles Mont was reciting mantras as an aid to meditation.

But already they were gathered together. In that moment when Jacqueline declined to make a phone call an invisible thread lassoed each of them, bound them one to another, related them more closely than blood.

# 3

George and Jacqueline were discreet people, and they didn't broadcast their coming good fortune. But Jacqueline did mention it to her friend Lady Royston who mentioned it to Mrs Cairne when the eternal subject of getting someone to keep the place clean came up. The news seeped through along the ramifications of Higgses, Meadowses, Baalhams and Newsteads, and in the Blue Boar it succeeded as the major topic of conversation over the latest excesses of Joan Smith.

Eva Baalham hastened, in her oblique way, to let Jacqueline know that she knew. 'You going to give her telly?'

'Give whom – er, television?' said Jacqueline, flushing.

'Her as is coming from London. Because if you are I can as like get you a set cheap from my cousin Meadows as has the electric shop in Gosbury. Fell off the back of a lorry, I reckon, but ask no questions and you'll get no lies.'

'Thank you so much,' said Jacqueline, more than a little annoyed. 'As a matter of fact, we're buying a colour set for ourselves and Miss Parchman will be having our old one.'

'Parchman,' said Eva, spitting on a window-pane before giving it a wipe with her apron. 'Would that be a London name, I wonder?'

'I really don't know, Mrs Baalham. When you've finished whatever you're doing to that window perhaps you'd be good enough to come upstairs with me and we'll start getting her room ready.'

'I reckon,' said Eva in her broad East Anglian whine. She never called Jacqueline madam; it wouldn't have crossed her mind. In her eyes, the only difference between herself and the Coverdales was one of money. In other respects she was their superior since they were newcomers, and not even gentry but in trade, while her yeomen ancestors had lived in Greeving for five hundred years. Nor did she envy them their money. She had quite enough of her own, and she preferred her council house to Lowfield Hall, great big barn of a place, must cost a packet keeping that warm. She didn't like Jacqueline, who was mutton dressed as lamb and who gave herself some mighty airs for the wife of the owner of a tin-can factory. All that will-you-be-so-good and thank-you-so-much nonsense. Wonder how she'll get on with this Parchman? Wonder how I will? Still, I reckon I can always leave. There's Mrs Jameson-Kerr begging me to come on her bended knees and she'll pay sixty pence an hour.

'God help her legs,' said Eva, mounting the stairs.

At the top of the house a warren of poky attics had long since been converted into two large bedrooms and a bathroom. From their windows could be seen one of the finest pastoral views in East Anglia. Constable, of course, had painted it, sitting on the banks of the River Beal, and as was sometimes his way he had shifted a few church towers the better to suit his composition. It was lovely enough with the church towers in their proper places, a wide serene view of meadows and little woods in all the delicious varied greens of early May.

'Have her bed in here, will she?' said Eva, ambling into the bigger and sunnier of the bedrooms.

'No, she won't.' Jacqueline could see that Eva was preparing to line herself up as secretary, as it were, of the

341

downtrodden domestic servants' union. 'I want that room for when my husband's grandchildren come to stay.'

'You'll have to make her comfortable if you want her to stop.' Eva opened a window. 'Lovely day. Going to be a hot summer. The Lord is on our side, as my cousin as has the farm always says. There's young Giles going off in your car without so much as a by your leave, I reckon.'

Jacqueline was furious. She thought Eva ought to call Giles Mr Mont or, at least, 'your son'. But she was glad to see Giles, who was on half-term, leave his voluntary incarceration at last to get some fresh air.

'If you'd be so kind, Mrs Baalham, we might start moving the furniture.'

Giles drove down the avenue between the horse-chestnut trees and out into Greeving Lane. The lane is an unclassified road, just wide enough for two cars to pass if they go very slowly. Blackthorn had given place to hawthorn, and the hedges were creamy with its sugary scented blossom. A limpid blue sky, pale green wheat growing, a cuckoo calling – in May he sings all day – an exultation of birds carolling their territorial claims from every tree.

Pretending that none of it was there, refusing, in spite of his creed, to be one with the oneness of it, Giles drove over the river bridge. He intended to get as little fresh air as was compatible with going out of doors. He loathed the country. It bored him. There was nothing to do. When you told people that they were shocked, presumably because they didn't realise that no one in his senses could spend more than a maximum of an hour a day looking at the stars, walking in the fields or sitting on river banks. Besides, it was nearly always cold or muddy. He disliked shooting things or fishing things out of streams or riding horses or following the hunt. George, who had tried to encourage him in those pursuits, had perhaps at last understood the impossibility of the task. Giles never, but *never*, went for a country walk. When he was compelled to walk to Lowfield Hall from the point where the school bus stopped, about half a mile, he kept his eyes on the ground. He had tried shutting them, but he had bumped into a tree.

London he loved. Looking back, he thought he had been happy in London. He had wanted to go to a boarding school in a big city, but his mother hadn't let him because some psychologist had said he was disturbed and needed the secure background of family life. Being disturbed didn't bother him, and he rather fostered the air he had of the absent-minded, scatty, preoccupied young intellectual. He was intellectual all right, very much so. Last year he had got so many O-levels that there had been a piece about him in a national newspaper. He was certain of a place at Oxford, and he knew as much Latin, and possibly more Greek, than the man who professed to teach him these subjects at the Magnus Wythen.

He had no friends at school, and he despised the village boys who were interested only in motor-cycles, pornography and the Blue Boar. Ian and Christopher Cairne and others of their like had been designated his friends by parental edict, but he hardly ever saw them, as they were away at their public schools. Neither the village boys nor those at school ever attempted to beat him up. He was over six feet and still growing. His face was horrible with acne, and the day after he washed it his hair was again wet with grease.

Now he was on his way to Sudbury to buy a packet of orange dye. He was going to dye all his jeans and tee-shirts orange in pursuance of his religion, which was, roughly, Buddhism. When he had saved up enough money he meant to go to India on a bus and, with the exception of Melinda, never see any of them again. Well, maybe his mother. But not his father or stuffy old George or self-righteous Peter or this bunch of peasants. That is, if he didn't become a Catholic instead. He had just finished reading *Brideshead Revisited*, and had begun to wonder whether being a Catholic at Oxford and burning incense on one's staircase might not be better than India. But he'd dye the jeans and tee-shirts just in case.

At Meadows' garage in Greeving he stopped for petrol.

'When's the lady from London coming, then?' said Jim Meadows.

'Mmm?' said Giles.

Jim wanted to know so that he could tell them in the pub that night. He tried again. Giles thought about it reluctantly. 'Is today Wednesday?'

343

' 'Course it is.' Jim added, because he fancied himself as a wit, 'All day.'

'They said Saturday,' said Giles at last. 'I think.'

It might be and it might not, thought Jim. You never knew with him. Needed his head seeing to, that one. It was a wonder she let him out alone at the wheel of a good car like that. 'Melinda'll be home to get a look at her, I reckon.'

'Mmm,' said Giles. He drove off, rejecting the green stamps.

Melinda would be home. He didn't know whether this was pleasing or disquieting. On the surface, his relationship with her was casual and even distant, but in Giles's heart, where he often saw himself as a Poe or Byron, it simmered as an incestuous passion. This had come into being, or been pushed into being, by Giles six months before. Until then Melinda had merely been a kind of quasi-sister. He knew, of course, that since she was not his sister, or even his half-sister, there was nothing at all to stop their falling in love with each other and eventually marrying. Apart from the three years' age difference, which would be of no importance later on, there could be no possible objection on anyone's part. Mother would even like it and old George would come round. But this was not what Giles wanted or what he saw in his fantasies. In them Melinda and he were a Byron and an Augusta Leigh who confessed their mutual passion while walking in Wuthering Heights weather on the Greeving Hills, a pastime which nothing would have induced Giles to undertake in reality. There was little reality in any of this. In his fantasies Melinda even looked different, paler, thinner, rather phthisic, very much of another world. Confronting each other, breathless in the windswept darkness, they spoke of how their love must remain for ever secret, never of course to be consummated. And though they married other people, their passion endured and was whispered of as something profound and indefinable.

He bought the dye, two packets of it called Nasturtium Flame. He also bought a poster of a Pre-Raphaelite girl with a pale green face and red hair, hanging over a balcony. The girl was presumably craning out of her window to moon after a lost or faithless lover, but from her attitude and the nauseous pallor of her skin she looked more as if,

344

while staying in an hotel in an Italian holiday resort, she had eaten too much pasta and was going to be sick. Giles bought her because she looked like Melinda would look in the terminal stages of tuberculosis.

He returned to the car to find a parking ticket on the wind-screen. He never used the car park. It would have meant walking a hundred yards. When he got home Eva had gone and so had his mother, who had left a note on the kitchen table for him. The note began 'Darling' and ended 'love from Mother' and the middle was full of needless information about the cold lunch left for him in the fridge and how she had had to go to some Women's Institute meeting. It mystified him. He knew where his lunch would be, and he would never have dreamed of leaving a note for anyone. Like all true eccentrics, he thought other people very odd.

Presently he fetched all his clothes downstairs and put them with the dye and some water in the two large pans his mother used for jam-making. While they were boiling, he sat at the kitchen table eating chicken salad and reading the memoirs of a mystic who had lived in a Poona Ashram for thirty years without speaking a word.

On the Friday afternoon Melinda Coverdale came home. The train brought her from Galwich to Stantwich, and the bus to a place called Gallows Corner two miles from Lowfield Hall. There she alighted and waited for a lift. At this hour there was always someone passing on his or her way home to Greeving, so Melinda hoisted herself up on to Mrs Cotleigh's garden wall and sat in the sun.

She was wearing over-long jeans rolled up to the knees, very scuffed red cowboy boots, an Indian cotton shirt and a yellow motoring hat, vintage 1920. But for all that there was no prettier sight to be seen on a sunny garden wall between Stantwich and King's Lynn. Melinda was the child who had inherited George's looks. She had his straight nose and high brow, his sharply sensitive mouth and his bright blue eyes – and her dead mother's mane of golden hair, the colour of Mrs Cotleigh's wallflowers.

An energy that never seemed to flag, except where Middle English verse was concerned, kept her constantly on the move. She lugged her horse's nosebag holdall up on

345

to the wall beside her, pulled out a string of beads, tried it on, made a face at the textbooks which hope rather than incentive had persuaded her to bring, then flung the bag down on the grass and jumped after it. Cross-legged on the bank while the useless bus passed in the opposite direction, then to pick poppies, the wild red poppies, weeds of Suffolk, that abound on this corner where once the gibbet stood.

Five minutes later the chicken-farm van came along, and Geoff Baalham, who was second cousin to Eva called, 'Hi, Melinda! Can I drop you?'

She jumped in, hat, bag and poppies. 'I must have been there half an hour,' said Melinda, who had been there ten minutes.

'I like your hat.'

'Do you really, Geoff? You are *sweet*. I got it in the Oxfam shop.' Melinda knew everyone in the village and called everyone, even ancient gaffers and gammers, by their Christian names. She drove tractors and picked fruit and watched calvings. In the presence of her father she spoke more or less politely to Jameson-Kerrs, Archers, Cairnes and Sir Robert Royston, but she disapproved of them as reactionary. Once, when the foxhounds had met on Greeving Green, she had gone up there waving an anti-blood-sports banner. In her early teens she had gone fishing with the village boys and with them watched the hares come out at dusk. In her late teens she had danced with them at Cattingham 'hops' and kissed them behind the village hall. She was as gossipy as their mothers and as involved.

'What's been going on in merry old Greeving in my absence? Tell all.' She hadn't been home for three weeks. 'I know, Mrs Archer's eloped with Mr Smith.'

Geoff Baalham grinned widely. 'Poor old sod. I reckon he's got his hands full with his own missus. Wait a minute, let's see. Susan Meadows, Higgs that was, had her baby. It's a girl, and they're calling it Lalage.'

'You don't *mean* it!'

'Thought that'd shake you. Your ma's got herself on the parish council, though I reckon you know about that, and – wait for it – your dad's bought colour telly.'

'I talked to him on the phone last night. He never said.'

'No, well, only got it today. I had it all from my Auntie Eva an hour back.' The people of Greeving are careless about the correct terms for relations. One's stepmother is as much one's ma or mum as one's natural mother, and a female second cousin, if old enough, is necessarily auntie. 'They're giving the old one to the lady help that's coming from London.'

'Oh God, how mean! Daddy's such a ghastly fascist. Don't you think that's the most undemocratic fascist thing you've ever heard, Geoff?'

'It's the way of the world, Melinda, love. Always has been and always will be. You oughtn't to go calling your dad names. I'd turn you over and tan your backside for you if I was him.'

'Geoff Baalham! To hear you, no one'd think you're only a year older than me.'

'Just you remember I'm a married man now, and that teaches you the meaning of responsibility. Here we are, Lowfield Hall, madame, and I'll take my leave of you. Oh, and you can tell your ma I'll be sending them eggs up with Auntie Eva first thing Monday morning.'

'Will do. Thanks tremendously for the lift, Geoff. You are *sweet*.'

'Cheerio then, Melinda.'

Off went Geoff to the chicken farm and Barbara Carter whom he had married in January, but thinking what a nice pretty girl Melinda Coverdale was – that hat, my God! – and thinking too of walking with her years before by the River Beal and of innocent kisses exchanged to the rushing music of the mill.

Melinda swung up the long drive, under the chestnuts hung with their cream and bronze candles, round the house and in by the gun-room door. Giles was sitting at the kitchen table reading the last chapter of the Poona book.

'Hi, Step.'

'Hallo,' said Giles. He no longer used the nickname that once had served for each to address to the other. It was incongruous with his Byronic fantasies, though these always crumbled when Melinda appeared in the flesh. She had quite a lot of well-distributed flesh, and red cheeks, and an aggressive healthiness. Also she bounced. Giles sighed, scratched his spots and thought of being in India with a begging bowl.

'How did you get red ink on your jeans?'

'I didn't. I've dyed them but the dye didn't take.'

'Mad,' said Melinda. She sailed off, searched for her father and stepmother, found them on the top floor putting finishing touches to Miss Parchman's room. 'Hallo, my darlings.' Each got a kiss, but George got his first. 'Daddy, you've got a suntan. If I'd known you were coming home so early I'd have phoned your office from the station. Geoff Baalham gave me a lift and he said his Auntie Eva'll bring the eggs first thing on Monday and you're giving our new housekeeper the old telly. I said I never heard anything so fascist in all my life. Next thing you'll be saying she's got to eat on her own in the kitchen.'

George and Jacqueline looked at each other.

'Well, of course.'

'How awful! No wonder the revolution's coming. *A bas les aristos*. D'you like my hat, Jackie? I bought it in the Oxfam shop. Fifty pee. God, I'm *starving*. We haven't got anyone awful coming tonight, have we? No curs or cairns or roisterers?'

'Now, Melinda, I think that's enough.' The words were admonitory but the tone was tender. George was incapable of being really cross with his favourite child. 'We're tolerant of your friends and you must be tolerant of ours. As a matter of fact, the Roystons are dining with us.'

Melinda groaned. Quickly she hugged her father before he could expostulate. 'I shall go and phone Stephen or Charles or someone and *make* him take me out. But I tell you what, Jackie, I'll be back in time to help you clear up. Just think, you'll never have to do it again after tomorrow when Parchment Face comes.'

'Melinda . . .' George began.

'She had got rather a parchment look to her face,' said Jacqueline, and she couldn't help laughing.

So Melinda went to the cinema in Nunchester with Stephen Crutchley, the doctor's son. The Roystons came to dine at Lowfield Hall, and Jacqueline said, Wait till tomorrow. Don't you envy me, Jessica? But what will she be like? And will she really come up to these glowing expectations? It was George who wondered. Please God,

348

let her be the treasure Jackie thinks she is. *Schadenfreude* made Sir Robert and Lady Royston secretly hope she wouldn't be, but cut on the same lines as their Anneliese, their Birgit and that best-forgotten Spanish couple.

Time will show. Wait till tomorrow.

# 4

The Coverdales had speculated about Eunice Parchman as to her work potential and her attitude, respectful or otherwise, towards themselves. They had allotted her a private bathroom and a television set, some comfortable chairs and a well-sprung bed rather as one sees that a workhorse has a good stable and manger. They wanted her to be content because if she were contented she would stay. But they never considered her as a person at all. Not for them as they got up on Saturday, 9 May, E-Day indeed, any thoughts as to what her past had been, whether she was nervous about coming, whether she was visited by the same hopes and fears that affected them. At that stage Eunice was little more than a machine to them, and the satisfactory working of that machine depended on its being suitably oiled and its having no objection to stairs.

But Eunice was a person. Eunice, as Melinda might have put it, was for real.

She was the strangest person they were ever likely to meet. And had they known what her past contained, they would have fled from her or barred their doors against her as against the plague – not to mention her future, now inextricably bound up with theirs.

Her past lay in the house she was now preparing to leave; an old terraced house, one of a long row in Rainbow Street, Tooting, with its front door opening directly on to the pavement. She had been born in that house, forty-seven years before, the only child of a Southern Railway guard and his wife.

From the first her existence was a narrow one. She seemed one of those people who are destined to spend their lives in the restricted encompassment of a few streets. Her school was almost next door, Rainbow Street Infants, and those members of her family she visited lived within a stone's throw. Destiny was temporarily disturbed by the coming of the Second World War. Along with thousands of other London schoolchildren, she was sent away to the country before she had learned to read. But her parents, though dull, unaware, mole-like people, were upset by reports that her foster mother neglected her, and fetched her back to them, to the bombs and the war-torn city.

After that Eunice attended school only sporadically. To this school or that school she went for weeks or sometimes months at a time, but in each new class she entered the other pupils were all far ahead of her. They had passed her by, and no teacher ever took the trouble to discover the fundamental gap in her acquirements, still less to remedy it. Bewildered, bored, apathetic, she sat at the back of the classroom, staring at the incomprehensible on page or blackboard. Or she stayed away, a stratagem always connived at by her mother. Therefore, by the time she came to leave school a month before her fourteenth birthday, she could sign her name, read 'The cat sat on the mat' and 'Jim likes ham but Jack likes jam', and that was about all. School had taught her one thing – to conceal, by many subterfuges and contrivances, that she could not read or write.

She went to work in a sweetshop, also in Rainbow Street, where she learned to tell a Mars bar from a Crunchie by the colour of its wrapping. When she was seventeen, the illness which had threatened her mother for years began to cripple her. It was multiple sclerosis, though it was some time before the Parchmans' doctor understood this. Mrs Parchman, at fifty, was confined to a wheelchair, and Eunice gave up her job to look after her and run the house. Her days now began to be spent in a narrow twilight world, for illiteracy is a kind of blindness. The Coverdales, had they been told of it, would not have believed such a world could exist. Why didn't she educate herself? they would have asked. Why didn't she go to evening classes, get a job, employ someone to look after her mother, join a club, meet people? Why, indeed. Between the Coverdales and the

Parchmans a great gulf is fixed. George himself often said so, without fully considering what it implied. A young girl to him was always some version of Paula or Melinda, cherished, admired, educated, loved, brought up to see herself as one of the top ten per cent. Not so Eunice Parchman. A big raw-boned plain girl with truculent sullen eyes, she had never heard a piece of music except for the hymns and the extracts from Gilbert and Sullivan her father whistled while he shaved. She had never seen any picture of note but 'The Laughing Cavalier' and the 'Mona Lisa' in the school hall, and she was so steeped in ignorance that had you asked her who Napoleon was and where was Denmark, she would have stared in uncomprehending blankness.

There were things Eunice could do. She had considerable manual dexterity. She could clean expertly and shop and cook and sew and push her mother up to the common in her wheelchair. Was it so surprising that, being able to do these things, she should prefer the safety and peace of doing them and them alone? Was it odd to find her taking satisfaction in gossiping with her middle-aged neighbours and avoiding the company of their children who could read and write and who had jobs and talked of things beyond her comprehension? She had her pleasures, eating the chocolate she loved and which made her grow stout, ironing, cleaning silver and brass, augmenting the family income by knitting for her neighbours. By the time she was thirty she had never been into a public house, visited a theatre, entered any restaurant more grand than a teashop, left the country, had a boy friend, worn make-up or been to a hairdresser. She had twice been to the cinema with Mrs Samson next door and had seen the Queen's wedding and coronation on Mrs Samson's television set. Between the ages of seven and twelve she four times travelled in a long-distance train. That was the history of her youth.

Virtue might naturally be the concomitant of such sheltering. She had few opportunities to do bad things, but she found them or made them.

'If there's one thing I've taught Eunice,' her mother used to say, 'it's to tell right from wrong.' It was a gabbled cliché, as automatic as the quacking of a duck but less meaningful. The Parchmans were not given to thinking before they spoke, or indeed to thinking much at all.

All that jerked Eunice out of her apathy were her compulsions. Suddenly an urge would come over her to drop everything and walk. Or turn out a room. Or take a dress to pieces and sew it up again with minor alterations. These urges she always obeyed. Buttoned up tightly into her shabby coat, a scarf tied round her still beautiful thick brown hair, she would walk and walk for miles, sometimes across the river bridges and up into the West End. These walks were her education. She saw things one is not taught in school even if one can read. And instincts, not controlled or repressed by reading, instructed her as to what these sights meant or implied. In the West End she saw prostitutes, in the park people making love, on the commons homosexuals waiting furtively in the shadows to solicit likely passers-by. One night she saw a man who lived in Rainbow Street pick up a boy and take him behind a bush. Eunice had never heard the word blackmail. She didn't know that demanding money with menaces is a popular pastime punishable by the law. But neither, probably, had Cain heard the word murder before he struck his brother down. There are age-old desires in man which man needs no instruction to practise. Very likely Eunice thought she was doing something original. She waited until the boy had gone and then she told her neighbour she would tell his wife unless he gave her ten shillings a week not to do so. Horribly frightened, he agreed and gave her ten shillings a week for years.

Her father had been religious in his youth. He named her after a New Testament character, and sometimes, facetiously, would refer to this fact, pronouncing her name in the Greek way.

'What have you got for my tea tonight, Eu-nicey, mother of Timothy?'

It riled Eunice. It rankled. Did she vaguely ponder on the likelihood that she would never be the mother of anyone? The thoughts of the illiterate are registered in pictures and in very simple words. Eunice's vocabulary was small. She spoke in clichés and catch-phrases picked up from her mother, and her aunt down the road, Mrs Samson. When her cousin married, did she feel envy? Was there bitterness as well as greed in her heart when she began extracting a further ten shillings a week from a married woman who was having an affair with a salesman? She expressed to no one her emotions or her views on life.

Mrs Parchman died when Eunice was thirty-seven, and her widower immediately took over as resident invalid. Perhaps he thought Eunice's services too good to waste. His kidneys had always been weak, and now he cultivated his asthma, taking to his bed.

'I don't know where I'd be without you, Eu-nicey, mother of Timothy.'

Alive today, probably, and living in Tooting.

Eunice's urges pressed her one day to get on a coach and have a day in Brighton, another to take all the furniture out of the living room and paint the walls pink. Her father went into hospital for the odd fortnight.

'Mainly to give you a break, Miss Parchman,' said the doctor. 'He could go at any time, he could last for years.'

But he showed no signs of going. Eunice bought him nice bits of fish and made him steak-and-kidney pudding. She kept up his bedroom fire and brought him hot water to shave in while he whistled 'The King of Love my Shepherd is' and 'I am the Lord High Executioner'. One bright morning in spring he sat up in bed, pink-cheeked and strong, and said in the clear voice of one whose lungs are perfectly sound:

'You can wrap me up warm and put me in Mum's chair and take me up on the common, Eu-nicey, mother of Timothy.'

Eunice made no reply. She took one of the pillows from behind her father's head and pushed it hard down on his face. He struggled and thrashed about for a while, but not for long. His lungs, after all, were not quite sound. Eunice had no phone. She walked up the street and brought the doctor back with her. He asked no questions and signed the death certificate at once.

Now for freedom.

She was forty, and she didn't know what to do with freedom now that she had it. Get over that ridiculous business

353

of not being able to read and write, George Coverdale would have said. Learn a useful trade. Take in lodgers. Get some sort of social life going. Eunice did none of these things. She remained in the house in Rainbow Street, for which the rent was scarcely now more than nominal, and she had her blackmail income, swollen now to two pounds a week. As if those twenty-three years had never been, those best years of all her youth passed as in the twinkling of an eye, she went back to the sweetshop and worked there three days a week.

On one of her walks she saw Annie Cole go into a post office in Merton with a pension book in her hand. Eunice knew a pension book when she saw one. She had been shown by her father how to sign his as his agent. And she knew Annie Cole by sight too, having observed her leaving the crematorium just before Mr Parchman's funeral party had arrived. It was Annie Cole's mother who had died, and now here was Annie Cole collecting her pension and telling the counter clerk how poor mother had rallied that day. The advantage of being illiterate is that one achieves an excellent visual memory and almost total recall.

Annie thereby became Eunice's victim and amanuensis, paying her a third of that pension and doing needful jobs for her. She also, because she bore no malice, seeing Eunice's conduct as only natural in a catch-as-catch-can world, became the nearest Eunice ever had to a friend until she met Joan Smith. But it was time now to kill Mother off finally as she was getting scared, only Eunice as beneficiary wouldn't let her. She determined to be rid of Eunice, and it was she who, having flattered her blackmailer to the top of her bent on her housewifely skills, produced as if casually the Coverdales' advertisement.

'You could get thirty-five pounds a week and all found. I've always said you were wasted in that shop.'

Eunice munched her Cadbury's filled block. 'I don't know,' she said, a favourite response.

'That place of yours is falling down. They're always talking about pulling that row down. It'd be no loss, I'm sure.' Annie scrutinised *The Times* which she had picked at random out of a litter bin. 'It sounds ever so nice. Why not write to them and just see? You don't have to go there if you don't fancy it.'

'You can write if you want,' said Eunice.

Like all her close acquaintances, Annie suspected Eunice was illiterate or semi-literate, but no one could ever be quite sure. Eunice sometimes seemed to read magazines, and she could sign things. There are many people, after all, who never read or write, although they can. So Annie wrote the letter to Jacqueline, and when the time came for the interview it was Annie who primed Eunice.

'Be sure to call her madam, Eun, and don't speak till you're spoken to. Mother was in service when she was a girl and she knew all about it. I can give you a good many of Mother's tips.' Poor Annie. She had been devoted to her mother, and the pension-book fraud had been perpetrated as much as a way of keeping her mother alive and with her as for gain. 'You can have a lend of Mother's court shoes too. They'll be about your size.'

It worked. Before Eunice could think much about it, she was engaged as the Coverdales' housekeeper, and if it was at twenty-five rather than thirty-five pounds a week, either seemed a fortune to her. And yet, why was she so easily persuaded, she who was as bound to her burrow and her warren as any wild animal?

Not for pastures new, adventure, pecuniary advantage, or even the chance of showing off the one thing she could do well. Largely, she took the job to avoid responsibility.

While her father was alive, though things had been bad in many respects, they had been good in one. He took responsibility for the rent and the rates and the services bills, for filling in forms and reading what had to be read. Eunice took the rates round to the council offices in cash, paid the gas and electricity bills in the same way. But she couldn't hire television or buy it on HP – there would have been forms to fill in. Letters and circulars came; she couldn't read them. Lowfield Hall would solve all that, and as far as she could see, receive her and care for her in the only way she was interested in for ever.

The house was rendered up to an amazed and delighted landlord, and Mrs Samson saw to the selling of the furniture. Eunice watched the valuing of her household goods,

355

and the indifference on the man's face, with an inscrutable expression. She packed everything she possessed into two suitcases, borrowed from Mrs Samson. In her blue skirt, hand-knitted blue jumper, and navy raincoat she made, characteristically, her farewells to that kind neighbour, that near-mother who had been present when her own mother gave her birth.

'Well, I'm off,' said Eunice.

Mrs Samson kissed her cheek, but she didn't ask Eunice to write to her, for she was the only living person who really knew.

At Liverpool Street Station Eunice regarded trains – trains proper, not tubes – for the first time in nearly forty years. But how to find which one to take? On the departure board, white on black, were meaningless hieroglyphs.

She hated asking questions, but she had to.

'Which platform for Stantwich?'

'It's up on the board, lady.'

And again, to someone else. 'Which platform for Stantwich?'

'It's up on the board. Thirteen. Can't you read?'

No, she couldn't, but she didn't dare say so. Still, at last she was on the train, and it must be the right one, for by now eleven people had told her so. The train took her out into the country and back into the past. She was a little girl again, going with her school to Taunton and safety, and her whole future was before her. Now, as then, the stations passed, nameless and unknown.

But she would know Stantwich when she got there, for the train and her future went no further.

# 5

She was bound to fail. She had no training and no experience. People like the Coverdales were far removed from any people she had ever known, and she was not accom-

modating or adaptable. She had never been to a party, let
alone given one, never run any house but the one in Rainbow Street. There was no tradition of service in her family
and no one she knew had ever had a servant, not even a
charwoman. It was on the cards that she would fail abysmally.

She succeeded beyond her own stolid hopes and Jacqueline's dreams.

Of course, Jacqueline didn't really want a housekeeper
at all. She didn't want an organiser and manager but an
obedient maid of all work. And Eunice was accustomed to
obedience and hard work. She was what the Coverdales
required, apparently without personality or awareness of
her rights or that curiosity that leads an employee to pry,
quiet and respectable, not paranoid except in one particular, lacking any desire to put herself on the same social level
as they. Aesthetic appreciation for her was directed to only
one end – domestic objects. To Eunice a refrigerator was
beautiful while a flower was just a flower, the fabric of a
curtain lovely whereas a bird or a wild animal at best
'pretty'. She was unable to differentiate, as far as its aesthetic value was concerned, between a *famille rose* vase and
a Teflon-lined frying pan. Both were 'nice' and each would
receive from her the same care and attention.

These were the reasons for her success. From the first
she made a good impression. Having eaten the last of
the Bounty bar she had bought herself at Liverpool Street,
she alighted from the train, no longer nervous now that
there was nothing to be deciphered. She could read Way
Out, that wasn't a problem. Jacqueline hadn't told her how
she would know George, but George knew her from his
wife's not very kind description. Melinda was with him,
which had floored Eunice who was looking for a man on
his own.

'Pleased to meet you,' she said, shaking hands, not smiling or studying them, but observing the big white car.

George gave her the front seat. 'You'll get a better view
of our beautiful countryside that way, Miss Parchman.'

The girl chattered nineteen to the dozen all the way,
occasionally shooting questions at Eunice. D'you like the
country, Miss Parchman? Have you ever been up in the
Fens? Aren't you too hot in that coat? I hope you like

stuffed vine leaves. My stepmother's doing them for to-night. Eunice answered bemusedly with a plain yes or no. She didn't know whether you ate stuffed vine leaves or looked at them or sat on them. But she responded with quiet politeness, sometimes giving her a small tight smile.

George liked this respectful discretion. He liked the way she sat with her knees together and her hands folded in her lap. He even liked her clothes which to a more detached observer would have looked like standard issue to prison wardresses. Neither he nor Melinda was aware of anything chilly or repulsive about her.

'Go the long way round through Greeving, Daddy, so that Miss Parchman can see the village.'

It was thus that Eunice was given a view of her future accomplice's home before she saw that of her victims. Greeving Post Office and Village Store, Prop. N. Smith. She didn't, however, see Joan Smith, who was out delivering Epiphany People literature.

But she wouldn't have taken much notice of her if she had been there. People didn't interest her. Nor did the countryside and one of the prettiest villages in Suffolk. Greeving was just old buildings to her, thatch and plaster and a lot of trees that must keep out the light. But she did wonder how you managed when you wanted a nice bit of fish or suddenly had a fancy, as she often did, for a pound box of chocolates.

Lowfield Hall. To Eunice it might have been Buckingham Palace. She didn't know ordinary people lived in houses like this which were for the Queen or some film star. In the hall, all five of them were together for the first time. Jacqueline, who dressed up for any occasion, got into emerald velvet trousers and red silk shirt and Gucci scarf to greet her new servant. Even Giles was there. Passing through at that particular moment, looking vaguely for his Hindi primer, he had been collared by his mother and persuaded to remain for an introduction.

'Good evening, Miss Parchman. Did you have a good journey? This is my son, Giles.'

Giles nodded absently and escaped upstairs without a backward glance. Eunice hardly noticed him. She was looking at the house and its contents. It was almost too much for her. She was like the Queen of Sheba when she saw King Solomon – there was no more spirit in her. But none of her wonderment showed in her face or her demeanour. She stood on the thick carpet, among the antiques, the bowls of flowers, looking first at the grandfather clock, then at herself reflected in a huge mirror with gilded twirls round the edge of it. She stood half-stunned. The Coverdales took her air for poise, the silent self-sufficient containment of the good servant.

'I'll take you to your room,' said Jacqueline. 'There won't be anything for you to do tonight. We'll go upstairs and someone will bring your bags up later.'

A large and pleasant room met Eunice's eyes. It was carpeted in olive drab Wilton, papered in a pale yellow with a white vertical stripe. There were two darker yellow easy chairs, a cretonne-covered settee, a bed with a spread of the same material and a long built-in cupboard. The windows afforded a splendid view, *the* view, which was better seen from here than from any other room in the house.

'I hope you find everything to your liking.'

An empty bookcase (destined to remain so), a bowl of white lilac on a coffee table, two lamps with burnt orange shades, two framed Constable reproductions, 'Willy Lott's Cottage' and 'The Leaping Horse'. The bathroom had light green fittings and olive green towels hung on a heated rail.

'Your dinner will be ready for you in the kitchen in half an hour. It's the door at the end of the passage behind the stairs. And now I expect you'd like to be left alone for a while. Oh, here's my son with your bags.'

Giles had been caught by George and coaxed into bringing up the two cases. He dumped them on the floor and went away. Eunice disregarded him as she had largely disregarded his mother. She was staring at the one object in those two rooms which really interested her, the television set. This was what she had always wanted but been unable to buy or hire. As the door closed behind Jacqueline, she approached the set, looked at it, and then, like someone resolved upon using a dangerous piece of equipment that may explode or send a shock up one's arm, but knowing still that it must be used, it must be attempted, she pounced on it and switched it on.

On the screen appeared a man with a gun. He was threatening a woman who cowered behind a chair. There was a shot and the woman fled screaming down a corridor. Thus it happened that the first programme Eunice ever saw on her own television dealt with violence and with firearms. Did it and its many successors stimulate her own latent violence and trigger off waves of aggression? Did fictional drama take root in the mind of the illiterate so that it at last bore terrible fruit?

Perhaps. But if television spurred her on to kill the Coverdales it certainly played no part in directing her to smother her father. At the time of his death the only programmes she had seen on it were a royal wedding and a coronation.

However, though she was to become addicted to the set, shutting herself up with it and drawing her curtains against the summer evenings, that first time she watched it for only ten minutes. She ate her dinner cautiously, for it was like nothing she had ever eaten before, and was taken over the house by Jacqueline, instructed in her duties. From the very beginning she enjoyed herself. A few little mistakes were only natural. Annie Cole had taught her how to lay a table, so she did that all right, but on that first morning she made tea instead of coffee. Eunice had never made coffee in her life except the instant kind. She didn't ask how. She very seldom asked questions. Jacqueline assumed she was used to a percolator – Eunice didn't disillusion her – while they used a filter, so she demonstrated the filter. Eunice watched. It was never necessary for her to watch any operation of this kind more than once for her to be able to perform it herself.

'I see, madam,' she said.

Jacqueline did the cooking. Jacqueline or George did the shopping. In those early days, while Jacqueline was out, Eunice examined every object in Lowfield Hall at her leisure. The house had been dirty by her standards. It brought her intense pleasure to subject it to a spring-cleaning. Oh, the lovely carpets, the hangings, the cushions, the rosewood and walnut and oak, the glass and silver and china! But best of all was the kitchen with pine walls and cupboards, a double steel sink, a washing machine, a dryer, a dishwasher. It wasn't enough for her to dust the porcelain in the drawing room. It must be washed.

'You really need not do that, Miss Parchman.'

'I like doing it,' said Eunice.

Fear of breakages rather than altruism had prompted Jacqueline to protest. But Eunice never broke anything, nor did she fail to replace anything to the exact spot from where she had taken it. Her visual memory imprinted neat permanent photographs in some department of her brain.

The only things in Lowfield Hall which didn't interest her and which she didn't handle or study were the contents of the morning-room desk, the books, the letters from George in Jacqueline's dressing table. Those things and, at this stage, the two shotguns.

Her employers were overwhelmed.

'She's perfect,' said Jacqueline who, parcelling up George's shirts for the laundry, had had them taken out of her hands by Eunice and laundered exquisitely between defrosting the fridge and changing the bed linen. 'D'you know what she said, darling? She just looked at me in that meek way she has and said, "Give me those. I like a bit of ironing." '

Meek? Eunice Parchman?

'She's certainly very efficient,' said George. 'And I like to see you looking so happy and relaxed.'

'Well, I don't have a thing to do. Apart from her putting the green sheets on our bed once and simply ignoring a note I left her, I haven't had a fault to find. It seems absurd calling those things faults after old Eva and that dreadful Ingrid.'

'How does she get on with Eva?'

'Ignores her, I think. I wish I had the nerve. D'you know, Miss Parchman can sew too. I was trying to turn up the hem of my green skirt, and she took it and did it perfectly.'

'We've been very lucky,' said George.

So the month of May passed. The spring flowers died away and the trees sprang into leaf. Pheasants came into the fields to eat the green corn, and the nightingale sang in the orchard. But not for Eunice. Hares, alert and quivering, cropped under the hedges, and the moon rose slowly behind the Greeving Hills, red and strange like another sun. But not for Eunice. She drew the curtains, put on the lamps and then the television. Her evenings were hers to do as she liked. This was what she liked. She knitted. But gradually, as the serial or the sporting event or the cops and robbers film began to grip her, the knitting fell into her lap and she leant forwards, enthralled by an innocent child-like excitement.

She was happy. If she had been capable of analysing her thoughts and feelings and of questioning her motives she would have said that this vicarious living was better than any life she had known. But had she been capable of that it is unlikely she would have been content with so specious a way of spending her leisure. Her addiction gives rise to a question. Wouldn't some social service have immensely benefited society – and saved the lives of the Coverdales – had it recognised Eunice Parchman's harmless craving? Given her a room, a pension and a television set and left her to worship and to stare for the rest of her life? No social service came into contact with her until it was far too late. No psychiatrist had ever seen her. Such a one would only have discovered the root cause of her neurosis if she had allowed him to discover her illiteracy. And she had been expert at concealing it since the time when she might have been expected to overcome it. Her father, who could read perfectly well, who in his youth had read the Bible from beginning to end, was her principal ally in helping her hide her deficiency. He who should have encouraged her to learn instead conspired with her in the far more irksome complexities not learning entailed.

When a neighbour, dropping in with a newspaper, had handed it to Eunice, 'I'll have that,' he had been used to say, looking at the small print, 'don't strain her young eyes.' It came to be accepted in her narrow circle that Eunice had poor sight, this solution generally being the one seized upon by the uneducated literate to account for illiteracy.

'Can't read it? You mean you can't *see*?'

When she was a child she had never wanted to read. As she grew older she wanted to learn, but who could teach her? Acquiring a teacher, or even trying to acquire one, would mean other people finding out. She had begun to shun other people, all of whom seemed to her bent on ferreting out her secret. After a time this shunning, this isolating herself, became automatic, though the root cause of her misanthropy was half-forgotten.

Things could not hurt her – the furniture, the ornaments, the television – she embraced them, they aroused in her the nearest she ever got to warm emotion, while to the Coverdales she gave the cold shoulder. Not that they received more of her stoniness than anyone else had done; she behaved to them as she had always behaved to everyone.

George was the first to notice it. Of all the Coverdales he was by far the most sensitive, and therefore the first to see a flaw in all this excellence.

# 6

They sat in church on Sunday morning and Mr Archer began to preach his sermon. For his text he took: 'Well done, thou good and faithful servant. Thou hast been faithful over a few things; I will make thee ruler over many things.' Jacqueline smiled at George and touched his arm, and he smiled back, well satisfied.

On the following day he remembered those exchanged smiles and thought he had been fatuous, perhaps over-complacent.

'Paula's gone into hospital,' Jacqueline said when George came home. 'It's really rather awful the way they fix a day for your baby to be born these days. Just take you in and give you an injection and Hey presto!'

'Instant infants,' said George. 'Has Brian phoned?'

'Not since two.'

'I'll just give him a ring.'

They would be dining, as they often did when alone, in the morning room. Eunice came in to lay the table. George dialled but there was no reply. A second after he put the phone down it rang. After answering Paula's husband in monosyllables and a final 'Call me back soon,' he walked over to Jacqueline and took her hand.

'There's some complication. They haven't decided yet, but she's very exhausted and it'll probably mean an emergency Caesarean.'

'Darling, I'm so sorry, what a worry!' She didn't tell him not to worry, and he was glad of it. 'Why don't you phone Dr Crutchley? He might reassure you.'

'I'll do that.'

Eunice left the room. George appreciated her tactful silence. He phoned the doctor who said he couldn't comment on a case he knew nothing about, and reassured George only to the extent of telling him that, generally speaking, women didn't die in childbirth any more.

They ate their dinner. That is, Giles ate his dinner, Jacqueline picked at hers, and George left his almost untouched. Giles made one small concession to the seriousness of the occasion and the anxiety of the others. He stopped reading and stared instead into space. Afterwards, when the suspense was over, Jacqueline said laughingly to her husband that such a gesture from Giles was comparable to a pep talk and a bottle of brandy from anyone else.

The suspense didn't last long. Brian called back twice, and half an hour after that was on the line to say a seven-pound boy had been delivered by Caesarean operation and Paula was well.

Eunice was clearing the table. She must have heard it all, George's 'Thank God!', Jacqueline's 'That's wonderful, darling. I'm so happy for you', Giles's 'Good', before he took himself off upstairs. She must have heard relief and seen delight. Without the slightest reaction, she left the room and closed the door.

Jacqueline put her arms round George and held him. He didn't think about Eunice then. It was only as he was going to bed and heard faintly above him the hum of her television that he began to think her behaviour strangely cold. Not once had she expressed her concern during the anxious time, nor her satisfaction for him when the danger was past. Consciously he hadn't waited for her to do so. At the time he hadn't expected a 'I'm so glad to hear your daughter's all right, sir', but now he wondered at the omission. It troubled him. Lack of care for a fellow woman, lack of concern for the people in whose home one lived, were unnatural in any woman. Well done, thou good and faithful servant. . . . But that had not been well done.

Not for the world would George have spoken of his unease to Jacqueline who was so happy and contented with her employee. Besides, he wouldn't have wanted a loquacious servant, making the family's affairs her affairs and being familiar. He resolved to banish it from his mind.

And this he did quite successfully until the christening of the new baby which took place a month later.

Patrick had been christened at Greeving; Mr Archer was a friend of the Coverdales, and a country christening in summer is pleasanter than one in town. Paula and Brian and their two children arrived at Lowfield Hall on a Saturday at the end of June and stayed till the Sunday. They had quite a large party on the Saturday afternoon. Brian's parents and his sister were there, as well as the Roystons, the Jameson-Kerrs, an aunt of Jacqueline's from Bury and some cousins of George from Newmarket. And the arrangements for eating and drinking, carried out by Eunice under Jacqueline's directions, were perfect. The house had never looked so nice, the champagne glasses so well polished. Jacqueline didn't know they possessed so many white linen table napkins, had never seen them all together before and all so freshly starched. In the past she had sometimes been reduced to using paper ones.

Before they left for the church Melinda came into the drawing room to show Eunice the baby. He was to be called Giles, and Giles Mont, aghast at the idea now, had been roped in to be godfather before he realised what was happening. She carried him in in the long embroidered christening robe that she herself, her brother and sister, and indeed George himself, had once worn. He was a fine-looking baby, large and red and lusty. On the table, beside the cake, was the Coverdales' christening book, a volume of listed names of those who had worn the robe, when and where they had been baptised and so on. It was open, ready for this latest entry.

'Isn't he *sweet*, Miss Parchman?'

Eunice stood chill and stiff. George felt a coldness come from her as if the sun had gone in. She didn't smile or bend over the baby or make as if to touch his coverings. She looked at him. It wasn't a look of enthusiasm such as George had seen her give to the silver spoons when she laid them out on the saucers. Having looked at him, she said:

'I must get on. I've things to see to.'

Not one word did he or Jacqueline receive from her during the course of the afternoon when she was in and out with trays as to the attractiveness of the child, their luck in having such a fine day, or the happiness of the young parents. Cold, he thought, unnaturally cold. Or was she just painfully shy?

Eunice was not shy. Nor had she turned from the baby because she was afraid of the book. Not directly. She was simply uninterested in the baby. But it would be true to say that she was uninterested in babies because there are books in the world.

The printed word was horrible to her, a personal threat to her. Keep away from it, avoid it, and from all those who will show it to her. The habit of shunning it was ingrained in her; it was no longer conscious. All the springs of warmth and outgoing affection and human enthusiasm had been dried up long ago by it. Isolating herself was natural now, and she was not aware that it had begun by isolating herself from print and books and handwriting.

Illiteracy had dried up her sympathy and atrophied her imagination. That, along with what psychologists call *affect*, the ability to care about the feelings of others, had no place in her make-up.

General Gordon, in attempting to raise the morale of the besieged inhabitants of Khartoum, told them that when God was handing out fear to the people of the world, at last he came to him. But by that time God had no more fear to give, so Gordon was created without fear. This elegant parable may be paraphrased for Eunice. When God came to her, he had no more imagination or affect to give.

The Coverdales were interferers. They interfered with the best intentions, those of making other people happy. If it

366

were not such an awful thing to say of anyone (to quote one of Giles Mont's favourite authors) one could say that they meant well. They were afraid of being selfish, for they had never understood what Giles knew instinctively, that selfishness is not living as one wishes to live, it is asking others to live as one wishes to live.

'I'm worried about old Parchment Face,' said Melinda. 'Don't you think she has a terrible life?'

'I don't know,' said Giles. Melinda was paying one of her rare visits to his room, sitting in fact on his bed, and this both made him happy and threw him into a panic. 'I haven't noticed.'

'Oh, you – you never notice anything. But I can tell you she does. She's never once been out, not all the time she's been here. All she does is watch television. Listen, it's on now.' She paused dramatically and turned her eyes up to the ceiling. Giles went on with what he had been doing when she first came in, pinning things up on the cork tiles with which he had covered half one of the walls. 'She must be terribly lonely,' said Melinda. 'She must miss her friends.' She grabbed Giles by the arm and swung him round. 'Don't you *care*?'

Her touch gave him a shock and he blushed. 'Leave her alone. She's all right.'

'She's not. She can't be.'

'Some people like being alone.' He looked vaguely round his room, at the heap of orange clothes, the muddle of books and dictionaries, the stacks of half-finished essays on subjects not in the Magnus Wythen curriculum. He loved it. It was better than anywhere else except possibly the London Library where he had once been taken by a scholarly relative. But they won't let you rent a room in the London Library, or Giles would have been at the top of their housing list. 'I like being alone,' he said.

'If that's a hint to me to go. . . .'

'No, no, it isn't,' he said hastily, and resolving to declare himself, began in a hoarse thrilling voice, 'Melinda. . . .'

'What? Where did you get that awful poster? Is she supposed to have a green face?'

Giles sighed. The moment had passed. 'Read my Quote of the Month.'

It was written in green ink on a piece of paper pinned to the cork wall. Melinda read it aloud. ' "Why should the generations overlap one another at all? Why cannot we be buried as eggs in neat little cells with ten or twenty thousand pounds each wrapped round us in Bank of England notes, and wake up, as the sphex wasp does, to find that its papa and mamma have not only left ample provision at its elbow but have been eaten by sparrows some weeks before?" '

'Good, isn't it? Samuel Butler.'

'You can't have that on the wall, Step. If Daddy or Jackie saw it, it'd absolutely freak them out. Anyway, I thought you were supposed to be doing classics.'

'I may not do anything,' said Giles. 'I may go to India. I don't suppose,' greatly daring, 'you'd want to come too?'

Melinda made a face. 'I bet you don't go. You *know* you won't. You're just trying to get off a subject that might involve you. I was going to ask you to come down with me and *confront* Daddy and make him do something about her. But I bet you'll say you won't.'

Giles pushed his fingers through his hair. He would have liked to please her. She was the only person in the world he cared much about pleasing. But there were limits. Not even for her would he defy his principles and flout his nature. 'No,' he said, and gloomily, almost sorrowfully, contorting his face in a kind of hopelessness, 'No, I won't do that.'

'Mad,' said Melinda and bounced out.

Her father and Jacqueline were in the garden, in the midsummer dusk, surveying what Jacqueline had done that day. There was a heavy sweet scent from the first flowers on the tobacco plants.

'I've been thinking, my darlings. We ought to do something about poor old Parchment Face, take her out, give her an interest.'

He stepmother gave her a cool smile. In some respects Jacqueline could fill the wasp role her son had meted out to her. 'Not everyone is such an extrovert as you, you know.'

'And I think we've had enough of that Parchment Face business, Melinda,' said George. 'You're no longer the naughtiest girl in the sixth.'

368

'Now you're evading the issue.'

'No, we're not. Jackie and I have been discussing that very thing. We're quite aware *Miss* Parchman hasn't been out, but she may not know where to go, and it's difficult without a car.'

'Then lend her a car! We've got two.'

'That's what we're going to do. The chances are she's too shy to ask. I see her as a very shy woman.'

'Repressed by a ruling class,' said Melinda.

It was Jacqueline who made the offer.

'I can't drive,' said Eunice. She didn't mind saying this. There were only two things she minded admitting she couldn't do. Hardly anyone in her circle had been able to drive, and in Rainbow Street it had been looked on as a rather bizarre accomplishment for a woman. 'I never learnt.'

'What a pity! I was going to say you could borrow my car. I really don't know how you'll get around without transport.'

'I can go on the bus.' Eunice vaguely supposed a red doubledecker trundled around the lanes with the frequency of the 88 in Tooting.

'That's just what you can't do. The nearest bus stop's two miles away, and there are only three buses a day.'

Just as George had detected a flaw in his housekeeper, so now Eunice sensed a small cloud threatening her peaceful life. This was the first time any Coverdale had shown signs of wanting to change it. She waited uneasily for the next move, and she didn't have to wait long.

Progenitor of Coverdales, George was the arch-interferer of them all. Employees were hauled into his office at TBC and advised about their marriages, their mortgages and the higher education of their children. Meadows, Higgs and Carter matrons were accustomed to his entering their cottages and being told to get the dry-rot people in, or why not grow a few vegetables on that piece of ground? Ever such a nice man was Mr Coverdale, but you don't want to take no notice of what he says. Different in my gran's time. The squire *was* the squire then, but them old days are gone, thank God. George went on interfering – for the good of others.

He bearded the lion in its den. The lion looked very tame and was occupied in womanly fashion, ironing one of his dress shirts.

'Yes, sir?' Her tabby-cat hair was neatly combed, and she wore a blue and white checked cotton dress.

All his life George had been looked after by women, but none of them had ever attempted the formidable task of washing, starching and ironing a 'boiled' shirt. George, if he ever thought about it at all, supposed that there was a special mystique attached to these operations, and that they could only be performed in a laundry by a clever machine. He smiled approvingly.

'Ah, I can see I'm interrupting an expert at a very skilled task. You're making a fine job of that, Miss Parchman.'

'I like ironing,' said Eunice.

'I'm glad to hear it, but I don't suppose you like being confined at Lowfield Hall all the time, do you? That's what I've come to talk about. My wife tells me you've never found time in your busy life to learn to drive a car. Am I right?'

'Yes,' said Eunice.

'I see. Well, we shall have to remedy that. What would you say to driving lessons? I shall be happy to foot the bill. We're doing well by you and we'd like to do something for you in return.'

'I couldn't learn to drive,' said Eunice who had been thinking hard. The favourite excuse came out. 'My sight wouldn't be up to it.'

'You don't wear glasses.'

'I should do. I'm waiting for my new pair.'

In-depth questioning elicited that Eunice should have glasses, had been in need of new ones when she came to Greeving, had 'let it slide', couldn't, even with glasses, read a number plate or a road sign. She must have her eyes tested forthwith, said George; he would see to it himself and drive her into Stantwich.

'I feel rather ashamed of myself,' he said to Jacqueline. 'All the time the poor woman was as a blind as a bat. I don't mind telling you now we know the reason for it, but I was beginning to find that reserve of hers quite off-put-ting.'

Alarm showed in her eyes. 'Oh, George, you mustn't say that! Having her has made such a difference to my life.'

'I'm not saying a thing, darling. I quite understand she's very short-sighted and was much too diffident to say so.'

'The working classes are absurd about things like that,' said Jacqueline, who would have suffered agonies struggling with contact lenses, would have bumped into walls rather than wear glasses. They both felt immensely satisfied with George's discovery, and it occurred to neither of them that a purblind woman could hardly have cleaned the windows to a diamond brilliance or watched the television for three hours every evening.


# 7


At forty-seven, Eunice had better sight than Giles Mont at seventeen. Sitting beside George in the car, she wondered what to do if he insisted on coming into the optician's with her. She was unable to concoct any excuse to avoid this happening, and her experience was inadequate to teach her that middle-aged conservative landowners do not generally accompany their middle-aged female servants into what is virtually a doctor's surgery. A sullen puzzled resentment simmered within her. The last man who sought to make her life insupportable got a pillow over his face for his pains.

A slight fillip came to her spirits at the sight, at last, of shops, those familiar and wonderful treasure houses that had seemed left behind for ever. They got an even greater lift when George showed no sign of accompanying her into the optician's. He left her with a promise to be back in half an hour and the instruction to have any bill sent to him.

Once the car had gone, Eunice walked round the corner where she had noticed a confectioner's. She bought two Kit-Kats, a Mars bar and a bag of marshmallows, and then she went into a teashop. There she had a cup of tea, a currant bun and a chocolate éclair, which made a nice change from *cassoulets* and vine leaves and all those made-up dishes she got at Lowfield Hall. The picture of respectability was Eunice on that Saturday morning, sitting upright at her table in her navy blue crimplene suit, nylon stockings, Annie Cole's mother's court shoes, an 'invisible' net on her hair. No one would have supposed her mind was racing on lines of deception – deception that comes so easily to those who can read and write and have IQ's of 120. But at last a plan was formed. She crossed the road to Boot's and bought two pairs of sunglasses, not dark ones but faintly tinted, one pair with a crystal blue frame, the other of mock tortoise-shell. Into her handbag with them, not to be produced for a week.

The Coverdales seemed surprised they would be ready so quickly. She was taken to Stantwich the second time by Jacqueline, who luckily didn't go with her into the optician's because of the impossibility of parking on a double yellow line. It was bad enough having to pay the fines incurred by Giles. Eunice bought more chocolate and consumed more cake. She showed the glasses to Jacqueline and went so far as to put the crystal blue pair on. In them she felt a fool. Must she wear them all the time now, she who could see the feathers on a sparrow's wing in the orchard a hundred feet away? And would they expect her to *read*?

Nobody really lives in the present. But Eunice did so more than most people. For her five minutes' delay in dinner now was more important than a great sorrow ten years gone, and to the future she had never given much thought. But now, with the glasses in her possession, occasionally even on her nose, she became very aware of the printed word which surrounded her and to which, at some future time, she might be expected to react.

Lowfield Hall was full of books. It seemed to Eunice that there were as many books here as in Tooting Public Library where once, and once only, she had been to return an overdue novel of Mrs Samson's. She saw them as small flattish boxes, packed with mystery and threat. One entire wall of the morning room was filled with bookshelves; in the drawing room great glass-fronted bookcases stood on either side of the fireplace and more shelves filled the twin alcoves. There were books on bedside tables, magazines and newspapers in racks. And they read books all the time. It seemed to her that they must read to provoke her, for no one, not even schoolteachers, could read that much for pleasure. Giles was never without a book in his hand. He even brought his reading matter into her kitchen and sat absorbed in it, his elbows on the table. Jacqueline read every new novel of note, and she and George re-read their way through Victorian novels, their closeness emphasized by their often reading some work of Dickens or Thackeray or George Eliot at the same time, so as later to discuss a character or a scene together. Incongruously, it was the student of English literature who read the least, but even so Melinda was often to be found in the garden or lying on the morning-room floor with one of Mr Sweet's grammars before her. This was not from inclination but because of a menace from her tutor – 'If we're going to make the grade we shall have to come to grips with those Anglo-Saxon pronouns before next term, shan't we?' But how was Eunice to know that?

She had been happy, but the glasses had destroyed her happiness. She had been content with the house and the lovely things in the house, and the Coverdales had hardly existed for her, so little notice had she taken of them. Now she could hardly wait for them to go away on that summer holiday they were always talking about and planning.

But before they went, and they were not going until the beginning of August, before their departure set her free to expand, to explore, and to meet Joan Smith, three unpleasant things happened.

The first was nothing in itself. It was what it led up to that bothered Eunice. She dropped one of Geoff Baalham's eggs on the kitchen floor. Jacqueline, who was there, said only, 'Oh, dear, what a mess!' and Eunice had cleaned it up in a flash. But on the following morning she went up to turn out Giles's bedroom, always a formidable task, and for the first time she allowed herself to look at his cork wall. Why? She could hardly have answered that herself, but perhaps it was because she was now equipped to read, made vulnerable, as it were, to reading, and because she had now become aware of the oppressive number of books in the house. There was a message on the wall beside that nasty poster. 'Why' it began. She could read that word without much difficulty when it was printed. 'One' she could also read and 'eggs'. Giles evidently meant it for her and was reproaching her for breaking that egg. She didn't care for his reproaches, but suppose he broke his silence – he never spoke to her – to ask her why. Why hadn't she obeyed his 'why' message? He might tell his stepfather, and Eunice was on tenterhooks whenever George looked at her unbespectacled face.

At last the message was taken down, but only to be replaced by another. Eunice was almost paralysed by it, and for a week she did no more in Giles's room than pull up the bedclothes and open the window. She was as frightened of those pieces of paper as another woman would have been had Giles kept a snake in his room.

But not so frightened as she was of Jacqueline's note, the third unpleasant incident. This was left on the kitchen table one morning while Eunice was at the top of the house making her own bed. When she came downstairs, Jacqueline had driven off to London to see Paula, to have her hair cut and to buy clothes for her holiday.

Jacqueline had left notes for her before, and had wondered why the otherwise obedient Miss Parchman never obeyed the behests in them. All, however, was explained by her poor sight. But now Eunice had her glasses. Not that she was wearing them. They were upstairs, stuffed into the bottom of her knitting bag. She stared at the note, which meant as much to her as a note in Greek would have meant to Jacqueline – precisely as much, for Jacqueline could recognize an alpha, an omega and a pi just as Eunice knew some capital letters and the odd monosyllabic word. But connecting those words, deciphering longer ones, making anything of it, that was beyond her. In London she would have had Annie Cole to help her. Here she had no one but Giles, who wandered through the kitchen to cadge a lift to Stantwich, to moon about the shops and spend the afternoon in a dark cinema. He didn't so much as glance at her, and she would rather anything than ask help from him.

It wasn't one of Eva Baalham's days. Could she lose the note? Inventiveness was not among her gifts. It had taken all her puny powers to convince George that the optician's bill hadn't come because she had already paid it, liked to be independent, didn't want to be 'beholden'.

And then Melinda came in.

Eunice had forgotten she was in the house, she couldn't get used to these bits of kids starting their summer holidays in June. Melinda danced in at midday, pretty healthy buxom Melinda in too-tight jeans and a Mickey Mouse tee-shirt, yellow hair in Dutch-girl pigtails, her feet bare. The sun was shining, a wind was blowing, the whole kitchen was radiated with fluttering dancing sunbeams, and Melinda was off to the seaside with two boys and another girl in an orange and purple painted van. She picked up the note and read it aloud. 'What's this? "Please would you be awfully kind and if you have the time press my yellow silk, the one with the pleated skirt. I want to wear it to-night. It's in my wardrobe somewhere up on the right. Thank you so much, J.C." It must be for you, Miss Parchman. D'you think you could do my red skirt at the same time? *Would* you?'

'Oh, yes, it's no trouble,' said the much-relieved Eunice with quite a broad smile for her.

'You are *sweet*,' said Melinda.

August came in with a heatwave, and Mr Meadows, the farmer whose land adjoined George's, began cutting his wheat. The new combine harvester dropped bales of straw shaped like slices of Swiss roll. Melinda picked fruit, along with the village women, in the cherry orchards, Giles put up a new Quote of the Month, again from Samuel Butler, Jacqueline weeded the garden and found a thorn-apple, poisonous but beautiful and bearing a single white trumpet flower among the zinnias. And at last it was time to go away, 7 August.

'I won't forget to send you a card,' said Melinda, recalling as she did from time to time that it was her duty to cheer old Parchment Face up.

'You'll find any numbers and addresses you may want in the directory by the phone.' This from Jacqueline, while George said, 'You can always send us a telegram in case of emergency.'

Useless, all of it, had they but known.

Eunice saw them off from the front door, wearing the crystal blue glasses to allay admonition. A soft haze lay over Greeving at this early hour, a haze thickened by smoke, for Mr Meadows was burning the stubble off his fields. Eunice didn't linger to appreciate the great purple dahlias, drenched with dew, or listen to the cuckoo's last calls before his departure. She went quickly indoors to possess what she had looked forward to.

Her purpose didn't include neglecting the house, and she went through her usual Friday routine, but with certain additional tasks. She stripped the beds, threw away the flower arrangements – more or less dead, anyway, nasty messy things, dropping petals everywhere – and hid, as best she could, every book, magazine and newspaper. She would have liked to cover the bookcases with sheets, but only madness goes that far, and Eunice was not mad.

Then she cooked herself a dinner. The Coverdales would have called it lunch because it was eaten at one o'clock. They were not to know how dreadfully their housekeeper had missed a good solid hot meal eaten in the middle of the day. Eunice fried (fried, not grilled) a big steak from the deep freeze, fried potatoes too, while the runner beans, the carrots and the parsnips were boiling. Apple pudding and custard to follow, biscuits and cheese and strong black tea. She washed the dishes, dried them and put them away. It was a relief not to be obliged to use that dishwasher. She never had liked the idea of dirty plates with gravy or crumbs all over them hanging about in there all day, even though the door was shut and you couldn't see them.

Mrs Samson used to say that a woman's work is never done. Not even the most house-proud could have found more work to be done in Lowfield Hall that day. Tomorrow she would think about taking down the morning-room curtains, but not today, not now. Now for a thoroughgoing indulgence in, an orgy of, television.

7 August was to be recorded as the hottest day of the year. The temperature rose to seventy-eight, eighty, until by half past two it touched eighty-five. In Greeving, jam-making housewives left their kitchens and took the sun on back doorsteps; the weir on the River Beal became a swimming pool for little Higgses and Baalhams; farm dogs

hung out their tongues; Mrs Cairne forgot discretion and lay on her front lawn in a bikini; Joan Smith propped her shop door open with a box of dog biscuits and fanned herself with a fly swat. But Eunice went upstairs, drew her curtains, and settled down in deep contentment with her knitting in front of the screen. All she needed to make her happiness perfect was a bar of chocolate, but she had long ago eaten up all those she had bought in Stantwich.

Sport first. People swimming and people racing round stadiums. Then a serial about much the same sort of characters as those Eunice had known in Rainbow Street, a children's programme, the news, the weather forecast. She never cared much for the news, and anyone could see and feel what the weather was and was going to be. She went downstairs and fetched herself jam sandwiches and a block of chocolate ice-cream. At eight o'clock her favourite programme of the entire week was due to begin, a series about policemen in Los Angeles. It is hard to say why Eunice loved it so much. Certainly she confounded those analysts of escape channels who say that an audience must identify. Eunice couldn't identify with the young police lieutenant or his twenty-year-old blonde girl friend or with the gangsters, tycoons, film stars, call girls, gamblers and drunks who abounded in each adventure. Perhaps it was the clipped harsh repartee she liked, the inevitable car chase and the indispensable shooting. It had irked her exceedingly to miss an episode as she had often done in the past, the Coverdales seeming deliberately to single out Friday as their entertaining night.

There was no one to disturb her this time. She laid down her knitting the better to concentrate. It was going to be a good story tonight, she could tell that from the opening sequence, a corpse in the first two minutes and a car chase in the first five. The gunman's car crashed, half-mounting a lamp-post. The car door opened, the gunman leapt out and across the street, firing his gun, dodging a policeman's bullets into the shelter of a porch, pulling a frightened girl in front of him as his shield, again taking aim. . . . Suddenly the sound faded and the picture began to dwindle, to shrink, as it was sucked into a spot in the centre of the screen like black water draining into a hole. The spot shone like a star, a tiny point of light that burned brightly and went out.

Eunice switched it off, switched it on again. Nothing happened. She moved knobs on the front of it and even those knobs on the back they said you should never touch. Nothing happened. She opened the plug and checked that the wires were all where they ought to be. She took out the fuse and replaced it with one from her bed lamp.

The screen remained blank, or, rather, had become merely a mirror, reflecting her own dismayed face and the hot red sunset burning through a chink between the closed curtains.

# 8

It never occurred to her to use the colour set in the morning room. She knew it was usable, but it was *theirs*. A curious feature of Eunice Parchman's character was that, although she did not stop at murder or blackmail, she never in her life stole anything or even borrowed anything without its owner's consent. Objects, like spheres of life, were appointed, predestined, to certain people. Eunice no more cared to see the order of things disturbed than George did.

For a while she hoped that the set would right itself, start up as spontaneously as it had failed. But each time she switched it on it remained blank and silent. Of course she knew that when things went wrong you sent for the man to put them right. In Tooting you went round to the iron-monger's or the electric people. But here? With only a phone and an indecipherable list of names and numbers, a useless incomprehensible directory?

Saturday, Sunday, Monday. The milkman called and Geoff Baalham brought the eggs. Ask them and have them tell her to look such and such a number up in the phone book? She was cruelly bored and frustrated. There were no neighbours with whom to pass the time of day, no busy street to watch, no buses or teashops. She took down the

378

curtains, washed and ironed them, washed paintwork, shampooed the carpets, anything to pass the slow, heavy, lumbering time.

It was Eva Baalham, arriving on Wednesday, who discovered what had happened, simply as a result of asking Eunice if she had watched the big fight on the previous evening. And Eva only asked that for something to say, talking to Miss Parchman being a sticky business at the best of times.

'Broke down?' said Eva. 'I reckon you'll have to have that seen to then. My cousin Meadows that keeps the electric shop in Gosbury, he'd do that for you. I tell you what, I'll leave doing the old bits of silver till Friday and give him a ring.'

A long dialogue ensued with someone called Rodge in which Eva enquired after Doris and Mum and 'the boy' and 'the girl' (young married people, these last, with children of their own) and finally got a promise of assistance.

'He says he'll pop in when he knocks off.'

'Hope he doesn't have to take it away,' said Eunice.

'Never know with they old sets, do you? You'll have to have a look at the paper instead.'

Literacy is in our veins like blood. It enters every other phrase. It is next to impossible to hold a real conversation, as against an interchange of instructions and acquiescences, in which reference to the printed word is not made or in which the implications of something read do not occur.

Rodge Meadows came and he did have to take the set away.

'Could be a couple of days, could be a week. Give me a ring if you don't hear nothing from Auntie Eva. I'm in the book.'

Two days later, in the solitude and silence and boredom of Lowfield Hall, a compulsion came over Eunice. Without any idea of where to go or why she was going, she found herself changing the blue and white check dress for the crimplene suit, and then making her first unescorted assay into the outside world. She closed all the windows, bolted the front door, locked the door of the gun room, and started off down the drive. It was 14 August. If the television set hadn't broken down she would never have gone. Sooner or later one of her own urges or the efforts of the Coverdales would have got her out of that house, but she would have gone in the evening or on a Sunday afternoon when Greeving Post Office and Village Store, Prop. N. Smith, would have been closed. If, if, if . . . If she had been able to read, the television might still have held charms for her, but she would have looked the engineer's number up in the phone book on Saturday morning, and by Tuesday or Wednesday she would have had that set back. On Saturday the 15th, Rodge did, in fact, return it, but by then it was too late and the damage was done.

She didn't know where she was going. Even then, it was touch and go whether she went to Greeving at all, for she took the first turn off the lane, and two miles and three-quarters of an hour later she was in Cocklefield St Jude. Not much more than a hamlet is Cocklefield St Jude, with an enormous church but no shop. Eunice came to a crossroads. The signpost was useless to her but she wasn't afraid of getting lost. God tempers the wind to the shorn lamb, and as compensation perhaps for her singular misfortune she had been endowed with a sense of direction almost as good as an animal's. Accordingly, she took the narrowest exit from the cross which led her down a sequestered defile, a lane no more than eight feet wide and overhung with the dark late-summer foliage of ash and oak, and where one car could not pass another without drawing deep into the hedge.

Eunice had never been in such a place in her life. A cow with a face like a great white ghost stuck its head over the hedge and lowed at her. In a sunny patch, where there was a gap in the trees, a cock pheasant with clattering feathers lolloped across in front of her, all gilded chestnut and fiery green. She marched on, head up, alarmed but resolute, knowing she was going the right way.

And so, at last, to Greeving and into the heart of the village itself, for the lane came out opposite the Blue Boar. She turned right, and having passed the terrace of cottages inhabited by various Higgses and Newsteads and Carters, the small Georgian mansion of Mrs Cairne and the discreet, soberly decorated neon-less petrol station kept by

380

Jim Meadows, she found herself on the triangle of turf outside the village store.

The shop was double-fronted, being a conversion of the ground floor of a largish, very old cottage, whose front gable was half-timbered and whose roof was badly in need of rethatching. Behind it was a garden which sloped down to the banks of the Beal that, at this point, curved out of the meadows to run under Greeving Bridge. Greeving Village Store is now efficiently run by Mr and Mrs Mann, but at that time the two large windows held a dusty display of cereal packets, canned fruit, and baskets of not very fresh-looking tomatoes and cabbages. Eunice approached one of these windows and looked inside. The shop was empty. It was often empty, for the Smiths charged high prices while necessarily stocking only a small selection of goods. Greeving residents with cars preferred the supermarkets of Stantwich and Nunchester, availing themselves only of the post office facilities of their village store.

Eunice went in. On the left the shop was arranged for self-service with wire baskets provided. On the right was a typical sub-post-office counter and grille with, beside it, a display of sweets and cigarettes. At one time there had been a bell which rang each time the door was opened, but this had gone wrong and the Smiths had never had it mended. Therefore, no one heard her enter. Eunice examined the shelves with interest, noting the presence of various commodities she well knew from shopping expeditions in South London. But she couldn't read? Yet who does *read* the name of a product or its manufacturer's name on a packet or tin? One goes by the colour and the shape and the picture as much if one is a professor of etymology as an illiterate.

It was a month since she had tasted a sweet. Now she thought the most desirable thing in the world would be to have a box of chocolates. So she walked up to the counter on the left of the grille and, having waited in vain for a few seconds, she coughed. Her cough resulted in a door at the back of the shop opening and in the appearance of a woman some few years older than herself.

Joan Smith was at this time fifty, thin as a starved bird, with matchstick bones and chicken skin. Her hair was the same colour as Jacqueline Coverdale's, each aiming, of course, at attaining Melinda's natural fine gold by artificial means. Jacqueline was more successful because she had more money to spend. Joan Smith's coiffure, wiry, stiff, glittering, had the look of one of the yellow metal pot-scourers displayed for sale on her shelves. Her face was haphazardly painted, her hands red, rough and untended. In her shrill voice, cockney overlaid with refinement, not unlike Annie Cole's she asked Eunice what she could do for her.

For the first time the two women looked at each other, small blue eyes meeting sharp grey ones.

'Pound box of Black Magic, please,' said Eunice.

How many thousands of pairs of people, brought together into a partnership for passion, for pain, for profit or for disaster, have commenced their relationship with words as mundane as these?

Joan produced the chocolates. She always had a sprightly manner, coy, girlish, arch. Impossible for her simply to hand an object to anyone and take the money. First must come elaborate flourishes, a smile, a little hop that almost lifted her feet out of her Minnie Mouse shoes, her head roguishly on one side. Even towards her religion, she kept up a familiar jolly attitude. The Lord was her friend, brutal to the unregenerate, but matey and intimate with the chosen, the kind of pal you might take to the pictures and have a bit of a giggle with afterwards over a nice cuppa.

'Eighty-five pee,' said Joan, 'if you *please*.' She rang it up on the till, eyeing Eunice with a little whimsical smile. 'And how are they all enjoying their holiday, or haven't you heard?'

Eunice was amazed. She didn't know, and was never really to know, that very little can be kept secret in an English village. Not only did everyone in Greeving know where the Coverdales had gone, when they had gone, when they were coming back and roughly what their trip cost, but they were already aware that she herself had paid her first visit to the village that afternoon. Nellie Higgs and Jim Meadows had spotted her, the grapevine was at work, and her appearance and the motive for her walk would be discussed and speculated about in the Blue Boar that night. But to Eunice that Joan Smith should recognize her and

382

know where she worked was little short of magical divination. It awoke in her a kind of wondering admiration. It laid the foundation of her dependence on Joan and her belief, generally speaking, in the rightness of everything Joan said.

But all she said then was, 'I haven't heard.'

'Well, early days yet. Lovely to get away for three weeks, isn't it? Chance'd be a fine thing. Ever such a nice family, aren't they? Mr Coverdale is what I call a real gentleman of the old school, and she's a real lady. Never think she was forty-eight, would you?' Thus Joan added six years to poor Jacqueline's age from no motive but pure malice. In fact, she heartily disliked the Coverdales because they never patronised her shop, and George had been known to criticise the running of the post office. But she had no intention of admitting these feelings to Eunice until she saw how the land lay. 'You're lucky to work for them, but they're lucky to have you, from all I've heard.'

'I don't know,' said Eunice.

'Oh, you're being modest, I can see that. A little bird told me the Hall'd never looked so spick and span. Makes a change, I daresay, after old Eva giving it a lick and a promise all these years. Don't you get a bit lonesome, though?'

'I've got the TV,' said Eunice, beginning to expand, 'and there's always a job wants doing.'

'You're right. I know I'm run off my feet with this place, it's all go. Not a churchgoer, are you? No, I'd have spotted you if you'd been to St Mary's with the family.'

'I'm not religious. Never seemed to have the time.'

'Ah, you don't know what you miss,' said proselytizing Joan, wagging a forefinger. 'But it's never too late, remember. The patience of the Lord is infinite and the bridegroom is ever ready to welcome you to his feast. Lovely weather he's sending us, isn't it, especially for those as don't have to sweat their guts out slaving for others.'

'I'll be getting back now,' said Eunice.

'Pity Norm's got the van or I could run you back.' Joan came to the door with Eunice and turned the notice to Closed. 'Got your chocs? That's right. Now, don't forget, if ever you're at a loose end, I'm always here. Don't be afraid of putting me out. I've always got a cup of tea and a cheery word for a friend.'

383

'I won't,' said Eunice ambiguously.

Joan waved merrily after her. Across the bridge went Eunice and along the white lane to Lowfield Hall. She took the box of chocolates out of the paper bag, threw the bag over a hedge, and munched an orange cream. She wasn't displeased to have had a chat. Joan Smith was just the sort of person she got on best with, though the hint of getting her to church smacked a little of interference in her life. But she had noted something exceptionally soothing about their talk. The printed word or anything associated with it hadn't remotely come up.

But Eunice, with her television set returned and as good as new, wouldn't have considered seeking Joan Smith out if Joan Smith had not first come to her.

This bird-like, bright-haired and bright-spirited little body was as devoured with curiosity about her fellow men as Eunice was indifferent to them. She also suffered from a particular form of paranoia. She projected her feelings on to the Lord. A devout woman must not be uncharitable, so she seldom indulged her dislike of people by straight malicious gossip. It was not she who found fault with them and hated them, but God; not she but God on whom they had inflicted imaginary injuries. Vengeance is mine, saith the Lord: I will repay. Joan Smith was merely his humble and energetic instrument.

She had long wanted to know more about the interior of Lowfield Hall and the lives of its occupants – more, that is, than she could gain by occasionally steaming open their post. Now was her chance. She had met Eunice, their initial chat had been entirely satisfactory, and here was a postcard come from Crete, come from Melinda Coverdale, and addressed to Miss E. Parchman. Joan kept it back from the regular postwoman's bag and on the Monday she took it up to the Hall herself.

Eunice was surprised and not a little put out to see her. She recoiled from the postcard as from an insect with a sting and muttered her usual defence:

'I can't see that without my glasses.'

'I'll read it to you, shall I, if I won't be intruding? "This is a super place. Temperature in the upper eighties. We have been to the Palace of Knossos where Theseus killed

384

the Minotaur. See you soon. Melinda." How lovely. Who's this Theseus? I wonder. Must have missed that in the paper. There's always a terrible lot of fighting and killing in those places, isn't there? What a lovely kitchen! And you keep it like a new pin. Eat your dinner off the floor, couldn't you?'

Relieved and gratified, Eunice came out of herself enough to say, 'I was just going to put the kettle on.'

'Oh, no, thank you, I couldn't stop. I've left Norm all alone. Fancy her writing "Melinda" like that. I will say for her, she's no snob, though there are sides to her life distressing to the Lord in his handmaiden.' Joan uttered this last in a brisk and practical way as if God had given her his opinion while dropping in for a natter. She peered through the open door into the passage. 'Spacious, isn't it? Could I just have a peep in the drawing room?'

'If you want,' said Eunice. '*I've* no objection.'

'Oh, they wouldn't mind. We're all friends in this village. And speaking as one who has been a sinner herself, I wouldn't set myself above those who haven't found the strait gate. No, you'll never hear me say, Thank God I am not as other men are, even as this publican. Beautiful furnishings, aren't they, and in the best of taste?'

The upshot of all this was that Joan was taken on a tour of Lowfield Hall. Eunice, somewhat overawed by all this educated talk, wanted to show off what *she* could do, and Joan gratified her by frequent exclamations of delight. They went rather further than they should have done, Eunice opening Jacqueline's wardrobe to display her evening gowns. In Giles's room, Joan stared at the cork wall.

'Eccentric,' she said.

'He's just a bit of a boy,' said Eunice.

'Terrible, those spots he has, quite a disfigurement. His father's in a home for alcoholics, as of course you know.' Eunice didn't, any more than anyone else did, including Jeffrey Mont. 'He divorced her and Mr Coverdale was the co-respondent, though his wife had only been dead six months. I don't sit in judgement, but I can read my Bible. "Whosoever shall marry a divorced woman, committeth adultery." What's he got that bit of paper stuck up there for?'

'That's always there,' said Eunice. Was she at last to discover what Giles's message to her said?

She was.

In a shrill, amazed and outraged tone, Joan read aloud:

' "Warburg's friend said to Warburg, of his wife who was ill, If it should please God to take one or other of us, I shall go and live in Paris." '

This quotation from Samuel Butler had no possible application to anything in Giles's life, but he liked it and each time he read it, it made him laugh.

'Blasphemous,' said Joan. 'I suppose it's something he's got to learn for school. Pity these teachers don't have more thought for a person's soul.'

So it was something he had to learn for school. By now Eunice felt quite warmly towards Joan Smith, sent by some kindly power to enlighten her and set her mind at rest.

'You won't say no to that cup of tea now, will you?' she said when, the carpet, bathroom and television set having been admired (though not, according to Joan, good enough for a superior housekeeper like yourself, more a companion really), they were once more in the kitchen.

'I shouldn't, not with Norm all on his own-io, but if you twist my arm.'

Joan Smith stayed for a further hour, during which time she told Eunice a number of lies about the Coverdales' private life, and attempted unsuccessfully to elicit from her hostess details of hers. Eunice was only a little more forthcoming than she had been at their first meeting. She wasn't going to tell this woman, helpful as she had been, all about Mum and Dad and Rainbow Street and the sweetshop, not she. Nor was she prepared to go with Joan to some prayer meeting in Nunchester on the following Sunday. What, swap her Sunday-evening spy serial for hymn-singing with a lot of cranks?

Joan didn't take offence.

'Well, I'll say thanks for the magical mystery tour and your generous hospitality. And now I must be on my way or Norm'll think I've met with an accident.'

She laughed merrily at this prospect of her husband's anxiety and drove off in the van, calling 'Cheeri-bye' all the way down the drive.

# 9

The relationship between Eunice Parchman and Joan Smith was never of a lesbian nature. They bore no resemblance to the Papin sisters, who, while cook and housemaid to a mother and daughter in Le Mans, murdered their employers in 1933. Eunice had nothing in common with them except that she also was female and a servant. She was an almost sexless being, without normal or abnormal desires, whose vague restlessness over the Eu-nicey, mother of Timothy, business had long ago been allayed. As for Joan Smith, she had exhausted her sexual capacities. It is probable that like Queen Victoria in the anecdote, Eunice, for all her adventurous wanderings, did not know what lesbianism was. Joan Smith certainly knew and had very likely experimented with it, as she had experimented with most things.

For the first sixteen years of her life Joan Smith, or Skinner as she then was, led an existence which any psychologist would have seen as promising to result in a well-adjusted, worthy and responsible member of society. She was not beaten or neglected or deserted. On the contrary, she was loved, cherished and encouraged. Her father was an insurance salesman, quite prosperous. The family lived in a house which they owned in the better part of Kilburn, the parents were happily married, and Joan had three brothers older than herself who were all fond of and kind to their little sister. Mr and Mrs Skinner had longed for a daughter and been ecstatic when they got one. Because she was seldom left to her own devices but talked to and played with almost from birth, she learned to read when she was four, went happily off to school before she was five, and by the age of ten showed promise of being cleverer than any of her brothers. She passed the scholarship and went to the high school where she later gained her school certificate with the fairly unusual distinction of an exemption from matriculation, as her results were so good.

The war was on and Joan, like Eunice Parchman, had gone away from London with her school. But to foster-parents as kind and considerate as her own. For no apparent reason, suddenly and out of the blue, she walked into the local police station in Wiltshire where she accused her foster-father of raping and beating her, and she showed bruises to support this charge. Joan was found not to be a virgin. The foster-father was charged with rape but acquitted because of his sound and perfectly honest alibi. Joan was taken home by her parents, who naturally believed there had been a miscarriage of justice. But she only stayed a week before decamping to join the author of her injuries, a baker's roundsman in Salisbury. He was a married man, but he left his wife and Joan stayed with him for five years. When he went to prison for defaulting on the maintenance payments to his wife and two children, she left him and returned to London. But not to her parents, whose letters she had steadfastly refused to answer.

Another couple of years went by, during which Joan worked as a barmaid, but she was dismissed for helping herself from the till, and she drifted into a kind of suburban prostitution. She and another girl shared a couple of rooms in Shepherd's Bush where they entertained an artisan clientele who paid them unbelievably low rates for their services. From this life, when she was thirty, Joan was rescued by Norman Smith.

A weak and innocent creature, he met Joan when she went to a hairdresser's in Harlesden for a tint and perm. One side of this establishment was for the ladies, the other a barber's shop, but there was much coming and going on the part of the assistants, and Norman often stopped for a chat with Joan while she was under the dryer. She was almost the first woman he had looked at, certainly the first he had asked out. But she was so kind and sweet and friendly, he didn't feel at all intimidated. He fell violently in love with her and asked her to marry him the second time he found himself alone with her. Joan accepted with alacrity.

Norman had no idea how she had earned her living, believing her story that she had taken in typing and occasionally been a freelance secretary. They lived with his mother. After a year or two of furious daily quarrels with old Mrs Smith, Joan found the best way of keeping her quiet was to encourage her hitherto controlled fondness for the bottle. Gradually she got Mrs Smith to the stage of spending her savings on half a bottle of whisky a day.

'It would kill Norman if he found out,' said Joan.

'Don't you tell him, Joanie.'

'You'd better see you're in bed then when he comes home. That poor man idolises you, he puts you on a pedestal. It'd break his heart to know you were boozing all day, and under his roof too.'

So old Mrs Smith, with Joan's encouragement, became a self-appointed invalid. For most of each day she was in bed with her whisky, and Joan helped matters along by crushing into the sugar in her tea three or four of the tranquillizers the doctor had prescribed for her own 'nerves'. With her mother-in-law more or less comatose, Joan returned by day to the old life and the flat in Shepherd's Bush. She made very little money at it, and her sexual encounters had become distasteful to her. A remarkable fact about Joan was that, though she had had sexual relations with hundreds of men as well as with her own husband, she had never made love for pleasure or had a 'conventional' illicit affair except with the baker's roundsman. It is hard to know why she continued as a prostitute. Out of perversity, perhaps, or as a way of defying Norman's extreme working-class respectability.

If so, it was a secret way, for he never found her out. It was she eventually who boldly and ostentatiously confessed it all to him.

And that came about as the result of her conversion. Since she was fourteen, and she was now nearly forty, she had never given a thought to religion. But all that was necessary to turn her into a raving Bible-thumper was a call at her front door by a man representing a sect called the Epiphany People.

'Not today, thanks,' said Joan, but having nothing better to do that afternoon, she glanced through the magazine, or tract, he had left on the doorstep. By one of those coincidences that are always happening, she found herself on the following day actually passing the Epiphany People's temple. Of course, it wasn't really a coincidence. She had passed it a hundred times before but had never previously noticed what it was. A prayer meeting was beginning. Out of curiosity Joan went in – and was saved.

The Epiphany People were a sect founded in California in the 1920s by a retired undertaker called Elroy Camps. Epiphany, of course, is 6 January, the day on which the Magi are traditionally supposed to have arrived in Bethlehem to bear witness to the birth of Christ and to bring him gifts. Elroy Camps and his followers saw themselves as 'wise men' to whom a special revelation had been granted: that is, they and only they had witnessed the divine manifestation, and hence only they and a select band of the chosen would find salvation. Indeed, Elroy Camps believed himself to be a reincarnation of one of the Magi and was known in the sect as Balthasar.

A strict morality was adhered to, members of the sect must attend the temple, pay a minimum of a hundred proselytising house calls a year, and hold to the belief that within a very short time there would be a second Epiphany in which they, the new wise men, would be chosen and the rest of the world cast into outer darkness. Their meetings were vociferous and dramatic, but merry too with tea and cakes and film shows. New members were called upon to confess their sins in public, after which the rest of the brethren would burst into spontaneous comment and end by singing hymns. Most of these had been written by Balthasar himself.

The following is an example:

As the Wise Men came riding in days long gone by,
So we ride to Jesus with hearts held up high;
Bearing our sins as they bore him presents,
That shall be washed white in his holy essence.

At first it seems a mystery why all this should have made an appeal to Joan. But she had always loved drama, especially drama of a nature shocking to other people. She heard a woman confess her sins, loudly proclaiming such petty errors as bilking London Transport, fraudulent practice with regard to her housekeeping money, and visits to

390

a theatre. How much better than that could she do! She was forty, and even she could see that with her faded fair hair and fine pale skin she hadn't worn well. What next? A grim obscure domesticity in Harlesden with old Mrs Smith, or the glorious publicity the Epiphany People could give her. Besides, it might all be true. Very soon she was to believe entirely in its truth.

She made the confession of the year. It all came out. The congregation were stunned by the revelation of Joan's excesses, but she had been promised forgiveness and she got it, as much as the woman who had travelled on the Tube without a ticket got it.

Joan the faithless wife opened her heart to a stunned and disillusioned Norman. Joan the evangelist went from house to house in Harlesden and Wood Lane and Shepherd's Bush, not only distributing tracts but recounting to her listeners how, until the Lord called her, she had been a 'harlot' and a scarlet woman.

'I was arrayed in purple and scarlet colour,' said Joan on the doorstep. 'I had a golden cup in my hand full of the abominations and filthiness of my fornication. I was the hold of every unclean spirit and a cage of every unclean and hateful bird.'

It wasn't long before some wit was making snide cracks while in the barber's chair about unclean and hateful birds. In vain did Norman ask his wife to stop it. He had suffered enough in learning of her former mode of life without this. The street buzzed with it and the boys called after him as he went to work.

But how do you reproach a woman who has reformed, who counters every reproof with total agreement? 'I know that, Norm, I know I was steeped in lowness and filth. I sinned against you and the Lord. I was a lost soul, plunged in the abominations of iniquity.'

'I just wish you wouldn't tell everyone,' said Norman.

'Balthasar said there is no private atonement.'

Then old Mrs Smith died. Joan was never at home and she was left all day in a cold and filthy house. She got out of bed, fell and lay on the floor for seven hours in only a thin nightgown. That night, not long after Norman had found her, she died in hospital. Cause of death: hypother-

391

mia; she had died of exposure. Again the street buzzed, and it was not only schoolboys who called after Norman.

His mother had left him the house and a thousand pounds. Norman was one of those people – and they are legion – whose ambition is to keep a country pub or shop. He had never lived in the country or run a grocer's, but that was what he wanted. He underwent training with the post office, and at about the same time as the Coverdales bought Lowfield Hall he and Joan found themselves proprietors of Greeving Village Store – Greeving, because the only other Epiphany temple in the country was in Nunchester.

The Smiths ran the store with disastrous inefficiency. Sometimes it opened at nine, sometimes at eleven. The post office was, of course, open during its prescribed hours, but Joan (for all her virtuous protestations to Eunice) left Norman in sole charge for hours and he couldn't leave his cubby-hole behind the grille to serve other customers. Those who had been regulars drifted away. The rest, compelled through car-lessness to allegiance, grumbled ferociously. Joan investigated the mails. It was her duty, she said, to find out the sinners who surrounded her. She steamed open envelopes and re-glued them. Norman watched in misery and despair, longing for the courage to hit her, and hoping against all odds and his own nature that he would one day find it.

They had no children and now Joan was passing through what she called an 'early change'. Considering she was fifty, it might have been thought that her menopause was neither early nor late but right on time.

'Norm and I always longed for kiddies,' she was in the habit of saying, 'but they never came. The Lord knew best, no doubt, and it's not for us to question His ways.'

No doubt, He did. One wonders what Joan Smith would have done with children if she had had them. Eaten them, perhaps.

# 10

For a long time George Coverdale had suspected one of the Smiths of tampering with his post. Only a week before he went on holiday an envelope, containing a letter from his son Peter, showed a glue smear under the flap, and a parcel from the book club to which Jacqueline subscribed had obviously been opened and re-tied with string. But he hesitated to take action without positive proof.

He hadn't set foot in the shop or used the post office since the day, some three years before, when, in front of an interested audience of farm labourers' wives, Joan had gaily reproached him for living with a divorced woman and exhorted him to abandon his sinful life and come to God. After that he had posted his letters in Stantwich and given Joan no more than a stiff nod when he met her in the village. He would have been appalled had he known she had been in his bedroom, fingered his clothes and toured his house.

But when he and his family returned from holiday there was no sign that Eunice had defected from her established ways.

'I don't believe she's been out of the house, darling,' said Jacqueline.

'Yes, she has.' Village gossip always reached them by way of Melinda. 'Geoff told me. He got it from Mrs Higgs, the Mrs Higgs who rides the bike; she's his grandma's sister-in-law. She saw her out for a walk in Greeving.'

'Good,' said George. 'If she's happy pottering about the village, I won't press her about the driving lessons. But if you should get it via the bush telegraph that she's got hankerings to learn, perhaps you'll let me know.'

Late summer, early autumn, and the vegetation seemed to become too much for man and nature itself to control. The flowers grew too tall and too straggly, the hedges overbrimmed with leaves, berries and tendrils of the bryony, and the wild clematis, the Old Man's Beard, cast

393

over all its filmy fluffy cloak. Melinda went blackberrying, Jacqueline made bramble jelly. Eunice had never before seen jam being made. As far as she had known, if it didn't exactly descend like manna from heaven, at least it was only available in jars from a shop. Giles picked no black-berries, nor did he attend the Harvest Festival at St Mary's. On the cork wall he pinned a text of his own, a line that might have been written for him: *Some say life is the thing, but I prefer reading*', and he went on struggling through the Upanishads.

Pheasant shooting began. Eunice saw George go into the gun room, take the shotguns down from the wall and, leaving the door to the kitchen open, clean and load them. She watched with interest but in innocence, having no idea of their being of future use to her.

George cleaned and loaded both guns, but not because he had any hope of Giles accompanying him on the shoot. He had bought the second gun for his stepson, just as he had bought the fishing tackle and the fat white horse, now eating its head off down in the meadow. Three autumns of apathy and then downright opposition on Giles's part had taught George to abandon hope of making him a sports-man. So the second gun was lent to Francis Jameson-Kerr, stockbroker son of the brigadier.

Pheasants were plentiful, and from the kitchen window, then from the kitchen garden where she went to cut a cabbage, Eunice watched the three of them bag four brace and a hen bird. A brace for the Jameson-Kerrs, a brace each for Peter and Paula, the remaining birds for Lowfield Hall. Eunice wondered how long the bloodied bundles of feathers were to be hung in the back kitchen before she had the pleasure of tasting this hitherto unknown flesh. But she wasn't going to ask, not she. A week later Jacqueline roasted them, and as Eunice tucked into the thick slice of breast on her plate, three little round pellets of shot rolled out into the gravy.

The shopping was always done by Jacqueline, or a list phoned by Jacqueline to a Stantwich store and the goods later collected by George. It was a chronic source of anxiety to Eunice that one day she might be called on to phone that list, and one Tuesday in late September this happened.

The phone rang at eight in the morning. It was Lady Royston to say that she had fallen, thought she had broken her arm, and could Jacqueline drive her to hospital in Nunchester? Sir Robert had taken one car, her son the other, and then, having taken it into her head to begin picking the apple crop at the early hour of seven-thirty, she had climbed the ladder and slipped on a broken rung.

The Coverdales were still at breakfast. 'Poor darling Jessica,' said Jacqueline, 'she sounded in such pain. I'll get over there straight away. The shopping list's ready, George, so Miss Parchman can phone it through when the shop opens, and then perhaps you'll be an angel and pick it up?'

George and Giles finished their breakfast in a silence broken only by George's remarking, in the interest of being a good stepfather, that such a brilliant start to the day could only indicate rain later. Giles, who was thinking about an advertisement he had seen in *Time Out* asking for a tenth passenger in a minibus to Poona, said 'Could it?' and that he didn't know anything about meteorology. Eunice came in to clear the table.

'My wife's had to go out on an errand of mercy,' said George, made pompous by Eunice's forbidding presence, 'so perhaps you'll be good enough to get on to this number and order what's on the list.'

'Yes, sir,' said Eunice automatically.

'Ready in five minutes, Giles? Give it till after nine-thirty, will you, Miss Parchman? These shops don't keep the early hours they did in our young days.'

Eunice stared at the list. She could read the phone number and that was about all. By now George had disappeared to get the Mercedes out. Giles was upstairs. Melinda was spending the last week of her holiday with a friend in Lowestoft. The beginning of a panic stirring, Eunice thought of asking Giles to read the list to her – one reading would be enough for her memory – on the grounds that her glasses were somewhere up at the top of the house. But the excuse was too feeble, as she had an hour in which to fetch those glasses herself, and now, anyway, Giles was crossing the hall in his vague sleepwalking way, leaving the house, slamming the front door behind him. In despair, she sat down in the kitchen among the dirty dishes.

All her efforts went into rousing some spark out of that atrophied organ, her imagination. By now an inventive woman would have found ways of combating the problem. She would have said she had broken her reading glasses (and trodden on them to prove it) or feigned illness or fabricated a summons to London to the bedside of a sick relative. Eunice could only think of actually taking the list to the Stantwich store and handing the list to the manager. But how to get there? She knew there was a bus, but not where it stopped, only that the stop was two miles distant; not when it ran or where precisely it went or even the location of the shop. Presently habit compelled her to stack the dishes in the washer, wipe clean the surfaces, go upstairs to make the beds and gaze sullenly at Giles's Quote of the Month which would have had a peculiarly ironical application to herself had she been able to understand it. Nine-fifteen. Eva Baalham didn't come on Tuesdays, the milkman had already been. Not that Eunice would have dared expose herself by asking for enlightenment from these people. She would have to tell Jacqueline that she had forgotten to phone, and if Jacqueline came back in time to do it herself . . . She glanced up again at the cork wall, and then into her mind came a clear picture of having stood there with Joan Smith.

Joan Smith.

No very lucid plan had formed. Eunice was just as anxious for Joan Smith not to know her secret as for Eva or the milkman or Jacqueline not to know it. But Joan too had a grocer's shop, and once the list was in her hands, there might be a way. She put her best hand-knitted cardigan on over her pink cotton frock and set off for Greeving.

'Long time no see,' said Joan, sparkling. 'You are a stranger! This is Norman, my better half. Norm, this is Miss Parchman from the Hall I was telling you about.'

'Pleased to meet you,' said Norman Smith from behind his grille. Enclosed by bars, he had the look of some gloomy ruminant animal, a goat or llama perhaps, which has too long been in captivity to recall its freedom but still frets dully within its cage. His face was wedge-shaped, white and bony, his hair sandy grey. As if he were sustaining the cud-chewing image, he munched spearmint all day long. This was because Joan said he had bad breath.

'Now to what do we owe the pleasure of your visit?' said Joan. 'Don't tell me Mrs Coverdale's going to patronise our humble abode at last. That *would* be a red-letter day.'

'I've got this list.' Looking vaguely about her at the shelves, Eunice thrust the list at Joan.

'Let me see. We *have* got the plain flour and the oats, that I do know. But, my goodness, kidney beans and basil leaves and garlic!' The bad shopkeeper's excuse came to Joan's aid. 'We're waiting for them to come in,' she said. 'But, I tell you what, you read it out and I'll check what we do have.'

'No, you read it. I'll check.'

'There's me being tactless again! Ought to remember your eye trouble, didn't I? Here goes, then.'

Eunice, checking and finding only two items available, knew that she was saved, for Joan read the list out in a clear slow voice. It was enough. She bought the flour and the oats which would have to be hidden, would have to be paid for out of her own money, but what did that matter? A warm feeling for Joan, who had saved her again, welled in Eunice. Dimly she remembered feeling something like this long ago, ages ago, for her mother before Mrs Parchman became ill and dependent. Yes, she would have the cup of tea Joan was offering, and take the weight off her feet for ten minutes.

'You'll just have to phone that Stantwich place,' said Joan, who thought she saw it all, that Eunice had come to the village store off her own bat. 'Use our phone, go on. Here's your list. Got your glasses?'

Eunice had. The ones with the tortoise-shell frames. While Joan bustled about with the teacups, she made her call, almost dizzy with happiness. Appearing to read aloud what she in fact remembered brought her a pleasure comparable to, but greater than, the pride of a traveller who has one idiomatic French phrase and chances to bring it out successfully at the right time without evoking from his listener a single question. Seldom did it happen to her to *prove* she could read. And, putting the phone down, she felt towards Joan the way we feel towards those in whose

397

presence we have demonstrated our prowess in the field where we least possess it – warm, prideful, superior yet modest, ready to be expansive. She praised the 'lovely old room', ignoring its untidy near-squalor, and she was moved so far as to compliment Joan on her hair, her floral dress and the quality of her chocolate biscuits.

'Fancy them expecting you to hump all that lot back,' said Joan who knew they hadn't. 'Well, they say he's a hard man, reaping where he has not sown and gathering where he has not stored. I'll run you home, shall I?'

'I'd be putting you out.'

'Not at all. My pleasure.' Joan marched Eunice through the shop, ignoring her husband who was peering disconsolately inside a sack as into a nosebag. The old green van started after some heavy manipulation with the choke and kicks at the accelerator. 'Home, James, and don't spare the horses!'

The van coughed its way up the lane. Joan took Eunice to the front door of Lowfield Hall. 'Now, one good turn deserves another, and I've got a little book here I want you to read.' She produced a tract entitled *God Wants You For A Wise Man*. 'And you'll pop along to our next meeting with me, won't you? Sunday night. I won't call for you, but you be in the lane at half five and I'll pick you up. OK?'

'All right,' said Eunice.

'Oh, you'll love it. We don't have a prayer book like those church people, just singing and love and uttering what comes into our hearts. And then there's tea and a chat with the brethren. God wants us to be joyful, my dear, when we have given our all to him. But for those who deny him there shall be weeping and gnashing of teeth. Did you knit your cardigan yourself? I think it's smashing. Don't forget your flour and your oats.'

Well content, Joan drove back to Norman and the store. It might seem that she had nothing to gain from friendship with Eunice Parchman, but in fact she was badly in need of a satellite in the village. Norman had become a cipher, not much more than a shell of a man since his wife's revelations of what his early married life had truly been. They hardly spoke these days, and Joan had given up pretending to her acquaintances that they were an ideal couple. Indeed, she told everyone that Norman was her

398

cross, though one that it was her duty as his wife to bear, but that he had turned his back on God and so could be no companion for such as she. God was displeased with him. Therefore she, as his handmaid, must concur in that displeasure. These pronouncements, made publicly along with others implying that Joan had the infallibility of God's personal assistant, had put off such Higgses, Baalhams and Newsteads as might have become her friends. People said good morning to her but otherwise ostracized her. They thought she was mad, as she probably was even then.

She saw Eunice as malleable and green. And also, to do her justice, as a lost sheep who might be brought to the Nunchester fold. It would be a triumph for her, and pleasant, to have a faithful admiring attendent to introduce to the Epiphany People and be seen by unregenerate Greeving as her special pal.

Eunice, flushed with success, turned out the morning room, and was actually washing down its ivory-painted walls when Jacqueline came back.

'Heavens, what a rush! Poor Lady Royston's got a multiple fracture of her left arm. Spring-cleaning in September? You're an indefatigable worker, Miss Parchman. I hardly like to ask if you saw to my shopping list.'

'Oh, yes, madam. Mr Coverdale will pick it up at five.'

'That's marvellous. And now I'm going to have an enormous sherry before my lunch. Why don't you have a break and join me?'

But this Eunice refused. Apart from a rare glass of wine at a relative's wedding or funeral, she had never tasted alcohol. This was one of the few things she had in common with Joan Smith who, though fond enough of a gin or a Guinness in her Shepherd's Bush days, had eschewed liquor on signing the Epiphany pledge.

*God Wants You For A Wise Man* necessarily remained unread, but Eunice went to the meeting where no one expected her to read anything. She enjoyed the ride in Joan's van, the singing and the tea, and by the time they were back in Greeving a date had been made for her to have supper with the Smiths on Wednesday, and they were Joan and Eunice to each other. They were friends. In the sterile existence of Eunice Parchman, Mrs Samson and Annie Cole had a successor.

Melinda went back to college, George shot more pheasants, Jacqueline planted bulbs and trimmed the shrubs and cheered up Lady Royston, Giles learned gloomily that the tenth place in the bus to Poona had been filled. Leaves turned from dark green to bleached gold, the apples were all gathered and the cob nuts ripened. The cuckoo had long gone, and now the swallows and the flycatchers departed for the south.

On Greeving Green the hunt met and rode down the lane to kill two hours later in Marleigh Wood.

'Good morning, master,' said George at his gate to Sir Robert Royston, George who would call him Bob at any other time.

And 'Good morning, sir,' said Bob in his pink coat and hard hat.

October, with its false summer, its warm sadness, mists and mellow fruitfulness and sunshine turning to gold the haze that lingered over the River Beal.

# 11

Melinda would have learned that when Eunice went out, as she now frequently did, it was to visit Joan Smith, and that when she set off in the dusk on Sunday evenings the Smith's van was waiting for her at the end of the drive. But Melinda was back at college, and had returned to her father's house only once in the month since her departure. And on that one occasion she had been unusually quiet and preoccupied, not going out, but playing records or sitting silent and deep in thought. For Melinda had fallen in love.

So although every inhabitant of Greeving who was not an infant or senile followed with close interest the Parchman-Smith alliance, the Coverdales knew nothing about it. Often they didn't know that Eunice wasn't in the house, so unobtrusive was she when there. Nor did they know that when they went out Joan Smith came in and passed many a pleasant evening with Eunice, drinking tea and watching television on the top floor. Giles, of course, was invariably in. But they took care not to speak on the stairs, the thick carpet muffled the sound of an extra set of footsteps, and they passed unseen and unheard by him into Eunice's bedroom where the incessant drone of the television masked the murmur of their voices.

And yet that friendship would have foundered in its earliest days had Eunice had her way. The warmth she felt for Joan cooled when her delight over the deciphering of the shopping list subsided, and she began to look on Joan, as she had always looked on most people, as someone to be used. Not to be blackmailed for money this time, but rather to be placed in her power as Annie Cole had been, so that she could always be relied on as an interpreter and trusted not to divulge her secret if she discovered it.

It looked as if Eva Baalham had delivered Joan into her hands.

Eva was disgruntled these days because, although she now had more rewarding employment with Mrs Jameson-Kerr, her working hours at Lowfield Hall had been reduced to one morning a week. And this demotion she blamed on Eunice, who did with ease all the jobs she used to groan over and, if the truth were admitted, did them a lot better. As soon as she thought she saw a way of needling Eunice she set about doing so.

'I reckon you're very pally with that Mrs Smith then.'

'I don't know,' said Eunice.

'Always in and out of each other's places. That's what I call very pally. My cousin Meadows that's got the garage, he saw you out in her van last week. Maybe there's things about her you don't know.'

'What?' said Eunice, breaking her rule.

'Like what she was before she came here. A street woman, she was, no better than a common prostitute.' Eva wasn't going to destroy the esoteric quality of this by saying it was generally known. 'Used to go with men, and her husband never knew a thing, poor devil.'

That night Eunice was invited to the Smiths for supper. They ate what she liked and never got at Lowfield Hall, eggs and bacon and sausages and chips. Afterwards she had a chocolate bar from the shop. Norman sat silent at the table, then departed for the Blue Boar where, out of pity, some Higgs or Newstead would play darts with him. Bumper cups of tea were served. Joan leaned confidingly across the table and began to preach the gospel according to Mrs Smith. Having finished the last square of her fudge wafer, Eunice seized her opportunity.

She interrupted Joan in her louder, more commanding, voice. 'I've heard something about you.'

'Something nice, I hope,' said Joan brightly.

'Don't know about nice. That you used to go with men for money, that's what I heard.'

A kind of holy ecstasy radiated Joan's raddled face. She banged her flat bosom with her fist. 'Oh, I was a sinner!' she declaimed. 'I was scarlet with sin and steeped in the foulest mire. I went about the city as an harlot, but God called me and, lo, I heard him! I shall never forget the day I confessed my sins before the multitude of the brethren and opened my heart to my husband. With true humility, dear, I have laid bare my soul to all who would hear, so that the people may know even the blackest shall be saved. Have another cup, do.'

Amazement transfixed Eunice. No potential blackmail victim had ever behaved like this. Her respect for Joan became almost boundless and, floored, she held out her cup meekly.

Did Joan guess? Perhaps. She was a clever woman and a very experienced one. If it were so, the hoisting of Eunice with her own petard must have brought her enormous amusement without in the least alienating her. After all, she expected people to be sinners. She wasn't a Wise Man for nothing.

The yellow leaves were falling, oak and ash and elm, and the redder foliage of the dogwood. What flowers that remained had been blackened by the first hard frost, and fungus grew under hedges and on fallen trees, the Oyster Mushroom and the Amethyst Agaric. Re-thatching began on James Newstead's cottage, his garden filled with the golden straw from a whole wheat field.

George in dinner jacket and Jacqueline in a red silk gown embroidered with gold went to Covent Garden to see *The Clemency of Titus*, and spent the night at Paula's. The Quote of the Month was from Mallarmé: 'The flesh, alas, is sad and I have read all the books'. But Giles, far from having read all the books, was deep in Poe. If, as seemed likely, he was never going to make it to India, he might ask Melinda to share a flat with him when they had completed their education. A Gothic mansion flat was what he had in mind, in West Kensington, say, a kind of diminutive House of Usher with floors of ebon blackness and feeble gleams of encrimsoned light making their way through the trellised panes.

But Melinda, unknown to him, was in love. Jonathan Dexter was his name and he was reading modern languages. George Coverdale had often wondered, though never spoken his thoughts aloud even to Jacqueline, whether his younger daughter was as innocent as her mother had been at her age. But he doubted it, and was resigned to her having followed the current trend of permissiveness. He would, in fact, have been surprised and pleased had he known Melinda was still a virgin, though anxious if he had guessed how near she was to changing that irrevocable condition.

Now that the ice was, as it were, broken, Eunice often went out walking. As she had roved London, so she roved the villages, marching from Cocklefield to Marleigh, Marleigh to Cattingham, through the leaf-strewn lanes, and as St Luke's Little Summer gave place to the deep of autumn, daring the still dry footpaths that crossed the fields and skirted the woods. She walked purposelessly, not pausing to look, through breaks in the trees, at the long blue vistas of wooded slopes and gentle valleys, hardly noticing the countryside at all. Here it was the same for her as it had been in London. She walked to satisfy some craving for freedom and to use up that energy housework could not exhaust.

She and Joan Smith never communicated by phone. Joan would arrive in the van when she was sure Lowfield Hall was empty but for Eunice. Whatever friend she visited, Jacqueline must pass through Greeving, and she seldom passed without being observed by Joan from the village store. And then Joan would drive up to the Hall, make her

403

way in through the gun room without knocking, and within two minutes Eunice had the kettle on.

'Her life's just one round of amusement. Sherry-partying with that Mrs Cairne she is this morning. One can just imagine what goes on in the mind of God when he looks down on that sort of thing. The wicked shall flourish like the green bay tree, but in the morning they were not, nay, they were not to be found. I've got four calls to make in Cocklefield this morning, dear, so I won't stop a minute.' By calls Joan didn't mean store or postal deliveries, but proselytizing visits. As usual, she was armed with a stack of tracts, including a new one got up to look like a comic and artfully entitled *Follow My Star*.

So fervid an Epiphany Person was she that often when Eunice called at the store during her walks, only Norman was found to be in charge. And then, from behind the bars of his cage, he shook his head lugubriously.

'She's off out somewhere.'

But sometimes Eunice called in time to be taken with Joan on her rounds, and from the passenger seat in the van she watched her friend preaching on cottage doorsteps.

'I wonder if you have time to spare today to glance at a little book I've brought . . .'

Or around the council estates that clung to the fringe of each village, red-brick boxes screened from the ancient settlement by a barrier of conifers. Occasionally a naïve householder asked Joan in, and then she was gone some time. But more often the door was shut in her face and she would return to the van, radiated with the glow of martyrdom.

'I admire the way you take it,' said Eunice. 'I'd give them as good as I got.'

'The Lord requires humility of his servants, Eun. Remember there are some who will be carried by the angels into Abraham's bosom and some who will be tormented by the flame. Don't let me forget to stop at Meadows', we're nearly out of petrol.'

They presented a strange sight, those two, to the indignant watcher as she dropped *Follow My Star* into her dustbin. Joan so spindly with bones like those of a starved child pictured in a charity appeal, her religion having done nothing to conquer her ingrained habit, almost unconscious now, of getting herself up in whore's garb: short skirt, black 'glass' stockings, down-at-heel patent shoes, great shiny handbag and fleecy white jacket with big shoulders. Her hair was like an inverted bird's nest, if birds ever built with golden wire, and on her pinched little face the make-up was rose and blue and scarlet.

Eunice might have been chosen as the perfect foil to her. She had added to her wardrobe since coming to Lowfield Hall only such garments as she had knitted herself, and on those chilly autumn days she wore a round woolly cap and a scarf of dark grey-blue. In her thick maroon-coloured coat she towered above Joan, and the contrast was best seen when they walked side by side, Joan teetering and taking small rapid steps, Eunice Junoesque with her erect carriage and steady stride.

In her heart, each thought the other looked a fool, but this did not alienate them. Friendship often prospers best when one party is sure she has an ascendancy over the other. Without letting on, Eunice thought Joan brilliantly clever, to be relied on for help whenever she might be confronted by reading matter, but mutton dressed as silly young lamb all the same, a hopeless housewife and a slattern. Without letting on, Joan saw Eunice as eminently respectable, a possible bodyguard too if Norman should ever attempt to carry out his feeble threat of beating her up, but why dress like a policewoman?

Joan made Eunice presents of chocolate each time she came to the shop. Eunice had knitted Joan a pair of gloves in her favourite salmon pink, and was thinking of beginning on a jumper.

All Saints, 1 November, was Jacqueline's forty-third birthday. George gave her a sheepskin jacket, Giles a record of Mozart concert arias. Melinda sent a card with a scrawled promise of 'something nice when I get around to coming home'. The parcel, containing a new novel, which arrived from Peter and Audrey, had obviously been opened and re-sealed. George marched off to Greeving Post Office and Village Store and complained to Norman Smith. But what to say in answer to Norman's defence that the book was half out of its wrappings on arrival, and that his wife

405

had re-packed it herself for safety's sake? George could only nod and say he wouldn't take it further – for the present.

That week he went for his annual check-up to Dr Crutchley and was told his blood pressure was up, nothing to worry about but better go on these tablets. George wasn't a nervous man or one who easily panicked, but he decided he had better make his will, a proceeding he had been procrastinating about for years. It was this will which has given rise to the litigation that still continues, that keeps Lowfield Hall ownerless and deserted, that has soured the lives of Peter Coverdale and Paula Caswall and keeps the tragedy fresh in their minds. But it was carefully drawn up, with all forethought. Who then could have foreseen what would happen on St Valentine's Day? What lawyer, however circumspect, could have imagined a massacre at peaceful Lowfield Hall?

A copy of the will was shown to Jacqueline when she got home from a meeting of the parish council.

' "To my beloved wife, Jacqueline Louise Coverdale," ' she read aloud, ' "the whole of my property known as Lowfield Hall, Greeving, in the County of Suffolk, unencumbered, and to be hers and her heirs' and successors' in perpetuity." Oh, darling, "beloved wife"! I'm glad you put that.'

'What else?' said George.

'But shouldn't it just be for my life? I've got all the money Daddy left me and what I got for my house, and there'd be your life assurance.'

'Yes, and that's why I've willed all my investments to the girls and Peter. But I want you to have the house, you love it so. Besides, I hate those pettifogging arrangements where the widow only gets a life interest. She's a non-paying tenant to a bunch of people who can't wait for her to die.'

'Your children wouldn't be like that.'

'I don't think they would, Jackie, but the will stands. If you pre-decease me, I've directed that the Hall is to be sold after my death and the proceeds divided between my heirs.'

Jacqueline looked up at him. 'I hope I do.'

'Hope you do what, darling?'

'Die first. That's what I mind about your being older than me, that you're almost certain to die first. I might be a widow for years, I can't bear the thought of it, I can't imagine a single day without you.'

George kissed her. 'Let's *not* talk of wills and graves and epitaphs,' he said, so they talked about the parish council meeting instead, and fund-raising for the new village hall, and Jacqueline forgot the hope she had expressed.

It was not destined to be gratified, though she was to be a widow for only fifteen minutes.

# 12

The Epiphany Temple in Nunchester is on North Hill just above the cattle market. Therefore, it is not necessary when driving there from Greeving to pass through the town, and Joan Smith could make the journey in twenty minutes. Eunice enjoyed the Sunday-night meetings. Hymn sheets were provided, but as anyone knows who has tried to give the impression that he has the Church of England morning service off by heart (actually to use the Prayer Book being to betray unpardonable ignorance) it is quite easy to mouth what other people are mouthing and muffle one's lack of knowledge in folded hands brought to the lips. Besides, Eunice had only to hear a hymn once to know it for ever, and soon, in her strong contralto, she was singing with the best of them:

'Gold is the colour of our Lord above,
And frankincense the perfume of His love;
Myrrh is the ointment, which with might and main,
He pours down from heaven to heal us of our pain.'

Elroy Camps was no Herbert or Keble.

After the hymns and some spontaneous confessing – almost as good as television, this bit – the brethren had tea and biscuits and watched films about black or brown Epiphany People struggling on in remote places (*in partibus*

407

*infidelium*, as it were) or delivering the Epistle of Balthasar to famine-stricken persons too weak to resist. Also there was friendly gossip, mostly about worldly people who hadn't seen the light, but uttered in a pious way and shoving the onus of censure and blame off on to God. Certainly the brethren honoured the precept of Come unto Me, all ye that are heavy laden, and I will give ye rest.

On the whole, they were and are a jolly lot. They sing and laugh and enter with gusto into their own confessions and those of new converts. They talk of God as if he were a trendy headmaster who likes the senior boys to call him by his Christian name. Their hymns are not unlike pop songs and their tracts are lively with comic strips. The idea of the elect being Wise Men who follow a star is not a bad one. The Camps cult would probably have been latched on to by young people of the Jesus freak kind but for its two insuperable drawbacks distasteful to anyone under forty – and to most people over forty, come to that. One is its total embargo on sexual activity, whether the parties are married or not; the other its emphasis on vengeance against the infidel, which means any non-Epiphany Person, a vengeance that is not necessarily left to God but may be carried out by the chosen as his instruments. In practice, of course, the brethren do not go about beating up their heretical neighbours, but the general impression is that if they do they will be praised rather than censured. After all, if God is their headmaster they are all prefects.

Eunice absorbed little of this doctrine which, in any case was implicit rather than proclaimed. She enjoyed the social life, almost the first she had ever known. The brethren were her contemporaries or her seniors; no one questioned her or attempted to interfere unpleasantly with her life or manipulated her into corners where she would be expected to read. They were friendly and cajoling and liberal with tea and biscuits and fruit cake because, of course, they saw her as a future convert. But Eunice was determined never to convert, and for her usual reason for not doing something. She wouldn't have minded the confessing because she would have confessed nothing beyond the usual run of evil thoughts and ambitions, but once she had taken that step she would be obliged to make the duty calls. And she knew only too well from her visits with Joan what that entailed.

Reading. Drawing the attention of the visited to points in *Follow My Star*, picking appropriate bits out of the Bible, arguing with frequent reference to the printed word.

'I'll think about it,' she said in her ponderous way when Joan pressed her. 'It's a big step.'

'A step towards Bethlehem which you would never regret. The Son of Man cometh like a thief in the night, but the foolish virgin has let her lamp go out. Remember that, Eun.'

This exchange took place one raw damp afternoon when Eunice had walked down to the village store for a cup of tea, a chat, and to collect her week's supply of chocolate bars which had again become an indispensible part of her diet. As they came out of the shop together, Jacqueline also came out of Mrs Cairne's house where she had been on some Women's Institute matter. They didn't notice her, but she saw them, and although Joan only came as far as the triangle of turf, it was obvious that what was taking place was no ordinary farewell of shopkeeper to customer. Joan was laughing in her shrill way, and while doing so she stuck out her hand and gave Eunice one of those playful pushes on the arm women of her kind do give to women friends in the course of making a joking reproof. Then Eunice walked off in the direction of the Hall, turning twice to wave to Joan who waved back quite frenziedly.

Jacqueline started her car and caught Eunice up just beyond the bridge.

'I didn't know you were friendly with Mrs Smith,' she said when Eunice, somewhat reluctantly, had got in beside her.

'I see a bit of her,' said Eunice.

There seemed no answer to make to this. Jacqueline felt she couldn't very well dictate to her housekeeper as to whom she chose for her friends. Not in these days. It wasn't Eunice's afternoon off, but they had all forgotten about those prescribed afternoons and evenings off since their holiday. She went out when she chose. After all, why not? It wasn't as if she neglected her duties at Lowfield Hall, far from it. But Jacqueline, who until now had had no fault to find with her housekeeper, who had been aghast when George, five months before, had voiced faint qualms, was suddenly made uncomfortable. Eunice sat beside her, eating chocolates. She didn't eat them noisily or messily, but wasn't it odd that she should be eating them at all, munching silently and not offering the bag? Nothing would have induced Jacqueline to eat a chocolate under any circumstances, but still . . . And hob-nobbing with Mrs Smith as if they were fast friends? Some awareness that George, if told of it, would concur rather too emphatically in her own view, stopped her mentioning it to him.

Instead, with her own particular brand of feminine perverseness, she praised Eunice to the skies that evening, pointing out how beautifully all the silver was polished.

In Galwich, Melinda Coverdale, wise or foolish, had surrendered her virginity to Jonathan Dexter. It happened after they had shared a bottle of wine in his room and Melinda had missed the last bus. Of course, the wine and the bus were not accidental happenings. Both had been inwardly speculating about them all the evening, but they were handy excuses for Melinda next day. She hardly needed consolation, though, for she was very happy, seeing Jonathan every day and spending most nights in his room. Sweet's Anglo-Saxon and Baugh on the history of the English language weren't so much as glanced at for a fortnight, and as for Goethe, Jonathan had found his Elective Affinities elsewhere.

At Lowfield Hall Jacqueline had made four Christmas puddings, one of which would be sent to the Caswalls who couldn't face the upheaval of bringing two infants to Greeving for the holiday. She wondered what to buy for George, but George had everything – and so had she. Eunice watched her ice the Christmas cake, and Jacqueline waited for her to make some remark, reminiscing or sentimental, when the plaster Santa Claus, the robins and the holly leaves were fixed to the frosting, but Eunice said merely that she hoped the cake would be large enough, and she only said that when asked for her opinion.

Disillusionment over India had killed oriental religion for Giles. It would never, anyway, have fitted in with his plans for himself and Melinda. He saw them sharing their flat, devout Catholics both, but going through agonies to maintain their chaste and continent condition. Perhaps he would become a priest, and if Melinda were to enter a convent, they might – say twice a year – have special dispensations to meet and, soberly garbed, have tea together in some humble café, not daring to touch hands. Or like Lancelot and Guinevere, but without the preceding pleasures, encounter each other across a cathedral nave, gaze long and hard, then part without a word. Even to him this fantasy seemed somewhat extreme. Before becoming a priest he must become a Catholic, and he was looking around Stantwich for someone to give him instruction. Latin and Greek would have their uses, so Virgil and Sophocles received more attention. He put that line from Chesterton up on the wall, the bit about the twitch upon the thread, and he was reading Newman.

Winter had stripped bare the woods and the hedges, and screaming gulls followed Mr Meadows' plough. The magical light of Suffolk became wan and opalescent, and the sky, as the earth turned its farthest from the sun, almost green with a streaking of long butter-coloured clouds. Blood is nipped and ways be foul and nightly sings the staring owl. From cottage chimneys the smoke of log fires rose in long grey plumes.

'What are you doing for our Lord's Nativity?' said Joan in the tone of someone asking a friend to a birthday party.

'Pardon?' said Eunice.

'Christmas.'

'Stopping at the Hall. They've got folks coming.'

'It does seem a shame you having to spend the Lord's birthday among a bunch of sinners. There's nothing to choose between the lot of them. Mrs Higgs that rides the bike, she told Norm that Giles is consorting with Catholic priests. God doesn't want you contaminated by the likes of that, dear.'

'He's only a bit of a boy,' said Eunice.

'You can't say that about his adulterous stepfather. Coming in here and accusing Norm of tampering with his post! Oh, how far will the infidel go in his persecution of the elect! Why don't you come to us? We'll be very quiet, of course, but I think I can guarantee you a goodly refection and the company of loving friends.'

Eunice said she would. They were drinking tea at the time in Joan's squalid parlour, and the third loving friend, in the shape of Norman Smith, came in looking for his

411

dinner. Instead of fetching it, Joan went off into a repetition of her confession which the slightest mention of others who had offended in a similar, or assumed by her to be similar, way was likely to evoke.

'You've led a pure life, Eun, so you can't know what mine has been, delivering up my body, the temple of the Lord, to the riff-raff of Shepherd's Bush. Submitting myself unheeding to the filth of their demands, every kind of disgusting desire which I wouldn't name to a single lady agreed to for the sake of the hard cash that my husband couldn't adequately provide.'

Courage came at last to Norman. He had had two whiskies in the Blue Boar. He advanced on Joan and hit her in the face. She is a very small woman, and she fell off her chair, making glugging noises.

Eunice rose ponderously to her feet. She went up to Norman and took him by the throat. She held the chicken skin of his throat like she might hold a hank of wool, and she laid her other hand hard on his shoulder.

'You leave her alone.'

'I've got to listen to that, have I?'

'If you don't want me shaking the life out of you.' Eunice suited the action to the threat. It was for her a wholly delightful experience and one which she vaguely wondered she hadn't indulged in before. Norman cringed and shuddered as she shook him, his eyes popped and his mouth fell open.

Joan's trust in her as a bodyguard had been justified.

She sat up and said dramatically, 'With God's help, you have saved my life!'

'Load of rubbish,' said Norman. He broke free and stood rubbing his throat. 'You make me sick, the pair of you. Couple of old witches.'

Joan crawled back into her chair to examine her injuries, a ladder in one of her stockings and what would develop into a mild black eye. Norman hadn't really hurt her. He was too feeble and, basically, too frightened of her to do that. Nor had she struck her head when she fell. But something happened to her as the result of that weak blow and that fall. Psychological perhaps, rather than physical – and connected also with the glandular changes of the menopause? Whatever it was, Joan was altered. It was

412

gradual, of course, it hardly showed itself on that evening except in a brighter glitter in her eyes and a shriller note to her voice. But that evening was the beginning of it. She had reached the edge of a pit in which was nothing short of raving madness, and she teetered there on the brink until, two months later, whipped-up fanaticism toppled her over.

# 13

'We'll go in the front way,' said Eunice, back from the Epiphany meeting. She sensed that Joan would be unwelcome at the Hall, though Joan had never told her so and had, on the contrary, at the time of her first visit said that the Coverdales would not object to her exploring their house because 'we're all friends in this village'. Eunice had never heard from George or Jacqueline a hint of their suspicions as to their post, but somehow, by means of her peculiar and often unreliable intuition, she knew – just as she was aware that had she brought home with her Mrs Higgs of bicycle fame or Mrs Jim Meadows, these ladies would have been graciously received by any Coverdale who chanced to see them.

Joan didn't mean to stop long, having only come to have her measurements taken for some secret plan of Eunice's to do with a Christmas present. They were already on the top flight when Giles's bedroom door opened and he came out.

'Looks as if he was backward to me,' said Joan in Eunice's room. She flounced out of her white coat. 'Bit retarded, if you know what I mean.'

'He won't say a word,' said Eunice.

But there she was wrong.

Giles wouldn't have said a word if he hadn't been asked. That wasn't his way. He had gone downstairs to fetch his Greek dictionary which he thought he had left in the morning room. There he found his mother alone, watching a concert of chamber music on the television. George had gone out for half an hour to discuss with the brigadier how to counter a proposal to build four new houses on a piece of land near the river bridge.

Jacqueline looked up and smiled. 'Oh, darling,' she said, 'it's you.'

'Mmm,' said Giles, groping under a pile of Sunday papers for his Liddell and Scott.

'I thought I heard someone on the stairs, but I imagined it was Miss Parchman coming in.'

Occasionally it flashed across Giles's brain that he ought, perhaps once a day, to utter a whole sentence rather than a monosyllable to his mother. He was quite fond of her really. So he forced himself. He stood up, spiky-haired, spotty, myopic, the mad young professor weighted down by a learned tome.

'You did,' he said in his vague abstracted way, 'with that old woman from the shop.'

'What old woman? What on earth do you mean, Giles?'

Giles didn't know the names of anyone in the village. He never went there if he could help it. 'The lunatic woman with the yellow hair,' he said.

'*Mrs Smith?*'

Giles nodded and wandered off towards the door, his dictionary already open, muttering something that sounded to Jacqueline like 'anathema, anathema'. Her patience with him snapped. Briefly she forgot what he had said, or the significance of it.

'Oh, Giles, darling, you must *not* call people lunatics. Giles, wait a minute, *please*. Couldn't you possibly stop down here with us sometimes in the evenings? I mean, you can't have that much homework, and you know you can do it with your eyes shut. You're turning into a hermit, you'll get like that man who sat on top of a pillar!'

He nodded again. The admonition, the request, the flattery, passed over him unheard. He considered very seriously, rubbing one of his spots.

At last he said, 'St Simeon Stylites,' and walked slowly out, leaving the door open.

Exasperated, Jacqueline slammed it. For a while, her concert being over, she sat thinking how much she loved her son, how proud she was of his scholastic attainments, how ambitious for him – and how much happier she would have been had he been more like George's children. And then, because it was useless trying to do anything about Giles, who would surely one day become normal and nice, she returned to what he had said. Joan Smith. But before she could dwell much on it, George came in.

'Well, I think we shall put a spoke in their wheel. Either this place is scheduled as an Area of Natural Beauty or else it isn't. If it comes to a public enquiry we shall all have to get together and brief counsel. You say the parish council are very much opposed?'

'Yes,' said Jacqueline. 'George, Mrs Smith from the store is upstairs. She came in with Miss Parchman.'

'I thought I saw the Smiths' van in the lane. How very unfortunate.'

'Darling, I don't want her here. I know it sounds silly, but it makes me feel quite ill to think of her being here. She goes about telling people Jeffrey divorced me and named you, and that he's a dipsomaniac and all sorts of things. And I *know* she opened the last letter I had from Audrey.'

'It doesn't sound silly at all. The woman's a menace. Did you say anything?'

'I didn't see her. Giles did.'

George opened the door. He did so at the precise moment Eunice and Joan were creeping down the stairs in the dark. He put on the light, walked along the passage and confronted them.

'Good evening, Mrs Smith.'

Eunice was abashed, but not Joan. 'Oh, hallo, Mr Coverdale. Long time no see. Bitterly cold, isn't it? But you can't expect anything else at this time of year.'

George opened the front door for her and held it wide. 'Good night,' he said shortly.

'Cheeri-bye!' Joan scuttled off, giggling, a schoolgirl who has been caught out of bounds.

Thoughtfully, he closed the door. When he turned round Eunice had disappeared. But in the morning, before breakfast, he went to her in the kitchen. This time she wasn't doing miracles with his dress shirt. She was making toast. He had thought of her as shy, and had blamed all her oddities on her shyness, but now he was aware, as he had been once six months before, of the disagreeable atmosphere that prevailed wherever she was. She turned round to look at him like an ill-tempered cow had once looked at him when he went too close to its calf. She didn't say good morning, she didn't say a word, for she knew why he had come. A violent dislike of her seized him, and he wanted the kitchen back in its disordered state, the saucepans still not washed from the night before, an *au pair* muddling through.

'I'm afraid I've got something rather unpleasant to say, Miss Parchman, so I'll make it as brief as possible. My wife and I don't wish to interfere in your personal life, you are at liberty to make what friends you choose. But you must understand we cannot have Mrs Smith in this house.'

He was pompous, poor George. But who wouldn't have been in the circumstances?

'She doesn't do any harm,' said Eunice, and something stopped her calling him sir. She was never again to call George sir or Jacqueline madam.

'I must be the best judge of that. You have a right to know the grounds of my objection to her. I don't think one can seriously say a person does no harm when she is known to spread malicious slanders and, well, to abuse her husband's position as postmaster. That's all. I can't, of course, prevent your visiting Mrs Smith in her own home. That is another matter. But I will not have her here.'

Eunice asked no questions, offered no defence. She shrugged her massive shoulders, turned away and pulled out the grill pan on which three slices of toast were burnt black.

George didn't wait. But as he left the kitchen he was sure he heard her say, 'Now look what you've made me do!'

He talked about it in the car to Giles, because Giles was there and his mind was full of it and, anyway, he was always racking his mind for something to say to the boy.

'You know, I've been very loth to admit it, but there's something definitely unpleasant about that woman. Perhaps I shouldn't be saying this to you, but you're grown up, you must be aware of it, feel it. I don't quite know the word I want to describe her.'

'Repellent,' said Giles.

'That's exactly it!' George was so delighted not only to have been supplied with this adjective but also because it had been supplied, quite forthcomingly, by Giles, that he took his eyes off the road and had to swerve sharply to avoid hitting Mr Meadows' ancient labrador which was ambling along in the middle of the lane. 'Look where you're going, you daft old thing,' he called after it in a kind of affectionate relief. 'Repellent, that's the word. Yes, she sends shivers up my spine. But what's to be done, Giles old boy? Put up with it, I suppose?'

'Mmm.'

'I daresay it's just made me a bit nervous. I'm very likely exaggerating. She's taken an enormous burden of work off your mother's shoulders.'

Giles said 'Mmm' again, opened his case and began muttering bits out of Ovid. Disappointed, but well aware that there was to be no repetition of that inspired contribution to this very one-sided discussion, George sighed and gave up. But a very nasty thought had struck him. If Eunice had been able to drive, if she had been driving this car five minutes before, he was intuitively certain she wouldn't have swerved to avoid the dog, or if it had been a child, to avoid that either.

Jacqueline left a note in the kitchen to say she would be out all day. She didn't want to see Eunice who was upstairs doing the 'children's' bathroom. It was a pity, she now thought, that Giles had told her about seeing Joan Smith, and an even greater one that she had been so impulsive as to tell George. Eunice might leave, or threaten to leave. Jacqueline drove off through the village to the Jameson-Kerrs' house, and when she saw the smeary windows, the dust lying everywhere, and her friend's rough red hands, she told herself that she must keep her servant at any cost and that the occasional presence of Joan Smith was a small price to pay.

Joan saw the car go by and put on her fleecy coat.

'Off to the Hall, I suppose?' said Norman. 'I wonder you don't live up there with Miss Frankenstein.'

Though she had once done so, Joan no longer unloaded her biblical claptrap on to her husband. He was the only person she knew who escaped it. 'Don't you say a word against her! If it wasn't for her I might be dead.'

Munching gum, Norman peered into one of his sacks. 'Stupid fuss to make about a little tap.'

'If it wasn't for her,' shouted Joan, with a flash of wit, 'you wouldn't be looking at mailbags, you'd be sewing them.'

She jumped into the van and roared up over the bridge. Eunice was in the kitchen, loading the washing machine with sheets and shirts and table linen.

'I saw her go off in her car, so I thought I'd pop up. Did you get into a row last night?'

'Don't know about a row.' Eunice closed the lid of the machine and put the kettle on. 'He says you're not to come here.'

Joan's reaction was loud and violent. 'I knew it! I could see it coming a mile off. It's not the first time the servants of God have been persecuted, Eun, and it won't be the last.' She swept out a spindly arm, narrowly missing the milk jug. 'Look what you do for them! Isn't the labourer in the vineyard worthy of his hire? He'd have to pay you twice what you're getting if you didn't have that poky room up there, but he doesn't think of that. He's no more than a landlord, and since when's a landlord got a right to interfere with a person's friends?' Her voice rose to a tremulous shriek. 'Even his own daughter goes about saying he's a fascist. Even his kinsmen stand afar from him. Woe to him whom the Lord despiseth!'

Unmoved by any of this, Eunice stared stolidly at the boiling kettle. No surge of love for Joan rose in her, no impulse of loyalty affected her. She was untouched by any of that passion which heats one when one's basic rights are threatened. She simply felt, as she had been feeling ever since the night before, that her life was being interfered with. At last she said, in her heavy level way:

'I don't mean to take any notice.'

Joan let out a shrill laugh. She was enormously pleased. She bubbled with excitement. 'That's right, dear, that's my Eun. You make him knuckle under. You show him it's not everyone that goeth when he says go and cometh when he says come.'

'I'll make the tea,' said Eunice. 'Have a look at that note she's left, will you? I've left my glasses upstairs.'

# 14

During term Melinda had only twice been home, but now that term had come to an end. Jonathan was going to Cornwall with his parents until after the New Year and she had been invited to go with them, but it would have taken more than being in love to keep Melinda from Lowfield Hall at Christmas. With promises to phone every day, to write often, they parted and Melinda got on the train for Stantwich.

Again it was Geoff Baalham who picked her up at Gallows Corner. No great coincidence this, as Geoff was always returning from his egg delivery round at about this time. But on 18 December it was dark at five, the windows of the van were closed and the heater on, and Melinda wore an embroidered Afghan coat and a big fur hat. Only the boots were the same.

'Hi, Melinda. You *are* a stranger. Don't tell me it's your studies been keeping you up in Galwich.'

'What else?'

'A new boy friend, or that's what I heard.'

'You just can't keep anything to yourself in this place, can you? Now tell me what's new.'

'Barbara's expecting. There'll be another little Baalham come July. Can you see me as a dad, Melinda?'

'You'll be marvellous. I'm so glad, Geoff. Mind you give my love to Barbara.'

'Of course I will,' said Geoff. 'Now, what else? My Auntie Nellie had a nasty fall off her bike and she's laid up with a bad foot. Did you hear about your dad throwing Mrs Smith out of the house?'

'You don't mean it!'

'It's a fact. He caught her sneaking down the stairs with your lady help and he told her not to come there again, and then he threw her out. She's got bruises all down her side, or so I heard.'

'He's a terrible fascist, isn't he? But that's *awful*.'

419

'Don't know about awful, not when you think what she says about your ma and opens their letters, according to what I hear. Well, here's where I leave you, and tell your ma I'll drop the eggs by first thing Monday.'

Geoff drove home to Barbara and the chickens, thinking what a nice girl Melinda was – that crazy fur hat! – and that the boy friend was a lucky guy.

'You didn't really throw Mrs Smith out and bruise her all down her side, did you?' said Melinda, bursting into the morning room where George, the carpet covered with a sheet, was cleaning his guns because it was too cold in the gun room.

'That's a nice way to greet your father when you haven't seen him for a month.' George got up and gave her a kiss. 'You're looking well. How's the boy friend? Now what's all this about me assaulting Mrs Smith?'

'Geoff Baalham said you had.'

'Ridiculous nonsense. I never touched the woman. I didn't even speak to her beyond saying good night. You ought to know village gossip by this time, Melinda.'

Melinda threw her hat on to a chair. 'But you did say she mustn't come here again, Daddy?'

'Certainly I did.'

'Oh, poor Miss Parchman! It's awfully feudal interfering with her friendships. We were so worried because she didn't know anyone or go anywhere, and now she's got a friend you won't have her in the house. It's a *shame*.'

'Melinda . . .' George began.

'I shall be very nice to her. I'm going to be very kind and caring. I can't bear to think of her not having a single friend.'

'It's her married friend I object to,' said George wickedly, and he laughed when Melinda flounced out.

So that evening Melinda began on a disaster course that was to lead directly to her death and that of her father, her stepmother and her stepbrother. She embarked on it because she was in love. It is not so much true that all the world loves a lover as that a lover loves all the world. Melinda was moved by her love to bestow love and happiness, but it was tragic for her that Eunice Parchman was her object.

After dinner she jumped up from the table and, to Jacqueline's astonishment, helped Eunice to clear. It was to Eunice's astonishment too, and to her dismay. She wanted to get the dishes done in time to watch her Los Angeles cop serial at eight, and now here was this great tomboy bouncing about and mixing gravied plates up with water glasses. She wasn't going to speak, not she, and perhaps the girl would take the hint and go away.

A kind of delicacy, an awareness of the tasteful thing, underlay Melinda's extrovert ways, and she sensed that it would be disloyal to her father to mention the events of the previous Sunday. So she began on a different tack. She could hardly have chosen a worse subject, but for one.

'Your first name's Eunice, isn't it, Miss Parchman?'

'Yes,' said Eunice.

'It's a biblical name, but of course you know that. But I think it's Greek really. Eu-nicey or maybe Eu-nikey. I'll have to ask Giles. I didn't do Greek at school.'

A dish was banged violently into the machine. Melinda, herself a habitual dish-banger, took no notice. She sat on the table.

'I'll look it up. The Epistle to Timothy, I think. Of course it is! Eu-nicey, mother of Timothy.'

'You're sitting on my tea towel,' said Eunice.

'Oh, sorry. I'll have to check, but I think it says something about thy mother Eunice and thy grandmother Lois. I don't suppose your mother's name is Lois, is it?'

'Edith.'

'Now that must be Anglo-Saxon. Names are fascinating, aren't they? I love mine. I think my parents had very good taste calling us Peter and Paula and Melinda. Peter's coming next week, you'll like him. If you'd had a son, would you have called him Timothy?'

'I don't know,' said Eunice, wondering why she was being subjected to this persecution. Had George Coverdale put her up to it? Or was it just done to mock? If not, why did that great tomboy keep smiling and laughing? She wiped all the surfaces viciously and drained the sink.

'What's your favourite name then?' said her inquisitor.

421

Eunice had never thought about it. The only names she knew were those of her relatives, her few acquaintances and those she had heard spoken on television. From this last, in desperation she selected, recalling her hero whose latest adventure she would miss if she didn't get a move on.

'Steve,' she said, and hanging up her tea-towel, marched out of the kitchen. It had been an intellectual effort which left her quite exhausted.

Melinda was not dissatisfied. Poor old Parchman was obviously sulking over the Joan Smith business, but she would get over that. The ice had been broken, and Melinda hoped confidently for a *rapport* to have grown up between them before the end of her holiday.

'Eu-nee-kay,' said Giles when she asked him, and, 'There was this man, you see, who got drunk at a party, and he was staggering home at about three in the morning when he landed up in the entrance to a block of flats. Well, he looked at all the names by the bells, and there was one called S. T. Paul. So he rang that bell, and when the guy came down, all cross and sleepy in his pyjamas, the man said, "Tell me, did you ever get any replies to your letters?" ' He let out a great bellow of laughter at his own joke, then abruptly became doleful. Maybe he shouldn't tell jokes like that with his conversion in view.

'You're crazy, Step,' said Melinda. She didn't appreciate, was never to appreciate, that she was the only person to whom her stepbrother ever uttered more than one isolated sentence. Her mind was on Eunice whom she sought out, armed with the Bible, next day with a dictionary of proper names. She lent her magazines, took her the evening paper George brought home, and obligingly ran upstairs to fetch her glasses when Eunice said, as she always did, that she hadn't got them with her.

Eunice was harassed almost beyond bearing. It was bad enough that Melinda and Giles were about the house all day so that Joan Smith couldn't come to see her. But now Melinda was always in her kitchen or following her about 'like a dog', as she told Joan. And she was perpetually on tenterhooks what with those books and papers constantly being thrust under her nose – which she didn't tell Joan.

'Of course you know what all that amounts to, don't you, Eun? They're ashamed of their wicked behaviour, and they've put that girl up to soft-soaping you.'

'I don't know,' said Eunice. 'She gets on my nerves.'

Her nerves were playing her up, as she put it to herself, in a way they had never done before. But she was powerless to deal with Melinda, that warm unsnubbable girl. And once or twice, while Melinda was haranguing her about names or the Bible or Christmas or family histories, she wondered what would happen if she were to pick up one of those long kitchen knives and use it. Not, of course, Eunice being Eunice, what the Coverdales would do or what would become of her, but just the immediate consequence – that tongue silenced, blood spreading over and staining that white neck.

On the 23rd Peter and Audrey Coverdale arrived.

Peter was a tall pleasant-looking man who favoured his mother rather than his father. He was thirty-one. He and his wife were childless, from choice probably, for Audrey was a career woman, chief librarian at the university where he had a post as lecturer in political economy. Audrey was particularly fond of Jacqueline. She was a well-dressed elegant bluestocking, four years older than her husband, which made her only seven years Jacqueline's junior. Before training as a librarian she had been at the Royal Academy of Music, which Jacqueline had attended before her first marriage. The two women read the same kind of books, shared a passionate love of Mozartian and pre-Mozartian opera, loved fashion and talking about clothes. They corresponded regularly, Audrey's letters being among those examined by Joan Smith.

They hadn't been in the house more than ten minutes when Melinda insisted on taking them to the kitchen and introducing them to Eunice.

'She's a member of this household. It's awfully fascist to treat her like a bit of kitchen equipment.'

Eunice shook hands.

'Will you be going away for Christmas, Miss Parchman?' said Audrey, who prided herself, as Jacqueline did, on having a fund of small-talk suitable for persons in every rank of life.

'No,' said Eunice.

'What a shame! Not for us, of course. Your loss will be our gain. But one does like to be with one's family at Christmas.'

Eunice turned her back and got the teacups out.

'Where did you get that awful woman?' Audrey said to Jacqueline later. 'My dear, she's creepy. She's not human.'

Jacqueline flushed as if she personally had been insulted. 'You're as bad as George. I don't want to make a friend of my servant, I want her the way she is, marvellously efficient and unobtrusive. I can tell you, she really knows her job.'

'So do boa constrictors,' said Audrey.

And thus they came to Christmas.

George and Melinda brought holly in to decorate Lowfield Hall, and from the drawing-room chandelier hung a bunch of mistletoe, the gift of Mr Meadows in whose oaks it grew. More than a hundred cards came for the Coverdales, and these were suspended on strings in a cunning arrangement fixed up by Melinda. Giles received only two personal cards, one from his father and one from an uncle, and these, in his opinion, were so hideous that he declined to put them up on his cork wall where the Quote of the Month was: 'To love oneself is the beginning of a lifelong romance.' Melinda made paper chains, bright red and emerald and shocking blue and chrome yellow, exactly the kind of chains she had made every year for fifteen years. Jacqueline took much the same view of them as her son did of his cards, but not for the world would she have said so.

On the Day itself the drawing room was grandly festive. The men wore suits, the women floor-length gowns. Jacqueline was in cream velvet, Melinda in a 1920s creation, rather draggled dark blue *crêpe de Chine* embroidered with beads which she bought in the Oxfam shop. They opened their presents, strewing the carpet with coloured paper and glitter. While Jacqueline unwrapped the gold bracelet that was George's gift, and Giles looked with something nearing enthusiasm on an unabridged Gibbon in six volumes, Melinda opened the parcel from her father.

It was a tape recorder.

# 15

Everyone was drinking champagne, even Giles. He had been prevailed upon by his mother to come downstairs, and was morosely resigned to staying downstairs all day. And it would be worse tomorrow when they would be having a party. In this view Melinda concurred – all those cairns and curs and roisterers – and she sat on the floor next to him, telling him how wonderful Jonathan was. Giles didn't much mind this. Byron, after all, was never perturbed by the existence of Colonel Leigh, and Christmas would be bearable if such conclaves with Melinda became the rule. He fancied that the others had noticed their closeness and were overawed by the mystery of it.

Far from noticing anything about her son except that he was there for once, Jacqueline was thinking about the one absent member of the household.

'I really do feel,' she said, 'that we ought to ask Miss Parchman to sit down to lunch with us.'

A spontaneous groan from all but Melinda.

'A female Banquo,' said Audrey, and her husband remarked that Christmas was supposed to be for merry-making.

'And for peace and goodwill,' said George. 'I don't find the woman personally congenial, as you all know, but Christmas is Christmas and it's not pleasant to think of her eating her lunch out there on her own.'

'Darling, I'm so glad you agree with me. I'll go and ask her and then I'll lay another place.'

But Eunice was not to be found. She had tidied the kitchen, prepared the vegetables, and gone off to the village store. There in the parlour, undecorated by holly or paper garlands, she and Joan and a gloomy sullen Norman ate roast chicken, frozen peas and canned potatoes, followed by a Christmas pudding from the shop. Eunice enjoyed her meal, though she would have liked sausages as well. Joan had cooked some sausages but had forgotten to serve them, and Norman, made suspicious by a peculiar smell, found them mouldering in the grill pan a week later. They drank water, and afterwards strong tea. Norman had got some beer in, but this Joan had deposited in the bin just before the dustmen called. She was in raptures over the salmon pink jumper Eunice had knitted for her, rushed away to put it on, and preened about in it, striking grotesque model-girl attitudes in front of the fingermarked mirror. Eunice received an enormous box of chocolates and a fruit cake from stock.

'You'll come back tomorrow, won't you, dear?' said Joan.

And so it happened that Eunice also spent Boxing Day with the Smiths, leaving Jacqueline to cope with food and drink for the thirty guests who came that evening. And the effect on Jacqueline was curious, twofold. It was as if she were back in the old days when the entire burden of the household work had been on her shoulders, and in Eunice's absence she appreciated her almost more than when she was there. This was what it would be like permanently if Eunice were to leave. And yet for the first time she saw her housekeeper as George and Audrey and Peter saw her, as uncouth and boorish, a woman who came and went as she pleased and who saw the Coverdales as so dependant on her that she held them in the hollow of her hand.

The New Year passed, and Peter and Audrey went home. They had asked Melinda to go back with them for the last week of her holiday, but Melinda had refused. She was a very worried girl. Each day that passed made her more anxious. She lost her sparkle, moped about the house, and said no to all the invitations she got from her village friends. George and Jacqueline thought she was missing Jonathan and tactfully they asked no questions.

For this Melinda was deeply thankful. If what she feared was true – and it must be true now – they would have to know sometime. Perhaps it might be possible to get through this, or out of this, without George ever suspecting. Children understand their parents as little as parents understand their children. Melinda had had a happy childhood and a sympathetic devoted father, but her way of

426

thinking was infected by the attitude of her friends to their parents. Parents were bigoted, prudish, moralistic. Therefore hers must be, and no personal experience triumphed over this conviction. She guessed she was George's favourite child. All the worse. He would be the more bitterly disappointed and disillusioned if he knew, and his idealistic love for her turned to disgust. She imagined his face, stern and yet incredulous, if he were even to suspect such a thing of his youngest child, his little girl. Poor Melinda. She would have been flabbergasted had she known that George had long supposed her relationship with Jonathan to be a fully sexual one, regretted it, but accepted it philosophically as long as he could believe there was love and trust between them.

Every day, of course, she had been having long phone conversations with Jonathan – George was to be faced with a daunting bill – but so far she hadn't breathed a word. Now, however, on 4 January, she knew she must tell him. This wasn't as bad as telling her father would be, but bad enough. Her experience of this kind of revelation had been culled from novel and magazine reading and from old wives' gossip in the village. When you told the man he stopped caring for you, he dropped you, didn't want to know, or at best shouldered his responsibility while implying it was all your fault. But she had to tell him. She couldn't go on carrying this frightening secret another day on her own, especially as, that morning, she had been violently sick on waking.

She waited until George had gone to work and Jacqueline and Giles to Nunchester in the second car, Jacqueline supposing that while she was shopping her son would be visiting a friend – a friend at last! – though, in fact, he was to receive his first instruction from Father Madigan. Eunice was upstairs making beds. There were three telephones at Lowfield Hall, one in the morning room, an extension in the hall and another extension by Jacqueline's bed. Melinda chose the morning-room phone, but while she was getting enough courage together to make her call, it rang. Jonathan.

'Hold on a minute, Jon,' she said. 'I want to close the door.'

It was at that precise moment, while Jonathan was holding the line and had briefly laid down the receiver to light a cigarette while Melinda was closing the morning-room door, that Eunice lifted the receiver on Jacqueline's bedroom extension. She wasn't spying. She was too uninterested in Melinda and too repelled by her attentions deliberately to eavesdrop. She picked up the receiver because you cannot properly dust a telephone without doing so. But as soon as she heard Melinda's first words she was aware that it would be prudent to listen.

'Oh, Jon, something awful! I'll come straight out with it, though I'm scared stiff to tell you. I'm pregnant. I know I am. I was sick this morning and I'm nearly two weeks overdue. It'll be frightful if Daddy or Jackie find out, Daddy would be so let down, he'd hate me, and what am I going to *do*?'

She was nearly crying. Choked by tears that would soon spill over, she waited for the stunned silence. Jonathan said quite calmly, 'Well, you've got two alternatives, Mel.'

'Have I? You tell me. I can't think of anything but just running away and dying!'

'Don't be so wet, lovey. You can have an abortion if you really want . . .'

'Then they'd be sure to know. If I couldn't get it on the National Health and I had to have money or they wanted to know my next of kin or . . .'

By now Melinda was hysterical. Like almost all women in her particular situation, she was in a blind unreasoning panic, fighting against the bars of the trap that was her own body. Eunice screwed up her nose. She couldn't stand that, lot of fuss and nonsense. And perhaps it was something else as well, some unconscious sting of envy or bitterness, that made her lay the receiver down. Lay it down, not replace it. It would be unwise to do that until after their conversation was over. She moved away to dust the dressing table, and thus she missed the rest.

'I don't like the idea of abortion,' said Jonathan. 'Do get yourself together, Mel, and calm down. Listen, I want to marry you, anyway. Only I thought we ought to wait till we've got our degrees and jobs and whatever. But it doesn't matter. Let's get married as soon as we can.'

'Oh, Jon, I do love you! Could we? I'd have to tell them even though we're both over eighteen, but, Jon . . .'

'But nothing. We'll get married and have our baby and it'll be great. You come up to Galwich tomorrow instead of next week and I'll hitch back and you can stay with me and we'll make plans, OK?'

It was very much OK with Melinda who, having wept with despair, was now bubbling with joy. She would go to Jonathan next day and tell George she'd be staying with her friend in Lowestoft. It was awful lying to him, but all in a good cause, better that than let him know, wait till they'd published the banns or got the licence. And so on. She wasn't sick on 5 January. Before she had packed her case she knew her fears had been groundless, the symptoms having resulted from anxiety and their cessation from relief. But she went just the same and took a taxi from the station to Jonathan's flat, so impatient to tell him she wasn't going to have a baby after all.

Being in possession of someone else's secret reminded Eunice of the days of blackmailing the homosexual and, of course, Annie Cole. It was a piece of information which Joan Smith would have delighted to hear, Joan who rather resented the way Eunice never told her anything about the private lives of the Coverdales. She wasn't going to tell her this either. A secret shared is no longer a secret, especially when it has been imparted to someone like Joan Smith who would whisper it to what customers she still retained in no time. No, Eunice was going to keep this locked in her board-like bosom, for you never knew when it might come in useful.

So, on the following night, when she climbed into the van that was waiting for her in Greeving Lane, she gave nothing away.

'I noticed the Coverdale girl went back to her college yesterday,' said Joan. 'Bit early, wasn't it? All set for a week of unbridled cohabitation with that boy friend she's got, I daresay. She'll come to a bad end. Mr Coverdale's just the sort of hard man to cast his own flesh and blood out of the house if he thought they'd been committing fornication.'

'I don't know,' said Eunice.

Twelfth Night, 6 January, Epiphany, is the greatest day in the calendar for the disciples of Elroy Camps. The meeting was sensational – two really uninhibited confessions, one of them rivalling Joan's own, an extempore prayer shrieked by Joan at the top of her voice, five hymns.

'Follow the star!
Follow the star!
The Wise Men turn not back.
Across the desert, hills or foam,
The star will lead them to their home,
White or brown or black!'

They ate seed cake and drank tea. Joan became more and more excited until, eventually, she had a kind of seizure. She fell on the floor, uttering prophecies as the spirit moved her, and waving her arms and legs about. Two of the women had to take her into a side room and calm her down, though on the whole the Epiphany People were more gratified than dismayed by this performance.

Only Mrs Elder Barnstaple, a sensible woman who came to the meetings for her husband's sake, seemed disquieted. But she supposed Joan was 'putting it on'. Not one of that company guessed at the truth, that Joan Smith was daily growing more and more demented and her hold on reality was becoming increasingly tenuous. She was like a weak swimmer whose grasp of a slippery rock has never been firm. Now her fingers were sliding helplessly down its surface, and currents of madness were drawing her into the whirlpool.

She hardly spoke as she drove the van home, but from time to time she let out little bursts of giggles like the chucklings of something unhuman that haunted those long pitch-dark lanes.

# 16

Bleak midwinter, and the frosty wind made moan. Eva Baalham said that the evenings were drawing out, and this was true but not that one would notice. The first snow fell in Greeving, a dusting of snow that thawed and froze again.

On the cork wall, from St Augustine: 'Too late loved I Thee, O Thou Beauty so ancient and so new, too late came I to love Thee!' For Giles the road to Rome was not entirely satisfactory as Father Madigan, accustomed until recently to Tipperary peasants, expected from him their ignorance and their blind faith. He didn't seem to understand that Giles knew more Greek and Latin than he and had got through Aquinas before he was sixteen. In Galwich Melinda was blissfully happy with Jonathan. They were still going to get married but not until she had taken her degree in fifteen months' time. To this end, because she would need a good job, she was working quite hard, between making love and making plans, at her Chaucer and her Gower.

The cold pale sun pursued a low arc across a cold pale sky, aquamarine and clear, or appeared as a puddle of light in a high grey field of cloud.

19 January was Eunice's forty-eighth birthday. She noted its occurrence but she told no one, not even Joan. It was years since anyone had sent her a card or given her a present on that day.

She was alone in the house. At eleven the phone rang. Eunice didn't like answering the phone, she wasn't used to it and it alarmed her. After wondering whether it might not be better to ignore it, she picked up the receiver reluctantly and said hello.

The call was from George. Tin Box Coverdale had recently changed their public-relations consultants, and a director of the new company was coming to lunch, to be followed by a tour of the factory. George had prepared a short history of the firm which had been established by his grandfather – and had left his notes at home.

He had a cold and his voice was thick and hoarse. 'The papers I want you to find are in the writing desk in the morning room, Miss Parchman. I'm not sure where, but the sheets are clipped together and headed in block capitals: Coverdale Enterprises from 1895 to the Present Day.'

Eunice said nothing.

'Now I'd appreciate it if you'd hunt them out.' George let out an explosive sneeze. 'I beg your pardon. Where was I? Oh, yes. A driver from here is already on his way, and I want you to put the papers into a large envelope and give them to him when he comes.'

'All right,' said Eunice hopelessly.

'I'll hold the line. Have a look now, will you? And come back and tell me when you've found them.'

The desk was full of papers, many of them clipped together and all headed with something or other. Eunice hesitated, then replaced the receiver without speaking to George again. Immediately the phone rang. She didn't answer it. She went upstairs and hid in her own room. The phone rang four more times and then the doorbell. Eunice didn't answer that either. Although she wasn't celebrating her birthday, it did strike her that it was very disagreeable having this happen today of all days. A person's birthday ought to be nice and peaceful, not upset by this kind of thing.

George couldn't understand what had happened. The driver came back empty-handed, the consultant left without the Coverdale history. George made a sixth call and at last got hold of his wife who had been in Nunchester having her hair tinted. No, Miss Parchman wasn't ill and had just gone out for a walk. The first thing he did when he got home was find the papers on the very top of the pile in the writing desk.

'What happened, Miss Parchman? It was of vital importance to me to have those papers.'

'I couldn't find them,' said Eunice, laying the dining table, not looking at him.

'But they were on the top. I can't understand how you could miss them. My driver wasted an hour coming over here. And surely, even if you couldn't find them, you could have come back and told me.'

'They cut us off.'

George knew that was a lie. 'I rang back four times.'

'It never rang,' said Eunice, and she turned on him her small face, which now seemed to have increased in size, to have swollen with resentment. Hours of brooding had filled her with gall, and now she used to him the tone her father had so often heard in the last weeks of his life. 'I don't know anything about any of it.' For her, she was quite voluble. 'It's no good asking me because I don't know.' The blood crept up her throat and broke in a dark flush across her face. She turned her back on him.

George walked out of the room, impotent in the face of this refusal to take responsibility, to apologise or even discuss it. His head was thick with his cold and felt as if stuffed with wet wool. Jacqueline was making up her face in front of her dressing-table mirror.

'She's not a secretary, darling,' she said, echoing the words he had used to her when she had hesitated about engaging Eunice. 'You mustn't expect too much of her.'

'Too much! Is it too much to ask someone to find four clearly labelled sheets of paper and hand them over to a driver? Besides, it isn't that which I mind so much. I never really knew what dumb insolence meant before, it was just a phrase. I know now. She doesn't give the number or our name when she answers the phone. If a pig could say "Hallo" it would sound just like Miss Parchman.'

Jacqueline laughed, smudging her mascara.

'And to put the phone down on me! Why didn't she answer when I called back? Of course the phone rang, it's just nonsense to say it didn't. And she was positively rude to me when I spoke to her about it.'

'I've noticed she doesn't like doing things which are – well, outside what she thinks of as her province. It's always the same. If I leave her a note she'll do what it asks but a bit truculently, I always think, and she doesn't like making phone calls or answering the phone.' She spoke quite blithely as if laughing off 'men's nonsense', humouring and soothing him because his cold was now worse than hers.

George hesitated, put his hand on her shoulder. 'It's no good, Jackie, she'll have to go.'

'Oh, no, George!' Jacqueline spun round on her stool. 'I

can't do without her. You can't ask that of me just because she let you down over those papers.'

'It isn't just that. It's her insolence and the way she looks at us. Have you noticed she never calls us by our names? And she's dropped that sir and madam. Not that I care about that, I'm not a snob,' said George, who did and was, 'but I can't put up with bad manners and lying.'

'George, please give her one more chance. What would I do without her? I can't face the thought of it.'

'There are other servants.'

'Yes, old Eva and *au pairs*,' said Jacqueline bitterly. 'I had some idea what it would be like at our Christmas party. I didn't enjoy it if you did. I was doing the food all day and running around all night. I don't think I spoke to anyone except to ask if they wanted another drink.'

'And for that I have to put up with a servant who would have been a credit to the staff at Auschwitz?'

'One more chance, George, *please.*'

He capitulated. Jacqueline could always win him over. Could he pay too high a price, he asked himself, to see his beloved wife happy and relaxed and beautiful? Could he pay too much for peace and domestic comfort and a well-run elegant home? Was there anything he wouldn't part with for that?

Except my life, he might have answered, except my life.

George intended to react by taking a firm line with Eunice in accordance with his calling, to manage and direct her. He wasn't a weak man or a coward, and he had never approved the maxim that it is better to ignore unpleasantness and pretend that it does not exist. She must be admonished when she returned his smile and his 'Good morning' with a scowl and a grunt, or he would have a quiet talk with her and elicit from her what the trouble was and how they had failed.

He admonished her only once, and then jocularly. 'Can't you manage a smile when I speak to you, Miss Parchman? I don't know what I've done to deserve that grim look.'

Beseechingly, Jacqueline's eyes met his. Eunice took no notice apart from slightly lifting her shoulders. After that he said no more. He knew what would happen if he tried a tête-à-tête with her. 'There's nothing wrong. It's no use talking about it because there's nothing.' But he realised, if Jacqueline did not, that they were conciliating Eunice Parchman, allowing her to manage and direct them. For Jacqueline's sake and to his own self-disgust he found himself smiling fatuously at his housekeeper whenever they encountered each other, asking her if her room was warm enough, if she had enough free time, and once if she would *mind* staying in on a certain evening when they had guests for dinner. His warmth was met by not a shred of reciprocation.

February came in with a snowstorm.

Only in pictures and on television had Eunice seen real country snow before as against the slush which clogged the gutters of Tooting. It had never occurred to her that snow was something that could bother people or change their lives. On the morning of Monday, 1 February, George was up before she was with an unwilling sleepy Giles, clearing two channels in the long drive for the wheels of the Mercedes. The first light had brought Mr Meadows out with his snow plough into the lane. A shovel and boots and sacks were put into the car's boot, and George and Giles set off for Stantwich with the air of Arctic explorers.

Against a livid sky the great flakes whirled, and the landscape was blanketed but for the dark demarcations of hedges and the isolated blot of a skeleton tree. No going out for Jacqueline that day or the next or the next. She phoned to cancel her appointment with the hairdresser, her lunch with Paula, the evening engagements. Eva Baalham didn't bother to phone and say she wasn't coming. She just didn't come. You took that sort of thing for granted in East Anglia in February.

So Jacqueline was imprisoned with Eunice Parchman. Just as she was afraid to use her car, so were her neighbours afraid to call on her. Once she would have seen the coming of the snow as a possible topic of conversation between herself and Eunice, but now she knew better than to try. Eunice accepted the snow as she accepted rain and wind and sunshine. She swept the paving outside the gun-room door and the front steps without comment. Silently, she went about her work. When Jacqueline, unable to repress herself, exclaimed with relief at the sound of George's car successfully returned through the thickening drifts, she reacted no more than if this had been a normal day of ordinary weather.

And Jacqueline began to see George's point of view. Being snow-bound with Eunice was more than disconcerting; it was oppressive, almost sinister. She marched doggedly through the rooms with her duster and her polishing cloths. Once, when Jacqueline was seated at the desk writing to Audrey, the half-filled sheet of paper was lifted silently from under her nose while a duster was wiped slowly across the surface of inlaid leather and rosewood. It was as if, Jacqueline said later to her husband, she were a deaf patient in a home for the handicapped and Eunice a wardmaid. And even when the work was done, and Eunice departed upstairs to watch afternoon serials, she felt that it was not the snow alone which pressed a ponderous weight on the upper regions of Lowfield Hall. She found herself treading carefully, closing doors discreetly, sometimes just standing in the strange white light that is uniquely the reflection thrown back from snow, gleaming, marmoreal and cold.

She was not to know, never dreamed, that Eunice was far more afraid of her than she was intimidated by Eunice; that the incident of the Coverdale History papers had made her retreat totally into her shell, for if she were to speak or allow them to speak to her, that arch enemy of hers, the printed word, would rise up and assail her. Reading in an armchair pulled close to a radiator, reading to please Eunice and keep clear of her, Jacqueline never guessed that she could have done nothing to please Eunice less or arouse her more to hatred.

Every evening that week she needed twice her usual allowance of sherry to relax her before dinner.

'Is it worth it?' said George.

'I talked to Mary Cairne on the phone today. She said she'd put up with positive abuse, let alone dumb insolence, to have a servant like Miss P.'

George kissed his wife, but he couldn't resist a dig. 'Let her try it then. It's nice to know Miss P.'ll have somewhere to go when I sack her.'

But he didn't sack her, and on the Thursday, 4 February,

something happened to distract them from their discontentment with their housekeeper.

# 17

Things were getting too much for Norman Smith. He also was snowbound with a fellow-being who was uncongenial to him, only the fellow-being was his wife.

Norman had often in the past told Joan she was mad, but in much the same way as Melinda Coverdale told Giles Mont he was mad. He didn't intend to imply she was insane. But now he was sure she literally was mad. They still shared a bed. They belonged in that category of married people who share a bed without thinking about it, who would have shared a bed even if they were not on speaking terms. But often now Norman woke in the night to find Joan absent, and then he heard her in some other part of the house laughing to herself, laughing maniacally, or singing snatches of Epiphany hymns or reciting prophecies in a shrill uneven voice. She had ceased altogether to clean the house or dust the goods in the shop or sweep the shop floor. And each morning she bedizened herself in bits of bizarre clothing saved from her Shepherd's Bush days, her face painted like a clown's.

She ought to see a doctor. Norman knew quite well that she was in need of treatment for her mind. A psychiatrist was the sort of doctor she ought to see, but how to get her to one? How to go about it? Dr Crutchley held surgery twice a week in Greeving in a couple of rooms in a converted cottage. Norman knew Joan wouldn't go of her own inclination, and he couldn't imagine going *for* her. What, sit in that waiting room among coughing and snuffling Meadowses and Baalhams and Eleighs, and then explain to a tired and harassed doctor that his wife sang in the night and bawled bits from the Bible at his customers and wore knee socks and short skirts like a young girl?

Besides, the worst manifestation of her madness he couldn't confess to anyone.

Lately she seemed to think she had a right, godlike or as God's censor, to investigate any of the mail that passed through Greeving Post Office. He couldn't keep the mail sacks from her. He tried locking them up in the outside lavatory, but she broke the lock with a hammer. And now she was an expert at steaming open envelopes. He winced and trembled when he heard her telling Mrs Higgs that God had punished Alan and Pat Newstead by killing their only grandchild, information Joan had culled out of a letter from the distraught father. And when she imparted to Mr Meadows of the garage that George Coverdale was in debt to his wine merchant, he waited till the shop was empty and then he struck her in the face. Joan only screamed at him. God would have vengeance on him, God would make him a leper and an outcast who dared not show his face in the haunts of men.

This was one of her prophecies which was to prove only too true.

On Friday, 5 February, when the thaw had begun and the lane between Greeving and Lowfield Hall could be negotiated without a struggle, George Coverdale walked into the village store at nine in the morning. That is, he walked in after he had banged peremptorily on the front door and fetched Norman, who was still at breakfast, out to open up.

'You're early, Mr Coverdale,' said Norman nervously. It was seldom that George had set foot on that threshold, and Norman knew his coming boded ill.

'In my opinion, nine is not early. It's the time I usually reach my place of business, and if I shan't do so this morning it's because the matter I have to discuss with you is too serious to postpone.'

'Oh, yes?' Norman might have stood up to George, but he quailed when Joan, her yellow hair in curlers, her skin-and-bone body wrapped in a dirty red dressing gown, appeared in the doorway.

George took an envelope from his briefcase. 'This letter has been opened and re-sealed,' he said, and he paused. It was horrible to him to think of Joan Smith spreading about the village that his wine merchant was threatening him with proceedings. And it was made all the more horrible by the fact that the letter was the result of a computer mistake.

George, having paid his bill in early December when it was due, had argued the whole thing out with the retailer by phone and obtained a fulsome apology for his error. But he scorned to defend himself to these people. 'There are smears of glue on the flap,' he said, 'and inside I found a hair which I venture to suggest comes from the head of your wife.'

'I don't know anything about it,' Norman muttered. He had unwittingly used Eunice Parchman's phrasing, and this inflamed George.

'Perhaps the postmaster at Stantwich will. I intend to write to him today. I shall lay the whole matter before him, not forgetting previous occasions when I have had cause for suspicion, and I shall demand an official enquiry.'

'I can't stop you.'

'Very true. I merely felt it was just to tell you what I mean to do so that you have warning in advance. Good morning.'

All this time Joan had said nothing. But now, as George moved towards the door, distastefully eyeing the dusty packets of cornflakes and baskets of shrunken mouldy vegetables, she darted forward like a spider or a crab homing on its prey. She stood between George and the door, against the door, her stick-like arms spread against the glass, the red wool sleeves falling back from flesh where the subcutaneous tissue had wasted away. She lifted her head and screamed at him:

'Generation of vipers! Whoremonger! Adulterous beast! Woe to the ungodly and the fornicators!'

'Let me pass, Mrs Smith,' said George levelly. Not for nothing had he seen service under fire in the Western Desert.

'What shall be done unto thee, thou false tongue? Sharp arrows of the mighty with coals of juniper.' Joan waved her fist in his face. 'God will punish the rich man who taketh away the livelihood of the poor. God will destroy him in his high places.' Her face was suffused with blood, her eyes white with the pupils cast up.

'Will you get your wife out of my way, Mr Smith!' said George, enraged.

Norman shrugged. He was afraid of her and powerless.

'Then I will. And if you care to sue me for assault, you're welcome.'

He pushed Joan and got the door open. Outside in the

car, Giles, the least involved of people, was actually watching with interest. Joan, only temporarily worsted, ran after George and seized his coat, shouting gibberish, her dressing gown flapping in the icy wind. And by now Mrs Cairne had appeared at her window, Mr Meadows by his petrol pumps. George had never been so embarrassed in his life, he was shaking with distaste and repulsion. The whole scene was revolting to him. If he had witnessed it in the street, an angry man, a half-dressed woman clinging to his coat, shouting abuse at him, he would have turned the other way, vanished as fast as possible. And here he was, one of the protagonists.

'Be quiet, take your hands off me,' he found himself shouting back at her. 'This is outrageous!'

And then at last Norman Smith did come out and get hold of his wife and manhandled her back into the shop. Afterwards, Meadows of the garage said he slapped her, but George didn't wait to see. With what shreds of dignity remained to him, he got into the car and drove off. For once he was glad of Giles's detachment. The boy was smiling distantly. 'Lunatic,' he said, before lapsing back into his own mysterious thoughts.

The incident upset George for the day. But he wrote his letter to the Stantwich postmaster without mentioning the scene of the morning or even that he had particular grounds for suspecting the Smiths.

'Let's hope we're going to have a quiet weekend,' he said to Jacqueline. 'What with battling to work through all this snow every day, and then this fracas this morning, I feel I've had enough. We're not going anywhere, are we, or having anyone in?'

'Just to the Archers tomorrow afternoon, darling.'

'Tea with the Rector,' said George, 'is just the kind of somniferous non-event I can do with at present.'

Melinda was not expected home, and Giles didn't count. It was rather like having a harmless resident ghost, Jacqueline sometimes thought sadly. It stalked the place, but it didn't bother you or damage things, and on the whole it kept quietly to the confines of the haunted room. She wondered from whose writings he had taken the Quote of the Month: 'I hope never again to commit a mortal sin, nor even a venial one, if I can help it.'

440

It was the last quotation Giles was ever to pin to his cork wall, and perhaps it was appropriate that the lines he had chosen, from Charles the Seventh of France, were said to be their author's dying words.

As it happened, Melinda did come home. Since 5 January she hadn't been back to Lowfield Hall, and her conscience was troubling her. Of course she would go home for the 13th, for that was George's birthday, but it seemed awful to stay away for five weeks. Also there was the matter of the tape recorder. George's present was her most prized possession, and because of it she was the envy of her college friends. Melinda didn't like to say no to people who asked to borrow it, but when someone took it to a folk concert, and afterwards left it all night in an unlocked car, she thought the time had come to remove it from harm's way.

Without having told anyone she was coming, she arrived in Stantwich as the dull red sun was setting, and at Gallows Corner after dark. She was just a little too late for Geoff Baalham, who had passed that way ten minutes before, and it was Mrs Jameson-Kerr who picked her up and told her George and Jacqueline had gone to tea at the Rectory.

Melinda went into the house through the gun room and immediately upstairs to find Giles. But Giles also was out. He had taken the Ford and, after a session with Father Madigan, gone to the cinema. The house was warm, spotless, exquisitely tidy and silent. Silent, that is, but for the muted tumult throbbing through the first-floor ceilings from Eunice Parchman's television. Melinda put the tape recorder on her chest of drawers. She changed into a robe she had made herself out of an Indian bedspread, put a shawl over her shoulders and a string of limpet shells round her neck, and, well pleased with the result, went down to the morning room. There she found a stack of new magazines which she took into the kitchen. Ten minutes later Eunice, coming down to remove from the deep freeze a chicken casserole for the Coverdales' supper, found her seated at the table with a magazine open in front of her.

Melinda got up courteously. 'Hallo, Miss Parchman. How are you? Would you like a cup of tea? I've just made it.'

'I don't mind,' said Eunice, the nearest she ever got to a gracious acceptance of any offer. She frowned. 'They're not expecting you.'

'I do live here, it's my home,' was what Melinda might have said, but she was not a prickly or defensive girl. Besides, here was an opportunity to go on being nice to Miss Parchman whom she had neglected along with her family since the New Year. So she smiled and said she had made her decision on the spur of the moment, and did Miss Parchman take milk and sugar?

Eunice nodded. The magazine on the table intimidated her as much as a spider might have intimidated another woman. She hoped Melinda would concentrate on it and shut up while she drank her tea which she rather regretted accepting. But it was evident that Melinda intended to concentrate on it only with her participation. She turned the pages, keeping up a running commentary, looking up from time to time with a smile for Eunice and even passing her the magazine for her to look at a picture.

'I don't like those mid-calf-length skirts, do you? Oh, look at the way that girl has done her eyes! It must take hours, I shouldn't have the patience. All those forties fashions are coming back. Did they really dress like that when you were young? Did you wear bright red lipstick and stockings? I've never possessed a pair of stockings.'

Eunice who still wore them and who had never possessed a pair of tights, said she wasn't much for dress. Lot of nonsense, she said.

'Oh, I think it's fun.' Melinda turned the page. 'Here's a questionnaire. "Twenty Questions to Test if You're Really in Love." I must do it, though I know I am. Now, let's see. Have you got a pencil or a pen or something?'

A firm shake of the head from Eunice.

'I've got a pen in my bag.' This battered holdall, literally a carpet bag made out of Turkey rug, Melinda had dumped in the gun room. Eunice, watching her fetch it, hoped she would take bag, pen and magazine elsewhere, but Melinda returned to her place at the table. 'Now, Question One: Would you rather be with him than . . . Oh, I can see the answers at the bottom, that's no good. I'll tell you what,

442

you ask me the questions and tick whether I get three marks or two or one or none at all. OK?'

'I haven't got my glasses,' said Eunice.

'Yes, you have. They're in your pocket.'

And they were. The tortoise-shell ones, the pair the Coverdales knew as her reading glasses, were sticking out of the right-hand pocket of her overall. Eunice didn't put them on. She did nothing, for she didn't know what to do. She couldn't say she was too busy – busy with what? – and nearly half a pint of hot tea remained in the mug Melinda had given her.

'Here.' Melinda passed her the magazine. 'Please do. It'll be fun.'

Eunice took it in both hands, and stumbled from memory through that first line Melinda had read. 'Would you rather be with him than . . .' She stopped.

Melinda reached across and picked the glasses out of her pocket. Eunice was cornered. A flush darkened her face to a deep wine colour. She looked up at the girl and her underlip trembled.

'What is it?' There was a let-out here if only Eunice had known it. For, instantly, Melinda jumped to a conclusion. Miss Parchman had reacted rather like this before, when asked what name she would have given her son if she had had one. Obviously there was something in her past that was still painful, and she, very tactlessly, had again touched the scar of that ancient disappointed love. Poor Miss Parchman, who had once loved someone and was now an old maid. 'I didn't mean to upset you,' she said gently. 'I'm sorry if I said something to hurt you.'

Eunice didn't answer. She didn't know what on earth the girl was talking about. But Melinda took her silence as a sign of unhappiness, and she was seized by a need to do something to make things all right again, to distract Eunice's mind. 'I really am sorry. Let's do the quiz on the opposite page, shall we? It's all about how good a housewife one is. You do it for me and see how hopeless I am, and then I'll do it for you. I bet you get top marks.' Melinda held up the glasses for Eunice to take them.

And now Eunice should have made capital out of Melinda's misapprehension. Nothing more would have been needed but for her to say yes, Melinda had upset her, and to have walked with dignity out of the room. Such conduct would have won for her the dismayed sympathy of all the Coverdales and have supplied George with his answer. What was the root cause of Miss Parchman's sullenness and depression? A womanly sorrow, a lost love. But Eunice had never been able to manipulate people because she didn't understand them or the assumptions they made and the conclusions they drew. She understood only that she was on the brink of having her disability discovered, and because of the awful crushing domination of that disability, she thought she was nearer to that brink than she actually was. She thought Melinda already guessed, and that was why, having mockingly said she was sorry, she was trying to test her out to confirm her assumption.

The glasses, held between Melinda's finger and thumb, hovered between the two women. Eunice made no move to take them. She was trying to think. What to do, how to get out of it, what desperate measure she could seize on. Puzzled, Melinda let her hand fall, and as she did so, she looked through them from a short distance and saw that they were of plain glass. Her eyes went to Eunice's flushed face, her blank stare, and pieces of the puzzle, hitherto inexplicable – the way she never read a book, looked at a paper, left a note, got a letter – fell into place.

'Miss Parchman,' she said quietly, 'are you dyslexic?'

Vaguely, Eunice thought this must be the name of some eye disease. 'Pardon?' she said in swelling hope.

'I'm sorry. I mean you *can't* read, can you? You can't read or write.'

# 18

The silence endured for a full minute.

Melinda too had blushed. But although she was aware enough to have guessed at last, her sensitivity didn't extend to understanding how appalling that discovery was for Eunice. She was only twenty.

'Why didn't you tell us?' she said as Eunice got up. 'We'd

have understood. Lots of people are dyslexic, thousands of people actually. I did some work on a study of it in my last year at school. Miss Parchman, shall I teach you to read? I'm sure I could. It'd be fun. I could begin in the Easter holidays.'

Eunice took the two mugs and set them on the draining board. She stood still with her back to Melinda. She poured the remains of her tea down the sink. Then she turned round slowly and, with no outward sign that her heart was drumming fast and heavily, fixed Melinda with her apparently emotionless, implacable stare.

'If you tell anyone I'm what you said, that word, I'll tell your dad you've been going with that boy and you're going to have a baby.'

She spoke so levelly and calmly that at first Melinda hardly understood. She had led a sheltered life and no one had ever really threatened her before.

'*What* did you say?'

'You heard. You tell them and I'll tell them about you.' Abuse wasn't Eunice's forte but she managed. 'Dirty little tart, that's what you are. Dirty interfering little bitch.'

Melinda went white. She got up and walked out of the kitchen, stumbling over her long skirt. Out in the hall her legs almost gave way she was shaking so much, and she sat down in the chair by the grandfather clock. She sat there with her fists pressed to her cheeks till the clock chimed six and the kitchen door opened. A wave of sickness hit her at the thought of even seeing Eunice Parchman again, and she fled into the drawing room where she fell on to the sofa and burst into tears.

It was there that George found her a few minutes later.

'My darling, what is it? What on earth's happened? You mustn't cry like this.' He lifted her and hugged her in his arms. There had been a quarrel, he thought, with that boy, and that was why she had come home to an empty comfortless house. 'Tell Daddy.' He forgot she was twenty. 'Tell me all about it and you'll feel better.'

Jacqueline said nothing but 'I'll leave you two alone'. George never interfered between her and Giles, and she never interposed her voice between him and his children.

'No, Jackie, you're not to go.' Melinda sat up and

scrubbed at her eyes. 'Oh, I am a *fool*! I'll tell you both, but it's so awful.'

'As long as you're not ill or hurt,' said George, 'it isn't awful.'

'Oh God.' Melinda swallowed, took a deep breath. 'I'm so glad you've come back!'

'Melinda, please tell us what's the matter.'

'I thought I was going to have a baby but I'm not,' said Melinda in a rush. 'I've been sleeping with Jon since November. I know you'll be cross, I know you'll be disappointed, but I do love him and he loves me and it's all right, really it is, and I'm not going to have a baby.'

'Is that all?' said George.

His daughter stared at him. 'Aren't you mad with me? Aren't you shocked?'

'I'm not even surprised, Melinda. For heaven's sake, d'you think me that much of a fuddy-duddy? D'you think I haven't noticed that things have changed since I was young? I won't say I don't regret it, I won't say I wouldn't rather you hadn't, and I shouldn't like you to be promiscuous. But I'm not in the least shocked.'

'You are *sweet*.' She threw her arms round his neck.

'And now perhaps you'll tell us,' said George, disengaging himself, 'why you were crying? I presume you're not sorry you aren't pregnant?'

Melinda managed a watery smile. 'It was that woman – Miss Parchman. It's unbelievable, Daddy, but it's true. She found out. She must have overheard me talking on the phone to Jon at Christmas, and when I – well, found out something about her, she said she'd tell you. She threatened me. Just now. She said she'd tell you I was pregnant.'

'*She did what?*'

'I said it was unbelievable.'

'Melinda, of course I believe you. The woman actually blackmailed you?'

'If that's blackmail, yes.'

'What were her exact words?'

Melinda told him. 'And she called me a tart. It was awful.'

Silent until now, Jacqueline spoke. 'She must leave, of course. Now. At once.'

'Darling, I'm afraid she must. I know what it means to you, having her, but . . .'

'It doesn't mean a thing. I never heard anything so odious and revolting in my life. To dare to threaten Melinda! She must be told at once. You'll have to do it, George, I couldn't trust myself.'

He gave her a glance that was passionate in his appreciation of her loyalty. And then, 'What did you find out about her, Melinda?'

Fatal question. It was a pity George hadn't waited to ask it until after he had dismissed Eunice. For his daughter's answer moved him as the substance of that answer had never moved her, and he was softened by pity.

Eunice believed that her threat had succeeded, and a pride in her achievement went a long way towards conquering distress. That great tomboy had looked really upset. She wouldn't give Eunice away, for, as Joan had said, her father would turn her out of the house. The television on for a variety show, she had watched for a quarter of an hour, knitting away, when there came a knock on her door. Melinda. They always came to you after the first shock was over to beg you not to tell. And even though you promised they kept wanting reassurance. It had been that way with the married woman and Annie Cole. Eunice opened the door.

George walked in. 'You can guess why I've come, Miss Parchman. My daughter naturally told me what passed between you. I'm sorry, but I cannot have a person who threatens a member of my family in my household, so you will, of course, leave as soon as possible.'

It was a tremendous shock to Eunice, who said nothing. The programme had been interrupted for the commercials, and the one currently showing consisted mainly of printed words, a list of East Anglian stores. George said, 'We'll have that off, if you don't mind. It can hardly be of interest to *you*.'

Eunice understood. He knew. She who was without sensitivity in all other respects had an acute delicate awareness in this one. And he, watching her, understood too. Her flush and the distortion of her face told him he had gone too far under gross provocation. He had committed that most uncouth of sins, mocked the hunchback's hump.

447

'You haven't a contract,' he said quickly, 'so I could ask you to leave at once, but all things considered, we'll say a week. That will give you the opportunity to look round for other employment. But in the meantime you will please keep to this room and leave the housework to my wife and Mrs Baalham. I am prepared to give you a reference as to your efficiency, but I could give no assurance of your personal integrity.' He went out and closed the door.

It would be hard to imagine Eunice Parchman in tears, and she didn't cry now. Alone in a place where she might have indulged her feelings, she gave no sign of having any. She neither shook nor sighed nor was sick. She turned on the television and watched it, though slumped a little more heavily than usual in her armchair.

Her illiteracy had been known to three people, but to none of them had it come as a sudden and shocking revelation. Her parents had never thought it important. Gradually Mrs Samson had come to know it and to accept it as she accepted that another child in Rainbow Street was a mongol, but it wasn't the kind of thing you talked about, certainly not to Eunice herself. No one had ever talked to her about it; no whole group of people had ever, all at once, become aware of it. In the days that followed, when she was more or less confined to her room, she thought not at all about where she should go or what she should do, what employment she could find or where she could live. She took very little thought for the morrow, for Mrs Samson or Annie Cole would take her in if she turned up on their doorsteps with her cases, but she thought exhaustively about the Coverdales' discovery which she believed must now be spread all over Greeving. It stopped her going out. It stopped her from going to the village store, and once, when Jacqueline was out and Joan called, she didn't respond to Joan's screeched greeting but stayed in hiding upstairs.

It seemed to her that the Coverdales must spend all their time discussing her disability and laughing about it with their friends. She was partly wrong and partly right, for George and Jacqueline were prevented from doing the latter by honourable feelings and also because it would have made them look very foolish not to have realized before that their housekeeper couldn't read. They told people they had dismissed her for insolence. But to each other they did talk quite a lot about it, and even laughed in a wondering way, and longed for next Monday, shutting themselves up in the drawing room when Eunice crept down for her meals.

Unmoved by any feelings of loyalty or duty to her friend, Eunice thought the best thing would be to avoid Joan and escape from Greeving without ever seeing her again. Things were bad enough without Joan's sympathy and solicitude and tedious questions, for by now Joan also must know. Joan, in fact, did know. Or, that is, she knew of Eunice's dismissal, for the Mrs Higgs, who was distinguished by *not* riding a bike, had told her about it on Tuesday. She waited for Eunice to come, she did her best to get into Lowfield Hall, and when she couldn't she took the only course open to her – even Joan was afraid to telephone – and sent a message.

That year St Valentine's Day fell on a Sunday, so Valentines needs must arrive on the Saturday. None came for the Coverdales, but one did arrive at Lowfield Hall among the birthday cards for George. It was addressed to Eunice, and Jacqueline handed it to her with a quiet 'This is for you, Miss Parchman'.

Both women flushed, both knew Eunice couldn't read it. She took it upstairs and looked in bewilderment at the gaudy picture of two cherubs twining a garland of pink roses around a blue heart. There were bits of writing all over it. Eunice threw it away.

George became fifty-eight on 13 February, and cards came for him from his wife and all his children. *All my love, darling, your Jackie. Many happy returns and love, Paula, Brian, Patrick and little Giles. Love from Audrey and Peter. Lots of love, Melinda – see you Saturday afternoon.* Even Giles had sent a card, inappropriately (or very appropriately) a reproduction of Masaccio's *Expulsion from Paradise*. He didn't go so far as to provide a present, though George got a watch to replace his twenty-five-year-old one from Jacqueline, and a record token and book token from his married son and daughter respectively. That night they were going to dine *en famille* at the Angel at Cattingham.

George drove to Stantwich and picked Melinda up at the station. She presented him with a rather awful scarf that looked as if it had come from the Oxfam shop, though it hadn't, and George thanked her lavishly.

'Time I forgot all this nonsense at my advanced age,' he said, 'but none of you will let me.'

'Well,' said Melinda, who had actually been giving a little time to studying one of her set plays, 'who's born the day that I forget to send to Antony shall die a beggar.'

'My God, the child's been doing some work for a change!'

As they entered the house she looked enquiringly at her father, and George understood. 'Upstairs,' he said with a jerk of his head.

Melinda smiled. 'Have you put her under house arrest?'

'In a way. She goes on Monday morning.'

They dressed up to go out, Jacqueline in the cream velvet, Melinda in her spangled blue, and they were an impressive sight as they walked into the hotel dining room. A handsome family, even Giles, who was at any rate tall and thin, not looking at all bad in his one suit and with his spots rather quiescent at the moment.

Afterwards the waiters and the other diners were to wish they had taken more notice of this happy family, this doomed family. They wished they had known, and then they would have listened to the Coverdales' light-hearted conversation, and paid more attention to Jacqueline's appearance, the evidences of Giles's superlative intellect, Melinda's charm, George's distinguished presence. They didn't know, so they had to confess ignorance when the newspaper reporters questioned them or – and this happened more often – invent all kinds of prognostications and doleful premonitions which they were convinced they had been aware of at the time. The police also questioned some of them, and their ignorance was proved by none of them recalling a discussion between the Coverdales that would have been of relevance in solving the case sooner than it was solved.

This conversation was on the subject of a television programme to take place on the following night, a film of a Glyndebourne production of *Don Giovanni*, due to last from seven until after ten.

'Do you have to get back tomorrow night, Melinda?' asked George. 'It seems a pity for you to miss this, it's supposed to be the television event of the year. I could drive you to Stantwich first thing on Monday.'

'I haven't got a lecture on Monday. Nothing till a tutorial at two.'

'What he really means, Melinda,' said her stepmother, laughing, 'is that he wants some moral support in the car when he drives the Parchman to the station.'

'Not at all. I shall have Giles.'

Jacqueline and Melinda laughed. Giles looked up seriously from his duck and green peas. Something moved him. His conversion? The fact that it was George's birthday? Whatever it was, he was inspired for once to say the perfect thing.

'I will never desert Mr Micawber.'

'Thank you, Giles,' said George quietly. There was an odd little silence in which, without speaking or glancing at each other, Giles and his stepfather approached a closeness never before attained. Given time, they might have become friends. No time was to be given them. George cleared his throat and said, 'Seriously, Melinda, why not stay for the film?'

It wasn't the prospect of missing work which made Melinda hesitate, but of missing Jonathan. They had been together every day and almost every night for weeks now. She would miss him painfully tonight. Must she now contemplate another night without him? It seemed selfish to refuse. She loved her father. How wonderful he and Jacqueline had been last week over that hateful business, how loyal and unwavering! And not a word of reproach for her, not even a warning to be careful. But Jonathan. . . .

She had come to a parting of the ways. Ahead of her the road forked. One path led to life and happiness, marriage, children, the other was a dead end, a cul-de-sac. No Through Road. She hesitated. She chose.

'I'll stay,' she said.


From the village store Joan Smith watched the Mercedes pass through the village on its way to the Angel. Five minutes later she was at the Hall, inside the Hall, for she had skipped in her new, thoroughly insane, way through the gun room to surprise Eunice as she sat devouring egg and chips and lemon cheesecake at the kitchen table.

451

'Oh, Eun, you must be broken-hearted. The base ingratitude after what you've done for them. And for a little thing like that!'

Eunice was not pleased to see her. The 'little thing' must surely be her inability to read. Her appetite gone, she glowered and waited for the worst. Eventually it was not the worst but the best that came, but she had to wait for that.

'All packed, are you, dear? No doubt, you've got plans of your own. Anyone with your skills won't have far to look for a brilliant situation, but I want you to know you're welcome to make your home with us. While Joanie has a spare bed and a roof over her head, you're welcome. Though the Lord only knows how long it'll be spared to us while the wicked man rageth.' Joan panted from her efforts, said breathlessly yet coyly, 'Did you get anything by the post today?'

Hard colour came into Eunice's cheeks. 'Why?'

'Oh, she's blushing! Did you think you'd got an admirer in the village, Eun? Well, you have, dear. Me. Why ever didn't you read my message on the back? I knew they'd be out; I said I'd pop up.'

Eunice had supposed Melinda had sent the mocking Valentine. But this wasn't the source of her overwhelming tremendous relief. Joan didn't know, it hadn't reached Joan. Relief threw her back, quite wan and weak, in her chair. She approached love for Joan in that moment, and she couldn't have done enough for her. Recovered and almost ebullient, she made tea, cudgelled her poor imagination to invent details of her dismissal to satisfy Joan, denounced the Coverdales with bitterness, promised Joan her attendance on the following night, her last night, at the temple in Nunchester.

'Our last time together, Eun. And I was counting on your company when Elder Barnstaple and Mrs come to us for supper on Wednesday. But God isn't mocked, dear. You'll rise again in all your glory when he's in the pit, when they're reaping the punishment of their iniquity – oh, yes, when they're heaped with retribution.'

Taking very little notice of all this, of Joan's ravings and prancings, Eunice nevertheless ministered to her like the Martha she was, pouring tea and slicing cheesecake and promising no end of things, like coming back to see Joan

452

at her first opportunity, and writing to her (of all things!) and swearing, in very un-Eunice-like fashion, undying friendship.

Joan seemed to have an instinct about when it was safe to remain and when to go, but this time, so vehement were they and with so much to talk about, that the van had only just turned out of the drive when the Mercedes came up it. Eunice tramped off to bed.

'Back to the grind on Monday,' said Jacqueline, leaving a satiny stripe in the dust where she had run her finger across the surface of her dressing table. 'I feel as if I've had nine months' holiday. Ah, well, all good things come to an end.'

'And all bad ones,' said George.

'Don't worry. I'm just as glad as you to see the back of her. Had a nice day, darling?'

'I have had a lovely day. But all my days are lovely with you.'

She got up, smiling at him, and he took her in his arms.


# 19


In church on Sunday morning, their last morning, the Coverdales murmured that they had done those things which they ought not to have done and left undone those things which they ought to have done. They uttered this in a reverent and quite sincere way, but they did not really think about what they were saying. Mr Archer preached a sermon about how one ought to be kind to old people, to one's elderly relatives, which had no bearing on anything in the Coverdales' lives, though plenty on the lives of Eunice Parchman and Joan Smith. After church they had sherry at the Jameson-Kerrs', and lunch was late, not on the table till three.

The weather was non-weather, windless, damp, the sky overcast, but already the first signs of spring had appeared. Early spring is not green but red, as each twig in the hedges takes on a crimson sheen from the rising vitalizing sap. In the garden of Lowfield Hall the snowdrops were coming out, first flowers of spring, the last flowers the Coverdales would ever see.

Melinda had phoned Jonathan before she went to church, speaking to him for the last time. For the last time Giles saw the Elevation of the Mass. Although he was not yet received into the Church, kind Father Madigan had heard his confession and shriven him, and Giles was perhaps in a state of grace. For the last time George and Jacqueline had a Sunday afternoon doze, and at five George moved the television set into the morning room, plugging in the aerial to the socket between the front windows.

When she woke up Jacqueline read the article on *Don Giovanni* in the *Radio Times*, and then she went into the kitchen to make tea. Eunice passed through the kitchen at twenty-five past five in her dark red coat and woolly hat and scarf. The two women pretended not to have seen each other, and Eunice left the house by way of the gun room, closing the door quietly behind her. Melinda fetched her tape recorder, and putting her head round the door of Giles's sanctum, told him she meant to record the opera.

'I suppose you won't even come down for it,' she said.

'I don't know.'

'I wish you would. I'd like you to.'

'All right,' said Giles.

The dark winter's day had slipped, without any apparent sunset, into dark winter's night. There was no wind, no rain, no stars. It was as if the moon had died, for it had not been seen for many nights. All around isolated Lowfield Hall the undulating fields, the deserted threading lanes, and the small crowding woods were enclosed by impenetrable blackness. Not quite impenetrable, for, from the Stantwich road, the traveller would be able to make out the Hall as a brilliant spot of light. How far this little candle throws his beams! So shines a good deed in a naughty world.

Joan and Eunice reached the Epiphany Temple at five to six, and Joan behaved peaceably, perhaps with an ominous quietness, during the hymn-singing and the confessing. Afterwards, while they were eating seed cake and Joan was recounting details of her sinful past to a new member, Mrs Barnstaple came up to her and said rather stiffly that she and the Elder would be unable to visit the Smiths on Wednesday evening. Now the Barnstaples lived in Nunchester, and efficient as the grapevine was, it didn't extend to Nunchester. Mrs Barnstaple had taken her decision because, although she knew Joan was a good Epiphany Person whom the Lord had pardoned, she couldn't (as she told her husband) stomach listening to any more of that stuff about goings-on in Shepherd's Bush while she was eating. But Joan took her refusal as reaction to the news of the enquiry set in train by George Coverdale, and she jumped up, giving a loud scream.

'Woe to the wicked man who spreadeth slanders in the ears of the innocent!' Joan didn't necessarily quote from the Bible. Just as often she ranted in biblical language what she thought ought to have been in the Bible. 'The Lord shall smite him in his loins and in his hip and his thigh. Praised be the Lord who chooseth his handmaid to be his weapon and his right hand!'

Her body was charged with a frenetic energy. She screeched, and spittle sprayed from her mouth. For a few seconds the brethren enjoyed it, but they were not mad, only misguided fanatics, and when Joan's eyes rolled and she began tugging at her hair, actually pulling some of it out, Mrs Barnstaple tried to get hold of her. Joan gave her a great push, and that lady fell backwards into the arms of her husband. Eunice was appealed to, but Eunice didn't want to do anything to antagonise Joan, who was now in control of the whole assembly, raving incomprehensible words and throwing herself backwards and forwards in a frenzy.

Then, as suddenly as she had begun, she stopped. It was mediumistic, the change that came over her. At one moment she seemed possessed by an enraged spirit, the next she had fallen spent and silent into a chair. In a small voice she said to Eunice, 'We'll be on our way when you're ready, Eun.'

They left the temple at twenty past seven, Joan driving like a cautious learner.

Grouped a suitable twenty feet away from the television set, George and Jacqueline sat together on the sofa, Me-

455

linda on the floor at her father's feet, Giles hunched in an armchair. The tape recorder was on. Having fidgeted with it during the overture, moving it about and watching it anxiously, Melinda grew less and less aware of its presence as the opera proceeded. She was all set to identify with every female character. She was Anna, she would be Elvira, and, when the time comes, Zerlina too. She leaned her head against George's arm of the sofa, for George, in her eyes, had become the Commendatore, fighting a duel and getting himself killed for his daughter's honour, though she didn't quite see her Jonathan as the Don.

Elegant Jacqueline, in green velvet trousers and gold silk shirt, pencilled a critical note or two on the margin of the *Radio Times*. Under her breath she whispered, following Ottavio, 'Find husband and father in me!' and she darted a soft look at George. But George, being a man, a handsome and sexually successful man, couldn't help identifying with the Don. He didn't want a catalogue of women, he only wanted his Jacqueline and yet . . .

'I will cut out his heart!' sang Elvira, and they laughed appreciatively, all but Giles. He was only there for Melinda's sake, and the age of reason and manners had never held much appeal for him. He alone heard a footstep on the gravel of the drive at twenty to eight while Scene Two and the Catalogue Song were ending, for he alone was not concentrating on the music. But of course he did nothing about it. That wasn't his way.

Looking indignant, Jacqueline added a line to her notes as Scene Three opened. The time approached five minutes to eight. As Giovanni sang, '*O, guarda, guarda!* Look, look!' the Smiths' van entered the drive of Lowfield Hall and crept, with only side lights on, almost to the front door. But the Coverdales did not look or hear any extraneous sound. Even Giles heard nothing this time.

Joan's driving had become erratic, and her jerky zigzagging from slow lane to fast was a frightening experience even for phlegmatic Eunice.

'You'd better calm down if you don't want us both killed.'

The admonitions of those who seldom remonstrate are more effective than the commands of naggers. But Joan was in no state to adopt the happy mean. It was neck or nothing for her, and she crawled along the lane to Greeving.

'Come in for a bit,' said Eunice.

'That'd be Daniel into the lion's den,' said Joan with a shriek of laughter.

'You come in. Why shouldn't you? A cup of tea'd calm you down.'

'I like your spirit, Eun. Why shouldn't I? They can't kill me, can they?'

Joan kangaroo-hopped the van in too high a gear up the drive. It was Eunice, the non-driver, who grabbed the gear lever and stamped on the clutch so that they could approach more quietly. The van was left standing on the broad gravel space, a little way from the streak of light that fell from between the drawing-room curtains.

'They're looking at the TV,' said Eunice.

She put the kettle on while Joan lingered in the gun room.

'Poor little birds,' she said. 'It doesn't seem right. What have they done to him?'

'What have *I* done?' said Eunice.

'Too right.' Joan took one of the guns down and levelled it playfully at Eunice. 'Bang, bang, you're dead! Did you ever play cowboys when you were a kid, Eun?'

'I don't know. Come on, tea's ready.' In spite of her defiant words, she was nervous that Joan's hysterical voice would penetrate to the drawing room and be heard above the music. They mounted the first flight of stairs, Eunice carrying the tray, but they never reached the attic floor. Never again was Joan Smith to enter Eunice's domain, and no final farewell was ever to be spoken between them. Jacqueline's bedroom door stood open. Joan went in and put the light on.

Eunice noticed that there was a patina of bedroom dust, composed of talcum and fluff, on the polished surfaces, and that the bed was less evenly made than when she had made it. She set the tray down on one of the bedside tables and gave the quilt a twitch. Joan tiptoed round the room, lifting her high heels an inch above the carpet and giggling soundlessly on a series of small exhalations like a person imitating a steam engine. When she reached Jacqueline's side of the bed she picked up the photograph of George and laid it face-downwards.

'She'll know who did that,' said Eunice.

'Doesn't matter. You said they can't do any more to you.'

'No.' After a small hesitation, Eunice laid the picture of Jacqueline face-downwards also. 'Come on, we'd better have that tea.'

Joan said, 'I'll pour.' She lifted the teapot and poured a steady stream into the centre of the counterpane. Eunice retreated, one hand up to her mouth. The liquid lay in a lake, and then it began to seep through the covers.

'You've done it now,' said Eunice.

Joan went out on to the landing and listened. She came back. She picked up a box of talcum, took off the lid and hurled the box on to the bed. White clouds of powder rose, making Eunice cough. And now Joan had opened the wardrobe.

'What are you going to do?' Eunice whispered.

No answer from Joan. She was holding the red silk evening gown on its hanger. She set her fingers in the circle of the neckline and ripped the dress downwards, so that she was holding the front in one hand and the back in the other. Eunice was frightened, she was appalled, but she was also excited. Joan's mounting frenzy had excited her. She too plunged her hands inside the wardrobe where she found the green pleated dress she had so often ironed, and she ran into its bodice the points of Jacqueline's nail scissors. The scissors were snatched from her by Joan who began indiscriminately slashing clothes, gasping with pleasure. Eunice trod heavily on the pile of torn cloth, she ground her heel into the glass of those framed photographs, she pulled out drawers, scattering jewellery and cosmetics and the letters which fluttered from their ribbon binding. It made her laugh throatily while Joan laughed maniacally, and they were both confident that the music from below was loud enough to drown any noise.

It was, for the time being. While Eunice and Joan were making mayhem above their heads, the Coverdales were listening to one of the loudest solos in the whole opera, the Champagne Aria. Jacqueline heard it out, and then she left the drawing room to make coffee, choosing this opportunity because she disliked the Zerlina and feared she would make a hash of *Batti, batti*. In the kitchen she noticed that the kettle was still warm, so Eunice must have come back, and noticed too the shotgun on the table. But she supposed George had put it there for some purpose of his own before they had begun to watch television.

The sound of the drawing-room door opening, and footfalls across the hall floor, sobered Joan and Eunice. They sat down on the bed, looking at each other in a mock-rueful way, eyebrows up, lips caught under upper teeth. Joan switched off the light, and they sat in darkness until they heard Jacqueline cross the hall and re-enter the drawing room.

Eunice kicked at a heap of mingled broken glass and nylon. She said, 'That's torn it,' quite seriously, not joining in Joan's laughter. 'Maybe he'll get the police on us.'

'He doesn't know we're here.' Joan's eyes gleamed. 'Got any wire cutters in the house, Eun?'

'I don't know. Could be in the gun room. What d'you want wire cutters for?'

'You'll see. I'm glad we did it, Eun. O, we have smitten him in his high places, in the bed of his lechery we have afflicted him. I am the instrument of the Lord's vengeance! I am the sword in his hand and the spear in his right hand!'

'If you go on like that they'll hear you,' said Eunice. 'I'm glad we did it too.'

They left the tray on the table, the teapot in the middle of the bed. The light was on down in the hall. Joan went straight to the gun room and rooted about in George's tool-box.

'I'm going to cut the phone wire.'

'Like they do on TV,' said Eunice. She had ceased to protest. She nodded approvingly. 'It comes in over the front door,' she said. 'Stop them phoning the police, that will.'

Joan came back, a silent smile glittering. 'What shall we do now, dear?'

It hadn't occurred to Eunice that they would do anything more. Breaking things down here must necessarily be heard in the drawing room, and, police or not, she and this frail stick of a woman could easily be overpowered by four strong adults. 'I don't know,' she said, but this time her habitual response had a wistful note in it. She wanted the fun to go on.

'May as well be hanged for a sheep as a lamb,' said Joan, picking up the shotgun and looking down one of its barrels. 'Frighten them out of their wits, it would, if I fired this.'

Eunice took the other gun off the wall. 'Not like that,' she said. 'Like this.'

'You're a dark horse, Eun. Since when've you been a lady gangster?'

'I've watched him. I can do it as well as he can.'

'I'm going to try!'

'It's not loaded,' said Eunice. 'There's things called cartridges in that drawer. I've often watched him do it. They cost a fortune, those guns, couple of hundred each.'

'We could break them.'

'That's what you call it when you open them to load them. Breaking the gun's what you say.'

They looked at each other and Joan laughed with a sound like a peacock's shriek.

'The music's stopped,' said Eunice.

It was twenty-five minutes to nine. Act One had come to an end, in the opera and in the kitchen.


# 20


In the lull between acts Jacqueline poured second cups of coffee for all of them. Melinda stretched and stood up.

'Marvellous,' said George. 'What do you think, darling?'

'Zerlina's awful. Too old and too tinkly. George, did you hear any sounds from upstairs during the minuet?'

'I don't think so. It was probably our *bête noire* slinking in.'

'The last thing she does is slink, Daddy,' said Melinda. 'Sneaking, maybe. Oh God, I've forgotten to stop the tape.'

'It wasn't slinking or sneaking I heard, but breaking glass.'

Melinda switched off her recorder. 'They were at a party,' she said, referring to the opera. 'I expect it was

460

sound effects.' The rest of what she was going to say was cut off by a thin shriek from somewhere outside the room.

'George!' Jacqueline almost shouted. 'It's that Mrs Smith!'

'I do believe it is,' said George, slowly and ominously.

'She's out in the kitchen with Miss Parchman.'

'Very soon she'll be out in the cold with her marching orders.' He got up.

'Oh, Daddy, you'll miss the beginning of Act Two. Nasty old Parchment Face is probably just having a farewell party.'

'I'll be two minutes,' said George. He went to the door where he paused and looked at his wife for the last time. Had he known it was the last time, that look would have been eloquent of six years' bliss and of gratitude, but he didn't know, so he merely cast up his eyes and pursed his mouth before walking across the hall and down the passage to the kitchen. Jacqueline considered going with him, but thought better of it and settled back against the sofa cushions as Act Two began with the quarrel between Leporello and his master. The tape recorder was on. *Ma che ho ti fatto, che vuoi lasciarmi?* But what have I done to you that you wish to leave me? *O, niente affatto; quasi ammazzarmi!* Oh, nothing at all, but almost killed me. . . .

George opened the kitchen door, and there he stopped in amazement. His housekeeper stood on one side of the table, her stripy hair coming away from its pins, her pale face flushed maroon, facing the crane-chick figure of Joan Smith, befeathered in green and salmon pink. Each was holding one of his shotguns which she pointed at the other.

'This is monstrous,' said George when he recovered his voice. 'Put those guns down at once!'

Joan gave a babbling shriek. 'Bang, bang!' she said. Some memory of war or war film came to her. '*Hände hoch!*' she shouted, and pointed the gun at his face.

'Fortunately for you, it isn't loaded.' Calmly Major Coverdale of Alamein looked at his new watch. 'I will give you and Miss Parchman thirty seconds to put those guns on the table. If you don't I shall take them from you by force, and then I shall call the police.'

'You'll be lucky,' said Eunice.

461

Neither woman moved. George stood stock-still for the full half-minute. He wasn't afraid. The guns weren't loaded. As the thirty seconds came to an end and Joan still pointed the gun at him, he heard faintly from the drawing room the beginning of Elvira's sweet and thrilling O, *taci ingiusto core!* Be silent, treacherous heart! His own was thudding steadily. He went up to Joan, grasped the gun and gave a sharp grunt as Eunice shot him in the neck. He fell across the table, flinging out his arms to grasp its edge, blood shooting in a fountain from the severed jugular. Joan scuttered back against the wall. With an indrawn breath, Eunice fired the second barrel into his back.

At the sound of the two shots Jacqueline sprang to her feet with a cry of alarm. 'For heaven's sake, what was that?'

'Mrs Smith's van back-firing,' said Melinda, and, dropping her voice because of the tape, 'It always does that. There's something wrong with the exhaust.'

'It sounded like a gun.'

'Cars backfiring do sound like guns. Sit down, Jackie, or we'll miss this, and it's the loveliest song of all.'

Be silent, treacherous heart. Beat not so in my breast. Elvira leaned from her window, Leporello and the Don appeared beneath it, and the great trio swelled on the two baritone voices and the soprano. Jacqueline sat down, glanced at the door. 'Why doesn't your father come back?' she said nervously.

'He's shot the lunatic,' said Giles, 'and he doesn't know how to tell us.'

'Oh, *Giles*. Darling, go and see, would you? I can't hear a sound.'

'Of course you can't, Jackie, with this on,' said Melinda with asperity. 'You don't *want* to hear him bawling Parchman out, do you? All this rubbish is going to be on my tape, isn't it?'

Jacqueline put up her hands, fluttering them in a little gesture of apology, yet of anxiety too, and Giles who had begun languidly to raise himself from his chair, slumped back into it. From the television came the softly plucked notes of Giovanni's mandoline. *Dei vieni alla finestra.* Then come to the window . . . Jacqueline, her hands clenched, obeyed his behest. She jumped up suddenly, went to the window on the left of the set and parted the curtains. The tape forgotten, she cried out:

'Mrs Smith's van is out there! It can't have been that we heard.'

She turned back to face them, a disgruntled Melinda, a bored exasperated Giles. Her face was puckered with distress, and even Giles saw it, felt it, her tension and her rising fear. 'I'll go,' he sighed, beginning to shift himself very slowly like an old man with arthritis. He lounged towards the door as Joan Smith and Eunice Parchman passed from the kitchen into the passage.

'We'll have to kill the others now,' said Eunice in the voice she used when speaking of some necessary measure, not to be postponed, such as washing a floor.

Joan, who needed no encouragement, looked back at George. He was dead, but his watch lived on, and since his death the minute hand had passed from the ten nearly to the twelve. It was almost nine o'clock. She looked back once, and then up at Eunice with a great face-splitting smile. There was blood on her hands and face and on the jumper Eunice had knitted for her. They passed into the hall and the strengthening music, music which met them with a blast of baritone voice and plucked strings as Giles opened the drawing-room door. He saw the blood and shouted out.

He shouted, 'Oh Christ!' and turned back, a split second before Joan told him to.

'Get back in there. We've got guns.'

Eunice was the first to follow him. A jumble of male voices singing roared in her head, and power, the chance at last to command and avenge, roared through her body. It strengthened her hands which had failed her a little back there in the kitchen. They were hard and dextrous now as she levelled the reloaded gun. Jacqueline's face, blanched and terrified, was to her only the face which had sneered a little while ago handing over that Valentine. Jacqueline's voice, screaming for her husband, was still the voice of a woman who read books and looked up from her letter-writing to murmur sarcastic courtesies. In those moments the words they cried and their pleas passed over her almost unheard, and by some strange metamorphosis, produced in Eunice's brain, they ceased to be people and became the printed word. They were those things in the book-cases, those patchy black blocks on white paper, eternally her enemies, hated and desired.

'You'd better sit down,' she said. 'You've got it coming to you.'

Joan's laughter cut across her words. Joan shouted something from the Bible, and then Joan fired her gun. Eunice gasped. Not because she heard the screams or saw the blood, but because Joan might do it first, Joan might beat her to it. She advanced, pointing her gun. She fired both barrels, reloaded while another shot rang in her ears, and then she emptied the two barrels into what lay on the Chinese carpet.

The music had stopped. Joan must have stopped it. The banging had stopped and the screaming. A silence more profound, more soothing to the mind and the savage breast, filled the drawing room like a thick tangible balm. It held Eunice suspended. It petrified this stone-age woman into stone. Her eyelids dropped and she breathed evenly and steadily so that, had she had an observer, he would have supposed her fallen asleep where she stood.

A stone that breathed was Eunice, as she had always been.

# 21

The exalted calm of one who has performed a holy mission descended upon Joan Smith. She surveyed what she had done and saw that it was good. She had scattered the enemies of God, and thus purified herself. If the M'Naghten Rules had been applied to her she would have passed the test, for though she had known what she was doing she did not know it was wrong.

She was innocent in the true meaning of the word. And now she would drive down into Greeving and tell the village what she had done, proclaim it in the streets and shout it aloud in the Blue Boar. It was a pity she had cut the phone wire, for otherwise she could have lifted the phone and announced it to the operator. Calmly, majestically, she laid down the gun and picked up the tape recorder. It was still on. She pressed something and the little red light on it went out. Inside it was a record of her achievement, and it is a measure of Joan's madness that at that moment she saw herself, at some future time, playing the tape for the edification of the Epiphany brethren.

Of Eunice she took very little notice. Eunice stood immobile, still holding her gun, staring implacably at the bodies of Giles and Melinda, who lay side by side in death, closer to an embrace than they had ever been in life. But Joan had forgotten who Eunice was. She had forgotten her own name, and the past, and Shepherd's Bush and Norman. She was alone, a titaness, an angel, and she feared nothing but that some malignant spirit, allied to the Coverdale interest, might yet intervene to prevent her from proclaiming the good news.

George's blood was on her jumper, on her hands and face. She let it dry there. Uncharacteristically, with a long slow stride, she walked towards the door and the hall, and Eunice was aroused from her contemplation.

'You'd better wash your face before you go,' she said.

Joan ignored her. She opened the front door and looked for demons in the darkness. The drive and the garden were empty, and to Joan they seemed friendly. She got into the van.

'Suit yourself,' said Eunice. 'Have a good wash before you go to bed. And mind you don't say a word. Just keep quiet.'

'I am the spear of the Lord of Hosts.'

Eunice shrugged. That sort of thing didn't much matter. Joan always went on like that, and the village people would only think she was more crazy than ever. She went back into the house where she had things to see to.

With only sidelights on, Joan drove the van euphorically out of the grounds of Lowfield Hall. She drove with her head held high, looking to the right and the left, anywhere but ahead of her, and she smiled graciously as if to an admiring throng. It was a miracle she even reached the gates. But she did reach them and got about a quarter of a mile along the lane. There, where the lane bent rather sharply to avoid a high brick wall that enclosed the front garden of Mr Meadows' farmhouse, she saw a white owl drop from one of the trees and flap heavily in front of her at windscreen level. Joan thought it was a demon sent by the Coverdales to get her. She stamped on the accelerator to smash through it and smashed instead into the wall. The front part of the van crumpled up like a concertina, and Joan's head crashed through glass into a twelve-inch thick bastion of concrete faced with brick.

It was half past nine. Mr and Mrs Meadows were visiting their married daughter in Gosbury, and there was no one else in the house to hear the crash. Norman Smith was in the Blue Boar where they had their own bit of excitement, although it wasn't until the following day that they realised how exciting it had been. He went home at ten-fifteen. His van wasn't parked between the village store and the triangle of grass, but he supposed Joan was still off somewhere with Eunice, it being Eunice's last night in Greeving, and a good thing too. No one came down Greeving Lane (or, at least, no one reported the crash) until the Meadowses got home at twenty-five past ten. When they saw their ruined wall and the van with Joan lying unconscious half in and half out of it, they phoned first for an ambulance and then they phoned Norman Smith. Joan, who was alive, though in a bad way, was taken to hospital where they weren't going to worry about whether the blood on her was all hers or not, there was so much of it. So Joan Smith, who ought to have gone into a mental hospital months before, ended up in an intensive-care ward for the physically injured.

This was the second time that evening Norman had been afforded the sight of blood. Very nearly three hours before he was fetched to the scene of his wife's accident, two young men had walked into the saloon bar of the Blue Boar, and the smaller and younger of them had asked the licensee, Edwin Carter, the way to the men's room. He wanted to wash his hands, for the left one appeared injured in some way, and blood had seeped through the handkerchief that bandaged it.

Mr Carter directed him to the lavatory, and his wife asked if there was anything she could do in the way of first aid. Her offer was refused, no explanation of the injury was given, and when the young man came back he had re-bandaged his hand with a cleaner handkerchief. Neither of the

Carters nor any of the patrons of the bar recalled actually having seen his hand, but only that there had been blood on the original bandage. The other witnesses were Jim Meadows of the garage, Alan and Pat Newstead, Geoff and Barbara Baalham and Geoff's brother, Philip, and Norman Smith.

Mrs Carter was to remember that the man with the injured hand drank a double brandy and his companion a half of bitter. They sat at a table, drank their drinks in less than five minutes, and left without speaking to anyone except to ask where they could get petrol at this hour, Meadows' garage being closed. Geoff Baalham told them there was a self-service petrol station on the main road past Gallows Corner, and describing how to find it, followed them out on to the Blue Boar's forecourt. There he noticed their car, an old Morris Minor Traveller, maroon bodywork in a wooden shooting brake frame. He didn't, however, notice the registration number.

They left the village by Greeving Lane, their route inevitably taking them past Lowfield Hall.

On the following day all those witnesses furnished the police with descriptions of these strangers. Jim Meadows said they both had long dark hair, were both dressed in blue denim and the one whose hand was not injured was over six feet tall. The Carters agreed that the tall one had long dark hair, but their daughter, Barbara Baalham, said both had brown hair and brown eyes. According to Alan Newstead, the one with the injured hand had short fair hair and piercing blue eyes, but his wife said that, though piercing, the eyes were brown. Geoff Baalham said the short one had fair hair and grey corduroy jeans, while his brother insisted both wore denim jeans and the tall one had bitten nails. Norman Smith said the fair one had a scratch on his face and the dark one was no more than five feet nine.

All of them wished they had taken more notice at the time, but how were they to know they would need to?

Left alone, Eunice, who had wanted to 'see to things,' at first saw to nothing at all. She sat on the stairs. She had a curious feeling that if she did nothing but just went off in the morning with her cases to the bus stop she had long ago located and got to London, it would all be all right.

They might not find the Coverdales for weeks, and when they did they wouldn't know where she was, would they?

A cup of tea would be nice, for she had never had that earlier one, Joan having poured the contents of the pot all over Jacqueline's bed. She made the tea, walking back and forth past George's body. The watch on his dead wrist told her it was twenty to ten. Now to pack. She had added very little to her personal property during those nine months apart from what were truly consumer goods, sweets, chocolate, cake, and these she had consumed. Only a few hand-knitted garments swelled her stock of clothes. Everything was packed into Mrs Samson's cases in much the same order as it had originally gone in.

Up here, in her room, it felt as if nothing had happened. Pity she had to go tomorrow really, for now there was no one to make her go, and she liked it here, she had always liked it. And it would be even better now that there was no one to interfere with her life.

It was rather early to go to bed, and she didn't think she would be able to sleep. This was exceptional for Eunice who knew she could always sleep as soon as her head touched the pillow. On the other hand, the circumstances were exceptional too, never had she done anything like this before, and she understood this. She understood that all the excitement was bound to keep her awake, so she sat looking round the room, looking at her cases, not feeling in the mood for television and rather wishing she hadn't packed her knitting at the bottom of the big case.

She was still sitting there at a quarter to eleven, wondering what time the bus went in the morning and hoping it wouldn't be raining, when she heard the wail of a siren in Greeving Lane. The siren was on the ambulance that had come to fetch Joan Smith, but Eunice didn't know this. She thought it must be the police, and suddenly, for the first time, she was alarmed. She went down to the first floor and Jacqueline's bedroom to see what was going on. She looked out of the window, but she could see nothing, and the wailing had died away. As she dropped the curtain, the siren started up again, and after a few moments some vehicle she couldn't see but for its light howled up towards the Hall, passed the Hall, and charged off towards the main road.

Eunice didn't like it. It was very unusual in Greeving. What were they doing? Why were they out there? Her television viewing had taught her a little about police procedure. She put a bed light on and walked about the room, absently wiping every solid article Joan had touched, the broken glass and the ornaments and the teapot. Steve, in her serial, when he wasn't shooting people or chasing them in cars, was a great one for fingerprints. The police would be here in a minute, though she could no longer hear their siren. She went downstairs. She went into the drawing room and again put a light on. Now she could see she had been silly, thinking the police wouldn't find out. If they didn't come now, they would come tomorrow, for Geoff Baalham would bring the eggs in the morning, and if he couldn't get in he would look through the window and see George's body. To stop them suspecting her, there were quite a lot of things she must do. Wipe Joan's prints off the wire cutters, for one thing, wipe clean the guns.

She looked around the drawing room. On the sofa, splashed with blood, was an open copy of the *Radio Times*, and along with the bloodstains was some writing. Eunice hated that, far more than the stains. The first thing she should have done was destroy that copy of the *Radio Times*, burnt it in the sink with matches, or cut it up and buried it, or pushed it scrap by scrap down the waste-disposal unit. But she couldn't read. She closed it and, in an attempt to make things look tidier, put it with the Sunday papers in the stack on the coffee table. It bothered her to leave those dirty cups there, but she felt it would be a mistake to wash them up. Putting the television back in its proper place in the morning room would also add to tidiness, and she lugged it across the hall, at last aware that she was quite tired.

There didn't seem anything else to be done, and the police car hadn't come back. Now, for the first time since she had wreaked this havoc, she looked long and steadily at George's body and then, re-entering the drawing room, at the bodies of his wife, his daughter and his stepson. No pity stirred her and no regret. She did not think of love, joy, peace, rest, hope, life, dust, ashes, waste, want, ruin, madness and death, that she had murdered love and blighted life, ruined hope, wasted intellectual potential,

469

ended joy, for she hardly knew what these things are. She did not see that she had left carrion men groaning for burial. She thought it a pity about that good carpet getting in such a mess, and she was glad none of the blood had splashed on to her.

Having spent so much time making things look all right, she was anxious that her good work should be seen. It had always brought her gratification, that the fruit of her labours was admired, though not by a smile or a word had she ever shown her pleasure. Why wait for the police to discover it when she herself was far away? They were about, she thought in her unclear way, they would come quite quickly. The best thing would be for her to tell them without delay. She picked up the phone and had started dialling before she remembered Joan had cut the wires. Never mind, a walk in the fresh air would wake her up.

Eunice Parchman put on her red coat and her woolly hat and scarf. She took a torch from the gun room and set off to walk to Greeving and the phone box outside the village store.

# 22

Detective Chief Superintendent William Vetch arrived in Greeving from Scotland Yard on Monday afternoon to take charge of the Coverdale Massacre Case, the St Valentine's Day Massacre.

He came to a village of which few people in the great world had ever heard, but whose name was now on every front page, blazed from every television screen. He found a village where on this first day the inhabitants remained indoors, as if afraid of the open air, as if that open air had changed its quality overnight and become savage, inimical and threatening. There were people in the village street, but those people were policemen. There were cars, police cars; all night and all day the drive to Lowfield Hall was jammed with the cars and vans of policemen and police photographers and forensic experts. But the people of

Greeving were not to be seen, and on that day, 15 February, only five men went to work and only seven children to school.

Vetch took over the village hall, and there he set up a 'Murder Room'. There, with his officers, he interrogated witnesses, examined evidence, received and made phone calls, spoke to the press – and had his first interview with Eunice Parchman.

He was an experienced officer. He had been a policeman for twenty-six years, and his career in the Murder Squad had been remarkable for displays of courage. He had personally arrested James Timson, the Manchester Bank Killer, and had led the group of officers who charged into the Brixton flat of Walter Eksteen, an armed man wanted for the murder of two security guards.

Among his juniors he had the reputation of fastening on to one particular witness in each case he handled, of relying on that person for support, and even, according to those who did not like him, of befriending him or her. In the Eksteen case this had paid off, and he had been led to the killer by Eksteen's ex-mistress whose trust he had won. The witness he chose for this role in the Coverdale case was Eunice Parchman.

No one had ever really liked Eunice. In their way her parents had loved her, but that is a different thing. Mrs Samson had pitied her, Annie Cole had feared her, Joan Smith had used her. Bill Vetch actually liked her. From the time of that first interview, he liked her. For Eunice didn't waste words or seem to prevaricate or show misplaced sentimentality, and she wasn't afraid to say when she didn't know.

He respected her for the way in which, having found four dead bodies in circumstances which had sickened the hearts of the police officers who first came, she had walked a mile in the dark to reach a call-box. Suspicion of her hardly touched him, and a faint doubt, present before he saw her, vanished when she told him frankly that she had not liked the Coverdales and had been dismissed for insolence. This, anyway, was no middle-aged woman's crime, nor could it have been committed single-handed. And already, before he saw Eunice, he had begun to mount the hunt for the man with the injured hand and his companion.

This is the statement which Eunice had made to the Suffolk officers on the previous night: 'I went to Nunchester with my friend, Mrs Joan Smith, at half past five. We attended a religious service at the Epiphany Temple on North Hill. Mrs Smith drove me back to Lowfield Hall and I got there at five to eight. I looked at the clock in the hall as I came in by the front door and it said five to eight. Mrs Smith did not come in. She had not been feeling well and I told her to go straight home. There was a light on in the hall and in the drawing room. You could see the drawing-room light from outside. The drawing-room door was shut. I did not go into the drawing room. I never did after I had been out in the evening unless Mr or Mrs Coverdale called me. I did not go into the kitchen either as I had had my tea in Nunchester after the service. I went upstairs to my room. Mr and Mrs Coverdale's bedroom door was open but I did not look inside. I did some knitting and then I packed my cases.

'Mr and Mrs Coverdale usually went to bed at about eleven on a Sunday. Giles spent most evenings in his own room. I did not know if he was in his room as the door was shut when I went upstairs. I did not think much about it. I was thinking about leaving on the next day, and I did not go out of my bedroom again until about eleven thirty.

'It was not necessary for me to go downstairs to wash as I had my own bathroom. I went to bed at eleven. The lights were always left on on the first-floor landing and on the stairs to the second floor. Mr or Mrs Coverdale turned them off when they came to bed. When I could see under my door that the lights were still on at eleven-thirty I got up and went to turn them off. I put on my dressing gown as I had to go down to the first floor to turn that light off. Then I saw some clothes on the floor in Mr and Mrs Coverdale's bedroom, and some broken glass. I had not seen this when I came up because then I had my back to the door. What I saw alarmed me and I went down to the drawing room. There I found the bodies of Mrs Coverdale and Melinda Coverdale and Giles Mont. I found Mr Coverdale dead in the kitchen. I tried to phone the police but could not get the dialling tone, and then I saw that the wire had been cut.

472

'I heard no unusual sounds between the time I came in and the time I found them. No one was leaving the Hall when I arrived. On my way home I may have passed cars, but I did not notice.'

To this statement Eunice adhered, changing it not in a single particular. Sitting opposite Vetch, her eyes meeting his calmly, she insisted that she had arrived home at five to eight. The grandfather clock had stopped because George had not been there to wind it at ten on Sunday night. Did that clock keep good time? Eunice said it was sometimes slow, she had known it as much as ten minutes slow, and this was confirmed by Eva Baalham and later by Peter Coverdale. But in the days that followed Vetch was often to wish that George's watch had been broken by shot, for of all elements in a murder case he most disliked confusion over time, and the difficulty of fitting the facts to the times was to cause him much frustration.

According to the medical experts, the Coverdales and Giles Mont had met their deaths after seven-thirty and before nine-thirty, rigor mortis having already begun when the bodies were first examined at a quarter past midnight. Its onset is accelerated by heat, and the drawing room and kitchen had been very warm, for the central heating remained on all night at Lowfield Hall in the depths of winter. Many other factors were taken into consideration: stomach contents, post-mortem lividity, changes in cerebro-spinal fluid, but Vetch could not persuade his experts to admit the possibility of death having occurred before half past seven. Not when that heat, a temperature of nearly eighty, was borne in mind, not in the face of Eunice's evidence that the meal the Coverdales had eaten at six – tea and sandwiches and cake – had been completely digested. And Vetch himself thought it odd that a family who had eaten at six should start drinking coffee at, say, seven.

Nevertheless, it could just be made to work out. The two youths in denim had come into the Blue Boar at ten to eight. That gave them fifteen minutes in which to kill the Coverdales – for what motive? For kicks? For some revenge against the social class the Coverdales represented? – and five minutes in which to leave the Hall and drive to Greeving. By the time Eunice came in at five to (or five past)

473

eight, they were a mile away, leaving death and silence behind them.

In that fifteen minutes they must also have ravaged the bedroom, though why they should have poured tea on the bed, Vetch couldn't imagine. Wanton damage, he thought, for none of Jacqueline's jewellery had been taken. Or had they been looking for money, and been surprised in their hasty plundering by one of the Coverdales? At some stage the man with the wounded hand must have removed one of the gloves he was wearing, for gloves had been worn as there were no prints, unless a glove had still been on the hand when shot grazed it. Fifteen minutes was enough, just enough in which to smash and tear and kill.

Vetch spent many hours questioning those patrons of the Blue Boar, among them Norman Smith, who had seen and had spoken to the two young men in denim. And by Monday evening every police force in the country was searching for that car and its occupants.

Joan Smith lay in a coma in Stantwich General Hospital. But Vetch believed she had never entered the Hall that evening, and with her he concerned himself only to check that Eunice had been correct in stating that the two of them had left the Epiphany Temple at seven twenty. The brethren confirmed it, but not one of them told Vetch's officers that Joan Smith had threatened George Coverdale's life shortly before her departure. They hadn't known it was George she was raving about, and if they had, the conduct and desires of the Epiphany People must be kept from policemen who were not of the elect.

Eunice was allowed to remain at the Hall, for she had nowhere else to go and Vetch wanted her on the spot. The kitchen was open to her but the drawing room was sealed up, and that copy of the *Radio Times* sealed up inside it.

'I don't know,' she said when Vetch asked her if George Coverdale had had enemies. 'They had a lot of friends. I never heard of anyone threatening Mr Coverdale.' And she made him a cup of tea. While she told him about the Coverdales' life, their friendships, their habits, their tastes, their whims, the murderess and the investigating officer drank their tea at the table, well scrubbed by Eunice, on which George had fallen in death.

What had happened at Lowfield Hall struck the inhabitants of Greeving with incredulity, with horror, and some of them with sick sorrow. Necessarily, nothing else was talked about. Conversations that began on practical matters – what should they have for dinner, how was someone's flu, rain again and bitterly cold, isn't it? – turned inevitably to this massacre, this outrage. Who would do a thing like that? You still can't believe it, can you? Makes you wonder what the world's coming to. Jessica Royston wept and would not be comforted. Mary Cairne had Eleigh's the builders to put up bars at her downstairs windows. The Jameson-Kerrs thought how they would never again go to Lowfield Hall, and the brigadier shuddered when he remembered pheasant shoots with George. Geoff Baalham, mourning Melinda, knew that it would be a long time before he could again bring himself to drive past Gallows Corner on a Friday or Saturday afternoon.

Peter Coverdale and Paula Caswall came to Greeving, and Paula, who was to stay with the Archers, collapsed from shock and grief within hours of her arrival. Peter stayed at the Angel in Cattingham. There, in the cold damp evenings, over the electric fire that inadequately heated his room, he sat drinking with Jeffrey Mont who was staying at the Bull at Marleigh. He didn't like Jeffrey, whom he had never met before and who got through a bottle of whisky a night, but he thought he would have gone mad without someone to talk to, and Jeffrey said that, without his company, he'd have killed himself. They went to the Archers together to see Paula, but Dr Crutchley had put her under sedation.

Jonathan Dexter, in Norwich, first learned of Melinda's death when he read of it in the paper. He did nothing. He did not check or get in touch with his parents or try to get in touch with Peter Coverdale. He shut himself up in his room and remained there, living on stale bread and milkless tea for five days.

Norman Smith went dutifully to visit his wife every evening. He didn't want to go. More or less unconsciously, he would have liked Joan to die because it was very pleasant on his own, but he would no more have said this to himself than he would have avoided going to see her. That was what a husband did when his wife was ill so he did it. But because Joan couldn't move or speak or hear anything, he couldn't tell her the news. Instead he gossiped about it with other visiting husbands, and thrashed it over incessantly in the Blue Boar where he was now able to spend as much time as he liked.

Nothing had been heard from Stantwich as to an enquiry into Joan's interference with the mail. Norman, who still retained some shreds of optimism in spite of what he had been through, supposed this was because the principal witness was dead. Or the postmaster had heard of Joan's accident and didn't like to harass him while his wife was ill.

His van had been towed to a garage in Nunchester. Norman went to Nunchester on the bus to find out about it and was told by the garage proprietor that it was a total write-off. A deal was done for the usable parts of the van, and the garage man said, 'By the way, this was under the back seat,' and gave him an object which Norman thought was a transistor radio.

He took it home with him, put it on a shelf with a pile of copies of *Follow My Star*, and forgot about it for some days.

# 23

Identikit pictures of the two wanted men appeared in every national newspaper on Wednesday, 17 February, but Vetch hadn't much faith in them. If a witness cannot remember whether a man's hair is fair or brown it is unlikely he will recall the shape of that man's nose or forehead. The attendant at the self-service petrol station a hundred yards from Gallows Corner remembered the taller dark one of them. But it was a self-service station, the dark youth had served himself, and had come into the glass-fronted office only to pay. The attendant had not even seen the other man, could not say that there had been another man, and remembered the car only because maroon is a fairly unusual colour for a Morris Minor Traveller.

It was from his recollection and that of Jim Meadows, Geoff Baalham and the other Sunday night patrons of the

Blue Boar that the pictures had been made up. They evoked hundreds of phone calls to the Murder Room in Greeving Village Hall from people offering sightings of grey or green or black Minor Travellers, or from those who possessed maroon coloured ones respectably locked up in garages. But each one of these calls had to be checked before they could be dismissed.

Appeals were made to every hotel keeper and landlady in the country as to whether any of their guests or tenants possessed a car answering to the description given by Geoff Baalham and the garage attendant. Had it been missing from its usual parking place on Sunday? Where was it now? These appeals resulted in hundreds more phone calls and hundreds of fruitless interviews that continued through Wednesday and Thursday.

But on Thursday a woman who was neither a landlady nor a hotel keeper phoned Vetch and gave him some information about a car answering the description of the wanted vehicle. She lived on a caravan site near Clacton on the coast of Essex, some forty miles from Greeving, and Vetch was talking to her in her own caravan not much more than an hour later.

Residents' cars were parked in a muddy and unsightly section of field adjacent to the entrance of the site, and Mrs Burchall, though possessing no car of her own, had often noticed there a maroon-coloured Traveller because it was the dirtiest vehicle in the park and, because of a flat rear tyre, had sunk lopsidedly into the mud. This car had been in its usual place on the previous Friday, but she couldn't remember whether she had noticed it since. However, it was not there now.

The owner of the car turned out to be, or have been, a man called Dick Scales. Scales, a long-distance lorry driver, wasn't at home when they called at the caravan where he lived, and Vetch and his men talked to a middle-aged Italian woman who called herself Mrs Scales but subsequently admitted she was not married. Vetch could get little out of her beyond cries of '*Mama mia!*' and expostulations that she knew nothing about any car and it was all Dick's fault. She rocked about on a broken chair while she talked, clutching in her arms a fierce-looking little mongrel terrier. When would Dick be back? She didn't know. Tomorrow, next day. And the car? They were not to ask her about cars, she knew nothing of cars, couldn't drive. She had been in Milan with her parents since before Christmas, had only returned last week, and wished now she had never come back to this cold, horrible, godless country.

Police waited for Dick Scales on the M1. Somehow or other they missed him, while Vetch in Clacton wondered uneasily about the set-up. If Scales were guilty, how could the Carters, the Baalhams, the Meadowses and the petrol-station attendant have mistaken a man of fifty for a tall dark youth?

At Lowfield Hall the drawing room remained sealed up, and several times a day, as Eunice came downstairs to the kitchen, she walked past that sealed door. She never thought of trying to get inside the room, although, had she wanted to, it would not have been very difficult. The french windows were locked, but the keys to them hung on their hook in the gun room. To such small oversights as these the police are sometimes prone. But in this respect their lack of caution neither damaged their case nor benefited Eunice, for she had no idea that the one piece of evidence which could incriminate her lay behind that door, and they had already dismissed that evidence, or what they had seen of it, as so much waste paper.

The one piece? Yes, for if she had secured it, been able to read what was written on it, it would have led her by now to that other. More precisely, she would have known what that other was, and when the time came would not have rejected it with unthinking indifference.

She was calm, and she felt herself secure. She watched television and she plundered the deep freeze to make herself large satisfying meals. Between meals she ate chocolate, more than her usual quota, for though unconscious of any real nervous tension, she found it a little disconcerting to encounter policemen daily. To maintain her stock of supplies, she walked down to the village store where Norman Smith presided alone, chewing gum from force of habit.

That morning he had had a phone call from Mrs Elder Barnstaple to say that she would drop in and collect such copies of *Follow My Star* as Joan had not had time to distribute. Norman took them down from the shelf, and with them the object that had been found in the back of his van. But he didn't show it to Eunice. He mentioned it while selling her three Mars bars.

'Joan didn't borrow a radio from you, did she?'

'I haven't got a radio,' said Eunice, refusing the gift of her future and her liberty. She walked out of the shop without asking after Joan or sending her love. Mildly interested to note that there were fewer police about than usual, she observed the absence of Vetch's car from its usual place outside the village hall. Mrs Barnstaple, just arriving, put hers there instead, and Eunice favoured her with a nod and one of her tight smiles.

Norman Smith took his second visitor into the parlour.

'That's a nice little tape recorder you've got there,' said Mrs Barnstaple.

'Is that what it is? I thought it was a radio.'

Again Mrs Barnstaple averred it was a tape recorder, and said that if it wasn't Norman's, to whom did it belong? Norman said he didn't know, it had been found in the van after Joan's accident, and perhaps it belonged to one of the Epiphany brethren. In Mrs Barnstaple's view, this was unlikely, but she would make enquiries.

Almost anyone with a spark of curiosity in his make-up would, after the object's function had been defined, have fiddled about with it and made it play. Not Norman. He was pretty sure he'd only get hymns or confessions out of it, so he put it back on the now empty shelf and went back to sell Barbara Baalham an air letter.

Some hours before, as a worried Dick Scales was beginning the drive from Hendon in north-west London to his home in Clacton, a young man with long dark hair walked into Hendon Police Station and, in a manner of speaking, gave himself up.

Friday, the day of the funeral.

It took place at two in the afternoon, and it was well attended. The press came along with a few carefully chosen policemen. Brian Caswall came from London and Audrey Coverdale from the Potteries. Jeffrey Mont, the worse (or perhaps the better) for drink, was there, and so were Eunice

Parchman, the Jameson-Kerrs, the Roystons, Mary Cairne, Baalhams, Meadowses, Higgses and Newsteads. Under a blue sky, as brilliant as on the day Giles Caswall was christened, the closest mourners followed the Rector from the church door along a little winding path to the south-east corner of the churchyard. Rugged elms and yew trees' shade, and an east wind blowing; George Coverdale had bought a plot under those yews, and in this grave his body and the bodies of his wife and daughter were laid to rest.

Mr Archer spoke these words from the Wisdom of Solomon: 'For though they be punished in the sight of men, yet is their hope full of immortality. And having been a little chastized, they shall be greatly rewarded . . .'

Giles, at his father's request, was cremated at Stantwich, and there were no flowers at the brief service that was held for him. The wreaths that came for the Coverdales never reached the destination for which Peter intended them, Stantwich Hospital – to decorate Joan Smith's bedside? – but shrivelled within an hour in the February frost. At the suggestion of Eva Baalham, Eunice sent a sheaf of chrysanthemums, but she never paid the bill the florist sent her a week later.

She was driven back to the Hall by Peter who advised her to go upstairs and lie down, a suggestion which met with no opposition from Eunice, thinking of her television and her Mars bars. In her absence and that of the police, in the terrible silence and the harsh cold, he took away the kitchen table, chopped it to pieces and burnt it down by the blackthorn hedge while the frosty crimson sun went down.

Vetch did not attend the funeral. He was in London. There he heard from Keith Lovat the story which had been told to the Hendon police, and accompanied by Lovat, he went to the house in West Hendon where Michael Scales rented one furnished room and Lovat another. At the end of the garden were three lock-up garages, surrounded by a high fence. On the concrete behind this fence and at the side of the garages, Vetch was shown what appeared to be a car concealed by a canvas cover. Lovat removed the cover to disclose a maroon-coloured Morris Minor Traveller which he told Vetch he had bought from Michael's father, Dick Scales, on the previous Sunday.

The car, Lovat said, had been for sale for eighty pounds, and he and Michael had gone up to Clacton by train to take a look at it. They arrived there at three and had a meal in the caravan with Dick Scales and the Italian woman whom Lovat called Maria and referred to as Michael's stepmother.

'Maria had this little dog,' Lovat went on. 'She'd brought it back with her from Italy in a basket with a cover over it, and she'd got it through Customs without them knowing. It was a snappy little devil, and I left it alone, but Mike kept playing with it, teasing it really.' He looked at Vetch. 'That was how it all happened, that was the cause of it.'

The flat tyre on the car having been changed for the spare one, he and Michael Scales decided to leave for home in it at seven, but not to take the A12 from Nunchester, a fast road which would have taken them in to East London. Instead they intended to go westwards to Gosbury and then south for Dunmow and Ongar, entering London by the A11 and the North Circular road to Hendon. But before they left Michael was again playing with the dog, offering it a piece of chocolate and snatching it away when the dog came to take it. The result of this was that the dog bit him on his left hand.

'We went just the same. Maria tied Mike's hand up with a handkerchief, and I said he'd better have it seen to when we got home. Dick and Maria got into a bit of a panic on account of her bringing the dog in like that, and Dick said they could get fined hundreds and hundreds if they got caught. Well, Mike promised he wouldn't go to a doctor or a hospital or anything, though the blood was coming through the bandage by then. We started off, and the fact is I lost my way. The lanes were pitch-dark, and I thought I'd missed the Gosbury road, though it turned out I was really on it. Mike didn't know anything about people not being allowed to bring animals into the country without putting them in quarantine, so I told him a bit about that, and when he said why not, I said it was on account of not spreading rabies. That really scared him, that was the beginning of it.'

They had turned into what was evidently Greeving Lane. The time? About twenty to eight, Lovat said. At the Blue Boar in Greeving Michael washed his hand and had a double brandy. They were directed to a self-service petrol station on the Gosbury Road which, Lovat realised, was the road they had mistakenly left half an hour before.

'Mike had got into a state by then. He was scared he'd get rabies and didn't want to go to the hospital in case he got his dad into trouble. We got home around eleven, I couldn't get more than forty out of the car, and when we got home I parked it down there and put that cover over it.'

Lowfield Hall? said Vetch. They must have passed Lowfield Hall twice on their way into and out of Greeving.

For the first time Lovat's voice faltered. He hadn't noticed a single house while driving along Greeving Lane. Strange, thought Vetch, when you remembered that Meadows' farmhouse on its raised ground loomed over the only real bend in the road. But for the time being he let it pass, and Lovat went on to say that on the Tuesday he had realised it was he and Michael Scales for whom the police were hunting. He begged Michael to go with him to their local police station, but Michael, who had been in touch with Dick Scales by phone, refused. His hand had begun to fester and swell, and he hadn't been to work since Wednesday.

On Thursday morning Dick Scales phoned the Hendon house from a call box in the north of England, and when he heard of his son's state he said he would call in on his way south. He reached Hendon at nine in the evening, and he and Michael and Keith Lovat had sat up all night, discussing what they should do. Dick wanted Michael to go to a doctor and say he had been bitten by a stray dog, mentioning nothing about the car or his visit to the caravan, and Michael was in favour of this. Lovat had been unable to make them see his point of view, that all the time they were getting themselves deeper into trouble, and could be charged with obstructing the police. Moreover, he was prevented from having repairs done to the car and, as far as he could see, from using it perhaps for months. At last he decided to act on his own. When Dick had gone he walked out of the house and went to Hendon Police Station.

It was a story not entirely consistent with this one that Vetch finally elicited from Michael Scales. Scales was lying

482

in bed in a filthy room, his arm swollen up to the elbow and streaked with long red lines, and at the appearance of Vetch and his sergeant he began to sob. When Vetch told him that he knew all about the car, the possibly rabid dog and the visit to the Blue Boar at Greeving, he admitted everything – and admitted something about which Lovat had evidently stalled. On their way into Greeving they had stopped at the entrance to the drive of a large well-lighted house, and Lovat had gone up the drive to ask for directions to Gosbury. However, before he reached the door his courage had failed him, on account, Scales said, of the clothes he was wearing and the dirt he had got on himself from tinkering with the car.

After some prevarication, Lovat admitted this. 'I never knocked on the door,' he said. 'I didn't want to scare the people, not at night-time and in a lonely place like that.'

It could be true. Lovat and Scales struck Vetch as being as pusillanimous and indecisive a pair as he had ever come across. Describe the house, he said, and Lovat said it was a big place with two long windows on either side of the front door, adding that he had heard *music coming from the house* as he hesitated on the drive. The time? Twenty to eight, said Lovat, and Scales said nearer a quarter to.

Vetch had Maria Scales charged with contravening the quarantine laws, and Michael Scales was removed to hospital where he was put into isolation. What to do with Lovat? There was as yet insufficient evidence to charge them with the murder, but by some string-pulling Vetch arranged with the resident medical officer to have Lovat taken into hospital also and kept in under observation. There, they were out of harm's way for the present, and Vetch, with a breathing space, considered what he had been told about the time and the music.

What music? The Coverdales' record player, radio and television set were all in the morning room. Therefore it looked as if the music had been an invention of Lovat's, though there seemed no reason why he should have invented it. More probably he and Scales had arrived much earlier at Lowfield Hall, and had killed the Coverdales for what reason? It wasn't up to Vetch to find a reason. But they could have entered the Hall to wash, to cadge a drink, to use a phone, and had perhaps met with physical opposition from George Coverdale and his step-son. It fitted, and the time, if Lovat were lying, also fitted. But Vetch had to be sure of one thing to start with, or as he told himself in the days that followed, face the music.

It was to the young Coverdales that he went for help, and at once Audrey Coverdale told him what had been perplexing her and yet what had seemed irrelevant to the discovery of the perpetrators of the crime.

'I've never been able to understand why they weren't watching *Don Giovanni*. Jacqueline wouldn't have missed that for the world. It's like saying an ardent football fan would miss the Cup Final.'

But the television set was in the morning room, and they couldn't have been in the morning room from seven onwards, for they had taken coffee in the drawing room, and no amount of juggling with time could make that coffee-drinking take place before seven. On the other hand, guilty or not, Lovat had said he had heard music. On Sunday afternoon Vetch broke the seals on the drawing-room door and revisited the scene of the crime. He was looking for signs that the television set had been in this room, but finding none, it occurred to him to check on the time the opera had begun. Vetch could easily have secured himself a copy of the *Radio Times* for that week from any newsagent. He still does not know to this day what made him pick up the *Observer* from the coffee table on the chance a *Radio Times* might have been underneath it. But it was. He opened it at the relevant page and noticed that page was splashed with blood. If anyone had previously observed this, he had not been told of it. In the margin, between and beneath the blood splashes, were three scribbled notes:

*Overture cut. Surely no ascending seventh in last bar of* La Ci Darem. *Check with M's recording.*

Vetch had seen enough examples of Jacqueline's handwriting to recognise that these notes had been made by her. And clearly they had been made by her while watching this particular broadcast. Therefore she had watched it or part of it. And, beyond a doubt, it had begun at seven. The only expert he had immediately to hand – and how much of an

484

expert she was he couldn't tell as he knew nothing of music – was Audrey Coverdale. He had the door re-sealed, and lingered for ten minutes to drink the tea Eunice Parchman had made for him. While he chatted with her and Eunice told him she had heard no music when she came in at five to (or five past) eight, that the television set was always in the morning room and had been in the morning room at the time of her discovery of the bodies, the *Radio Times* was a few feet from her, shut up in his briefcase.

Audrey Coverdale was preparing to leave, for she had to be back at work in the morning. She confirmed that the notes were in Jacqueline's hand and quailed at the blood-stains, glad that her husband was not present to see them.

'What does it mean?' said Vetch.

'*La Ci Darem* is a duet in the third scene of the first act.' Audrey could have sung every aria from *Don Giovanni* and told Vetch, within minutes, the precise time at which each would occur. 'If you want to know when it comes, it'd be – let me see – about forty minutes after the beginning.'

Twenty to eight. Vetch simply didn't believe her. It was useless consulting amateurs. On Monday morning he sent his sergeant into Stantwich to buy a complete recording of the opera. It was played on a borrowed player in the Murder Room in the Village Hall, and to Vetch's astonishment and dismay, *La Ci Darem* occurred almost exactly where Audrey had said it would, forty-two minutes after the commencement of the overture. *Overture cut*, Jacqueline had written. Perhaps the whole opera had been cut. Vetch got on to the B.B.C. who let him have their own recording. The opera had been slightly cut, but only by three minutes in the first three scenes of the first act, and *La Ci Darem* occurred in the recording at seven thirty-nine. Therefore, Jacqueline Coverdale had been alive at seven thirty-nine, had been tranquil, at ease, concentrating on a television programme. It was impossibly far-fetched to suppose that her killers had even entered the house by that time. Yet Lovat and Scales had been seen in the Blue Boar at ten to eight by nine independent witnesses. Someone else had entered Lowfield Hall after Lovat's departure and before five past – it now had to be five *past* – eight.

485

Vetch studied Jacqueline's notes, almost the only piece of concrete evidence he had.

# 24

Looking through the Wanted column in the *East Anglian Daily Times*, Norman Smith found an insertion from a man who was seeking a second-hand tape recorder. He didn't hesitate for long before picking up the phone. Mrs Barnstaple's enquiries had not found the tape recorder's owner, Joan still lay speechless, unable in any way to communicate, but it didn't cross Norman's mind to take the thing to the police. Or, rather, it crossed his mind only to be dismissed as too trivial when the police were obviously occupied with matters of more moment. Besides, he might get fifty pounds for it, and this would be most welcome in his present penurious car-less state. Fifty pounds, added to the miserable sum for which the van had been insured, would just about buy him a replacement of much the same vintage as the wrecked green one. He dialled the number. The advertiser was a freelance journalist called John Plover who told Norman he would drive over to Greeving on the following day.

Which he did. Not only did he buy the tape recorder on the spot, but he also gave Norman a lift into Stantwich in time for the hospital visiting hour.

In the meantime, Vetch was extracting more information from the notes in the margin of the *Radio Times*. *Check with M's recording* didn't seem of much significance. He had already checked with two recordings – though not in pursuit of a spurious ascending seventh, whatever that might be – and nothing could shift that aria or put it ten minutes before the time it had actually occurred. Unless Jacqueline had made the note *before* she heard the aria on television, had been listening during the afternoon to a record of Melinda's, and wanted to check with the televised opera. But what she had written was the very reverse of that.

Moreover, he was unable to find any record of *Don Giovanni* or any part of it in Lowfield Hall.

'I don't think my sister had any records of classical music,' said Peter Coverdale, and then, 'but my father gave her a tape recorder for Christmas.'

Vetch stared at him. For the first time he realised that a recording need not necessarily mean a black disc. 'There's no tape recorder in the house.'

'I expect she took it back to university with her.'

The possibility which this opened to Vetch was beyond any realistic policeman's dreams – that Melinda Coverdale had actually been recording when the killers came into the house, that the time might thus be precisely fixed, and the intruders' voices preserved. He refused to allow himself to speculate about that aspect of it. The first thing the killers would have done was remove the tapes and destroy them, then rid themselves of the recorder itself. The invaluable Eunice, the star witness, was called in.

She said, 'I remember her dad giving it to her at Christmas. It was in her room in a leather case, and I used to dust it. She took it to college when she went back in January and she never brought it home after that.' Eunice was speaking the truth. She hadn't seen the tape recorder since the morning she had listened in to Melinda's phone conversation. Joan had carried it out from the Hall, Joan who in her madness was a thousand times more sophisticated than Eunice would ever be, and Eunice had not even noticed she had anything in her hand.

While Vetch's men were scouring Galwich for that tape recorder, interrogating everyone Melinda had known, Eunice marched the two miles to Gallows Corner and caught the bus for Stantwich. In a side room off the Blanche Tomlin ward she found Norman Smith sitting by his wife's bedside. She hadn't bothered to tell him she was coming. She had come for the same reason that he came, because it was the thing to do. Just as you went to the weddings and the funerals of people you knew, so you went to the hospital to see them when they were ill. Joan was very ill. She lay on her back with her eyes closed, and but for the rise and fall of the bedclothes, you would have thought she was dead. Eunice looked at her face. She was interested to see what that stretched canvas looked like without paint on it. Stretched canvas was what it looked like, yellow-brown, striated. She didn't speak to it.

'Keep it nice, don't they?' she said to Norman after she had made sure there was no dust under the bed. Perhaps he thought she was speaking of his wife who was also 'kept nice', anchored to her drip-feed, tucked up under a clean sheet, for he made no reply. They were both hoping, for different reasons, that Joan would go on like that for ever, and going home together on the bus, each expressed the pious wish that such a vegetable existence would not be prolonged.

In forlorn hope, Vetch ordered a search of Lowfield Hall, including the long-disused cellar, and when that brought nothing to light, they began digging up the frost-bound flowerbeds.

Eunice didn't know what they were looking for, and she was very little concerned. She made cups of tea and carried it out to them, the policemen's friend. Of much more moment to her were her wages or, rather, the lack of them. George Coverdale had always paid her her month's money on the last Friday in the month. That last Friday, 26 February, would be tomorrow, but so far Peter Coverdale had given no sign that he intended to honour this obligation inherited from his father, which seemed to Eunice very remiss of him. She wasn't going to use the phone. She walked over to Cattingham and enquired for him at the Angel. But Peter was out. Peter, though Eunice didn't know this, was driving his sister back to London to her husband and her children.

Vetch appeared at the Hall on the following morning, and Eunice resolved that he should be her go-between. Scotland Yard's Chief Superintendent, Vetch of the Murder Squad, was only too happy to oblige. Of course he would get in touch with Peter Coverdale during the day, with pleasure he would apprise him of Miss Parchman's dilemma.

'I've baked a chocolate cake,' said Eunice. 'I'll bring you a bit with your tea, shall I?'

'Most kind of you, Miss Parchman.'

As it happened, it wasn't a bit but the whole cake which Eunice was forced to sacrifice, for Vetch had chosen eleven o'clock to hold a conference in the morning room with three high-ranking officers of the Suffolk Constabulary. She left him with a quiet 'Thank you, sir', and returned to the kitchen to think about getting her own lunch. And she was eating it at noon sharp, eating it off the counter in the absence of the table, when Vetch's sergeant walked in through the gun room with a young man Eunice had never seen before in tow.

The sergeant was carrying a large brown envelope with something bulky inside it. He gave Eunice a pleasant smile and asked her if Mr Vetch was about.

'In the morning room,' said Eunice, knowing full well whom you sir-ed and whom you didn't. 'He's got a lot of folks with him.'

'Thanks. We'll find our own way.' The sergeant made for the door to the hall, but the young man stopped and stared at Eunice. All the colour had gone out his face. His eyes went wide and he flinched as if she'd sworn at him instead of speaking perfectly normally. He reminded her of Melinda in this same kitchen three weeks back, and she was quite relieved when the sergeant said, 'This way, Mr Plover,' and hustled him out.

Eunice washed the dishes by hand and ate up her last bar of chocolate. Her last bar, indeed. She wondered if Vetch had yet done anything about Peter Coverdale and her wages. Outside they were still digging up the garden, in the east wind, under occasional flurries of snow. Her favourite serial tonight, Lieutenant Steve in Hollywood or maybe Malibu Beach, but she would enjoy it far more if she could be sure her money was forthcoming. She went out into the hall and heard music.

Music was coming from behind the morning-room door. That meant they couldn't be doing anything very important in there, nothing that wouldn't bear a polite interruption. The music was familiar; she had heard it before. Sung by her father? On the television? Someone was singing foreign words, so it couldn't have been one of Dad's.

Eunice raised her fist to knock on the door, let it fall again as a voice from within the room shouted above the music:

'Oh Christ!'

She couldn't identify that voice, but she knew the one that came next, a voice silenced now by massive brain injury.

'Get back in there. We've got guns.'

And the others. And her own. All blending with the music vying with it, drowning it in frenzy and fear.

'Where's my husband?'

'He's in the kitchen. He's dead.'

'You're mad, you're crazy! I want my husband, let me go to my husband. Giles, the phone . . . ! No, no . . . Giles!'

Eunice spoke to Eunice across the days. 'You'd better sit down. You've got it coming to you.'

A cackle from Joan. 'I am the instrument of One Above,' and a shot. Another. Through the music and the screams, the sound of something heavy falling. 'Please, please!' from the girl, and the reloaded guns fired for the last time. Music, music. Silence.

Eunice thought she would go upstairs and repack her things before retribution came from whatever it was in there that acted out, in some way beyond her understanding, the deaths of the Coverdales. But a numbness stunned her mind, and she was less than ever capable of reasoning. She began to walk towards the stairs relying on that strong body that had always done so well by her. And then that body, which was all she had, failed her. At the foot of the stairs, on the very spot where she had first stood on entering the Hall nine months before, where wonderingly she had seen herself reflected in a long mirror, her legs gave way and Eunice Parchman fainted.

The sound of her falling reached Vetch who was nerving himself to play the tape once more to an audience of policemen, white-faced now and rigid in their chairs. He came out and found her where she lay, but he could not bring himself to lift her up or even touch her with his hands.

# 25

Joan Smith still lies speechless and immobile in Stantwich General Hospital. She is in a machine which keeps her heart and lungs functioning, and the medical powers-that-be are at present deciding whether it might not be a mercy to switch that machine off. Her husband is a clerk in a post office in Wales, and he still keeps the name of Smith. There are, after all, a lot of them about.

Peter Coverdale still lectures on political economy in the Potteries. His sister Paula has never recovered from the deaths of her father and Melinda, and she has had three sessions of electro-convulsive therapy in the past two years. Jeffrey Mont is drinking heavily and almost qualifies for the destination in which Joan Smith placed him at her second meeting with Eunice Parchman. These three are engaged in continuous litigation, for it has never been established whether Jacqueline pre-deceased her son or he her. If she died first, Giles briefly inherited Lowfield Hall, and thus it must now be his father's the property of his next-of-kin. But if he died before his mother the Hall should pass to George's natural heirs. Bleak House.

Jonathan Dexter, tipped for a first-class Honours degree, got a third. But that was in the early days. He teaches French at a comprehensive school in Essex, has nearly forgotten Melinda, and is going steady with a member of the science department.

Barbara Baalham gave birth to a daughter whom they called Anne because Melinda, which was Geoff's original choice, seemed a bit morbid. Eva cleans for Mrs Jameson-Kerr and gets seventy-five pence an hour. They still talk about the St Valentine's Day Massacre in Greeving, expecially in the Blue Boar on summer evenings when the tourists come.

Eunice Parchman was tried at the Old Bailey, the Central Criminal Court, because they could not find an unbiased jury for the Assizes at Bury St Edmunds. She was sen-